The
MX Book
of
New
Sherlock
Holmes
Stories

Part V – Christmas Adventures

Part V - Christmas Adventures

THE MX BOOK OF NEW
SHERLOCK HOLMES
STORIES

EDITED BY
DAVID
MARCUM

1/-
NET

A. Conan Doyle

A NEW **SHERLOCK HOLMES** STORY

ISBN Hardback 978-1-78092-995-8
ISBN Paperback 978-1-78092-996-5
AUK ePub ISBN 978-1-78092-997-2
AUK PDF ISBN 978-1-78092-998-9

Published in the UK by MX Publishing
335 Princess Park Manor, Royal Drive,
London, N11 3GX
www.mxpublishing.co.uk
Cover Design by Brian Belanger
www.belangerbooks.com and *www.redbubble.com/people/zhahadun*

CONTENTS

(Continued on the next page . . . .)

(Continued on the next page . . . .)

**These additional Sherlock Holmes adventures
can be found in the previous volumes of**
The MX Book of New Sherlock Holmes Stories

(Continued on the next page . . . .)

PART III: 1896-1929

PART IV: 2016 Annual

(Continued on the next page . . . .)

COPYRIGHT INFORMATION

(Continued on the next page . . . .)

(Continued on the next page . . . .)

Editor's Introduction:
The Compliments of the Season
by David Marcum

"I had called upon my friend Sherlock Holmes upon the second morning after Christmas, with the intention of wishing him the compliments of the season."
– "The Blue Carbuncle"
The Adventures of Sherlock Holmes

It has been said that Charles Dickens invented our modern idea of how to celebrate Christmas. In the early days of Victoria's reign, Christmas was a subdued affair in England, a time for quiet reflection, worshiping at church, and staying around one's hearth. But Dickens, perhaps trying to rewrite his own bleak childhood memories, almost single-handedly gave people the idea that December 25th was something more than another somber religious date on the calendar. It could be a time of festivity, of mystery and merriment and wonder.

In his first novel, *The Pickwick Papers* (1836-1837), which so captured England's heart, Dickens portrays scenes of a season filled with holiday festivities and good will as the members of the Pickwick Club celebrate with their friends. And there is even a Christmas ghost story, in which a bitter old man is changed on Christmas Eve by a supernatural encounter. No, it's not the more famous *A Christmas Carol* (1843), the story that everyone knows about Ebenezer Scrooge and his amazing redemption. Rather, it's "The Story of the Goblins Who Stole a Sexton", a shorter tale related by Mr. Wardle to the Pickwickians, in which bitter church sexton Gabriel Grub learns that "setting all the good of the world against the evil . . . it was a very decent and respectable world after all."

Dickens refined his ideas of a proper Christmas, with decorations and singing and wishes for snow and a fat goose, in his later more famous story, wherein Ebenezer Scrooge is taken here and there across London and elsewhere, through his past, present, and future. It's an amazing story that has resonated from the time it was written to the present day – so much so that it's one of the most filmed of all narratives, with dozens upon dozens of adaptations. Some of the more notable are the musical version starring Albert Finney – a personal favorite of mine: *"Thank you very much!"*, the much grimmer variant with a heavy-set Scrooge played by George C. Scott (who also once played a mentally ill character who erroneously believed that he was Sherlock Holmes), the

1

old classics with Alistair Sim or Reginald Owen (who listed among his many roles a heavy-set Holmes), and more recently that of Patrick Stewart and the unique animated version starring Jim Carrey.

Whenever one of these versions is on television, I have to stop and watch – not so much at this point to see the very familiar story, which I know by heart backwards and forwards, especially as I re-read *A Christmas Carol* nearly every December. No, the big reason that I watch now is to see how each of these films portrays the dark, narrow, and very atmospheric streets of Victorian London.

And since this book is about Sherlock Holmes – and *not* Dickens (or Scrooge or even Gabriel Grub) – that seems to be a good place to begin the pivot to Our Heroes, the Detective and the Doctor. Although Dickens was writing his great works decades before Holmes and Watson first appeared in print, fittingly in the *Beeton's Christmas Annual* of 1887, there are a great many similarities between the Dickensian London and that in which Holmes carried out his business. Can anyone doubt that the opium dens and the dangerous little streets along the Thames, so ably described in "The Man With the Twisted Lip", weren't directly related to the same vile alleys memorialized by Dickens? And the unique and larger-than-life people who wander through Dickens's stories could be the very parents and grandparents of some of the clients and policemen and Irregulars who climbed the seventeen steps to Holmes and Watson's Baker Street sitting room.

So if one such as myself sees Dickens's London and then looks for foreshadowing of that Great Cesspool that Watson described so well, then how can one *not* see a connection between that same kind of Dickensian Victorian Christmas and Sherlock Holmes?

Of course, this isn't a new idea. There have been quite a number of previously related adventures telling about what Mr. Holmes of Baker Street was up to during those various Christmases in the latter decades of the Nineteenth Century, and so on into the Twentieth. The first that come to mind must be those two well-known and highly respected volumes, *Holmes for the Holidays* (1996) and *More Holmes for the Holidays* (1999), each edited by the late Martin H. Greenberg, Jon L. Lellenberg, and Carol-Lynn Waugh. Containing fourteen and eleven stories respectively, these were the first anthologies of their kind to feature stories specifically sharing Holmes's Christmas-related cases. (There are even a couple of tales that feature descendants of individuals involved in *A Christmas Carol*.) I remember how enthusiastic I was when I first discovered *Holmes for the Holidays* on a book store shelf. This was in those dark days when finding new stories about The Master was almost always a surprise, a rare and difficult thing, as one couldn't learn the release dates for upcoming Holmes books for the next year simply by looking on the internet – one had to rely on frequent trips to the bookstore and serendipity.

In addition to these fine additions to any Holmes library, there have been a number of other stories spread throughout different collections. Probably the best of them all is Denis O. Smith's "The Christmas Visitor". Val Andrews brought us one of his finer efforts in *Sherlock Holmes and the Yuletide Mystery.* A lesser known novel is *Sherlock Holmes's Christmas* by David Upton. John Hall produced "The Christmas Bauble", featured both as a short story in the new *Strand Magazine*, and then adapted for broadcast on radio's *Imagination Theatre.*

Elsewhere on radio was "The Night Before Christmas" (1945, with Basil Rathbone and Nigel Bruce), and "The Christmas Bride" (1947, with John Stanley and Alfred Shirley). And then there was the film *Young Sherlock Holmes,* released in early December 1985, and also set around Christmas-time – although it wasn't explicitly a Christmas story – and that *wasn't* Watson featured in the story, but someone else entirely. (Ah, but that's an essay for a different book.)

There isn't space here to tell of all the other impressive stories relating what Holmes and Watson did during this-or-that Christmas. And what has appeared in print doesn't even begin to match the level of excellent writing about Holmes and Christmas that one can find at fan-fiction sites on the web. In fact, for the last several years there has been a writing activity at *fanfiction.net* in which a group of authors each compose and post something for the entire month of December, for every turn of the calendar, either a complete story, ranging from very short to full-length, to something serialized across the whole month.

So, if there are already so many of them out there, why *another* book of Holmes Christmas adventures? Well, that requires a two-part answer. The first and shortest is that, for someone like me – and hopefully you too! – there can *never* be enough traditional tales about Holmes and Watson, two of the best and wisest men whom I have ever known. (And after reading and collecting literally thousands of stories about them for over forty-one years, I do feel like I know them.)

The other reason relates to the ever-increasing popularity of these MX Anthologies.

When I first had the idea for a new Holmes anthology in early 2015, the plan was to contact possibly a dozen or so "editors" of Watson's notes and see if they were interested. The idea grew and grew until the first collection was three volumes – really one big book spread out under three covers – and containing more new Holmes stories than had ever been assembled before in one place at one time. A big part of what made the project so special was that the authors donated their royalties to the Stepping Stones School for special needs students, then planning to move into one of Sir Arthur Conan Doyle's former homes, Undershaw. By the time the first three books were released in October 2015, renovations were well under way at the school's future home, and it also quickly became apparent that the need for future volumes of *The MX Book of New Sherlock Holmes Stories* was very strong. The process for producing more anthology volumes was in place, a desire for more traditional Holmes stories is always there, the school can always use more funding as provided by the sale of the books – and more and more authors wanted to participate.

Therefore, it was announced that there would be another anthology, the next in what would now be an ongoing series. But there was so much interest that it was quickly determined that *two* volumes would be necessary in 2016. Consequently, *Part IV – 2016 Annual* came out in the spring of 2016, and a second book, *this* book, was planned for the fall. But it couldn't simply be the *Part V – 2016 Annual – Part II.* It needed something to set it apart. And then it hit me – by releasing it in the fall, in time for the holidays, this book could be a new Christmas collection. After all, it has been twenty years since *Holmes for the Holidays* and its sequel. It was time.

And many authors and friends of the project answered the call, as seen by the thirty stories contained in this volume. As always, I've arrange them chronologically, as that seems to work best. In almost every case, the stories are completely new for this volume. (In typical Watsonian Obfuscation, there are a couple that have previously appeared, but in substantially different or shorter versions on the internet, and the scripts by Bert Coules and Jim French have been broadcast on radio, but they have never appeared in print as text versions. And it's very interesting to see the styles of how each script is presented.)

Some of the stories are inextricably plotted with the trappings of Christmas. Others are set during late December, and even though they could have occurred at any time of the year, they are certainly influenced by the season that surrounds them. In some tales there is festivity, and in others tragedy. Watson might be having a bad year in this one, and Holmes in that one – the same as each of us have high and low Yuletide seasons.

You may notice that some years seem to have more than one adventure taking place concurrently around Christmases in the same year. Don't let that worry you – it can all be rationalized. As someone who has kept a massive and detailed Chronology of both Canon and traditional pastiche for over twenty years, I can assure you that it all fits neatly together. When Watson pulls out this or that relevant thread from the Great Holmes Tapestry to construct a self-contained narrative, he doesn't necessarily include what else was happening at the same time. He's also been known at times to slide the facts around a little bit, to protect an identity – or in this case to avoid confusion. Think how twisted and intertwined are the events in a normal person's everyday life – how much more convoluted, then, were those of Our Heroes? I'm thankful that Watson has taken the time to separate these events into digestible and self-contained pieces.

I'm happy to report that the anthology series' popularity continues to grow, and that there are already two more volumes planned for 2017, the *Part VI – 2017 Annual* to appear in the spring, and *Part VII – Eliminate the Impossible* in the fall, in which Holmes and Watson will investigate a number of seemingly supernatural tales. However, I can assure you that I insisted, as did Holmes, that "No ghosts need apply." Time will tell if that turns out to be the case. I'm already receiving stories from literally all over the world for both volumes, all of amazing quality, and I can't wait to share them with everyone.

And perhaps most exciting of all is that, of this writing, the Stepping Stones School has finished the long-time-coming renovation of Doyle's Sussex home, Undershaw, and the children and teachers are there. How exciting that they will benefit in some small way from this and the other anthology volumes – because in the end, isn't part of the wonder of Christmas about children, both those who are of the appropriate age, and also the children that are still deep down – or maybe *not* so deep – in all of us grown-ups?

As always, I want to thank with all my heart my patient and wonderful wife of over twenty-eight years (as of this writing,) Rebecca, and our son, Dan. They are everything to me. I love you both!

And then there is that wonderful crew of people who listen to my complaints and manic enthusiasms, read my Sherlockian thoughts and dogma, and offer support, encouragement, and friendship, sometimes on a nearly daily basis. So I offer many many thanks to (in alphabetical order): Derrick Belanger, Bob Byrne, Steve Emecz, Roger Johnson, Mark Mower, Denis Smith, Tom Turley, Dan Victor, and Marcia Wilson.

I can't ever express enough appreciation for all of the authors who have donated their time and royalties to this project. I am so glad to have gotten to know all of you through this process. It's an undeniable fact that Sherlock Holmes authors are the *best* people!

Many thanks to Jonathan Kellerman for his generous participation, which will no doubt increase the attention on these books and the cause they support, and also for providing insight on how he became a writer – as one of Mr. Kellerman's very big fans for a long time now, I knew how he was influenced by Kenneth Millar (a.k.a. Ross Macdonald – in fact, Mr. Kellerman is *the* literary heir to Millar), but I had no idea that Doyle had played a part along the way as well.

I want to especially thank (again) Roger Johnson and his wife Jean Upton for so graciously hosting me during my 2015 Pilgrimage to England, and Nick Utechin for giving me the ultimate insider's tour of Oxford. I very much recognize the setting of his story in this book and recall the amusing anecdote that he related there.

Also, my thanks go to Melissa Farnham, the Head Teacher at Stepping Stones, for joining this party once again, and for all that she and everyone else accomplishes there every day.

And last but certainly *not* least, **Sir Arthur Conan Doyle**: Author, doctor, adventurer, and the Founder of the Sherlockian Feast. Present in spirit, and honored by all of us here.

As always, this collection has been a labor of love by both the participants and myself. As I've explained before, once again everyone did their sincerest best to produce an anthology that truly represents why Holmes and Watson have been so popular for so long. These are just more tiny threads woven into the ongoing Great Holmes Tapestry, continuing to grow and grow, for there can *never* be enough stories about the man whom Watson described as "the best and wisest . . . whom I have ever known."

David Marcum
August 7th, 2016
The 164th Birthday of Dr. John H. Watson

Questions or comments may be addressed to David Marcum at
thepapersofsherlockholmes@gmail.com

6

Foreword
by Jonathan Kellerman

I'm frequently asked which writer I consider the primary influence on my own career as a novelist. My answer is always the same: the American master of crime fiction, Kenneth Millar, writing as Ross Macdonald. Macdonald's meld of Southern California malice-amid-the-palms and stunning psychological insights helped me develop my own voice.

On the rare occasion when I'm asked about a secondary influence, I cite Sir Arthur Conan Doyle.

The Holmes stories, discovered during my pre-teen years, awed me with their wondrous mix of elegant language, rich sense of place, spot-on plotting and characterization, and cutting-edge (Victorian) science. The world to which Sir Arthur granted me entry kick-started my earliest attempts to write fiction.

But my debt goes beyond that.

In 1981, while working as a 31-year-old hospital psychologist and medical school professor, I learned from a colleague who was a devoted Sherlockian that Doyle had penned his earliest stories while waiting for patients to show up at his surgery – a less than booming enterprise.

Hmm.

The preceding decade had seen me hunched in an unheated garage from 11 p.m. to 1 a.m. writing bad novels that, mercifully, remained unpublished. But I persisted – ah, the virtues of the obsessive-compulsive personality! – and that year, spurred by the image of Doyle scratching away in a quiet office, I quit a tenured position and went into solo private practice.

I set up a typewriter in my consulting room, expecting scads of spare time – the country was gripped by a recession. Instead, my practice booked up in two weeks and back to the garage I went, finally getting it right and completing the first Alex Delaware novel, *When the Bough Breaks*. Forty novels later . . . .

Which brings us to the notion of pastiche.

When approached by David Marcum to write this introduction, I had reservations about the appropriation of a writer's character and style by others. Like most professional novelists, I'm protective of my characters, find the idea of someone else "borrowing" them curious, and would assertively challenge any attempt to profit monetarily from such.

But upon reading the stories in this compilation, I realized that no ill intent or mercenary aims were at play. Quite the opposite; these tales are love letters to Doyle, Holmes, Watson, and the entire Sherlockian world. Even better, this book is a charitable endeavor benefiting a cause dear to my heart and endorsed by Sir Arthur's descendants – a school for children and adolescents with special needs, situated at Undershaw, Doyle's long-time home.

Reassured by all that, I set about reading the stories and grew impressed by their quality. This is, for the most part, an impressive display of The Collective Baker Street Unconscious.

So here it is, an introduction. Read, enjoy, take a few moments to pay silent homage to one of the greatest writers of our time. And thank you, Sir Arthur, for spurring me to quit my job.

Jonathan Kellerman
May 2016

"This bids fair to be the merriest of Christmases."

– "The Adventure of the Stone of Scone"

by Roger Johnson

Of course, when it comes to Sherlock Holmes, there is only one Christmas story.

Isn't there?

Well, it's true in a way. Arthur Conan Doyle wrote only one Holmes story set at Christmas time, so "The Adventure of the Blue Carbuncle" is the only *Canonical* example. Christopher Morley's description of it as "a Christmas story without slush" is perceptive and understandably famous, though I can't agree with his assertion that "as a story 'The Blue Carbuncle' is a far better work of art than the immortal *Christmas Carol*." Not that I rank Conan Doyle's tale lower than Dickens's, but it does have one serious flaw.

We may reasonably assume, I think, that Holmes intends Mr. and Mrs. Peterson to be the beneficiaries of the Countess of Morcar's £1,000 reward for recovering the celebrated jewel, which is only right. Nevertheless, he appears blithely optimistic in thinking that the case against the unfortunate John Horner would necessarily "collapse" if James Ryder didn't testify against him. I find myself wondering whether, after all, the circumstantial evidence would have been strong enough to secure a conviction.

In any case, the number of suspects seems to have been limited. If he did decline to appear against Horner, then Ryder himself would surely be the obvious suspect. How would he explain his *volte face*, especially as his original story had been backed up by her ladyship's maid, Catherine Cusack?

As you'll have realised, my affection for "The Adventure of the Blue Carbuncle" is not blind, but I love it anyway, and so do innumerable others – most obviously the many who have decided that one Christmas story is not enough for the Holmes devotee.

Before his creator's death in 1930, nearly all the unofficial fiction about the great detective was humorous or satirical. The earliest volume to contain a substantial amount of pastiche along with the parody was Ellery Queen's ill-fated anthology *The Misadventures of Sherlock Holmes*, published in 1944. Among the many delights in that rare collection is a short play called "Christmas Eve", written by the great Holmesian scholar S.C. Roberts. More was to follow. Personal favourites include "The Adventure of the Christmas Visitor" by Denis O Smith, "The Christmas Client" by Edward D Hoch, *Holmes in Time for Christmas* by Ross K. Foad, "Sherlock Holmes and the Ghost of Christmas Past" by David Stuart Davies . . . but there are many more.

Mention of "Christmas Eve" reminds me that the combination of Holmes and Yuletide remains irresistible to dramatists. "The Blue Carbuncle" has been adapted many times, of course, for stage, screen and radio. I'm hoping that the popular American play *Sherlock Holmes and the Case of the Christmas Goose* will make it across the Atlantic before long.

The Granada Television film with Jeremy Brett and David Burke is excellent, and so is the early BBC production with Peter Cushing and Nigel Stock. Mention of Nigel Stock reminds me that in 1970 he played Watson to Robert Hardy's Holmes in an admirable audio dramatisation. The story always seems to work well in sound alone, whether the protagonists are portrayed by Carleton Hobbs and Norman Shelley, John Patrick Lowrie and Lawrence Albert, or – and you can read Bert Coules' superb script in this very book – Clive Merrison and Michael Williams.

Also on radio, one of the most bizarrely entertaining of the classic 1940's series starring Messrs Rathbone and Bruce is "The Night Before Christmas", in which Holmes and Watson encounter a member of the Moriarty gang whose distinctive feature inspired his nickname, Lou the Lisper. Even more distinctive to the British listener is his strong Californian accent, but that seems to pass unnoticed by the denizens of Victorian London!

I'm taking up too much of your time, so I'll just mention another play that I hope one day to see: John Longenbaugh's *Sherlock Holmes and the Case of the Christmas Carol*, an ingenious amalgam of Conan Doyle and Dickens which has proved popular in America and did tour England last year – but without coming anywhere near me, alas.

Ah! There is one other thing. If you're wondering about the story that gives this little homily its title, then you should acquaint yourself with the exploits of the Master's greatest protégé, Mr. Solar Pons of Praed Street, as chronicled by August Derleth. As far as Christmas stories are concerned, even better that "The Adventure of the Stone of Scone" is "The Adventure of the Unique Dickensians". If you'll forgive the pun, it's a cracker!

That's something to look out for. Meanwhile, in the pages of this book is a literary feast to keep you satisfied during these long winter evenings!

Roger Johnson, BSI
Editor, *The Sherlock Holmes Journal*
July 2016

Undershaw:
An Ongoing Legacy
for Sherlock Holmes
by Steve Emecz

Undershaw
Circa 1900

The authors involved in this anthology are donating their royalties toward the restoration of Sir Arthur Conan Doyle's former home, Undershaw. This building was initially in terrible disrepair, and was saved from destruction by the *Undershaw Preservation Trust* (Patron: Mark Gatiss). Today, the building has been bought by Stepping Stones (a school for children with learning difficulties), and has been restored to its former glory.

Undershaw is where Sir Arthur Conan Doyle wrote many of the Sherlock Holmes stories, including *The Hound of The Baskervilles*. It's where Conan Doyle brought Sherlock Holmes back to life. This project will contribute to specific projects at the house, such as the restoration of Doyle's study, and will be opened up to fans outside term time.

You can find out more information about the new Stepping Stones School at *www.steppingstones.org.uk*

A Word From the
Head Teacher of Stepping Stones
by Melissa Farnham

How humbling to sit and write this short piece from the very room where Sir Arthur Conan Doyle composed such literary success. I feel that if a time machine were to bring his good self to the present, here today, he would be sitting across from me with a smile upon his face, emanating gratification and thanks . . . .

> *"Thank you for bringing my home to life again; a home where I could fulfil my passion and write. I can see a host of staff members that also have a passion, a passion to ensure that every young person now here, has an equal chance in life by way of academic endeavour and social grace."*

Society has not changed so much and neither has Undershaw. The enhancements that have come merely bring back to life an inspiring part of the Surrey landscape, whilst now accommodating aspirational young people to work and develop to become the changing faces of society. These/those young people that some have said "won't get there" are, thanks to this wonderful legacy, really achieving their true potential under our watch.

Melissa Farnham
Head Teacher, *Stepping Stones,* Undershaw
July 2016

Sherlock Holmes (1854-1957) was born in Yorkshire, England, on 6 January, 1854. In the mid-1870's, he moved to 24 Montague Street, London, where he established himself as the world's first Consulting Detective. After meeting Dr. John H. Watson in early 1881, he and Watson moved to rooms at 221b Baker Street, where his reputation as the world's greatest detective grew for several decades. He was presumed to have died battling noted criminal Professor James Moriarty on 4 May, 1891, but he returned to London on 5 April, 1894, resuming his consulting practice in Baker Street. Retiring to the Sussex coast near Beachy Head in October 1903, he continued to be involved in various private and government investigations while giving the impression of being a reclusive apiarist. He was very involved in the events encompassing World War I, and to a lesser degree those of World War II. He passed away peacefully upon the cliffs above his Sussex home on his 103rd birthday, 6 January, 1957.

Dr. John Hamish Watson (1852-1929) was born in Stranraer, Scotland on 7 August, 1852. In 1878, he took his Doctor of Medicine Degree from the University of London, and later joined the army as a surgeon. Wounded at the Battle of Maiwand in Afghanistan (27 July, 1880), he returned to London late that same year. On New Year's Day, 1881, he was introduced to Sherlock Holmes in the chemical laboratory at Barts. Agreeing to share rooms with Holmes in Baker Street, Watson became invaluable to Holmes's consulting detective practice. Watson was married and widowed three times, and from the late 1880's onward, in addition to his participation in Holmes's investigations and his medical practice, he chronicled Holmes's adventures, with the assistance of his literary agent, Sir Arthur Conan Doyle, in a series of popular narratives, most of which were first published in *The Strand* magazine. Watson's later years were spent preparing a vast number of his notes of Holmes's cases for future publication. Following a final important investigation with Holmes, Watson contracted pneumonia and passed away on 24 July, 1929.

The MX Book
Of
New Sherlock Holmes Stories

PART V
CHRISTMAS ADVENTURES

The Ballad of the Carbuncle
by Ashley D. Polasek

Since time unknown I had untouched slumber,
Crystalizing in faraway China.
I awoke to an ecstatic finder;
Thus began troubles of untold number.

I have seen nearly twenty Christmas days –
Murders, suicide, thievery join them.
In truth, to the season I've grown quite numb;
I'd lost hope I'd overcome my malaise.

In recent years I'd settled myself
In the care of the Countess of Morcar:
A gift from her lover who'd died afar
A *momento mori* to sorrow and wealth.

In early December, through frosted air,
I overheard a wicked scheme laid:
A lecherous man and a covetous maid
Planned a most un-Christmas-spirited snare.

A mere three days from the holiday morn –
How I wished I could have made the alarm –
An earnest young plumber came to harm
As on false evidence to jail was bourn.

This I witnessed from James Ryder's waistcoat,
Where the sweaty-palmed rifler had earlier slipped me.
He called the Yard and named Horner guilty,
Then rushed into the chill, I thought, to gloat.

Instead, we dashed madly down alley and street
As his breathing grew ever more ragged;
He cringed from each face we passed, the blackguard,
And slid wildly on ice under his feet.

The smell of cheap tobacco was acrid,
Mingled with that of impending snow,
While we paced a garden to and fro,
Sweating although the evening grew frigid.

Then, without warning, the villain freed me,
Pried open the bill of a struggling goose,
And though I have suffered much abuse,
Never have I felt such indignity!

With a squawk and a gulp I travelled down,
And with a ghastly, flapping drop,
Came to rest in a mythical crop,
Where, no doubt, he hoped I'd not be found.

To my surprise, he left me behind,
And soon after another came to call,
Took me to his Covent Garden stall,
Where the market bustled as Christmas bells chimed.

My foul new home was near frozen solid
When we moved next I was cosseted within;
At the end I overheard, "Alpha Inn,"
And hoped for a new home rather less squalid.

It had been two days, though felt much later –
The chatter told me it was Christmas Eve –
I hoped for a miracle; I mustered belief;
What I got was a chap called Henry Baker.

"Here," thought I, "is the fellow I've longed to meet,
"Surely he'll free me from my poultry prison,"
But no sooner had a ruckus arisen,
Than a crash left me, goose and all, in the street.

I lamented that there I would surely rot,
Alone and forgotten, buried in frost,
But, once again, I was not yet lost,
Rather gathered up by another, and off we shot.

A woman's voice spoke an incantation,
As though its spell could solve every ill,

22

"Take it to Mr. Holmes," she said with a thrill,
"Sherlock Holmes!" a man answered with elation.

After bumping and banging up seventeen stairs,
The tale was recounted of fight, flight, and bird,
"Leave the hat, eat the goose," came the crisp, cool word;
Just like that, I exited with the commissionaire.

That cold Christmas night my last hope had gone
All light had vanished without a trace;
Then my eyes beheld a warm womanly face –
The darkness had fled from my salvation's dawn!

A full day Peterson spent amazed,
Then back we went to the Baker Street marvel,
A haze of pipe smoke marked our arrival,
"A thousand pounds," Peterson muttered, dazed.

In Holmes's strong box, I felt safe and secure
Though still I was lonely and far from home;
I'd never realized how fond I'd grown
Of my Countess – I wished to fly back to her.

Later that evening a familiar voice
Came to collect his own Christmas goose;
I gathered it was part of a ruse
To learn whether he was involved in my heist.

Sent happy and hatted upon his way,
The sharp Mr. Holmes and his kindly friend
Made Baker's clue their next Christmas errand –
Silence fell as they scurried away.

Three sets of footfalls later entered the room
As soon as he spoke, I knew they'd found him:
The rat-faced weasel – that squirrely villain –
Who'd secreted me out of my lady's home.

Holmes held me up to Ryder's greedy eyes;
His tone was as icy as the winter outdoors,
"The game's up, this gem is clearly not yours,
"Tell the truth – it's straight to the docks if you lie."

He recounted to business, and spoke it all true,
Shocked, I heard, "Get out," spoken tersely,
And warmed in the light of Christmas mercy,
In that moment, I realized that now I knew.

Though I had suffered a wicked trial,
My suffering was a Christmas gift;
A husband still mended his marriage rift;
Another can treat his family in style.

A third, though it was a nasty business,
Is vindicated despite sins of old;
The last man is broken, but retains his soul,
And I understand the season of forgiveness.

The Case of the
Ruby Necklace
by Bob Byrne

I have told you, dear reader, of the first case I shared with Sherlock Holmes, which occurred in March of 1881. I recall well his comments to me just before we received Inspector Gregson's summons to Lauriston Gardens:

"Well, I have a trade of my own. I suppose I am the only one in the world. I'm a consulting detective, if you can understand what that is. Here in London we have lots of Government detectives and lots of private ones. When these fellows are at fault, they come to me, and I manage to put them on the right scent. They lay all the evidence before me, and I am generally able, by the help of my knowledge of the history of crime, to set them straight. There is a strong family resemblance about misdeeds, and if you can have all the details of a thousand at your finger ends, it is odd if you can't unravel the thousand and first."

"And these other people?" I asked, regarding the many strangers that visited our rooms for private sessions with Holmes. I had wondered if he were not some kind of fortuneteller and too embarrassed to tell me so.

"They are mostly sent on by private enquiry agencies. They are all people who are in trouble about something, and want a little enlightening. I listen to their story, they listen to my comments, and then I pocket my fee."

"But do you mean to say," I said, "that without leaving your room you can unravel some knot which other men can make nothing of, although they have seen every detail for themselves?"

"Quite so. I have a kind of intuition that way. Now and again a case turns up which is a little more complex. Then I have to bustle about and see things with my own eyes. You see I have a lot of special knowledge, which I apply to the problem, and which facilitates matters wonderfully. Observation with me is second nature."

I was at his side when he demonstrated his special knowledge and observational skills as he shone light on the mysterious deaths of Enoch J. Drebbor and his secretary, Joseph Stangerson. Inspectors Gregson and Lestrade of Scotland Yard were no closer to solving the mystery than was our not as yet long-suffering landlady, Mrs. Hudson.

25

While we became more comfortable as lodging mates, we still lived largely separate lives as that year wore on, though I confess I myself had little to occupy my time. The Army examined me and declared my health to be beyond serviceable status and I was discharged. With no possibility of being posted again as a military doctor, my ends could not have been looser.

Often, I had no idea where Holmes was, though he seemed uninterested in running here and there without what he deemed a specific purpose. I myself was prone to walks about the park as I attempted to recover from the wounds I had received at Maiwand. Holmes rarely accompanied me on these jaunts, and my solitary existence meandered along aimlessly.

221b certainly saw many comings and goings, though. Rarely did a week pass without at least one or two persons visiting our lodgings and asking Holmes for advice or guidance. Thus our Spring turned into Summer, Summer into Fall, and then the holiday season was upon us.

The cold weather caused my shoulder to ache and a feeling of listlessness seemed to have overtaken me the week before Christmas. Holmes had little use for the holiday, but I had allowed Mrs. Hudson to decorate our rooms a bit with a few pine spruces, pieces of holly, and some red bows. There were no stockings hung from the mantel, of course, but with a roaring fire, it was a cozy place with a little of the holiday spirit.

One evening I was comfortably ensconced in my chair, a copy of Anthony Trollope's *The Eustace Diamonds* in my hands. I found the tale to be less than compelling, though I admit I was hoping that Lizzie Greystock received her comeuppance. I fear I was making little progress, dozing off and on while attempting to continue my reading.

Holmes slouched in his own chair, puffing absentmindedly on his briar pipe. Since I had quickly learned that he chose the clay for deep meditation and his cherry-wood when he felt particularly disputative, I guessed that he was bored: his machine-like brain spinning to no purpose.

A knock at the door brought him out of his reverie and me out my half-sleep. "Come in, Jamison," he called out as I attempted to escape my state of torpor.

The door opened and in stepped a mustached man, wearing a bowler and a heavy overcoat. Both were wet from the light drizzle outside. "How could you know it was me, Holmes?"

Holmes waved a hand dismissively. "It's nothing, really. Were it not a member of the official force, Mrs. Hudson would have announced you herself, not merely sent you up on your own. And you always skip the seventeenth step. Thus I knew it was not Lestrade or Gregson."

He removed his hat, revealing thinning hair, showing gray around the edges. "Well then, nothing clever, I see."

Holmes smiled bleakly. "Merely observation and deduction. Two things in short supply. No, no, Watson, please stay." This was in response to my rising awkwardly and starting towards the door. It was my custom to leave when Holmes's visitors arrived.

"Inspector Jamison, you have not had the pleasure of meeting Doctor John Watson, late of her Majesty's Afghan service. He is my flat mate."

Jamison offered his hand, which I took. "Hello, Doctor." I exchanged a greeting and looked curiously at Holmes.

"I assume you have come with some little problem. Watson's advice could be of aid. He will respect your confidences, won't you, Watson?"

I admit that I straightened my shoulders with some pride as I returned to my seat. "Yes, yes, of course. Be glad to help if I can," I told the inspector earnestly.

He nodded his head politely and took off his coat, revealing an ill-fitting suit. Such seemed to be required of inspectors at the Yard. He draped the coat on a table and took a seat himself, declining my offer of a drink.

"Good of you, Doctor." He turned away from me. "Holmes. You know of Lord Bragington?"

The name was vaguely familiar to me, but Holmes instructed me to get the index book he kept which included subjects under the letter "B". These books, into which he pasted various articles and bits of information, were a valuable resource to him.

Book in his lap, he leafed through it. "Bar of Gold – there's an opium den of ill repute. Bertillon – brilliant fellow, though I believe there is a less cumbersome system yet to be developed. Oh. The Marquise de Brinvilliers. Poisoned her own family members. But that's too far. Ah, here it is."

He mumbled fragments aloud. "Wilifred Bragington. Financier. Trusted advisor to the government. Hmm . . . mm . . . mm."

He clapped the book shut and tossed it carelessly aside. "I see nothing to indicate trouble emanating from Bragington himself. What is your concern?"

Jamison stared into the fire. "Lord Bragington, his wife, and daughter were here at their London home for Christmas when he was summoned to Burma on the Crown's behalf. Lady Bragington and the daughter, Melissa, remained in town, with three other guests. The first was Alice Hitchcock, formerly Melissa's nurse, and now a friend."

"Nurse, you say? What is the young girl's condition?" I interjected. Holmes made no objection, so Jamison turned to me.

"Formerly, she was very depressed and laid about all day. Her mother said she had no energy or interest in anything."

I nodded my head. "Ennui. It is a lack of interest in life. Not fatal in itself, but if left untreated, the body is susceptible to various ailments. And of course, it can lead to serious depression, culminating in suicide attempts."

"The young lady had overcome her affliction, I presume, as this Miss Hitchcock is now her companion, rather than her nurse," Holmes added.

Jamison turned his attention back to him. "You've got it right, Holmes. Lady Bragington said they remained friends, and that seems to have helped keep her daughter's spirits up."

"And the other two guests?" So focused was I on the medical aspect of Jamison's tale I had forgotten about the other players in this unrevealed mystery.

"Yes, yes." Jamison removed a dog-eared notebook from his breast pocket and leafed through a few pages. "Jonathon Radwell. Late twenties, served in the military. He is quite glib. He is free and easy with his words, of the 'hail – well met' variety. He seems to be some kind of deal broker, but I've yet to determine what he actually does."

Holmes puffed on his pipe, sending blue smoke drifting towards the ceiling. "A source of mine at the Foreign Office has warned me to be wary of this new breed of financial brokers. Often there is no real foundation at the base of the 'propositions' into which they connive to draw their investors. There is much talk but little substance. Great amounts of money are apt to be lost." He paused. "I wonder if our Mister Radwell is one such?"

Holmes had mentioned an acquaintance at the Foreign Office once before, but he had provided no details. I wondered what position such a person might hold and how Holmes knew him.

"That's as may be, Mister Holmes, but I couldn't say. He's the one with this ruby necklace."

So saying, he handed Holmes an envelope. I watched my friend remove a silver necklace adorned with stunning rubies. The light from the fire reflected off a few of them and they seemed to burn from within. Holmes reached out for his magnifying glass and subjected the necklace to a thorough investigation. "I see that the setting has recently been worked upon."

Jamison nodded. "You have a good eye, Holmes. Radwell had just returned from Scotland, where he had the silver setting replaced." The detective returned the necklace to the envelope and handed it back to Jamison.

"Indeed, indeed. Most interesting."

I admit I found nothing at all interesting in this but remained silent.

"It seems that Radwell intimated that if Melissa Bragington accepted his suit, the necklace would be hers. Perhaps as a Christmas present or as an engagement gift. I don't believe that was made clear. But it was taken from his room and later found in Miss Hitchcock's room."

Holmes leaned forward, his eyes twinkling. "Excellent. You have my interest, Inspector. Everything in its order. What of the other guest?"

Jamison went back to his notebook. "Godfrey Stalwinn, employed by the firm of Hammersby, Odeon, and Nickwich." He paused to reflect upon the young man, looking for the right words. "I wouldn't call him taciturn, Holmes. Nor is he quite unfriendly. But his responses are always brief, and conversations with the man are filled with long pauses. I daresay a talk with him is the complete opposite of one with Radwell."

I snorted. "A man who does not like talk may not be best suited for a career at law, eh, Holmes?" Though I immediately thought of several solicitors whom I would prefer to be less voluble.

"Indeed, Watson."

"Did he have some gift for the young lady as well?" I interjected, wanting to contribute something more substantive.

"Nothing more than flowers, Doctor."

"Ah," I said, warming to the task. "Might not the morose young man have been upset with Radwell's extravagant one-upsmanship? Perhaps he snatched the necklace to stir things up and take some of the shine from the presence of the rubies?"

Holmes smiled. "A valid point, Watson, though what would he gain by hiding it in Miss Hitchcock's room?"

"Perhaps someone came down the hall and he was forced to duck into her room and hide it there?" I said, tentatively.

"No, no, Watson. That won't do at all."

Somewhat miffed, I resolved to remain silent for the next few minutes.

Holmes emptied his pipe into a copper bowl on the table next to him and set it down. "It all seems rather straightforward from your point of view, Jamison. Why have you sought me out?"

The inspector moved about in his chair. I wouldn't quite call it "squirming", but he seemed uncomfortable. "Yes, here's the thing. Miss Hitchcock is a niece of Sir William Gull."

"Aha!" Holmes fell back into his chair with a loud laugh.

"Really Holmes," I cried, my vow of silence discarded by need. "That's hardly a matter for joviality."

Inspector Jamison looked back and forth between Holmes and I, wondering what he had found himself in the middle of.

"Come now, Watson. If this were just some common nurse, I certainly doubt that Inspector Jamison would be seeking my help. But a relative of the Physician in Ordinary to the Queen? I daresay he needs to be absolutely certain that the case is airtight before prosecuting the young lady."

Jamison cleared his throat uncomfortably and leaned forward, iron in his voice. "Now see here, Holmes. If you're implying that I would see an innocent person . . . ."

Holmes raised a hand, palm outward, to stay Jamison. "No, no, Inspector. I assure you I am not besmirching your honor. But I know the, shall we say, difficulties and complexities when such an august personage may be involved. No matter how tangentially."

A smile of gratitude crossed the inspector's face and he sat back, voice softening. "You've got it exactly right, sir."

"She denies taking the necklace, of course?"

"Naturally, Holmes. She has no idea how it got in her room. Or so she says." Jamison's tone of voice indicated that he was not fully convinced of her innocence.

"She used to be a governess, found herself unemployed, and discovered a calling as a nurse. She apparently is a good one and worked wonders in bringing Melissa Bragington back to health. The two stayed friends, which is why she was invited for Christmas."

"Very close friends," I observed.

"Definitely so, Doctor. Lady Bragington is understandably unhappy with Miss Hitchcock. She told me that they treated her as if she were their own daughter."

"That is trusted, indeed. Why would she take the necklace?"

Jamison went back to his notebook. "Radwell presented the necklace after dinner one evening. Melissa Bragington tried it on, then gave it to Alice Hitchcock to do the same. Apparently the latter was quite taken with it. Lady Bragington even commented that it was better suited to her darker skin than to her daughter's."

Holmes began fiddling with his pipe again, tamping the tobacco in the bowl and lighting it once more. "I see," he said quietly between puffs.

Jamison stared at him blankly. "I don't see a thing, Holmes."

"You see, but you do not observe, Inspector. Just another piece of clay as we make our bricks to fashion a wall of evidence"

I was stunned to see Holmes look askance at me and wink! "Tell me: Did Alice Hitchcock or Lady Bragington report any change in behavior in young Melissa? Perhaps during her friend's visit?"

Jamison's jaw dropped. "It's witchcraft, it is. How could you know?"

"I am merely analyzing the data and making conjectures from it, Jamison. What one must always remember is that if the conjecture does not fit the data, one must either re-examine the data or discard the conjecture. I fear failure to do so is one of the greatest flaws in many of your colleagues."

Jamison puzzled out that he had not just been insulted. "Yes, it seems that the young lady began acting a bit erratic during the holiday visit. Her mood would swing between irritable and lethargic."

Holmes looked to me. "Your milieu, Doctor.

I paused for a moment of reflection. "It sounds as if she were in danger of a relapse. However, the irritability indicates that something specific was bothering her, preventing a malaise from completely overtaking her."

"Tell me, Jamison. Do you know when the changes in her personality occurred?"

More flipping through the notebook. "I believe the problems began shortly after Radwell shared the necklace."

"As I thought. Things take shape."

He gazed thoughtfully at the ceiling and silence reigned for several moments. "If, in fact, young Miss Hitchcock is guilty, then you already have enough evidence to convict her, Jamison. So let us posit that she is innocent and someone else took the necklace."

He quieted again as Jamison and I watched him, surprised at this change in direction.

"You have looked into the servants, of course?"

Jamison nodded. "Yes. That was our first thought, but we found nothing along that path."

"Was the necklace locked up in Radwell's room, Inspector?"

"Yes, in a drawer. Before you ask, there were only two keys. One kept in the butler's office and one with Radwell, who insisted he never left it off his chain."

"So, anyone with opportunity could have removed it from the butler's office, used it, and returned it?"

"I suppose so, Holmes, though the butler says that was unlikely."

"He would." We were silent and I took the opportunity to light a cigar. I did not yet prefer a pipe.

"I cannot imagine Lady Bragington stooping to theft from a guest, Holmes. And then, why would she hide the necklace in Miss Hitchcock's room?"

"Nobility is no bar to crime, Watson. But she does seem a less likely suspect. Of course, you have ascertained whether or not the necklace was insured?" Holmes asked, eyebrows raised.

"Well, err, not quite yet, Holmes. That was next on our list."

Holmes smiled at the inspector but chose not to comment on the man's obvious dereliction of duty.

"Radwell may have hidden the necklace to gain the proceeds of an insurance policy. But we shall proceed with our explorations."

"I should think that the other suitor, Stalwinn, would be a likely candidate."

"Oh you do, do you, Watson? Pray, elaborate."

I detected no insincerity in his comment, so I continued. "Well, as a suitor he seems to pale in comparison to Radwell. Less sociable and charming."

"Very good. Continue."

"And the introduction of the necklace most certainly injured his position. But if it were to disappear, he would regain some semblance of footing in the race to pursue Melissa Bragington."

Holmes smiled. "Well thought out, Watson. Though he certainly put himself at great risk. Were he caught, he would not be able to woo her from prison. I think he would need more motivation than that."

I sat back, a bit rankled at the dismissal of my theory. Jamison said nothing.

"Do you not see it, Jamison?"

"I see nothing, Mister Holmes. Nothing you've said makes it less likely that Alice Hitchcock is the thief."

"Really, Inspector." He shook his head sadly. "This is why you come to me. You have all the evidence I do. More, actually. Yet you fail to see the entire matter. Alice Hitchcock is guilty of nothing. Here is what you must do, just as I instruct."

Jamison and I listened as Holmes laid out the entire matter, to our stunned surprise.

It was the next evening that Jamison stopped by our rooms, accepting a cup of tea. Mrs. Hudson had left the service and I took one myself. Upon hearing our visitor, Holmes had come out of his room, wearing his purple dressing gown.

"What news, Jamison?"

The inspector put his cup on the side table at his elbow and smiled broadly. "It was just as you foretold, Mister Holmes. I gathered Alice Hitchcock, Radwell, Stallwin, and Lady and Melissa Bragington at the latter's house, just as you instructed.

"I told Radwell that we knew the stones were fakes and we were inquiring after his confederate in Scotland. Before he had a chance to deny it, Melissa Braginton wailed like a banshee and attacked him. He made to dash away before she reached him, but Stallwin, standing near the door, put him down with as nice a punch to the chin as I've seen in many a day."

Had Holmes not revealed his deductions to us the prior night, I would have been dumbstruck with surprise at this recounting of events.

"Alice Hitchcock moved to comfort her friend, but young Miss Bragington then began shrieking at her."

Here he paused and nodded approvingly at Holmes. "It was as you figured out. She had come to hate her friend. She accused her mother of loving Miss Hitchcock more than her, and said other unpleasant things. She had removed the spare key from the butler's office unnoticed, taken the necklace, hidden it in Miss Hitchcock's cabinet, and returned the key."

He shook his head. "But when she found out that she would be getting fake rubies by choosing Radwell, she broke down completely. Of course, we released Miss Hitchcock immediately."

"What made you suspect that the rubies were fakes, Holmes?" I asked. For he had not explained that last night.

"When the good Inspector related that Radwell had gone to Scotland to have the setting reworked, I considered the possibility. It would be perfectly natural to have such work done here in London. But if he wanted to replace the genuine rubies with fakes, then sell the originals, taking them north of the border would be sensible. My examination showed they were fine work, but still fakes."

Jamison nodded. "And as you suspected, Holmes, he had insured the necklace for a hefty amount."

"The scoundrel," I said. "So he likely planned to falsify their theft, so he would reap the benefits of secretly selling the genuine rubies and then collecting the insurance on the fakes."

"Yes. But then Melissa Bragington stole the necklace and pointed the finger of guilt to Alice Hitchcock by having it found in her room. He still would have profited from the sale of the actual rubies, but we put an end to that."

"What of the Bragington girl, Inspector?" I asked.

"Well, of course, the Bragingtons are quite an important family. And though she did not know it, the necklace she stole was a fake."

"Yes. One might say that in taking the necklace, she was preventing a crime, as it brought the matter to our attention, which prevented Radwell from proceeding with his insurance ruse."

At this early stage in our friendship, I could not yet read Holmes very well, and I often failed to distinguish when he was serious and when he was subtly goading.

Clearly, the inspector did not know, either. "Yes, I suppose that's one way to look at it sir."

I detected a twinkle in Holmes's eyes for just a moment.

"Anyways, Radwell wasn't in much of a position to proffer a charge." Jamison added.

"I hope that Lady Bragington realizes that her daughter needs specialized medical attention," I stated.

Jamison nodded gravely. "She certainly does, Doctor. If you had seen the lass attack Radwell." He shook his head and sighed. "She clearly was not in control of herself. Obviously, Miss Hitchcock will not be returning to her duties with the girl. I believe there was some discussion of sending young Bragington to a rest home in the country."

"Not a very merry Christmas, for that family, I daresay."

"No indeed, Doctor Watson. I understand that a summons was sent to Lord Bragington, but it will be some days before he returns from Burma. Lady Bragington is understandably not in a festive mood. Nor will Radwell be joyous. We have his accomplice in Scotland and will know all the details very soon."

"Fine work, Jamison. The Yard is unequalled at such tasks. I believe that Alice Hitchcock, though likely shaken by her experience, will have a better Christmas than she feared when she was in the cell."

Jamison talked for a time longer, and we learned that he had recently become a father. "He's going to be an inspector at the Yard, just like his old man, you can wager." He thanked Holmes one final time and departed. Later that evening, I complimented Holmes on how deftly he had solved the crime and saved an innocent woman from prison.

He paused from rosining his bow and gazed wistfully out the window. "You know, Watson, I grow tired of this armchair detecting. Perhaps if I was a grossly overweight genius with no ambition or desire to interact with the world around me, it would be suitable. Though I imagine such a person would be quite irritable."

He put away the rosin and scraped the bow across the strings. "But I crave more of a challenge. Such as the discoveries I made in that room at

Lauriston Gardens. I think that this case of the ruby necklace may be the last I take in which I merely analyze data and give advice."

He paused. "Imagine – had I revealed my deductions with all the parties in attendance. It would have resembled theater."

This gave me the first intimation that acting was in Holmes's soul, and as future cases proved, he embraced the drama inherent in his profession.

"Henceforth, I shall undertake cases which involve our leaving Baker Street."

I looked up in surprise. "'Our leaving', Holmes?"

He smiled. "If you are willing, of course. I find your stolidity a whetstone to my sharp-edged intellect."

You, good reader, will recognize the first incarnation of a sentiment that grew less than flattering over the years.

"Certainly. Any way that I can assist."

"Excellent. I think this is the beginning of a profitable partnership, Watson." With that, he began playing a medley of Christmas songs. To this day, I have never heard a more poignant version of "We Three Kings of Orient Are". Holmes could easily have been a first chair violinist in a leading orchestra if he had dedicated himself to the art.

I will add that on Christmas morn, we had a visit from Alice Hitchcock, accompanied by her fiancé. She could not have been more complimentary to Holmes for saving her, and the young couple gave each of us a pound of Fribourg and Treyer's finest tobacco!

Holmes was as good as his word, and he began undertaking more active cases, for which I am most grateful, as I cannot imagine my accounts of his exploits would have garnered the attention they have, had he simply reasoned from our sitting room at 221b Baker Street. Upon reflection, I would have to say it was the finest Christmas present I ever received.

So, I give you *The Case of the Ruby Necklace*. It was the last case in which Holmes was truly what he himself referred to as a consulting detective.

The Jet Brooch
by Denis O. Smith

During the years I shared chambers with Mr. Sherlock Holmes, the well-known criminal investigator, he handled many cases which involved the intimate private concerns of families whose names would be recognized by most readers of the daily Press. I have included but few of these in this series of records I have laid before the public, for obvious reasons. I would be guilty of gross indiscretion and a very great breach of confidence were I to even hint at the nature of some of these adventures, let alone provide a detailed account. Occasionally, however, when some time has elapsed since the events in question, and when I am able with a few little changes to disguise the identities of those involved, it is possible for me to give an account of one or two of these narratives, if I judge that the facts of the matter are of sufficient interest to warrant it. Such a tale is the one I shall now recount, an odd little tangle with a mysterious package at one end and a well-known song at the other.

It was the week before Christmas. The weather was cold, and I had awoken that morning to the rapid rat-a-tat-tat of hail against my bedroom window. Our breakfast finished, Sherlock Holmes had pulled the sofa a little nearer to the fire, and now lounged there in his old mouse-coloured dressing-gown, examining a small, flat package, about an inch in depth and three or four inches square, which had been delivered that morning.

"I wonder what this can be?" he remarked, turning it over in his hand, as I sat down on the other side of the fireplace. "I was not expecting anything today, so it is probably from a stranger."

"Why do you not open it and see?" I suggested.

"All in good time," said he. "I prefer to examine the outside first. It is easier to extract any information that may be there while the package is still intact. What do you make of it, Watson?" he asked, tossing it across to me.

"It is a little lighter than I had expected," I said, weighing it in my hand. "I thought it might have been a tin of tobacco, but I don't think it is heavy enough for that. It is wrapped in rather dull brown paper. This is not gummed in any way; it is simply fastened with string. It feels as if there is a small cardboard box inside the wrapping," I added, as I gave the package a gently squeeze.

"Anything else?"

"Not that I can see."

"The address?"

I looked again at the address. "Why," I said in surprise, "the house number has been missed off. It simply says 'Mr. Sherlock Holmes, Baker Street, London'."

"Precisely. We benefit from the fact that the postman has delivered so many letters to me in the year we have been living here that he knows where to find me, even when the address is incomplete. Now, I can't imagine that anyone who knew it would forget to include the house number in the address. It therefore seems likely that it was not known by the sender, who just trusted to luck that the parcel would find me. This supports my initial supposition that it is from a stranger, and someone, moreover, who was not in a position to find out my full address. Are there any more clues in the wrapping?"

"I don't think so," I replied after a moment.

"What about the string?"

"It is just a commonplace piece of thin twine," I said as I examined it.

"Not quite," said Holmes with a shake of the head. "It is certainly commonplace, but it is not one piece but three, which have been knotted together to make a suitable length."

"That is true, but is that of any significance?"

"Well, it suggests either someone who is very parsimonious with his string – using short pieces that most people would probably have thrown away – or perhaps a servant or other employee who has used discarded string – perhaps rescued from a waste-paper basket – to avoid being accused of using his employer's property for his own purposes."

"It is possible."

"Next we come to the handwriting itself, which, as you see, is in pencil. It seems to me it is a woman's hand. Why the handwriting of men and women should differ in so distinctive a way, I do not know – it is a mystery I have not yet solved – but that they do so differ is undeniable. Of course, each hand has its own idiosyncrasies and not all women write in this way, but I have never yet encountered a single man whose hand was like this. Therefore, we are probably justified in saying it is the hand of a woman. It is clear enough, but not very regularly formed, so it may be the hand of a young person, although that inference cannot be drawn with the same degree of confidence. As to what you describe as dull brown paper, I think it is simply ordinary brown paper turned back to front, with the shiny side on the inside and the dull side on the outside. This suggests someone using old paper, and accords with the inferences we drew from the knotted string. Let us now open the package and see what it contains!"

He took a small pen-knife from the little table by his elbow, neatly cut the string, and slipped it from the packet. Then he unwrapped the brown paper and examined it closely for a moment. "This piece has been cut – rather hurriedly to judge from the irregular shape – from a larger sheet. It is indeed a used piece of paper, for on the other side there is another address, written in ink, in a different hand. I rather fancy that my mysterious correspondent has used this ingenious method to indicate where the package has come from."

He passed me the paper and I saw that the address on the back of it was *"Sir George Datchett, 8 Cumberland Gardens, Kensington"*, although the name on the first line had been crossed through with a pencil. Holmes, meanwhile, was carefully lifting the lid from the cardboard box which had been wrapped in the paper. As he did so, he let out a cry of surprise, and I saw that the box was full to the brim with some white powder. He licked his finger, pushed it into the powder and tasted it.

"It is flour," said he, "perfectly ordinary flour. If you would pass me a piece of paper from the desk, Watson, I will tip it out and see if there is anything else beneath the flour."

I laid the sheet of paper on the hearth-rug and watched as my companion carefully tipped the flour onto it. All at once, a small, dark object fell out onto the little heap of flour. He picked it up, blew off the loose flour, then rubbed it on the sleeve of his dressing-gown. As he held it up, I saw that it was an ornate brooch. In the centre was a circular black disc, the size of a large coin, its surface faceted so that it caught the light with each slight movement, and around the edge was a golden rim in which the metal was teased into fantastic little twirls and curls.

"The stone in the middle looks like jet," I said.

My friend nodded his head. "Yes, and the setting is gold. It looks quite a valuable piece of jewellery." He passed me the brooch, and lifted the lid of the box to his nose. "There is a distinctive smell to this box," he said.

"Of what?"

"Soap. Scented soap. Quite expensive, I should say, as might be used in a fairly well-to-do household. Now, why should anyone send me a jet brooch without explanation, packed in flour in an old soap-box? Ah!"

He leaned over and extracted a tiny scrap of paper from the little heap of flour on the floor. The paper was of a rough, irregular shape and appeared to have been torn from the edge of a sheet of newspaper.

"Perhaps this will make things clearer," said my companion, but his face remained impassive as he examined it, and, with a frown, he passed it to me.

Upon the scrap of paper, just three words were written in pencil: *"Please help me"*.

"That does not tell us much," I remarked.

"No," said Holmes. "It is written in the same hand as the address, and with the same pencil, but that is no more than one would expect."

"I wonder why the box has been filled with flour."

"Presumably to prevent the brooch from rattling about. The use of flour suggests someone who has access to a kitchen, or, to look at it another way, someone who does not have access to any more usual packing material, such as cotton wool. To sum up, then, our mysterious correspondent is probably female, probably young, and probably a domestic servant in a well-to-do household, who has read or heard my name somewhere and believes I may be able to help her. In what way she requires help we cannot say. It may have something to do with this brooch, but that is not certain. The brooch may be simply a deposit to secure my services – although it seems an unlikely piece of jewellery for a young housemaid to have in her possession."

"I was just thinking the same," I remarked. "It looks like something an older woman might wear."

As I was speaking there came a ring at the front-door bell. A few moments later, our landlady appeared in the doorway to inform us that a lady had called to see Mr. Sherlock Holmes, but had declined to give her name.

"One moment, Mrs. Hudson," said Holmes, springing to his feet. "I shall just restore a little order, and then you can show her up." Carefully, he picked up from the floor the sheet of paper on which lay the little heap of flour and carried it over to his desk. I gathered together the brown paper, string and cardboard box and handed them to him. These, together with the brooch and scrap of paper, he also placed on his desk and closed the lid. "Now," said he, as he pulled the sofa back from the fire, "I think we are ready to receive our visitor."

The woman who was shown into our room a few moments later was tall and stately in her bearing. Although of middle age, she had retained the figure and posture of a younger woman. She was wearing a very smart dark blue costume with yellow piping on the edges.

"Pray, take a seat," said Holmes, indicating the chair beside the hearth, "and let us know what we can do for you."

"No, thank you," returned our visitor in a firm tone. "I shall not be here for more than a few moments. I have simply called to collect something."

"Oh?" said Holmes in surprise. "And what might that be?"

"A brooch," said she. "My brooch. It has been sent here in error. The wrong address was written on the package."

"Did you address it yourself?"

"No. Someone else did."

"To whom should it have been sent?"

"To the jeweller. The clasp needs repairing."

"Well," said Holmes, "so far as I am aware, we have received no misaddressed parcels here."

"You must have; it was posted yesterday."

Holmes shook his head. "It is but a few days to Christmas, madam," said he, "and you must know what that means for postal deliveries. The sorting-offices have mailbags piled up to the ceiling, and everything takes longer than usual. If you would give me your name and address," he continued, taking up his note-book and pencil from the table, "I shall let you know if any misaddressed parcel arrives here."

The woman hesitated. "No," said she. "I shall call again tomorrow."

She had turned to leave us, but stopped as Holmes spoke again.

"It seems strange to me," said he, "that you should have my address at all. Do you – or anyone in your household – wish me to look into some problem for you?"

"Absolutely not," she returned sharply. "It is no concern of yours how the mistake was made. I simply wish you to return to me the package when I call again. Do you understand?"

"Understanding is not the issue here, madam," returned Holmes in an urbane tone. "Rather, it is a matter of proof. You will call again and expect me to hand over to you something I have received in the post. But how do I know you have any right to the object in question? For all I know, the brooch may have been stolen – possibly by you. If so, the rightful owner would scarcely thank me for handing it over to someone I have never met before and who refuses to give me her name."

Our visitor's face blanched perceptibly. "How dare you make such an impertinent remark!" she cried in a sharp tone. She appeared about to say more, but bit her lip and was silent for a moment, breathing very heavily. "I shall return tomorrow," she said at length, scarcely able to get the words out as her breast rose and fell with emotion, "and shall bring a pair of ear-rings with me that you will see exactly match the brooch." With that, she turned on her heel and left the room, slamming the door as she did so.

"What a very entertaining interview!" said Holmes after a moment.

"She appeared to be one used to having her instructions obeyed," I remarked, "but she also seemed very emotional about something."

Holmes nodded his head. "More than that," said he; "she is in a state of extreme anxiety. About what, I do not know – but I intend to find out. Of course, what she told us is a tissue of lies: there is nothing wrong with the clasp on the brooch, as I could see when I examined it."

"Will you follow her, to see where she goes?" I asked.

Holmes shook his head. "I am confident that the address on the reverse of that brown paper is pertinent to the matter. That is where I shall go."

He disappeared into his bedroom and did not emerge again for fifteen minutes. I looked up from the newspaper I was reading as he did so and received a shock. In the place of the neatly turned out fellow-lodger I had expected to see, there stood a disreputable-looking figure with a tangled beard, wearing an old, threadbare jacket and cap and a pair of ill-fitting corduroy trousers. The appearance was completed by a bright check muffler that was knotted round his neck.

"Is that you, Holmes?" I queried, not entirely in jest.

"Yes, Watson, it is I," returned he. "It is not only villains who can adopt disguises in order to pursue their ends. I am off to do a little research, and have adopted the character of Jack Brown, itinerant knife-grinder, which I believe will serve me the best."

"Knife-grinder?" I cried with a chuckle. "But you haven't got a grinding-wheel!"

"True, but that is not an insuperable obstacle. I have a small grindstone, at least," he continued, producing a cylindrically-shaped stone from an inside pocket. "That may suffice for my purposes. Now, I can't say when I shall be back, but I should be obliged if you would save me a little bread and cheese from your mid-day meal, as I may not have much opportunity to eat while I am out!"

With a little salute he was gone, and I was left to wonder what it was he intended to do. For a time I tried to distract my thoughts with the day's newspapers, but they contained little of interest and I soon found my thoughts returning once more to the strange business my companion was involved in.

It seemed likely to me that the brooch really did belong to our morning visitor, but as Holmes had remarked, it did not appear to be in need of repair. Why, then, had it been sent anywhere at all, and why, in particular, had it been sent to Holmes? Our visitor did not appear to have sent it herself, but how, then, did she know it had been sent to our

41

address? Who had sent it and why? Did our visitor know who had sent it or not? Why was she so determined to withhold her own name?

One thing that seemed evident was that she did not want Holmes to learn anything of the facts surrounding the brooch, but Holmes, it was clear, was equally determined that he would uncover these facts. He had had a tiny message in the package he had received, pleading for his help, and he needed no further persuasion than that. As I was beginning to learn, it was only rarely that he refused his help when it was sincerely requested. This generosity of spirit put enormous demands upon his constitution, demands that would have quite exhausted another man, but which seemed only to spur my friend on to greater industry.

I should not wish my readers to think that I was excessively self-absorbed, but as I reflected on my fellow-lodger's intense and energetic activity, I was led inevitably to a consideration of my own contrasting circumstances. Little more than a year had passed since I had been invalided home from the war in Afghanistan, and I had stepped onto the jetty at Portsmouth with my health seemingly ruined forever. That had, in truth, not proved to be the case: I was definitely in somewhat better health now than I had been twelve months previously; but the slightest over-exertion was still likely to reduce me to the state of a limp rag. In these circumstances, I had come to look to Sherlock Holmes and his work to provide the zest and interest in my life which I could not provide for myself. I had begun to keep notes of his cases and had on a few occasions been able to accompany him on his investigations, although that was not always possible. Now, as I pondered the mystery of the jet brooch, I found myself glancing frequently at the clock on the mantelpiece, wondering when my friend would return, and if he would have managed to learn anything of the matter.

It was the middle of the afternoon before I heard Holmes's characteristically rapid footsteps ascending the stair. I could see at once, from the expression on his face, as he burst into the room like a whirlwind, that he had had some success.

"The bread and cheese is on the table, under the cloth," I said.

"Good man!" said he. "I am famished! I shall just remove this beard, which has begun to irritate me, and be with you in a moment. Do you know if we have any beer in the house at present?"

"Yes," I said. "There are some bottles of pale ale in the cupboard. I'll open one for you."

A few minutes later, he returned from his bedroom. The beard had gone, along with the grimy jacket and cap, and he had donned his old dressing-gown once more.

"Now," said he, as he laid into his simple meal with gusto, "I dare say you are wondering what I have discovered."

"I have been able to think of little else."

Holmes laughed. "Yes, it is an intriguing little problem, is it not! You will be interested to know, then, that I have learned a great deal – although there are still one or two small points that are not clear to me.

"I made my way to Cumberland Gardens, in Kensington. It is a short, handsome street, with plane trees along the sides. The houses are very smart, all in white stucco, and clearly the homes of the wealthy. I began my investigation by simply loafing about there and striking up a conversation with anyone who seemed likely to respond. I make a grand loafer, Watson, even if I say so myself. It seems to come naturally to me. Gradually, through conversation with some of the ostlers in the nearby mews, a man delivering vegetables from his cart, and numerous other people, I was able to accumulate information about the occupants of Number Eight. Needless to say, I also gathered information about the occupants of Numbers Two, Four, Six and Ten, which I endeavoured to forget as soon as I had heard it.

"Head of the household at Number Eight is Sir George Datchett, who was one of the founders of the Sea Eagle Marine Insurance Company, and who was knighted just two months ago for his services to commerce. His wife is Lady Hilary Datchett, and from the description I was given of her, I am fairly certain it was she who called upon us this morning. The family is completed by a son, Michael, aged about twenty, who is up at Oxford but returned home for the Christmas vacation two weeks ago, and a daughter, Olivia, who is seventeen and in her final year at the Cheltenham Ladies' College. She returned home last week. The domestic staff at the Datchett household consists of a butler, who organizes the household, a cook, a kitchen-maid, and a chambermaid.

"Having amassed this information, I abandoned my loafing about and called at the tradesman's entrance of Number Eight, where I offered my services as a knife-grinder. This was rejected, much as I had expected, but I did not give up.

"'My dear lady,' I said to the cook, who had answered the door to me. I was about to extol the benefits of having sharpened knives, but she interrupted me.

"'Don't you be so bold,' said she. '"Dear lady" indeed!' But she laughed nonetheless, and I could see that by amusing her I had gained a small foothold. I thereupon offered to sharpen a pair of scissors for her free of charge, 'to demonstrate the worth of my technique', as I put it. This she assented to, in grudging fashion, and I had thereby gained a few more minutes of standing in the kitchen doorway, which was of course my aim.

"As I did my best to sharpen the scissors a little, I chatted with her and watched as she and the kitchen-maid – who appeared to be called Lily – bustled about their work. When I'd finished, I declared that it was 'thirsty work' and asked if I might have a cup of water, which she brought me. Up to that point, to speak frankly, I hadn't really learned anything very useful, but all at once things changed. Another girl came into the kitchen in a maid's uniform. She was there for only a few moments, picked something up and left again, but in that few moments I thought I might have found my way to the heart of the mystery. I was already fairly confident, if you recall, that the brooch and the request for help had been sent to me by someone who was young, female, and a domestic servant. Neither the cook nor the kitchen-maid looked likely to be so imaginative or enterprising, and the butler could surely be ruled out. But in the few moments the other housemaid had been in the kitchen, she had glanced across to where I stood, in the doorway. For half a second, our eyes had met, and in that half-second I had seen an unusual depth and intelligence in her eye. Surely, I thought, this was my mysterious correspondent! I might also add that she was quite exceptionally pretty and attractive."

"I thought you always said," I interrupted, "that the appearance of your clients was a matter of complete indifference to you."

"Yes, of course, that is true when their appearance is irrelevant to the case, as it generally is; but there are odd occasions when a woman's appearance is not simply an irrelevant, peripheral matter, but a central feature of the case, and I found myself wondering if this might not be one such instance. Sometimes, a pretty face in a household or other group of people can have an effect akin to the tossing of a small pebble into a placid mill-pond: ripples are created which, although sometimes scarcely discernible, can reach a long way.

"'That girl who was in here just now,' I said to the cook as I sipped my cup of water, 'I believe I may know her. Is it not Susan, who used to be in the household of Lady Darlington?'

"'No, it ain't,' said the cook. 'It's Jane, who didn't use to be in anybody's household.'

"'Of course,' I said, 'but I do know her from somewhere. Is it Jane Robinson?'

"'No it ain't. It's Jane Page – and how would a shabby-looking fellow like you know someone as sweet as Jane?'

"I was saved from having to answer that question by the reappearance of the girl herself.

44

"'Here, Jane,' said the cook. 'This dirty-looking scoundrel reckons he knows you from somewhere. Do you know him?'

"The girl looked across the kitchen at me, a very dubious expression on her face. 'I don't think so,' she said.

"I glanced at the cook. She had turned away to put something in the sink, and I took the opportunity to take a card from my pocket and held it out so that the girl could see it.

"She took a step closer. 'You don't look like I thought you would,' she said in a doubtful tone.

"I leaned in at the kitchen door. The cook and the kitchen-maid were still occupied at the other side of the room. I dropped the rough accent I had assumed in my guise as a knife-grinder and, lowering my voice, I said, 'I'm in disguise. I've come in answer to your request for help. Quickly! Tell me what has happened!'

"She came to the kitchen-door and stuck her head out so that she would not be heard by the others. 'That brooch,' she began.

"'Yes? Is it Lady Hilary's?'

"'Yes. Someone put it in my box.'

"'Where was that? At the foot of your bed?'

"'Yes. And then Lady Hilary found it was missing from her jewellery-case, and asked me if I had seen it anywhere. I said I hadn't, but it was in my pocket. I was walking round all day with it in there, trying to think what to do with it. I couldn't tell her where I'd found it – she'd just think I'd stolen it. But I couldn't just put it back in her room, either, as she told me she'd looked all round there – on the dressing-table and on the floor underneath it. Then I thought of you. Mr. Boardman – '

"'Is that the butler?'

"'Yes. He'd read us out a report in the newspaper one evening of how Sherlock Holmes of Baker Street had solved some mysterious burglary when nobody else could, and I thought perhaps you could help me.'

"'I'll try. Who do you think might have put the brooch in your box? Are any of the other servants jealous of you?'

"'Oh, no,' she returned in surprise. 'We all get on famously. Hardly ever a cross word.'

"'Your master and mistress?' I asked. 'Do they treat you well? Are you happy here?'

"'Oh, yes,' she replied quickly. 'It's like Heaven. Sir George is the kindest man I've ever known.'

"'And Lady Hilary?' I asked as she paused.

"'She can be a bit sharp sometimes,' Jane replied, lowering her voice a little more, 'but I think she's quite nice underneath.'

"'The children?'

"'I never see much of Miss Olivia. She's been away at school all the autumn and only came home at the end of last week. She seems nice enough.'

"'And the son?' I asked as the girl hesitated.

"'He's very good looking, and they tell me he's quite clever.'

"'But?'

"'He's a bit bold sometimes. One night last week, I think he'd had a little too much to drink and got a bit over-familiar with me, if you know what I mean. I told him it was wrong, but he wouldn't take "no" for an answer, and I had to push him away. I was worried after that that I'd get into trouble.'

"'When did you find the brooch in your box?'

"'Just yesterday morning. Then, about tea-time, Sir George gave me some letters to post for him. I put them on the hall table and went downstairs to get my hat and coat. While I was downstairs, I had the idea of sending the brooch to you, so I put it in an old soap-box, filled it up with flour to stop it rattling about, and wrapped it up.'

"'Could anyone have learned where you sent it? Did anyone see you writing the address?'

"'No, I'm sure they didn't.'

"'Did you perhaps leave it somewhere unattended for a few moments?'

"'No – wait! – I did! When I got back up to the hall, I realized I'd not got my gloves, so I put the little packet on top of Sir George's letters and ran back downstairs to get them. It was only for a few seconds, though, and there was nobody about in the hall.'

"'But someone might have passed through the hall, and seen the packet lying there?'

"'I suppose so. But I didn't see anyone.'

"At that moment, the butler, Boardman, entered the kitchen and put an end to our discussion by asking what I wanted. I told him I was a knife-grinder, he said they didn't need any knives grinding and that was that. I thanked them for the water, gave the cup back to Jane, and wandered off.

"I then loitered near the end of the street for some time, sitting on a low wall, smoking my old clay pipe. I was just deciding what to do next when my mind was made up for me. The front door of the Datchett's house opened, and out stepped a smart and fashionably-dressed young man who proceeded along the pavement, tapping his cane as he went. I followed him until I judged we were far enough from the house that our encounter would not be visible from there.

"'Excuse me,' I said.

"'No, I haven't got any small change that I can spare,' he responded, scarcely glancing in my direction, and evidently taking me for some sort of beggar.

"'I don't want any,' said I.

"'Then you should be very happy that I'm not going to give you any,' said he, without breaking stride.

"I could see that the only way I could halt his progress long enough to speak to him would be to surprise him, so I again dropped my rough accent and in my ordinary voice simply said, 'Michael Datchett?'

"He stopped abruptly and turned to me. 'Who the devil are you, and how do you know my name?' he demanded.

"'It is my business to know things,' I said, and gave him my card.

"'Well, Mr. Sherlock Holmes,' said he as he handed back my card, 'what is it you want?'

"'I am looking into a matter concerning Jane Page.'

"'What, Jane the housemaid?' he cried in surprise. 'What has she done?'

"'She hasn't done anything. On the contrary, things have been done to her.'

"'Such as?'

"'You have recently forced your unwanted attentions upon her.'

"'Oh, I see,' said Datchett. 'That is what she told you, is it? Well, Mr. Sanctimonious Holmes, you don't want to believe everything you are told.'

"'Do you deny it?'

"'No. Why should I? What I dispute is the term "unwanted". The whole matter is, in any case, an utter trifle.'

"'And now someone has stolen something from the house and placed it among Miss Page's possessions, with the evident intention of getting her accused of theft and thus dismissed, or even charged with the matter in a court of law.'

"'Surely it is more likely, if anything is stolen, that she has stolen it herself.'

"'If so, she would hardly have told me about it.'

"'You might think that, but you can never tell what people might do. Look, if she's taken a silver tea-spoon from a cutlery drawer in the kitchen, or whatever it is, just tell her to put it back where she found it and no-one will be any the wiser. I certainly won't mention it to anyone. Now I really must be off.'

"He turned away, but I persisted. 'It would be natural to wonder if the attempt to incriminate her was a form of revenge, perhaps perpetrated by someone whose advances had been rebuffed.'

"'"Revenge"?' he repeated in an incredulous tone, then burst out laughing. 'Why on earth should I want dear Jane dismissed? Christmas is coming. In two or three days, there will be bunches of mistletoe hanging up, and then she will be obliged to accept a kiss from me. You can't go against the venerable traditions of antiquity, you know! You'll see – or, at least, she will!' With that, he turned away once more, and I was left to ponder the matter further."

"With any result?" I asked.

My friend shook his head. "There are several possibilities," he replied, "with little in the way of evidence to indicate which is true."

"What will you do, then?"

"I really think I shall have to go round to the Datchetts' house this evening and try to force matters to a conclusion. If I don't, Lady Hilary will call here again tomorrow morning and I shall have to give her the brooch. She will then take it away with her and the mystery will remain unresolved. For all we know, Miss Page might then be dismissed from her position, and that is not something I can contemplate with equanimity."

Holmes fell silent then for several minutes, and it was apparent he was considering the matter from every different point of view. "Would you care to accompany me?" he asked abruptly.

I was somewhat taken aback by this sudden and surprising invitation. "I think I should like that," I replied, "if I would not be in your way."

"Not at all," said my friend. "I think it would be interesting for you to see what I hope will be the final act in this little drama. It will be best if we call when the family are all present, but before they sit down to dine, so be ready to leave just after six. Make yourself as neat as possible, Watson, and I will do the same. We must make a favourable initial impression or we may not be seen at all."

It was starting to snow as we took a cab from Baker Street, and as we rattled along through the dark, raw evening, the street lamps we passed served only to illuminate the whirling and tumbling snowflakes which filled the air. By the time we reached Kensington, just after half-past six, I could see that the snow was beginning to settle.

The front door of the Datchetts' house was opened to us by a large and imposing-looking butler who took Holmes's card into a room on the left while we waited in the hall. A moment later, the door opened and the butler re-emerged, followed by a pleasant-faced, grey-haired man of about fifty, who held Holmes's card in his hand.

"What is this about, gentlemen?" he enquired in a puzzled tone, as he closed the door behind him.

"Something odd has happened to a member of your household," replied Holmes, "and I have been trying to help. I am here to conclude the matter."

Datchett frowned. "Perhaps we should continue this discussion in the study," said he, indicating a door on the opposite side of the hall.

"Excuse me, Sir George, but are your family all in the drawing-room?"

"Yes, they are, as it happens. We were just chatting, and are about to dine shortly. Why do you ask?"

"I think it would be better if I said what I have to say in front of everyone. It will not take very long."

"Who is principally concerned in the matter?"

"Your maid, Jane Page."

"Has she done something she shouldn't have?"

"No."

"Very well," said Datchett after a moment's hesitation, "if you think it best. But be aware that I am only agreeing to this because I have heard something of you, and your reputation is that of a gentleman. I do not want any unpleasantness. My wife detests anything of that sort, and my daughter is still a schoolgirl. Do you understand?"

Holmes nodded his head but did not reply, and, after a moment, Datchett opened the drawing-room door and we followed him into the room.

"This is Mr. Sherlock Holmes and his colleague, Dr. Watson," said Datchett, as his wife, son, and daughter turned towards us, their features expressing surprise. "They have something to tell us. Go ahead, Mr. Holmes," he continued as he seated himself on a sofa.

"I will be as brief as possible," Holmes began. "Your maid, Jane, found a valuable piece of jewellery – a jet brooch – among her own possessions the other day, which she recognized as belonging to her mistress. She had no idea how it got there. Before she could do anything about it, Lady Hilary found that the brooch was missing. Frightened that she would be accused of stealing it, and unable to think what to do with it, Jane, on the spur of the moment, parcelled it up and sent it to me. This removed the immediate danger from her, by getting the brooch out of the house. No doubt she also thought that my involvement might lead to the truth being revealed.

"Unfortunately for her, Lady Hilary learned where she had sent the brooch. I assume, madam," he continued, addressing Lady Hilary, "that you saw the package lying on the hall table."

"That is correct. I happened to pass through the hall, and as I did so I glanced at some items on the table that were awaiting posting. Most of them, I could see, were letters my husband had written, but there was also a small package which appeared to have been addressed in a different hand. When I mentioned it to my husband later, he said he knew nothing about it."

"You then conjectured that it might have contained the brooch?"

"Yes, from the size and shape of the package."

"When you called at my chambers this morning and gave me some rigmarole about the brooch needing repair, you did not assume I was involved in the theft of the brooch, or consider calling the police?"

"No, of course not. Like others, I have heard of you as one who solves crimes, not commits them."

"And yet, you presumably felt sure by then that it was Jane who had sent the brooch to me."

"Yes. What of it?"

"Do you believe that Jane stole the brooch?"

"No."

"Why not?"

"Because I don't believe it is in her character to do such a thing."

"Well, if Jane did not place the brooch under her own pillow, then someone else did. She was led, understandably, to the conclusion that someone had deliberately tried to incriminate her, so she would be accused of theft and dismissed, a conclusion with which I entirely concur. If you did not believe that Jane had stolen it, you must surely have reached the same conclusion. There is no other possibility."

Lady Hilary hesitated a moment, and glanced at her husband as if for support, but the expression on his face was one of complete mystification, and it was evident she could receive no assistance from that quarter.

"I repeat," Holmes persisted, "if Jane did not remove the brooch from your jewellery-case, then someone else did, and I believe you know who that someone is, which is why you were so keen to hush the matter up, and had no intention of pressing charges against Jane."

"Oh, all right," said Lady Hilary abruptly in a sharp tone, rising to her feet. "I took the brooch myself. I was looking for a way of dismissing her. I felt my husband was becoming too fond of her, and that she was almost eclipsing his own children in his eyes."

"What nonsense!" cried her husband.

"But when I realized she had sent the brooch to you," Lady Hilary continued, ignoring the interruption, "I decided it had all got out of hand. I just wanted to get the brooch back, brush the whole business under the carpet, and forget about it."

"So, let us be clear about it," said Holmes. "You yourself took the brooch from your jewellery-case, and you yourself placed it under the pillow on Jane's bed?"

"Yes, I did. So now you know everything."

"Unfortunately, I do not."

"What do you mean?"

"Madam, you are not speaking the truth."

"How dare you call me a liar in my own house!"

"The house is irrelevant. I know you are not speaking the truth, madam, because you say it was you that placed the brooch under Jane's pillow, and I know you did not do so. I know you did not do so because no-one did so: Jane did not find the brooch under her pillow, but in the box at the foot of her bed."

"It is no good, Mother," said Olivia Datchett, speaking for the first time since we had entered the room. "He has tricked you." She rose to her feet. "Mother is trying to protect me," she said, addressing Holmes, her voice breaking with emotion. "It was I that took the brooch, and I that placed it in Jane's box."

"Olivia!" cried her father. "Surely you would not stoop to such a low, mean trick!"

At this, the girl burst into tears. "It's true," she said, between sobs. "It was mean of me, and stupid, and I am very, very sorry."

I took a handkerchief from my pocket and passed it to her, as no-one else seemed to be doing so, and she dabbed her eyes.

"Can this really be true, Hilary?" asked Datchett.

"Yes," replied his wife. "Olivia came to me and asked if I had seen the jet brooch recently, as she said she had been trying to find it and couldn't see it anywhere. But there had been an odd expression on her face as she spoke to me, and all the time I was looking for the brooch, I suspected that she herself had had something to do with its disappearance. Eventually, in the evening, I confronted her with my suspicions and she admitted the truth. I then remembered the package I had seen on the hall table, and told her I was fairly certain I knew where the brooch had gone. I said I would try to get it back the next morning, so we could put the matter behind us and forget it had ever happened. Unfortunately, things did not work out so simply as that."

The room fell silent for a moment then, until, with a bewildered shake of the head, Datchett addressed his daughter. "Whatever can have possessed you, Olivia, to do such a thing? What has Jane ever done to cause you displeasure?"

"Mother told me in a letter that you have arranged for a special tutor to come in to coach Jane in English and arithmetic."

"And you were jealous of the attention? It is only one afternoon a week, Olivia – I am not sending her to the Cheltenham Ladies' College! She is an intelligent girl, and works very hard. I thought it was the least I could do. She has great potential, and could make someone a good housekeeper one day – or a good wife."

"Then, in Mother's last letter, she said that Jane had been singing so beautifully that it had made you cry."

"Oh, that!" Lady Hilary interrupted. "I only put that in the letter to amuse you, Olivia. You know what Father is like: he cries when he hears sad songs, he cries when he sees a sad play, and sometimes he even cries when he sees a happy play! It is just his way, and I am sure we would not want him any different!"

"He never cries when I sing," said Olivia through her sobs.

"Ah! I see!" said her father in a tone of enlightenment. "Now I think I understand! Sit down, sit down, both of you – and you, too, gentlemen – and I will tell you something you do not know. Perhaps then you, too, will understand matters a little better." He closed his eyes for a few moments, as if gathering his thoughts, before continuing.

"When Jane was just a tiny baby," he began at length, "she was left at the foundling hospital. Neither she, nor anyone else, has any idea who her mother and father were. She was simply left one morning on the doorstep in a little wicker basket. A few months later, she was adopted by an elderly couple called Page from the East End, who gave her the name of Jane. The man worked as a cobbler, and apparently did all right for himself, but just a few years later, both Mr. and Mrs. Page fell ill and died within a few months of each other. Thus, the only family little Jane had ever known had been taken from her. She was only five years old at the time. Mrs. Page's sister took her in for a little while, but she herself was elderly and could not cope with the child, and less than a year later she gave her up and she was placed in an orphanage. After a time, she was moved from that orphanage to another, and, later, to a third. In all, she remained in such institutions for nearly ten years.

"Two years ago, when we needed a new chamber-maid, Jane was recommended to me. I agreed to take her almost as soon as we had met, for I could see at once that she showed great promise, and I have not been disappointed. Despite her unfortunate and unhappy childhood – which might have embittered or spoiled the character of some people –

she has fitted in to our household very well, and gets along well with everyone.

"Now I come to what occurred two weeks ago. I was in my bedroom early one evening, changing for dinner. My bedroom, as you know, overlooks the back garden, and through the window I could see that it was a dark, cold evening. All at once, as I stood before the mirror, buttoning my shirt, I heard someone singing in the garden below. I looked out, and there, illuminated by a light from the kitchen window, was Jane. She was putting some rubbish in the dustbin – not the most pleasant of jobs at the best of times – and singing softly and sweetly to herself. And do you know what she was singing, this girl who has never had any family, nor anywhere she could ever call her home? She was singing *Home, Sweet Home* – 'Mid pleasures and palaces though we may roam; be it ever so humble, there's no place like home.'

"As I stood there listening, I knew that the home she referred to was our house, that we had, without particularly intending it, given Jane the first real home she had ever had in her life. At that realization, as much as at her voice, I admit I began to weep, but I am not ashamed of it. Your mother came into the room then, and asked me why I was crying. I told her I had been listening to Jane singing, but it was getting late, we had visitors coming, and there wasn't time for me to explain all the circumstances to her. There," said Datchett in conclusion. "That is the story of how Jane's singing brought me to tears, and I hope, Olivia, that you will understand the matter a little better now."

The room had fallen silent, save for the girl's quiet sobbing, and remained so for several minutes. Then Sherlock Holmes rose to his feet and took from his pocket the jet brooch, which he handed to Lady Hilary.

"That, I believe, concludes the matter, from my perspective at least," said he.

"Thank you for unravelling it all for us," said Sir George Datchett as he stood up and shook my companion by the hand.

We had turned to leave when there came a sharp pull at the front-door bell, and I heard the sound of singing from outside the house. A moment later, the butler entered the room to announce that the carol-singers from St Mary's had called, collecting for the parish charity.

"Oh!" cried Olivia. "I forgot it was tonight. I wanted to go with them! May I go? Please, Father? I can get a bite to eat later."

"Of course you may," said Datchett. "But you must wrap up warm, Olivia. It is a very cold night."

"And may I take Jane with me?" she asked. "I know from something she said to me this morning that she would dearly love to go carol-singing."

"Certainly, certainly," said Datchett, "but see that she, too, wraps up well. Now I must speak to the carol-singers."

With a cry of delight, the girl ran from the room, and I heard her footsteps clattering down the stair to the basement. We followed her father to the front door and stood for several minutes, listening to the carol-singers. Behind them in the cold night air the snow was now falling heavily. As they finished their carol, Datchett spoke to their leader, but I was distracted by the arrival behind me in the hall of two girls in overcoats, hats and mufflers. I turned to see them, but they slipped quickly past us and ran down the steps to join the carol-singers outside.

Presently, as the carol-singers made their way out of the gate and along the street, Sir George Datchett turned to us and thanked my friend again for his help. "Please send me your account for the trouble you have been put to," he said.

Holmes shook his head with a smile. "That won't be necessary," said he. "Sometimes the elucidation of the truth is itself more than adequate recompense."

As we made our way down the street, we came to where the carol-singers had stopped before another house, and paused a moment to listen. A girl at the back of the group glanced our way and I had an impression of a pair of bright, piercing eyes in a happy face, framed in tight dark curls. Holmes made a little gesture and she left the group and ran over to where we stood.

"I am confident everything will be all right now, Jane," said he, leaning over to speak closer to her.

"Yes," she returned in a breathless voice. "Miss Olivia has explained it all to me. It's all right now."

"But," he continued, "if at any time you find yourself in difficulty once more, do not hesitate to write to me again."

She nodded her head, then, raising herself on her tip-toes, she gave my companion a little peck on the cheek. "You look better without your beard," said she in a gay tone, and ran back to re-join the carol singers.

"I feel I should point out to you, Watson," said Holmes in a tone of embarrassment, as we resumed our progress down the street, "that that is not a regular occurrence at the conclusion of my cases."

I laughed. It amused me greatly to see my logical friend, usually so cold and unemotional, discomfited by a young girl, and I confess that I teased him about it for some time afterwards. Trivial incident though it may have been, I thought it worthy of mention here as being the only occasion in all of my records when my famous friend received payment from his client in the form of a kiss.

54

The Adventure of the Missing Irregular
by Amy Thomas

"**M**r. Holmes, Eccles is missing."

It was with these words that the intrepid captain of my friend's irregular force greeted us on the morning three days before Christmas. Wiggins stood slightly forward on the balls of his feet, eager to share his news, his chest puffed out by the importance of it.

Holmes eyed him calmly. "For how long?"

"Three days."

"And you've done the usual?"

Wiggins nodded. "Checked all the places twice."

"What about her mother?"

I had been listening to this conversation with what I like to think was a normal level of concern, but when I heard the unexpected pronoun, I fixed my friend with a pointed look of disapproval.

Wiggins, meanwhile, tipped his hand up to his mouth in a drinking motion. "Not in a state to notice who's been in or out."

"Thank you, Wiggins," said Holmes. "I see that you're freezing and haven't eaten today. Go and get something from Mrs. Hudson while I gather my things."

The boy hopped off to do as told, and my friend rose to gather a small kit of supplies. "If only adults were as sensibly amenable as children," he muttered, whilst, beyond the closed door, I heard Mrs. Hudson's exclamations of horror at the boy tramping dirt through the building.

"Holmes," I said sharply, "am I correct in assuming that Eccles is a girl?"

"Yes," he answered briefly.

My indignation only grew. "I gather why these children are helpful to your work. Truly I do. I've even said it was noble of you to provide an income. But girls, Holmes? It's not natural."

My friend stopped and stared at me for a moment, as if deducing the most expedient way to proceed. "I could speak to you of the competence of many women, such as our own landlady, that extends far above their station, but instead I will tell you about Maria Eccles, ten years old. Wiggins brought her to me two years ago. She and her mother had just been thrown out of the miserable space they occupied atop a chemist's, for failing to pay the rent the proprietor requires for them to subsist in a rat-infested closet. The father deserted them long ago. Before alcohol became her only employment, the mother used her beauty to earn enough of a pittance for herself and her daughter to live upon. They were both half-frozen when Maria came to me. I paid her enough to keep the room, and she became part of my force. She's certainly as clever as the boys, cleverer than quite a few of them. More importantly, she has a home with her mother because of what I pay.

"Should I have let them starve, Watson, or foist them on the charity of the public, which is about the same thing?"

I shook my head. "Of course not."

He continued. "Yes, Watson, I employ girls. They're good at the work, and the pay keeps them just as alive as their male counterparts."

Needless to say, I was silenced by my friend's words, and I nodded my assent. "You're quite right."

"Yes," he said. "I am."

Just then, Wiggins burst back in, effervescent with food and attention. "Here, put this on." Holmes handed him one of his own jumpers, and the boy put it on over his shirt, pushing up the too-long sleeves and putting his threadbare jacket over both, until he looked like a miniature old man. He didn't seem to mind. As usual, he gazed at us both with a cocky stare.

"We'll go to the room first," Holmes said brusquely.

"I knew you'd say that," said our young visitor. "I've been there, but of course, you'll find more than I did." He looked downcast for a moment.

"I shouldn't worry about that," said my friend, wrapping a scarf around his neck. "You've plenty of time to learn."

I followed them outside, wrapping my coat tight against the chill. My relatively short acquaintance with Holmes meant that most of the other children hadn't yet warmed to me, but Wiggins's frequent visits to my friend had created a stronger acquaintance between us. He was an unusual child, precocious beyond his years, a bit cheeky, but an uncannily capable captain. I didn't envision him following in Holmes's footsteps, though he certainly picked the work up quickly. He was far more suited to a profession like barrister, which would utilize his talents of human understanding and, as he grew older, most likely, manipulation. I had little experience of such things myself, but my mind was ever less averse to speculation than that of the man who shared my flat.

Predictably, Wiggins, who was used to walking the city in shoes so worn he was practically barefoot, was thrilled at the novel prospect of riding in a hansom cab. He hopped in between Holmes and myself, brimful of questions about the conveyance and horse, which Holmes answered with equanimity. He considered, I had already learned, that curiosity in the young was an admirable quality which should be encouraged at every possible turn. I did not disagree, but I still found it dissonantly peculiar to see Sherlock Holmes exhibiting utmost patience when dealing with a human being of any sort.

We arrived at a disreputable-looking chemist's within the half-hour. It was exactly as I'd imagined it to be, considering the unfortunate prospects of Eccles and her mother, complete with peeling paint, a half-faded sign offering dubious "Medicinal Remedies", and windows thick with grime. A Dickensian sort of place, which, I could not help thinking, had a peculiar appropriateness considering the time of year.

Upon entry, we were greeted by Eaker, a man whose appearance did not in any way personify the narratively-pleasing stereotype of wizened and cunning proprietor. He was a pleasant-looking, squarely-built man whom I supposed to be near his fortieth year, smiling in a friendly way. "May I assist you gentleman with a compound?" Just then, he saw Wiggins, who came in behind Holmes, and his expression changed to one of pure malevolence.

"I told you not to come back here, you little filth," he hissed. "Leave these gentleman alone, or I'll take a broom handle to you." He looked at us as if he intended to apologize for the imposition of such a lowly creature, but he found Holmes staring back at him in white-faced fury. I had, as yet, seen my friend truly angry very few times, but I knew the signs. He was not a man to let another person rob him of his composure, but he was also relentless when his ire was truly raised.

"This boy is in my employ," he said coldly. "I have no intention of patronizing your miserable establishment, but I wish to gain access to the room upstairs, where Mrs. Eccles and her daughter reside."

For a moment, the man looked as if his temper might be turned on my friend and me, but he apparently thought better of angering two determined-looking men any further and instead jerked his head in the direction of a narrow staircase off to one side of the room.

"Thank you," said Holmes, quite as if he meant the opposite, and we proceeded up the wooden stairs.

"I've had a couple of bruises off him before," said Wiggins, bobbing up the stairs. "I'm quick on my feet, but he got me by surprise once. Thanks for telling him off."

"Good lad," said Holmes, but I could tell that his attention was engaged in deducing the details of our surroundings. What looked like an ordinary unkempt stairwell to me no doubt contained far more for my friend's eyes. I knew from experience that he could read worlds in what I only saw as dust and grime.

At the top of the stairs, we entered a close, musty corridor which had closets and storage rooms, but only one area designed for habitation. I use the description imprecisely. Had I entered the room rented by Eccles and her mother without knowing its use, I would have assumed it was another cramped closet. As it was, we came in and found an almost-empty room with a tiny stove against one wall and a worn quilt on the floor. There was certainly nothing in this mean little chamber that would suggest to anyone that it was nearly Christmas. "Where's Dorothea, her mother?" asked Holmes, walking around to each wall and corner and using his magnifying glass to check footprints in the dirt on the floor.

"She goes out once a day," said Wiggins. "If Loo's given her money, she buys bread and gin. If not, she begs until she gets enough for the gin, if not the food. I didn't think she'd be up."

"All the better for my purposes," said Holmes, still scouring the room for information long after I'd given up on deducing anything other than the obvious presence of empty bottles and an overlay of dust on every surface.

"The mother's been gone for more than a few hours," said Holmes tersely, touching the top of the stove with his fingers. "Is that unusual?"

"Not when she's drunk off her head," said Wiggins, immediately closing his mouth on any other observations he might have had. He knew that my friend did not appreciate being distracted by extraneous discussion.

"I don't suppose our friend downstairs would have any light to shed on the matter, but I wish to search the shop for whatever details it might present. Wiggins, you'd better go. If Eccles contacts any of you, go to Baker Street at once and leave word with Mrs. Hudson."

"Can't I stay?"

"No," said Holmes, not unkindly. "You'll be of much more use away from us. Here." He took a coin out of his pocket, and the boy accepted it soberly and turned on his heels and left without another word.

"You've quite a way with him," I said.

Holmes looked up from his contemplation of the far left corner of the small room. "I treat him exactly as if he's a human being."

I followed my friend back downstairs, where the proprietor looked, if not benevolent, at least slightly less infuriated with Wiggins out of the way. "Sir," said Holmes, "I need to search the rest of the premises. I will pay you, since I'm under no illusion that the idea of a missing woman and child will be enough inducement in itself to entice your cooperation."

The man flushed at this. "Well, Sir, I – " he fumbled for words. "I was not aware of your identity when you first appeared. You are, I believe, Mr. Sherlock Holmes of Baker Street." Rather than appearing pleased at this, Holmes gave the man a look of supreme irritation, as if he would rather have remained unknown to such a repugnant character. Nevertheless, he answered, "I am that man."

"Then there's certainly no need for payment," said the other man hurriedly, clasping and unclasping his hands nervously, his demeanor entirely different from what it had previously been.

"I insist upon it," said Holmes with steel in his voice. "I won't be indebted to the likes of you." With that, he put a pile of coins on the counter in front of the chemist. "Come, Watson, we must search."

I followed my friend to the far corner of the shop, but not before, I confess, I had stolen a look at the proprietor's stormy countenance. I have always been a man of simple pleasures. I count my enjoyment of Holmes's effect on others to be one of them.

"Why would this have anything to do with the girl's disappearance?" I asked, as soon as I'd joined Holmes behind a bottle-laden shelf.

"Looking for a trail, Watson," he said enigmatically, doing his usual work of scanning each nook and cranny and corner, as I followed and tried to observe more than the usual collection of chemical remedies both useful and otherwise.

After ten minutes of this, Holmes straightened up from his perusal of a bottle of pills. "I suppose this is about as much as we're likely to gain," he said quickly, and began to lead the way out the creaky wooden door.

"Mr. Holmes!" The proprietor's voice arrested us. "I – might know something about the girl."

"Oh, yes?" Holmes stared at him coolly.

"She – hasn't been here for three days," he answered quickly. "The mother has, but not the little girl."

"When did you last see her?" Holmes asked.

"Three days ago, around eight in the morning," he replied.

"Thank you," said Holmes, "and when her mother reappears, please direct her to 221b Baker Street, if you would be so kind."

The man nodded, and I could see his desire to be helpful to the detective from the newspapers warring with his annoyance at being treated like an unimportant part of the drama.

When we were back outside on the busy street, I turned to Holmes. "Did you find anything of interest in the shop? I confess I saw little."

"For once," he replied, "I agree with you. I wanted to search the place, but my other aim was to give the unpleasant owner some time to contemplate his own involvement in the matter and decide if he wanted to remain antagonistic. I deduced correctly that his pride would win out, and he wouldn't be able to settle for keeping silent."

"But surely," I put in as we re-entered our cab, "he knew very little."

Holmes smiled. "Quality is more important than quantity, Watson, when one cannot have both. What he told us is very useful. We now know that Eccles disappeared in the early hours of the morning, which Wiggins did not know, since he meets with her in the afternoon."

"But surely she goes out early each day," I said.

"Indeed," Holmes answered, "but it rules out the possibility that she came back and left again in the evening for an unusual errand from which she did not return. You observed the door to the chemist's apartment behind the shop, I am sure. The walls of the place are thin, and I trust that he'd have known if either the girl or her mother had taken a late-night stroll."

"Do you really intend to speak to the mother?" I asked, as we neared Baker Street once again.

"Certainly," Holmes answered, "if she appears. Even her drunken recollections may assist us in formulating an idea of events."

We did not have to wait long to find out what Dorothea Eccles did or did not know, for as soon as we arrived, we found her in our flat, sitting across from Wiggins with a cup of tea in her hand. "I found her after I left you, at one of her usual places," said the boy. "Thought you'd want to see her."

"Very good," said Holmes. "You anticipated me, which can't be said for many people." He handed over another shiny coin, which Wiggins pocketed after twirling it around in his fingers for a moment.

The woman was a pitiful sight. Her dress, which had started out as some other color, was now brown and dingy with accumulated dirt, and she stared at us with blank, sad eyes.

"Mrs. Eccles," said Holmes, "when did you last see your daughter?" As Wiggins had assured us, she was hardly in a condition to provide veracious testimony, but she nodded slowly after a few moments.

"Mrs. Stubbs," she said. "I saw her go there yesterday. She never came home."

"Who is Mrs. Stubbs?" Holmes asked, but she had fallen silent, and she stared into the fire, as if hoping to regain her wits there.

"I know the answer," said Wiggins, suddenly and unexpectedly. "Mrs. Stubbs sells old bread on the corner of this street, but she didn't go there yesterday, or we would have seen her, since we started watching the street two days ago – when she missed two of our meetings in a row."

Holmes again turned his attention to the boy. "We have reason to believe her last visit there was three days ago. Does she go there often?"

"Not until lately," Wiggins answered. "The bread she sells is terrible, but Maria started going a few months ago. I thought it was because her mother was taking more of her money, so she couldn't afford better." He spoke about Dorothea Eccles as if she wasn't there, but I couldn't really blame him, so absent and lost did she seem.

"Have you ever been there with her?" Holmes asked, and I wondered to what on earth his questions were tending.

Wiggins shook his head. "No, but Colin's seen her going there."

"Then we'll speak to Mrs. Stubbs," said Holmes, rising. "Come along, Watson and Wiggins. Mrs. Eccles, you may use our fire while we're gone, if you wish," said Holmes, and, turning to me, "We'll make sure Mrs. Hudson looks in on her."

With that, the three of us wrapped up against the chill again and hailed another cab to take us where we'd already been. This time, we stopped at the end of the street, where Wiggins assured us that Mrs. Stubbs resided when she was not peddling her repugnant wares, which she only did in the earliest part of the day, long before the hour of our arrival.

Within a moment, the rickety door was opened to us by the proprietress herself, a woman whose faded finery appeared to be making a valiant effort at respectability but was, on the whole, failing. "What?" She asked. "Not open now. Bread tomorrow."

Holmes stepped forward and handed her a coin. "A little girl comes here. Maria Eccles. Do you remember her?"

"A lot of little girls come here," she said, "and boys," but her tone was not uncivil, and she held the money like a treasure.

"Ten years old, brown hair, exceptionally intelligent," said Holmes. "Wears a silver locket."

Mrs. Stubbs made a show of thinking long and hard about her answer. "Yes," she finally replied. "Comes every three or four days – for the last half-a-year or so."

"What does she buy?" asked Holmes. "How much bread? Enough for how many people?" I had been trying to follow Holmes's line of enquiry, but I found myself baffled by the question.

"Barely enough for one, I should think," she answered, and my friend nodded.

"As I expected," he said. "Which way does she go when she leaves, if you can recall?" She jerked her head in the direction away from the shop where mother and child lived. "That way. Always."

"Thank you. You've been most helpful."

The woman's face registered disappointment that she could think of no other way to extort money from Holmes, but she called after us. "Come in the morning for the best bread in town, Dearies!"

Wiggins snorted at this, but knew better than to cause a scene that would halt Holmes in his progress, and he followed us like an obedient, if highly excitable, puppy.

"Bread for one," said Holmes. "For half-a-year, she buys bread for one and goes outside the area she's meant to keep her eyes on for me. Finally, one day, she disappears in that direction and doesn't return."

"There is any number of reasons a young girl might not return home in this part of London," I said, my mind filled with grave conjectures.

"But the bread, Watson!" said Holmes. "Think of the bread."

"It makes every kind of sense for a child with limited means to purchase cheap bread for her meals," I answered.

"Aha," said my friend, "but only for one, and only every few days, at that? As Wiggins has asserted, she provides for herself and her mother. They may not be living a luxurious existence, but neither has died of starvation. Does she buy bread in two different places?"

I was quite flummoxed at this, and I shook my head. "I don't understand it."

"Wiggins," he continued, "do you know the story of Maria's father?"

The boy nodded, his eyes wide and serious. "She told it to me once, but made me promise not to tell anyone."

"Excellent," said Holmes. "You may tell us, since Dr. Watson and I are quite far outside the realm of 'anyone'." I smiled at this, but Wiggins spent a moment of serious thought before he spoke again.

"She said when she was small, her father was a bricklayer, but he was hurt when part of a wall fell onto him. He couldn't work, so he didn't have any money for food. And – he stole so Maria and her mother could eat. Someone found out, and they threatened to turn him in to the police if he didn't pay them off, but he couldn't, so he went away to avoid going to prison."

"The fog begins to clear, Watson," said Holmes, though I couldn't see how. "Very good, Wiggins. Your memory serves well." The boy, who for all his enthusiasm had been uncharacteristically sober as a result of worry for his friend, smiled widely at this, but quickly returned to his former state of solemnity.

"Will you send her away?" he asked curiously. "Will you stop letting her work for you?"

"That," said Holmes, "will depend on the reason and mode of her disappearance, but I very much doubt that it will be necessary." Wiggins visibly relaxed at this, and I was touched by his evident trust in my friend and concern for his comrade.

"From whom did her father steal the money?" Holmes asked, continuing his mode of questioning.

Wiggins shook his head. "She never told me."

"Very well," said Holmes. "Go and attend to your usual activities, and I'll send a message to you when I need you again."

This seemingly cold dismissal was met with cheerful acquiescence by Wiggins, who scampered off as if he hadn't a care in the world.

"Excellent!" said Holmes, turning to me. "We will return to Baker Street and find out from Mrs. Eccles who her husband's debtor is."

"And if she doesn't know?"

"One thing at a time, Watson," he answered.

We reached home in the early afternoon and found the lady in question speaking to Mrs. Hudson, with a plate of scones in hand and looking less famished, at any rate. As soon as we entered the flat, our landlady offered us a warming libation against the chill and retired to her own rooms.

"Mrs. Eccles," said Holmes, "I believe I will have the opportunity to reunite you with your daughter very soon, and perhaps more, but I need you to tell me whom your husband robbed before he disappeared, if you know." He spoke abruptly, to astonish the lady into replying before any natural reticence could encumber her.

She stared at him for a moment, and there was intelligence somewhere in her eyes, I thought, that circumstance and desperation hadn't quite succeeded in eradicating. "Do you know how it happened?"

"Not yet, but I'd be very glad if you would tell me," Holmes answered, sitting opposite her with uncharacteristic patience.

Dorothea Eccles clutched a glass of the same liquid that was warming the insides of Holmes and myself. "My husband is – was, I suppose – a clever man. He worked as a bricklayer, but he was also acquiring education to become a chemist. That is how he met Eaker, the horrible man who owns the house where Maria and I live."

"Aha," said Holmes. "I suspected that there was more than general unpleasantness behind the man's demeanor."

"James worked for him to learn the trade, for two years after the accident that hurt his arm. He asked Eaker to take him on full-time, since he could no longer lay bricks, but the man refused and said that my husband ought to owe *him* money for all he'd taught him, not taking into account any of the time James had spent doing his work for him." She stopped speaking for a moment, her face filled with deep indignation.

"My husband had pride, but he was desperate, so he asked for a small loan. But Eaker also refused him there. I believe – he was jealous, because my husband was more intelligent than he, and the customers had begun to prefer him. He'd begun to fear that James would eclipse him in skill and take his business, which he certainly would have done. He'd have kept a far better establishment.

"At that time, Maria was a small child, and she became ill. We spent the remaining money we had on the doctor. Mr. Holmes, you will already know that she still has a weakness in her breathing – she falls ill very easily. At any rate, my husband was driven to near-despair over this. For several weeks, we thought we would lose her, and he blamed his inability to provide a better home and better food.

"Then, late one night, he went to Eaker's and came home with more money than I'd seen since his injury. I asked him where it was from, and he told me his master had decided to pay all he owed him for the work he'd done. I didn't believe him, and he finally confessed that Eaker had left him in charge that night, and he'd purposefully omitted the last several orders of the day from the record." As she said this, she looked away from Holmes, and I could tell that the shame was still keen, even though the event was long past.

"I was surprised, because James had always been an honest man, and it nearly killed him to admit the deed to me, but once he had, I didn't know what to do. Our need for the money was so great that I could not bear the thought of returning it and facing exposure.

"It seemed, for three weeks, like James had succeeded, but my husband was a cleverer man than criminal, which I suppose does him more credit than otherwise. One of the orders he'd failed to record was a close friend of Eaker's, who came back when the proprietor was in the shop and referred to his purchase, a purchase Eaker didn't know about. From there, he figured out what had happened. My husband begged for mercy – for time to pay him back – but he said that if the whole sum wasn't returned by the following day, he would turn James in to the police.

"We could not pay back what we had already spent, so James fled, and that was the last time I saw my husband. When Eaker found out, he purported to be deeply sorry for me and my daughter, and he offered us the room we now occupy. The truth, I believe, is that he was hoping my husband would return, and he wanted to have us underfoot so that if James tried to do so, he could exact his revenge.

"Two years ago, he threatened to put us out onto the street, for I believe he had realized, as I have, that my husband was probably no longer in this world. At that time, Maria began working for you to pay what he required, because my – earnings – were only enough to feed us, barely, and I am not a young woman."

"And one not overmuch concerned with temperance, as I understand it," said Holmes, startling me with his harshness.

"Yes," she agreed, "I have not endured our situation as bravely as I ought to have done, and our Maria does greater credit to James and me than either of us deserves."

"I expect to have this matter resolved within a day or two," said Holmes, just as Mrs. Hudson knocked lightly at the door and entered.

"Mrs. Eccles, I have a room ready for you. I won't hear of you going back out in this chill. I do hope you're finished with her, Mr. Holmes. She needs rest."

"Yes, excellent," said Holmes. "I would not have had her return to Eaker's this night."

Dorothea looked at our landlady in wonder and stood to follow her, but she turned back to us. "I have not always been as I am now."

After she had left, I dined, while Holmes wrote out a long paper in his best hand. He spoke not a word, and I could not fathom what he was doing, but after an hour or so, he arose, folded it, and put it into his pocket. "Come, Watson! We must away to that accursed street once again."

"Whatever for?" I asked, following obediently.

"To settle the man's debt, of course," he replied.

"This is what is owed to you from the theft of James Eccles, with heavy interest," said Holmes, standing in front of the counter in Eaker's shop and showing the shocked man a pile of notes. The chemist reached out to take the money, but my friend held it back and produced a folded document from his coat. "Before I will release the money to you, you will sign this letter absolving Eccles of the accusation of any crime against you, and vowing that you will pursue no legal action against him. I suggest you accept the offer, for you'll not get another."

Eaker looked at Holmes's affidavit, which was written in plain, unadorned language, and left no doubt of its meaning. As he perused it, I could sense the internal war between his desire for vengeance and his pure, unadulterated avarice. Finally, he took out a pen and signed with precision, not handing back Holmes's paper until he had the money in hand, easily five times as much as he was actually owed.

My friend pocketed the signed document, then turned and left the shop without another word. I followed, noting how pleased he seemed as soon as we were outside. "Well, Watson, we're nearly to the end of the matter now," he said cheerfully.

"I fail to grasp your meaning," I answered frankly. Though I had not known him overlong, I was, by this time, well aware that he did not expect me to share his powers of deduction or to reach conclusions nearly as quickly as he did.

"Why do you suppose I paid the man's debt?" he asked, as we secured a cab to return us to Baker Street.

"For the child," I answered. "I supposed that she had fled because of some sort of threat from Eaker, and that your intention was to secure her freedom from his endangerment."

"Aha," he answered. "Not the worst surmise of your short career, Watson, but what of the stale bread? If the girl was fleeing danger, why stop for a mite's worth of nearly-inedible bread?"

I had no answer to this and shook my head. "I can't account for it."

"The solution to any mystery, as you know, must encompass all the facts," said Holmes. "The bread is what put me on the right track in the first place, and it is there that the heart of the matter may be deduced.

"When Wiggins first came to me, I considered Eccles's situation. She is an extremely clever girl and aptly skilled at evading danger. She also has ample allies in Wiggins, the other children, and myself, of course, if she had found herself or her mother in any kind of danger. I also considered the strangeness of her change in habit regarding the bread. If, as Wiggins assumed, she was simply responding to financial straits, the quantity of bread she was buying wouldn't have been enough to keep herself and her mother alive. Yet alive they are, and in decent health, considering. In addition, she neither took the bread home nor ingested it immediately, which would be the expected action of a starving person, instead taking it in a direction away from home and away from the area where she is paid by me to keep watch."

"Was she taking it to someone?" I asked, my mind expanding to admit a new angle of thought.

Holmes smiled. "You're getting there now, Watson. I believe the elder Eccles has returned, and that, if we lie in wait for Maria's next visit to the bread-seller, we may find both of them and deliver the news to Mr. Eccles that he is no longer in danger if he returns to his family."

"But if she's been buying him bread for six months, why did she just now disappear from her usual duties, and why do you think she'll come back?" I asked.

"Excellent questions," said Holmes complacently. "I do not yet know what changed in the past few days. From the facts, it appears that the father has been giving money to her to secure food for him, just enough to keep him from absolute starvation. Though I abhor guessing, I suspect the girl hasn't been home because of her mother's absence. Perhaps the only reason she hadn't gone to her father before was to care for her. She may have intended to return if her mother did."

"As for returning to Mrs. Stubbs's miserable establishment, she has not been absent any longer than her usual interval of days, and she has no reason to consider the place unsafe. Waiting for her there may prove fruitless, but we will know within a day or two, because if more than a day or two past the usual interval elapses, we may safely deduce that she no longer intends to frequent the place."

In truth, my medical duties not yet copious enough to make the waste of a morning or two much of a hardship, and early the next day, just one before Christmas Eve, Holmes and I met Wiggins one street beyond the chemist's and took our place on the first floor of an abandoned building across from Mrs. Stubbs.

As it turned out, we did not have to waste more than an hour-and-a-quarter, for Maria appeared soon after the woman had opened sales for the day. I did not know the girl's appearance, but Holmes and Wiggins both spotted her face and figure beneath her ill-fitting coat.

From our vantage point, we watched the girl purchase stale bread, then turn in the direction Mrs. Stubbs had indicated that she usually went. Holmes held us back for a moment before leading the way downstairs and out the back of the house.

Had he intended to follow for a long period of time without being seen, Holmes would no doubt have left Wiggins and me behind, for following in a group of three is an unwieldy business. As he'd suspected, however, we did not need to keep Maria in view for many streets before we followed her around a corner and found the little girl and a man entering a crumbling lodging house, hand-in-hand. Upon seeing us, she gave a violent start and hung her head, her eyes downcast.

"Now, Eccles, there's no need for that," said Holmes quickly. "We fully understand the matter."

As the five of us lingered outside, Wiggins bristled. "You could've left some kind of word. We've wasted days looking for you." Holmes put a hand on his shoulder to quiet him.

"Mr. Eccles," said my friend, "I believe the easiest way to resolve this matter is to inform you that no criminal accusations exist against you any longer; you're free to return home."

The man, who, I realized from Holmes's speech, was Maria's father, stared in open amazement. "How?"

It was the girl's turn to speak, and she looked up with tears in her eyes and did so in a shaky voice. "Mr. Holmes – paid him off, didn't you?"

My friend looked back at her steadily. He was still a young man then, one possessed of a character filled with right angles and sharp edges, but he smiled. "It would have been a great inconvenience to me to lose an assistant as capable as yourself, and I deduced that the easiest way to retain your services was to facilitate your father's return."

Wiggins understood and was finally mollified. He nodded to Maria, and she nodded back, and that was the end of the matter as far as any animosity was concerned.

"Papa," said the little girl, turning toward her father, "this is Mr. Holmes, Dr. Watson, and Wiggins."

The man bowed his head slightly. "I thank you gentlemen for your care of my daughter, and for your kindness to me."

"I wish to know the story of your return," said Holmes.

Eccles answered with great feeling. "When I left my wife and child, I spent every moment wishing to God I hadn't, but I believed it would be worse for them to have a father and husband in gaol than one who'd disappeared. It's a long and tedious story, but my arm finally healed, and since then I have been a nameless nomad, staying nowhere long and working every possible moment, with the idea that someday I might come home and pay back what I owed, and, perhaps, be reunited with my family. Six months ago, I came back to London with nearly enough money and a job that would pay the rest. I had no intention of seeing my Dorothea or Maria until I was ready to fix it with Eaker, but I went to buy bread at the cheapest place I could find, and while I was there, I saw the face of my little girl passing by on the street. I have not seen her for many years, but she looks so much like my wife that I was in no doubt. I tried to restrain myself, but I could not resist speaking to her, and she – my Maria – remembered her father's face after all these years."

"She met you daily and bought bread for you from then on," said Holmes. "That much I understand. But why did you disappear three days ago?" He looked at the girl, who held her father's hand tightly.

James spoke again. "Four days ago, I had enough money to pay back the debt, with ten-percent extra, hoping that he would accept it after all this time. I had not known until my return that my wife and daughter lived above that horrible man's establishment, and when I found out, I determined to bring Dorothea and Maria to my lodgings when I was ready to pay him, in case he turned violent or the police were called. However, when Maria came to me that day, she told me that her mother was nowhere to be found – which, I understand, is not uncommon. I convinced Maria to remain with me, and I watched the shop to see when her mother might return, not willing to chance Eaker until I'd hidden her in my lodgings with Maria. It has – been a great hardship to be so close to my family for these six months but to be separated from them. That is the apology I offer for my daughter's disappearance."

"Your wife is safe," said Holmes. "She lodged with my landlady overnight, and she awaits you on Baker Street. You will not find her in the best of health, but you will find her alive."

"I will, of course, pay you the sum I'd intended to pay Eaker," Eccles added.

Holmes shook his head. "Your daughter's services are invaluable to me, and you will require the money for Christmas, so we'll say no more about it." The man seemed about to argue, but he saw the sense of it after a while and merely nodded. We five made our way to Baker Street a happy, if sober, company.

The Eccles family spent Christmas in James's Spartan lodgings. Dorothea had a long journey before her to reach true soundness of mind and body, but her face was less drawn, and she spent a portion of the day sober. In spite of what time and circumstance had done to her, her husband's eyes held nothing but adoration. Maria perched herself on her father's knee and refused to let go of him all day long, and he did not seem any more eager to relinquish his hold on her.

I know these things from personal observation, for Holmes, Wiggins, and I were invited guests at the event. Mrs. Hudson, generous soul that she was, prepared a repast for us to share, and we partook of it in dismal conditions made cheerful by the bonds of family and friendship and the promise of a more hopeful future.

I said nothing to Holmes when we returned home, but I stored the memory of the Eccles Case in my mind, and it informed my opinion of him thereafter. The man I had supposed to be brilliant but unbending was, I had come to know, capable of deep generosity toward his fellowman. Much time would pass before I understood the true depths of his regard for my friendship, but that Christmas, I learned that the man the world knew as an infallible reasoning machine had far more within him than it would ever realize.

I pondered these same things on a rainy afternoon many years later whilst sitting in church, with Holmes beside me, as Wiggins and Eccles were united in holy matrimony. They were married on Christmas Day, which I thought was very fitting, and though my friend did not expound on the subject, I believe he shared my opinion. His smile, still rare, though less so than it had once been, told me so without words.

The Adventure of the
Knighted Watchmaker
by Derrick Belanger

As I sit in my heated room and watch the wonderful winter rains envelope the streets of London through my window, see automobiles splash through the puddles, and hear the weathermen on the radio warn that the storm will not abate for another twenty-four hours, I am reminded of my first winter with Sherlock Holmes at our rooms on the first floor of 221b Baker Street over forty years ago.

Of course, that year the rain was much fiercer and caused terrible damage around all of England. It was in late December, 1881. Harsh gale winds pummeled the country from the coast to the hills. The Thames rose and nearly overflowed into the streets, and with the wretched weather came a lack of business for Holmes and myself. Indeed, for most of December, Holmes found himself without a case. London's citizens were not yet familiar with the name Sherlock Holmes nor his intellectual skills. The police, however, had already grown tired of Holmes's smug attitude towards them. Though he was correct in all the cases he worked alongside the Yard, most of the force, besides inspectors such as Lestrade and Gregson, who were able to put aside their pride and recognize my dear friend's superior skills, kept their distance from the consulting detective, preferring to use their own methods of deduction, as bumbling and incompetent as those methods were at the time.

With the foul weather, my few patients had dwindled as well. No one wanted to brave the wretched rains, preferring to stay home sick rather than to pay a call to the office where, at the time, I was filling in as a locum. So it was that Holmes and I found ourselves penniless just a few days before Christmas. While I assisted Mrs. Hudson with decorating our Baker Street residence, hanging garlands of mistletoe and holly throughout the house, adding candles in the windows, and a wreath with a red velvet bow upon the front door, the detective had been turning more and more within himself to assuage his boredom.

On December 23rd, I was able to pull Holmes out of his melancholic slump to assist me in standing the spruce, which Mrs. Hudson had ordered cut and delivered in order to be her Christmas tree.

"In my opinion, this is a waste of a perfectly proper tree," Holmes lamented as he stood it upright in the tin bucket while I poured in the sand that would hold the spruce in place. Mrs. Hudson directed us, noting if we were off by a quarter-inch in keeping the tree perfectly upright.

"Come now, Holmes. It gives us something to do to occupy our time," I said, putting my best foot forward. "It may be wretched weather outside, but Mrs. Hudson has kept it jolly and warm in here."

Holmes muttered, "There is nothing comforting about following modern customs. Just a few years ago, Christmas was a raucous time for drinking and merriment, not for exchanging gifts and singing out-of-tune carols. We'll see how joyful Mrs. Hudson is when we turn out our pockets come time to pay our rent."

"What was that, Mr. Holmes?" Mrs. Hudson asked, still eyeing the very tip top of the tree and ensuring there was no slant.

"I was only noting how you've picked a particularly lovely tree for Christmas this year. Do you always get a seven footer?"

"I always try to get a tree to fill the front room," Mrs. Hudson answered. Fortunately, she had not heard Holmes's concerns over money.

As we finished setting up the tree, there came a sharp rapping at the front door. "Now who could that be?" wondered Mrs. Hudson aloud.

She went to get the door and returned with a squat, elderly woman wearing a dark blue mantelet and carrying a matching fringed parasol. Mrs. Hudson asked the woman about the flooding.

"Weather is still damp out there, but I hasten to say that the worst of the storm is over. Bags of sand are holding up the Thames and most of the water has drained away. If you do not need to leave your domicile, then I would stay inside with the warmth and leave the soggy streets for tomorrow. I am certain the streets will be dried out by then," she answered in a sharp, cold tone of voice reminiscent of the commanding officers of the Fusiliers.

Mrs. Hudson took the woman's hat, mantelet, and parasol, and I noted that our visitor was well-dressed despite the dreary weather. She wore gold rimmed pince-nez glasses which gave her face an owl-like feature. Her hair was short, white, and curled. Her attire was a long-sleeved gray chiffon dress which was supported by a whale bone corset, so popular with the ladies of the time.

"Yet you did leave the comforts of your own home and brave the streets of our fair city to come visit me. The matter concerning your husband must be one of great urgency," stated Holmes, who had moved away from the Christmas Tree to introduce himself to the visitor.

"Ah, so you must be Mr. Holmes."

"Yes, and though I do not know your name, I do know that you are the wife of a watchmaker, that you work alongside your husband assisting and creating time-telling devices, and that some information you have received in the post has greatly disturbed you."

The woman's expression did not show the slightest sign of surprise at Holmes's observations. She merely gave a slight nod and introduced herself as if Holmes did nothing more than welcome her into his study.

"My name is Mrs. Nicholas Ehrly. I understand you solve problems which people cannot puzzle out themselves. My friend, Mrs. Greta Taylor, says you were able to tell her of her husband's indiscretions and to whom he was having his indiscretions with, without ever leaving your flat in Montague Street."

"Miss Greta's problem was a rather simple one, Mrs. Ehrly, and one where all the evidence was before her, yet she lacked the will to see the conclusion until the obviousness of the answer was explained to her. I believe your problem will not be quite so simple, but please, let us go upstairs to the comforts of my sitting room. We will give Mrs. Hudson the space she needs to decorate her home for the upcoming holiday." Then, my flat mate turned to me. "Dr. Watson, will you also accompany us? It helps to have your opinion on difficult problems."

I asked Mrs. Hudson if she could spare my assistance for a time, and she shooed me away with Holmes and Mrs. Ehrly. I had noticed that when a member of the fairer sex appeared at her door and wished for Holmes's assistance, Mrs. Hudson always made sure Holmes and I had time to hear their case. When a man, or worse, a member of the Yard appeared, Mrs. Hudson always muttered about the time she had to take out of her daily chores to show riff-raff up to Holmes's rooms.

We ascended the stairs to our sitting room. All the time I wondered how Holmes could have determined so much about Mrs. Ehrly's situation from such a brief introduction. Since I had only known Holmes for not quite a year at the time of this case, I still had yet to fully realize my dear friend's powers of observation.

After we entered into the sitting room, Holmes offered Mrs. Ehrly a seat at the settee, and Holmes and I took to our chairs. Before Mrs. Ehrly began her tale, I ventured to ask Holmes how he came to know so much about the woman.

I expected Holmes to answer, but he nodded towards Mrs. Ehrly, who answered the questions for him. "It is quite obvious to me how Mr. Holmes knew about my work and my husband. I am wearing a wristlet, yet my dress also has a side pocket which I use to hold a pocket watch."

"Oh, yes, now I see you do have a pocket on your dress. That is quite unusual for a lady. But why would you need two watches?" I asked, a little flustered.

"Why, Watson," Holmes answered, "Mrs. Ehrly needs to make certain that her watches are keeping accurate time. By having the pocket for her larger watches and wearing one upon her wrist, she can make certain that they both strike five at the exact same moment."

"You are correct, Mr. Holmes," the lady answered. "I have my tailor add a pocket to all of my outer garments to ensure that I have space for at least two watches upon my body at all times. I'm sure you noted the oil on my gloves when I entered your domicile, and when I removed my gloves, you most likely saw the slight nicks on my fingers from the tiny gears I insert into the devices."

"And what of the worry about your husband?" I asked Mrs. Ehrly, for she seemed just as knowledgeable as my friend about how he drew his conclusions.

"Mr. Holmes knew that from this." Here, Mrs. Ehrly took a wrinkled letter from her pocket. The envelope had been crumpled up and then smoothed out again. "I kept my hand over my pocket when I entered the room. Mr. Holmes could tell I had the watch in my pocket, but from where I was holding my hand and double checking, it was easy to determine that there was something else in my pocket, something thin; a letter made the most sense. As to the concerns with my husband, I'm sure if a lady comes to see Mr. Holmes, it most likely concerns either a husband or a lover."

Holmes burst into applause. "Bravo, Mrs. Ehrly! You have the eye of an observer and the mental skills of a logician. I am glad that you have found a way to use your powers, even if it is towards solving problems which are mechanical and not criminal.

"Now," Holmes said while leaning back in his chair and steepling his fingers before his silver eyes, "please tell us of your case. I am most intrigued as to how someone as knowledgeable as you can have a problem worthy of skills beyond your own."

Mrs. Ehrly removed her pince-nez for a moment, rubbed her eyes, put the spectacles back on and started her tale. I was surprised at how blunt the woman was, never once acknowledging the high praise which my detective friend had bestowed upon her. I was also relieved to see the warmth and intensity return to Holmes's visage. With his hawkish features and Mrs. Ehrly's owl-like face, I felt as if two birds of prey were in the room, sizing each other up, and pleased to find they were equals who were not rivals.

"About ten years ago, I met my husband, Nicholas, at his shoppe in First Avenue. A family heirloom which had been bestowed to me by my grandfather was his gold hunter. The watch had stopped working, and while I tried my best to fix the duplex escapement, I could not get the balance wheel to swing properly. Hence, I found Mr. Ehrly."

I gave Holmes a quick side glance to let him know I did not understand much of what Mrs. Ehrly had just said.

"Just a moment, Mrs. Ehrly," Holmes said with a flick of his wrist to stop the woman's tale. Then he said to me, "A duplex escapement is used in many pocket watches to keep time, Watson. They use two sets of teeth, locking teeth and impulse teeth, which move the pallet and balance wheel to keep accurate time. They are going out of fashion now, being replaced by the more accurate lever escapements.

"But Mrs. Ehrly, you are telling us of events which occurred nearly a decade ago." Here Holmes paused and covered up a long yawn from his mouth probably to emphasize his boredom.

"I am not one to tell a meandering tale, Mr. Holmes. I only wish to allow you to see the relationship between my husband and me.

"When I brought the watch to Mr. Ehrly, I explained the trouble and my own attempt to repair it. Rather than dismissing me as a member of the fairer sex meddling in mechanics, he talked to me as an equal. He was impressed with my knowledge and pointed out that one of the locking teeth had worn away just enough as to make the watch unworkable. When he showed me the problem, I felt ridiculous for not catching it myself. He then showed me a wristlet he was designing and asked for my advice about the watch. I strapped the device to my wrist and found it to be too heavy for most women.

"We tinkered with several watches that afternoon, and by the time I left his shoppe, we had already made plans for a dinner engagement. Not a month passed before we were married."

"How romantic," Holmes stated with an obvious air of sarcasm.

Mrs. Ehrly ignored my friend. "It was romantic, Mr. Holmes, and for two widows so much in tune to find each other later in life was miraculous. Since that time, I have worked by the side of my husband in his shoppe, and we have grown the business together. All was fine until the summer of last year.

"During that August, a change came over my husband. Where he had been open and communicative with me, I found him suddenly reticent. My husband, who always talked warmly with me, was now cold and taciturn."

"Did he give you any indication as to why he so suddenly changed his temperament?" I asked. With my own involvement with women, I knew men often became uninterested in a relationship if it continued for many years. There were many happy marriages in the world, but some were due to wives turning a blind eye to their husbands' indiscretions.

"His rationale for his behavior, Dr. Watson, was that he was performing poorly in his chess club."

Holmes suddenly sprang up in his seat, his spine stiffened like a sitting soldier at attention. "Ehrly...of course! The great Nick Ehrly of the Paddington Chess Players. I knew your husband's name sounded familiar. Watson, Mr. Ehrly is a bit of a celebrity in chess circles, holding his own in a match against the great Wilhelm Steinitz. He also was a key player when the London Chess Club defeated the Vienna Chess Club in a telegraph match which lasted well over a year. Your story has just become much more intriguing," admitted the detective.

"I'm glad you think so, Mr. Holmes," answered Mrs. Ehrly, and I wondered if I detected a note of derision in her statement. "I thought perhaps my husband just needed some time to work through whatever problems were running through his mind, so I did not press him beyond his ridiculous answer about poor chess games.

"We remained that way for about a month, working and living quietly together. Then, the first odd turn of events occurred."

"The first?" I inquired. Holmes raised up his lanky left arm and with his hand motioned me to be silent.

"Yes, the first, Doctor. One day while working on the latest incarnation of his own wristlet, my husband became frustrated while inserting a wheel into the device. His face turned beet red, his hands shook, and he tossed down his tools. I thought he just needed a moment to compose himself. Instead, he broke down into loud sobs. I inquired as to what was the matter, and he told me that his son had recently passed away."

"And you had no indication that this son existed?" questioned Holmes.

"None at all, Mr. Holmes. He had mentioned no kin beyond his deceased parents, certainly no offspring. After my husband had calmed down and I served him a cup of Darjeeling, he explained to me that his son had been a major fighting in the Afghan war. He was killed in late July from wounds incurred at a battle at Maiwand."

Here I started and gripped my shoulder which still gave me trouble from being hit by a Jezail bullet. "Madame, I also was in that bloody battle. It grieves me to hear of your step-son's demise on so great and terrible a battlefield."

"Thank you, Dr. Watson. Did you know of any Ehrlys?"

"I did not. There were many regiments there, but there was no Ehrly in my own, the Fifth Northumberland Fusiliers."

"I understand. It would be nice to meet someone who saw my step-son on the battlefield. My husband shared with me the one photograph he

76

had of the boy, a profile featuring him in his uniform, a strapping lad yet with much more brooding features than my husband. The Major clearly resembled more of his mother's side of the family.

"Nicholas told me that his son's name was Marcus and that he was buried just a few blocks from the shoppe in the Anglican section at Kensal Green. We walked there after closing up for the day, and my husband explained that he and Marcus had become estranged from each other. There had been no funeral for the boy, and my husband was devastated that he never had the opportunity to say goodbye to his son.

"Having learned what truly ailed my husband, I knew how to attempt a remedy. When my husband needed distance, I provided it. When he needed warmth, I provided that as well. Over the next few months as I nursed Nicholas, he slowly began to return to his normal self. I thought time and my love were all he needed to heal from this open wound."

"Then you received the letter in the post," stated Holmes, accurately predicting the next part of Mrs. Ehrly's tale.

"Yes, a week before Christmas last year, my husband received a strange letter in the post. The letter was addressed to Sir Nicholas Ehrly, KCB. There was no other address, no post mark, or indication as to whom the letter was from. Just my husband's name and supposed honorary title.

"I brought the letter to my husband and assumed someone he knew was having a lark. Maybe one of his chess friends.

"When Nicholas saw the letter, his face turned ashen. He snatched the letter from my hand, ripped it open, and removed a single sheet of paper. On the paper was a rather crude pencil drawing of two girls sitting at a table, drinking tea. The art looked to be created by a child no older than five or six years of age.

"My husband tore the paper and envelope asunder and tossed the paper pieces into the fireplace, where they were set aflame.

"I asked my husband what it was all about, but he just shook his head and muttered a queer word. It sounded like he said *Dirgleby*."

"Dirgleby?" I inquired.

"Yes, that's what it sounded like, and I heard it enough. For the next few weeks, my husband refused to talk about the letter, and would constantly be muttering the word Dirgleby under his breath.

"Again, I gave my husband distance, and after about a month or so, he again began returning to his normal self, though if I mentioned the letter to him, he would have a black day.

"After several months, my husband had improved. He talked more to me, and I felt that I had my old Nicholas back. I did not refer to the letter, and I began to forget about it."

"Until your husband recently received another letter in the post," said Holmes.

"Yes, five days ago, I returned home from the grocer to find my husband in a dark and foul mood. He was sitting in his favorite arm chair, brooding. On the parlour table, I saw an open letter and a picture, both were identical to the ones sent a year before.

"I asked my husband what the letter could mean, why it ailed him so. He simply muttered Dirgleby in response, and he then rose from his seat and left our home to go for a walk. This time, he did not destroy the letter."

Here, Mrs. Ehrly paused and removed the crinkled envelope containing the letter from her dress pocket. She handed it to Holmes, who eyed the writing, sniffed the envelope, and turned the paper between his hands.

"It is a plain envelope, Mr. Holmes. It is the content inside which you will find of interest," Mrs. Ehrly said, clearly wanting the detective to see the crude drawing.

"This plain letter has many details to tell, Mrs. Ehrly. While you are correct that the envelope has no obvious information, such as the letter's place of origin, I can tell you that the letter was not delivered by the man who wrote your husband's address, that the man who delivered the letter is left-handed, possibly working as a cab driver, and residing here in London.

"Now, let us look at the message itself." Holmes removed the paper from the envelope. Inside was a most childish illustration of two girls sitting for tea. The primitive figures were a mix of blob heads and bodies with triangle shaped dresses, stick hands, stringy hair, dot eyes, and curved line smiles. The table was a block with four straight rectangle legs, and the tea cups rested in the air above it. The cups were half circles and the pot a blob with a curved shaft next to it representing the spout.

Holmes rose, went to his desk, and returned with his magnifying glass in hand. He inspected the lines in the drawing, the smudge marks around the edges, and studied the picture up close and at a distance.

"This is certainly a unique case you have brought to me, Mrs. Ehrly," Holmes said with a clear sense of joy in his tone. "Now, let us discuss my fee."

After Mrs. Ehrly left the premises, Holmes sent a message to a Mr. Ignatius Cobbleton, a member of the Paddington Chess Players, who resided in one of the newer stucco homes in Tyburnia.

"Ah, excellent news, Watson," Holmes said after receiving a telegraph response. "Mr. Cobbleton will see us at his residence late this afternoon. That gives us time to visit the gravesite of Marcus Ehrly beforehand."

We had a light lunch of an assortment of breads and cheeses, plus a fine bottle of merlot between us. Holmes had persuaded Mrs. Ehrly to pay him half of his fee in advance, so while not wealthy, we now did not want for money. Holmes paid Mrs. Hudson the rent owed, and we then hailed a cab and were on our way to Kensal Green.

During the ride, Holmes kept inspecting the envelope and crude drawing of the letter.

"Whatever does it mean, Holmes?" I asked my friend.

"I am not certain as of yet. I need more time to evaluate all of the possibilities. I can assure you, Watson that this drawing is more than a drawing. It contains a message. Whether the message is symbolized by the drawing or hidden as a code within the crude lines of the pictures, I am not certain."

"And is the message 'Dirgleby'?" I inquired.

"Again, Watson, I do not know." And here Holmes actually grinned. "It is a puzzle which will take time to piece together. Yet, I will piece it together. Perhaps in time for Christmas, perhaps by the New Year. I believe that once I have deduced the message of the picture, the other parts of this problem will fall into place, and all will be revealed. Ah, we are at our destination."

We exited the four-wheeler, and Holmes asked the driver to stay, in order to bring us next to the residence of Mr. Cobbleton. The driver agreed with a shrug of his shoulders, and Holmes and I wandered off through the cemetery entryway. The pathway was still damp, and cloudy brown pools of water were all around us as we trudged along the path, our boots sinking slightly into the mud. "This way," Holmes told me. "She said that he is buried in the Anglican portion of the cemetery."

As we wandered along, I noted the ornate stone mausoleums, the intricate designs of angels on headstones, hand carved crosses, and Latin etched in stone. It made me feel that the dead here were honoured, and I was proud that a fellow fighter at Maiwand was buried in such a place as Kensal Green.

We weaved our way through the headstones and then came to a tiny gravesite with a stone laid in the ground. In Latin, the engraving roughly said, *Here lies Marcus Ehrly. May his memory live on.*

I lowered my head at the site and said a prayer for my fallen comrade. I started thinking of all of my friends whom I lost that day, the horrors of the infirmary where limbs were lopped off and stacked like logs. I shuddered as the battle began replaying in my mind, and I would have probably stood there reliving my memories for many moons, had I not heard a harsh cough somewhere behind me.

I turned and was shocked to see Holmes a good distance away, amidst a conversation with one of the working grave diggers. *How long had I been lost in my memories?* I wondered. I saw Holmes tip his deerstalker and hand the man a sovereign. "Bless ya, sir," said the grave digger, and he sauntered off, carrying his rusty steel shovel and pickaxe with great effort.

"I apologize, Holmes. Standing at this gravesite brought back many unpleasantries from my military career," I said as the gaunt form of my companion rejoined me, his Inverness cape billowing softly in the light wind.

"No need to apologize, Watson. I could tell you needed a moment of solitude, and I had a very interesting conversation with Mr. Lory, there."

"You gleaned some useful information about Marcus Ehrly?"

"Perhaps. I noted how small this gravesite appeared compared to the others around it, and noting its close proximity to the other gravesites, determined that the grave could be no more than a length of five feet."

"Five feet?" I stammered. "Why, he must have been rather short for a major, or else he was severely injured in the war. Perhaps," and here I choked on my own words, "perhaps not all of his body made it back to England."

"A dark possibility, Watson. Mr. Lory said he buried a rather small casket, more like the size of a dispatch box."

"Why, that's absurd. Isn't it? I've never heard of such a thing. Even with the man's remains severely reduced, they would have the common courtesy to, at the very least, bury him in a child-sized coffin."

"Ah, Mr. Lory believes that young Mr. Ehrly may have been cremated."

"Cremated?" I snapped, derision now rising in my voice. "Holmes, that isn't even legal. I've heard of such things in the Far East, but in London? Why, that's not Christian."

"Oh, come now, Watson. It is a common burial method in Italy, and it has been gaining its supporters in London. I've even heard that the Queen's physician, Sir Henry Thompson, is a promoter of this form of burial."

"Ridiculous, Holmes. We are a far more civilized society than to allow for such barbarism. Why, if we are to sanction such treatment of our bodily remains, we will soon be living like savages and returning to the Dark Ages." I stilled my tongue, for I had worked myself into a tirade, and seeing the amused expression upon my friend's visage made me stop. If I hadn't regained my composure, I may have raged at him. Finally, after huffing for a moment, I asked sharply, "Besides, what bearing would this have on the case?"

"An excellent question, Watson, and I am happy to report that I do not know the answer as of yet."

"Happy to report? Why, Holmes, I believe that you are enjoying yourself."

"I am, Watson. This is the first time in over two months where a case hasn't supplied an obvious answer. Though I do believe that once I have enough information, the veil will clear, and the answer will reveal itself as rather elementary. For now though, I will enjoy this mental exercise. Come now, for we should away to see Mr. Cobbleton."

During our brief travel from Kensal Green to Tyburnia, I asked Holmes about the letter and drawing that Mr. Nicholas Ehrly had received, and how Holmes had concluded that the deliverer of the letter was a possibly a cabbie who was *not* the artist of the contained drawing.

"Ah, those were rather basic deductions. I'm sure you noted that there were a few smudges on the back of the envelope. They were not very large, but they indicated that the letter was carried between the left thumb and index finger. Who, but a left-handed man, carries a letter in such a way?

"Contrasting this is the slight slant of the words on the envelope's address. It is easy enough to conclude that the writer of the address was a right-handed man."

"Remarkable, Holmes. You make it seem as simple as a rudimentary problem for a schoolboy. How about the occupation of the messenger?"

"It is quite clear that the letter was not sent in the post. There is no label stating the letter's place of origin. This means that someone slipped it in with other letters on both occasions. There are several people and occupations who would have the opportunity to deliver such a letter undetected. In fact, I may have had to leave it at fifteen different possibilities, such as a commissionaire, or even a post officer. However, I noted two thin strands of hair stuck in the envelope's glue. On close examination, I could see that these were hairs from cob horses. It was very easy to determine who, other than a cabbie, would have cob horse hairs on his body. Since the message was delivered from a cab driver, it is easy to ascertain that the letter originated in London."

"Fascinating, Holmes. I'd say it was incredible, even inhuman, but when you explain your reasoning, it seems like all of London should be able to see as you do."

"All can, Watson. It just takes mental training to not just see, but to observe. Ah, we are at Mr. Cobbleton's residence. Let us find out if he can add any information to our endeavor."

We exited the taxi, and Holmes again requested that our driver remain. After a quick talk, Holmes was by my side, and we left the horse-drawn carriage and approached the elegant stucco home of Mr. Cobbleton. Holmes rapped on the door, and we were greeted by a young manservant who ushered us into the waiting room.

The servant supplied each of us with a glass of brandy and then left to fetch his master.

"How do you know Mr. Cobbleton?" I asked Holmes.

"Last year, I helped clear the name of one of his maids. Several pieces of jewelry had gone missing from his home, and the maid had been accused of the crime. She was the only known person with access to the room besides Cobbleton's wife and mother. In the end, I revealed that the mother, in her old age, was becoming frightful and forgetful. She was the first to accuse the maid of the crime. I was able to show the matriarch had moved the jewelry to a safe location, or what she *thought* was a safe location, due to her suspicion of the maid and really the entire staff. Her safe spot was an old mouse hole in the back of her room behind a sofa.

"Mr. Cobbleton was very grateful, and ended up getting his mother her own home with staff to watch over her. Ironically, the maid was hired at increased wages to help care for Mrs. Cobbleton."

"That worked out nicely," I said and added, "You know, that would make for a good book, the type like Dickens writes. A grand mystery, a smart detective – maybe just add in a romance."

Holmes looked aghast at my suggestion. "This is the real world, Watson, not some cheap romance one can have for a penny. Besides, we must be careful with Cobbleton."

"Why is that Holmes?"

"Because he is a chess player, and there is no one so cunning or scheming as a master of that game. I hear footsteps, Watson. Please let me do the talking. I have not been completely honest with Mr. Cobbleton as to the nature of our visit."

Before I had a chance to ask my friend what he meant about his honesty, the young manservant ushered in a charming man of excessive height. He must have been well over six-and-a-half feet tall, with broad shoulders, well-groomed cropped white hair, and a thick and bushy mustache. He wore a fluffy red bow tie which added expression to his dour looking black suit. The man exuded the power of his class, and his form seemed to symbolize the strength of his station in life.

"The great Sherlock Holmes! Welcome! Welcome!" boomed the gentleman. He first grabbed Holmes's hand and shook it, then with a vice-like grip, he grabbed my own and shook vigorously.

"I'm Mr. Ignatius Cobbleton, but please call me Iggy. That's what my friends do. And to whom do I have the pleasure?"

"My name is Dr. Watson." I answered.

"Doctor, aye. Good show! How do you come to know Mr. Holmes?"

I told him of our status as flat mates.

"Splendid," Iggy said. "Not a bad idea, a detective and a doctor living together. You must have some of the safest rooms in all of London. Now, tell me, what do you need to know about Sir Nick?"

Holmes and I jumped at this statement and gave each other knowing looks.

"Thank you, Iggy," said Holmes, with a look of dissatisfaction at calling Mr. Cobbleton by his nickname. "As you know, we are here representing an elite club that is interested in offering membership to Mr. Ehrly. The club has requested that its name be withheld throughout this process."

"Secrets, aye?" said Iggy. "Oh, you boys made a good choice then in offering a spot to Sir Nick. The man's a master of secrets."

Again, Holmes and I looked at each other with surprise. Mr. Cobbleton, I thought, might provide Holmes with everything he needed to know.

"We just have some routine questions for you, Iggy, and then we shall be on our way. We have dinner plans for this evening, and so cannot dawdle."

"Understand, Mr. Holmes. Completely understand. What would you like to know about Sir Nick? I can vouch for the man's character. Excellent! All around a good man. He is the least well-to-do member of the Paddington Players, but please do not hold that against him. He's a good lad and an excellent craftsman. Plus, he's smart. One of the best chess players I've met. That's why we call him 'Sir Nick'."

"Why is that?" asked Holmes.

"Because the man is a genius on the chessboard. During his match against Wilhelm Steinitz, he beat the man twice. The second time in a rather routine move using his rook, but in the first game, he was able to use both his knights to corner Steinitz's king in a checkmate. After that game, he was always known as 'Sir Nick'."

Holmes then asked a few routine questions on Mr. Ehrly's character. The answers were straightforward and unremarkable. After about a half-of-an-hour, Holmes thanked Iggy for his time.

"Always a pleasure, detective. Anymore questions for me?"

"Just one. Can you tell me anything about Mr. Ehrly's son?"

Here Iggy grumbled and shook his head a bit. "Now, Mr. Holmes, remember you are looking to invite Sir Nick into your club, not his relations."

"So you've met his son, Marcus."

"I have, Mr. Holmes, and the fruit could not have fallen further from the tree. It must have been twelve or more years ago that Nick brought his son to the chess club. He only brought him along a few times. He said his son rivaled him in his capabilities, and that he was an exceedingly shrewd player."

"Then, what was the problem?" I asked.

"Dr. Watson, it was not his ability to play the game, but his attitude towards others. When he would win, he would gloat over his opponent. When he would lose, he would rage, using his arm to fling all the pieces off of the chess board. Ridiculous behavior! After a few showings like that, Sir Nick never brought his son back. Maybe he took him over to his other club."

"Mr. Ehrly belongs to another chess club?" Holmes inquired.

"Not a chess club exactly. A smaller group called the Paddington Puzzlers. They solve all sorts of codes and puzzles. I don't have much interest in that sort of thing, but a few members of the chess club belong. I can give you some names if that would be helpful."

"Most helpful," answered Holmes.

The next morning, while breakfasting, I inquired as to whether Holmes was going to spend the day interviewing members of the Paddington Puzzlers.

"First, my dear Watson, I am going to finish my cup of Oolong, read *The Times*, and enjoy my breakfast." Mrs. Hudson had provided a delightful light meal of tea, porridge, and pastries. "After that, I'm going to pay a visit to Inspector Gregson at the Yard."

"I see. Then, will you interview the Puzzlers?" I asked, assuming that would be the logical next step in this case.

"Only if need be. I do think this case is almost closed."

"Why, Holmes, I am just as baffled as ever. Please enlighten me as to how our work yesterday has led you to this conclusion."

84

"Ah, not quite yet Watson," Holmes said, and took a sip of his tea. "There is still the possibility that Gregson might provide information which will lead me to a different conclusion. Though, I feel fairly certain that this puzzle will be solved by early this afternoon."

"My word, Holmes," I ejaculated. "And all I've been able to figure is that Mr. Ehrly is not an actual knight."

Holmes had a mischievous expression on his face, and he let out one of his odd, silent laughs.

"You mean," I stammered, "that the man is a *real* knight."

"While Mr. Ehrly may be called 'Sir Nick' by his chess playing comrades, he is an actual knight, for the envelope was not only addressed to Sir Nicholas Ehrly but was followed by the letters KCB. This means that Sir Nicholas is a Knight Commander in the Most Honourable Order of the Bath."

I was startled by this news, for I had forgotten about the letters upon the envelope, but I did remember some information about the Order of Bath. "But Holmes, isn't that order strictly for members of the military?"

"Not anymore, Watson. Queen Victoria has allowed for civilian appointments for over a decade now. For some reason, which I intend to learn, Mr. Ehrly was knighted. Now, Watson, how is your patient schedule today?"

"I have a full morning ahead of me, Holmes, but as of now, a light afternoon."

"Very good. I shall send you a telegram early this afternoon. If all goes as I believe that it will, then I will ask you to meet me at Mr. Ehrly's shoppe. At that point in time, all will be revealed. If I am wrong, then we shall have a fine dinner at home, and I shall give you a full update."

"I look forward to hearing from you."

The telegram arrived at precisely one o'clock in the afternoon. Holmes said all had gone as he expected, and he requested my presence at Mr. Ehrly's shoppe at four. This was a perfect time, as my schedule for the day had filled – which was auspicious, for it meant that my coffers had filled as well. My last appointment was to end at three. With it being Christmas Eve, I believed that those who wanted to see me, but had delayed because of the flood, made it a priority to visit me before I closed for the holiday. After treating an unexpected late patient with a debilitating cough, I hailed a hansom and was on my way to rendezvous with Holmes.

On my way to the watchmaker's shoppe, I kept running the events of the last two days through my mind. *According to Holmes, Sir Nick*

85

was a true *knight, but what could have caused him to earn such an honor? Could it have something to do with the Paddington Puzzlers or, more likely, the death and cremation of his son? Perhaps he was knighted for allowing his son to be the first man to be officially cremated. Could it be that the Crown, church, and government were going to announce new burial expectations? With the millions of people living in London, we could be running out of cemetery space.* Here, I shook my head and scoffed. I could not believe that our leaders would take such a horrid course of action, and yet, I had seen many horrors in my day. Changes in the battlefield, changes in social customs . . . . Well, I for one, I decided, was not going to change with these strange times. I would hold steady to my traditional decorum, no matter the social pressures.

By the time I arrived at Sir Nick's shoppe, I was quite agitated and upset with the possible solutions I had concocted for this case. As my carriage dropped me on First, I saw Holmes strolling along the sidewalk. He must have walked a good deal of the way.

"Ah, Watson, your timing is impeccable," my friend told me as he met up with me and vigorously shook my hand.

"Did Gregson have all the answers you needed?" I asked gruffly. My mind was still imagining all of Britain's headstones being replaced with urns of ashes.

"He did, my dear fellow, but that was only at the start of my morning. The man who was most helpful was not a Yarder, but a warden at Newgate Prison. It was through his influence that I was able to ascertain the conclusion to this mystery. After spending half of a day in that dreadful, dark pit on the corner of Old Bailey, I felt a good walk in the air was necessary. But let us not dally." Holmes opened the door to the watchmaker's shoppe and a little bell jingled. He ushered me inside. "After you, Watson."

The establishment was a small yet tidy business. Mr. Ehrly was a squat man with bushy sideburns, standing at the counter, winding a large copper pocket watch. There were several glass display cases showing off his wares, and I made a mental note that if I ever needed a watch, this would be a good place to purchase one.

"Hello, gentlemen. We are closing up soon, what with it being Christmas Eve and all." Mr. Ehrly looked up at us and he had a warm smile. "Is there anything in particular you gentlemen are seeking, or perhaps you are here for a repair?"

"Indeed, there is something which we are seeking." Here, Holmes paused and took a bow. He then glared at me. "Watson, you are forgetting your manners. Please give a little bow to Sir Nicholas. It is not often one finds themselves in the company of a Knight Commander from the Order of Bath."

Sir Nicholas stumbled backwards a few steps, clearly shocked by Holmes's statement. "Whoa! What do you want?" he asked, his bottom lip quivering, and his face a ghostly white.

"Actually," Holmes smiled. "I've come to collect my fee."

The color quickly returned to Ehrly's features as his fists clenched and his cheeks turned a bright crimson of rage. "I'll have none of that! None of that! You get out of my shoppe! Get out this instant!!" he shouted.

"What's all this about?" came a call from a back room. Through a doorway behind the counter entered Mrs. Ehrly, who looked confused at hearing her husband's shouts and at seeing Holmes and me before him. "Why Mr. Holmes. Dr. Watson. Whatever are you doing here?"

"You are familiar with these scoundrels, Marigold?" Mr. Ehrly asked his wife.

"Yes, dear," Mrs. Ehrly told her husband and put her hand on his back to comfort him. "Mr. Holmes is a detective."

"Detective?" Sir Nicholas asked. His face was a flurry of confusion and emotions.

"Please, let me explain," said Holmes. "As your wife said, my name is Sherlock Holmes, and I am a detective. Mrs. Ehrly hired me to discover who was sending you anonymous letters, containing what appeared to be crude children's drawings."

"Nothing crude about them," Sir Nicholas grumbled.

"No, there is not," stated Holmes, and he removed from his coat pocket a folded piece of paper which he handed to Sir Nicholas Ehrly.

Ehrly unfolded the paper revealing a different crude drawing, one in the same style as the two girls at tea, but this one was of a boy and a girl standing in a meadow. Mr. Ehrly's eyes ate up the drawing, looking over every square inch of the paper.

Finally, the man let out a long sigh. "Very well, Mr. Holmes, you have my attention. What is this about?"

"Like I said, your wife hired me to discover the author of the letters. I have done so. I have also spoken with the man."

"He's no man," spat Sir Nicholas. "He's the Devil."

"Your son has committed many wrongs in his lifetime, but he is certainly not the Devil."

"Son?" both Mrs. Ehrly and I said in a shocked tone.

"But he's dead, Mr. Holmes," Mrs. Ehrly explained.

"Yes, at Maiwand," I said, again thinking of the atrocities committed there.

"He is not dead. At least, he is still made out of living breathing flesh and blood, though he is officially declared dead," Holmes said, looking squarely at Sir Nicholas Ehrly. "Should I explain all, or should you?"

Sir Nicholas looked ill, his anger turned to worry. Beads of sweat coated his face. He swallowed hard, turned to his wife, turned back to Holmes, nodded, and said, "Please go on."

"Very well," Holmes began. "When Mrs. Ehrly brought this case to me yesterday, I was most intrigued by the picture. I could tell that there was something hidden in it, whether it was a coded message, or the picture itself represented the message. I was not certain. I needed more data.

"Dr. Watson accompanied me, and then we went to pay a visit to your son's grave. Interesting gravesite, that. The grave was small, the size of a child's. Whether you are aware of this or not, it is far too small to be one for a full-bodied adult. Then, I spoke with one of the gravediggers at the site who was certain that he had buried cremated ashes and not a man's body.

"Knowing that ashes are not often buried in a grave, they are more often kept in an urn or scattered, and the fact that cremation remains illegal in England, I surmised that the gravesite contained not a body, but materials representing a symbolic death."

"That it does, sir. That it does," admitted Sir Nicholas.

"Now, at this point, there were two logical possibilities. The first, that Marcus Ehrly was alive, and for some reason his death had been faked. Second, that Marcus Ehrly had perished in the battle at Maiwand as reported, and that his remains had never been recovered – hence the need for a symbolic burial.

"I concluded the former reason was the solution after Dr. Watson and I paid a visit to Mr. Ignatius Cobbleton."

"You saw Iggy," groaned Sir Nicholas.

"He knows nothing. We explained that we were inquiring about you for membership to a private club. Iggy spoke highly of your character, but much less so about the character of your son. He also spoke of the Paddington Puzzlers, and that is when I began to see the full picture of your son's crimes.

"I remembered that during a criminal surveillance with some Yarders in which I was a participant, two inspectors spoke in harsh whispers about a bungled conspiracy against the Crown in which the villains were caught due to their secret code being broken.

"This morning, I went to see Inspector Gregson of the Yard with your son's drawing. He instantly recognized it and asked how it came into my possession. As usual, I told him very little, and he told me quite a lot. It appears, Mrs. Ehrly, that there was a conspiracy to murder the Queen of England and destroy the House of Commons in a move reminiscent of the Gunpowder Plot.

"The plot was suspected when two of the conspirators were seen exchanging crude drawings. A rather impressive guard thought there was something suspicious in the way the two men kept exchanging the pictures, and the guard was able to confiscate several of the illustrations.

"Gregson explained to me that the secret code within the drawings was cracked and the conspirators apprehended before they could do any damage. All of the thirteen men involved were sentenced to death and hanged in July of last year."

"Not all of them," stated Sir Nicholas with a deep frown.

"No, not all of them," agreed Holmes. "After speaking with Inspector Gregson, I was able to conclude that you, Sir Nicholas, were crucial in breaking the conspirators' code, that you were knighted for your efforts. Yet you kept this honor a secret. It led me to the conclusion that your son was involved in the conspiracy and that you were granted the request of having your son's life spared. If he *was* spared, he certainly was not allowed to go free. No, he would spend the remainder of his years in prison. Which one? Newgate was the logical choice, as it is the most secure to hold such a prisoner.

"I tested my theory by going to the delivery drivers who frequented the prison. It did not take me long to ascertain that there was only one left-handed driver, a milkman, who entered the prison regularly.

"I approached the delivery man and gave him one of my crude drawings. He was cautious in talking with me, but using my knowledge of the conspirators as well as my deductions, I was able to gain his trust. I explained I was an outside man working against the Queen, and just recently learned of Marcus still being alive. We struck up a conversation, and the driver explained he was also an outside man, that he did not know too much beyond his role as a messenger of notes. He did inform me that Marcus was in prison under the name Bartholomew Huggins, and that his father was responsible for this turn of events. The man was very nervous upon meeting me, and even more so as I continued asking him questions. I asked him to keep silent about our meeting. The man gave me his assurances and then took off on his route.

"So, I knew that Marcus was inside Newgate Prison and that he was incarcerated under the name Bartholomew Higgins. Fortunately, I know the warden at Newgate, and I soon found myself in a private meeting with Marcus, now Bartholomew."

"And I'm sure upon meeting him, you saw a scoundrel the likes of which you've never laid eyes upon before. He is a horrible man, a wretched human being whose actions would have caused a reaction that could have destroyed the Commonwealth. He's been a wretch for years, Mr. Holmes. It's why he was estranged from me since before I met my dear wife. He has been in the criminal world for many years and has worked along the most insidious scoundrels ever to walk the earth. He deserved to be executed along with his miserable lot, Mr. Holmes."

"Yet," my friend said gently, "you could not bring yourself to allow him to die."

"No, sir, and I now realize it was weakness on my part. The Queen was kind enough to grant my request to have my son's execution commuted and sentenced to life in prison. Many years ago, before I took Marcus to the Paddington Players, he had been dismissed from the service on account of his fighting. Because of his military career, though brief and disorderly, his history was rewritten to state that he was killed at Maiwand.

"I wanted him dead to the world, wanted the son I knew who was a good boy to rest in peace. I took all the memories I had of that boy, the childhood letters and photographs, and had them buried at Kensal Green. This new person, this horror he grew into – he deserved Newgate. It is better that he rots there."

"Sir Nicholas, your son has done treasonous acts and deserves his punishment. When I met with him, he knew of your work in destroying the conspiracy. He is also aware that you were behind his life imprisonment, but he did not know that your actions spared his life. He was taken aback by this information, and by the time I left, I had gained his assurances that he will no longer send you an annual letter."

"If only that were true, Mr. Holmes."

"I believe that it is, Sir Nicholas. Your son has done a very bad deed, probably many of them, but he is a human being, and I could see the remorse in his manners over what he had done. Your son will spend the remainder of his life behind bars, of that I am certain; however, he does not need to do it alone."

"What are you saying, Mr. Holmes? You want me to visit that traitor! He is dead to me!" bellowed Sir Nicholas.

"No, Nicholas," Mrs. Ehrly interjected. "Your son is alive. Perhaps with time . . . ."

"Perhaps nothing!" Sir Nicholas raged.

"I believe your wife is correct, Sir Nicholas, though you do not see it now. With time, eventually, I feel that you should visit your son. He is not dead, and the good son you remember is still alive inside of him."

Sir Nicholas fumed, but he let out a long sigh. With a tone of utter sadness and regret, he whispered. "Perhaps, there is hope."

"Of course there is hope, Sir Nicholas," explained Holmes, and he had a warm smile when saying this. "After all, it is Christmas Eve. 'Tis the season of hope."

The next morning, Christmas morning, Holmes answered some last few questions I had about the case, mainly what was meant by the term Dirgleby.

"The code, Watson, is a rather difficult one. If I had not known the word 'Dirgleby', then I probably could not have cracked it. After we met with Iggy, I knew that the drawing must contain a secret message. I stayed awake most of the night determining how the lines met to represent letters. Once I was able to determine the code, I read within the tea party drawing the word 'Dirgleby', but it was actually broken in two as *Dir Gilby* with *Dir* representing *yer* or *you're*, and *Gilby* representing *guilty*. So, each year, Marcus planned on sending his father a message saying *'You're Guilty'*, that he was guilty of sending his son to prison for life. I do believe that the letters will stop, and with the aid of Mrs. Ehrly, the two men will reconcile over time. An appropriate start to Christmas. Aye, Watson, which reminds me . . . ."

Holmes paused and pulled out a box from beneath the dining table, which he handed over to me.

"What is this?" I asked.

"Please, open it Watson. It is the quickest way to find out."

I did as he asked and was shocked to find a cleaning kit for my Webley. "Why, Holmes, thank you. I did not expect . . . ."

"I believe that is the point, Watson. A Happy Christmas to you!"

"But," here I was embarrassed, "I fear that I did not get you a gift. I never really have done a gift exchange at Christmas."

"Actually, Watson, there is something I would like from you."

"Name it."

"I find that on my cases, when you are an active participant, my mind moves in directions which do not come naturally to my thinking process. Sometimes it is an expression upon your face or a muttering under your breath. You may not have known it, Watson, but I believe your role in solving this case, of getting my mind to the right path, was crucial."

"Thank you, Holmes, though you are correct. I do not see what help I was to you."

"That is fine, my dear Watson. You do not need to see, though I believe over time you will. You will begin to have some of my gifts with practice, and that's what I would like from you for Christmas.

"What is that?"

"I would like for you to continue to be my companion on cases, Watson. What say you?"

"Holmes," I chuckled. "That is a Christmas present that I am more than happy to provide."

The Stolen Relic
by David Marcum

I paused in the doorway of 221 Baker Street, anxious to make my way inside and out of the bitter wind, but held in place by the sound of the approaching carolers. They were singing "The Moon Shines Bright", a song I remembered from my youth, and the lilting refrain brought bittersweet memories to mind, despite the cheery major key. It recalled times long gone when, as a child, our family had traveled south to visit my mother's people during the Christmas season. It was only then that I was able to see a traditional English celebration, and with it all that I missed during those other years while being raised in Scotland, where Christmas is not celebrated as such.

As the carollers came closer, I heard the words more clearly: *The moon shines bright and the stars give a light, little before it is day; Our Lord our God he called on us, and bids us awake and pray.*

I took another step into the building, but caught myself as they began the next verse, which I also recalled and which seemed to reflect my thoughts from this seemingly grim December: *The life of a man it is but a span, it's like a mourning flower; We're here today, to-morrow we are gone, we are dead all in one hour.* Shaking my head at this decidedly dark sentiment, and trying to imagine how it could possibly fit into a Dickensian holiday, I went inside and shut the door.

I had not intended to return home so early that Christmas Eve, having meant to spend the morning at Barts, followed perhaps by a rare afternoon at some theatrical entertainment, and then possibly a meal. I was feeling distinctly antisocial, and sought solitude. However, I was not needed at the hospital, and I found that I wasn't in the mood for the rest of my plans. With nowhere left to go, I glumly returned home.

While hanging my coat, I could see light shining at the top of the stairs, indicating that the sitting room door was open. But even as I watched, the stairwell darkened when the door closed with a solid thud, followed immediately by Mrs. Hudson's determined descent. I had only known our landlady for slightly less than a year, but I recognized this as the tread she made when irritated.

Seeing me standing there, she said, "Doctor Watson, I am *so* sorry. I've tried to do what I could to make your sitting room more festive, but *he* will have none of it." And with that, she cast an angry look back over her shoulder.

"It's quite all right," I said. "As you know yourself from being raised in the north, all of this Christmas merriment is, even now, still occasionally somewhat foreign to me."

"I felt that way as well, when I was younger," Mrs. Hudson replied. "But I've grown to love it. The decorations and the songs. The food and the tree. It's certainly better than how we did it when I was growing up in Scotland, where Christmas was just another day."

"I suppose," I agreed halfheartedly and, with a nod to her, started up the stairs. The truth was that I had enjoyed the British version of the holiday at times in the past. But this year, I was finding it more difficult to embrace any celebratory feelings whatsoever.

When I was a child, my parents' marriage had never set well with my maternal English grandfather, and in spite of his widely read experience and knowledge, he simply could not understand why Christmas wasn't observed in Scotland. My father would attempt to explain how the Church of Scotland, strictly Presbyterian as it was, had no use for Christmas, or *Christ's Mass*. Long before, it had been decided to be a Catholic affair, and thus anything remotely "Popish" was abolished in Scotland in the 16th century. And so it has remained.

But my mother was English through and through, and she had made sure that in our home, at least, some sort of Christmas was acknowledged. It was nothing like that which we saw on those few occasions celebrated at Grandfather's, and her efforts did little to otherwise alleviate the dour northern winter that held the rest of our town in its grip every December.

After I came to London to study medicine, I truly found myself in the midst of the seasonal excitement. In my student days, while living in Bloomsbury, there was no happier celebrant than myself, though perhaps for all the wrong reasons. I was in the thick of every party, and it was said by many that no one kept Christmas better than John Watson. But then came the army, and Afghanistan.

Now, in that late December of 1881, I found myself at the end of a difficult year. In July of '80, I was wounded at Maiwand, and then sent back to England, my health irretrievably shattered. I was set ashore on the Portsmouth jetty during a wet snow, with neither kith nor kin left in England. After that rather miserable Christmas had passed, I was acknowledging Hogmanay with a drink at the Criterion, and sourly contemplating the need to find cheaper lodgings to reflect my limited half-pay, when I was hailed by an old acquaintance, Stamford. What followed was an introduction to Sherlock Holmes, and the amazing series of events that had come over the past year.

94

Amazing they had been, but some had also been disappointing. Just months earlier, following a great portion of the year spent enduring a painful recovery, I had been notified that the army officially had no further need for my services. Each day that had passed since then reminded me in some way that I was marking time, and not going forward with my life. I had made myself useful, filling in as a *locum*, or assisting at Barts and a few of the other hospitals. But I knew that I should be devoting myself to something more permanent. The thought would not leave me.

And now, standing in the doorway of the sitting room, I felt the same thing. I was too happy to return here, when I should be looking for a more effective and prosperous alternative.

I only paused in the doorway for an instant before propelling myself forward. My friend was there, lounging in his chair by the fire and puffing on his cherry-wood pipe, and scowling at a veritable mound of holly and ivy lying across the mantelpiece.

"Ah, Watson. Come warm yourself by the fire. You'll see that Mrs. Hudson just brought tea, along with this pestiferous sampling of *Ilex Aquifoliaceae* and *Hedera Araliaceae*, detritus from some forest that has been killed before its time to rot above our fireplace."

"*We're here today, to-morrow we are gone, we are dead all in one hour,*" I muttered to myself.

"What was that?"

"Nothing," I replied. "Nothing at all."

"My dear fellow," said Holmes, rising suddenly. "You're freezing. Sit down, while I pour you some tea." And he moved to the table, showing that hidden compassion of his that appeared in the most unexpected moments.

Soon I was thawing out, and my mood increased exponentially. I was even able to look with appreciation at the difference made by having the decoration draped in front of Holmes's criminal relics that still rested, now hidden, upon the mantel.

We sat in companionable silence for a while, both looking into the fire with our own thoughts. Therefore, it was with some surprise when the bell rang. Holmes glanced at me. "Rather late in the day for the usual clients who help me earn my bread and cheese."

"Perhaps it is a crony of Mrs. Hudson's, here to wish her the compliments of the Season."

"True enough. We shall soon see."

It quickly became apparent that the caller was not there to visit our landlady, as we heard steady footsteps ascending the stairs. In a moment there was a knock, and Holmes called for the visitor to enter.

95

As we stood, the door opened, revealing a man in his mid-thirties, dressed in the habiliments of a plain priest's cassock. He wore no coat, paying no deference to the British cold, and he was clearly a stranger to our shores.

"Mr. Holmes?" he said, looking from one to the other of us, and speaking in an accent that betrayed his Italian origins. Holmes nodded, and gestured the man towards the basket chair facing the fire.

"May we offer you some refreshment?" I asked.

"Nothing, thank you."

"This is my friend, Dr. Watson. You may speak freely before him."

The man greeted me with a friendly and open countenance. I revised my opinion of his age. Upon closer inspection before the light from the fire, I could see that he was in his early forties.

"My name," said the priest, "is Father Abele. I am of the order located at the *Basilica di San Nicola*, in Bari."

Holmes nodded and stood. "One moment if you please, Father." As he walked over to the shelf where he kept his indexes, the Father smiled patiently, glancing my way in a friendly manner before turning his eyes to the fire. As he warmed, I could see him visibly relax.

Returning to his chair, Holmes sat and began to leaf through the volume. "Hmm. Interesting indeed," he murmured. Then, looking back at the priest, he said, "And how can we help you?"

"You were recommended to me, Mr. Holmes, by a man to whom you provided a previous service, Father Gregor, of the Orthodox Church, regarding the recovery of some stolen icons."

Holmes nodded. "I remember the case." Glancing my way, he said, "Quite before your time, Watson."

Father Abele continued. "I hold a unique position within the *basilica*. It is my duty there to be something of a roving agent, tasked to deal with those issues which might have cause to require a more substantial . . . interaction with the outside world." He looked from one to the other of us. "In short, I am here because a relic from the church has been stolen."

Holmes's eyes brightened, and he tapped his finger on the index. "Indeed. Might I ask – ? But no, let me not anticipate your story. Please tell it in order, from the beginning."

The priest nodded. "As I said, I represent the church of *San Nicola*, or as you would call him, Saint Nicholas."

My eyes widened. "Saint Nicholas. *The* Saint Nicholas? As in Father Christmas?"

Father Abele smiled. "There is that connection, of course," he said. "Even as the Americans have corrupted his name into the garbled appellation of *Santa Claus*."

"The Americans are not completely to blame," added Holmes. "The Dutch called him *Sinterklaas*, and carried that name with them when they immigrated to the United States."

The priest nodded. "As you can imagine, we are quite aware of the different iterations and adaptations of our patron's name throughout the world. But you are correct, Dr. Watson. I am referring to the *true* Saint Nicholas, of historical fact, and so canonized by the Church.

"Quite odd," I said, "the way a man who lived and breathed can, over time, come to be perceived as a make-believe character."

"Indeed," the man continued. "If I may, I would share a bit of history with you. I assure you that it is relevant, and I will not waste too much of your time." With a nod from Holmes, Father Abele continued.

"In case you were not previously aware, Saint Nicholas was born in the year 270 A.D. in Myra, an Asian part of what is now Turkey, and in what was then the Roman Empire. From an early age, he was quite religious, and entered the church while still a boy. Throughout his life, his kindness for both children and sailors was highly recognized, and it was through stories spread across the known world at that time by these very sailors that his fame grew.

"Throughout his life, he performed a number of miracles, including resurrecting the dead, feeding the hungry from food stores that did not decrease as they were used, no matter how much was used, and performing acts of great kindness and then directing the gratitude to God. An example of this was when he provided the dowries for a man's three daughters when the man could not provide it himself. The story goes that the Saint did so," continued the priest, looking at us significantly, "by dropping gold coins down the man's chimney and so into the daughters' stockings, hanging there to dry – hence, the variant form of receiving gifts now credited to Santa Claus.

"When the Saint was in his mid-fifties, he was quite respected within the church, and was invited by Emperor Constantine himself to attend the first Council of Nicaea, where he was one of the signers of the Nicene Creed. He died in 343, and within a few hundred years from his death, he was recognized as one of the Saints of the Church.

"At the time of his death, his body was entombed in Myra, where – for over six-hundred years – his grave was a destination of pilgrims and worshipers from all over the world.

"But in 1087, following several decades of unrest, sailors from Italy, fearing that access to Nicholas's tomb would become unreachable for pilgrims, seized a number of the bones from his tomb in Myra and brought them back to Bari, where the *Basilica di San Nicola* was constructed, and where pilgrims have journeyed ever since."

"A number of the bones, you say," interrupted Holmes. "But not all of them, I believe."

"That is correct. The others, initially left behind in Myra, were later seized by Crusaders and taken to Venice, where they are also kept in a church dedicated to the Saint."

Holmes nodded. "And you mentioned that a relic from the church has been stolen. Are we to assume then that one or more of the bones of St. Nicholas has been taken?"

"One bone," replied our visitor.

"And you need our assistance to locate it."

"That," said Father Abele, "is somewhat accurate. I know who took the relic. But I have not yet located where he is in London, and as a stranger in your country, I do not have the authority to retrieve it from him."

"I'm afraid that you're mistaken, sir, if you believe that I have any such authority."

The priest nodded. "That is understood, Mr. Holmes. But your involvement in helping me to locate him will go a long way toward clearing the matter up, and will prevent me from blundering in and making a bad situation worse by my ignorance of your customs."

"So," I interrupted, "you simply wish to retrieve the relic, then? And by not involving the police, as you clearly do not wish to do, you do not intend to prosecute?"

Father Abele nodded. "My only interest is in retrieving the object. The thief's punishment is beyond my influence."

"And you are certain the thief is in London?"

"Yes. I believe that you will be able to help me determine his location."

"And this relic?" said Holmes. "You said it is a single bone?"

"Yes. A *distal phalange*, as I think you would call it, from the Saint's left hand."

"The tip of a finger, then," I said.

The priest inclined his head. "More specifically, that of his left thumb. It was stolen more than a week ago. We must retrieve it as soon as possible, before any of the *manna* is lost."

I raised my eyebrows, but Holmes's lips tightened. "My index mentions this phenomenon. I will be happy to help you reacquire the object, but I'm afraid that I cannot give any credence to this supposed miracle."

98

"Miracle?" I asked. "*Manna*?"

Holmes gestured toward the priest, indicating that he should elaborate upon the matter. "Following the Saint's death, his tomb in Myra was always said to have a sweet smell resembling roses. And it has excreted a liquid, known as *manna* or *myrrh*, which has healing powers."

"I'm afraid that – " interrupted Holmes, but the priest continued.

"I understand your disbelief, Mr. Holmes. It is difficult sometimes to have faith in the manifestation of God's miracles. But I have often seen this for myself. After the bones were brought to the *basilica* in Bari, the smell of roses from the tomb has continued, as well as the appearance of the liquid, to the present day. And I have watched how it has been used to perform many miracles."

"And the tomb with the other bones in Venice? Does it also produce this *manna*?"

"I have not been there myself, but it is my understanding that they also have vials of the liquid."

"But surely," said Holmes, "there is another explanation. Seepage of groundwater into the tomb, perhaps? Or condensation?"

The priest shook his head, a tolerant smile dancing upon his lips. "No, Mr. Holmes. The tomb has been verified to be watertight, and no water is entering through the stones. The bones themselves ooze the liquid, much more than could be accounted for by simple condensation. Enough, as a matter of fact, that it is bottled in vials for use, along with Holy Water, in the performance of miracles."

Holmes frowned, as if looking for another argument. Finally, he shook his head. "That is all neither here nor there," he said, "in terms of recovering the bone. As you say, it is important to you to do so sooner, rather than later, but the idea of this *manna's* existence in and of itself has no impact on the actual recovery. What were the circumstances of the theft?"

The priest nodded, as if some sort of accord had been reached, and there was now enough to be going on with. "A little over a week ago, a British ship was docked in Bari. St. Nicholas always had a special relationship with sailors, so it is not unusual for them to visit the *basilica* in order to honor the tomb. Many are simply curious, but a few are genuine pilgrims who wish to worship.

"On the day in question, a group of sailors were there, including one who was recognized as having been there before on several occasions. On previous visits, he was always reverent and respectful, and had asked a number of intelligent questions. This time, however, he did something unusual.

"One of the novitiates noticed that this sailor, a Russian who had previously introduced himself on an earlier visit as Grigori Golov, had stayed behind when his compatriots departed. No other visitors in the *basilica* were present at the time. The novitiate thought nothing of it until, a few minutes later, he returned from an errand to discover that the stone cover of the tomb had been shifted. He called for help, and a number of priests, including myself, quickly determined that the thumb bone had been removed. It was obvious that only Golov could had taken it. There was no damage to the tomb itself, and no other relics were moved.

"As I indicated, it is my position within the church to act in matters relating to the outside world. I quickly made my way to the docks, only to determine that the ship upon which Golov served, *The Good Catherine*, had just left port for England. Obviously, Golov had planned his theft to the minute, allowing for a successful escape.

"Not wanting to involve the police, I decided to follow Golov on my own to retrieve the relic. There were no ships leaving immediately, and I did not want to take the time to follow in so leisurely a manner in any case. Therefore, upon returning to the *basilica*, I arranged to travel by rail, setting foot here three days ago.

"I had just missed the arrival of *The Good Catherine*, but I was able to determine that Golov had disembarked from the ship. It is scheduled to sail again in two days. I have been unable to locate him, although I suspect that he lives in the East End of London. The officials at the shipping office became decidedly uncommunicative when I pressed my questions, and rather than wait for him to reappear at his ship, I decided to see if someone else could help me locate him sooner. I had been given your name, Mr. Holmes, and here we are."

Holmes patted his hand twice upon his index, and then stood abruptly, as he was wont to do upon making a decision. "I believe that I can assist you." He walked around the two of us, replacing the scrapbook. "If you will come back in three hours, I should have the information that you need."

If the priest was surprised at this sudden burst of activity or the promise of a quick solution, he did not show it. He rose from his chair, and I did so as well. With a nod and a small bow, the priest agreed to return, and walked from the room.

Holmes moved into his room, removing his dressing gown as he did so. "Watson, I shall be back in time to meet our client. Do continue to warm yourself in front of the fire." And then, reappearing and wearing clothing suitable for the cold, he departed.

Rather than reseating myself, I stepped over to the shelf holding Holmes's scrapbooks, pulling out the one that he had recently replaced. I found the entry on the Saint, but it gave no more additional information than that which had been recently provided by Father Abele. Unsatisfied, I returned to my seat.

Growing up, I had been exposed to the stories of St. Andrew, that Galilean fisherman who accompanied Christ during his lifetime, and who later carried on the work of the church. I knew about the story of the miracle associated with his name, in which King Angus had seen a vision of St. Andrew's Saltire Cross in the rising sun, and it had inspired him and his men to win a decisive victory over the opposing Saxons, thus leading to the adoption of that Cross as the Scottish symbol. But, in spite of this tale, stories of miracles like the healing fluid produced from the bones of St. Nicholas were not regularly part of the strict Church of Scotland Presbyterian fabric of my boyhood.

I was still brooding upon these questions nearly three hours later when Holmes reappeared, followed almost immediately by the priest. "I have found your sailor," said Holmes as we stepped outside.

"I had no doubts," said Father Abele.

Soon, we were in a four-wheeler, making our way to the south and east. Looking at the priest, sitting across from me in the bitter cold, and without a coat but seemingly indifferent to the fact, I began. "This *manna* . . . ."

The man nodded. "I understand, Doctor. You are curious about the healing properties. You perhaps believe that there is not a true power within the liquid, but rather that the ills are cured by the power of suggestion, and the patient's own desperate desire to be well once again."

"Such things are not unknown," I said. "I could tell you stories of men on the battlefield, during times when we had completely exhausted our supplies. They were given water and told that it was, in fact, morphine. Their belief was enough to convince them that their pain, sometimes from horrible wounds, had been reduced or even eliminated."

Father Abele nodded, and with a kind smile stated, "God has blessed us with minds that have great powers indeed. After all, these minds are created in His own image. One does not realize what the mind is capable of, whether in terms of great reasoning, or the expression of beautiful art or music, or even in terms of healing. But," he added, his face now quite serious, "none of that negates in any way the actual power of a true miracle, which is a separate and distinct thing from that which is conceived of within the mind. A miracle is a gift, granted to us by the Grace of God." And he settled back with finality.

Holmes had a slightly troubled look upon his face, and he was silent throughout this conversation, remaining so throughout the journey. I wondered what he was thinking, although I could imagine. The priest and I also sat quietly, and soon we were at our destination.

We stepped down from our cab, and Holmes led us to a dark arch, from which we signaled for our cabbie to wait. We passed through a tunnel-like passage into a tiny court, and inside were several doors. Holmes stopped in front of the second on the left. It was part of a mean cluster of dark brick buildings, yet surprisingly well kept, considering the neighborhood in which it had been built. "Golov lives on the third floor," said Holmes as we entered the building and climbed the stairs.

Inside, the air was somewhat warmer, although not much, and there was the stale smell of cooked cabbage that is so often found in buildings in that part of London. The stairwell was quite dark, but the treads appeared to be solidly placed, and there was an absence of the refuse that clutters buildings of this sort.

Stopping at the door indicated by Holmes, we caught our breath. From beyond it, we heard quiet conversation. Then the priest knocked solidly, and the voices stopped immediately. After a very short wait, there were heavy footsteps, and the door opened.

We were faced by a tall man, wrapped in a pea coat to ward off the chill. Behind him, we could see a woman with a sad face, standing beside a table where she had apparently been sitting. The man, undoubtedly the sailor Grigori Golov, looked from one to the other of us before settling on Father Abele. A look of sadness crossed his face as he identified the priest's cassock, and he said, with only a trace of accent, "So. You have come, then."

"Was there ever a doubt?" asked the priest, not unkindly. "You did nothing to hide your tracks, my son. We knew your name from when you visited the *basilica* on previous occasions. You waited until no one was there before you opened the tomb, so that it was unavoidably certain that you would be the one identified as the taker of the relic. You made no effort to hide your return to the ship, and your action was apparently planned so as to be able to leave with the vessel at its planned departure time."

Golov nodded. "As you say. But you must understand. I had no choice."

"May we come in?" asked Holmes. "Then, you can explain your reasons."

Golov stepped back, gesturing for us to pass by him. Shutting the door, he said, "This is my wife, Maria."

We nodded at the woman, who simply looked at us, a fearful expression upon her face, pinched with a kind of dread and terror.

"Are these policemen, then?" asked Golov of the priest, looking from Holmes to me. "Are you here to arrest me?"

"No, my son. These men are from here in London. I requested them to help me find you, as I do not know this city very well." He looked around. "Do you still have it? The relic?"

Golov nodded. "I do. And you must believe me that, after I had used it, I intended to return it. I would not have taken it for anything. But, you see, I had no choice."

Holmes nodded. "Is it your child?"

Golov nodded, while the priest looked to his side at my friend. "Child? What do you mean, Mr. Holmes?"

Pointing to several items that I had also spotted on the table in the center of the room, Holmes stated, "Surely it is obvious, from the medical accoutrements placed here and there, that there is illness in the home. There is indication of a child's presence from some of the objects in the room, but he or she – yes, a girl, I believe – is not present. Based upon the various icons placed on the walls, this is a family of deep faith. No doubt Mr. Golov intended to use the power of the relic to heal someone who is ill. Neither Mr. nor Mrs. Golov appears to be sick, so the relic was taken to aid someone else, most likely the child."

Father Abele looked back at the sailor. "Is that so?"

Golov nodded, and his wife began to cry softly.

"And did it help?" asked the priest. "Has your child been healed?"

"No," said Golov sadly. "She has been too ill to even be aware that the Saint's bone is now here."

"Surely," said Father Abele, "she does not need to know it is here for its healing power to make itself manifest."

"That may be," said the big sailor. "And yet, from the time that I returned with it, she has been asleep, suffering from a fever, and unaware that I brought it, as she had asked. I believed that she would know of its power if she recognized that it was here."

"Your daughter requested for you to bring the relic?"

"She did. Many has been the time that I've told her of my visits to the tomb of the Saint, when I've had the opportunity to travel to Bari. When she was scratched several weeks ago, the wound quickly became much worse than one would expect. The doctor came and speculated that the scratch might have simply brought to light some other illness that might prove to be incurable. When it did not seem to get any better, and it appeared as if the doctor could be proven right, our daughter mentioned that perhaps one of the bones of the Saint could be used to heal what the doctor could not.

"I do not know if she really meant for me to bring it, but I resolved that I would do so. Thus, on my last journey, I made my way to the tomb, and as you know, removed the bone." He swallowed, and continued. "I swear, Father, that I was as respectful and as careful as I could be. I would not have desecrated the tomb under any other circumstance, but . . . . but . . . ." He broke off with a sob and hung his head. His wife took a step closer and pulled him to her.

"We are afraid," she said, speaking for the first time, "that she will die."

"I am a doctor," I said, stepping forward. "May I see her?"

At the same time, the priest also said, "The relic? Is it with your daughter?"

Golov looked up, from one to the other of us, and nodded. "In here."

He led us into the other room of the tiny flat, a dark chamber with most of the space taken by a small bed. Lying in the middle of it was a wee girl, probably about seven or eight, but appearing more insignificant due to a likely lack of nutrition during the early years of her life. She was huddled under several blankets, her breathing raspy and labored while she shifted from side to side, moaning lightly with each exhalation. Asking "May I?" and receiving a nod from both her parents, I leaned down and felt of her forehead. She was burning.

While I began to examine the girl, I heard the others talking softly behind me. "The relic?" asked the priest. "Where is it?"

"Here," said Golov, reaching for a small tin on a shabby table beside the bed. "I have not opened it since taking it," he said. "I wanted to keep it safe in transit, as you will understand, and there was no need to see it once I arrived, as Alina was too ill to take note of it."

"Then surely there may be enough . . ." said the priest softly to himself.

I glanced over my shoulder to see the Russian handing the tin to the priest. Father Abele took it and carefully raised the lid. Then he turned it slightly from side to side, in order to catch the faint light from the single-paned window. He stopped turning it when he found the angle he wished, and then he simply looked at it for a long moment. I continued to watch him, curious as to the apparent mesmerization that the object seemed to hold over him.

Finally, he looked up at Holmes, and then toward me. "Gentlemen? Would you like to see?"

He held it out, and I rose, even as Holmes took a step forward. Leaning in, we both saw inside the tin. It contained a small whitish nub, undoubtedly the bone from the tip of a thumb. It rested in the corner of the tin, nearly covered by an oily looking liquid. Even as I realized it, the scent of roses seemed to fill the room.

The priest smiled. "Mr. Golov," he said. "Did you also take any of the liquid that was in the tomb when you removed the relic?"

The sailor shook his head emphatically. "No, Father. I was careful to reach in and retrieve only the bone. I was praying as I did so, in order to be as respectful as possible. Some of the liquid lying around the bones in the bottom of the tomb got on my fingers as I picked out the bone, but I shook it off before I put it in the container. It was damp, but that was all." Suddenly, with a realization crossing his face, he asked, "Why?"

Turning slightly, the priest showed the girl's parents what Holmes and I had just seen, the fragment of St. Nicholas, nearly covered with a fluid that it had apparently excreted between the time it was taken in Bari and now. If one believed that sort of thing.

"But surely, Mr. Golov," said Holmes, stubbornly trying to make sense of what he had seen, "you added the liquid at some point. Or your wife."

"We did not!" cried the Russian, while his wife shook her head emphatically.

"Then someone on the ship from Bari," said Holmes. "Some other sailor who knew what you carried, and got at it at some point."

"No one knew that I had it. I did not tell anyone. I did not want to take the chance that it might be taken from me before I could return with it to Alina."

"A miracle, Mr. Holmes," said the priest simply. "A miracle."

Turning away from the frowning expression on my friend's face, I returned to my examination of the girl. She had a long scratch on her leg, quite infected, and suppurating. Around it, her leg was swollen, with streaks stretching above and below. I had seen this before, and knew that there was more going on beneath the skin than was easily seen.

"She fell," said her mother. "Outside. She said that as she did so, her leg dragged itself across a broken board."

I nodded. "No doubt there are splinters buried in the wound, adding to the injury. This and the fever are the body's way of fighting back. How long has she been like this?"

"She became ill about two weeks ago, not long after the injury. The doctor gave us this." She reached behind to a cabinet affixed to the wall and turned back with a brown bottle. I examined it with disgust, seeing that it was among the worst of the patent medicines available to the ignorant, prescribed by charlatans.

"Which doctor gave you this?"

"Doctor Anglesey," replied the girl's mother.

I snorted. I was aware of the man. In the year that I had been back in London, while volunteering my services at Barts, I had more than once come across the victims of this mountebank's practice.

"This concoction will not help her," I said, shaking the bottle and then handing it back. "She is in danger." I saw no reason to keep them from knowing the truth. "The treatment she received from your Doctor Anglesey did not help. In fact, letting her go for so long without true medical attention has only made the problem worse. She has blood poisoning, and . . . and there is a danger that she might lose her leg."

Golov's eyes widened, while his wife gave forth a sob. "Will she die?" asked the women quietly.

I shook my head. "It is not too late. She can be treated, but we must get her to hospital immediately."

I leaned down and began to wrap her tightly in the thin blankets. But as I was doing so, Father Abele spoke. "Doctor? If I may?"

I turned to see him holding the tin, a questioning look in his eyes. I knew what he was asking.

"Father, I simply cannot. We do not know what is in that liquid."

"We do not know what is in it, but we do not need to. We know from whence it comes."

"It may do more harm than good," I answered with exasperation. "It has been in contact with a bone, for goodness' sake."

"Exactly," said the priest. "For goodness' sake."

I hesitated, uncertain as to whether to allow it. I noticed the girl's father staring intently at me. He nodded. "Let him, Doctor," he said. "Please."

I straightened and glanced at Holmes. His eyes were in a frown, but, sensing my uncertainty, he nodded. With a sigh, I stepped back, allowing the priest access.

He sat himself on the edge of the bed and, laying a hand across the girl's brow, began to pray in low, even tones. Mr. and Mrs. Golov bowed their heads, silently mouthing the words to the prayer as well. Meanwhile, Holmes watched intently.

Father Abele took his open palm from the girl and brought it to the tin, held in his other hand. Placing a finger carefully inside, he brought it back out, now damp from the liquid *manna* within. Moving carefully, so that none of it would drop off, he extended his hand back to Alina's forehead, where he traced the figure of a cross, lengthwise and then side to side, still praying as he did so. Suddenly, almost the instant that he had finished and lifted away his fingertip, the girl gave a gasp and flickered

106

her eyes, but then settled back into the same condition in which she had been when we found her.

Pulling aside the blankets, he then repeated his actions, carefully tracing the length of the girl's wound with the oily substance from the tin. This time, the girl gave no reaction, and the liquid simply shone in the dim light from the window before gradually losing its sheen as it dried.

With a solemn "Amen," the priest arose and made room for me. Not wanting to disturb the fluid, still faintly outlined on the girl's forehead, I placed a hand against her cheek. Was her fever already lessened? Surely not. And yet, I could not be sure in that cold room, and I did not want to take time to find out otherwise. Bundling her up, I rose and carried her out of the bedroom, and so on until we reached the street, where our four-wheeler was waiting.

Talking to our cabbie was another driver, apparently a friend of his, who had tarried for a while during the time that we were inside. The two were talking and smoking, while the second driver's hansom was parked nearby. "*How fortunate to find a second cab in this neighborhood,*" I thought to myself as I climbed with the girl into the four-wheeler. "*Almost a miracle,*" my mind added as I settled back on the seat, carefully holding my patient. I was joined by the girl's parents, while Holmes engaged the hansom for him and the priest to follow.

"The Royal London Hospital, Whitechapel Road," I called to our driver. "And hurry!"

"Right away," the man answered, gigging his horse. Within minutes we were in transit, and not long after, I was carrying the girl inside, explaining the situation, and being directed to a room in order to begin treatment.

Even as we had traveled, the girl had inexplicably and impossibly begun to show signs of recovery. I would like to believe that it was due to the uncomfortable shock of being taken from the womb-like atmosphere of the bedroom and out into the cold December day. How could she not react in some way? But a part of my mind could not help but wonder if the priest's ministrations had not had something to do with it.

Within an hour of our arrival at the hospital, the girl's wound had been debrided and treatment was being given for the fever. Careful probing had revealed a long nasty splinter, black and slick, invisible from the surface and resisting to the end as it was pulled from the girl's wound. The streaks of blood poisoning had already unexplainably commenced to recede back toward the puncture. And, in all honesty, the fever had already started to abate well before the efforts at the hospital began. Within a short while, it was with a great feeling of satisfaction that I was able to call in the sailor and his wife, who joyfully reunited with the now conscious and smiling girl at her bedside.

Some time later, in the hallway outside, Holmes and I stood with the priest.

"She will be fine," I said. "They will be able to take her home within a few hours."

"And now, Doctor? Mr. Holmes?" asked Father Abele. "Now do you see the power of the miracle?"

I wanted to answer, but my response was torn. As a doctor, I could credit the effect of the mind in letting the body cure itself. As a man of science, I wanted to reject the moonshine associated with a miracle. In the end, I said nothing, looking toward my friend.

With a tight smile, Holmes simply said, "There are all sorts of miracles, Father."

Seeing that this was the best that he was going to get, the priest nodded. "Your fee, Mr. Holmes?" He reached within his cassock, pulling out a worn leather purse that jingled with heavy coins. Holmes waved his hand.

"Not necessary, Father. My assistance was minimal."

"Nevertheless," said Father Abele. "I insist."

"If you must," said my friend, "then use it to assist the poor. Perhaps the Golov's could benefit from it. Anonymously, of course."

"Of course. And Doctor? May I compensate you for your troubles?"

"Not at all," I said. "Add my portion to Holmes's. For the Golov family."

"Very good," he replied. He replaced the purse and patted his chest, where the container holding the relic of the Saint now rested. "Then I must get this back to where it belongs. May you both go with God."

"And you, Father," I replied, while Holmes simply nodded.

Later, as we were leaving Whitechapel behind, I turned to Holmes, sitting beside me in the hansom. "Father Abele," I said with a false heartiness, as I attempted to place these events in some sort of container in which they could be examined and understood, "certainly believes in the power of this supposed miracle."

"Indeed. He has dedicated his life to such an idea."

I was silent for a moment, before I felt the need to say, "I must confess, Holmes, that the girl's response following the touch of the liquid, and the subsequent and unexpectedly immediate improvement in her condition, is unheard of. It seems to give some validity to the Father's argument."

"There are all sorts of miracles," said my friend, repeating his comment of a few minutes earlier.

I smiled. "I'm surprised, Holmes. You are the ultimate defender of the scientific and rational explanation over that of superstition. What credence do you give to miracles?"

Holmes was silent for so long that I thought he had chosen not to answer. The sound of the horse's steady tread went on for quite a while before he spoke. And then, finally, "Ah, Watson, how can I explain it? I seek rational explanations to questions, because if I cannot define a mystery within the known rules and laws by which we exist on a daily basis, what hope do I have? No ghosts need apply. If the possibility for a supernatural explanation *does* exist, then when do we choose to carry on and find the truth if a human agency is responsible, and when do we abandon our efforts and throw up our hands, declaring that the problem has no solution, for it is the fault of a spirit or god beyond our understanding, and therefore the solution cannot be perceived by our mere mortal minds?

"If I am to function within my chosen field, I have to believe that there is a rational and worldly explanation for every action. There have to be some defined parameters within which I can work. If a person believes himself to be haunted, I must determine who is doing whatever is being done to make him *think* that, and then relieve him of the problem. I cannot simply assume that the possibilities are endless. You, as a doctor, must do the same thing. You must seek the cause of a disease, and treat it with the best defined methods in order to achieve real results, rather than stepping back and simply counting on the effort of a prayer, hoping that some magical culmination to the situation will be achieved."

I started to reply, but Holmes added, "But, as I said, Watson, there are all sorts of miracles."

"That," I said, "is contradictory, and does not seem to fit with your previous statement."

"But it does. I cannot refuse to make an effort to find a solution, simply on the surrendering assumption that it is beyond my powers. Nevertheless, as a scientist, I must also be aware of the smallness of man in the great scheme of the Universe, and how little we truly know. We have so much more understanding of the physical world than we did even a hundred years ago, but it would be foolish to think that we now understand all of it, and that all the mysteries of existence are now solved. There are so many things that we think we know with certainty that we probably have wrong, and so much more that we do not even *know* that we do not know. Our understanding of the actual world is like that of an ant's knowledge of the workings of a steam engine."

"You astound me, Holmes. I was certain that you would have had a much different point of view."

"I'm happy that, even after a year, Watson, I can still surprise you. Would it also astonish you to learn that I believe in the human soul?"

"Frankly, yes it would."

"And yet, given my statement that we really know nothing about the Universe around us, how could I not? For what is it that gives us a self-awareness? What is it that takes all of the various separate substances that make up our bodies, each a miniscule dead piece of matter that has never been alive and will never be alive as we understand it, and brings it all together into a unit that functions together for a while as a cohesive unit, with thought and action and purpose, before separating again into dead pieces, each one going its own way. And for that matter, what is it that allows us to change the world around us, with or without a plan, in violation of all the natural laws of the Universe?"

I found myself fascinated as this conversation spiraled from the discussion of a sick girl to the laws of the Universe. "What do you mean by that?"

"Simply that the Universe works by following a defined set, as we understand them, of natural entropic laws. Heat disperses into coolness. Higher energy decreases into levels of lower energy. The force of gravity pulls a smaller object towards a heavier one, but with a mutual attraction always existing between both of them. Any random particle in the Universe will follow these natural laws governing its motion and behavior.

"But this," he said, raising a hand in front of us, "this simple action of raising my hand and holding it there because I *choose* to do so, defies all the laws of the Universe. The Law of Gravity states that I should not be able to voluntarily and decisively raise my hand, going against the pull of the entire planet. Everything in the Universe says no. And yet . . . I choose to do so, and then I so accomplish it.

"What is it that makes me decide to do this, to take this random collection of dead substances held together for a while as *me*, and place them in opposition to the will of the Universe? As a scientist, I see this action accomplished. It has happened, and happens everywhere, every day, whether raising a hand or a pyramid. It must be achieved by something. For lack of anything else better to call it, it must be a *soul*."

"But animals choose to move independently," I countered. "Plants grow in opposition to gravity. Are you saying that they have souls as well?"

110

He shrugged. "Who is to say? Perhaps we all have a fragment or spark of the Divine within each of us, to a greater or lesser degree. I know as little about it as an ant knows of a steam engine.

"But let me give you another example: If I choose to roll a boulder up to the top of a hill, something that would never happen naturally in this entropic universe, gravity immediately wants to pull it back down to the bottom. Suppose then that I brace it, where it cannot roll away. My action has thus defied one of the basic natural laws of the Universe. Wind and weather – both caused, by the way, by convection currents and other phenomena related to natural laws – will wear at the boulder and the earth beneath it for countless ages. They may do so for so long that the hillside itself erodes away, thus allowing the boulder to be freed again from its support, whereupon it will follow the natural laws and again roll back to the bottom. But in the meantime, during all those years, the boulder has been sitting where *my* own will and *my* energy and *my* choice placed it, where it never would have been located before, according to every natural law in the Universe. The same is true for a statue or a building made up of bricks and alloys and other materials that never would have been combined or formed together in that particular way or shape if someone had not intentionally done so, defying the laws and will and intent of the Universe.

"Knowing all of that, and additionally realizing how small we are in the great scheme of things, how can I doubt that there must be different sorts of miracles?"

I was quiet for a moment, contemplating the vast scope of his statement. Finally, I said, not knowing how else to reply, "I never knew that you felt this way."

"It has never come up. But how can we ignore it? When trying to determine that which is greater than us, there is nothing so necessary as deduction. And if we believe that existence is essentially good, as I do – in spite of much that I have seen – then the greatest assurance of that goodness seems to rest in the extras that we are given, such as flowers, for instance. Their beauty is an extra, an embellishment of life, and not a condition, and one that I am thankful for.

"But, even if I am thankful for this extra, I must conduct my work with a degree of separation from it, so that I do not end up counting on miracles. Yet, I do believe them, and the events of today convince me of that even more."

"How so? In what way?"

"We may or may not believe in the power of the *manna* from the St. Nicholas relic, although '*there are more things in heaven and earth, Watson, than are dreamt of in your philosophy*', to paraphrase the Bard.

111

The relic's liquid could have contributed to the girl Alina's recovery, or not. But I do believe that your unexpected return today, allowing you to be present in order to participate in our trip to Stepney, was part of a bigger plan. For you, a doctor, were with us when we visited this girl who needed medical attention. You had, I believe, intended to spend the day at Barts, and then at other pursuits. What if you hadn't been at home when Father Abele arrived? I would have found the Golovs, but would we have known to seek immediate additional treatment for the girl? Would we have recognized the seriousness of her illness? Or that her wound was much graver than it appeared from the surface? Perhaps the anointment of the *manna* would have healed the girl, but I have to believe that she needed the immediate attention of a physician as well – and you were there."

"The second cab," I said softly. Holmes raised his eyebrows. "I thought at the time that it was unusually fortunate that a second cab was waiting in that neighborhood when we carried the girl outside."

He nodded. "Another minor miracle, perhaps?" Then, lowering his voice, he continued. "And then there is the other occurrence, which might also be something of a miracle."

A silence fell as he ruminated for a moment, until I prodded him to continue. "I didn't tell you about how I located the Golovs," he said.

"I had assumed it was a straightforward investigation."

"I should have been. I was able to speak to my various contacts near the docks, and I was quickly given the man's address. But then . . . then I *couldn't find it.* Watson, you know that I have an encyclopedic knowledge of London, but in this case, it failed me. And everyone that I asked was uncertain as well as to the location of the little court where the sailor and his family lived.

"Time was passing, and soon I would need to return to Baker Street to meet the priest. Just when I was feeling most frustrated, I heard a soft voice behind me. Turning, I discovered a tall old man, with a white beard and a high forehead, smiling at me with a most warming expression. He spoke with an unusual accent that I couldn't quite place, clearly foreign, and with something of the Mediterranean about it. 'The house you seek is there, my son.' And he raised his arm, pointing toward that same dark passage, previously unnoticed by me up to that moment, where I later returned with you and Father Abele. Then he lowered his hand, his smile becoming possibly even more filled with pure joy than before. I wanted to speak, to ask a question, to thank him, but I found that I could not. And as he turned and walked away into the gloom, I was aware of his eyes, Watson. They were perhaps the kindest eyes that I have ever seen . . . ."

His voice faded, and I knew the unspoken thought between us. Who could the man have been who knew just where to direct Holmes in his moment of desperation? Someone from that neighborhood, perhaps, who had heard Holmes's attempts to locate the address, and had simply offered assistance. *Or could it have been . . . ?* But no – for that would be impossible. Still, one somehow knows that at Christmas, above all other times of the year, the possibility of miracles might somehow truly exist.

I raised my eyes to find Holmes smiling at me, obviously reading my thoughts. "So there are different sorts of miracles, Watson, and I think that today's events count. Most fittingly, they were Christmas miracles."

And as we rode in silence, I found, with further examination, that I agreed with him. I recalled my feelings of just a few hours before, as I had looked about me with a sore lack of appreciation for the season. In fact, considering the circumstances in which I might have found myself at this point in my life, had I not met my friend when I did, I was very fortunate indeed. If, in fact, there is an overall plan, as Holmes espoused, one that is greater than our understanding, I could only be thankful that I could dimly recognize and appreciate my place in it, and thus count my many blessings.

"Merry Christmas, Holmes," I was moved to say.

"Indeed, my friend. Indeed it is."

A Christmas Goose
by C.H. Dye

During the earliest years of my friendship with Mr. Sherlock Holmes, when he had not yet been recognized by the broader public for his unique genius and I was still dependent upon my wound pension for my needs, there were times when either he or I found ourselves unfortunately light in the pocket – he due of a lack of cases and therefore income, and I because, despite my best intentions, money had a tendency to slip through my fingers. Having failed to recover my health sufficiently for a return to my duties, either as a soldier or as a doctor, my one useful occupation soon became accompanying Holmes upon his investigations and taking notes in the background so as to leave him free to perform without interruption. When he lacked cases, I lacked occupation, and not infrequently his malodorous chemical investigations or silent brooding drove me back to my haunts near the Criterion and the wastrel habits I had tried to forswear. Still, for some time it chanced that our periods of insolvency failed to coincide, and between us we managed to pay Mrs. Hudson for our room and board each quarter, each of us making up the difference as necessary with the certainty that the other would pay him back as soon as either work or wound pension became available.

It was on the 22nd of our second December at Baker Street that the hammer finally fell. Holmes had not had a case since Guy Fawkes Night and I, in a disastrous attempt to recoup my finances, had allowed myself to be inveigled by an acquaintance into a notorious gambling hell, wherein I proceeded to lose the bulk of my meagre savings, my watch, my cufflinks, and my fare to Baker Street. And this with the rent coming due on Christmas Day!

As I trudged home through a freezing rain, I contemplated my options. Holmes, I knew, was low in funds, or he would not have allowed his tobacco pouch to grow so disastrously flat. An appeal to Mrs. Hudson's better nature was precluded by the cost of the impending coal bill, or so I told myself. I'd had too much to drink, and my pride was as sore as my head. I was not yet so low as to give the river more than a passing thought, and any chance of vanishing into the anonymity of the gutter was precluded by the certainty that Holmes would find me, no matter where in London I might try to hide. Still, I had yet a few possessions which I could pledge until the New Year brought my stipend and I might, by a stricter exercise of economy, redeem them.

114

Resigned to the loss, however temporary, of my winter coat and my books, I turned the corner onto Baker Street and discovered Holmes outside our door in his dressing gown, wielding a large umbrella, and ushering our landlady into a cab, despite the hour being well past midnight.

"Ah, there you are, Watson!" he called as I approached. "You see, Mrs. Hudson, you can set your mind at rest."

"Doctor!" Mrs. Hudson cried in a distracted tone, stepping away from the cab to come and take my hands in hers. "You're sopping wet. And you're shivering. Whyever didn't you get a cab home?"

"I . . . I felt like walking," I stammered, having made no plan to excuse my condition. Fortunately, our good landlady didn't press me for a better explanation.

"You must take him upstairs and stir up the fire straightaway, Mr. Holmes," she ordered my fellow lodger, as imperious as any Duchess. "The water in the kitchen boiler should still be warm. Have Polly . . . oh, bother," she interrupted herself. "Polly's gone off to see her mother."

"And you must be off to see to your daughter," Holmes interrupted, steering her once again towards the growler. By a tip of his head, he invited me to assist him in handing her up to the seat, all the while assuring her that he and I would be more than capable of tending ourselves until the maid returned upon the morrow, and reminding her that if she delayed, her first grandchild would be in Croydon before her.

I took up the thread, no longer baffled by this midnight departure. Mrs. Hudson's daughter had been expecting to deliver on or near Twelfth Night, and in the usual way of things, our good landlady would have departed Baker Street on Boxing Day, leaving us in the care of her cousin, Mrs. Turner. But the child, as children are wont to do, was arriving early, throwing all of Mrs. Hudson's plans into disarray. Despite the potential for concern that must attach to a premature birth, I felt nothing but relief. Once in Croydon, Mrs. Hudson would no doubt stay for the entire Christmas season, and I might never need explain the gaps in my closet and shelves. "There's nothing so joyous as a Christmas baby," I said, settling the rug over Mrs. Hudson's lap. "You'll be able to have a nice visit and save your daughter the cooking."

"Oh, good heavens, the cooking!" It was only my hand upon her sleeve which kept her from leaping up again. "I forgot all about the cooking!"

"Polly can manage for a few days," Holmes said, with utter confidence. "And if she does not provide the feasts which would have come from your hands, I assure you our suppers will still be a vast improvement upon the meals I suffered when I was at Montague Street."

"Her cooking is getting better," Mrs. Hudson agreed, as if mesmerized by Holmes's assertion. "And she can always consult Mrs. Beeton."

"There, you see? All will be well. And now I need to get Dr. Watson inside before he shivers himself out of his skin." Holmes stepped back, drawing me with him. "Give our best to your family!" he called to her and, "Drive on!" to the cabby, who snapped his whip. The horse, glad to move again in the relentless wind, stepped off briskly, and all Mrs. Hudson could do was wave a last farewell before the night and rain obscured her from our view.

"Come inside," Holmes said, tugging at my arm as if I might be reluctant to obey. "I want to get out of these wet slippers. Did you have any supper in your wanderings tonight?"

"Yes." Bread and a bit of cheese, to go with the wine still muddling my head, and hours past, but Holmes did not enquire after details. After securing the front door, he merely stopped to light his candle at the gas fixture still burning in the hallway and then led me back to the darkened kitchen. I stumbled after him, wondering why I was shivering all the harder now that I was inside, and tightening my jaw to keep my teeth from chattering.

"Even with the fire banked, the kitchen is warmer than every other room in the house," Holmes said, as he reached up to drop a penny in the box for the kitchen gaslight. "And as there's not a female in the place, you can bathe right next to the stove. Much simpler than carrying the tub and water upstairs to our sitting room, don't you agree?" He turned in the blossom of light and his manner changed as he cast his suddenly sharpened gaze over me. "Oh, Doctor. You have had a night of it, haven't you? Even your cab fare?"

"I was winning," I protested as I felt my cheeks heat with shame. I should have realized how impossible it was to keep my impoverished state from Sherlock Holmes's notice.

"Yes, and then you were losing." He made a moue of frustration. "I take it that it would be futile of me to apply to you for assistance in paying my share of this quarter's rent?"

"I shan't be able to pay even my share without pawning half my wardrobe," I admitted. "I shouldn't have taken my cheque book with me."

Holmes waved away the consideration with one fine sweep of his hand. "And I shouldn't have turned down that case from Gregson," he confessed. He thrust his fists into his pockets and scowled at the floor. "Mrs. Hudson is not going to be pleased with either of us. But it sounded so confoundedly *dull*."

For a moment we both sulked like schoolboys waiting to be dressed down by the teacher, but then a stray thought occurred to me and I found myself trying not to laugh.

"What?" Holmes asked, looking up with an answering smile tugging at the corner of his mouth.

"Father Christmas is going to be terribly disappointed."

Holmes laughed with me and held up one sodden foot. "Father Christmas wouldn't want to touch these long enough to put in the coal," he said. "Here, Watson, you stir up the fire in the stove and strip off those wet things, and I'll fill the tub from the boiler and then fetch down some dry things for you and some dry stockings for me."

Come morning, the rataplan of rain against the windowpanes had been replaced by the hiss of driven snow and the whistle of the wind down my chimney. A perfect day to stay abed, had not the aches in my head and my wound combined with the harsh jangling of the bell below to drive me out into the sullen grey light. I threw on my dressing gown and slippers and stumbled downstairs, but Holmes had also been roused, and he was sufficiently ahead of me that I heard him answering the door to the messenger boy, even before I reached the first floor landing. A moment later he came bounding up the stairs, the telegram in his hand.

"Word from Mrs. Hudson?"

"A girl child, safely delivered, and weighing six pounds, three ounces," Holmes said, "and we are to remind Polly that she should do the laundry on Saturday if she wishes to enjoy Christmas Monday."

I rubbed at my arms, hoping to counter the bitter cold in the hall. "Where is Polly?" I asked. "Shouldn't she have answered the door?"

"Delayed by the storm, no doubt," Holmes said. "She'll turn up. In the meantime, see what you can do about warming up the sitting room while I investigate the larder."

I fussed with the leavings of the sitting room coal scuttle and the clinkers from the night before, but I am the first to admit it was not my best work. Not that Holmes did much better in the kitchen! He and I breakfasted together next to a sputtering fire, toasting bread cut from the end of the loaf, spooning out the remainder of a jar of plum jam, and drinking tea brewed strong enough for a brave man to walk upon. Holmes sipped at his cupful with a dubious expression, but I had tasted far worse in my time in the Army and was only grateful for the chance to sweeten my drink with a dollop of the jam.

"I think I put in too many leaves," Holmes decided, after another assay.

"That or we let it steep too long," I said. Brewing tea seemed sufficiently like making an infusion of medicine that I thought I could diagnose the error. "Haven't you kept the preparation of a proper pot of tea in your brain attic?"

"Why should I?" Holmes replied, leaning back in his chair and stretching his long legs in front of the hearth. "Mrs. Hudson is a mistress of the art. And if Polly proves not to have acquired the skill, then we can find out which of our neighbors is this Mrs. Beeton to supply the deficiency."

I could not help but laugh. Holmes's odd gaps in what was otherwise an extensive body of knowledge gave me the advantage upon occasion. "Mrs. Beeton is not a neighbor, Holmes, she's a book. Or rather an author, who has written a book of cookery and household management." At his look of inquiry I added, "I've often seen it at the bookshop. It's practically a standard reference on the topic."

"It must be, for a bachelor like yourself to know of it," Holmes said. He set aside his teacup, still mostly full, and leaned on his elbows, steepling his fingers before his face as he mused. "Mrs. Hudson must have a copy of it, then, somewhere in the house."

"Presumably," I agreed. I drank more tea at a gulp, wanting the stimulation, but having no desire to savour the drink itself.

Holmes eyed his cup with a wry smile. "Cookery book or no, I think we shall find ourselves missing Mrs. Hudson before long. Still, perhaps we should be glad that we've been granted a reprieve. I doubt she will come all the way back to Baker Street to collect the rent money before the New Year. You'll have received your wound pension by then."

"And you'll have solved that case for Inspector Gregson," I said. "But Holmes, shouldn't we be prepared to pay her on Christmas Day, regardless? She might send her son-in-law, even if she doesn't come herself."

He nodded agreement. "Indeed we should. Fortunately, I have made a study of the pawnbrokers of London, and I think, if you'll entrust the errand to me, I know where we might best pledge those of our belongings we are willing to do without for the most profit."

"Temporary profit," I amended. For all that the ache had diminished, my head was still not right and I propped it up with one hand as I doggedly finished my tea.

His plans made, Holmes repaired to his room to dress and to assemble the belongings he meant to pawn. I made a similar foray up to the chill of my bedroom, but found the pickings slender. I have never been a man who bedecks himself with extraneous jewelry, and such tiepins and cufflinks as I owned were rather plain. The curiously carved box in which I kept them – one of my few possessions to survive the siege of Candahar – seemed to me to be more valuable than its contents, even with my compass and military medals to supplement them. My evening wear and heavy winter coat were still waterlogged from the previous night, so I left them on the clothes horse, and drew out my summer linens and the new tweeds I had bought in a burst of profligracy the previous September. I was staring hopelessly at the bookshelves, wondering which volumes might be of interest to anyone but myself, when Holmes came clattering up the stairs with a half-filled valise in one hand. "Here you go, Doctor. If I'm to pawn the case, it can at least do its duty first."

I glanced at the contents as I began to add my own belongings. "Your microscope, Holmes?" I asked, frowning. "Surely you can raise sufficient funds for your share of the rent without hobbling your investigations?"

He settled onto the bed and began folding the linen suit. "Any clues Gregson has failed to observe are going to be blazingly obvious or already obliterated by police boots. And I would rather not count on the generosity of his fee being sufficient for our requirements."

"What shall you do if he's already solved his case?" I asked, placing some books around the microscope case to add a layer of protection. Scientific instruments, as I knew all too well, were susceptible to damage when being transported from place to another. My time in Afghanistan had seen the demise of my own microscope during a storm much like the one which still raged outside our window. "Gregson won't pay you at all if he doesn't need your help."

"Then I shall find the correct solution," Holmes said airily. "And save some poor soul the ignominy of being tried for a crime he did not commit in the hopes of a modest reward." He reached up to lay a hand on my arm. "Don't fret, Doctor. If by some chance I can't get a fee from Gregson before Christmas, I'll borrow the sum required."

That hardly seemed fair. "And pay some outrageous rate of interest? If it comes to that, I'll go to the moneylenders myself. After all, it was my foolishness that landed us in these straits." I could feel myself beginning to tremble at the thought of it. Debts he could not afford to redeem has sent my brother on his downward path, and I had no desire to emulate him.

Holmes frowned and stood, resting one pale hand on my forehead for a moment. "I don't think you should go out in this weather, Watson," he said. "You don't feel feverish, but I think that long walk in the pouring rain did you little good last night. Then again, it's so cold in this room, I'm not sure you'd feel warm, even if you did have a fever." He waved at the ice which had formed on my washbasin.

"I'm not sick," I told him brusquely. After all, I was the one with the medical degree. "I just have a headache. And how else are you to carry this lot to the pawnshops with that going on?" I waved a hand at the window, where the snow was rapidly accumulating on the sill.

"Oh, the Underground should be running," said he. "And I'll recruit a few of my Irregulars to help carry. It will make a pleasant change for them from sweeping the snow for pennies."

"But if you keep them from earning pennies, how will you recompense them?" I asked.

"With a share of our Christmas goose, what else?" His eyes twinkled merrily at the thought.

I stared at him, wondering if I had missed some essential part of the conversation. "We have a goose?"

"We have a goose." He got to his feet. "Come, Doctor. I'll show you."

I followed him down to the larder, where a magnificent fowl dangled in all its wingspread glory from the highest hook.

"Good heavens," said I, blinking up at it. "Mrs. Hudson must have been planning quite a feast. Or do you think she meant to take it with her to Croydon?"

Holmes made gesture of irritation. "Doubtful. Despite the chill, there's no reason to believe that the bird will be in any condition to be consumed by the New Year, much less Twelfth Night. No, Watson, it is our own Christmas dinner you see before us, and more than enough to share with any of the lads who might come to our assistance. After all, Mrs. Hudson isn't here to scandalize. And I doubt Polly will object to their company."

"Not if young Robinson is among them," I had to agree. Polly, at that time, had not yet celebrated her sixteenth birthday, and while diligent in her duties and of real assistance to Mrs. Hudson in the kitchen, like many another young servant, she was always happier in the company of her peers than in the presence of her employers. I had often heard her in early morning conversation with one or another of Holmes's street Arabs whilst she beat out the rugs beneath the plane tree outside my window. I should perhaps note that Robinson was not in any way her particular *amour*, being not yet four feet tall. But he was a cheerful little fellow, and often turned up in a useful way when Polly had work to be done outside, as much because he liked her as for the sake of the ginger biscuits she kept in her apron pocket.

Holmes clapped me on the shoulder. "That's settled then. I'll take our gleanings to McGregor – after that business with the wedding rings he should remember both of us – and see if I can't get a decent price. And you, old chap, can take a nap by the sitting room fire."

"I have a perfectly good bed," I grumbled, having a mulish desire to ignore Holmes's peremptory advice and take whatever sleep I needed in my own bed, however cold.

In the end, I did sleep in the sitting room. I told myself that it was because my wound ached from the cold, and I didn't wish to climb another flight of stairs after helping Holmes carry everything we meant to pawn down to the front door. And in the end, it was just as well. I doubt the snowballs that thudded on the windowpane to waken me could have reached much higher.

I stumbled to the window and looked out to find Baker Street deserted but for the coal wagon, its driver muffled to the ears and standing in snow nearly up to his knees. He waved a mitten hopefully, and I threw open the sash. Before I could ask what he meant by attacking our windows, he called up, "Sorry about the snowball, mister, but the bell ain't working, and I saw the light up there. I've got a delivery for Mrs. Hudson, and a bill due, too."

"She's not here," I said. "She's in Croydon."

"Croydon?" he echoed. "How's she's going to pay me when she's in Croydon?"

"Wait," I told him. "I'll come down to the door."

I closed the window and fetched my cheque book, stuffing it into my dressing gown pocket with a glance at the clock and hoping Holmes might have already deposited sufficient funds into my account to cover the price of the coal.

The hall outside our sitting room was so cold I could see my breath, and the banister so icy that I made my way down our stairs without its assistance. The doorknob gave me pause, but I pulled my handkerchief from my sleeve to protect my hand from the cold metal. Even so, I had to tug hard to get the door open. There was ice in the gap between the door and the jamb, and ice on the doorbell wire.

The man was waiting on the step, hugging himself and jigging up and down to combat the snow-laden wind. "Come in," I told him, having no desire to conduct our transaction with the snow piling up on Mrs. Hudson's carpet.

"Thanks, mister," he said, and stepped inside. He started to unfold and then wrapped his arms back up. "Cor, it ain't half cold in here. Looks like I've come just in time."

"Indeed!" I said. It was never warm in the hallway in the winter, but it was seldom this cold. "Polly!" I called, back toward the kitchen. "Polly! The coal man is here!" I called. But there was no answer.

Holmes, still bundled up against the snow, his face white and his lips blue with the cold, found me in the coal cellar that evening, refilling the scuttle. I had stirred up the kitchen fire by then, which had ameliorated conditions somewhat, but the stove was a voracious beast, and it was in need of another feeding. My fellow lodger took the heavy scuttle from me without a word. It wasn't until we were both settled in the kitchen, and I had supplied Holmes with a portion of brandy, that he thawed sufficiently to speak.

"No sign of Polly then," he said, and it was not a question. "And no message from her."

"Not a word," I agreed, pulling the potatoes I had set to baking out of the oven. Potatoes in the coals and fresh trout on a stick over a fire were the extent of my culinary skills, but Holmes seemed glad enough when I passed his share to him in a bowl and nodded to the salt and pepper.

"If she sent a telegram, it may have gone astray," Holmes said. "A gas line exploded near the Central Office this morning, and took out many of the wires leading to the main exchange. That's why I had to do my researches in person."

"That can't have been easy in this weather." I took the blanket I'd been warming by the stove and threw it over my friend's shoulders, grateful for the chance to return the favour he had done me the evening before. "Perhaps the storm has prevented Polly from returning, and she is unaware that we do not know why."

"Possibly." Holmes frowned, his eyes narrowed in thought. "Her surname is Hunter, is it not?"

"As far as I know, yes." I poured myself half-a-glass of brandy. My shoulder was aching, and I did not need to look at the barometer to know why. The storm seemed to me to be more than enough reason for an intelligent girl to avoid travel.

Holmes put down his fork, and looked at me, "What have I told you about Gregson's case, Watson?"

"Only that it is dull," I said. "A series of thefts, I believe."

Holmes nodded. "And in each case," he added pointedly, "a disappearing maid. Gregson, and for that matter, I, have assumed that the two are related. But if young girls are disappearing from homes and hotels across London, then there might be something far more sinister afoot than a bit of Faginy."

122

"But there has been no theft here," I objected, despite my alarm. "Surely your case has nothing to do with our maid."

"Perhaps, and perhaps not." Holmes drew his notebook out from his pocket. "There have been a total of eight thefts, each of them following a celebration, be it an elaborate dinner or a ball. For the most part, the thieves have targeted small jewelry set with exceptionally precious stones. Not every bit of jewelry is stolen, curiously enough, which is what caught Gregson's eye. The repeated pattern suggests a single mind behind the thefts, even though the servants who have gone missing have little more in common than youth and sex. My investigation suggests that the thieves have somehow gained access to empty jewelry cases and replaced the hinge pins with cheap brass, whilst the gems are bedecking their owners. Later, it is the work of a moment to regain access, even if the case has been locked. The girl who polishes the fire irons, or the boy who refills the scuttle, may both visit a room more than once. But the common method suggests a controlling mind."

"We've had no ball or grand dinner here," I objected. "Polly doesn't fit the pattern."

"No, she doesn't. But Gregson has not been gathering data concerning the disappearance of young girls, regardless of thefts, and it may be that the two patterns are actually unrelated. And there is this; this afternoon when I visited the St. Pancras Hotel to look into the theft of Lady Waterston's ruby eardrops yesterday, the concierge told me that three of his maids had failed to appear this morning. Mary Mitchell, Ann Smith, and Elizabeth Hunter." He tapped the page with his notes. "It's a common enough name, I grant you. And the storm might be explanation enough. But I've heard Polly speak of a sister called 'Betsy'."

As had I. "Betsy, who works in a hotel. Robinson would know which one, I expect." I looked around. As much as it dismayed me to think that Polly might be in difficulties, I was nearly as concerned by the shambles I had made of the kitchen in my attempt to provide a meal. "Holmes, what shall we do? We shouldn't alarm Mrs. Hudson prematurely. We can't expect Mrs. Turner to forego her Christmas plans to come early when we don't know if Polly might turn up at any time. And we can hardly afford to dine in restaurants until Boxing Day."

"We may end up living on bread and jam like half of London does for a few days – not that it would do us any harm." Holmes scowled at the prospect. "But I promised the boys a Christmas goose, and I should hate to go back on my word."

"How many boys?" I asked.

"Four. Wiggins, Robinson, Clarence, and Brown." Holmes pushed away his plate and got up to warm himself by the stove. "They did a yeoman's work today. The streets and pavements are icy beneath the snow, and I think the promise of a goose dinner was all that kept them going."

"You're the one who promised a goose," I pointed out. "If Polly doesn't turn up, you'll just have to roast the goose and hope for the best."

"Oh, no," Holmes said. "You agreed that we should use the goose as payment for the boys."

"That was when I thought Polly would be doing the cooking!" I protested.

We discussed our quandary for some time, coming to no real agreement except that Mrs. Hudson should not be disturbed unnecessarily. At last Holmes exploded with frustration. "This is ridiculous, Watson. We're two intelligent men, fully grown, and experienced. One of us ought to be able to roast a fowl without feminine assistance."

That struck a chord. "Feminine assistance!" I said, with a snap of my fingers, and "*Mrs. Beeton!*" we both said together.

Mrs. Beeton, upon consultation (we found her in the pantry cupboard) took scarcely a page to describe the process of transforming a raw goose into our dinner. Holmes and I both took heart from that, and our discussion, which had consisted of reasons from each of us why the other should undertake to prepare the goose, became a discussion of why each of us thought that he had a likelier chance of succeeding. At last we agreed that each of us would do our best to provide a meal or two in Polly's absence from the contents of the larder. Whichever one of us best succeeded would be the cook on Christmas Day and the other would play scullion.

"Mind you," Holmes said. "I shall have to concentrate my efforts more on finding the girl than on attempting to take up her duties. Not to mention Gregson's case!"

"If my shoulder is right," I said, rubbing at the ache, "you shall have more than enough time to experiment in the morning. I doubt anyone in London shall be venturing far."

There is an art to even so simple a thing as cracking an egg, as I discovered the next morning, and, as Holmes demonstrated, a certain amount of time and attention which cannot be scanted even in so minor a procedure as restoring dried peas to an edible state. But hunger is a powerful motivator, and neither pea soup nor shirred eggs are so difficult to contrive. By the time the storm finally began to abate, it is fair to say that we stood in no danger of starvation.

By then, it was but a scant hour past noon. We had spent the morning in near isolation; between the howling of the wind and the thick veil of snow, the streets were all but empty. Holmes had spent the idle hours adding to his commonplace books and attempting to construct a pipeful of tobacco out of the dried dottles and plugs he had lined up upon the mantelpiece, whilst I took notes out of Mrs. Beeton, and hoped for a clarification as to precisely which organs constituted "giblets" when it came to making gravy. Our only visitor had been a dutiful postman, carrying letters and cards for Mrs. Hudson, which we duly forwarded on to Croydon before retreating once more to the comfort of our sitting room. But with the faint glow of sunlight fighting through the thinning clouds, the sturdiest of London's denizens took heart, and we soon heard voices and the scrape of shovels and brooms from without.

"I think I shall go over to the telegraph office," Holmes said, after observing the street from our bay window. "And perhaps fetch a few groceries before returning to my case. I am certain we will have a few shillings to spare once Gregson has paid my fee."

"Does this mean you concede the role of cook tomorrow?" I asked, surprised. "Because you know the scullion is going to have to peel the vegetables and pluck the goose, as well as clean up after the meal."

"I thought we might get the boys to help us," Holmes said. "They'd be much warmer here than trying to find a corner at St. Cyprian's. And we've plenty of oatmeal in the bin if they want a bite of breakfast." He stripped off his dressing gown and went into his room to dress more warmly.

"And what will you be doing, if the boys and I are preparing Christmas dinner?" I called.

"Oh, I expect you'll still need my assistance," Holmes said blithely, returning a moment later with his scarf hung round his neck and his eyes alight with mischief. "But it is clear that you have read more of that cookery book than I, and therefore I shall be at your command."

"And when does this felicity begin?" I asked, for the occasions when Holmes was willing to let anyone else take charge of his affairs were vanishingly rare.

"Whenever you begin to require my services," he said, buttoning up his coat. "Why do you ask?"

"Because it so happens that I have a list," I said, producing the fruit of my efforts with book and larder. Holmes stared at it for a moment, and then drew himself up to attention and threw me a parade ground salute.

"Reporting for duty, sir!" he said, as straight-faced as a man can be who has just struck himself in the forehead with his gloves. "I'm ready to run up the sails!"

"Here are your orders, Private," I said, playing the game as best I could with a grin wishing to break out on my face. Holmes was not the only one who could mix a metaphor! "And when you've come back, you can raise the deck and swab the yardarm."

He saluted elaborately again, and then took a look at the page I handed him and sobered. "What, no pudding?"

"I can't see how we can afford one," I replied. "I'm not even certain you can purchase everything on the list. Start at the top and work down, and when you've run out of money, stop."

"Bread, onions, sage . . . no oysters either, I see."

"We have neither the lemon rind nor the pinch of mace for that recipe." Holmes was not the only one to regret that we could not try Mrs. Beeton's receipt for a "savoury oyster stuffing". I had every intention of pointing out the page to Mrs. Hudson someday soon, and a number of other recipes as well.

"Butter. Only half-a-pound?"

"That should be sufficient, if we're careful."

"Apples, potatoes. This will be a feast, Doctor, if you intend to give us apple sauce and mashed potatoes with our goose. A quarter-of-a-pound of currants and four oranges?" At the last two items on my list, Holmes drew his eyebrows together. "Oranges for the boys, yes. Children should get oranges at Christmastide. But currants?" He looked a question at me.

"Something to set afire in lieu of a Christmas pudding," I said. "I have a gill of brandy left for Snap Dragon."

Holmes tucked the list into his pocket with a nod to me. "That should be interesting," he said. "I've never played it, and I doubt the boys have either."

It was my turn to be surprised. Snap Dragon had been a regular feature of my family's Christmas celebrations, and the taste of hot brandied currants, as well as the glee of knowing that one had snatched the treat from the fire without having burned a finger, were as much a part of Christmas to me as holly and mistletoe. Not that we had holly or mistletoe. Our mantel was quite bare. I thought for a moment about asking Holmes to find some evergreens for decoration, but discarded the notion. I had a better idea. "I may take a short turn around the park," I told Holmes, as he reached for his hat. "I'd like to enjoy the sun while it lasts."

"Be careful, then," Holmes ordered, in his usual commanding way, and then paused on the doorsill to bow. "Be careful then, *sir*," he repeated, his obeisance undone by the amused tilt of his eyebrows. "And if you don't wish to get caught, I suggest that you cut your branches from the cedar behind the bandstand."

I made one other stop besides the park, at Bradley's, where my frequent patronage was sufficient to persuade that excellent tobacconist into extending me the courtesy of providing a pouch of Holmes's favorite shag pipe tobacco on the promise that I would bring the funds in the New Year. That delicate negotiation delayed me sufficiently so that, by the time I returned to Baker Street, Holmes had come and gone. I found the small pile of groceries in the kitchen, along with a note from Holmes and sixpence.

"*Watson,*" it read, "*I have dispatched Wiggins to Aldgate to discover if Polly's family knows her whereabouts. I was able to reach Scotland Yard by police telegraph, and have learned that the Christmas Eve ball at the Langham Hotel will be held as planned at eight this evening. Gregson has arranged for both of us to attend. Supper will be provided at seven. Use my obsidian cufflinks. Holmes.*"

I groaned, thinking of the condition of my evening clothes, still draped over the clothes horse in my room, and reached for Mrs. Beeton. Ironing, I suspected, was as much a skill as cooking, and I had very little time to learn the art.

The sun was long gone when I reached my destination, but the light streaming from every window of the magnificent facade of the Langham rewarded my diligence. Londoners of every age and description were out and about, bundled up against the cold and enjoying the crisp clean air, temporarily free of its usual burden of soot. Every shop I had passed was open, and the pavements were mostly clear. The streets, of course, were still packed in snow, and it was an enterprising sleigh owner who received my sixpence and thanks as I stepped down.

Inspector Gregson was directing his forces from a small alcove set in back of the lobby, his expression dour. His fair hair was slicked back and his attire as formal as my own. "Thank you for coming, Doctor," he said, when I reported to him. "Have you seen Mr. Holmes about?"

"I thought I would meet him here," I said.

"And so you have," came Holmes's soft voice from behind me, and I turned to discover a lanky footman in the hotel's livery, his now-auburn hair and freckled face quite altered from their usual appearance. He touched a gloved finger to his lips to prevent me from exclaiming. "I've a message for you, sir," he said at normal volume, and offered Gregson a note on a salver.

Gregson took the note with a grunt of thanks, but as he read it his face cleared. "That seems feasible," he admitted, and then glanced at me. "I hope you weren't looking forward to the dancing, Doctor Watson."

"Only the supper," I confessed cheerfully. It had been a very long time since luncheon, and given the state of the kitchen, my "tea" had been two digestive biscuits taken with water. Holmes coughed behind his hand, hiding a smile.

The corner of Gregson's mouth tugged upwards too, and he waved a hand at Holmes. "This fellow can no doubt show you what to do. I'll be along as soon as I've spoken to Lord Lindsay about our arrangements."

I followed Holmes, who led me through the spacious lobby and the glittering celebrants to a discreet green baize door, and on into the kitchens, where servants in half-a-dozen liveries darted to-and-fro under the direction of an imperious cook. Holmes didn't even glance at her, but went on until he came to a small chamber, where a tureen of stew and a plate of buttered bread awaited. Holmes ushered me in, and then checked to be sure no one was paying him attention before joining me and closing the door. "You look festive, Watson," he said, cheerfully, slinging himself to the chair opposite me as I sat down to my meal.

"You said we were invited to a ball," I reminded him. "If I'd known the hotel would provide my attire, I would have saved myself the ironing. Have you had any word of Polly?"

Holmes smiled, "Wiggins reported back to me not an hour ago. Polly and her family are on the *Atlas.*"

"The *Atlas?*" I exclaimed, surprised by his air of content. The quarantine ship anchored downstream from London was the last place I would hope to find an acquaintance. "They have the smallpox?"

"It is a precautionary quarantine only," Holmes said, producing a newspaper from the pocket in his coattails. He placed the story before me. "A sailor visited the Cathedral of St. Paul shortly before his symptoms appeared, and as a consequence, the boys of the choir school were possibly exposed. They had scattered to visit their families before the holiday services commenced, and as it turns out, one of their number is called Peter Hunter, brother to both Polly and Betsy Hunter. The authorities were alerted just as the storm worsened, and are indeed thanking their lucky stars that none of the boys dawdled on their ways home during the rain."

"So we will be without her services for another ten days," I calculated. "Longer if the disease takes hold, but at least we can tell Mrs. Hudson where she is now."

"I've sent a note to the *Atlas,*" Holmes said. "They should send confirmation tomorrow. Then, if we manage to solve our case tonight, we can visit Mrs. Hudson in Croydon with both the news and our rent."

"Do we stand a good chance of solving it then," I asked.

"Well, if nothing else, we may prevent the theft of Lady Lindsay's diamond brooch. His Lordship is likely to reward us on that account alone." Holmes clapped me on the shoulder. "Now, eat your supper while I explain the plan."

My role, as it turned out, was to position myself to observe which servants used the back stairs during the dancing. Holmes had scouted out a corner window with a seat where I could be stationed, with a little rouge on my cheeks and nose and a half-empty bottle of whisky as a prop to provide me an excuse to linger there. "You can even have your pen and notebook in hand. Tell anyone who asks that you are contemplating rhymes for 'Aurelia'," he suggested, standing back to consider his handiwork. "Just try not to wipe at your nose."

It was not a lonely vigil. Holmes passed me now and then, as well as a stolid fellow whose boots below his livery betrayed him as a constable. I saw Gregson once, although he passed by without speaking to me. And the maids. Tall, short, thin, stout, a few older, but most young enough, carrying clean linen upwards and dirty linen down, or armed with brush and pan, rag and polish. Never in my life have I been so aware of the work required to provide us cleanliness and comfort, or the women and girls who see that it is daily done.

The music of the ball had been drifting upwards for an hour, and my bottle was growing emptier as I attempted to keep the chill from the window from seeping into my bones, when there was a shout from the flight of stairs above me. "Watson! Stop him!"

I stumbled to my feet, stiff from the sitting and clumsy with the whisky, and raised my fists, but the first person to come pelting down the stairs was a maid, the tall fair one who had passed me twice before. I hesitated, and she picked up a fist, driving it into my chin with all the force at her command. Or his command, I should say, for as I fell I grabbed for my assailant and to my dismay the crown of yellow braids came away in my hand!

Astonishment prevented me from retaining my grasp, and the boy scrambled to his feet and disappeared down the stairwell, followed a moment later by Holmes, his face bloody from a blow. I followed as soon as I found my feet, and reached the kitchen in time to watch as the chase dodged around the tables, the cries of "Thief!" and "Stop him!" coming from every side. The young criminal dodged skillfully, throwing aside platters and cutlery and lobbing vegetables at his pursuers. He wasn't stopped until the scullion, sitting near the larder with a table of plucked turkeys by her side, overturned the buckets which were sitting at her feet. The slippery deluged tripped him up at last, and Holmes reached him a moment before the constable.

A burst of applause from the far doorway heralded the arrival of Gregson and several of the guests from the party who had been attracted by the shouts. Holmes, ever the showman, gave them a bow, and released his captive into the custody of the disguised constable. "You shall find the pins in his pocket," he told Gregson, "and a prybar in his sleeve, which should be sufficient to hold him on a charge of burglary. I caught him coming from Lady Lindsay's room, and if you examine her jewel case, it will no doubt be altered."

"We'll have her ladyship check for damage," Gregson said, looking over the prisoner with a contented eye. Even with cropped dark hair, the lad's clean cheeks and delicate colouring lent him a feminine air. "However did you spot this scoundrel, Mr. Holmes?"

Holmes swept off his own wig. "I know something of disguise," he said simply, and earned himself another round of applause.

It was nearing midnight when we returned to Baker Street, with Gregson's fee safely tucked into Holmes's pocket and a five pound block of paraffin from the hotel cook, which my friend had requested after a short discussion with the heroic scullery maid. My medical skills had come into play, not only for the cut over Holmes's eye, but also for other small injuries to the hotel staff, although I had been saved the trouble of making the sort of lengthy statement which delayed Holmes. But we were content. The case was solved, our rent assured, the fate of our maid in other hands, and nothing remained of our difficulties but our Christmas goose.

The sun had risen by the time I descended to the sitting room to find Holmes kneeling on the hearth, blowing the fire back to life. He had our Christmas breakfast, a simple matter of bread and jam to tide us over, already set out upon the table. Quickly, I drew his Christmas present out of my dressing gown pocket and set it by his plate while he was still occupied. "Good morning, Holmes," I called. "Happy Christmas to you."

"And a Happy Christmas to you, Watson," he said, rising and dusting his hands against his trousers. Far from donning "gay attire" as the old song says, he was dressed in a disreputable suit that was mostly useful as a disguise, although it quite matched the bruises on his face. "You're up early." He waved at the window, where the grey light of dawn was just showing.

"You're earlier," I pointed out, pulling out my chair. I discovered a package sitting on it, brown paper tied with a blue ribbon. "What's this?"

"The fruit of my labors yesterday afternoon," Holmes said. "And the boys. You shall have to thank them. They're much better carolers, than I." He came to the table and picked up the packet I had left for him.

We unwrapped our presents and then had a good laugh, because he had gone to Bradley's too, and purchased for me a tin of Ship's. Our after-breakfast pipes were much appreciated!

By nine o'clock, we were in the kitchen. Holmes was making his preparations for plucking the goose, and I was distributing my pilfered evergreen branches around the room when the doorbell rang. I went to answer it and found all six of the Baker Street Irregulars, who burst into "Hark the Herald Angels Sing" the moment I opened the door. Holmes came to listen too, watching from over my shoulder. When the boys finished the first song, they went on to "The Holly and the Ivy", and Wiggins pulled out a berryless branch of holly from behind his back and presented it to me when the song ended.

"Here, Doctor. Mr. Holmes said you didn't have no holly this year, so we brung you some. And we was wondering if we could share our dinners like with Jimmy and Billy, even if they didn't help carryin', acos they were sweeping snow for toffs that day, and we don't mind them eating some off'n our plates if you don't."

I glanced at Holmes, but he shook his head just a bit, to indicate that he bore no responsibility for the boys' request. "You're in charge, my dear fellow," he murmured. "It's up to you."

I looked at young Smith and even younger Jones and knew that I could never be so hard hearted as to turn them away. "Very well, boys," I said, and then raised an admonishing finger before their celebrations could begin. "But, there's one condition. You must all, every one of you, *wash*."

It says much about the conditions under which our poor live that the boys had to confer before agreeing to remove the layer of dirt that they thought of as protective. And it undoubtedly complicated the process of preparing our Christmas dinner to have those six rapscallions dancing around the kitchen in Holmes's shirts while their own clothes hung from ropes we'd strung up as clotheslines. (It was hardly worth washing the boys if we didn't wash their clothes.) But many hands make light work, and they all pitched in with a will.

Holmes, true to our agreement, took his direction from me for the most part, but could no more resist taking center stage for demonstrating the paraffin method of removing pinfeathers than he could fly. I was as interested as the boys, however, and we all applauded when the paraffin, cooled by a dip into a pot of cold water, cracked away, leaving the goose's body clean and bare.

Then it was my turn to be observed as I dismembered and gutted the goose. One or two of the boys were surprisingly knowledgeable about the viscera, having taken work now and then as scullions at the mission or workhouse, and I set them to cleaning the gizzard and digestive organs while I named the other organs for the curious. I made certain to dispose of the gall bladder, after letting young Robinson taste a tiny bit of the bile when he protested my wastefulness.

Holmes, in the meanwhile, had assembled the stuffing, in consultation with Mrs. Beeton. He read aloud the directions for beating the breastbone and skewering the bird whilst I did the work, and soon our goose was ready to be roasted. The boys raised a cheer as I set it into the oven, and I felt like cheering myself.

That was not the end of my work, of course, as I had still the gravy, the applesauce, and the potatoes to prepare, but now I could get the boys out from underfoot. I set them small tasks of peeling or chopping, which they could do at the table, and told Holmes to find something to keep their hands and minds occupied once those tasks were complete. He chose to fetch down needles and thread to repair the worst of the rents in their clothing. By the time I had the last pot on the stove, they were sufficiently absorbed to have fallen quiet. Young Clarence, usually the quietest of the lot, was handier with his needle with the rest, and as I sat down to pour myself a well-earned cup of tea, he began to sing "I Saw Three Ships", and the rest of us joined in.

Despite his deprecations, Holmes had a pleasant tenor that blended well with the boys' high voices. My own baritone was rusty. I had not sung a Christmas carol since Afghanistan, had not sung at all since Maiwand, and I kept my contributions soft as we sang carol after carol. It wasn't until "We Three Kings" that I found myself singing alone. Wiggins had sung about gold, and Holmes about frankincense, which left me myrrh, and although I got through the verse without stumbling, I found myself overwhelmed with memories that seemed to me to have no place at a Christmas celebration. As soon as the song was done, I excused myself to go and stir my pots and turn and baste the goose.

The giblets needed additional water, the apple sauce as well, and the potatoes were nearly soft enough to mash. But when I opened the oven door, it was clear that the dripping pan I had chosen was going to be far too small for the amount of grease coming off the goose. I wrapped my hands in towels and began to lift it out, calling to Holmes to fetch me a substitute pan.

I had underestimated the boys' restlessness, for three of them jumped up from their seats, volunteering to bring the pan in Holmes's stead. Robinson, left alone on the end of a bench, suddenly had it tip up from his weight, and he gave a yell and fell off of it, rolling into my feet. I managed to avoid spilling hot grease all over him, but only by dint of letting it slop over my covered hand and past him onto the middle of the floor. The other boys, still barefoot, jumped up onto the table to avoid the grease, and would have tipped it too if Holmes hadn't flung his weight onto it as counterbalance. His chair, abandoned, fell, and struck the buckets nearby, spilling the larger goose feathers into the air and paraffined pinfeather lumps across the greasy floor.

Perhaps a quarter of the grease was still in the pan, and I hastily set it down on the stovetop so that I could unwrap the hot greasy towel from my hand. Robinson was squealing like a stuck pig at my feet, so I hauled him up and carried him over to the sink, where I doused us both with cold water, all the while shouting for everyone to stop making noise and sit down in terms that I blush to recall. For right in the middle of my diatribe, the door to the front passage opened up, and there stood Mrs. Hudson in her coat and hat, holding a Christmas pudding, still in its bag.

I think, if the Irregulars had been wearing their clothes, they would have run for it. I would have run for it myself, if I hadn't just drenched half my side in cold water. Robinson, writhing with the pain of a grease-splashed shoulder, was still making a noise, but the rest of us swallowed our shouts and held still as Mrs. Hudson advanced into the room.

"Doctor," she said, as she paused at the edge of the puddle of grease. "Is the child badly hurt?"

"No," I said, for there wasn't any blistering I could see. "He'll be fine."

"Good." Her regal gaze turned upon my fellow lodger. Between the stitches on his face, the roughness of his knuckles, and the disheveled condition of his attire, he was not a prepossessing sight. I found myself wishing I could spare a hand to conceal the bruise upon my own chin. "Mr. Holmes?" If she had been shouting, she would have seemed far less dangerous.

But Holmes collected himself and addressed her with as much aplomb as if he weren't being used as a hiding place by two small boys. "Mrs. Hudson. What an unexpected pleasure. We thought you would be in Croydon celebrating Christmastide with your family."

"So I surmise," she intoned. She drew an envelope out of her pocket, which I recognised as one of the letters we had forwarded the previous day. "And at what juncture were you planning to inform me that Polly was in quarantine, Doctor?"

I did not carry off my turn at being interrogated with nearly the same insouciance as my friend. "We didn't know where she was ourselves until yesterday evening," I said. And then, knowing it disastrous to elaborate, went on, "Given the storm and all, however, we thought it best not to worry you."

133

"After all," Holmes leapt into the fray. "We are two grown men, and perfectly capable." He smiled his most charming of smiles.

Mrs. Hudson let her eyes turn up deliberately to the hanging clothes, and then down to the grease and flour bedecked floor.

"And we had Mrs. Beeton," I said, pointing to the book, having only just then realising that when Holmes had sat down to keep the boys amused, he had been too busy to keep up with the detritus of my cooking efforts. This was far from being the neat kitchen which Mrs. Hudson had left in our care!

"A most useful volume." Holmes carefully made his way to the stove, so as to lift the roasting pan's cover and display the bird inside. "And as you can see, our goose is nearly cooked."

"No, Mr. Holmes," Mrs. Hudson said, signalling for Brown to bring her a chair. She settled into it and began to unpin her hat. "Your goose is, I assure you, *entirely* cooked. But since I am here to give you your pudding, I shall see that you may get the chance to eat it as well."

The Adventure of the
Long-Lost Enemy
by Marcia Wilson

From *Cox & Kings* (formerly *Cox & Co.*), August18[th], in the Year of Our Lord, MCMXXX:

> *It is rare to discover a case that demonstrates the editing between Dr. Watson's natural verbose style and the final, polished result from Sir Arthur. The following may be the only one of its kind, being complete in the Doctor's original voice and in possession of no "failed" feats of deduction, nor the other alleged "failures" that led to so many adventures' consignment to the limbo of Cox. From the perspective of History, the worthy Detective will doubtless argue that this case is a paltry show of his abilities. We respectfully posit this manuscript is an insight into the unique methods that he used in solving crimes.*

It was late on December the 18th, the Thursday before Christmas. It was my custom to pay my patients a last call before the holidays, and my rounds were circuitous. Frost sprinkled over the black ice-piles in the gutters like anthracite, and it was all any light could do to cast some feeble glow into the black lumps for my safe passage. My old wounds stung as a sour wind blew from the North, bringing flakes the size and texture of Brittany's bitter grey salt to gently rest a carpet over the cobbles. A haze grew around the nimbus of light hissing about the street-lamps as distant carolers practiced their arts, their songs and bells echoing softly back and forth over the valleys and mountains of brick and stone. Here and there winked the few brave lights of Christmas, and wafts of fresh greenery cleansed the nose of soot. More vocal proofs of midwinter rested on the countless playbills: tonight was the night to pay respects for Sebastian among the Eastern Orthodox. A newspaper pasted to the door of a Confectionary's advertised the feast of Winibald, brother of Walpurgis; a crude painting of the saint with his bricklayer's trowel in hand stood by a pretty little ikon of his sister cradling her corn dolly – doubtless a petition for her gentling hand against the storms that had plagued our city from the sea.

The closed-down Indian spice shops were liberally painted with festival. Thanks to my military days, I could read the praises for a peaceful Al-Hijra that had passed on the fourth, and in gold paint were notices of the Day of Ashura, so reminiscent to the Occidental eye of the Jewish Hanukkah. A child from somewhere in the high tenants' housing was singing a high, sweet ululation in praise of the Prophet. Typical of the tolerance of the sub-Continent, across the street the devout were winding down their day-long fast of Durgashtam. Lord Shiva's day had been on the Wednesday, and I could see his serene form behind beaded curtains. A plump Ganesh smiled in a tiny sill, the tip of his broken tusk winking by the light of a single butter-lamp.

In the Chut quarters, the prayers and fastings had ended with rich aromas that would have set an aesthetic's stomach growling. Earlier that day, I had passed this spot and paused to listen to two lively children excitedly relating to their younger siblings the moment when Adam created fire with two stones in blessing to God for the way of the world turning to darkness, then light. Now these children were in bed, their door-way empty but for a curled-up beggar, sleeping with a new loaf of bread inside his arms and two dozing moggies curled for warmth inside the folds of his oversized coat. A Rabbi prayed in a sing-song voice in an attic glowing from tiny seven-tier candelabras.

I passed from one country's street to another: The Irish feted their Saint Flannán with happy toasts. Strains of *O Adoni* wafted through the air where an Armenian chapel practiced late Vespers. I was surprised to find a Zoroastrian colony on my way, and stopped for a moment to regard the humble scenes in the barred glass, thinking of my wanderings between India and the East. These quiet folk were preparing for *Shab-e-Yaldā*, for they see Christmas as the first day of winter. Red being felicitous, they had arranged a brilliant display of tiny Christmas apples and the holly wreaths that could scarce be seen for the amount of scarlet berries and red marzipan pears and pomegranates. They must have been long residents of England, for they knew the trick of forcing the pale pink cherry blossoms to bloom in water. In accordance to their custom, this was the season for beaus to declare their sincerity to their fair maids, and I watched as three laughing sisters hurried out with baskets of fruits and nuts in response to the courtesy of their swains.

I was in a splendid mood despite the weather. London can demonstrate great beauty, and it is possible to discover such treasures if one is willing to see it. I never failed to feel that this season was the one time of year in which all hostilities are suspended; one can feel, in the slimmest hours between the old year and the next, that the entire world is resting content. It is indeed a time where one ought to believe in Peace on Earth.

I opened the door of our sitting room to discover Holmes organising his impressive collection of books.

My friend was well-read. When needs must, he attacked the unknown with gusto, questioned the experts without thought to his incommodities, and absorbed the smallest detail to be used at some unknown moment in the future. The urge to know drove him in the same way that food's finest sauce was the hunger of its diner. The thickest and most obscure tome could be devoured by his hungry eyes in mere days. The dullest sums were easily immortalized in the notes which were never thrown away, for he preferred to move ever-forward in his cases, and ordered his papers to keep memory for him as he cleaned his brain-attic for the next case to come. In concession to this voracity, Mrs. Hudson had granted him an unused room, and he was wasting no time in this advantage. A ziggurat of dictionaries teetered on the bearskin; natural history smothered most of the carpet. In the odd corners and inconvenient nooks, I could see the titles that had caught his fancy: foreign language, climate, bones of long-dead beasts, arguments of colour-vision, mental studies, and many other examples, some too fantastic to mention here. It was a tactile exhibit of his learning, which he preferred to call an omnivorous diet to feed the mind.

"Ah, I thought I heard you," Holmes said. As I navigated the rough seas to my sofa, he emerged laden with more books. These joined the pile on the bearskin and a cloud of dust curled up to rest upon the ceiling.

"I should think that will be enough for the night." He declared, and stepped back to better admire his achievement. With that, he rang for supper and changed the subject for a discussion of the weather and how it was affecting travel. London was always ripe for dull crime, he felt, but the wintry avenues harvested broad challenges for the cleverer brain, and it was to these that he wished to test his mettle.

Our usual after-supper custom was to enjoy one last conversation before the fire. Tonight, this required a bit of meandering around books, and I had to clear out my chair.

Holmes was mellow. He plucked up a small calabash that he prized but never used. He often smiled when he examined it, its secrets known only to him. "There is something about the element of fire which brings out my personal philosopher."

"I suppose that is part of being man, Holmes. We have ever gathered around fire for thought."

"Perhaps the season makes me more contemplative, but I find that strangely comforting." Holmes polished the pipe as he spoke. "I shall be sorting the last shelves this week-end; after that I may require some assistance in moving the boxes, should you feel Marcini's a proper payment."

"I would be pleased to help after I finish my two days for Dr. O'Neill. He is an interesting fellow, if a bit absent-minded, and he has a way of attracting patients with *outré* cases."

The following morning, I found myself standing on the steps of my patron's office with white sheets in the windows and a QUARANTINE card on the door. Through the mail-slot, the housekeeper assured me that the practice was indisposed for the week and I would be free to call upon the gentleman of the house by the following Monday – Wednesday the latest.

As I wryly observed this twist in my funds, a voice called from the London throng. I turned to see Inspector Lestrade, straining his small body in the crowd to get my attention. My second surprise in as many minutes left me speechless and worse the wear for descriptive powers, for he reminded me of nothing so much as a stubborn salmon flailing against the dominant current. In seconds, he was panting on the same lower step as I.

"Heavens! Is this why we couldn't reach Dr. O'Neill?"

I assured him he would eventually return.

"Well, that's a relief!" he exclaimed. "But here, do you know someone who could help the Yard in a pinch?"

"What is the problem?"

"We need a death confirmed to legally cart the remains to our Coroner. We're so overworked, we have been relying on outside contracts, and we pay a day's wage for each trip out."

I assured him that I would be pleased to be useful, if he felt it within my capacity.

The little detective looked up in surprise from batting a cloud of dust off his bowler.

"Bless you, but we'd be pleased to have you any day. I assure you we don't have a lot of cases that deserve your attention, that's true; our medical folk see humdrum work most the time."

I was still absorbing the fact that I had the reputation of being the surgeon's version of Sherlock Holmes in the eyes of the police when Lestrade put his hands to his mouth and whistled for his police cab. Without further ado, I followed him inside and we set off to an inconsequential slum tucked away on the opposite side of Clerkenwell.

The poorer slums of central London have an inexplicable lack of concern compared to the sensationalism of our city's "East of Aldgate". Since Elizabeth's time, the area has quietly upheld admirable creativity with lawlessness. This early an hour, the stacks were fresh and blankets of soot bathed the clouds, turning the day into a dark and sinister forest of buildings. Here and there, windows wanted glass and roofs dearly lacked for new slate, giving the impression of winking, ragged-cropped giants.

"They usually send Gregson over here," Lestrade complained as he kept up a futile dusting of his coat. "But he's out with the same sick, sulphur onions piled up to his chin! I am sorry this won't be a very interesting bit, but most of our days are thus."

"I shan't complain for the chance to work, and you feel it is within my abilities."

"It is unpleasant if simple. We have a matter of a long death."

"A long death?"

"A man died and his brother didn't take him from their rooms out of fear the body would be put to infernal use – oh, you needn't look so! I didn't mean cults. That's really quite rare. Tends to be the spoilt-up lads that conduct that sort of nonsense, and they hardly ever kill anyone on purpose."

I felt Lestrade's profession was not as boring as he believed. "What did he fear?"

"Oh, the usual. Those ghoulish students, or collectors wanting a fresh corpse to study. What with the recent stories of cremation, there's *that* worry amongst the poor." Lestrade stared out the window with a lordly air. "The newspapers think they can't afford to properly put the dead to rest, you know. But I know that's not the case. They'll starve if it sets a loved one to rights. And here of all places? No, they have been hard-used by others, and will do their best to keep one final indignity from the grave. This poor fellow was a common faith-healer of sorts, and he had some regard in the back-alleys for his way with thrush. It would be most unlikely someone would steal his remains – they're more likely to nick a piece of his clothing or a clip of his hair."

I wondered at his angry expression, which with his suddenly jutted-out jaw and crimped brow, gave the impression of a short-tempered bulldog. "His brother hid him from burial?"

"Who is now dead himself. Oh, not inside the room! Dear me, I've gotten ahead of myself, just like Holmes says." He shook his head sadly. "Tommy Shenk was a coal-swinger. Brother Jonas stayed home and earned a few bits with his faith-healing. It was an odd arrangement but it worked for them, but last night Tommy was killed at the docks. Too many new sailors fresh to the port and too much green beer and raw rum. Four dead in all, and six more abed! We thought we were taking poor Jonas news of his brother's death when we found out the hard way he was already talking to him from his side of Creation." In agitation, the little detective slapped his gloves upon his knee. "What a mess! We're worn thin enough as it is. Shenks' body was being kept in an old earthen cellar, and that whole map is bad for outbreaks. Typhoid, cholera, measles, every pox . . . what would happen if the waters were tainted again?" We both shuddered. "And it is Grim House, to make things worse."

I confess I felt a thrill, for everyone in London knows that place. A hundred years ago, the Grim name was revered in our architecture, but that respect ended with the last of the line's two sons. The eldest, Basil, was considered "The Good Brother" for his tireless kindness, but younger brother Garland was made of sterner stuff and dabbled, it was whispered, in the lucrative trade of child-selling. Many swore he was the true inspiration for Dickens' Scrooge, and the treatment of his four sons had been the stuff of legends.

Basil eventually grew sick enough of his family that he set his fortunes in Australia. Before leaving forever, he bound his brother by his last will to properly house his nephews. Garland had salved his fury by carving their house into four meagre-thin tenements. The sons reacted to this largess by following their uncle's example and dispersing. Grim spent the rest of his days as Scrooge would have done without Marley: alone, unloved, and unmourned. His solicitors tried to gain some financial solace from his work, and the curious came for miles to look upon this lump of stone, a fitting mausoleum to the absence of charity. I myself had glimpsed the nefarious James Tracks, his surviving partner in their vile trade. Tracks used his rat-catching trade to discover – and then steal – promising children from families too poor to protest. His breeding of yellow rats as pets for the wealthy gave him the chance to look over a house from the inside, and return later to rob it clean. Such was the terror behind his name that none dared help the Yard or even Holmes in hunting him.

We soon set our feet upon a crumbling street too narrow for the cab. Our way was overcast with a double row of glowering brick buildings and plain-scrubbed panes, and the air reeked of carbolic and boiled vinegar.

I prided myself in knowing London, but this was the first time I saw rats in broad daylight, if daylight this could be called, pinched to starving skeletons. Hoardes flowed over the kerb and street and paused in the narrow alleys to stare us with cold red eyes. In the thick fogs and stifling atmosphere, these streets were more congenial for the spirits and melancholy than the living. Rarely have I seen any slum without a congestion of humanity, but the people ran before us into the fog, and dogs barked incessantly.

"They know me," Lestrade muttered. The little detective scowled at dark nooks as though they meant something to him. "This is the worst of it. The sewer was closed on a cholera outbreak and they started rinsing the rats out, but the cold weather damaged the pipefittings . . . people are staying inside now until the vermin's cleared out, but right now I have more faith in rat-catchers like old Tracks supplying the pits." He sunk deeper into the scarf about his throat, angry that a man of the law would be forced to support an illegal cruelty. "If these buildings were wood, I fear someone would have cleansed it with fire long ago."

"Do they fear you more than the rats?"

"Not likely. Mind you, they are proud and often straight as a tack! They work hard to help themselves. You'd be amazed at the cleverness they possess, for they'll run right at a problem to solve it. But it is cold, most of the able-bodied are away on any jobs they can find, and . . . well. Times are hard." He shook his head in pity. "Christmas is the one time they can hope to make the year's money, and the rent will rise on Boxing Day."

The dirty mist parted to show four impossibly narrow, rib-thin houses. There was barely enough room for the stairs and a stingy bottle-window on each floor.

Lestrade rightfully understood my expression.

"They say good and evil both lives on after the man dies, but I've never heard a single good thing about Garland Grim." The detective shuddered. "He built this over a freshet that fed the Stamford, so no-one owns the building further than its earthen floor! In other words, small as his sons' rooms would be, they couldn't lengthen it by digging further down – and there's no means by which they could add further rooms on top. The neighbors still refer to him as "Grudging Garland.""

It was unlike Lestrade to deviate from business into personal gossip, but I could tell he was at the end of his wits over the affair. "We'll be going to the one on the far end there." He pointed with his chin, where two Constables guarded the doorway.

Up close, Grim House was dull with filth piled upon the paths between the listless street-sweepers and crawlers. The stench was marked and Lestrade warned me to keep my handkerchief across my face. He scurried over the slimy cobblestones to halloa. Lestrade's Constables straightened as we drew closer and tapped their brims.

"There you are, Balan. What news?"

"Some of the neighbors were nosin' about agin, but Ardalean and I put 'em back, sir."

"They should have nosed about weeks ago! This is a hazard!"

As they spoke, I caught the stench from inside the building and held my breath. "How could anyone have not reported this?" I cried. "Is there no Inspector of Nuisances?"

"They cannot come in without permission," Lestrade said through the muffling of his face. "The other tenants' wishes are not good enough when everything is all legally hide-bound. I appealed to the Magistrate as soon as I could, but until this is settled, these poor folk are living all doubled up like bees in a hive in the untainted three quarters of the house."

As this was being relayed, a bony driver squeaked up with a narrow van marked for the city's mortuary. It must have been designed for these alleys, for it was mostly canvas and too lean for more than the horse, the driver, and a coffin.

"Finally!" The little detective clapped his gloved hands in relief and rocked on the balls of his feet. "I'm taking Dr. Watson down. Tell them to be ready, for there shall be no time to waste!"

The constables looked at me in admiration. I was certain it was undeserved.

I followed Lestrade down a yard-thin flight of stairs. He had to inch slowly with Ardalean's bull's-eye, for it was dark and the wood creaked and moaned under our lightest steps. In the darker corners, I gleamed an astounding number of cobwebs. A dusty rope caught me in the face.

"They spin as soon as we walk through 'em too," Lestrade grumbled. "The poorest folk still use cobwebs for bandages." He lifted his walking-stick to knock down a large netting. "Especially for stab wounds. One sees a lot of blood around here. Here we are."

The cellar was small and rude and empty, save for a heavy red carpet upon which perched the coffin on a crude sawbucks bier. A single candlestick rested at the wall, prepared to light for a Christmas that would never come.

"I couldn't tell you if he died by fair means or foul, but I'm hoping you can verify that he has died. From there we can take the remains to our morgue." With that he set his jaw and lifted the lid of the coffin, holding his breath and hastily backing away.

I held my handkerchief over my nose and made a quick work of it. "He is clearly dead, Mr. Lestrade."

"Thank you!" Lestrade rolled his eyes in comical relief. "Thank you, and thank you. I am not asking you to make the determination of death – that shall be Dr. Pennywraith's duty, if the court deems it necessary. They might freeze him first to keep the air down."

"I would not know where to begin in determining cause of death." One last glance at the unsightly contents of the box and Lestrade returned the lid. "Most signs would be erased."

"I never know what the court will want from the Yard," was the weary sigh. "Lord help us! I simply do not understand." He shook his head from side to side. "The things people do. And those neighbors – pah!"

"Curiosity is normal, is it not?"

"I'd agree, but they were probably nosing about because of the rumours old Ghastly left a fortune in his house. They couldn't find it in their quarters, so they have decided it must be here, and as I said, they know their rent is upping."

"Lestrade, you appear to be very suspicious of human nature."

"Thank you." The little detective grunted as was forced to step closer to the coffin in order to put the lid back. He stopped across the clasp, and a strange look came over his pale face.

"What is the matter?"

"My foot just went down in something. Well, there's nothing for it."

I bent to see that his left foot was inside a depression in the carpet directly under the centre of the coffin. "For what, Lestrade?"

"I'm going to see what that is as soon as the lads take the coffin out of here."

The stairs were narrow and the coffin, awkward. At long last the wagon was off and the Constables were back on duty outside the front step.

I held the lantern as Lestrade moved the sawbucks and slowly rolled the carpet a bit at a time across the hard-packed floor. He suddenly gave a cry of satisfaction: below the spot where the corpse rested, a deep-set brick had been removed and replaced with hasty hands, allowing a half-inch gap between.

"Look at that, Doctor!" He pointed to the brick.

I did not understand his triumph. The brick had been written on with a sharp implement, such as a nail-tip. Hours of labour had gone into the careful engraving of a complex rune that, once I adjusted the lantern, could read:

Thou horseman and footman, you are coming under your hats; you are scattered! With the blood of Jesus Christ, with his five holy wounds, thy barrel, thy gun and thy pistol are bound; sabre, sword, and knife are enchanted and bound, in the name of God the Father, the Son, and the Holy Ghost Amen

"What does it mean?"

"The missing fortune, I'll be bound. This is an old rune against thieves." The little professional sought with his gloved fingers, then yanked upwards, bringing the brick out of the little pit. At the bottom was a grimy oilskin. "Dear me, I wasn't expecting this." Lestrade tugged open the throat of a musty purse and shook out a handful of tarnished coin. "Real guineas! And eight of them! More than enough to slit a throat."

"A low enough sum against a life."

"Oh, I agree, but this won't be the end of it." Lestrade sighed and dropped the purse to his lap. "If one fortune is found in the cellar, there'll be rumours that two more are hiding in the walls, and who's to say? Desperation makes a person clever. But this is likely the Shenks' fortune, and not Grimey's."

"How can you be so certain?"

"He hated banks. There would be much more than this. Also, this swag-hole has been freshly used." Lestrade rapped on the brick. He sadly replaced the money in the purse and tied the throat up tight. "I suppose that explains why no one ever saw both brothers outside – one was staying home to guard the money."

"But he died."

"Tommy used his body to guard the money." Lestrade nervously fidgeted with his walking-stick. "Sanctity of death is one of the few things people respect here. They wouldn't have disturbed him . . . I might have known when I saw this carpet in a basement . . . too nice for a dirt floor."

"This carpet is not too fine for a brother's funeral parlour."

"It drew my attention when we came down here – I should have listened to my eyes." Lestrade was very glum at his self-chastisement, and it was all I could do not to tell him that I had seen this expression many times by Holmes.

"What happens to the money?"

"Escheats to the Crown, if it isn't disqualified as being disproven as their property."

"But it is under their floor!"

144

"And the property line ends at the earth. *Bona vacantia* is a nightmare, but it will see to their proper burial!" He tucked the purse inside a large pocket sewn inside the lining of his coat and looked in the crevice one last time. "Now what is this?"

I peered down. A whiff of something indefinably musty, and mildewed like a long-abandoned grave, blew into our faces. Cobweb wobbled before our eyes and Lestrade brushed it aside, angling the lantern without much hope. At last we succeeded when I pulled out the hand-mirror used for my examinations and we reflected the lamp-light into the hole, which I could see, was not a hole at all but a black wooden pipe.

"This is one of the original pipes of London!"

"An alderwood?" I marveled, for I had heard of but never seen the log pipes built to ferry water throughout the older parts of the city. "It is in poor enough condition that I can believe it was set over a hundred years ago."

"Alderwood's still being used in the cow-country where I was born. It stays good if wet and never splinters. It only falls apart when it dries out."

"It must have dried when a stream was diverted."

"Yes." Lestrade was scowling, and even though I could not see his face, I could hear his unhappiness. "This is very queer, Doctor. There appears to be something clogging it up . . . ." He poked and prodded with a persistence I found puzzling, and I said so.

"You wouldn't believe some of the swags we've found." With a grunt, he pulled out a well-preserved walking-stick of ebony, a matching peg-leg, and finally a wad of many-waxed and oiled skins well wrapped around a small book bound of cracked and crazed black leather, the pages uneven and thin.

Pow-Wows
Or
The Long-Lost Friend

"Someone wasn't taking chances, eh, Doctor? Saw a lot of these during the American War."

"But what is it?"

"Oh, just a spellbook." Lestrade coughed. "Let's get out of this! I'll beg to the Inspector of Nuisances to get on down here with his zymotic steam-oven . . . ."

Outside, the light was better. "Some of this appears to be a low form of German."

145

"It might be that, Doctor. It might also be a cipher. Those books are private, you know. They don't like the wrong eyes reading personal words." Lestrade shrugged. "A lot of countries have them banned outright. Or they'll just burn them. They – " He suddenly jumped back and swore as a blotched rat with a short tail staggered out of a narrow hole in the foyer wall and ran out the door in terror.

I chuckled and expected Lestrade to make a comment about rats, but he was staring where it had vanished with a strange expression.

"Lestrade?"

He laughed self-consciously and rubbed at his eyes. "Up too many hours, that's what. Eyes playing tricks."

"I can assure you that really was a rat."

"So it was!" He laughed again and it was a forced, false gaiety before his entire face changed to dread. "Doctor, do you think Mr. Holmes might be available for a bit of work? There's something about this that I don't like. He could make sense of it all, I'm sure."

I bade my farewells, accepting Lestrade's offer of a cab as part of my fee for the day and a promise to return, with or without Holmes, as an answer. The weather had lightened somewhat, but a light dance of ice had touched that larger streets. At a snail's crawl we half-slid, half-hobbled to Baker Street, where Holmes was finishing up a linseed-oil application to his now empty bookshelves.

"I do apologise for the smell, Watson."

My composure shattered. After a few minutes, I was calm enough to explain myself.

"You earned your pay after all, and with a story."

"A story and perhaps a diversion from your books?"

"It is a case with some interesting points about it."

"I wish I knew why. Lestrade was badly affected, but it was only a rat!"

"There is no knowledge without effort." Holmes rose. "You are chilled to the bone, and have time for a sandwich and coffee as I review a few notes." With that he plucked up a small brown journal perching on the books and paged through it. I followed his advice and had barely finished when Holmes leaped to his feet with a laugh of satisfaction.

"Watson, would you mind accompanying me to this puzzle? We need only to make a brief stop and send a wire to an old friend whom I feel will be most helpful!"

There was a peculiar smile to his face that I found untranslatable. When I asked he only shrugged.

"The best Christmas gifts can be years in the making, Watson."

Lestrade was waiting outside when we returned, and his countenance had taken a turn for the worse since our brief parting.

"I am all right." He tried to wave me off, but the open concern from his Constables compelled me to examine him. He was grey-green from some sort of shock, and the sweat on his brow was ice-cold. It was almost unthinkable to imagine him so moved after his stoicism in the cellar. "It's . . . we just found another body."

"Not much of one, if I may say," Balan spoke up. "All sticks inside a bag of skin."

"Too true." Lestrade suddenly sank to the bottom step and put his head in his hands. It was quite unlike the little professional to demonstrate any weakness before his Constables, but they were looking ill themselves.

"I assure you Watson and I will not place ourselves in any risk. If you could describe to me what you saw?"

"There wasn't much to see," Lestrade protested weakly.

"Nevertheless, I would trust your eyes."

Lestrade took a restorative breath of smelling salts and braced himself. "After Dr. Watson left, I was worried about that alderwood pipe. It isn't strictly the building's property, but we have a very ticklish Inspector of Nuisances, and if I couldn't convince him this wasn't a case of just another poor wretch and a long death, he'd be slower to bring down the disinfectors. There are at least twenty children living in the rest of the rooms, plus the elderly ones who can't get out, so I was hoping to find more proof in case it all came down completely to the Magistrate."

"You were trying to prevent an epidemic," I assured him. "Disease sweeps through these places like fire."

"Yes, well, that was what I was thinking, and there was at least one rat running in and out. So I took the lamp and your mirror and poked around that pipe again. I didn't see a thing, but I ran my walking-stick into it, and found something giving way. It looked like old leather. It took almost a quarter-hour, but I finally fished up a corner close enough that I could grab it and pull it up to the hole. What I thought was a leather bag wasn't a bag. It was a loose flap of skin. This poor soul, whoever it was, had been stuffed down that pipe years ago."

"You were quicker than I expected, Lestrade. But I must congratulate you for being quick and resourceful. I shouldn't worry about finding the missing leg – Basil Grim had it buried with a proper funeral at St. Mary's graveyard forty years ago after that unfortunate accident with the horse. The peg-leg you found was undoubtedly his."

Lestrade went from green to white. The police turned looks of dumbfounded awe upon my friend.

147

"Mr. Holmes," Lestrade said very slowly and clearly once his breath returned, "Had you been born sooner, they would have hanged you with the Yorkshire Witch."

"How did you know that was Basil Grim, sir?" Balan gasped. "And the missing leg?"

"Come, come, you know my methods." Holmes rose to his feet. "Now I believe I see our old friend Shinwell Johnson puffing up. He was the last man to see Basil Grim alive, and I am certain he is quite capable of identifying the remains."

"Porky Johnson?" Lestrade jumped up as the old criminal staggered to us, a swarm of dirty little urchins chattering and clustering about his battered working-slops.

"Is it true?" Johnson gasped. His tiny blue eyes blinked frantically under a fringe of hair that had he had been in the process of combing when Holmes's news came. Dried shaving-lather spotted his neck, and a flannel night-shirt peeped at the neck of his hastily-bound coat. "Did you find him?"

"I shall not take credit for another man's work, Porky. We have Lestrade for the credit."

The little detective could not have been more astonished when the old criminal grabbed up his hand and pumped it in gratitude.

"Bless you, bless you!" he cried.

"For what?" Lestrade shouted. "Holmes, what?"

"It means I was right and poor Mr. Basil was murdered all those years ago!" The stocky old criminal mopped at his face.

"His disappearance was suspect." Holmes added. "Johnson was one of the 'sons' and heirs to Grim House. Rather, one of the children kidnapped and made to serve Garland and his loathsome partner, Tracks the Rat-Catcher."

"Is this true?" Lestrade demanded hotly. "Man, why did you never say anything to us?"

"I am not from nice society, as you well know," the man answered with dignity.

"I know old Carpet-Tracks," Lestrade scowled. "I assure you we are always looking to catch him in the act!"

"He must have known you were too close to his old crime," Johnson grumbled. "No-one's seen a whit of him in weeks. Gone to ground, I'll be bound!"

"If his infernal rats are around, he can't be far. We'll find him, Porky." Lestrade pulled at his hat in agitation. "But you are positive you can identify the remains as Basil Garland's?"

"Just look close upon the head, sir. He had a left green glass eye."

"It would be common knowledge if he had one."

"It was Thuringian-made, with the stamp in the back. Two loops over a squat crossed T. 'Twas my job as a boy to wash it for him every night."

Lestrade's expression became positively stone-like, and even Holmes was surprised when he reached into his pocket and pulled out a shattered green glass eye.

"You have convinced me," he said quietly. "Mr. Holmes, if I may beg your pardon, I shall be asking questions of my witness."

Holmes was wordless until we returned home. After a quiet meal, he again plucked up his calabash for polishing. I joined him before the fire.

"Thirty years is a long time to solve a case, Watson." Holmes finally spoke. "The rat-catcher is still free, but I have my nets out as well as the police and he cannot be far. Betrayed by the special rats he breeds with pale fur and short, furry tails for fine ladies – we will find that beast before the year is finished, I'll be sure of that."

"Lestrade was as eager to snare him as you.'

"The child-sellers are beyond redemption. Fagin was an angel compared to the Tracks of the world, and I had no choice but to watch and wait. Were I endowed with powers of authority to match my intellect, there would be no criminal free from my hand.'

"How did you know of this?"

"I first met Porky as a torn man, wanting to reform, but also resigned that he could not find the proof that his kindly old master, Basil Grim, had been murdered. Who believes such an unworthy child? He was stolen with no memory of his past outside of his name, which comes from the Jewish quarters. His memory was much eroded from time, and what I suspect was the trauma of witnessing Brother Garland striking his own flesh and blood dead – dead, he recalls, because Basil wrote the will to provide for Porky and the other children.

"After the murder, Garland enlisted his partner James Tracks the Rat-Catcher to hide the body, and Porky was forced to help. Suspecting his own end, he ran away with his mind fogged in terror. It was years before he could recall a few details, other than Basil was stowed inside a large wooden pipe with his ebony walking-stick. The best I could do was keep a written record of what he could remember, and slowly piece together the smallest clues in hopes of drawing a larger picture."

"I begin to see. The Shenks must have dug into the cellar to hide their small wealth and re-discovered the pipe. They used it as a cache, not thinking that anything else was inside the pipe."

"To be discovered in turn by Lestrade."

"But you were the only one capable of seeing this for what it was."

Holmes held up the little brown book. "I am proud of my library, Watson, but I confess my vanity for what I have written. This is a compendium of all the Porky Johnsons in my life, all the murders, thefts, and imaginable crimes witnessed by the un-witnessable. Crime being what it is, the wicked often repeat themselves, and many are the cases where I have solved a crime because I have taken the word of a little street-urchin seriously, or listened to the babble of a woman in a madhouse. A parallel incident here – a suspiciously familiar circumstance there – and I have a new crime solved with an old crime. If not solved, at least brought to some sort of justice. There are many hard-earned victories, Watson, in which I can tell my applicant that justice of a sort has been served, if not the justice they had hoped to see.

"For I am the judge, Watson. And it is my right to declare if a person's testimony is worth hearing." He was smiling as he rested the little brown book upon a world atlas. "My belief in him aided Porky immensely in his departure from crime. Now he may rest this Christmas, vindicated that he was not imagining murder. To-night is the night of *O Radix Jesse*, and I am struck by the poetry of the closing lines, '*come and deliver us, and delay no longer*'."

"It would seem that you have granted yourself a Christmas gift, Holmes – I have rarely seen you so content."

"Ah, my gift will be the pinch of Tracks! But Lestrade has given me a nice consolation." Holmes produced the cracked book of *The Long-lost Friend*. "I asked him if I might keep this, and he was all too eager to oblige. It was below the legal property-line, and a policeman who brings in a book of witchcraft will not be taken seriously by his peers! The rats would soon eat up the paper and glue. I have always wanted one of these books, but they are guarded jealously . . . aha! Here is a fine one, Watson! A charm to immobilise thieves! Shall we try it out? But is that the bell? At this hour?"

We turned to our open doorway, for we could already hear Mrs. Hudson's exclamations and Lestrade's uneven stride hammering up the steps.

"Holmes!" Lestrade clutched the door-frame for support. "You said you wanted word as soon as we found Tracks! Well, we found him when the disinfectors followed the alderwood to the next building over! Dead as can be, picked clean by his own rats! Pennywraith said he must have died in his sleep, and the disinfectors have threatened to quit because the rats found we'd unblocked the pipe when we removed Basil's remains and they're running all over the place now and – I say! Do you think this is funny, Holmes?"

Addendum

Dr. Watson attached notes to the back of this manuscript explaining that a strange sort of justice had prevailed on behalf of the poor tenants of Grim House. Trask's unique rats were swiftly captured and, with the notoriety of the case, became more valuable than ever, leaving the people with the financial means to keep up with the higher rent upon Boxing Day. He understood that they made meek enough pets, but were absolute terrors in the rat-fighting rings. Eventually Shinwell Johnson was deemed the heir and lowered the rent even further, wishing no profit from a terrible past.

The Case of the
Christmas Cracker
by John Hall

Even his best friends and greatest admirers could not in all honesty say that Mr. Sherlock Holmes would be the first choice for the stage portrayal of one of Charles Dickens's more convivial Christmas characters, Mr. Pickwick, say, or Scrooge after his instructive visits by the ghosts.

None the less, some short time after my marriage, I called upon him a day or two after Christmas, with the object of instilling in him some seasonal cheer. It was ten o'clock in the morning when I arrived, and I found him seated in an armchair, smoking one of his old briar pipes, and staring somberly at the fire in the grate. His breakfast lay untouched upon the table.

"No case in hand just now, Holmes?" said I, for I knew these symptoms well.

"Not at the moment, Doctor."

"Well, let me see if I can break the monotony. Here is a box of cigars – rather decent – and this – " and I produced the object to which I referred from an inside pocket, " – this is a new thing. The latest novelty. A Christmas cracker. An American invention, I believe, and very appropriate to the season."

He groaned.

"At least give it a chance, Holmes!"

He took the object and stared at it. "A curious shape, tubular, with a covering of a garish red paper – "

"Just pull it, Holmes!"

"Doctor?"

"Each person – you and I in this instance – holds one end, different ends of course, to be pedantic, and then we pull."

"And then?"

"Then the thing makes a loud bang, or crack – hence the name . . . ."

"Why?"

"Why?" Holmes has a knack of asking pertinent questions which can sometimes be very wearying. "Why, ah – why, to cheer up those doing the pulling, of course!"

152

"It seems a very inadequate way of producing geniality," said Holmes. "Could one not simply snap one's fingers, or – "

Frankly, I had heard enough of this drivel. I seized the free end of the cracker and tugged it viciously. As you might expect, there was no loud "Bang!", but merely a feeble rasping or whimpering sound, rather like a match being drawn over sandpaper.

Holmes smiled ironically.

"Perhaps the actual construction still needs some development," I suggested weakly.

"Perhaps so." But Holmes regarded the sorry fragment of paper in his hand with at least the beginnings of animation. "Intriguing. It is evidently fulminate of mercury, or some such substance. I wonder – " And he glanced toward the old chemical bench.

"There is more, Holmes. We have not yet considered the contents. After that, you may conduct your chemical analysis if you so wish."

"Indeed. Contents, you say?"

I produced a couple of scraps of paper from the body of the cracker. "A hat, Holmes."

"You are ahead of me, Doctor. Ah!" said he as I unfolded the thin sheet of coloured paper. "A hat of sorts indeed, though neither Mr. Lock nor Mr. Bowler would care to acknowledge it, I fear."

"A paper hat, Holmes. Most appropriate for the festive board, I think. And there is a motto, as well."

"Ah! Something inspirational for the young people, no doubt! 'Discipline for Service' perhaps, or boastful '*Floreat Etona*', say?"

"Not so much a motto, Holmes – "

"Or '*Resurgam*' perhaps?" and he laughed. "Most appropriate for a man in my profession, would you not agree?"

"As I was about to remark, it is less a motto in the usual sense, but more of a joke, or riddle."

"Ah."

"And before you ask, I have no idea why is should be called a motto when it is not," I told him firmly. "Now, Holmes, a challenge to even your powers of deduction, this! 'Why is an afternoon caller like an ardent lover?'"

Holmes frowned. "Is that entirely suitable for reading aloud at a family gathering?"

"Rubbish, Holmes! Of course it is. Well?"

By way of an answer, he sat upright in his chair, and for a moment I thought that he was seriously considering the little conundrum I had posed. But then he smiled, and remarked, "Your problem must wait, I fear, Watson. That is certainly the ring of the doorbell, and a client."

"I heard the bell, but a client?"

"Assuredly. And a woman, by the sound of it.

A moment later, Mrs. Turner – for Mrs. Hudson was visiting friends, as indeed was my wife, a not infrequent occurrence – showed the client, for such indeed it was, into our humble sitting room, and announced, in her broad Glaswegian accent, "Miss Beatrice Denby here to see you, Mr. Holmes."

"Ah, thank you, Mrs. Turner. Perhaps Miss Denby would care for a cup – no, a pot – of your famous strong tea? Unless you would like a true Scotch breakfast? For I observe, Miss Denby, that you are somewhat agitated and in need of a calming beverage, if nothing more substantial."

"You are right, Mr. Holmes. I have had something of an unpleasant experience. Tea will be more than adequate." Miss Denby seemed about to say more, but was evidently reluctant to speak before Mrs. Turner, who mumbled something about tea and breakfast, then made a great clatter as she cleared the untouched dishes from the table and left the room.

I felt that my position was a delicate one, and rose to leave with a word of apology.

Holmes, however, waved me back into my chair. "This is Doctor John Watson, whose name is doubtless familiar to you," said he, "a true friend and valued colleague, before whom you may speak freely."

Miss Denby nodded at me, but still seemed disinclined to tell her story. I busied myself clearing the table of its residual clutter of papers, whilst covertly studying our client, for so I know thought of her. She was perhaps some thirty-five years of age, not conventionally pretty in any girlish way, but with a handsome and determined face with spoke of independent means and a masterful character. There was, however, something of reticence about her which struck me as foreign to her nature, and I could see how Holmes had deduced some powerful shock, some unexpected upset.

Mrs. Turner soon returned with a tray of tea and the like, and as our client sipped the strong and refreshing brew and nibbled upon a shortbread biscuit, her true nature reasserted itself, and she was able to state her case. Somewhat to my relief, I may add, for Holmes was by this time showing unmistakable signs of impatience.

"To make matters brief, Mr. Holmes, the facts are these. My parents unfortunately died some ten years ago, and since then I have lived alone. Alone, but not lonely, for I have a large circle of friends. I have, however, never had occasion to think about matrimony, or indeed the married state, save to knit the usual small articles when my female friends have – ah, the usual thing."

"But that has changed lately, I deduce?"

"You are right, Mr. Holmes." Miss Denby sipped her tea, then went on with some reluctance. "Some weeks ago, quite by chance, I met a – a gentleman – by the name of Omerod. Silas Omerod. He was kind enough – or so it seemed then to me – to pay me some attentions, entirely courteous and gentlemanly, and – well, to be plain, I found myself attracted to him."

There was nothing in Holmes's demeanour to show it openly, but I, who knew his every mood, could tell that he was mentally grinding his teeth. "He had, I am sure, some gainful employment?" he managed at last.

"Ah – he represented to me that he had some private means, as I do myself."

"Just so," said Holmes with an effort. "And doubtless there was some investment, some sure-fire speculation . . . ?" He left it hanging in the air.

Miss Denby blushed delicately, and sipped her tea, rather to gain a little time than from any epicurean reason. "You have it exactly, Mr. Holmes. But I have heard such tales, and have known foolish women in the same situation, and – well, I promised to think the matter over before making any financial commitment."

Holmes heaved a sigh of relief. "You undoubtedly did very well to act as you did," said he. "However, beyond commending your prudence, I do not see – "

"I had not finished, Mr. Holmes," said our client with some asperity. When Holmes had apologised, Miss Denby went on. "Mr. Omerod's mention of this – investment opportunity – came the day after Christmas. The following day, that is to say yesterday, as we walked through the snow of London, looking at the shops and so forth, he did not mention it again, but I could not help thinking about it, becoming more and more certain that it was but my money that had attracted him. These sad thoughts, however, were entirely thrust from my mind when – here, at the very corner of Baker Street, Mr. Holmes – my attention was drawn to a – a woman, evidently of the poorer classes, who stared at the two of us in a most curious manner. I drew Mr. Omerod's attention to her with some remark or the other, and to my astonishment, when he glanced at her, he cried out, 'Oh! My wife!' and turned and raced away."

It takes a good deal to throw Holmes, but this simple account managed it. For myself, I have some recollection that I muttered some expression which no gentleman should utter in mixed company, but fortunately Miss Denby did not catch it. To make amends for this, I ventured, "You are certain that he said 'wife' and not, perhaps, 'My life!' or some similar expression of astonishment?"

Miss Denby smiled at me. "You are very kind to try to make me feel less foolish, Doctor Watson, but there can be no mistake as to his words."

"You say that Omerod took to his heels," said Holmes, as practical as ever, "but did you not perhaps think to query the matter with the other lady concerned?"

"I did, Mr. Holmes, but by the time I had quite recovered my wits, she too had vanished from sight."

"Did you have time to remark upon her appearance?" asked Holmes. "Pray think carefully, for what seems but the merest detail may have some significance."

Miss Denby shook her head. "Beyond remarking that she was of the poorer class, there – but wait! I recall that she wore a hat of a peculiar red shade, and there was a small, inexpensive brooch or pin in the side, in the form of a violet."

"Oh!" said I, "that is surely the 'flower girl', as they call them, though many are advanced in years. You know, the one who stands at the end of Baker Street. You will have seen her, Holmes. Although I did not notice her there today. The Christmas season, I suppose, or the inclement weather, for it is perishing cold outside! And of course, there are few flowers to sell at this time of year. Holly or mistletoe, perhaps or – " and I stopped under Holmes's stern gaze.

"Thank you, Watson. Yes, I know the lady, though only by sight. I wonder – " and he broke off in his turn, and smiled at Miss Denby. "Well, Miss Denby, you have, I think, given us enough to work on, and I am in hopes that we may – " and he broke off a second time, a frown appearing on his face. "Ah – I quite forgot to ask, but just what is it that you would wish to do in the matter? You can hardly want the return, as it were, of a suitor who already has a wife to his credit."

Miss Denby managed a laugh. "Hardly! No, sir, it is something more serious. The fact is, when I returned home, my maid informed me that Horace – Mr. Omerod – had called a few minutes previously."

"Ah."

Miss Denby nodded. "He had presented to her that I had sent him on some small commission – a pocket handkerchief – and my maid, being used to seeing him around the place – for I had pretty much given him a free run of my house – left him alone in my room. When I looked into my jewellery box, a valuable diamond ring and a good string of pearls were missing."

156

"Indeed? Then, as I feared, the matter is more serious than a mere breach of promise marriage?"

"Much more," said Miss Denby emphatically. "I care nothing for the wretch, but a good deal for my jewellery!"

Holmes nodded his approval. "We shall try to return the one, whilst leaving the other where he is! Unless, that is to say, you would wish to press charges against him?"

Miss Denby considered this, a look of distaste upon her face. "If it were simply a case of trifling with my affections, I should have thought nothing more about it – or him. But theft is another matter altogether. Yes, Mr. Holmes, I will give evidence against this villain, though it may expose me to ridicule as a foolish woman."

Again Holmes nodded approvingly. "A couple of points only remain. Why, since this encounter took place in Baker Street itself, did you not contact me yesterday?"

"I did not think, Mr. Holmes. But when I mentioned the incident, and the loss of jewellery to my maid, who is an intelligent girl, she reminded me of you, and I resolved to contact you on the morrow, that is to say, today. I spent a wretched night thinking about the whole sordid affair, and half determined to leave it alone, but my maid reminded me of my original intention, and – well, here I am!"

"Just so. Well, then, if you would give Doctor Watson here a note of your address? And we shall hope to be in touch with you very soon."

When our visitor had left, Holmes rang the bell. Mrs. Turner appeared, and he said, "I believe that you might be of inestimable help to me, for your knowledge of the environs of Baker Street is second only – that is to say, it is supreme. Tell me, do you have any acquaintance with the lady in a red hat, wearing a violet pin – "

"Lizzie, sir! Mrs. Norton, or rather Mrs. Cruikshank as she is now, on account of her having remarried – what she was a widow woman you know, sir – and her marrying a Mr. Cruikshank. And him a bad lot, by what I understand."

I frowned, and Holmes glanced at me, but I shook my head.

"Well, then," Holmes went on, "you should not happen to know Mrs. Cruikshank's address, by any chance?"

"Not to say *know*, Mr. Holmes, but I do know she lives in Dorset Mews, at the back of Baker Street here."

"I know it."

"And if you was to ask at the corner shop, they'd just as like know her house number."

"Just so. Thank you, Mrs. Turner, that was most helpful. And now, Watson," he added as she left, "I think a brisk walk around the corner might be in order."

"Indeed."

"By the way, Doctor, you seemed to recognize the name 'Cruikshank' just now."

"Something rang a bell, as they say, Holmes. Popular illustrator of that name, of course. But still – no, can't recall it. It'll come to me, no doubt."

"Quite." And Holmes led the way to the back of Baker Street, and a narrow lane of small cottages. Enquiry at a little tobacconist's shop revealed the number of the Cruikshank establishment, and Holmes was very soon knocking on the door.

It was answered by a little woman with a worried expression on her face. Not much above middle age, she nonetheless bore every sign of a hard existence. "Yes, sir?"

"Mrs. Cruikshank? I wondered if I might have a word with Mr. Cruikshank. I should very much like to speak to him on an urgent matter."

Mrs. Cruikshank smiled, a thin and ironic smile. "You and me both, sir!" The smile quickly vanished. "It wasn't about money, was it, sir? Only there isn't above sixpence in the house."

"No, we are not the bailiffs," said Holmes with a smile. "Might I prevail upon you to allow us inside, for it is very cold in the street?"

Mrs. Cruikshank muttered something or the other, but stood aside to allow us in. The house was scantily furnished, and I noticed two or three thin children staring at us from various hiding places. The place was freezing cold – I almost said colder than the street, if that were possible, for the only heating was a tiny and smoky coal fire burning in a huge fireplace.

Holmes rubbed his hands together for warmth, and said, "I gather that your husband has – ah – "

"Legged it, sir, is what 'e's done. Yes. And taken all my Christmas club savings with 'im, or it would've done, 'ad 'e not blotted 'is copybook pretty badly!" Mrs. Cruikshank sniffed loudly, whether from cold or emotion I could not well judge. "And that's not the worst of it, sir! Only yesterday, as I was trying to work out how I might find the rent for the rest of the week, I spotted 'im, large as life and twice as nasty, strolling down Baker Street, nice as you please, and with another woman!" Mrs. Cruikshank seemed inclined to say more, but her feelings overcame her, and I was obliged to offer her my clean handkerchief.

Holmes, practical as ever, asked, "And when exactly did he vanish, madam?"

"Oh, let me see. Five week, six? That was bad enough in all conscience, your husband leaving without a word, but then when I came to collect the Christmas money, I was told 'e'd drawn it out already, every brass farthing!" And her emotions too over again.

"Do you mean to tell me," I asked with some warmth, "that your few savings for Christmas have entirely gone? What did you do as to Christmas dinner, then?"

"You may well ask, sir. A mighty lean time we 'ad of it, I can tell you! Why, I'm ashamed to say what I put – or rather, didn't put – on the table, and me with four children to feed, if you'd credit it, sir!"

"The poor mites!" I felt in my pockets and, despite her protestations, handed her some few coins. "For the children, you know."

"Tell me," said Holmes, "how much was involved?"

"Five pounds, all upon, sir. And 'e 'ad it, every penny."

"And you have no idea where he might have gone? Where he might be now?"

Mrs. Cruikshank shook her head. "Not an inkling, sir."

"Well, thank you all the same." Holmes followed my example, and some silver changed hands. "Come, Watson." To Mrs. Cruikshank he said, "I cannot promise you anything, madam, but we shall try to ensure you do not lose your savings."

As we left, he said with some anger in his voice, "This is dreadful, Watson! We might not have too much sympathy for Miss Denby, who already had her suspicions, but to rob what is effectively a widow and orphans! I shall not hesitate to turn this rogue over to the police."

"Assuming we can lay hands upon him, Holmes."

"Assuming that. But I am in hopes that we may. Consider, Watson, that both his victims have been in the near vicinity of Baker Street. Why, then, not a third upon our very doorstep?" He shook his head. "If we but knew the name he might be using. Cruikshank, Omerod – "

"Belvedere!" I cried.

Holmes stared at me as if I had lost my senses. Then he laughed out loud. "Of course! Cruikshank, Omerod, and Belvedere, Solicitors and Commissioners for Oaths! The firm of lawyers at the end of Baker Street! Well done, Watson!"

"Nothing, Holmes. I should have got it sooner, for they drew up my will when I got married, and the lease on my practice. Although it wasn't any of those names I saw, probably all dead last century anyway, but a fellow named Chapmen, nice young man with a fine taste in beards. Anyway," I finished as Holmes gave some indication of impatience, "this villain is evidently going through the partners, and thus I predict he is now calling himself Belvedere. Doesn't get us any nearer to finding him, though."

"Does it not? I think you underestimate our combined intelligence, Doctor. A few enquiries of the local tradesmen, and I fancy that we shall have him."

In any event, it took a dozen queries at a dozen local shops, but in the end we found that a widowed lady by the name of Granby had recently remarried a man called Belvedere, and the address, in another poor mews, was forthcoming.

Holmes led the way through the streets, which already showed signs of the early winter evening's closing in. I asked, "Suppose the bird has already flown, though? He may have moved on to Mrs. Cruikshank, rather than away from her."

"True. But let us remain optimistic, Watson, for we have not done so very badly in the course of but one day."

Arriving at the house in question, Holmes paused. "There is, you observe, a passage at the side of the house, which may indicate a back door. Would you mind, Watson, going through and stationing yourself in readiness for a hasty exit? I shall knock on this door, and we shall see what may occur."

I went down the narrow and dirty passageway, and found that there was indeed an even narrower and dirtier back lane, a tiny back yard, and a back door to the house. I turned up my collar, for there was ice in the yard, and the snow was beginning to fall.

The houses in the mews were tiny, and I could hear Holmes's knock and his high-pitched voice, evidently enquiring after a Mr. Belvedere. There was a clatter from inside the house, the back door shot open, and a small man came running out.

I stuck out my foot. The man tripped over it, slipped on the ice, and slid over the little yard until he was abruptly halted by colliding with the outer wall of a small but convenient brick building. I hauled him to his feet as Holmes appeared in the doorway, and together we escorted him into the house.

Mrs. Belvedere, another thin and worried looking woman, regarded the three of us with sardonic amusement. "Just as I thought!" she said, together with some further remarks as to her husband's habits and character, which I shall take the liberty of omitting.

"Has he had money from you, madam?" asked Holmes.

"Not likely! Though it's not from want of trying. Is it a police matter?"

"I much fear it is. Watson, if you would be so kind as to call a constable?"

I did so. We discovered Miss Denby's jewellery, which slightly surprised me until Holmes pointed out that the pawnbrokers were probably shut over the holidays. Mrs. Cruikshank's Christmas savings were gone, but Holmes and I agreed that we would make up that trifling amount between us.

"By the way, Holmes," said I, as we returned to the warmth of 221b, "that little adventure reminded me forcibly of my riddle earlier today. Might have been written for it, in fact. You know, 'Why is a lover like an afternoon caller?' wasn't it? You see it?"

Holmes stared at me. "Alas, no, Watson."

"Well, with you at the front door, and me at the back, you see."

"I fear you have lost me, Doctor. Perhaps if you revealed the answer to the riddle?"

"Ah, yes. Forgot it had you puzzled, Holmes. Afternoon caller, ardent lover. 'Because they both go to a door,' you see."

Holmes patted his pockets and took out his silver cigarette case.

"It's a play on words, Holmes. 'To a door,' three words, and 'to adore,' two words. Do you see it?"

Holmes lit a cigarette and blew out a cloud of smoke. Then he patted me kindly on the shoulder. "In view of the season, with its spirit of forgiveness and goodwill to all men, I shall overlook this lapse, Watson."

"Thank you, Holmes."

"Just this once."

NOTE

I refuse to accept responsibility for this riddle, which really is late Victorian or early Edwardian, from 1901 or 1902. Age, of course, does not make it any better. – J.H.

The Queen's Writing Table
by Julie McKuras

As I look back on my long association with Sherlock Holmes, I believe that 1887 was an exceptional year for both my friend and the British Empire. It was the year of Queen Victoria's Golden Jubilee, and that milestone celebrated her rule over a vast number of the world's human beings and our Empire's position as the most powerful country on earth.

As for Sherlock Holmes, the year 1887 saw him engaged in a number of his most remarkable cases. While many of these successful adventures are known to my readers, there were several which occurred at that time which, for one reason or another, have never been made public. In the adventure which I titled "The Five Orange Pips", I recounted those untold cases, which included ". . . the Amateur Mendicant Society, who held a luxurious club in the lower vault of a furniture warehouse . . . ." It was this case which required such delicacy and diplomacy that I dared not make further mention of it at the time. In the intervening ten years since I noted that unrecorded adventure, Her Majesty Queen Victoria has celebrated her Diamond Jubilee, several of those who played important parts in it have passed on, and those once-secret alliances have changed. There is no longer a reason to keep it secret.

Despite his many intriguing problems that year, the waning days of 1887 presented nothing which captured Holmes's imagination. The lethargy which overtook him when he was unchallenged threatened to consume him as the New Year drew near. Upon my return from my medical practice each day, I often found Holmes still in his dressing gown, surrounded by clouds of tobacco smoke and scattered papers. The upcoming Christmas holiday offered no promise to relieve his morose behaviour; he complained that even the criminal element of London had left the city to celebrate.

In the week before Christmas, I saw the usual last minute rush of patients, anxious to be restored to health before holiday celebrations began. I've found that children who are uncomfortable or upset by a visit to their physician can generally be distracted when asked what Father Christmas might bring them on that most blessed of days. It was after one such day, when several young patients excitedly told me their hopes for a new doll, toy soldiers, or a jump rope, that I returned to Baker Street, my spirits buoyed by their innocent, expectant faces. On my cold and wet walk home, I passed holiday shoppers and store windows decorated with the usual holiday greenery and suggested gifts. I longed to spend a quiet evening by the fire after dinner, with a restorative brandy, a good book, and contemplation of all that Christmas represented.

Considering my long association with Sherlock Holmes, I should hardly have been surprised when I saw a carriage standing in front of our door. Unexpected visitors were more often the expected when one shared rooms with Holmes. Mrs. Hudson met me in the foyer, and confirmed my assumption that a visitor had called. Already resigned to the fact that my peaceful evening was not to be, I entered our rooms and, as I hung up my coat and hat, stole a brief look at our visitor. He was a tall and thin man of middle age, elegantly dressed, with a look of grave concern upon his face. Holmes introduced me to our caller.

"Watson, I'd like to you to meet Sir Max Michaels."

I extended my hand and introduced myself. "Dr. John Watson, at your service."

"I dislike calling on you after a long day, particularly this close to Christmas, but I am afraid it is unavoidable. Both of you are held in the highest regard by the people I represent, and there is no one else we deemed able to help us in this sensitive matter." With those words, Sir Max crossed the room to the fire, the very spot where I had envisioned myself in repose. He seemed to bear a great weight, and after a brief moment to collect his thoughts, he began to relate the problem which had led him to our door.

"Gentlemen, I come to you on behalf of Lord Edward Clinton, who serves the Queen as Master of the House. He is in charge of the Royal Household, which includes the employees of the Palace, such as the kitchen workers, the pages, the footmen, the housekeeper, and her staff. Late this afternoon, he called at my office and requested that I assist him, on behalf of the Queen, in this concern which demands the highest discretion. I spent the afternoon looking into the situation as it was described to me, and as asked, I am here tonight to enlist you in helping to save a worthy gentleman's reputation and career."

To say that he had our attention is an understatement. "The Queen will shortly announce her New Year's Honours List, which has been prepared before her removal to Windsor Castle for the holidays. Among the names of those deemed worthy for these honours, decorations, and medals is a man known for many years to those at the Palace. He isn't a diplomat or a military man, but instead, is engaged in commerce. His name has been brought forward for The Royal Victorian Order, given for Services to the Crown."

163

"And that gentlemen would be . . . ?" asked Holmes who moved to the mantel and retrieved his pipe and tobacco before taking a chair. I could tell his curiosity was already aroused and he was prepared to listen carefully.

"His name is Richard Atwell, of Atwell and Sons Furniture Restoration. The Palace utilizes his services for unique furniture repairs and construction of the most delicate nature, and the work they do is of the highest quality. While that in itself is a valuable contribution, it is hardly worthy of such an honour as I mentioned. His real service is to the poor of our great city. For many years, he has hired people in dire circumstances and trained them as skilled woodworkers. Under his tutelage, their acquired talents enable them to provide for themselves and their families. Their loyalty to Atwell is evident, as most remain in his employ. A modest man, he has saved many a family from abject poverty."

Atwell Furniture vans were seen frequently on the streets of London, but his work with the poor wasn't as well known, at least to those of us in more comfortable surroundings than those he helped. Taking advantage of Sir Max's momentary silence, I asked, "Why would such a man be in danger of losing his reputation?"

Our visitor bowed his head before replying. "I'm afraid I may have understated things. It isn't just his reputation and business at risk, but his freedom as well. You see, he may stand accused of the theft of several of the Queen's personal items."

Holmes stirred and asked, "Can you tell us the circumstances of such a theft? Or is it thefts? In order to assist you, we will need details. And please, what may on the surface appear irrelevant might prove to be of the utmost importance in discerning the truth."

Sir Max exhibited the first flicker of a smile. "Yes, I've heard that you would ask that. Recently, a large luggage cart damaged one leg of the Queen's writing table. It is at this table in her private rooms where she reviews matters of government concern, writes personal letters, and displays some of her valued keepsakes while she is in residence. Atwell and Sons were called to the Palace to evaluate the necessary repairs. As you can imagine, anyone entering this portion of the palace is subjected to the highest scrutiny, and is always accompanied by a trusted staff member."

Holmes chose to make what I deemed to be a rather sarcastic remark. "Yes, several of my cases have made me aware of the nature of the scrutiny and security government officials occasionally provide." Fortunately, our guest failed to miss the thinly veiled criticism entirely.

164

"Yes, yes, I'm sure you agree how necessary it all is. Atwell and Sons have been frequent visitors to the Palace and are familiar with our practices. All such repairs are done within the Palace."

"Please, tell me what was stolen." I could tell that Holmes was getting somewhat impatient at this point and wanted to hear the particulars.

"Mr. Atwell and an assistant came for a brief time on Monday, the nineteenth, to review the damage and assess what was necessary to repair the table. Shortly after this visit, Her Highness could not find her copy of a book of poetry by Alfred, Lord Tennyson, a favorite of the late Prince Albert, inscribed by the Queen to the Prince. She wanted to take the book with her to Windsor, and felt certain it had been on her desk. It was believed that the book had been merely misplaced and no alarms were raised." Sir Max's face indicated a certain amount of regret as he related this.

Holmes looked up from his study of his pipe and asked, "And the nature of the second theft? Or are there more than two?" The sarcasm was evident to Sir Max by this time.

"There are just the two. Atwell and an assistant returned this morning to make the actual repairs. It was done to everyone's satisfaction, but once they left, the staff realized a wedding photograph of Her Highness and Prince Albert was gone. It figured prominently on her table and its absence was evident. Mr. Holmes, calling the police is out of the question. We cannot guarantee their inquiries will be kept quiet, and if Atwell became known as the suspect, not only would his honour be doubted, but Her Majesty's decision to name him to the Honours List would be questioned as well. While the first is undesirable, even if he is proved innocent, it is the second point, that of the Queen's judgement, that cannot come into question. It is an unhappy state of affairs. Hence, you find me here in Baker Street this evening."

Holmes rose from his chair and put his pipe aside. He crossed to Sir Max and took his hand. "Sir, you have my promise, as well as Watson's, that we shall exercise all prudence necessary to keep this matter private. I believe from the impending announcement of the list, which I recall appears on January second, that we should make haste in our inquiries."

"Mr. Holmes," replied Sir Max, his relief evident, "you have grasped the urgency of the situation. Please, leave no stone unturned and report directly to me at the Palace. We have pursued no inquiries of our own, not wanting to alert Atwell of our suspicions until you could speak to him."

Although I had kept quiet during this exchange, I could not fail to note one question which had not been addressed. "Sir Max, do you know if the same associate accompanied Atwell each time?"

"I recall the staff indicated they were two different young men."

"Watson, you have certainly struck upon a most important point. And was either of these young men one of Atwell's 'and sons'?" Holmes began his pacing, which I associated with his engagement in a case.

Sir Max looked at the two of us and answered. "No, neither. I don't know their names, but I feel certain the staff does. The Head Butler at the Palace has been instructed to discuss these thefts with you. You may call upon him at your earliest convenience."

Our visitor left and we heard the carriage draw away from Baker Street. I turned to Holmes, and I'm sure my disgust that someone would steal from our Sovereign was evident. "Holmes, can you imagine that such a person exists who would stoop to take personal items from Her Majesty?"

Holmes turned to me and with a somewhat satisfied look and said, "Watson, can you imagine that such highly placed officials would stoop to lie to us about such a theft? While I have no doubt that those items were stolen, do you really think that they would have such an elevated concern for a book and a photo? If that was the extent of it, despite what Sir Max said, the police would have approached Mr. Atwell and the two assistants. No, there is something more at stake here, and they have chosen not to reveal what else has been taken. I hope you noticed that Sir Max told us to report to him at the Palace, yet he left no card and did not inform of his actual role in government affairs."

It was certainly not the first time that Holmes surprised me with his ability to see beyond the obvious. There were deeper currents to this situation, which led me to believe that Holmes was receiving what he truly wanted for Christmas. I could see the lethargy and apathy slip from his shoulders as he contemplated the true nature of what transpired. "Tomorrow morning, Watson, we go to the Palace – that is if you can be away from your patients. I feel certain it will be a busy day." With that, he was off to his room.

It wasn't a difficult task to forego my office hours, as I had only two appointments which were easily referred to a fellow physician. Holmes rose early, and we were soon at the imposing gates of Buckingham Palace. The sky was a dreary gray and it felt like snow was in the air. Despite the weather, Holmes was in good spirits as we were led to the Palace office of the gentlemen.

"Mr. Holmes, Dr. Watson, I am Zachary James, Head Butler." He bowed slightly and ushered us to his office where he offered tea or coffee, which we refused. James was a sturdily built man with red hair and a military air about him. "I have been informed that I am to speak frankly with you and am prepared to do so. I accompanied Mr. Atwell and his assistants on each visit, so I hope I can aid in the recovery of the items." We were anxious to determine the truth beyond what we believed to be subterfuge, and Holmes quickly came to the crux of the matter.

"Mr. James, I would like to see the room where the table sits and hear your version of the events when the thefts occurred. As you indicated, your frankness will be appreciated." James nodded in agreement and we were soon inside the Queen's private residence, a somewhat unnerving prospect for a mere former military surgeon.

Holmes had no such reservations. "Mr. James, could we begin with the details about this room, the writing table's damage, and the visit by Atwell?"

"Certainly." James moved to the table. "As you will note, there are only two possible entrances into this room, with doors at each end of the chamber. The writing table is kept primarily for the Queen's correspondence, both personal and that related to the government. When the luggage cart hit, it caused a major crack in the wood of the table's leg, which you can see is rather ornate. We were unsure if the damage could be repaired by our own staff, so we called in Atwell. He arrived at the appointed time and with his assistant, a Mr. Jonathan Davies, examined the leg, and decided it required replacement. I remained with them, and only one other member of staff, a maid named Miss Vivian May, was in the room while they were here."

Holmes stopped him. "You have an eye for details, Mr. James."

James allowed himself a slight smile. "One does not remain as Head Butler here at the Palace if one fails to note the little things."

"Just so. And can you tell me where the articles normally kept on the table were placed?"

"We put a temporary table in that corner and moved everything to it."

Satisfied, he indicated James should proceed. "When they finished, they repacked their satchels and took the table leg with them in order to duplicate it. Before you ask, I did not personally examine their bags, but watched them as they stored their equipment. I will swear that neither man put the book into their bags. Atwell made an appointment for the completion of the repair and the two left."

"And how long did it take before anyone realized the book was gone?"

"Just one day, on Tuesday. But as Her Majesty's eyesight isn't what it used to be, the staff assumed she had carried it to another room and it would eventually be located. We searched, as the Queen was quite disturbed, but to no avail. Yesterday, Thursday morning, Atwell and another assistant, a Mr. Phillip Ellis, returned. They replaced the broken leg and left us with instructions to keep the table on its top until the glue dried and it could safely bear weight. Again, I was with them the entire time, but no other staff entered the room. By that time, we were beginning to pack the items that the Queen likes to have with her while at Windsor Castle, and it was after Atwell left that Miss May realized the wedding photograph was no longer on the temporary table."

"Had Atwell been gone for long by then? And who else would have had access to the room in the interval?" Holmes asked.

"He'd left about three hours previously. I was summoned to the residence and realized that, while one book might have been simply misplaced, another loss meant something entirely different, and I reported my suspicions to the Master of the House. As for who had access, only the regular staff who serve in that part of the Palace. I would stake my reputation that none of them are involved."

Holmes asked, "Is it possible to have a word with the maid?"

James nodded and rang the bell near the far door. Soon, an apprehensive young woman entered the room and curtsied. "Sir? You need to see me?" She was a bright young thing with clear blue eyes and blonde hair.

"Miss May, these gentlemen have only a few questions for you," James told her, trying to put her at ease.

Holmes could be quite gentle with the fair sex. "Miss May, I'm told that you were in the room with the workmen from Atwell and Sons on the occasion of their first visit. Did you notice anything untoward while they were here?"

"No sir. They spread out their tools and made sure not to get anything dirty. They turned over the table and talked a bit about what they needed to do. They weren't here very long, and I was in and out of the room a few times."

Holmes considered her answer and continued his questioning. "What were you doing in the room?"

She thought for a moment before responding. "The first time I just walked through the room. The second time, I brought in a jug of water and added some of it to the vases. Her Majesty likes fresh flowers, even during the winter." She pointed to two large vases on either end of the mantel.

"Carrying a jug with enough water for those two vases must have been quite heavy."

"Yes sir, it was. Mr. Atwell was kind enough to help me. He lifted the vases down so I could add the water, then returned each to the mantel. He's ever so polite. Then I left and didn't see them again."

"Thank you, Miss May. You've been quite helpful." Holmes nodded to James that the interview with her was complete, and he dismissed her.

Holmes seemed content with the inquiries and relayed that to the Head Butler. "Mr. James, could you show us to the office of Sir Max Michaels?"

"His office? He has no office here. Sir Max did stop in earlier and advised me that he will be here at the Palace today, in the offices of the Master of the House, Lord Edward Clinton, should you want to speak to him."

Holmes cast a sidelong glance at me, as if to confirm his suspicions that a more complicated crime was at play. After Holmes's notice that Sir Max failed to supply him with a card and that he had no office in the Palace, I was beginning to see why he doubted this was a simple theft.

James led us from the private apartments, and we were soon ushered into the office of The Master of the House. Introductions followed, and we each took a chair as he addressed us.

"Gentlemen, what have you to report? Do you feel you've obtained the information required from the Palace to proceed with your questioning of Atwell?"

Sherlock Holmes was never one to hold his tongue when faced with those in positions of authority. "No, sir, I most certainly do *not* feel I have all the information I need. Rest assured that the fault does not lie with the Head Butler, who gave a most excellent report. The failure belongs to the two of you, and the fact that you have lied to us."

One could have heard a pin drop. I realized I was holding my breath, waiting for the order to come for us to be forcibly ejected from the Palace, perhaps to new quarters at the Tower of London. Holmes, however, appeared in control of the situation. The two gentlemen did not move or speak for a moment but finally, Sir Max gathered his wits. "Sir! How dare you accuse of us of lying!"

Holmes was at his best in such a verbal duel. "Sir, how dare you enlist help from both Dr. Watson and myself, and yet lie to us about the true nature of what happened here? How do you expect us to recover the stolen items under such a transparent web of falsehoods? I have no doubt those two items are missing, but I maintain serious misgivings that they are the full extent of the theft. No, gentlemen, something else is missing, or you would not have asked for our help. It is time to tell us the truth."

By this time, I was imagining those Tower of London quarters and wondering if they served meals as satisfying of those cooked by Mrs. Hudson. Yet Holmes remained calm, maintaining eye contact with the Master of the House. Which one would flinch first?

Lord Edward stood, placing both hands on his desk, and silently took the measure of Sherlock Holmes. He must have realized that full disclosure was the only avenue left open to him. "I apologize if you are offended by our version of the events. You must realize that what I am about to tell you cannot leave this office." Holmes nodded his agreement, as did I. "Gentlemen, the portion of the story that we told you is the truth. It just isn't the *entire* truth."

Holmes looked completely unsurprised by this revelation and added, "It normally isn't. Please, let's not waste any more time."

Lord Edward and Sir Max exchanged glances, and Lord Edward completed the story for us.

"We didn't reveal there was a third item stolen from The Queen's private residence. Her Majesty reviews correspondence from many government offices. At the time of the second visit by Mr. Atwell, there was such a folder present, set aside from her writing table. Inside that folder was a letter relating to several agreements among nations. As you are probably aware, The League of Three Emperors – Germany, Russia and Austria-Hungary – collapsed earlier this year over the question of influence exerted in the Balkans. In June, the Reinsurance Treaty was signed by Germany and Russia, guaranteeing that the two countries will remain neutral if the other goes to war with another world power, with two exceptions. One of the exceptions to their sworn neutrality is if Russia attacks Austria-Hungary."

I had not heard of such a pact. "Has this treaty been made public?"

Sir Max answered. "Absolutely not. I'm sure you understand why we could not reveal anything about this secret treaty, as it would mean the life of the person who disclosed this agreement to us."

"Dr. Watson and I pledge our discretion." The situation was taking an increasingly serious tone.

"To further complicate matters, our country signed The Mediterranean Agreement with Italy, Spain, and Austria-Hungary this spring, and have just this month exchanged communications with these allies. Our agreement seeks to keep the Russians from expanding into the Balkans and controlling waterways. As you can see, our agreement and their treaty are certainly at cross purposes. Our foreign office received information about events in that chaotic part of the world and it was that letter, describing our role in potential events, which was in The Queen's residence. Revealing our knowledge of their secret treaty or a potential

Russian war with Austria-Hungary could bring about our engagement in the hostilities. I requested Sir Max to assist me in this matter, as I am aware of any confidential communiques brought to the Palace."

War. As one who saw such suffering in Maiwand, and suffered myself, I could hardly endure such a horrible thought. I looked at Holmes, hopeful that he understood the necessity of their ruse. It was apparent that he did.

"Then we shall proceed as if we are simply pursuing the loss of those two items. From the description provided by Mr. James, I feel confident that the loss of this folder took place at the same time as the other thefts. Atwell or one of his men is in possession of all three items. Gentlemen, Dr. Watson and I will visit the premises of Atwell and Sons, and hopefully will soon have a good report for you."

Standing outside the Palace gates, I must admit that I was pleased to remain a free man and that Holmes's outburst had served to elicit the truth instead of an arrest.

He began walking with a definite purpose, striding quickly from that fashionable part of London toward what I knew must be a less than elegant part of the city. Looking straight ahead while he walked, he began, "Although I never guess, here is what I believe must have happened, from the scant evidence we have. I feel relatively certain that the esteemed Mr. Atwell had no part in the thefts. I cannot say the same for his two assistants, although which one is behind it remains unknown. It is possible that when surrounded by the Queen's personal memorabilia, temptation might have proved too much for one of these young men. Perhaps one saw a way of adding funds to his account and engaged the other to steal an additional item or two. These are murky waters, Watson, yet I cannot imagine our thief had any idea in advance that such a secretive diplomatic letter was in the room. No, I think this was a crime of opportunity."

The prediction for snow was proving true; large flakes were falling and accumulating on the streets and sidewalks. One could feel that the temperature had fallen as we made our way through the busy streets. "Holmes, which first? A visit to Atwell and Sons, or the pawnbrokers not far from here?"

"First to Atwell's, and from there, to the pawnshops, with a possible stop to see a gentleman who knows a thing or two about stolen goods."

Our walk took us to the warehouse area and a large, tall building of several stories adorned with the sign "Atwell and Sons Furniture Restoration". We stood outside and Holmes studied the exterior. Once inside the noisy building, the smell of cut wood, paint, oil, and varnishes filled the air. We asked to speak to the head of the firm and were led to his office. Richard Atwell was a tall gentleman, slim with a full head of silver hair and a short beard and mustache. He rose and shook hands as introductions were made.

"I cannot say that I ever expected to meet the famous Sherlock Holmes and Dr. Watson! This is indeed an unexpected pleasure. How may I help you?"

Holmes had a somber expression, which conveyed this was a visit of serious import. "Mr. Atwell, I'm sorry to tell you that there has been some unpleasant business requiring your attention."

Atwell crossed the room and closed the door, either to keep out the noise or to keep our conversation private, or perhaps both. "Please, sit and tell me why some unpleasant business necessitates a visit to my company."

We took our seats, as did Atwell. Holmes began immediately. "Sir, I am aware that you and an associate visited Buckingham Palace twice this week in order to repair a writing table in the Queen's private residence. After each departure, certain articles belonging to Her Majesty were found to be missing. It is believed they were stolen, and the efforts to regain these pieces have focused on this firm."

The colour drained from the owner's face. Taking a deep breath, he answered the accusation. "Mr. Holmes, I assure you that I proudly serve the Queen in whatever capacity asked of me and my associates. The thought of stealing anything from her is an abomination. I have no reason to doubt either of the men who accompanied me, but I will cooperate fully so that the stolen items can be returned, and any doubts regarding this company can be resolved."

"Then let us work together to discover the truth. First, we've learned that you were initially accompanied by a Mr. Jonathan Davies and later, by Mr. Phillip Ellis. Please tell us what you know about these men."

Atwell seemed resigned to the thought that nothing good would come of our visit. "Mr. Davies has been with me for five years, and Mr. Ellis, for four. They both came to me through our hiring program. I don't know if you're aware of this, but coming from meager circumstances myself, I provide job training for the unskilled poor."

Without revealing how we learned of this, we both nodded. He continued, "They both took to the training and proved themselves capable and trusted workmen." He stopped; obviously he saw the potential irony of that statement. "Or so I thought. They came to me as relatively young men, as many do. Our program includes simple lodgings for our trainees, as many are without a roof over their heads when they arrive. For those with families, they are welcome to stay here as well, until such a time when they can afford to pay their own expenses. It is difficult for a man to concentrate on learning a skill, knowing that his family is suffering from inadequate shelter or diet. Some of the workmen and their families remain lodgers here for years as they, in turn, work to train others. It has been a most satisfying program."

I was overwhelmed with Atwell's generosity to those less fortunate. His chequebook might show a far greater balance without these expenditures. "Mr. Atwell, you are most charitable."

He smiled. "I must admit that when I was a young man, I was greatly influenced by a statement made by a Mr. Jacob Marley to Ebenezer Scrooge. It is a passage I have never forgotten. 'Mankind was my business. The common welfare was my business; charity, mercy, forbearance, and benevolence, were, all, my business.' I have endeavored these years spent in commerce to help those in need."

I could not believe that this man had a hand in the thefts, and looking over at Holmes, I felt he shared that thought.

"Please tell us more." Holmes settled back in his chair. One would never know from his appearance what urgency had brought us to his office.

"I converted this building into my furniture warehouse. This floor houses the woodworking shop and dock, plus a few offices. The first floor is where the furniture is painted or varnished, and the top two floors have the quarters for the workmen and their families."

Holmes was now out of his chair, walking back and forth in the office, intent on the sounds his boots made on the wooden floor. "And is there nothing below this floor?"

"There is a large cellar, but only a portion of it was ever used for storage. It sits empty, but for a few pieces of old equipment."

"Thank you. And now Mr. Atwell, could you point out these two gentlemen without raising any alarms? They must not be made aware of our investigation."

We rose, and followed Atwell to the workroom floor. There were several dozen men scattered throughout the space, some obviously serving as instructors to those who either listened or followed their example, while others were working independently.

Atwell seemed painfully aware that nothing should appear out of the ordinary. He smiled, a smile which did not quite reach his eyes, and without any indication of who he was talking about, said, "See the dark-haired man with the scar on his cheek on my right? That is Ellis. The man about twenty feet from him, with light brown hair and holding the chisel, is Davies."

Holmes thanked him, appearing to be discussing nothing more serious than a broken side chair. We left the workshop, and as we neared the front door, Holmes stopped. "Mr. Atwell, thank you for your assistance. With your permission, might we inspect your cellar?" Atwell seemed perplexed by this request, but gave his assent before wishing us good luck in our endeavours.

Still shaking my hand, he looked me in the eye and said, "Gentlemen, I hope against hope that neither Ellis nor Davies is involved, but if they are, then do whatever is necessary. I trusted them, and it will be a painful thing to their mothers if either proves to be a criminal. But I will pray those two good women will comfort each other as sisters do."

"Their mothers are sisters? Ellis and Davies are cousins?" It was evident that this bit of information might be the connection we sought. Atwell seemed surprised at Holmes's reaction, but had no time to ask further questions as we bid farewell and left.

Once outside, we walked to the side of the building as he had directed, and saw a separate entry to the lower level. We went down the steps and stopped at the entrance door, being careful to ascertain that no one saw us. The door was unlocked, and he signaled for me to stay quiet as we walked through the cellar, taking note of the disturbances in the dusty floor. It was apparent there had been considerable activity, and as I looked up from the floor, I saw that Holmes was pacing the exterior of the room. After looking around the room, we left as quietly as we entered, and were soon on the street.

"Watson, the situation is not what Atwell thinks, for I believe him to be an honest man."

I indicated my agreement and asked "I saw you walking along the outside walls. Unless I'm mistaken, the room we were in isn't nearly as large as the floors above it."

"You are correct, and if you noted the direction of the footprints, you'll find they didn't lead to those few pieces of dusty equipment along one wall, but instead led toward the far wall. There is a door behind some shelves holding stacks of old wood and paint cans, and I noted a semi-circular pattern in the dust larger than the door, leading me to believe that the shelves are on a platform which is easily pulled aside to provide access to what I suspect is another room. We might yet return to that room, but there is much to be done yet today."

We were now in a part of London that did not reflect the upcoming gaiety of the holiday, and instead seemed to be even more dirty and distressed than usual, despite the fresh coating of snow. In an area full of gin shops and tenements, the pawn shop windows reflected the desperation that drove many to their doors. There was brisk business, both buying and selling being conducted, as it was only two days until Christmas. It didn't take us long to decide that a man in need of pawning royal items would find no takers in a shop full of miserable items which the former owners could no longer afford. Display racks with cheap teacups and cheaper jewelry would not hold a silver-framed wedding photo of the Queen or her book.

After a brief discussion outside the last shop we visited, Holmes decided that it was time to consult with Shinwell Johnson, a recently rehabilitated criminal who still had an ear to the ground for unlawful activity in our great city. We found him at home, and when Holmes gave him an abridged overview of what we were seeking, he perked up and put his finger along the side of his nose.

"Ah, Mr. Holmes. You might be looking for a few royal trinkets, but I'm guessing you're fishing for something bigger. Or am I mistaken?"

"Mr. Johnson, you are correct, but the exact nature of what we seek is best left unsaid. But it is of the utmost urgency that we locate this 'bigger fish'. What have you heard?"

"I heard from one of my sources that a youngish man approached him last night trying to sell a photo and a book. While this someone might have been interested in them, because of who they belonged to, he most certainly had no interest in a leather folder with a letter inside which he was also trying to sell. Are we talking along similar lines Mr. Holmes?"

"We are indeed."

"Then you should know your young man was unsuccessful with the regular sales avenues and was directed to one who deals in more specialized pilfered trifles, a Mr. Thaden. Thaden told our light-fingered young man that what he wanted to sell was something very few would buy, including himself. He told him to go to a Mr. Drumpf in Grosvenor Gardens. I would have let you know about this had I thought you were interested, but I didn't know what was in the letter, and still don't. Thaden played that close to his chest."

"When did this happen?"

"Just after 11:30 last night, so I heard. The young man probably didn't call then. Maybe he tried this morning."

We had the information we needed. As we thanked Johnson and left his flat, I told Holmes, "I hope we're not too late, but we know both men were at work today." He looked at me, nodding in agreement. We had gone from Buckingham Palace to a warehouse, to the slums to Johnson's flat; it was hard to believe it was only 2:30 in the afternoon. I stepped out into the street and hailed a hansom cab to take us to Grosvenor Square.

By the time we arrived at the Square, the snow was falling heavily. The gaslights had been lit as the gloom worsened, and I drew my scarf tighter around my face while Holmes seemed oblivious to the cold. Both aware of what the two cousins looked like, we took up discrete posts on opposite sides of the square. For the first time that day, I wished I had my revolver in my pocket, as I wasn't sure what we would face when the thief, or thieves, were confronted with their deeds.

The minutes turned into an hour and the sidewalks began to fill with people on their way home when I heard a sharp whistle. Turning, I saw Holmes nearing me and pointing to an advancing "Atwell and Sons Furniture Restoration" wagon which stopped in front of an elegant home. We were off in a flash, arriving to meet the van driver before he had a chance to leave his seat.

"Ah, Mr. Davies. We meet again, or didn't you notice us at your place of business today?"

Davies looked alarmed and seemed unsure of his next move. I grasped the reins of the horse in the hopes that he would not raise the whip to either me or the horse. Holmes grabbed the sleeve of Davies' coat, throwing him off-balance enough that he fell from the seat onto the street.

"Mr. Davies, this is not the time to play coy with us. We are aware of what you stole and what you plan to do with your swag. I can guarantee that we will find it, and you, sir, will go to either jail for theft or the gallows for treason, as will your cousin. He is your cohort, is he not?

I thought that Davies might be sick. His was the face of an amateur, embroiled in something that had taken on a life of its own. "Please, you've got to help me. I didn't mean for it to go this far."

That was enough for me. "What do you mean you didn't mean for it to go this far? You're near the property where you've heard you can sell a secret document that you stole from the Queen! How did you think this would end? With your pockets full?"

Holmes put his hand on my arm, knowing I was dangerously close to hitting the man. "Watson, please. Davies, you've got only a moment to decide how this will end. Make your decision."

As I looked up, I saw a man staring at us from a window in Drumpf's home, and realizing we were attracting too much attention and with a subtle gesture in his direction, told Holmes, "We should leave immediately."

176

Holmes fixed his gaze on the man, who had a distinctly unpleasant expression on his face, and readily agreed. Together with Davies, we climbed into the van and Holmes took the reins, leaving Grosvenor Square behind. Once we were away into the flow of traffic, Holmes demanded an exact accounting of what had transpired.

Davies began. "I have been a faithful worker for Mr. Atwell for five years now, and I owe him everything. He's taken in many a wretch like me, if you'll pardon the reference to the hymn, including my cousin. But there were others there before us. They weren't bad men, you understand, but poor. Poor in a way you can't imagine. Even after they had a roof and enough for them and their families to eat, it was hard to shake that feeling that you could lose it all.

"One of them went to the cellar one day and found out that nobody ever went down there. Since so many lived at the building, and being family men or so inclined, they didn't like going to those cheap gin joints, and decided they could go down there for a drink and a laugh after the business closed for the day. They took over a part of the cellar that nobody ever checked and hid the door. They met many an evening, after their families were asleep. 'Why, we ain't beggars no more' was the saying one had and what started it all. They moved some the furniture no one was ever going to use into the room and started calling themselves 'The Amateur Mendicant Society' to show just how far they'd come. Sounded better than beggars. Didn't take too long before it was outfitted pretty posh through purchase or pilfering. 'Course, once me and Phillip were there for a while, we joined them.

"Then, just the other day, I got to go to Buckingham Palace with Mr. Atwell. Me, who hadn't had a penny to my name not so long ago, here I was inside the Palace. So many pretty things that I thought nobody would miss a thing or two. I took my chance when Mr. Atwell was helping that sweet maid with them heavy vases. I grabbed the book and stuffed it in the back of my trousers, under my jacket. It was so easy, and I thought what a laugh it would give the lads back at the Society. I told my cousin, and he volunteered to go with Mr. Atwell the next time, figuring if anyone even noticed something was gone, they'd never suspect us, since it was different helpers each time."

"And if they'd suspected Atwell? And arrested him? What then?" Holmes face was grim.

"Honest, I'd have made up some story and tried to get them things back to the Palace. Maybe just leave them with a note, unsigned and all. I wouldn't have let nothing happen to him."

Perhaps there was honor among thieves after all.

"Anyways, Phillip went the next time and I told him to take something flat that could be hidden the same way I hid the book, under the back of my jacket. He saw that leather folder with the crest on it and took it along with the picture. Honest, he didn't know what was in it. He can't even read. By the time I saw it and realized it wasn't just an empty folder, it was too late."

Holmes looked at me, then back at Davies. "You will serve time for this, but if you can return it all, you'll avoid the gallows. Where is it?"

Davies hung his head but reached under the seat to retrieve the three items which had caused so much consternation. We were literally on top of what we sought.

"Mister, I understand what I did was wrong and I'm ready to pay the piper for it. My ma will be ashamed but she'll get by. There's only one thing in this world that depends on me and that's my dog. He's a good young pup that don't deserve to be thrown out on the streets or worse. My ma can't have a dog where she lives, and nobody at Atwell's needs another mouth to feed. Can you help me?"

"You have my word."

Davies and Ellis were arrested, and through the intervention of my friend and the Palace, which had no desire to make the exact nature of the theft public, they received light sentences for minor theft. Holmes kept his word to the Palace officials, returning the Queen's stolen treasures and the letter which might have caused the death of an informant, or even our engagement in a war. Mr. Atwell was delighted to be named on the Honours List only a week later, and remained forever indebted to the two of us for saving his reputation. If he ever learned of the Amateur Mendicant Society, it was not from us.

Holmes also kept his promise to that young man. We returned to Atwell's that very night and rescued the friendly pup. "Watson, I don't believe Mrs. Hudson has ever gotten over losing her terrier. I do believe this little dog will make a good companion for her."

The next day was Christmas Eve. Holmes and I presented Timmy the pup to Mrs. Hudson, who received it with open arms. He stayed with her for many a happy year. The next morning as the church bells chimed to commemorate the day of Our Lord's birth, Mrs. Hudson served us a special breakfast. "Mr. Holmes, Dr. Watson, it would be my great honor if you would accompany me to church this morning. I have much to be grateful for. I'll be leaving for St. Bride's within the hour."

So that morning Holmes, Mrs. Hudson, and I went to celebrate the day at St. Bride's on Fleet Street. Holmes was rarely seen within a church, but that day he seemed as happy as I had ever seen him. It was indeed a Merry Christmas.

The Blue Carbuncle
by Sir Arthur Conan Doyle
Dramatised for Radio by Bert Coules

After kicking off with *A Study in Scarlet* and *The Sign of the Four*, the BBC's ground-breaking complete audio Canon moved on to tackle Doyle's short stories in book publication order, so "The Blue Carbuncle", which comes from the first collection *The Adventures of Sherlock Holmes,* was one of the earliest episodes to be written and recorded. Looking back at the script now for this anthology, I don't think it shows; I hope not, anyway. It's true that everyone was feeling their way slightly, concerned about establishing a house style and laying down guidelines as to what we could and couldn't do with the stories, but from the very beginning, the brief was to be 'imaginatively faithful', to be aware that a dramatisation had to be exactly that: dramatic. What was required – and on the whole what was expected, too, by a modern audience – was not simply the original prose text parcelled out to a bunch of different voices and tied together with a lot of straight-off-the-page narration, but a true recreation, a reinvention making full use of all the possibilities of a different medium. I'll leave you to decide how well or otherwise I succeeded with this particular example.

Technical terms: a *teaser* is a short scene before the opening credits designed to establish the mood and hopefully to hook the audience. The *sig* is the signature tune, in our case a haunting solo violin passage from Mendelssohn's Sonata, *Opus 4 in F Minor. Int* and *Ext* in the scene headings stand for *Interior* and *Exterior*, an important distinction, since the sound-picture of each as conjured by the acoustic, the effects, and the actors' performances is markedly different. *Cut to* is the customary way of denoting the end of a scene in a script, though in production hard cuts are rare and tend to be used purely for an occasional shock effect: mixes or fades are more usual and help to create a seamless flow of action.

And that's all you need to know, and probably more. Unleash your imagination and try to hear what you read; I hope you enjoy the experience.

First broadcast on the BBC on January 2ⁿᵈ, 1991

THE CAST
in order of speaking

HOLMES Sherlock Holmes.

WATSON Doctor John Watson.

COLLECTOR A female Salvation Army tin-rattler.

HORNER John Horner. A rising young plumber, determined to go straight after his one lapse ten years ago.

MRS. HORNER Alice, John Horner's wife.

BRADSTREET Inspector Bradstreet of Scotland Yard. A determined detective.

RYDER James Ryder. The upper-attendant (which is to say glorified dogsbody) at the rather ritzy Hotel Cosmopolitan. *"What a shrimp it is . . . Not enough blood in him for felony."* (Holmes).

BAKER Henry Baker. A once dignified, scholarly gentleman who has come down in the world and sought solace in drink. Now very hard-up and shabbily dressed, but retaining something of his old pride. Rather a sad figure.

WINDIGATE The host of the Alpha Tavern in Bloomsbury, and typically bluff and outgoing.

1st ROUGH On the London street.

2nd ROUGH A chum of the above.

PETERSON A member of the Corps of Commissionaires, a well-respected body in Victorian London. The higher end of the working class and almost certainly an ex-serviceman. A man with a keen sense of what's right and what's wrong.

BRECKINRIDGE A goose-dealer at Covent Garden street market. A keen betting man with a short temper.

MRS. OAKSHOTT Sister of James Ryder, but a rather more balanced individual.

CONSTABLE A constable with little to say for himself.

It is the 23rd of December, 1889.

TEASER. MUSIC: SOMETHING EERIE AND MYSTERIOUS.

Over it, perhaps with very slight echo:

HOLMES: (*Close, intense*) Look at it. Just see how it glints and sparkles. It is a nucleus and focus of crime. There have been two murders, a vitriol-throwing, a suicide, and several robberies brought about for the sake of this forty-grain weight of crystallised charcoal. It's a bonny thing.

The music swells into the opening sig.
Opening announcements.
The music fades into:

WATSON (*narrating*): The winter of 1889 was bitterly cold. After dark, the stars shone stark and bright in a cloudless sky and the breath of the late-night Christmas shoppers blew out into smoke like so many silent pistol shots, while their footfalls rang out crisp and loud. But for all the inclement weather, there was a sense of collective goodwill in the air as if the people of the capital had agreed to lay aside their differences and petty squabbles for a few short days and unite in celebrating the season of forgiveness.

SCENE 1. EXT. A BUSY LONDON STREET. LATE AFTERNOON.

Horse traffic, the buzz of people, the shouts of children, have faded up under the end of Watson's narration.
Now, a Salvation Army brass band strikes up "God Rest Ye Merry, Gentlemen".
After a few moments, a collecting lady rattles her tin. The music recedes a little.

COLLECTOR: Support the Mission, won't you sir? A warm Christmas meal for the poor and needy.

HORNER: Yes, yes, of course. There.

He sorts through his small number of coins, donates one.

COLLECTOR: Lord love you sir. A Merry Christmas to you and your good lady.

HORNER: Thank you.

MRS. HORNER: And to you.

COLLECTOR: Bless you ma'am. (*Moving off*) Support the poor at Christmas. Thank you sir, thank you . . . .

MRS. HORNER: (*Amused*) Well, "sir".

HORNER: Yes, "ma'am"? (*He chuckles*) Sounds good, don't it? I suppose she gets more money that way.

MRS. HORNER: Now John, don't be like that. Why shouldn't you be shown a bit of respect?

HORNER: True enough. John Horner, plumber and builder by Royal Appointment, that's me after today's little job. Mind you, they was careful to call me in when Her Ladyship was out the way. Couldn't have her clapping her eyes on a working man.

MRS. HORNER: But it paid well.

HORNER: Very handsome. Course I told them I ought to take less.

MRS. HORNER: You never did!

HORNER: That's right – I never did.

MRS. HORNER: (*Laughing*) Get on with you.

HORNER: So I reckon we can treat the kids to a present apiece and have enough left over for a bit of something tasty for the table. It's going to be a good Christmas, girl.

MRS. HORNER: Well, God bless the aristocracy.

HORNER: May they never learn to do their own plumbing.

BOTH: (*Chuckle happily*)

The moment is killed by a heavy hand clamping down on Horner's shoulder.

BRADSTREET: John Terence Horner?

HORNER: Who wants to know?

BRADSTREET: Inspector Bradstreet, Scotland Yard.

MRS. HORNER: John!

HORNER: What do you want?

BRADSTREET: What I want, my friend, is you. You're under arrest.

Cut to:

SCENE 2. INT. A JAIL CELL.

The door is unlocked and thrown open.

BRADSTREET: In here please, Mr. Ryder.

RYDER: Inspector.

HORNER: Thank God you're here, mate. He'll tell you, copper, he was the one what engaged me.

BRADSTREET: Well sir?

RYDER: Oh yes. That's him all right.

HORNER: See? I don't know what all this is about, but you've got the wrong man.

RYDER: I was a fool to leave you alone in that room.

HORNER: Do what?

RYDER: I found the jewel-case all broken open, where you left it.

HORNER: (*Going for him*) You bloody liar!

Bradstreet grabs Horner and there is a brief struggle. Bradstreet throws Horner down.

BRADSTREET: Any more of that and I'll have you chained. Understand?

HORNER: I am not a thief!

BRADSTREET: Clarke and Sons, Dealers in Gemstones, Holborn. March, eighteen seventy-nine.

HORNER: That was ten years ago! I've been straight since then. God's truth.

BRADSTREET: Save your breath, Horner. There's only one thing I want to hear from you: (*Moving close*) Where have you hidden the Countess of Morcar's blue carbuncle?

Cut to:

SCENE 3. INT. A LONDON PUB.

Much merriment. Raucous singing of "We Wish You A Merry Christmas".
In a quieter corner Mr. Henry Baker drains his glass and plonks it down. He's somewhat drunk but retains his dignity.

BAKER: Good night, landlord. The compliments of the season to you.

184

WINDIGATE: And to you, Mr. Baker. And to your good lady wife.

BAKER: (*Unenthusiastically*) Oh . . . yes.

WINDIGATE: I hope you enjoy your Christmas dinner.

BAKER: Assuredly, my good sir. Thanks to you.

He pats a bulky newspaper-covered parcel.

Good night and good health to you. (*Walks off unsteadily*) Good tidings I bring . . . Good tidings I bring . . . .

WINDIGATE: Take care, Mr. Baker. And a Merry Christmas.

BAKER: (*Way off*) Merry Christmas!

Cut to:

SCENE 4. EXT. A QUIET LONDON SIDE STREET. 4 a.m.

Baker's footsteps echo eerily as he approaches.

BAKER: We won't go until we've got some, so bring some out here. Glad tidings I bring . . . . (*Suddenly wary*) Who's there? Come out into the light. (*A moment*) I warn you, I have a stick!

Suddenly, very close and menacing:

1st ROUGH: Hello, my friend.

BAKER: What? Who are you?

2nd ROUGH: He doesn't know us, Harry.

1st ROUGH: We're the poor and needy. How'd you like to give us a present?

BAKER: You're nothing but a couple of roughs. Get out of my way, or

185

I'll summon a constable.

2nd ROUGH: (*Taking it*) Nice hat, this.

BAKER: Give that back at once!

2nd ROUGH: (*Disgusted*) 'S'too big. (*He flings it away with a grunt*) Flies nice, though.

BAKER: My hat!

1st ROUGH: What's in the parcel, then?

He grabs it.

BAKER: No!

2nd ROUGH: Oh, something precious, is it? Let's have a butcher's.

They begin to tear off the paper.
The object is revealed.
The roughs are impressed.

1st ROUGH: Well now, that's what I call a handsome present. Go down a treat, that will.

BAKER: Very well. I gave you fair warning. Much as I deplore violence
. . . .

2nd ROUGH: Oh – we'd better give it back to him, Harry. He's got a stick!

BAKER: Take that!

He swings back his stick with a grunt – and puts it straight though a shop window.

Oh my good God.

A frozen moment. Then the roughs burst out laughing.

1st ROUGH: Congratulations, me old chum. Welcome to the wrong side of the law.

Suddenly, from a distance:

PETERSON: Here! What's going on?

2nd ROUGH: It's a copper!

BAKER: Oh no.

1st ROUGH: Shift yourself Fred!

The roughs drop the parcel and run off.

PETERSON: (*Still off*) That's right. Get off out of it!

BAKER: Oh my life.

He gathers himself together and runs.

PETERSON: (*Approaching*) Not you! I didn't mean . . . . (*To himself*) Oh God. (*Calling*) What about your hat?

His foot catches the partly-wrapped bundle.

What the devil's this?

He picks it up with a grunt. It's not light. He pulls aside the wrapping.

Good Lord.

A solo violin flourish takes us to:

SCENE 5. INT. THE SITTING-ROOM AT 221b BAKER STREET. 8 a.m.

A fire blazes. Holmes is barely awake.

PETERSON: . . . so, to cut a long story short, Mr. Holmes –

HOLMES: Yes, do that by all means, my dear fellow.

PETERSON: Yes, well, as I say, to cut a long story short . . . I brought both items straightway round to you as soon as I could. Knowing as how you're always interested in any little problems.

HOLMES: Yes. Quite right. (*He yawns, involuntarily*) Excuse me, Peterson.

PETERSON: It's not too early for you sir? I mean I could come back again later on.

HOLMES: (*It's not that interesting*) No, no! (*He makes an effort*) Very well, Commissionaire. You've told me the story in admirable detail, pray unveil the trophies.

BAKER: The trophies? Oh, I see what you mean. Well, the hat, you've seen that.

HOLMES: Yes, I've seen that. But what exactly do you have wrapped up in yesterday's *Echo*, second edition?

BAKER: Well, sir . . . .

He clears his throat and, in the manner of a magician producing a rabbit, pulls away the paper wrapping from the mysterious object. A moment.

HOLMES: (*Laughs*) Oh my dear fellow, I congratulate you. That is a most unimpeachable goose.

PETERSON: There's no call to congratulate me, Mr. Holmes. It's not mine. Look here, there's a label:

He indicates a label tied to the bird's leg.

HOLMES: "*For Mrs. Henry Baker*".

PETERSON: The old gent what run off last night – mistaking me for a constable, like I said – well, he must have been taking it home. And you see my problem, sir.

188

HOLMES: Your problem is the price of your honesty, Peterson. A lesser man would be counting his good fortune.

PETERSON: Well that's as maybe. But I know my duty, and that's to return both the hat and the bird. But how, Mr. Holmes? That's the question.

HOLMES: How indeed. Do you sincerely want my advice as to what to do with the goose?

PETERSON: Well, yes sir, I do.

HOLMES: Take it home, cook it and eat it.

PETERSON: Mr. Holmes!

HOLMES: There are . . . (*He sniffs*) signs that delay would be unwise.

Holmes lifts the package and gives it to Peterson.

PETERSON: Well, perhaps . . . .

HOLMES: Most definitely. It is high time for it to fulfil the ultimate destiny of a goose. I trust you and Mrs. Peterson will enjoy it.

PETERSON: But the rightful owner, sir!

HOLMES: (*Moving off*) You may leave him – and his hat – to me.

He opens the door.

(*Approaching*) Good morning to you, Peterson.

PETERSON: (*Moving slowly off*) Well, er . . . and to you, sir. And a very Merry Christmas to you.

HOLMES: (*Grunts a reply*)

The door shuts.

(*Sighs*)

Cut to:

SCENE 6. INT. A JAIL CELL.

BRADSTREET: I'm rapidly running out of patience with you, Horner.

HORNER: (*Wearily*) Look, Mr. Bradstreet. If I knew where it was, I'd tell you. But I've never laid eyes on it, my word on the book.

BRADSTREET: Your word?

HORNER: Can I see my wife?

BRADSTREET: Oh it's prisoner's privileges you're wanting, is it? Listen Horner, the Countess of Morcar's been pulling strings. I've got the Commissioner looking over my shoulder, and I don't like that one little bit. Where's that jewel?

Cut to:

SCENE 7. INT. THE SITTING-ROOM AT 221b BAKER STREET.

The fire crackles.

WATSON: A very Merry Christmas to you, Holmes!

HOLMES: (*Not quite a groan*) Thank you, Watson.

Watson rubs his hands at the fire.

WATSON: Cheer up, old man. It's supposed to be the season of goodwill. (*He shivers*) It must be close to freezing out there. (*A moment*) This is for you.

He gives him a small package.

HOLMES: Oh, my dear fellow.

He starts to unwrap it.

WATSON: Now you mustn't open it until tomorrow.

HOLMES: I shouldn't dream of it.

He puts it down.

How is Mrs. Watson?

WATSON: Very well, thank you. In her element. Mrs. Forrester – you remember, Mary's old employer? She's staying with us.

HOLMES: And her charming children?

WATSON: Oh yes. All three of them.

HOLMES: Congratulations on effecting your escape.

WATSON: (*Slightly ashamed of himself*) I hope my motives weren't as transparent to them as they are to you. I do find a little goes a long way, I must say. Gives one new respect for the patience of womankind.

HOLMES: (*Snorts – "respect" and "womankind" are not related terms in his book*).

WATSON: I mustn't stay away too long. They are guests, after all. And anyway, they're eagerly awaiting the lurid details of your latest triumphs.

HOLMES: Well I'm sure your powers of invention will rise to the occasion.

WATSON: Oh – been quiet has it? What about the Hotel Cosmopolitan robbery? Haven't they called you in on that?

HOLMES: I'm afraid you overestimate Scotland Yard's eagerness to admit their inefficiency. Would you care for a drink?

WATSON: Thank you.

Holmes pours two drinks.

WATSON: You know, I'd never heard of this blue carbuncle until I read the report in *The Times* this morning. The word has a very different connotation for me.

HOLMES: And you accuse me of single-mindedness. (*Giving him his drink*) Here. Your very good health.

WATSON: The compliments of the season.

HOLMES: (*Winces audibly*)

WATSON: Sorry.

They drink. A moment.

HOLMES: A carbuncle is a precious stone, usually a garnet, cut in the *en cabochon* or domed-top shape, and invariably deep ruby red in colour.

WATSON: Ah, so that's why this *blue* specimen is so valuable.

HOLMES: It's unique. It was found in the banks of the Amoy River in Southern China, just over nineteen years ago.

WATSON: The things you know.

HOLMES: It's generally considered to be worth at least twenty-thousand pounds.

WATSON: Good God.

He drinks up and puts down his glass.

Thank you. Look, it's been good to see you, but I really ought to be getting along. Perhaps they'll have tired themselves out by now.

HOLMES: Can you spare a few moments more?

WATSON: (*Not really*) Well . . . .

HOLMES: No, you're quite right. Domestic responsibilities come first. And it's only a very minor investigation.

WATSON: (*Hooked*) Investigation?

HOLMES: (*Chuckling*) Before I tell you the story, have a look at this. What do you think of it?

Holmes picks up and passes over the hat.

WATSON: Another gift?

HOLMES: Hardly. There are those in this bustling capital with good cause to wish me ill, but I fancy most of them have in mind something rather more drastic than insulting me with shabby items of headgear.

WATSON: Well then? (*Deliberately over the top*) Does it have some deadly story linked to it? Is it the clue that will lead you to the solution of a mystery and the punishment of a terrible crime?

HOLMES: No, the matter is a perfectly trivial one.

WATSON: Oh.

HOLMES: It's just one of those whimsical little incidents which will happen when you have four million human beings all jostling each other within the space of a few square miles.

WATSON: You're right, it is shabby.

HOLMES: Look on it, not as a battered billycock, but as an intellectual problem. What can you deduce about its owner?

WATSON: Deduce? From this old felt?

HOLMES: You know my methods.

WATSON: Observation and deduction . . . Well . . . It's an old, round hat with a brim.

HOLMES: Very good, Watson.

WATSON: (*Coughs meaningfully*)

HOLMES: A thousand apologies, my dear fellow. Pray continue.

WATSON: The lining used to be of red silk. No maker's name . . . Ah, the initials "H.B" scrawled on the inside. It's cracked, exceedingly dusty, daubed with ink here and there to hide the discoloured patches, and the brim has been pierced for a hat-securer, though the elastic's missing. It's a very ordinary black hat. I can see nothing.

HOLMES: On the contrary Watson, you can see everything, as you just proved with that excellent description. You fail, however, to reason from what you see. You're too timid in drawing your inferences.

WATSON: Well what inferences can you draw?

HOLMES: The man is highly intellectual. That's obvious, of course. He was fairly well-to-do, although within the last three years he has fallen upon evil days. He had foresight, but has less now than formerly, pointing to a moral retrogression. This, taken with the decline of his fortunes, seems to indicate some malign influence at work upon him, possibly drink. This may account also for the obvious fact that his wife has ceased to love him.

WATSON: (*Disbelief*) My dear Holmes!

HOLMES: He has, however, retained some degree of self-respect. He is a man who is out of training entirely, is middle-aged, has grizzled hair which he has had cut within the last few days, and which he anoints with lime-cream. (*A moment*) Also, it is extremely improbable that he has gas laid on in his house.

WATSON: (*Amused*) Surely you're joking?

HOLMES: Not in the least. Can you truly not see how I arrived at these conclusions?

WATSON: I've no doubt I am very stupid.

HOLMES: Watson.

194

WATSON: Well then, how did you deduce that this man is intellectual?

HOLMES: It's a question of cubic capacity. Put the hat on.

WATSON: (*Puzzled*) Very well.

He does so, and it comes down over his eyes.

(*Exclaims in amusement*)

HOLMES: You see? Or rather, you don't see.

Watson removes the hat.

WATSON: It's huge.

HOLMES: And a man with so large a brain must have something in it.

WATSON: The decline of his fortunes?

HOLMES: This hat is three years old. These flat brims curled at the edge came in then. And it's of the very best quality. You remarked that the lining was once excellent, and look at the band: ribbed silk. If this man could afford so expensive a hat three years ago but has had no hat since, then he has assuredly gone down in the world.

WATSON: Perhaps he just prefers wearing an old hat. He may well have a wardrobe full of new ones.

HOLMES: A favourite hat would be merely well-worn. This one is positively repellent.

WATSON: Yes, I noticed that. All right. But what about the foresight and the moral retrogression?

HOLMES: Here is the foresight.

WATSON: The holes for the hat-securer?

HOLMES: They're never sold on hats, they have to be ordered specially. Hence, foresight – he went out of his way to take precautions against the wind. And less foresight now than previously, because –

WATSON: Because he hasn't bothered to replace the broken elastic. And you see that as moral retrogression?

HOLMES: A weakening nature. On the other hand – and again, as you pointed out – he's attempted to hide these stains with ink, so he hasn't entirely lost his self-respect. That he's middle-aged with grizzled hair, lime-creamed and recently cut, you can see from a close examination of the lower lining.

WATSON: And out of training? Ah, I've got it: he perspires copiously. Something else I learnt when I had it on.

HOLMES: Exactly. And finally, the matter of the gas. Five tallow stains can hardly come by chance. Tallow stains mean tallow candles. Are you satisfied?

WATSON: Well, you have an answer for everything. No, wait a minute: how on earth do you know his wife has ceased to love him?

HOLMES: When I see you, my dear Doctor, with a week's accumulation of dust on your hat, and when Mrs. Watson allows you to go out in such a deplorable state, I shall fear that you also have been unfortunate enough to lose your wife's affection.

WATSON: (*Triumphantly*) He might be a bachelor!

HOLMES: (*Chuckling*) Look at this label.

WATSON: "*For Mrs. Henry Baker*". Well?

HOLMES: It was tied to the leg of the goose.

WATSON: (*Completely thrown*) What goose?

HOLMES: The goose that Mr. Henry Baker – H.B. – was taking home as a peace offering to his wife.

WATSON: Well, I think you might have mentioned that before I started.

A frantic knock at the door. It bursts open.

PETERSON: Mr. Holmes!

HOLMES: Peterson! What have you found this time?

PETERSON: (*Approaching*) No, no, sir. The goose! The goose!

HOLMES: What of it, man? Has it returned to life and flapped off
through the kitchen window?

PETERSON: See here, Mr. Holmes. See what my wife found in its crop!

He unwraps tissue paper from a small object.

WATSON: Good heavens, Peterson.

HOLMES: (*Whistles*) This is treasure trove indeed. I suppose you know
what you've got?

PETERSON: It cuts into glass as though it were putty. It's some sort of
precious stone.

HOLMES: It's more than a precious stone. Just at the present, it's *the*
precious stone.

WATSON: It's the Countess of Morcar's blue carbuncle.

Cut to:

SCENE 8. EXT. COVENT GARDEN STREET MARKET. MIDDAY.

Traders shouting, people milling about.
A barrel-organ plays yet another Christmas carol.

*Breckinridge's angry monologue doesn't give the person he's talking
to any opportunity to butt in.*

BRECKINRIDGE: Now listen. I told you last night and I'm telling you
again now: I come by that merchandise fair and square, and I'll not

197

have anyone saying otherwise. You got no call snooping round here prying into my business. Who I sell my goods to, that's private between them and me, see? If you wanted one, you should have got here earlier. Don't you know it's Christmas? Now clear off out of it.

Cut to:

SCENE 9. INT. THE SITTING-ROOM AT 221b BAKER STREET.

As before.
Glass chinks as Watson pours a drink.

WATSON: Here you are Peterson. Drink this.

PETERSON: (*Weakly*) Thank you, Doctor.

He drinks, splutters and coughs. Eventually:

That's better.

WATSON: Sit there for a moment. Get your breath back.

PETERSON: You are sure, Mr. Holmes? You wouldn't say it if you weren't sure, would you?

HOLMES: (*Occupied, a little off*) Perfectly sure. The reward was announced today. One-thousand pounds.

WATSON: You're a rich man, Peterson.

PETERSON: The shock'll kill my Elsie.

HOLMES: Then you'd better break it to her gently.

He finishes what he's been writing.

There. (*Approaching*) You see, Watson? Our little deductions have suddenly assumed a much less innocent aspect. Here is the gem, the gem came from the goose, and the goose came from the gentleman with the

198

bad hat and all the other characteristics with which I bored you.

WATSON: And now we must locate him. What were you writing?

HOLMES: "*Found at the corner of Goodge Street and the Tottenham Court Road, a goose and a black felt hat. Mr. Henry Baker can have the same by applying at 6:30 this evening at 221b Baker Street.*" That is clear and concise.

WATSON: Very. But will he see it?

HOLMES: He's sure to keep an eye on the papers. Don't forget, he's a poor man; the loss must have been a heavy one. Peterson, are you recovered?

PETERSON: Yes, Mr. Holmes.

HOLMES: Good. Run down to the advertising agency and have this put in the evening papers.

PETERSON: Which ones, sir?

HOLMES: Oh, *The Globe, Star, Pall Mall, St. James's Gazette, Evening News, Standard, Echo,* and any others that occur to you.

PETERSON: Very well, sir. And the stone?

HOLMES: Ah, yes. I shall keep the stone.

PETERSON: Ah.

HOLMES: And Peterson, stop off on your way back and buy a goose. We must have one to give to Mr. Baker this evening.

PETERSON: Certainly sir. Er . . . .

Holmes fishes out a coin, passes it over.

HOLMES: Here's a sovereign.

PETERSON: Mr. Holmes. (*Moving off*) Thank you very much, gentlemen. (*Stopping at the door*) A thousand pounds . . . .

The door shuts.

WATSON: He won't forget this Christmas in a hurry. (*A moment*) Holmes?

HOLMES: (*Lost in the jewel*) Look at it, Watson. Just see how it glints and sparkles. It is a nucleus and focus of crime. Every good stone is. They are the devil's pet baits. There have been two murders, a vitriol-throwing, a suicide, and several robberies brought about for the sake of this forty-grain weight of crystallised charcoal. Who would think that so pretty a toy would be a purveyor to the gallows and the prison? It's a bonny thing.

WATSON: What will you do with it? Are you going to tell the police that it's been found?

HOLMES: All in good time, my dear Doctor. All in good time.

Cut to:

SCENE 10. INT. A JAIL CELL.

Keys and mechanism jangle as the door is unlocked.

BRADSTREET: Someone to see you, Horner. In here.

HORNER: Alice!

BRADSTREET: (*Moving off*) You've got two minutes. (*Low, to her*) Remember what I said.

The door bangs shut.

HORNER: (*Going to her*) Thank God you're here.

MRS. HORNER: Oh John.

They embrace.

HORNER: What did he mean? What did he say to you?

MRS. HORNER: I'm supposed to ask you where you stashed it.

HORNER: So that's why they let you see me.

MRS. HORNER: Why don't you tell them, John?

HORNER: What?

MRS. HORNER: They said it'll be easier for you if you do.

A frozen moment.

HORNER: You think I did it. You really think –

MRS. HORNER: Oh John! How could you be such a fool?

Cut to:

SCENE 11. INT. THE SITTING-ROOM AT 221b BAKER STREET.

The fire, as usual. The door opens.

HOLMES: Ah, come in, Doctor. I was beginning to think you were going to miss the excitement.

WATSON: Unfortunately, my patients haven't yet learned to be ill only between the hours of nine and five-thirty.

He warms himself. Holmes pours him a drink.

HOLMES: Here. Some restorative medicine.

WATSON: Thank you. The compli – Your very good health.

He knocks it back, appreciatively.

That's excellent.

The doorbell rings.

HOLMES: Mr. Henry Baker. He's admirably punctual.

WATSON: Do you think he did have anything to do with the robbery?

HOLMES: Why speculate? Soon, we shall know.

WATSON: What about the man Bradstreet's arrested? Is he innocent?

HOLMES: I can't tell.

WATSON: He has a wife and two children.

HOLMES: And a previous conviction.

WATSON: He's continued to protest his innocence. Suppose he's not the thief. What sort of Christmas are his family going to have?

HOLMES: I'm interested in facts, not suppositions. Come in!

The door opens. There was no knock – Holmes's timing is impeccable.

BAKER: Good evening, gentlemen.

HOLMES: Mr. Henry Baker, I presume?

BAKER: Correct, sir.

He closes the door.

HOLMES: Pray come and sit by the fire, Mr. Baker. It's a cold night, and I observe that your circulation is more adapted for summer than for winter.

BAKER: (*Approaching*) Thank you, Mr . . . ?

HOLMES: Holmes. And this is my friend and colleague, Dr. Watson.

WATSON: Good evening, sir.

BAKER: Doctor. (*Sits*) I saw your advertisement in *The Echo*, gentlemen.

HOLMES: Excellent. Is that your hat, Mr. Baker?

BAKER: Yes sir, that is undoubtedly my hat. I thought never to see it again. Or my specimen of *ansa ansa domesticus*.

HOLMES: Ah yes, your goose. I'm afraid we were compelled to eat it.

BAKER: To eat it!

HOLMES: Yes. It would have been no use to anyone had we not done so.

BAKER: Oh dear.

WATSON: Chin up, Mr. Baker. Look on the sideboard.

BAKER: The sideboard, sir? (*He looks around*) Ah!

HOLMES: I presume that that goose, which is about the same weight –

WATSON: And perfectly fresh.

HOLMES: – will answer your purpose equally well?

BAKER: (*With a sigh of relief*) Oh certainly, certainly.

HOLMES: Of course, we still have the feathers, legs, crop, and so on of your own bird, if you so wish . . . ?

BAKER: (*Laughing*) They might serve as relics of my adventure, but beyond that, I can hardly see what use the *disjecta membra* of my late acquaintance are going to be to me.

HOLMES: Here is your hat then.

WATSON: (*Lifting it*) And here is your bird.

BAKER: (*Rising*) Thank you, gentlemen.

HOLMES: By the way . . . .

BAKER: Mr. Holmes?

HOLMES: Would it bore you to tell me where you got the other goose from? I am something of a fowl-fancier, and I have seldom seen a better-grown bird.

BAKER: Certainly sir. (*Taking his bird*) Thank you, Doctor. There are a few of us who frequent a particular tavern near the British Museum – we are to be found in the Museum itself during the day, you understand . . . studying.

HOLMES: Quite so.

BAKER: Yes. Well, this year, our good host, Windigate by name, instituted a goose-club, by which, on consideration of some few pence every week, we were to receive a bird at Christmas.

WATSON: An admirable arrangement.

BAKER: Indeed, sir. For one such as I, to whom shillings are not so plentiful as once they were, it was a Godsend. And then to have both bird and headgear snatched from my person . . . . (*He pulls himself together*) Well, enough of that.

HOLMES: And what is the name of this excellent hostelry?

BAKER: Ah yes. The Alpha Inn.

HOLMES: Thank you.

WATSON: A very good evening to you, Mr. Baker.

He opens the door.

BAKER: (*Going*) Goodnight Mr. Holmes. Doctor Watson.

HOLMES: Goodnight.

BAKER: And the compliments of the season to you both.

HOLMES: (*Grunts*)

WATSON: And to you, sir.

He closes the door and returns.

Well. It's quite certain that he knows nothing whatever about the matter. Poor old soul. Why was he so embarrassed about his studies?

HOLMES: I fancy he values the Museum as much for its warmth and its comfort as for its books. (*A moment. Then suddenly all action*) Now, Doctor, what are your plans for the evening? Is Mrs. Watson standing anxiously in the window, awaiting your return to home and hearth?

WATSON: Not now I've told her what happened this morning. She knows you far too well. "Tell Mr. Holmes I'd appreciate having you back by the New Year," she said.

HOLMES: (*Laughs delightedly*) Splendid! Come along then.

Cut to:

SCENE 12. INT. THE ALPHA INN. EVENING.

Crowded and noisy. More carol-singing.

WINDIGATE: Evening, gents. What's your pleasure?

WATSON: Two glasses of your best beer, please landlord.

WINDIGATE: Straight away, sir.

HOLMES: Your beer should be excellent if it's as good as your geese.

WINDIGATE: (*Surprised*) My geese?

HOLMES: Yes. I was speaking only half-an-hour ago to Mr. Henry

Baker, who was a member of your goose-club.

WINDIGATE: Oh, I see, yes. But them's not my geese.

WATSON: Indeed? Whose then?

Cut to:

SCENE 13. EXT. COVENT GARDEN STREET MARKET. EVENING.

Still busy with last-minute shoppers.
The tireless barrel-organ operator is still churning out his carols.
But the first thing we hear is:

BRECKINRIDGE: (*Curt*) Yes?

HOLMES: Good evening. It's a cold night. Sold out of geese, I see.

BRECKINRIDGE: Let you have five-hundred tomorrow morning.

HOLMES: That's no good.

BRECKINRIDGE: Well he's got some over there.

HOLMES: Ah, but I was recommended to you.

BRECKINRIDGE: Who by?

HOLMES: The landlord of the Alpha Inn.

BRECKINRIDGE: (*Instantly suspicious*) I sold him a couple of dozen.

HOLMES: Fine birds, too. Now: where did you get them from?

BRECKINRIDGE: Now then mister, what's all this about? Let's have it straight, now.

HOLMES: It's straight enough. I should like to know who sold you the geese which you supplied to the Alpha.

BRECKINRIDGE: Well I'm not going to tell you.

HOLMES: I don't know why you should be so warm over such a trifle.

BRECKINRIDGE: Warm? You'd be warm if you were as pestered as I am.

WATSON: Pestered, Mr. Breckinridge?

BRECKINRIDGE: When I pay good money for a good article, there should be an end of the business; but it's "where are the geese?" and "who did you sell the geese to?" and a lot more besides. You'd think they were the only geese in the world, the fuss that's been made over 'em.

HOLMES: Well I have no connection with any other people who have been making enquiries.

BRECKINRIDGE: Makes no odds to me who you're connected with. I didn't tell them and I won't tell you.

HOLMES: Just as you like. I'm sorry, Watson, the bet's off.

WATSON: The bet? (*Falling in*) Oh, right. Too bad.

BRECKINRIDGE: Bet? What bet?

HOLMES: I have a fiver on it with my friend here, that the bird I ate was country bred. Isn't that right, Watson?

WATSON: Absolutely. And I say I know a town-bred bird when I taste one.

BRECKINRIDGE: Got it from the Alpha, did you?

HOLMES: From Mr. Windigate's own hands.

BRECKINRIDGE: Then you've lost your fiver. Those geese was town bred.

HOLMES: They were nothing of the kind.

BRECKINRIDGE: I say they were.

HOLMES: I don't believe you.

WATSON: Come on, Holmes, don't be a sore loser. (*To Breckinridge, confidentially*) He's always like this. Won't take anyone's word for anything.

HOLMES: Please, Watson. Mr. Breckinridge, you'll never persuade me that those birds were town bred.

BRECKINRIDGE: Do you want to bet?

HOLMES: No, I'd just be taking your money.

BRECKINRIDGE: How much?

HOLMES: A sovereign.

BRECKINRIDGE: Done. Look here, Mr. Cocksure.

He gets a large ledger from under the stall, plonks it on the counter and flips the pages.

This is a list of my suppliers. Country folk first, then town. There. What does that say at the top of the page?

HOLMES: "*Mrs. Oakshott, 117 Brixton Road*".

BRECKINRIDGE: Town, right? And what's the latest entry?

HOLMES: "*Twenty-four geese at seven-and-six*".

BRECKINRIDGE: Thank you. And underneath that?

HOLMES: "*Sold at twelve shillings each to . . . Mr. Windigate, Alpha Inn, Bloomsbury*".

BRECKINRIDGE: Right. So what do you say now?

HOLMES: (*Exclaims in disgust*)

He fishes out a sovereign and slams it down.

Good night to you.

He strides away.

WATSON: You see? Terrible loser. (*As he moves rapidly off*) Holmes! I say! What about my fiver?

Cut to:

SCENE 14. EXT. A QUIETER CORNER. EVENING.

The hum and bustle of the market is now slightly muted.

WATSON: Well done, Holmes!

HOLMES: Thank you for your contribution. A masterly performance. Your after-dinner recitation tomorrow should be excellent. What is to be? "Billy's Rose"? "Christmas Day in the Workhouse"?

WATSON: Please. (*A moment*) "'Twas the Night Before Christmas".

HOLMES: (*Laughs*)

HOLMES: All right, all right. Look, how did you know that that would work?

HOLMES: When you see a man with whiskers of that cut and a sporting paper protruding out of his pocket, you can always draw him with a bet.

WATSON: Do we have to go out to Brixton? How much longer is this trail going to stretch?

HOLMES: Remember Watson, a man will certainly get seven years' penal servitude unless we can establish his innocence.

WATSON: Oh, so you do think he's innocent?

209

HOLMES: Well, it's possible. Wait a moment. Look.

Slightly distant, raised voices sound from Breckinridge's stall.

BRECKINRIDGE: Right, I've had enough of you and your geese. If you show your face here again, I'll set the dog on you, see if I don't.

RYDER: But all I want to know is – (*who you sold them to . . . .*)

BRECKINRIDGE: Did I buy them off you? Did I sell them to you?

RYDER: No, of course not.

BRECKINRIDGE: Then it's none of your business, is it? Now be off.

RYDER: But Mrs. Oakshott told me to ask you.

BRECKINRIDGE: You can ask the King of Proosia for all I care, I've had enough. Are you going?

RYDER: Don't hit me, don't hit me! (*He comes closer to us, calling back:*) I didn't mean no harm! Honest I didn't! It's just that one of them was mine, that's all . . . Mine . . . .

HOLMES: (*Suddenly close*) Good evening.

Ryder jumps out of his skin.

RYDER: Who are you? What do you want?

HOLMES: I couldn't help overhearing. I think that I could be of assistance to you.

RYDER: You? Who are you? How could you know anything about it?

HOLMES: It's my business to know what other people don't know. My name is Sherlock Holmes.

RYDER: (*Whimpers*)

A violin passage takes us to:

SCENE 15. INT. THE SITTING-ROOM AT 221b BAKER STREET.

The fire still blazes merrily.

HOLMES: (*Cheerily*) Here we are! The fire looks very seasonal in this weather.

WATSON: You look cold, sir.

HOLMES: Perhaps that accounts for your silence during the cab journey.

RYDER: Well, I . . . That is to say . . . .

HOLMES: Quite. Now then! Pray tell me who it is that I have the pleasure of assisting.

RYDER: My name is John Robinson.

HOLMES: (*Sweetly*) No, no, the real name. It's always awkward doing business with an alias.

RYDER: (*Groans*)

He collapses into a chair.

HOLMES: Yes, do please take a seat. You too, Watson.

WATSON: (*Sitting*) Thank you.

HOLMES: (*Sitting with a sigh*) Isn't this cosy? Oh – I believe you were going to tell us your name.

A moment.

RYDER: My real name is James Ryder.

HOLMES: Precisely so. Watson, you saw the account in the papers?

WATSON: (*Realising*) You're the head attendant at the Hotel Cosmopolitan.

RYDER: Yes sir, yes I am. The business there – it's upset me terribly.

HOLMES: I'm sure it has. Now: you're interested in some geese?

RYDER: Oh, yes sir.

HOLMES: Or rather, I fancy, in one particular goose. White, with a black bar across its tail.

"Ryder quivers with emotion."

RYDER: Oh sir! Can you tell me where it went to?

HOLMES: It came here.

RYDER: Here?

HOLMES: Yes, and a most remarkable bird it proved. It laid an egg after it was dead.

RYDER: (*Whimpers*)

HOLMES: The bonniest, brightest little blue egg that ever was seen. (*Suddenly cold as ice*) The game's up, Ryder.

RYDER: No! No . . . .

He staggers to his feet, swaying perilously.
He knocks the fire-irons to the hearth. They clatter.

(*Reacts with a start*)

Watson rises and catches him.

WATSON: Hold up man, or you'll be in the fire.

HOLMES: That's it, Watson, give him an arm back into his chair.

WATSON: (*Doing so*) There. Easy, now.

A moment.

RYDER: (*Pants weakly*)

HOLMES: Look at him. He's not got enough blood in him for felony.
What a shrimp it is, to be sure. Give it some brandy, Doctor.

WATSON: Very well.

He pours some, passes it across.

Here.

RYDER: (*Almost inaudibly*) Thank you.

He drinks, splutters, quietens down.

HOLMES: Now, Ryder. I have almost every link in my hands, and all
the proofs which I could possibly need. You had heard of this blue
gemstone of the Countess of Morcar's, and – (*contrived a plan to
steal it . . . .*)

RYDER: It was Her Ladyship's waiting-maid told me about it. Cathy –
Catherine Cusack. She put me up to it! She said if I got it, she would
. . . she would . . . .

He can't go on.

HOLMES: Yes. So what did you do? Somehow or other, you knew that
this man Horner had been concerned in some such matter before.
You made some small job in my lady's room and sent for him. Then
you rifled the jewel-case, raised the alarm, and had this unfortunate
individual arrested.

*Ryder "throws himself down upon the rug and clutches at Holmes's
knees."*

RYDER: For God's sake have mercy! Think of my father! My mother! It
would break their hearts!

WATSON: For goodness' sake, man.

213

RYDER: I never went wrong before! I never will again, I swear it. I'll swear it on a Bible. Oh don't bring it into court! Say you won't!

HOLMES: (*Very angry*) Get back into your chair! It's very well to cringe and crawl now, but you thought little enough of this poor man Horner, in prison for a crime of which he knew nothing.

RYDER: I'll fly, Mr. Holmes. I'll leave the country, sir. Then the charge against him will break down.

HOLMES: Hmm. We'll talk about that. But first, I want to hear a true account of this matter. How came the stone into the goose and the goose onto the open market? Tell us the truth, for there lies your only hope of safety.

RYDER: Oh Mr. Holmes. Sir.

HOLMES: Get on with it.

RYDER: (*Collecting himself*) Well, it happened just like you said. As soon as Horner had gone, I smashed open the jewel-case and got the stone. Then I ran out to the street and found a constable. When we got back to the hotel, the old lady – that is, Her Ladyship – had got back and was screaming the place down. Course a constable wasn't good enough for her, she had to have an Inspector at the very least.

HOLMES: Friend Bradstreet of B Division.

RYDER: Yes . . . Proper put the wind up me, he did. Made me identify Horner.

HOLMES: Where was the gem while you were perjuring yourself at Scotland Yard?

RYDER: In my pocket. As soon as I could get away I high-tailed it for my sister's house. In Brixton.

WATSON: Mrs. Oakshott.

RYDER: That's right. All the way there, every man I met seemed to me to be a policeman or a detective, ready to put the finger on me. The sweat was pouring down my face by the time I got there.

We move to a flashback:

SCENE 16. EXT. THE BRIXTON ROAD. EVENING.

Ryder knocks frantically at a door. It opens.

MRS. OAKSHOTT: Why Jem! Hello.

RYDER: Hello Maggie.

MRS. OAKSHOTT: Whatever's the matter with you, Jem? Are you sick?

RYDER: There's been some trouble at work, Maggie.

MRS. OAKSHOTT: What have you been and done?

RYDER: Nothing! It's just upset me, that's all.

MRS. OAKSHOTT: Well you better come in. Come on.

RYDER: Right. Yes.

The street fades under:

RYDER: (*Over*) I told Maggie I wanted to get a bit of air, and I went through to the backyard and tried to think what it would best to do.

The background has mixed to:

SCENE 17. EXT. THE BACKYARD. EVENING.

Two dozen geese are milling about, happy in their ignorance of imminent doom.

RYDER: (*Over*) I sat there, looking at the geese that my sister fattens up

215

for the market. And suddenly, an idea came into my head which showed me how I could beat the best detective that ever lived.

HOLMES: (*Over, contemptuously*) Ha.

A sudden flurry from the geese.

RYDER: Come here, you . . . Stand still, you stupid bird! (*He corners it*) Ah, now I've got you . . . .

An anguished squawk from his victim.

Keep still, blast you. That's it. Now, look what your Uncle Jem's got for you, then . . . .

RYDER: (*Over*) I caught one of the geese: a fine big one, with a barred tail, and I thrust the stone as far down its throat as I could reach with my finger. Then the bird gave a gulp and I felt it pass down into its crop.

RYDER: That's right. Let's see 'em find it in there, then.

MRS. OAKSHOTT: (*Off*) Jem! What are doing with that bird?

RYDER: (*A guilty start*) What? Ah!

He loses his grip on the goose and it escapes to join the others. They welcome it back honkily.

Oh no . . . .

MRS. OAKSHOTT: What on earth were you up to?

RYDER: Well, er . . . You said you'd give me one for Christmas. I was just feeling which one was the fattest.

MRS. OAKSHOTT: Oh, we've got one set aside for you. Jem's bird, we call it. We've been feeding it up special.

RYDER: But . . . .

MRS. OAKSHOTT: What?

RYDER: Well if it's all the same to you, Maggie, I'd rather have that one. The one with the barred tail.

MRS. OAKSHOTT: But yours is a good three pound heavier.

RYDER: (*Desperately*) No, I really like that one.

MRS. OAKSHOTT: Well, if you're sure.

RYDER: And I'll take it now.

MRS. OAKSHOTT: But . . . Oh very well. Kill it and take it with you.

RYDER: Thank you, Maggie, thank you. Come here, you brute . . . .

He attacks the geese. They retaliate.
We move back to the present:

SCENE 18. INT. THE SITTING-ROOM AT 221b BAKER STREET.

A match flares as Holmes lights a pipe.

RYDER: Well, I did what she said, Mr. Holmes, and carried the bird off to my place in Kilburn. Then I got a knife and cut it open. My heart turned to water – there was no sign of the stone.

And again to a flashback:

SCENE 19. EXT. THE BRIXTON ROAD. EVENING.

As before.

MRS. OAKSHOTT: Jem! Whatever now?

RYDER: (*Pushing past her*) 'Scuse me, Maggie.

MRS. OAKSHOTT: Well!

Mix to:

SCENE 20. EXT. THE BACKYARD. EVENING.

Not a goose to be heard. The back door flies open. A long pause.

RYDER: (*Yells in anguish. Then sobs.*)

Back to the present:

SCENE 21. INT. THE SITTING-ROOM AT 221b BAKER STREET.

As before.

RYDER: They'd gone. They'd all gone.

WATSON: To Breckinridge's of Covent Garden.

HOLMES: And there had been more than one with a barred tail.

RYDER: There were two. Maggie told me she couldn't ever tell them apart. I went to Breckinridge as fast as I could run, but not one word would he tell me about where they'd gone. I went back again and again – and to Maggie's too, to see if she knew. She thinks I'm going mad. Sometimes I think she's right. And now . . . and now I am a branded thief, without hardly having touched the wealth I sold my character for. God help me! God help me! (*Sobs*)

A long moment.

HOLMES: Get out.

RYDER: What, sir?

HOLMES: Get out.

RYDER: Oh, heaven bless you.

HOLMES: No more words. Get out!

Panting heavily, Ryder rises.

RYDER: I, er . . . .

But he thinks better of it, and bolts for the door. He opens it, scoots through, slams it behind him. A moment.

HOLMES: (*A weary sigh*)

WATSON: Well, well. My dear Holmes.

HOLMES: I am not retained by the police to supply their deficiencies.

He relights his pipe.

I suppose I am compounding a felony, but it is just possible that I am saving a soul. Send him to jail now and you make him a jailbird for life. (*A throwaway*) Besides, it's the season of forgiveness.

WATSON: Holmes, you amaze me sometimes.

HOLMES: I'm delighted to hear it. (*Springing up*) Come on – get your hat.

A violin passage takes us to:

SCENE 22. INT. A JAIL CELL.

Clanking keys as the door is unlocked.

HORNER: Now what? More questions?

BRADSTREET: You're free to go.

HORNER: What?

BRADSTREET: Come on, come on.

HORNER: But what's happened?

BRADSTREET: You've got this gentleman to thank.

HOLMES: Good evening, Horner.

HORNER: Do I know you sir?

HOLMES: My name would perhaps be familiar to you.

HORNER: Well then . . . ?

HOLMES: It's of no importance. I suggest you leave before the worthy
Inspector changes his mind.

HORNER: Yes, yes, right. (*Leaving*) God bless you sir, whoever you are.

HOLMES: (*Grunts a reply*)

BRADSTREET: (*Calling off*) Constable, take Mr. Horner up and give
him his belongings.

CONSTABLE: (*Off*) Sir. This way.

And they're gone. A moment.

BRADSTREET: Mr. Holmes, I swear I still don't know how you
persuaded me to do that.

HOLMES: Really, Bradstreet. You have the stone, you have the
Commissioner's good grace, and you have my assurance that I'm on
the trail of the true thief. What more do you want?

BRADSTREET: Well, a little hard and fast evidence wouldn't come
amiss.

HOLMES: My dear fellow. It's Christmas.

Cut to:

SCENE 23. EXT. A LONDON STREET. THE EARLY HOURS.

If we can take it, a Salvation Army band two streets away plays one last carol.
Slightly distant, a hansom cab goes by, the horse's hooves crisp in the cold air.
Then:

HOLMES: (*Approaching*) My apologies for keeping you waiting, Doctor.

WATSON: It was worth it to see the expression on Horner's face when he came out. Well done, Holmes.

HOLMES: (*A vocal shrug*)

WATSON: No, I mean it. There he was, off back to his family and friends . . . Did my heart good.

HOLMES: I await with interest your heart-wringing prose version.

WATSON: Really, old man. Can't you let it drop for a second? (*A moment*) Well. I must be getting home. It's certainly been a Christmas Eve to remember. And tomorrow I dare say I'll even find the children tolerable.

Holmes says nothing.
Watson breaks the silence.
He rubs his hands together, ready to leave.

Ah well. Goodnight, then.

Holmes desperately wants him to stay.
He drops the mask for the barest moment:

HOLMES: Watson. Wait.

Watson stops dead.
To him, the plea was unmistakeable.

He's not sure how to handle this.

WATSON: Holmes?

And neither is Holmes.
A moment.
Way off, Big Ben strikes the quarter.
Watson looks at his pocket-watch.

Good Lord. I'd no idea it was so late. Early.

HOLMES: Watson . . . .

An awkward silence. Watson takes charge.

WATSON: Holmes . . . this is damnably rude of me, but . . . well, I know
you dine very late, as a rule.

And Holmes realises what he's doing and is grateful for it. The mask
goes back up.

HOLMES: Absolutely true, Doctor. Are you about to tell me that I'm
ruining my digestion?

WATSON: Actually, I was wondering if Mrs. Hudson might stretch to
providing for two.

HOLMES: For two?

WATSON: Mary will have gone to bed hours ago. The whole household.
I realise it's a dreadful imposition.

HOLMES: I believe I can tolerate it.

WATSON: Thank you, Holmes.

And again, the mask disappears . . . .

HOLMES: Thank you, my friend.

But not for long. After a moment:

222

Come along, Doctor. Faces to the north and quick march!

They begin to walk, their footsteps echoing in the early-morning stillness.
The scene is overtaken by the closing sig.
Closing announcements.
The music ends.

The Man Who Believed in Nothing
by Jim French

T his script has never been published in text form, and was initially performed as a radio drama on December 23, 2001. The broadcast was Episode No. 26 of The Further Adventures of Sherlock Holmes, one of the recurring series featured on the nationally syndicated Imagination Theatre. Founded by Jim French, the company has currently produced over one-thousand multi-series episodes, including one-hundred-and-twenty-two (as of this writing) Sherlock Holmes pastiches. In addition, Imagination Theatre has also recorded the entire Holmes Canon, featured as The Classic Adventures of Sherlock Holmes. This is the only version in which all the episodes have been written by the same writer, Matthew J. Elliott, and with the same two actors, John Patrick Lowrie and Lawrence Albert, portraying Holmes and Watson, respectively.

THE CAST

SHERLOCK HOLMES – John Patrick Lowrie

DR. JOHN H. WATSON – Lawrence Albert

REVEREND KENNETH PAIGE – Frank Buxton: *Distinguished Vicar of a small old Anglican church in the town of Harrow. Well-educated, British, Age 60*

ALICE VAN METER – Kate Fleming: *Choir director and organist for the church. Age 37, single*

REVEREND HENRY LANTRY – Dennis Bateman: *Assistant Pastor. Mild-mannered, frail, Age 35*

MRS. HUDSON *and* **MATRON** – Lee Paasch: *Head nurse of a British Mental Hospital. Age 60's*

MUSIC – OPENING, *DANSE MACABRE* AND UNDER

WATSON: My name is Doctor John H. Watson. To some of you who have followed my stories about Sherlock Holmes, it may seem that his services were always in constant demand. However, in the fall of 1889, despite having solved the hideous killing in the Tuttman Gallery several weeks earlier, Holmes experienced a period of inactivity. In the first week of December, I had just attended a patient whose condition had worsened, and now required immediate admittance to a sanitarium. Being only half-a-mile or so from Baker Street – and needing a change of mood – I decided to stop around at 221b for a visit with Holmes.

MUSIC – OUT

SOUND EFFECT – SEGUE TO STREET SOUNDS. DOOR OPENS

MRS. HUDSON: Oh, it's Doctor Watson! Come in, Doctor! How nice to see you!

WATSON: It's good to see you, Mrs. Hudson. How have you been?

SOUND EFFECT – DOOR CLOSES. STREET SOUNDS DOWN

MRS. HUDSON: Oh, still hale and hearty, thanks be. And yourself? You're looking fine!

WATSON: I've been quite busy lately. Is Holmes in?

MRS. HUDSON: Yes, he's in. I was just going up to collect his breakfast dishes. (LOW) You know, Doctor, for the past fortnight, he's been in one of his gloomy spells. But then a letter came this morning, and I think he's back to his old self.

WATSON: A letter, eh?

MRS. HUDSON: By special messenger, at six a.m.! It must have been good news, because he began to bustle about, and I even heard him whistling. He never whistles.

WATSON: Well, we know he has his moods, but give him a juicy case, and he's right as rain.

MRS. HUDSON: And how is your wife these days?

WATSON: Mary? She's in excellent spirits, I'm glad to say. Today she's poring over a cook book, planning what to serve for Christmas.

MRS. HUDSON: Ah, then she likes to cook, does she?

WATSON: (CHUCKLES) Can't you tell? I've had to buy new suits!

SOUND EFFECT – STEPS STOP. MRS. HUDSON TAPS ON DOOR. PAUSE, THEN DOOR OPENS

HOLMES: Watson! Come in. I was just thinking about you.

WATSON: Hello, Holmes. I was just in the neighbourhood –

HOLMES: – visiting a highly contagious patient.

WATSON: Now how on earth can you tell?

HOLMES: (CHUCKLES) The marks from the sanitary mask are still impressed on your face.

WATSON: Eh? They are? I must have tied it too tightly.

HOLMES: And by the evidence of your new clothes, your practice must be flourishing. Feel free to take the breakfast tray, Mrs. Hudson

MRS. HUDSON: (MOVING OFF) Yes, I'll only be a moment.

WATSON: And how is it with you, Holmes?

HOLMES: My life has become a study in boredom. Scarcely a whisper of interest from anyone since that museum horror. But then this morning, a glimmer. A letter came from out of town, making me think of you and your predilection for idylls in the country.

MRS. HUDSON: (FAR OFF) Well! I see for once you ate every scrap!

226

HOLMES: And Mrs. Hudson, I shan't be dining here for the rest of the day, so you are now free to go and buy out the stores.

MRS. HUDSON: Buy out the stores, indeed!

SOUND EFFECT – (UNDER ABOVE) MRS. HUDSON WALKS OFF, PLATES JIGGLING. DOOR OPENS. SHE GOES OUT. DOOR CLOSES.

WATSON: You *are* in a chipper mood. Is it the letter?

HOLMES: Like to hear it?

WATSON: Certainly.

SOUND EFFECT – NOTE HANDLED

HOLMES: (READING) *"Dear Mr. Holmes: Knowing of your most excellent reputation in solving all manner of difficulties, may I trouble you to consider helping us locate one of our clergy who is missing? He is quite disturbed, and I fear he may try to harm himself. It is urgent that he be found before a tragedy takes place, and it is equally urgent that this matter remain confidential, for reasons which I will explain in detail if you will grant us the goodness of your help. I prayerfully await your earliest reply, for time is of the essence, and a life may hang in the balance. May God bless you. Most sincerely, The Reverend Kenneth Paige, Vicar of the Anglican Church of Harrow."*

WATSON: Well. What do you think?

HOLMES: I sent a telegram this morning, telling him I would be there this afternoon. You wouldn't like to come with me, would you? I may need your medical knowledge, and I am almost certain that you won't be chased by a crocodile this time. Of course, with a busy practice like yours . . . .

WATSON: Nonsense. Old Jackson would be glad to take my patients for a day or so, and Mary is so busy with her shopping, I doubt she'd even notice I'm gone. Of course I'll come with you, Holmes! With pleasure!

MUSIC – UNDERCURRENT

WATSON: It was late afternoon when Holmes and I arrived in the Middlesex town of Harrow. The church stood on a road of gabled houses. On one side was a small cemetery, and on the other was a large two-story house. It was here that the Reverend Paige had arranged to meet us. He welcomed us into a darkly-panelled study, warmed by a wood fire.

MUSIC – OUT

PAIGE: So terribly good of you to come so promptly. May I offer you tea or coffee? Or we do have some hot mulled wine.

WATSON: Well! After a chilly trip, that would make me most wel–

HOLMES: Perhaps later, thank you. Now, about the missing man. How long has he been gone?

PAIGE: Since last night.

HOLMES: You've called the police?

PAIGE: No, as I mentioned in my letter, this is a . . . delicate matter.

HOLMES: Delicate in what way?

PAIGE: Well, Father Lantry certainly wasn't in his senses when he left?

HOLMES: Oh?

PAIGE: Miss Van Meter tells me she found him in a despairing mood last evening, before our service. They spoke for a few minutes, then went their separate ways. Then, at just before seven, when I entered the sanctuary to prepare for Vespers, I discovered the gold altar cross and a pair of silver candlesticks were missing. Well, of course the first thing that entered my mind was that we'd been robbed!

HOLMES: The church isn't kept locked when it's not in use?

PAIGE: No. Parishioners may need to come into the sanctuary at any time for prayer or meditation. But, thinking we'd had a burglar, I immediately went to the sacristy to see if anything there was missing, and a silver communion chalice was gone, along with the morning's collections!

WATSON: Oh, I say. What a shame.

HOLMES: And what about the missing man?

PAIGE: Father Lantry didn't turn up for Vespers, so I conducted the service by myself. But immediately after the benediction, I hurried up to his room to see if he was ill. And there . . . I found the missing items. Now you see why I must shield Father Lantry form any public shame.

HOLMES: Tell me all you can about him.

PAIGE: Well, he grew up in this parish, and came out of the seminary and served as a deacon. Then he accepted a call to replace the chaplain at Blackwall Prison, but that turned out to be too much for him.

HOLMES: In what way?

PAIGE: Associating with that low class of men every day caused him to doubt his faith, and that brought on a nervous collapse. He resigned his post as chaplain, and the Diocese decided it would be best if he were put under treatment at a mental hospital. Parkhurst Hospital, in the West End.

HOLMES: Be more specific about what brought on his condition and what it did to him.

PAIGE: Well, many of the prisoners he ministered to – or tried to minister to – had committed unspeakable crimes. They were such brutal men, that no matter what Henry did, it seemed to do no good. The anger and the violence he encountered eventually broke his spirit. But in hospital, he seemed to have convalesced well, so we welcomed him back to the parish, and found quarters for him right here in the vicarage.

HOLMES: I take it he's unmarried?

PAIGE: Oh, yes.

ALICE: (OFF) Father Paige?

PAIGE: Oh, yes, Alice, come right in. Gentlemen, our choir director and organist, Miss Alice Van Meter. Alice, these are the gentlemen who so graciously came up from London to help us. May I present Mr. Sherlock Holmes and Doctor –

ALICE: Doctor Watson? It's Doctor Watson, of course! (MOVING ON) Excuse me, I can't believe I'm actually in the same room with Sherlock Holmes and Doctor Watson! I've read everything about you, Mr. Holmes!

HOLMES: Most kind of you.

WATSON: I'm glad you enjoy the stories.

PAIGE: Now, Alice, I've been telling the gentlemen about what happened last night, and I thought they might have some questions for you.

ALICE: I'll tell you all I can, gentlemen.

HOLMES: The Vicar was saying Mr. Lantry spent some time in mental hospital.

ALICE: Ten months and a week, to be exact.

PAIGE: But he gradually improved, and seemed to be anxious to resume his duties in the Parish. We thought he was getting along rather well.

HOLMES: The Vicar tells me you spoke with Mr. Lantry last night, shortly before he turned up missing.

ALICE: Yes.

HOLMES: Did you have any concerns about him at that time?

ALICE: Yes, I did. But . . . well, he spoke to me in confidence.

PAIGE: If you can throw any light on our search for him, my child, you ought to realize that his safety is of paramount importance. Please tell us what he said.

ALICE: Well, as you know, he'd been struggling with his faith, and . . . and he'd had another of his blank spells. He's been having them right along, but he didn't want you to know.

HOLMES: Describe these spells.

ALICE: He forgets whole hours of time. He . . . he won't remember doing this or that . . . . It's as if his mind went to sleep for a short time, and then woke up again.

HOLMES: Watson? Have you ever heard of this?

WATSON: Well, it's rare, but not unheard-of. The literarure mentions it from time to time, but I haven't seen it personally. It may be what they call a "fugue" state.

PAIGE: Is it considered a form of insanity?

WATSON: Well, you know there's no reliable measure for insanity. There's a broad line between normal and abnormal behaviour.

HOLMES: What brings on these "fugues"?

WATSON: Sometimes it's a shock of some sort. And typically he won't remember the cause when he comes out of it.

HOLMES: And so Mr. Lantry confided in you that he was having these mental lapses. What else?

ALICE: He . . . he was terribly disillusioned by his work with the prisoners. I think he questioned why God would permit Man to do such horrible acts.

HOLMES: Are you saying he lost his faith?

ALICE: I . . . Yes. I supposed that's what it comes down to.

HOLMES: May we see his room?

PAIGE: Certainly. Just follow me.

ALICE: May I come too?

PAIGE: Of course.

<u>SOUND EFFECT – (UNDER) GROUP ASCENDING STAIRS</u>

WATSON: The priest's room was upstairs in the back. It had a thin rug on the floor, curtains at the window, a narrow cot, a chair, and a writing desk, with a painting of "The Last Supper" hanging on the wall. The room was dominated by a heavy mahogany armoire.

<u>SOUND EFFECT – STEPS STOP</u>

HOLMES: Where did you find the missing goods?

PAIGE: There, in the armoire. Go on, open the wardrobe doors. You see, all his clerical garb is hanging there. Two complete sets – that's all he had. So he left here wearing layman's clothing.

<u>MUSIC – UNDERCURRENT UP AND UNDER</u>

WATSON: Holmes pulled open the drawers beneath the wardrobe. They were empty. He stood quietly in the middle of the room for several seconds. Then, he walked to the cot and carefully lifted the blanket, then the pillow, and then the thin mattress, and there – under the mattress – lay a single sheet of paper. He picked it up.

<u>MUSIC – OUT</u>

<u>SOUND EFFECT – SINGLE PAPER FLEX</u>

HOLMES: Half-a-sheet of cheap writing paper, torn in half down the middle. Would you recognize Mr. Lantry's handwriting?

PAIGE: I think so.

ALICE: *I* would.

232

HOLMES: Is this his writing?

SOUND EFFECT – PAPER FLEX

ALICE: Yes, it's his. But what's this he's written?

HOLMES: It appears to be a list.

PAIGE: What does it say? "*God, self, humanity, country, royalty . . . .*"

ALICE: ". . . *Government, education, money, science, intelligence,* (PAUSE) . . . *love . . . .*"

PAIGE: "*Law, loyalty, honesty, sympathy, and service to others.*" What is this?

HOLMES: Things people believe in, it would seem.

PAIGE: Why would he have written this?

HOLMES: I'm more interested in what he wrote on the half that was torn away.

WATSON: How do you know he wrote anything on the other half of the paper?

HOLMES: Because, Watson, here . . . on the very edge where he tore it, is the start of another line of writing. You see it?

WATSON: Oh! I'd missed that.

PAIGE: He may have thought better of what he wrote and thrown the other half away.

ALICE: Mr. Holmes, how in the world did you know to look under his mattress?

HOLMES: I thought he might have left a note before he left, and the only place to hide one in this room – if not in the armoire – was in or under the bed. Now: would you, by any chance, remember what Mr. Lantry was wearing when you saw him last night, Miss Van Meter?

233

ALICE: Why, he was still in his vestments.

HOLMES: Does he own a coat?

ALICE: Yes.

HOLMES: And a hat?

ALICE: Yes.

HOLMES: Then where are they?

ALICE: Why, I don't know.

HOLMES: Well, I think, for the moment at least, we may discard any fear that he's taken his life. He would hardly go to the trouble to dress against the weather if he went outdoors only to commit suicide.

MUSIC – UNDERCURRENT

WATSON: But the question remained, where *had* the Reverend Lantry gone – and why? Holmes requested a private interview with Alice Van Meter, and the two of them went down to the sitting room by themselves for a few minutes while I had coffee with the Vicar. Afterward, Holmes joined me in the study. The Vicar excused himself to attend to some parish business. Holmes paced around the study in an impatient mood, puffing on his pipe. And then suddenly, he whirled and smote his forehead.

MUSIC – OUT

HOLMES: Of course! I think I know where he is!

WATSON: Where?

HOLMES: Watson, make our goodbyes to the Vicar, while I see about hiring a carriage to take us to the train station.

SOUND EFFECT – FADE UP: TRAIN IN MOTION

WATSON: We were able to catch a southbound train at 5:05 p.m., which made many stops on its way to London. During the trip, Holmes appeared to have fallen asleep. But then he said, without opening his eyes –

HOLMES: Go on, Watson. I'm not asleep, and you're about to burst like a tea kettle. I can feel the pressure from here, so ask away.

WATSON: Well! To begin with, where are we going?

HOLMES: To Notting Hill. To the Parkhurst Hospital. That's where I believe we shall find Reverend Lantry.

WATSON: What makes you think that?

HOLMES: The hospital was his first place of refuge after quitting his job as a prison chaplain. But when he left there, he may have still felt he'd lost his faith. No doubt he feels a great confusion and guilt. Where else to go but back to Parkhurst? But Watson, if I'm right and we find him, I have reason to believe we can help him!

MUSIC – UNDERCURRENT

WATSON: We got off the train at Notting Hill Station and took a hansom to Ladbroke Road, where there stood a manor house with a sign saying "Parkhurst Hospital". We approached the matron on duty at the front desk.

MUSIC – OUT

MATRON: May I help you?

HOLMES: We are here to visit a patient. Henry Lantry.

MATRON: Your names?

HOLMES: Sherlock Holmes.

WATSON: Doctor John H. Watson.

MATRON: Oh. Has Reverend Lantry been your patient, Doctor?

WATSON: Uh, why, uh . . . .

HOLMES: Doctor Watson is here in a consulting capacity. He is a specialist, as am I.

MATRON: I see. Well, if you'll excuse me for a moment, gentleman –

<u>SOUND EFFECT – SHE GETS UP AND WALKS OFF. DOOR OPENS/CLOSES</u>

WATSON: (LOUD WHISPER) Consulting capacity?

HOLMES: Perfectly truthful. We *are* consulted by clients all the time, aren't we?

WATSON: Well, yes, I suppose that's right. But what if they don't let us see him? He may be too ill . . . or he may not want to see anyone.

HOLMES: Our mission was to find him, and apparently we've done that. But there is more to learn about this, which will be of some use to he Vicar . . . .

<u>SOUND EFFECT – (OFF) DOOR OPENS/CLOSES. WOMAN WALKS ON</u>

MATRON: This way please.

<u>MUSIC – UNDERCURRENT</u>

WATSON: She led us into a comfortably appointed office, where we waited a moment or two, and then she returned, with a pale, thin, haunted-looking man. He barely spoke as we were introduced. The matron remained in the room.

<u>MUSIC – OUT</u>

LANTRY: What do you want with me?

HOLMES: We want to help you.

LANTRY: They all want to help me, but there is no help, not for me. How did you know where to find me?

HOLMES: A fortunate assumption. Reverend Lantry, I think I –

LANTRY: Don't call me that! Don't call me Reverend, not any more.

HOLMES: Very well, Mr. Lantry. I think I know why you left the parish so suddenly. You believed you had stolen money and valuables from the church while you were not aware of what you were doing. And when you came to your senses and found these things in your room, you decided to leave and come back here before you did something else, perhaps something worse.

LANTRY: I don't know how you would know that.

HOLMES: We found the note you left.

LANTRY: The note?

HOLMES: This.

SOUND EFFECT – PAPER CRINKLES

HOLMES: You did leave this under your mattress?

LANTRY: I . . . forgot I left it there.

HOLMES: What did you do with the other half of the page?

LANTRY: How did you know there was another half? I was going to burn it. Destroy it! But I kept it. I don't know why. The madness, perhaps.

HOLMES: Do you still have it?

MATRON: It's with his things. Do you want me to get it, Henry?

LANTRY: Yes, you might as well.

MATRON: I'll be right back.

SOUND EFFECT – A STEP. DOOR OPENS. STEP OUT. DOOR CLOSES.

237

HOLMES: Are you treated well here?

LANTRY: As well as I deserve.

WATSON: Look here, Mr. Lantry . . . Holmes has information that will relieve your mind.

LANTRY: Nothing will relieve my mind! I've been cursed by Blackwall Prison! I went there to bring God to the inmates, but the inmates took God away from me!

HOLMES: But they couldn't do that, could they? Didn't Saint Matthew quote God as saying, "*I am with you always*"?

LANTRY: Matthew 28, Verse 20. *"I am with you always."*

HOLMES: *"Even unto the end of the world."*

<u>SOUND EFFECT – DOOR OPENS. STEP IN. DOOR CLOSES</u>

MATRON: Is this what you want?

<u>SOUND EFFECT – PAPER UNFOLDED</u>

LANTRY: Yes.

HOLMES: May I see it?

LANTRY: Here.

HOLMES: Hmm. Now it makes sense. The list I found on the left hand side of the paper has a list of things to believe in.

LANTRY: Things I *ought* to believe in . . . things I *used* to believe in! Mr. Holmes, I left the chaplaincy in Blackwall with no believe left in me! It was burned out of me! I struggled day after day, but I felt like an empty shell! So one night, I wrote down the things I ought to believe in, starting with God, so I could think and pray about them. Then, on Sunday evening, after talking with Alice . . . Did you meet Alice . . . ?

238

HOLMES: Yes, we met her.

LANTRY: Well, I went up to my room and took out the list . . . and I saw that I had written something opposite each of the objects of believe! While I was out of my senses! It was so horrible, I tore it away!

HOLMES: But look, Mr. Lantry. Look at these two lists. The right column isn't your handwriting.

LANTRY: Oh, I'm afraid that it was my hand, guided by the Devil! Look what I wrote! Opposite *"Service to Others"*, I wrote *"Waste of Time"!* "Opposite *"Law"*: *"A contrivance of the ruling class"*! Opposite *"Love"*: *"Animal Emotion"*; and worst of all, opposite *"God"*: *"Superstition"*! I came back to my room and found what I'd done – stolen the cross and the rest – and knew I had to leave right then!

MUSIC – UNDERCURRENT

WATSON: We were allowed to spend the night talking with Lantry. It wasn't until eight o'clock the next morning that the doctor in charge permitted us to take Henry Lantry back to Harrow with us. And it was noon when we got back to the church, and Holmes asked the Vicar to meet with Lantry and me in the study, and for Alice Van Meter to join us and bring her notes for the upcoming Christmas program.

MUSIC – OUT

PAIGE: I'm overjoyed to have you back with us, Henry, and we shall do everything possible to make things just as they were before.

HOLMES: Or possibly not.

PAIGE: What do you mean? Father Lantry seems to be quite himself again!

LANTRY: I may still have occasions when I go blank, but my doctor tells me these will gradually go away. But during the past few hours, Mr. Holmes made several things clear to me, and now I must make *everything* clear. Alice?

ALICE: Yes, Henry?

LANTRY: I told Mr. Holmes about our conversation on Sunday.

ALICE: You did what?

HOLMES: He told me how you had thrown yourself at him, Miss Van
Meter.

ALICE: Why, you surely don't believe that!

HOLMES: Didn't you tell him that you could bring him health and
happiness if you would marry?

ALICE: We discussed our understanding, yes, but –

LANTRY: We had no understanding, Alice, but you were so
determined that we should be married –

ALICE: Don't think I haven't had a lot of chances! Every bachelor in
this parish wants to marry me! But I saved myself for you, Henry!

HOLMES: And how did this conversation end, Mr. Lantry?

ALICE: You won't tell him that, Henry! You mustn't!

LANTRY: She kissed me. I didn't expect it, but . . . she kissed me!

HOLMES: And then what happened?

LANTRY: I was so dazed, I didn't remember anything until I found
myself back in my room. And I opened my armoire and I saw the
cross and the chalice and the candlestick! Of course, I thought I'd
taken them from the sanctuary myself, without realizing it. So I knew
I should leave and go back where I couldn't do any more harm. I went
back to Parkhurst.

HOLMES: How did those items get from the church and into Mr.
Lantry's room, Alice?

ALICE: He took them! He'd been in the prison too long, you see, and it
turned him into a criminal! I tried to protect you, Henry!

240

HOLMES: May we see your notes for the Christmas service?

ALICE: What?

HOLMES: The notes you shared with me during our talk a few minutes ago.

SPECIAL EFFECT – RUSTLE OF PAPERS

ALICE: Here.

HOLMES: Now, Mr. Lantry, the half page you tore away because you thought you had written it?

LANTRY: Yes, here it is.

SPECIAL EFFECT – SINGLE RUSTLE OF PAPER

HOLMES: Compare the handwriting, Reverend Paige.

PAIGE: (PAUSE) The writing on the right half is different.

HOLMES: Now, compare it to Alice's writing.

PAIGE: This *is* Alice's writing!

HOLMES: Mr. Lantry listed the things he believed in. He'd shown you his list. He told you where he kept it. You took the opportunity to add to it, at the time you hid the objects from the church in his armoire, hoping Mr. Lantry would think he had written it, just as you hoped he'd think he'd stolen the goods! It was all part of your plan of revenge because Mr. Lantry refused to marry you. Isn't that right?

ALICE: (PAUSE) I forgive you, Henry. You're not in your right mind. After we're married, I'll take care of you.

PAIGE: Alice . . . my child . . . you'd better come with me now.

ALICE: (FADING OFF) You don't need to be afraid anymore, my darling. I'll protect you. I love you! I've always loved you . . . .

PAIGE: (OFF) Come along, Alice

ALICE: (OFF) They're evil men, Henry! Like the men in the prison –

SPECIAL EFFECT – DOOR CLOSES

MUSIC – UNDERCURENT

WATSON: The Vicar had a long talk with Alice Van Meter. More than that we weren't told. But it was enough to satisfy Holmes, and we returned to London on the next train. A few days later, we received an invitation to come back to Harrow for the Christmas Service at the church. To my surprise, Holmes said that he'd be there . . . if my wife and I would come with him. Which, I'm happy to say, we did.

MUSIC – *DANSE MACABRE*

NARRATOR: You have heard *"The Man Who Believed in Nothing"*, written and directed by Jim French. "The Further Adventures of Sherlock Holmes" features John Patrick Lowrie as Holmes and Lawrence Albert as Doctor Watson.

WATSON: And this is Doctor John H. Watson. I had many more adventures during our long friendship, and I'll tell you another one – when next we meet!

The Case of the
Christmas Star
by S.F. Bennett

Glancing through the correspondence I regularly receive concerning my friend, Mr. Sherlock Holmes, I find that chief among the requests are those that ask for some account of his investigations which had a festive flavour. I suspect this may be borne of some whimsical notion that the season lends itself to cases involving merry carol-singers, cherubic children, and happy endings all round. Nothing could be further from the truth, I have found, but if I have been reticent, with one notable exception, it is not due to any curmudgeonly reluctance on my part, but rather, to use Holmes's words, because of a paucity of stimulating material.

It has been my experience that, in general, the professional criminal classes enjoy Christmas as much as the average man, leaving the field open for petty thefts and minor indiscretions by the opportunist, few of which have afforded Holmes with anything but a passing interest. Indeed, it has been the period which follows the festivities that has proved most fruitful, and one day I may gain Holmes's permission to give an account of the Duelling Debutantes of Doncaster and the wishbone which was pivotal to the solution of the mystery.

I say in general, because there are always exceptions to the rule, and one in particular which I have good reason to recall, as the experience nearly proved fatal to all concerned. But for the timely intervention of a remarkable woman, it is not an exaggeration to say that none of us would be alive to tell the tale, and London would have been prematurely deprived of the talents of the foremost detective of his day.

So it was that on the Christmas Eve of the first year of my marriage, I was obliged to call at Baker Street on an errand. Whilst away with my new bride, I had impetuously purchased a wax anatomical model for three shillings from a pawn shop in Aberdeen, with the intention of having it displayed as a curiosity in my surgery. The shopkeeper had promised to despatch it without delay and, anticipating that it would reach London before I did, I gave my old address. I was to learn later that he was not a man of his word, and many weeks passed before Mrs. Hudson informed me of the arrival of a crate.

It had been my intention to call on Holmes in any case, for I was mindful that several weeks had passed since we had last spoken. Armed with a decent brandy, I thought to spend a few hours at Baker Street in convivial companionship, sharing the memory of old times and hearing of his new cases, before returning to home and hearth.

After a dreary journey in unceasing rain, I arrived at my former lodgings to find that Holmes was absent, having left several days before. Mrs. Hudson, too, was on the point of departure, for she answered the door already clad in coat and gloves. I gathered from the bulging carpet bag at the bottom of the stairs that she was to be gone for some time.

"I'm spending a few days with my niece at Margate," she explained. "She had a little girl last month. As it is the baby's first Christmas, I thought I should pay them a visit."

"A holiday for you, Mrs. Hudson," I said brightly.

She looked dubious. "I doubt that, Doctor. It's her first and, between you and me, I think she's struggling. If she's anything like her sister when she had her first, I know who's going to be left doing the cooking and cleaning."

"Mr. Holmes has made other plans for Christmas, I take it?"

"He told me he would be returning this afternoon, Doctor," said she, looking in the hall mirror to adjust her hat. "I offered to leave him a cold collation for tomorrow, but he wouldn't have it. Told me he was perfectly capable of fending for himself for a few days. Well, he'll have to, that's all I can say. I let the maid go home to her parents, so he'll be here on his own."

"Will he?" That prospect troubled me more than I cared to say. The devil makes work for idle hands, and Holmes, without a case, would be idle enough to turn to other diversions. "You don't mind if I wait for him upstairs?"

Mrs. Hudson smiled warmly and patted my arm. "You're always welcome, Dr. Watson. Just remember to take that crate with you when you leave."

It was rather larger than I had anticipated. Five feet by four, made of sturdy wooden slats, it dominated the narrow hallway and almost blocked the bottom of the stairs.

"It's heavy too," Mrs. Hudson went on. "It took two deliverymen to carry it in. I thought the older gentleman was going to pass out. He went a very funny colour."

"I'll have removed by tonight," I promised. "I apologise if it has been an inconvenience."

"No trouble at all, Doctor. I wouldn't have bothered you this side of Christmas, except it has a *peculiar* smell. What is it?"

"A wax model."

"Flowers?"

"A man's torso. Here, let me show you."

She waited patiently with a polite, if puzzled expression on her face while I prised the lid open. The contents had been closely packed with straw and it took me a moment or two to locate the head. It was the face of an older man, realistically rendered, with the skin slightly marbled and the eyelids, with their delicate lashes, closed as if in sleep. There was something unnerving about it when viewed in the gloom of the grey afternoon and flickering gaslight. Perhaps I was imagining it, but I was sure that the hair of the torso I had purchased had been brown, whereas this was iron grey. Some time had lapsed since I had last seen it, however, and I dismissed my uncertainties as mere fancies.

Mrs. Hudson glanced down at it, only to shudder and tighten her scarf about her neck. "Why anyone would want that ghastly thing in their home I don't know. I could understand it if it was Mr. Holmes. He leads you into bad ways, Dr. Watson, I'm sure of it."

I chuckled at her censure. "I had my wife's approval."

"Then she was being diplomatic," said she. "Don't be surprised if an accident befalls that monstrosity. Whatever is that dreadful smell?"

With the lid removed, the odour of putrefaction was stifling. "A rat crawled in and died, I suspect."

"A *legion* of rats from the smell of it. Put the lid back on, Dr. Watson, before the neighbours start complaining. Now, I must be off or I'll miss my train. Will you call me a cab?"

I managed to attract the attention of a passing four-wheeler and, after seeing Mrs. Hudson safely installed inside with cases and umbrella, waved her goodbye. Left alone, I investigated my purchase with greater care. Probing further, I had only to touch the skin to realise my mistake. This was no model of wax, but a deceased person of flesh and blood.

I withdrew in horror, colliding with the hallstand in my haste. At that same moment, the bell rang. In my confusion, I opened it, expecting Holmes, only to find a genial policeman on the doorstep with a sprig of holly in his buttonhole and that patient expression that only comes after years of dealing with the foibles of his fellow man.

"Good afternoon, sir," said he, smiling benignly. "I'm collecting for the Christmas Fund for Police Widows and Orphans. This time of year, we like to look after those less fortunate than ourselves." He shook the collecting tin he was holding vigorously when I was slow to respond. "All donations gratefully received."

"By all means," I said, delving into my pocket and finding a handful of coins.

"Most generous of you, sir," said the sergeant, as the money rattled into the tin. "You know what they say, it's better to give than have it taken from you." He must have seen my agitation, for his smile faded. "Just my little joke, sir." His eyes narrowed with concern. "If you don't mind me asking, sir, are you all right?"

I assured him, somewhat distractedly, that I was.

"I'm glad to hear that." He sniffed. "Blocked drain, is it?"

"What?"

"That queer smell. You've got a blocked drain."

"I dare say."

"I may be able to help you there, sir. My old dad is a plumber. I know a thing or two about pipes."

"Thank you, Sergeant, I can manage," I said, pulling the door shut behind me and trapping myself on the doorstep.

A questioning look came into his eye when he saw my reaction. He craned his head to one side and tried to squint through the narrow crack between door and frame into the gloom of the hallway. "Is there something you don't want me to see in there, sir?"

"Not at all."

"Then you won't mind me taking a look, will you?"

He pushed past me and stepped inside, taking in his surroundings with the practised eye of an expert. As I knew he would, he came to the crate and parted the straw to investigate the contents. I saw the colour promptly drain from his face.

"Just when you think you've seen it all," said he, hurrying to join me outside and taking deep, gulping breaths to clear his lungs. A sheen of cold perspiration shone on his face and he took a moment to mop his forehead with his handkerchief. "Is that what I think it is?"

I nodded. "I am afraid so."

"What's he doing in there?"

"I couldn't say. I thought it was a wax model that they use to teach anatomy to medical students."

"An understandable mistake, sir, under the circumstances. And you have no idea who he is?"

"I've never seen him before in my life."

Something about his manner changed. The sergeant took out his notebook and licked the end of his stubby pencil. "Then why were you trying to hide him from me, sir?"

"I thought you might jump to the wrong conclusion."

"What conclusion might that be?"

I laughed nervously. "I was concerned you might think . . . well, that I had something to do with the poor fellow's death."

"Now why would I think that?" he pressed, one eyebrow now raised in accusation. "Let's start by having your name, sir."

246

"Dr. John Watson."

"And this is your address?"

"No. I live in Paddington, although I am looking for premises to set up my practice."

The sergeant glanced at me curiously. "Well, you won't find any here, sir. Or did you think this fellow in the box was a potential patient?"

"I came to visit Mr. Holmes. He lives here."

"Oh, so it's his crate, is it? Perhaps this Mr. Holmes did away with this here gent, and you're his accomplice." He snapped his notebook shut. "I think you should accompany me to the police station, Dr. Watson. We'll talk this over with my inspector."

I envisaged spending Christmas Day locked in a cell with my wife passing beef sandwiches to me through the bars.

"I fear there has been a misunderstanding," I said. "Do you know Inspector Lestrade?"

"By reputation," he grunted.

"Could you send for him? He would vouch for me."

"Known to the police, are you? I thought so. You've got that shifty look about you." He suddenly paused, took a step back and eyed me thoughtfully. "You're not *that* Dr. Watson, are you?"

"Yes, I am."

"And I suppose this Mr. Holmes is . . . ?" He sighed when I nodded in agreement. "I'll send for the inspector. He can deal with it. I'm off-duty in an hour anyway. You stay here, sir. And try not to touch anything."

He went on his way and I retreated upstairs to pour myself a drink to steady my nerves. No sooner had I downed the contents of a second glass than I heard Holmes's key in the door. I descended to find him entering in the guise of an elderly clergyman, complete with grey wig and whiskers, warts and a prominent overbite.

"Watson, this is unexpected," said he, when he saw me. "Well met, my dear fellow. I was going to call on you this evening to pay you the compliments of the season. One should always observe the usual proprieties, even in these changing times." He paused, his nose wrinkling. "Dear me, is the sewer gas escaping again?"

"Holmes, I have bad news."

"So I see. Was it one brandy or two?"

"Two. However did you know?"

"There is a wet stain upon your lapel. As to the substance, I have always known you to recommend brandy in cases of shock. Your hands were shaking then as they are now, and you spilled it."

"That much is true. As to the rest, something has happened, and I'm expecting Inspector Lestrade."

"Ah, that *is* bad news," said he, removing his hat. The wig came away with it and he stowed it in his pocket. "To what do we owe the pleasure? Confound this crate!" He had collided with it and was giving it further inspection. "Is this yours?"

"It is. I ordered it during our trip to Aberdeen and had it sent here. It was not what I was expecting."

Tentatively, I removed the lid. Holmes caught his breath and drew back.

"I see what you mean, Watson. Most curious. Do we know who he is? No? Then, if would permit me."

So saying, he drew a handkerchief from his pocket, tied it around his head, covering both nose and mouth, and delved into the crate.

"Dead five days, wouldn't you say?"

"About that," I agreed.

"And you've sent for Lestrade?" he asked, lifting the dead man's hand for a closer examination. "He is undoubtedly the man to ask, for unless I am mistaken, this fellow died in police custody. As to the cause, we are left with speculation. Further investigation would necessitate removing the body, and that we should reserve for surroundings other than these."

"That seems unlike you, Holmes."

"I do live here, Watson," said he, straightening up and pulling the handkerchief away. "This corpse has not been embalmed. Or perhaps you would care to explain to Mrs. Hudson why we had to discard the hall carpet?" He looked at me with an expression somewhere between sympathy and amusement. "This is hardly the reaction of an old campaigner. It is not the first corpse we have encountered."

"It is the first sent to me through the post."

"That is a little out of the ordinary, I grant you."

"What you said about where he died, Holmes – why police custody?"

He gestured to me to draw nearer. "How often have I told you that a man's trade may be reflected in his hands? See here, at these new scars overlaying the old. Repeated burns suggest a pattern, in this case of contact with a volatile, unpredictable material. His trade depends upon it. Were it not so, he would have ceased to use it long ago, considering the extent of his injuries. Observe the left hand, two fingers truncated at the second joint. Those he lost in an explosion, I'll wager."

"An old soldier, perhaps?"

"A careless one, if so. On the contrary, I should say he was an amateur. Given his age and uneven muscle tone, consistent with someone in the past who has endured hard labour, my first thought is that he was by profession a cracksman. Not a very good one, admittedly; his latest escapade ended in his capture by the police."

"How do you know he died after being arrested?"

With care, Holmes lifted the head of the corpse and tilted it towards the light. "He was plagued by an ear infection. There is a trace of discharge by the entrance to the ear canal. The same can be seen under his nails, the result of inserting his finger into this ear to scratch the irritation. Note, however, how generally clean the ear is in relation to the rest of his face. After he was arrested, he complained of pain and a doctor was summoned. He died some time after the examination. That is evident from how little new discharge has escaped the ear canal. So much we can ascertain for now. Time and Inspector Lestrade shall tell."

He gently lowered the man's head back onto the straw and returned the lid to the box. "Let me rid myself of these vestments and prepare for our visitor. Help yourself to another brandy, Watson."

"Holmes, why are you dressed like that?" I asked, as I followed him upstairs. "Was it a case?"

"I *had* a case," said he, over his shoulder. "A trifling affair in Somerset. But that is not the reason. At this time of year, my garb has a practical purpose. Tradesmen increase their prices depending on the social standing of their customers, but I find there are few who are willing to take advantage of a man of the cloth."

I was somewhat taken aback by this revelation. "Do you mean to say you impersonated a Vicar to get a discount?"

"To pay a fair price, Watson. There is a difference. I object to paying double simply because it is Christmas. If something was sixpence yesterday, I do not see why I should have to pay three shillings for it today. It is a day like any other. The price should be consistent."

"The police might not see it that way," I suggested.

"Then do not tell them," he called from the depths of his room. He returned a moment later, wiping his face on a towel. He still wore the knee-length clerical frock coat and gaiters, although he had removed the collar. "Are you staying?"

"I think I should."

"I dare say you have other calls upon your time. The last time you were here, you regaled me with tales of horror concerning the state of your present accommodation."

"I may have found something permanent. There is a decayed practice a few streets away from my current address."

"Then it should be ideal. I have never known you to shy away from a challenge."

"We may have to wait a few months before it becomes available. It has other problems too."

"Which you shall no doubt overcome," said Holmes, as he swept past. "Now, forgive me, Watson, I have a dead man in the hall and an inspector of Scotland Yard imminent. Your domestic trifles shall have to wait."

I did not take offence. It has been my experience, as a rule, that a man's household arrangements are of little interest to any save himself.

"All the same, I shall stay until Lestrade arrives," I replied. "I am curious about the man myself."

"As you wish. If you are hungry, there are biscuits in the tin and walnuts in the bowl. That is the best I can offer. Mrs. Hudson has gone to Kent."

"You'll be dining with your brother, I dare say."

A flurry of papers cascaded to the floor, followed by a glove, a penknife and an ancient candle-snuffer as Holmes rifled through the clutter on the mantelpiece for a cigarette. Lighting it, he threw the spent match into the grate, from where it bounced onto the rug and smouldered into nothingness.

"Mycroft has gone to ground until the New Year," he explained. "The Diogenes Club has closed its doors on the world until the Lord of Misrule is again in his box. The members shall be fed and watered, secure in the knowledge that they will be protected from the spirit of Christmas for yet another year."

"Then you will be here alone?"

"Unless a client comes calling." Veiled by the smoke of his cigarette, his expression was unreadable. "There has been precious little of late, however, so that possibility seems unlikely. There was that business of the theft of the Christmas Star last week, but Scotland Yard seems to have that well in hand."

"In that case," I began, sensing that his answer was likely to be a refusal, "would you care to join us tomorrow?"

"I fear I must disappoint you, Watson. I have to leave for Milan on Thursday. Before then, I have two days to learn all I can about the painting techniques of Caravaggio. There is a question of provenance concerning a depiction of St. John the Baptist which may explain the deaths of three art critics, a nun, and a Spanish grandee."

Our conversation was interrupted by the sudden clatter of the bell. Downstairs, we found Lestrade on the doorstep, looking disgruntled. He cast a critical eye over Holmes's apparel and his frown deepened.

"What's this? You off to a fancy ball, Mr. Holmes?"

"If so, Lestrade, it is a *Danse Macabre*. Come in."

"I'm not in the mood for your little games," said the inspector, wearily. "I have to be home by five. The wife is expecting me. Good afternoon, Dr. Watson. I had a message from a Sergeant Shaw, something about you having an unexpected guest."

"A most irregular one," said Holmes. With a flourish, he removed the lid from the crate. Lestrade wandered over, took a cursory glance and withdrew sharply, suppressing the urge to vomit.

"I see what you mean," said he, covering his mouth with a handkerchief.

"Are you missing a body, Lestrade?" asked Holmes.

A look of annoyance flashed in the inspector's eyes. "How the devil do you know that?"

A fleeting smile lifted the corners of Holmes's mouth, although he said nothing.

Lestrade stifled a sigh. "It wasn't meant to be public knowledge, but, yes, the boys of E Division did lose a body a couple of nights ago. It appears the remains in question vanished late in the evening, while the orderlies were out at the local public house. One of them had had a windfall and bought everyone a drink. The next morning, they found they were missing a corpse."

"Stolen," Holmes stated.

"I should say so," said Lestrade with a dry chuckle. "It didn't get up and walk out on its own."

"Who would steal a corpse?" I asked.

Our friend looked imperiously down his nose. "Ever heard of Burke and Hare, Dr. Watson?"

"The Anatomy Act of 1832 put paid to that particular practice."

"I suppose you have some theory, Mr. Holmes?" Lestrade enquired grudgingly.

"Several, all of which depend on the identification of this individual. Do you know him?"

Lestrade nodded. "'Honest' Harris Henderson, petty villain of this parish. Blowing up safes is his speciality. Almost blown himself to kingdom come a few times too. He's been in and out of prison more times than you've had hot dinners."

"Hardly honest then," I said incredulously.

"Ah, that's just our name for him," Lestrade explained. "Whenever he's arrested, the first thing he always says is: 'It weren't me, guv'nor, *honest* it wasn't'." His humour faded. "Not that he'll be saying it any more, poor old devil."

"How did he die?" asked Holmes.

"From what I was told, he was arrested in Hatton Garden on suspicion of theft. You've heard about the disappearance of the Christmas Star, I suppose?"

Holmes nodded, but I shook my head.

"We're talking about twelve diamonds, cut from a single stone," Lestrade explained. "They were to be mounted in a setting surrounding a blue diamond. The shape suggested the name, as you can imagine. It was to be presented to Her Majesty on Christmas Day as a gift from certain of her loyal subjects."

"Henderson was suspected of stealing the diamonds from the jeweller's workshop," said Holmes.

"He was there. They caught him red-handed. He had a housebreaker's kit in his pocket and a jemmy down his trouser leg."

"But no diamonds."

"The theory was he had hidden them somewhere before he was arrested. They tried the usual tactics – said they would have a word with the judge, the promise of a lighter sentence, and such like – but he wasn't telling. Then he starts complaining of pain, first in his ear and then in his stomach. The next thing they knew, he was dead."

Holmes started abruptly. "When was this?"

"Thursday."

"And the body went missing?"

"Four days ago."

"When did the crate arrive?"

"Mrs. Hudson sent word this morning," I told him.

"They are hours ahead of us!" he exclaimed. "We should take precautions. To delay would be foolish in the extreme."

"We can't abandon the body," Lestrade protested.

"Inspector, this crate was intended for somebody. That person will know by now that there has been a mistake. Looking at the way the name and address has been chalked on the lid, I should say the error occurred at a railway station."

"That is probably true," I said. "It was sent from Aberdeen."

"Envisage a situation where the labels came off two boxes which were almost identical," Holmes continued. "A porter, trying to be helpful, attempts to match names to crates, with the resulting confusion. Whoever was expecting the body of Henderson now has Dr. Watson's box. In his place, I should ask the deliverymen if they had any crates of a similar dimension. Ah," he breathed; "but it may already be too late."

I followed his gaze to the open doorway to where two men had appeared. The elder was a stern, hard-faced man of impressive stature with receding hair and dark, restless eyes burning beneath shaggy grey brows. His companion, an ugly, misshapen individual, with a nose as bent and twisted as a wind-blown tree, was short and stocky, his mouth curled in a perpetual grin that revealed sharp, pointed teeth.

The sight of them was enough to make Lestrade catch his breath. Tension rolled across his shoulders, and he moved to put himself between us and the newcomers.

"Well, well, gentleman," said the older man, strolling in with the casual air of someone doing nothing more remarkable than taking a walk in the park. "It seems you've got something of ours. And look who's here, Lestrade of the Yard."

"Now, Georgie, there's no need to be hasty – "

"That's *Mr. Fowler* to you," he snapped. "Respect, Inspector. I always demand it."

"Stuffing a dead man in crate doesn't sound like respect to me," Lestrade retorted.

A smooth smile creased the lines about his mouth. "Everyone ends up in a box sooner or later," said Fowler. "Ain't that the truth, Vicar?" He glanced at Holmes. "Shouldn't you be in church? This is your busiest time of year, ain't it?"

The ruffians chuckled before Fowler's gaze turned to me.

"You must be Dr. John Watson. We've got your . . . what would you call it, Bailey?"

"A wax doll, Mr. Fowler," said the younger man.

"A wax doll, yes. Imagine our surprise. Gave us quite a turn, didn't it, Bailey?"

"Yes, guv'nor, quite a turn."

"There's us expecting old Harris and all we got was a glorified candle with a bad wig. Now, I don't say it was your fault, Doctor. There was a mix-up at King's Cross. You got ours and we got yours."

"Take him and go," said Lestrade.

"Now wait a minute," I protested, only to feel Holmes's hand close about my arm in warning.

"Yes, don't be hasty, Inspector," said Fowler. "That's not very hospitable, what with it being Christmas. No room at the inn, eh, Vicar?"

Holmes managed a weak smile. "All the same, the inspector has a point. Convey the gentleman to his final resting place, with our blessings."

"I would, Vicar, but you see, this delay has caused me problems. It's a good thing we've a doctor on hand. Happy coincidence, you might say. You're going to help us, Dr. Watson."

"The devil I am."

253

"Reconsider."

The revolver that had appeared in his hand was persuasive.

"What's through there?" said he, gesturing down the hallway.

"The kitchen," I replied.

"Good, then that's where we'll go. Now don't try anything, Vicar. I know the Lord helps them what helps themselves, but getting shot won't help you none unless you feel like getting closer to your maker. And just to be sure . . . ."

He grabbed Lestrade around the neck and pressed the muzzle to the side of his head.

"Try something," he hissed in his ear.

"I wouldn't give you the satisfaction."

"Oh, you will, Inspector. Believe me, you will."

With Bailey leading the way, we were marched down the corridor and into Mrs. Hudson's domain. The kitchen, as always, was clean and tidy, a perfume of lavender in the air tempered with undertones of carbolic. In the centre of the room was the table with its fresh white cloth and striking red poinsettia, and around it, four wooden chairs, smelling strongly of beeswax.

"Sit down, Vicar," Fowler ordered. "Bailey, tie him to the chair."

"Is this really necessary?" said Holmes, assuming a placative tone of voice. "Violence is never the answer, my son. It is the season of forgiveness."

"You think the inspector here'll be so forgiving with his brains spread across the wall? I said, sit down!"

Holmes was obliged to do as he was told. Bailey produced a length of twine from his pocket and expertly bound his hands behind his back. The procedure was repeated on me and then finally on Lestrade. Satisfied we were in no position to cause trouble, the pair returned to the hall.

"It's always a pleasure coming here," said Lestrade gruffly.

I could not blame him for the bitterness in his voice.

"I take it you know these ruffians?" I asked.

"Yes, I know them," he grunted. "Georgie Fowler is a nasty piece of work. Born rotten, if you ask me. He's the worst sort, a villain with ambition."

"Then why is he still at large?"

Lestrade's eyes flashed with irritation. "It's not through want of trying, Dr. Watson. 'Innocent until proven guilty', that's the law of the land. It's a question of proof. There's always someone else to take the blame."

"You have proof now."

"Much good it'll do me." Lestrade spared me a pitying glance. "Why do you imagine he isn't behind bars? Fowler doesn't like policeman."

"How does he feel about doctors?"

"The same way he feels about clergymen, I imagine. And private detectives. You're lucky he doesn't know how to read, Mr. Holmes."

"I fear our 'luck' is in short supply, Lestrade." Holmes had been fidgeting in his chair and now paused, his breath coming quickly. "It may be possible to break these bonds. A sharp implement would be better, but as you see, Mrs. Hudson is tidy to a fault. Failing that, the uprights of this chair may go some way to fraying the twine. Unfortunately, it is of excellent quality. Our visitors came prepared."

"A pity we weren't," Lestrade grumbled.

"You can hardly lay the blame at our door," said Holmes. "From the moment Henderson died, it should have been obvious what had happened."

"It was not my case!"

"And yet here we are."

"I don't understand," I spoke up. "What does Fowler want with me?"

Holmes managed a tight smile. "Very soon, Watson, Fowler is going to ask you to do something. Whether you comply or not is entirely up to you. Both Lestrade and I would prefer that you did, for you may buy us some time. Whatever you choose, however, know that the end result may be the same. Do not blame yourself."

"Whatever I can do, I will, Holmes, you know you can rely on me. What is this task?"

"He is going to ask you to perform an autopsy, my dear fellow. Here, on the kitchen table, I shouldn't wonder."

I stared at him. "But that's monstrous! Why?"

"Because Henderson had the diamonds all along. He swallowed them. A hard object may pass through the digestive system without causing damage. I dare say you will discover, however, that the diamonds of the Christmas Star have sharp edges. They would have ripped through his gut like a knife through paper, causing catastrophic internal bleeding. A terrible death."

"Save your sympathy for us, Mr. Holmes," said Lestrade. "We're going to need it."

"But surely," I said; "once Fowler has what he wants – "

"He'll kill all of us. He never leaves witnesses. I was hoping he'd take the body and leave. I don't think much of our chances once he tells us about the diamonds."

It was a sobering thought. We sat there in silence, Holmes still struggling with his bonds and Lestrade in grim acceptance of what was about to happen. From the hall came the sounds of activity, the scraping of wood across the floor and grunts of exertion.

"Some Christmas this is turning out to be," said the inspector dolefully. "This was meant to be my day off. I only came in today because the wife's parents are staying. Her father's a good sort, a bit too fond of his drink, but her mother has a tongue like a whiplash. It's bad enough without her lecturing me about Frederick."

"Who?" I asked.

"Her other son-in-law. An accountant, doing well for himself. Got his own business and employs fourteen people. And then there's me. She wants to know why I'm not a superintendent."

So saying, Lestrade glanced up at the clock. The hands stood at five minutes to five.

"Right about now, the children will be dressing the tree. I said I'd be home to help them." He gave me a rueful smile. "The wife's nagging mother suddenly doesn't seem so bad, after all. How are you getting on with that twine, Mr. Holmes?"

"I believe I am almost free," came his breathless reply.

"Try harder. They're coming back."

The door was kicked open, and Bailey entered, walking backwards and carrying the feet of the unfortunate Harris Henderson, with Fowler holding his shoulders. With effort, they heaved the naked body onto the table, knocking the plant onto the floor, where it spilled earth and scarlet petals across the polished tiles.

Decay was well advanced. The body was marbled and bloated, with the abdomen grotesquely distended. In the confines of the kitchen, the smell was suffocating.

"Now, Doctor," said Fowler, gesturing to his accomplice to untie my hands. "I'm in need of your professional services. You see, Mr. Henderson here has something of mine and I want it back. I had a doctor waiting to open him up back home, but since he's here and not getting any fresher, I want you to do it. Thirteen diamonds, that's what he's got in there."

"What you are asking me to do is barbaric," I retorted.

Fowler's eyes held a hard gleam of spite. A jerk of his head caused Bailey to rummage through the kitchen drawers. Finding a large knife, he grabbed Holmes by the hair, pulled back his head and held the blade to his exposed throat.

"What do you say, Vicar?" said Fowler, almost conversationally. "Do you find it barbaric?"

256

"I'll tell you what's barbaric," spoke up Lestrade. "Killing a man for a handful of diamonds."

Bailey released Holmes, and we all breathed again. Fowler turned his cold gaze on the inspector.

"Who says I killed him?"

"You had him so scared he would have died rather than hand those gems over to us."

A slow smile spread across Fowler's face. "You couldn't be further from the truth. He came to me, Henderson did, a few weeks ago. His lungs were rotten, he told me. Said he had weeks to live. Asked me if I could help him, one last job, he said. Well, I didn't like to refuse. When I told him what I had in mind, he jumped at the idea. He wanted his daughter to get his share of the money. You didn't know he had a daughter, did you, Lestrade?"

"No, I did not," he answered.

"And didn't care none, either," Fowler spat. "Well, he wasn't much of a father. He knew that. He'd left her and her mother when she was a babe in arms. Hadn't given them a thought since, so he said. But when a man knows his time is up, his thoughts turn to family. He had a conscience, and he knew the girl was in need. She's got a young 'un of her own. I'll see she gets her share."

"Are you saying he swallowed the diamonds on purpose? I don't believe it."

"And broken glass too, just to be sure it killed him. There was no other way to get the diamonds out of the workshop. He knew he would be caught. The plan was that once he was dead, we would get his body and retrieve the goods." Fowler sneered at the inspector. "You're a family man, Lestrade. What would you do for your children? Shall we find out?"

"Fowler," I called to him. "I'll do what you want."

"Good. Hold that thought, Inspector." He patted Lestrade's shoulder before wandering over to me. "If it's any consolation, Dr. Watson, he died a happy man."

"I find that hard to believe."

"He was adamant he wanted to go this way. Said he didn't want to die alone in some hovel where he wouldn't be discovered for weeks. No one cared about him, you see. No friends, no family, no one to notice when he wasn't around any more. So he got his wish. I dare say the police looked after him at the end. They even cleaned out his dirty ears. Now, get on with it."

"I do not have a scalpel."

Fowler grabbed another knife from the drawer and slapped it down hard on the dead man's chest. "Improvise."

I had no choice. My soul revolted at what I had to do. Against that, I had to weigh the lives of Holmes and Lestrade. I picked up the knife and tested it. Mrs. Hudson was meticulous about keeping a keen edge on her blades, and I was not disappointed. I thought for a moment about trying to turn the tables. Fowler must have seen my hesitation, for again he gestured to Bailey to place the knife at Holmes's throat.

"Just in case, Doctor. Don't you go getting any clever ideas."

I steeled myself and took a deep breath. Before I could make the first incision, from the hallway came the sound of a key in the front door. Fowler took a step back, his finger to his lips, warning us to stay silent. I could hear Mrs. Hudson muttering to herself about the state of the carpet before the footsteps started determinedly in our direction. The door opened and Fowler started forward with the revolver.

"Stay where you are," he growled.

Mrs. Hudson was momentarily taken aback, and then, with a deft move that took us all by surprise, hit him over the head with her umbrella. He reeled back, stunned, and in that moment, Holmes pulled his hands free of his bonds and grabbed Bailey's arm. While they struggled, with the knife inches from his face, I hurried to help Mrs. Hudson, but she had proved to be more than capable of fending off the villain. She picked up the gun that he had dropped and, pointing it at the ceiling, pulled the trigger. The shot made us all pause.

"You, young man, put down that knife and leave Mr. Holmes alone," she ordered.

Bailey quailed and did what he was told. Holmes rounded on him and knocked him to the ground, while I freed the inspector from his bonds. Lestrade took the revolver from Mrs. Hudson and trained it on Fowler.

"Your turn to sit down, *Mr.* Fowler," said he. "Keep your hands where I can see them. That's right. Dr. Watson, tie him up, and his friend too."

"Mr. Holmes, what has been going on here?" Mrs. Hudson said with evident displeasure. "Look at my plant. And my best tablecloth too. Cover that poor man up. Let him have some dignity."

"Mrs. Hudson, we are indebted to you," said Holmes, removing his coat and placing over the corpse Mr. Henderson. "Your assistance has proved invaluable."

"Yes, indeed," I agreed. "Where did you learn to use a revolver?"

She blushed a little. "Before I met my late husband, I was a nurse at a Seamen's Hospital, Doctor. They all kept mementoes of their travels;

258

I've seen more guns in my time than I care to say. And I've had plenty of experience of dealing with troublesome men, too," she added, with a sideways glance at Fowler.

I laughed. "Then we are most fortunate that you returned. But why are you here? I thought you'd gone to Margate."

"I got all the way to the station and I realised I'd forgotten the bonnet I'd knitted for the baby." She opened a drawer and took out a parcel neatly tied with string. "I'll be going on my way now, gentlemen. My train leaves in half-an-hour." She nodded to the covered mound of the dead man. "I shall expect a new tablecloth, Mr. Holmes. And that table will need scrubbing with carbolic."

With that, she turned on her heel and left.

"Remarkable woman, your Mrs. Hudson" said Lestrade with something approaching awe. "Well, I'd better send word to the local constabulary. These two will be spending Christmas in the cells."

"I should have killed you," muttered Fowler.

"You won't get the chance again. Nor you, Bailey. As for Mr. Henderson here, I'll have the mortuary send the cart. Keep an eye on them."

The inspector left, and shortly thereafter we were overwhelmed with policemen. Fowler and Bailey were taken away, and a stretcher was brought in to remove the body. Several constables set to work with scrubbing brushes, and soon it was as though the drama of the afternoon had never occurred.

"I'll be going home now, Mr. Holmes," said Lestrade when the last of the constables had departed. His gaze was drawn back to the table. "Makes you think, doesn't it? What *would* we do for our children if we were in his shoes?"

"Pray that we never have to find out," I said.

He nodded. "Good evening to you both. Merry Christmas."

"Lestrade," Holmes called after him. "What of the daughter? I understand there was a reward for the return of the diamonds."

"Seeing as how it was her father that took them, I can't see any money being forthcoming."

"And yet he has returned them."

Lestrade shrugged. "I'll see what I can do. Is there anything else?"

"Your wife's mother may praise her other son-in-law, yet she chooses to spend Christmas with you and your family. What are we to make of that?"

The inspector stared at him for a long moment before departing with a thoughtful expression. We followed him to the front door and watched him stride away down the darkened street, collar turned up against the penetrating drizzle. Suddenly devoid of people, the house felt cold and echoing.

"Holmes, about tomorrow," I began. "Will you not reconsider?"

"I do not share Mr. Henderson's fears about solitude, if that is your concern," said he firmly. "Nor have I been seized by any maudlin sentiment because of the events of earlier. It was not without certain features of interest."

I failed to suppress a shudder. "You may call it that. I thought the whole business was thoroughly disturbing."

"That is because you are focusing on the method of the man's death and not the motive. 'It is a far, far better thing that I do, than I have ever done' may be applied as equally to Harris Henderson as to Sydney Carton. The concept of noble sacrifice," he added; "may take many forms."

He laid his hand consolingly on my shoulder.

"There is nothing like a brush with death to sharpen the intellect. We are none the worse for our ordeal. As for you, my dear fellow, you should return to your home. Your wife will wonder what has happened to you. Merry Christmas, Watson."

"You too, Holmes."

I left, feeling somewhat reassured. Events and the demands of a new practice would conspire to keep us apart, and it was to be some time before I saw Holmes again.

I did, however, learn a little more of the case from accounts in the press. Lestrade naturally took the credit for the recovery of the Christmas Star diamonds, although I was to discover later that a portion of the reward money had been paid to Mr. Henderson's daughter as a gesture of goodwill. My wax bust was found at the Fowler residence and sent to me. It resided in my surgery for a number of years, and I could never look upon it without counting my blessings and remembering the events of that Christmas Eve. Then one day, while we were moving to our new home in Kensington, the model suffered a mysterious accident and was damaged beyond repair. How Mrs. Hudson predicted this I cannot say, but it would not surprise me at all if she was able to list foresight among her many and considerable talents.

The Christmas Card Mystery
by Narrelle M. Harris

On a squally day in the second week of December, and being in the neighbourhood to visit a patient, I called upon Baker Street to convey my regards to my old friend, Mr. Sherlock Holmes. Mrs. Hudson ushered me into the hall with warm greetings and the news that Holmes was out on a case.

"I shouldn't intrude, then . . ." I began.

"No intrusion, Doctor Watson," she promised me, "And it's wet enough out there, and cold enough, for you to stop by the fire a while. You're a busy man and mustn't make yourself unwell with a chill." Mrs. Hudson deftly relieved me of my hat, scarf, gloves, and coat so gently and relentlessly that I was in 221b and before the fire without offering a single protest.

In truth, I was glad to be out of the blustery, sleeting wind, and with my wife away a week visiting the lately mourning Mrs. Forrester, her old employer and friend, it was lonely at home. I missed, too, the old days of mysteries and liked to see, from time to time, if I might be of assistance again. Perhaps if he was on a case, I might be so fortunate again today.

I stood in front of the hearth warming my hands, noting that Holmes had left my old chair exactly where it had always been, beside his. I dared fancy he might at times miss my company in his endeavours, too, and hoped that I may visit.

The mantelpiece was as cluttered as ever with pipes and the Persian slipper, a few stray plugs of tobacco held against his morning smoke, unopened correspondence, the clock, a collection of curved wooden shapes of obscure function, and a retort containing pale yellow fluid sitting in a cradle – some half-completed or completely forgotten experiment, no doubt. The morocco case was thankfully not to be seen. An engaging case, then.

Sitting among all of this habitual detritus were five Christmas cards, each depicting scenes of a macabre humour. A frog that had stabbed its fellow, two naked-plucked geese with a man on a roasting spit, a wasp chasing two children with the unlikely subtitle *A Joyous New Year*, a savage white bear crushing an explorer in *A Hearty Welcome*, and a dead robin which read *May yours be a joyful Christmas*. The latter at least hearkened to the Christ story, the rest to a certain black wit about Holmes's profession.

It seemed likely to me that one card had been sent by Lestrade, others by Gregson or Jones. I took up the card depicting the frog-murder but found it inscribed merely with *To my dear friend* at the top and *Mrs. Inke Pullitts* underneath. The script was disorderly, as though done in haste, and struck me as more a masculine than a feminine hand.

I was startled out of my examination when the door flew open and Sherlock Holmes strode through it, a dozen newspapers under his arm.

"Ah, Watson, I see you are making yourself at home! No, no, my dear fellow, go right ahead, and tell me what you make of my Yuletide correspondence while I pour us a brandy. It's a cruel day out, and my blood's in need of warming."

He abandoned the papers over the arm of his chair. His pale cheeks were rosy with the cold he'd just escaped, and his grey eyes sparkled with the merriment I had long associated with an intriguing case.

"I had thought our friends at Scotland Yard were sending you cards," I admitted, "But I realise I must be quite wrong. They've never sent you any before now." In fact, Holmes rarely received such personal missives, except from me and Mary or his brother, Mycroft Holmes. "Did you retain the envelopes?"

Holmes placed two glasses on the table and fetched five envelopes from beneath a book on folklore. The topmost he gave to me. I examined it closely – it was addressed in the same untidy hand as the card to the attention of *Mr. S Holmes*, though scrawled so untidily as to appear to read "Mrs. Hulmes". The paper was inexpensive, matching the quality of the card, and bore no return address. The corner of the envelope was marked, fore and aft, with a peculiar indentation, as though it had contained something other than the greeting. I saw a similar mark upon the matching card. I sniffed the paper, as I had seen Holmes do in his investigations, but it told me nothing and made me feel foolish. I couldn't bring myself to dab the tip of my tongue to the paper, another of Holmes's investigative techniques.

"What was in it?" I asked.

He selected two of the wooden shapes from the mantel and held them between thumb and forefinger for me to see. The first was like a misshapen peg, three inches long, and almost a teardrop shape when viewed from the end that was rough with bark. The piece tapered slightly here – perhaps the top of the piece – though the other end was only a fraction thicker. The second piece, when viewed from the bark end, formed a rough U. They appeared to be carved from oak, as did the other pieces on the mantel when I examined them, though the wood was marred in places with a dark stain.

The remaining cards and their envelopes were alike in their particulars: addressed *To my dear friend* as from *Mrs. Inke Pullitts* and variously dented from the inclusion of the odd peg.

"Who is Mrs. Pullitts?" I then asked. With a broad smile, he told me he knew no such lady, and all his enquiries, made with advertisements in the papers and the gossip-gathering prowess of the Irregulars, had uncovered no person of that name who might seek him.

I was tempted to dismiss it all as a meaningless prank, but was too wise to say so. If this prank had stirred Holmes to the point of broad smiles and the spark of merriment in his eye, then it was a puzzle worth his attention.

A puzzle. I turned again to the mantel and took up the wooden pegs and U-shapes that lay there in a pile so that I might examine them more closely. Holmes beamed his approval at me as I set them on the table, and I confess I felt it as a high praise. He sipped on the brandy, but I ignored mine in favour of the puzzle of the pegs.

"These pieces seem to fit together," I said, "And this third." The three pieces indeed sat snugly together, bar the slender gaps created by the tapering. The grain of the wood and gnarled pattern of the external part betrayed their origin. "Hewn from the same oak log."

"Splendid," said Holmes. "What else?"

"Mrs. Pullitts is sending you this puzzle in a strangely piecemeal fashion, though for what reason I cannot surmise, unless it's to keep the sending of it secret from a member of her household – Mr. Pullitts perhaps? She has even attempted to disguise your name, unless it's simply that her handwriting is terrible. It would be so much easier to send a discreet letter, so I must conclude it's a vital secret."

"Well done, Watson, though as I've said, I know of no Mrs. Inke Pullitts, or of anyone of the name of either Inke or Pullitts. I don't think this letter comes from a woman at all."

"I did wonder at the more mannish stroke of the pen. A pseudonym, you think?"

"Perhaps, or a clue in itself."

"A clue?" I frowned. "How so?"

Holmes clapped me on the shoulder. "Drink your brandy and I'll show you." He fetched fifteen squares of paper from beneath the book of folklore to show where he had written the individual letters of his correspondent's name.

"Having ascertained that I knew of no *Inke*," he said, "I thought to look at the name in the light of one of the simplest codes. The little scenes on the cards and what appears to be parts of a child's wooden puzzle led to me think along a certain path." I must have looked quite blank for he added, "Consider it an anagram, Watson, and it may lead you to my own conclusion."

I placed my brandy aside and spent some time shifting squares of paper about the table. It was only by separating the letters of the word 'stilts' that the solution came to me. The letters spelled out *Rumpelstiltskin.*

"This really makes it no clearer to me, Holmes," I said, exasperated.

"No?"

"No. A fairy tale character is sending you macabre Christmas greetings and a child's wooden puzzle, but to what end? Your Rumpelstiltskin may be simply trying to test his wits against yours to pass the tedium of the season."

"Oh, Watson." His disappointment was palpable. "Taken alone, these cards may signify a certain pawky sense of humour, but taken as a collection, sent by the same nameless person taking such pains to keep their communiques secret, I fear it adds up to something sinister. Don't you recall the story of Rumpelstiltskin?"

"Yes, yes. The girl whose father swears she can spin gold from straw, and the King threatens to kill the girl if the boast isn't proven. Rumpelstiltskin uses magic to accomplish the feat for her, and demands her firstborn. But Holmes, this is mere childish nonsense. In any case, Rumpelstiltskin is the villain of the piece."

"That story has several villains in it, Watson, but for our purposes, I think we may reasonably hypothesise that our correspondent doesn't identify as the goblin, but uses the name to signal to us his dilemma."

"Which is?"

"What's the crux of the story, Watson?"

"A girl's held prisoner until she performs an impossible feat. She dupes her way out of death with fairy assistance, and then has to outwit her helper to save her child."

"Exactly!"

"How does this help?" My confusion was leading to annoyance.

Holmes shook his head at me. "You are a teller of tall stories, Watson. You should surely see the artistic licence in this one."

I was too used to his teasing references to my stories to be stung, but a reminder that I was sometimes required to alter details in my chronicles to protect certain parties (occasionally ourselves) suggested the solution.

"Your correspondent is held against his will – perhaps to achieve some difficult feat – and has found a way to send to you this plea for assistance."

Holmes clapped his hands and grinned. "Indeed! He must be held under some very tight scrutiny, to be unable to send a clearer message, yet with sufficient freedom to slip a card into the mail. He's very careful to disguise its destination, so he must feel certain that his gaoler would intercept anything that's too obvious."

I frowned and picked up one of the pegs. "I can't see how this will help you find the poor fellow."

"Have faith, Watson! And patience, and if you'll be kind enough to help me examine these papers, you might join me in a rescue mission. If you have the time, of course."

"All the time in the world, my dear fellow," I declared. I took up several of the papers, flung myself into my old chair, and opened the *Bromley and District Times*. "What am I looking for?"

Holmes sat opposite me with the *London Evening Standard*. "Anything that may strike you as relevant to a wooden puzzle, Watson, or any other unusual feature."

We began to go through each newspaper. I scanned smaller items as well as large, and even the advertisements, my efforts going much more slowly than Holmes's. He whipped impatiently through each page. He flung each paper aside with a grunt of irritation as he completed his search, while I folded them more neatly to drop on the floor beside me.

"These are all local papers, I see," I said after a moment, "What if he's from farther afield?"

"No, no! The postmark, Watson!" He softened his irascibility a little, "Though you couldn't know when each card arrived. I do, however, and the time between the postmark and delivery is so short that the sender *must* be within the metropolis. Oh, this is promising." He tore the page from the paper and rose, thrusting it at me. As he reached once more for his coat, hat and gloves, I read the obviously related story, a small piece in the corner of page five of *The Echo*.

> *Would anyone knowing the whereabouts of Mr. Silas North, cabinetmaker and carpenter of Chester Street, Lambeth, missing now for fifteen days, please make this known to his employer, Mr. Abel Sudbury. Mrs. North would also be pleased to hear from her husband.*

Our hansom deposited us before a row of three smart terraces that had once been more uniform, but now displayed a variety of railings, eaves and other decorative touches. The first's embellishments were primarily in woodwork, the next in ironwork and a third, ceramics.

"This will be Mr. North's home, I think," said Holmes. This house was trimmed in intricately carved wooden eaves and elegant window frames and shutters.

"These terraces are all owned by Abel Sudbury," explained Holmes as we headed for the door painted in fine, fresh blue, "Accommodation for the master craftsmen in his employ in the building trade. You'll note how he uses the buildings to showcase the skills he can offer his clients. This particular house offers the finest examples of woodwork. The right home for a master carpenter, wouldn't you say?"

Holmes's knock was answered by a harried looking woman of middle age. A small child with a round, sticky face hung upon her skirts and an older girl bustled towards them. "Here, now Bess, what did I say? Leave Mam alone for the door."

Little Bess gazed widely at us. I smiled at her and she ran away to hide behind her sister.

Holmes gave the woman a small bow. "Mrs. North. My name is Sherlock Holmes. I – "

"Oh, I know of you, Mr. Holmes!" said Mrs. North with a breathy sigh of relief, "Judy, my eldest, read out that story in *Beeton's*! Have you come to tell us where Silas has gone?"

"I'm afraid not, Mrs. North – but I have come in an endeavour to *find* him."

We were welcomed into the tidy little home and shown to the parlour while Mrs. North went to instruct the maid to prepare tea. Beyond the door, I heard the piping of young voices, and a motherly admonishment to hush and be good children.

While we waited for refreshment, Holmes prowled around the parlour, gleaning all he could about the family and their missing patriarch.

My efforts to follow Holmes's methods led me to conclude that the Norths had five children – two girls and three boys – and that Mr. North was a highly skilled craftsman, if it was his work that had furnished their home. The joinery and finishes were the best I had ever seen, and through my association with Holmes I had been in a good many exquisitely furnished apartments. The parlour was also filled with beautiful hand-made toys, many scuffed with loving use and age. On the top of a small bookshelf – filled with books by the likes of Ballantyne and Stevenson – was an unusually designed wooden castle and a regiment of painted soldiers.

The parlour spoke of a warm and loving family life, and I confess I felt a pang of envy. Mary and I had hoped before now to have our own home so filled with happy children.

Mrs. North and her maid returned with tea, and Holmes remained remarkably patient until all was settled to our hostess's satisfaction. Mrs. North sat on the edge of a chair commonly used for needlepoint, judging by the basket of work to one side. Her hands were clasped tightly together in an attempt to settle her agitation. Holmes sat opposite her, touching her wrist briefly in a gesture of reassurance, before leaning forward attentively, elbows on knees and fingers steepled.

I sat across from them with my tea and my notebook.

"When exactly did your husband disappear?" Holmes began, ignoring the cup at his elbow, "Tell me everything you recall about that day."

Mrs. North pressed her lips together, met his gaze with resolve and told her tale.

"He left us fifteen days ago today, on November the 29th. He had his breakfast as usual, waved us goodbye on the stoop and walked towards Kennington Station – he was catching the tube to a house in Angel, where he and Mr. Sudbury were to meet with a client, a Mrs. Babcock. Silas never arrived at the house. I knew nothing of it until Mr. Sudbury came to the door, very cross too, to see why he hadn't come."

"What did you do?"

"I sent Freddie with Mr. Sudbury to walk to the station, but nobody there knew anything, nor had they seen Silas."

"What steps did you take then?"

"We went to the police of course, but they've found nothing. Someone near the station thought they'd seen Silas get into a hansom with someone, but they couldn't be sure, and one hansom looks much like another. The police haven't found a cabman who'll own it they picked him up, and there's been nothing since. Except this."

Mrs. North rose to pluck a Christmas card from her mantelpiece. It depicted two owls on a bench, one in a top hat, the other in a bonnet. The inscription read *"Maudie"* at the top and *"I'll be home soon, God willing, S."* at the bottom.

Holmes examined the card minutely then held it out to me. The only thing clear to me was that the handwriting matched that of Holmes's mysterious Rumpelstiltskin.

"When did this arrive?"

"A week ago, only the police could make nothing of it. They say it only means he has run off for his own reasons and will be back or not as he pleases. They gave up looking. But Mr. Sudbury, who is a good man, knows my Silas as well as me, and we know he wouldn't just take off like this. There must be a reason he's away, and if he could come home he would. Only I've no notion why he can't!" Her harried look, kept at bay, returned, heralded by anxious tears. "If you can only tell me where he is, Mr. Holmes, I'll go and fetch him myself, or Mr. Sudbury will send a lad. This isn't like him! Please don't tell me, like that Inspector Bartle did, that Silas has run off. If he'd done so, why would he write?"

Holmes hushed her with a pat on her wrist. "I can assure you, Mrs. North, your husband is trying to return to you. Do you have the envelope this card came in?"

"No. Oh! Should I have kept it?"

"It may have been instructive, but I shall persevere without it. Now, can you tell us of the days before your husband disappeared? Did he seem preoccupied or anxious?"

"He was his usual self. He's a man of few words, my Silas, and soft-spoken when he has something to say. Though there was the gent, came to the door the week before. Silas wasn't pleased with his being there, but no hard words were exchanged that I know. I heard none of their conversation, and when I asked, Silas only said, 'The persistent fellow offers a fascinating commission, but I work for Mr. Sudbury, and that's that.' His contract with Mr. Sudbury is very watertight on that point – Silas isn't allowed to work for others."

Mrs. North was unable, however, to describe this "persistent fellow", beyond that he was tall and pale and "had the most penetrating blue eyes."

"One last thing, Mrs. North," said Holmes as we rose to leave, "The toy castle on the shelf – is this your husband's work?"

"Oh, yes. He learned the trick of it from his grandfather, and makes them for all the children around here who want them." Mrs. North brushed her fingers over the turrets of the toy, and all of a sudden the towers collapsed with a friendly clatter into the base. Then she lifted the base block and with a flick of her wrist, the carved pieces shot out, creating a concertina of shapes that built three extending layers of tower.

"Made all from a single piece of wood, I see," said Holmes, showing it to me. The tower pieces all had that peculiar curved shape, teardrops and U-shapes, tapering finely so that they fell snugly into place when flicked out, yet would collapse neatly into the base after. "Thank you, Mrs. North. You have been most helpful. I expect to have news for you within a day or so."

She pressed a hand urgently to his elbow. "He'll come home, you think? He isn't . . . ." she steeled herself, ". . . hurt or ill?"

"Not at this moment, and I've every hope he'll continue in good health until found. Come, Watson!"

As we strode back to Kennington Road in the wind, but thankfully not the rain, Holmes withdrew a wooden peg from his pocket. It was one of those sent with the cards, oak bark still attached to the crown of it.

"That castle design shown to us by Mrs. North is most unusual, Watson. Rumpelstiltskin is undoubtedly this vanished Mr. Silas North, and wherever he is, and if he willingly went, he almost certainly did not willingly stay."

"Perhaps he took on that fascinating commission," I ventured. Holmes flagged a hansom for our return to Baker Street.

"I'd be surprised if that persistent gentleman were not involved. The timing is too close to be a coincidence."

"Then perhaps Mr. North decided to take on the job, and keeps his silence as a way of avoiding questions from his regular employer, Sudbury."

"In that case, why send me these cards and castle pieces? Which, you'll note, are not carved as smoothly as the toy he made for his son. No, Watson. Silas North is held against his will, although not yet, I think, in any real physical danger. He has freedom enough to both make and send these tokens, but not enough to send a clear message. He has been allowed to reassure his wife, too, which means his warder isn't beyond humanity."

"You think he'll be released in due course, when whatever this commission is has been completed?"

"I'm not as certain as all that, Watson. If the report of Mr. North willingly getting into a hansom cab is correct, it's likely he was tricked into entering the vehicle, perhaps on the pretext of getting a ride closer to his intended destination, and waylaid that way. If no driver has come forward, either he has been paid well for his silence, or laid up in some fashion. Any legitimate business offer would surely not involve such secrecy, and would certainly not keep Mr. North from communicating with his family. No, Watson, I fear there may yet be some threat to Mr. Silas North, once he has completed whatever work is required of him."

"What can we do?"

"I must examine those cards and envelopes again, Watson, and consult a directory or two. You are most welcome to join me, if you have no other calls upon your time."

"None at all," I assured him, "Though, Holmes, do you think I should return home for my revolver?"

"I don't believe it will be necessary," he said thoughtfully, "But you should be ready with that strong left hook of yours, as needed."

Once more at Baker Street, we found a new delivery from the Royal Mail, and a new card. This, like all the others, was postmarked Bethnal Green, and was addressed scrawlingly to either Holmes or Hulmes. Within was a Christmas card depicting the head of a dog which threw a distorted shadow of a policeman. The inscription was identical to the previous missives, addressed *To my dear friend,* and signed with the anagram of Rumpelstiltskin. Holmes put the enclosed U-shaped peg with all the others and gave them to me.

"See what you can make of the addition, now that we know what they're for." He dashed to his shelves to withdraw several business directories and a map of Bethnal Green, and flung the lot over the table.

I sat in my old chair, placed the small side table in front of me and arranged the wooden castle pieces on it. This sixth piece filled the gap and now all six fit, with that slender fissure that showed how the pieces tapered towards the top.

Of course, these pieces lacked the unifying base that had held the North's toy castle together, and replicating that foundation might prove tricky. Of course, I need not have the solid base in order to flick out the towers and turrets as Mrs. North had done. It would be sufficient to have a pedestal that could hold the towers steady.

"Do you still have a plentiful supply of putty in your disguise kit, Holmes?" I asked.

He waved me towards the box where he kept such things, intent as he was on his directory. I retrieved a largish selection of putty and sat once more with my puzzle. As I considered it, Holmes leapt to the door, called for Mrs. Hudson, and sent her away with a telegram for Billy to take. "Tell him to wait for an answer!"

It struck me, turning over the pieces of carved oak and remembering the intricacies and layers of that toy castle, that surely Mr. North was only part way through sending his message to Holmes. Nevertheless, I slotted the pieces together and then, using the putty to hold each layer steady, I made the pieces jut up as intended.

Looking from above, the puzzle meant nothing. I was disappointed, having hoped for some secret message to be spelled out in the bark.

Holmes crouched by my side. He peered at the result – a crude selection of rising towers. I could imagine what the base must be like, and reckoned it'd be a handsome thing when completed, quite a neat little carpenters trick to make turrets that could stack high and then compact down again like that.

"I'm sorry, Holmes," I said, "I thought there might be more . . . ."

But Holmes grinned and clapped me on the shoulder. "Look again, Watson. I believe we have found our missing carpenter."

He rose as I peered at the pieces. It was a moment before I could see with new eyes, to find the clue I had missed, but there it was. Parts of the curved shape were stained a slightly darker colour, and now that I looked at the thing front-on, it was possible to read those marks as more than flaws in the wood. With a little imagination, I could see the letters *F* and *O*.

"I still don't see how this helps."

Holmes dropped a directory into my lap and leaned over my shoulder to jab at an entry with a long, elegant forefinger.

FOX BROS: Toymakers. Artful Constructions, Tricks and Trinkets for the Curious Child.

The address was in Bethnal Green.

"And here," added Holmes, dropping the second directory on top of the first. "By the fine print on the back, all of our cards and Mrs. North's owls were printed by Fox Brother's neighbours, Calico Press. I think we can be on our way and learn more of the 'why', once we have located our Rumpelstiltskin!"

The day had become dark, though the wind had dropped, as we made our way by hansom to the fringes of Old Nichol Street Rookery, a slum filled with workhouses and dilapidated tenancies. The rookery was notoriously crowded, damp and unsanitary, and I had professional cause to know that a child contracting whooping cough or diphtheria within its boundaries were significantly more likely to be lost to the disease than their counterparts a mere half-mile away.

The toymaker's store with its cheerful green door stood at the corner of Bethnal Green Road and a row leading to the warren of the rookery beyond. Its windows were crammed with all manner of bright and colourful trifles – dolls and sailing boats, tops and tea sets, tennis rackets and drums, puzzles and hoops, and books and soft felt rabbits. Nothing like the unusual castle we had seen at the North home could be seen, but Holmes was undeterred.

"That isn't why Mr. North's liberty has been taken from him. No, Watson, there's clearly a much bigger game at stake."

We didn't enter the toyshop, as I imagined we would, but turned down the row to the shop's perpendicular neighbour, Calico Printing. Its goods, too, were on display: posters for concerts, magic shows, and theatrical events, as well as prettily spread fans of pamphlets and monographs. A wide range of its fantastical and humorous Christmas cards were hung upon a string in its window.

"Be a good fellow," said Holmes, "And take a turn along this adjoining lane. I'd like to know if the Fox Brothers have a workshop at the back of their shop premises. We'll meet again at the corner."

I drew my coat and scarf closer against the cooling day and did as I was bid. I concluded, from the depth and height of the building, that the shop front and living quarters above it concealed modest space at the rear for at least some of the toy-making labour of the business. I met again with Holmes, who smiled in satisfaction at my report.

"Calico did indeed supply a modest number of cards to the Brothers Fox, which perforce have been delivered only to their premises here. So come, Watson, let's go shopping."

His ebullience was infectious, and we strode through the front door of Fox Brothers together, as two friends seeking Christmas gifts for their families. It was not so much pretence for me, as we had hopes, Mary and I, that this time she would carry to term. Her health was robust enough for her week away with Mrs. Forrester, early as she was in her condition, and from there I would ensure the best of care for her confinement. As Holmes spoke to the proprietor, I lingered at the blocks, dollies, and felt rabbits, thinking, *perhaps one day for my sons or daughters.*

"I understand your workshop can make special items on commission," Holmes said to the man at the counter, undoubtedly one of the Fox brothers. He was a slender fellow with a jolly face and gingery side whiskers that suited his name.

"It's possible," jolly Mr. Fox conceded, "It may depend upon your needs. We buy from local craftsmen around here, of course – one tries to support good local workers – but we can arrange special requests too."

"I was thinking of a type of toy castle," said Holmes, "Carved from a single piece of wood. The interlocking pieces unfold with a flick of the wrist to make towers . . . ."

"Oh, I do believe I know the design you mean. My youngest boy has a friend with the very toy. The other boy's father is a carpenter and makes them for local children. My brother approached the carpenter in question, North by name, to see if he'd make them for us, but he declined."

"That's a shame."

"Very much so, but you know, the fellow works exclusively as a cabinet maker for Sudbury Furnishing and Trimming, if you've heard of them."

"I believe I've heard them highly spoken of," offered Holmes cautiously.

"Their reputation is unparalleled," Mr. Fox assured him, "But Sudbury aims to keep it that way. He snatches up all the best craftsmen and their contracts are very strict."

"Surely the making of a trifle like a child's toy wouldn't constitute a problem."

"Constantine offered very generous terms, but North refused to work around his obligations. A very conscientious fellow, it seems."

272

"Ah well," said Holmes, feigning disappointment, "Perhaps North might consider that a one-off wouldn't violate his honour. Do you think he would?"

"Possibly," said Mr. Fox agreeably, "Although he also declined Constantine's request for another one-time commission."

"A pity," said Holmes. He looked to me. "Has something caught your eye?"

I placed a felt rabbit on the counter, which may have been precipitate of me, considering our previous loss, but I chose to look on it as an act of faith. "These seem well made."

Holmes gave me the most searching look, but I was well used to being under his scrutiny and it rarely bothered me.

"Our sister makes those," said Mr. Fox proudly, "She has a very fine hand and their little faces are very dear."

The felt rabbit did, indeed, have a very dear little face, and I happily handed over my coin for it.

"Are all your magnificent toys crafted by your talented family?" asked Holmes with generous admiration.

Mr. Fox beamed. "Not all, no, but they all contribute something. Well, Constantine isn't a craftsman, it's true, but he often designs some of our more clever toys for the artisans to make. He's a magician, you know, and does conjuring tricks for the customers. He's a great admirer of Maskelyne and would dearly love to follow in that great man's footsteps. He has been engaged for some house parties, and has hopes of gaining a following. He has hired a week at the Piccolo Theatre for the spring."

"Didn't we see a poster for *The Astounding Constantine*?" I asked Holmes: the poster had been displayed in the window at Calico's.

"Did you?" asked Holmes, though I knew full well we both had.

I turned to Fox. "My wife likes magic shows. Perhaps I should take her. What's his act?"

"My friend's wife is something of a connoisseur," expanded Holmes, "She would hope for something more than card tricks and disappearing coins."

Mr. Fox seemed mildly offended. "My brother's only starting out, but he takes the craft very seriously. Levitation, mind-reading, all of the best expected from the province of magic."

"A Cabinet of Wonders?" suggested Holmes. "I myself am fond of a good disappearing act."

"The very thing he's perfecting over the winter." Mr. Fox's familial pride had returned. "He saw a most excellent disappearing act last summer and has been designing an ingenious cabinet for the purpose."

"Oh, I'd like to see such a thing. These devices are splendid pieces of engineering. Would he let us see his workshop, do you think? Is it far?"

Mr. Fox shook his head. "He works in the shop behind the house, but he won't even let me see what he's up to. It's very secret stuff." He waggled his eyebrows at us, showing how charming he found his brother's eccentricities.

"You haven't seen him working?"

"Oh no," Mr. Fox assured us, "He's been nigh on living there for two weeks now, though he comes out to eat with the family. Many days he even sleeps in the workroom. Apparently, rival magicians are apt to sneak about and steal ideas."

"And you don't see him otherwise? He must be very dedicated."

"Oh he is, though he doesn't neglect his family duties. I told Constantine, 'if you must spend time sequestered on your art, you must, but at least you can address all the festive cards for our customers, clients, and suppliers, and save me the time!' And so he has done."

Mr. Fox's affectionate enthusiasm for his brother's preoccupation with magic and the making of a cabinet bordered, I thought, on the foolish. Certainly, he had a fool's propensity for wittering on about the brother with strangers, as though Constantine Fox was a precocious child who deserved to be indulged.

Holmes beamed upon the garrulous Mr. Fox. "I have friends in theatrical circles," he said, "Should your brother be in need of an agent. I shan't be this way again for a while, but I'd be happy to exchange a word with him now to confirm if he would like a letter of introduction."

Mr. Fox was so tickled by my friend's generosity and kindness, that he felt sure, he said, that Constantine would spare him a moment.

Holmes cast me a glance which spoke volumes. I tucked the felt rabbit, which Mr. Fox had wrapped in brown paper, into my pocket and followed the two men behind the counter, beyond the shop door to a corridor. The passage led left to stairs and the living quarters for the Fox family, and right to a firmly shut door.

Mr. Fox tapped on it. "Constantine! I have a visitor for you! A wonderful fellow who can recommend an agent for your show." He turned the handle, but the door was locked.

A sudden flurry of noise behind the door included what seemed a throttled cry, a dull thud and the sound as of a door slamming.

"What say you, Ezekiel?" came a strained voice, "Haven't I told you not to disturb me at work?"

274

Mr. Fox gave us an apologetic look, as though to excuse his brother's rudeness. "You have, but this man may be of great benefit to your career, and I thought you might make an exception."

Silence greeted this pronouncement, broken at last with a querulous: "You know an agent for a magic act?"

"Certainly," said Holmes with a flourish. "The great Allendale himself, who I am sure you know, acts on behalf of many of the great stage artists. He's a personal friend of mine, and was saying only the other day that he wished he had some new up-and-coming performer for whom to play Midas. *His* words. He tends towards vanity, though it seems well founded upon his successes."

"Yes," came the voice, "I've heard he's a bit of a peacock, but he's very good."

"He is," said Holmes, "And it'd delight to me to deliver him a new *protégé*. I owe him a good turn."

The key turned in the lock. The door opened a fraction.

A wan face looked out at us. Younger and shorter than his jolly brother, his thinness speaking of frailty, Constantine Fox had anxious blue eyes and a trembling mouth. Had he come to my door for professional services, I would, on that face alone, have prescribed bed rest in the country for a month. He seemed a man on the verge of nervous collapse.

Holmes acted on the instant, placing his foot in the narrow space between door and frame and pushing his shoulder against the door itself. With a yelp, Constantine Fox tried to slam the door shut. The violence of the action must have caused Holmes some pain, but he held fast and at the next moment I was using my own strength to push the door wide.

Ezekiel Fox shouted an ineffectual protest as Holmes and I stumbled into the room beyond. For his part, brother Constantine shouted at us about the invasion of his privacy while standing before a great wooden box placed on a wooden platform.

"It isn't any good, Mr. Fox," said Holmes sternly, "We know that you are keeping Mr. Silas North a prisoner here, and it's very easy to see the work you have been making him do." Holmes gestured grandly towards the box – the height of a man, with a pyramid roof, sturdily built and covered in chalk marks outlining so-called mystic symbols. I supposed this was the sketch for later decoration.

Constantine Fox went pale as a ghost and stumbled so that Holmes reached to catch him, but he righted himself and drew himself up defiantly.

"What nonsense!" Fox declared. "Ezekiel, who are these impossible intruders? I warned you about my rivals who would try to steal my idea!"

"I'm not your rival, but a detective," said Holmes crisply, "My name is Sherlock Holmes and you, Mr. Fox, are in dire trouble. If you tell me where you are keeping Mr. North prisoner, and you have done him no harm, I may yet persuade him and the authorities to press no charges."

A strange spark came into the magician's eyes. "I challenge you to find such a man, Mr. Holmes."

I could have warned him how foolish it was to issue such challenges to my friend, but I confess I rather enjoy the effect of their learning such foolishness for themselves.

Holmes immediately strode around the raised platform, heading for the back of the workshop. Constantine Fox appeared very smug about it, until Holmes, having walked a semicircle around it, leapt lightly onto the planks to investigate the box.

"I shall call the police this instant!" cried Ezekiel Fox.

"That's up to you," I said, watching as Holmes circled the cabinet now, his hands trailing across the four panels, "But I expect that will obviate Mr. Holmes's efforts to have no charges pressed, once he finds Mr. North."

"You are offensive, sir," said Ezekiel Fox haughtily. "Constantine hasn't seen Mr. North since approaching him about the toy castles. Have you, Constantine?"

"Of course not!" But there was something furtive about his reply, and as I had failed ever to keep a secret from my late brother Henry when we were boys (and indeed, ever from Holmes now), the elder brother knew instantly that the younger lied.

"Oh, Constantine, what have you done?"

"Nothing. Nothing!"

Holmes pressed the front panels of the cabinet and it sprang open. It was empty. Holmes immediately fell to his hands and knees and explored the floor of the thing, but no trapdoor was revealed. With a snarl of disappointment, Holmes stood inside the cabinet and felt all the walls of it, again without satisfaction. He fell still and closed his eyes, thinking, and when he opened them again, the gleam in the grey told me that he had solved it.

Holmes reached up to the ceiling of the box, which came some fourteen inches below the peak of a square hip-roof atop it. The four sides of that little pyramid were chalk-marked with symbols and the name *The Astounding Constantine*.

Holmes pushed. The ceiling clicked. Constantine Fox cried out in horror and fainted as the ceiling section yielded.

At that moment I suddenly had three patients on my hands – Constantine Fox in a swoon, and Sherlock Holmes on the floor, half under the man who had fallen from the tiny cavity in the roof of the cabinet – no doubt Mr. Silas North.

It was a simpler triage than many I had made on the battlefield, and I leapt at once to Mr. North's aid. His breathing was laboured with him, a tall man, having been folded up into so small a space for some minutes. He was curled in on himself with a bruise on his forehead.

Holmes scrambled out from underneath him, following my instructions to stretch out the patient on the floor. I set about raising North's arms above his head before bringing them down to his chest and repeating the action until his breathing regained regularity. North groaned and I checked his pupils. He'd have a very nasty headache, and perhaps a slight concussion, but would recover.

"Rest easy, Mr. North," I said in my most soothing tone, "You are rescued and will be home soon."

"Constantine!" I heard Ezekiel Fox cry in despair. "Constantine!"

I knelt by Constantine Fox's side, but there was nothing more wrong with him than exhaustion and the fear of the consequences of his own selfish madness. Already he was moaning, rather more theatrically than his condition warranted.

"That's enough of a fuss," I told him sternly, "You'll sit up and confess all."

Strangely, this is precisely what he did. He sat, pale and trembling, and told us the story as though seeking, if not absolution, then at least validation.

"Silas North is the best cabinet maker in London, and he refused to help, no matter how much I promised to pay, so I *made* him do it," he said. "That cabinet is the only thing I needed to begin my career. I designed it so *perfectly*, but I don't have the skill to make it myself. Twice North refused me. I took a hansom to see him, to ask again, and offer more money, and again he refused. Well, I had gone prepared for his stubbornness. I offered him a ride in my hansom, since he was heading over the river anyway. Once he was inside the cab, I overpowered him with chloroform, as I once read about in a book. When we were near home, told the driver my mate was taken ill and I carried North right in here with hardly a murmur. I didn't even pay the cabman extra, as that would have drawn attention to us."

Constantine Fox looked at us with a shining, beseeching face, but none, not even his indulgent brother, could give him absolution for his actions.

"I was good to him," he continued, "I let him write to his wife so that she wouldn't think him dead in a ditch. I told him he could go home when the cabinet was done, but he couldn't get it right. The floor, you see, is false. At the compression of the concealed switch, it springs up to become the ceiling, while I curl into the space, vanishing in a trice! Then my assistant closes the doors, the ceiling drops, and once again I appear in the box, to the amazement of all. Wonderful, don't you see? But the spring mechanism is supposed to be soundless, and lift very quickly, and North couldn't get it *right*. So I made him stay until he could. I'd have let him go after. *I would have*."

"You have nearly *killed* him," said Holmes darkly, which wasn't much of an exaggeration. Another few minutes in that crushing chamber and Silas North might have suffocated.

This observation set the elder brother to roughly shaking the younger by the shoulders.

"That is enough from you, Constantine!" snapped Ezekiel Fox, all jollity vanished, as Constantine might say, in a *trice*. "And enough of this ridiculous business. You have spent all your savings on this madness and it is done. You'll be lucky if you don't go to prison for this! Oh, you wretched idiot. I've been too forbearing with your stage-struck follies."

Constantine Fox wept, but it was very difficult to summon any sympathy for him.

We agreed to leave him in his disapproving brother's care until Mr. North was in a condition to choose his next steps. Scotland Yard should perhaps have been called immediately, but Mr. North wished only to return home to Lambeth, to his long-suffering wife and his little ones.

We escorted Mr. North home, where I completed a second examination to satisfy myself that he suffered no permanent injury.

"My messages reached you!" Mr. North said to Holmes, throat still hoarse from his ordeal.

"They did indeed," said Holmes, "Though I wonder how you smuggled them out. Even a man as overtaken with obsession as *The Astonishing Constantine* should have noticed what you were doing."

Mr. North shook his head. "He left me alone many nights, chained like a dog in the workshop and gagged so that I couldn't cry for help. But then he brought in boxes of cards he was to address for his brother's business, and decided that it was good use of my time to aid him with this so that we could together resume work on the magic box sooner. When he left to eat in the evening with his brother, he'd leave me to work, under the most dreadful threats if I made any sound. I was able then to work on the castle pieces that I sent you, from a piece of firewood, but it was very hard going.

278

"Still, he wasn't very observant. I took some of the cards and was able to slip them and their contents among the many piles of cards to post – some of which contained little trinkets. I disguised the messages, of course, in case someone in the household read them. I had no idea how many of them were in on the scheme. I'm lucky it is so successful a toy business that my little messages were able to leave my prison so easily and often."

"It's a clever man who can make the use of a good opportunity," Holmes assured him, and we left Mr. North in the embrace of his wife and loving family.

In truth, Holmes didn't try particularly hard to persuade Mr. North against pressing charges, but Ezekiel Fox paid a handsome compensation to him and gave many boxes of toys to Mr. North and all his neighbours. He also sent his wayward brother to South Africa to see if that might make him more sensible.

Within the week, Mary returned home, looking bright and healthy for her time in the country. I showed her the felt rabbit. She exclaimed upon its pretty face and said, "I do feel quite strong this time, John. I'm certain all will be well." She placed her hand over her belly, which held our hopes, and I kissed her cheek.

We invited Holmes to join us for Christmas lunch, and I was honoured that he came, bearing a box of fine chocolates for Mary, whose sweet tooth had become insistent since she was with child. I hadn't told him of her condition, so he must have deduced it – along with the fact that I had changed my brand of tobacco only a month before, as he brought me a tin of the new blend. Mary had knitted him a fine scarf, which he admired with all sincerity. He smiled too, at my gift to him of Kendal Mint Cake, which I knew he carried with him for quick energy while working on a case.

After an excellent roast dinner, Holmes played carols for us upon the violin. And so we three kept our Christmas together with an excellent meal, good cheer, and much hope for the future.

The Question of the
Death Bed Conversion
by William Patrick Maynard

Cold rain drizzled against the window as I looked down onto Baker Street.

"Jedidiah Enright is dead."

I turned upon hearing my friend's voice. Sherlock Holmes was still seated at the table, reading the newspaper as he had been before I momentarily lost my sense of place and time while watching the rain collect in dark pools on the pavement below.

"Good Heavens! The old codger has finally gone to meet his Maker, has he? He certainly lived to a ripe old age."

Holmes shrugged, "He was eighty-two years old. Not what one would consider ancient, but certainly long-lived."

"Imagine having to face God's Judgment when you've lived a life as depraved as his. Jedidiah Enright, the notorious womanizer who made his fortune creating scandal for others to feast upon for their reading pleasure. Every day for decades, countless Londoners have delighted in the vicarious thrill of revelling in every sordid detail his salubrious publication saw fit to print. What a ghastly business."

"Yes, quite," Holmes sighed and folded up his newspaper, "and here we sit finding pleasure reading about the poor man's passing. I fear it is only human nature to find comfort in others' misfortune. There may be no honour in such behaviour, but it is the mark of modern man. It is what makes us civilized, Watson."

"You're in an ill humour this evening," I laughed. "I see no harm in failing to grieve for such a contemptible rotter as that blackguard. A fit company for devils, that one is, and I don't regret saying so in the least."

Holmes said nothing in response. He merely smiled to himself and then returned to his newspaper.

The sun was shining a few days later when I next paid a visit to my old friend.

"Damn!" I heard Holmes swear as I entered the apartments we had shared together for so many years.

"That's a fine way to greet an old friend, Holmes."

"Listen to this, Watson," he said, paying me no mind as he sat in his chair reading from the morning newspaper.

"'*Notorious Publisher Has Deathbed Conversion. Miss Claire McKendrick, employed as Mr. Jedidiah Enright's nurse for the past three years, stated that Mr. Enright experienced a deathbed conversion and repented of his many sins just hours before his death on Saturday.*'"

He stopped reading and dropped the newspaper in his lap.

"Well, what do you make of it?"

I shrugged my shoulders, "What would you like me to say? I'm happy for him."

"You believe it then?"

"Why shouldn't I believe it? You just read it to me."

Holmes smiled, and I had the distinct impression he was in one of his difficult moods.

"I could be lying. I might have made the words up while staring at a completely different article."

"Then you would have tricked me and shame on you."

"No, but I wasn't lying."

"No, of course you weren't."

"But *she* might have been."

I felt myself growing cross.

"Who might have been, Holmes?"

"Miss Claire McKendrick, the nurse who claims Jedidiah Enright had a change of heart just before dying."

"Really now, Holmes! The things you get wound up about! Why should she lie? What possible reason would the woman have to make up such a story about a man who was vilified far and wide?"

"I can think of several possibilities."

"Such as?"

"Attention."

"You're joking, of course."

"No, no. I'm quite serious, Watson."

My old friend stood up and began pacing the room as he continued.

"Think of it. Long-suffering and doubtless attractive young nurse, employed by that lecherous old man who finally passes away. Now she has a story that puts her in the limelight and restores her doubtless tarnished reputation among her friends and family. They can't have been happy for whom she has worked these past three years."

My mind reeled listening to him speak.

"Holmes, calm yourself. How do you know she is a young woman and that her reputation is in question?"

Holmes stood up and made his way to the mantel where he proceeded to load his briar in evident irritation.

"There are times, Watson, when one might conclude you learned little to nothing of my methods in the years you have known me. Jedidiah Enright was well-known as a womanizer for decades. Had he not been a wealthy, powerful, belligerent newspaper publisher, then doubtless his scandalous behaviour would have been the ruin of him long ago. Would you consider it likely that such a man employing a live-in nurse would choose a matronly sister or a young and foolish slip of a girl in need of work and naïve enough to believe she could handle herself in his company?"

I clapped my hands together in exasperation as I sat back in the settee.

"Listen to yourself, Holmes! I admit you're very clever and your logic is as faultless as ever, but you've all but condemned the poor girl without ever having set eyes upon her or spoken to her even once."

My old friend stared at me beneath his furrowed brow and puffed contemplatively at his pipe.

"You misunderstand me, Watson; it's not the young lady's virtue I question."

"Come again?"

"Human nature, Watson. Jedidiah Enright was too embittered to change after all those years. 'The leopard doesn't change its spots', I believe, is how the saying goes."

I paused for a moment and considered his meaning.

"One supposes there might always be exceptions to every truism, Holmes."

"That's the point, Watson. It isn't an exception."

"I don't follow you."

"It is a weakness inherent in Christianity. After thinking the worst of your neighbour for years and years, one must suddenly paint a rose-coloured portrait of an eleventh hour conversion to inspire those who are lax in their faith to do the same. It's a fairy tale, of course, but all too typical of the Western mind. I suspect if we paid a visit to the library, we would find countless similar stories. Every time some old miser passes away, out trots a well-meaning churchwoman with a tale of how they made peace with the Lord just before giving up the ghost."

I waved him away and crossed my arms in consternation.

"I won't speak to you when you're like this. You're just miserable."

"You won't speak to me because you know I'm right and that makes you miserable."

"Really, Holmes, you are hopelessly cynical and chronically in need of an audience to impress with your brilliant deductions."

He scoffed at my response and sat down in the chair across from me and picked up the newspaper again. Twenty minutes or more passed in silence before I could bear it no longer.

"You could prove it, you know."

"What was that?" he said, putting the paper down in his lap.

I smiled in the knowledge he had taken the bait.

"You could prove which of us is correct."

"And how would you have me do that? Should I go and interrogate the poor woman?"

Holmes simply lifted his newspaper and continued reading as if I had said nothing.

Mrs. Hudson entered the room after a fashion and asked if we would like more tea.

"Not at present, Mrs. Hudson," Holmes replied, not looking up from his paper. "Watson was just leaving. Get his hat and coat, won't you?"

My dismissal had been final. When I left our old apartments that day, I thought it very likely that I might never return. I said little to my wife about our falling out. Happily, my practice was brisk and I had much with which to occupy my mind.

Nearly a fortnight later and I found myself out shopping for Christmas presents for Mary one evening. I was crossing Henrietta Street whilst delicately balancing three large parcels in my arms when I collided with an individual rounding the corner from Garrick Street.

"Good Heavens, my dear fellow!" I exclaimed as my parcels scattered along the kerbside.

"Watson!"

The bent figure before me straightened and handed a parcel back to me when I saw it was none other than Sherlock Holmes. I stammered for a few seconds with words failing to adequately express the emotion I felt at seeing him so unexpectedly. His face broke into a joyous smile, and at once I realized all of his irritability and petty mean-spiritedness had left him.

"You must come round to Baker Street with me . . . oh dear," he caught himself. "Of course you must be on your way home. Well, perhaps tomorrow or the day after then?"

"Certainly, Holmes," I assured him whilst reaching for the last of the parcels. "I would be quite pleased to do so."

Our reunion had been brief, but the awkwardness had dissipated, just as our foolish anger had been forgotten. We were, first and last, the best of friends, and all of our hard-headedness could not weaken that bond for long.

It was just after nine the following morning when I called on my old friend in Baker Street. The note of exasperation in Mrs. Hudson's voice made it evident that Holmes had been hard at work on his experiments through the night. The poor woman started upon a coughing fit and moved the handkerchief over her nose. The odour was strong, but Mrs. Hudson had always been particularly sensitive. It was a wonder she had managed to tolerate Holmes's scientific experiments for so many years. I climbed the stairs and knocked upon the door several times before at last it opened, and my old friend greeted me with a confused expression as if he had forgotten my invitation to join him.

"Come in, come in, Watson," he said as he ushered me inside. "Don't just stand there gawking. It is imperative I finish my work tonight."

I followed him into the sitting room which, as was his wont, had been converted into a laboratory. The breakfast table had been cleared and glass beakers now covered its surface. Yellow, grey, and green-coloured fluids bubbled within, releasing the odour that filled the house. Holmes took turns grasping the beakers with tongs to measure their level, which he then dutifully recorded in a journal after carefully replacing the beaker. This routine was repeated for a quarter-of-an-hour, until finally he had finished his experiments and carefully discarded the contents of the beakers.

Returning to the room, he stood in the doorway and sighed, "Now then, Watson, what brings you here so late at night?"

"It is half-past-nine in the morning, Holmes."

"Is it?" he sounded genuinely startled. "Well, all the more reason you come to the point then. I must get to bed."

"You asked me here only yesterday, Holmes."

"Did I?" he stopped and seemed to cast his mind back to recall the events. "So I did. It was about the McKendrick woman."

"Who?"

"The one who witnessed the death bed conversion. We shall go and see her tomorrow as you wished."

He amazed me at times like this. It was as if he did not recollect that weeks had passed, but believed we had just concluded our heated discussion only a few hours earlier.

"To what do I owe this change of heart, Holmes? Could it be an uncharacteristic spot of Christmas cheer?"

He looked at me as if I had said something distasteful and snapped, "Of course not. I am only going to prove to you that the alleged conversion of Jedidiah Enright is sheer nonsense. It's the only way you'll give me any peace. Now off with you. I very much need to rest. Come back in the morning."

I shook my head in bewilderment, but could only chuckle at my friend's eccentricities.

The morning drizzle did nothing to shake my mood that it just didn't feel like Christmas. As I made my way to 221 Baker Street, I was surprised to see my old friend waiting by the front steps for me.

"We haven't time to dawdle this morning, Watson. According to our ever reliable Master Wiggins, our prey is about to take wing."

He left me not a moment to question him as he took me by the arm and steered me in the direction of the nearest cab. A short time later and we were deposited before the great house on Serpentine Avenue that had belonged to Jedidiah Enright. Even when the sun shone, that imposing edifice cast a pall over the entire neighbourhood. I felt a shiver of dread as we approached the door and rang the bell. The door was opened by an aged figure who seemed frightfully fragile.

"May I help you, gentlemen?" the old man spoke with a strong Irish brogue.

"Certainly you may, McCarron," Holmes replied. "It is Mr. McCarron, is it not?"

The painfully frail old man inclined his head.

"Excellent. Please tell Miss McKendrick that Sherlock Holmes and Dr. Watson have arrived. She is expecting us."

The old man's lined face betrayed surprise for barely a moment before he regained his composure.

"I believe Madame was expecting you to join her for a luncheon appointment, sir."

"That is correct, McCarron, but seeing as Madame was hoping to be on her way to the station by then, you will kindly let her know we will see her now, if you please."

This time the old man's jaw hung slack and quivered for a moment, before he nodded and started to turn, leaving us standing in the rain. A woman's voice, clear and youthful called out from inside the great house.

"Who is it, Eoghan? It can't be my cab yet."

At the sound of her voice, Holmes boldly stepped forward and entered the house. Hesitantly, I followed suit.

"Good day, Miss McKendrick," Holmes bowed and removed his deerstalker in one deft motion. "We are fortunate to have caught you before your departure; only we were in the neighbourhood so I thought it best we drop by."

As I stepped inside the foyer, I beheld a very pretty and smartly dressed young woman with flashing brown eyes and chestnut hair to match. She was standing facing us at the foot of the stairwell. Three traveling bags were at her feet. Her eyes blazed at the realization she had been caught unawares.

"I don't believe I have had the pleasure," she spoke in a quiet, halting voice.

"Mr. Sherlock Holmes of Baker Street and my companion, Dr. Watson. I rung you a few days ago and we set an appointment for today. Clearly you failed to recall your travel plans, so it is fortunate we have arrived before your cab."

She gulped hard before finding the words to attempt a response.

"Yes, well it is not very convenient I'm afraid, Mr. Holmes. You see, I was just about to walk out the door."

"No coat just before Christmas?" Holmes's angular profile seemed even more severe than normal. "Certainly it would be more prudent to wait for your cab indoors where it is warm."

"Madame?" the old man asked, raising his eyebrows quizzically.

"Yes, that will be all, McCarron," Miss McKendrick replied irritably and, with a slight inclination of his head, the old man shut the front door and withdrew into the great house.

"I can spare you a quarter-of-an-hour and no more, Mr. Holmes," the young woman snapped. "You and your companion may join me in the sitting room."

Leaving her bags behind, she stalked out of the foyer as we followed.

The sitting room had the musty smell of age and disuse. It occurred to me that the colourful old Irishman, Eoghan McCarron, was likely the only servant in the declining years of his late master's health. The house, like both men, had been mummified with decay and the memories of too many passing decades. Miss Claire McKendrick, in contrast, was bright and vibrant and full of life and energy. She must have made the household surge with a vibrancy lacking these many years.

"What is it you wish to know, Mr. Holmes? I have told my stories to the newspapers and to Scotland Yard and to so many people, I question whether it is real or merely a story after so many tellings."

Holmes smiled and did his best to set her at ease.

"You know of my reputation as a consulting detective, Miss McKendrick. I have a client who is sceptical about your claims that Mr. Enright repented upon his deathbed."

I am uncertain who was more shocked, for both Miss McKendrick and I registered outrage at this suggestion. Her integrity had been called into question, while I feared the embarrassment of being identified as my friend's sceptical client.

"Have no fear, Madame. I do not doubt the veracity of your account for a moment," Holmes could appear positively charming when he wished it as he did now. "I only wish to ask a few questions to be able to lay the matter to rest with my client, who enjoyed a long and prosperous professional association with your late employer and finds the very notion of his mending his ways to be farcical."

The young woman's eyes narrowed to mere slits.

"I suspect I know just the professional associate you refer to, Mr. Holmes, but I will not ask you to violate a client's confidence. I respect you and your integrity far too much, and thank you for assuring me I have your support. I don't think I could address the matter if I thought otherwise."

My mind was reeling. I did not doubt the girl's sincerity for a heartbeat, but unless my old friend was deceiving me, he was behaving in a very callous and cavalier fashion by pretending to be her friend.

"I understand completely," Holmes said and patted his right knee as he spoke. "Now, kindly relate to us how you came into Mr. Enright's employment, if you don't mind."

There was just the slightest indication of trepidation before she responded to the question.

"Well, you see, I had arrived in London nearly three years ago. I am from County Kildare, originally. McCarron, our servant, was an old friend of the family and provided me with an introduction to Mr. Enright. He was in ill health and in need of a daily nurse, so I accepted the position, as I had trained as a nurse for several years in Dublin."

"I see," Holmes nodded as he listened. "That must have been quite daunting, a young girl coming to London by herself and taking employment from a notorious old womanizer such as Jedidiah Enright."

Her face flushed with emotion at his words.

"Oh no, not at all, Mr. Holmes. You see, Mr. Enright may have been all that when he was younger, but he was always a perfect gentleman to me."

She looked away for a moment and did not make eye contact with either of us as she spoke.

"He was a bit crotchety at times, of course, but he was like a grandfather to me. Truly."

She now held our glance with wide eyes that appeared filled with wonderment.

"As I understand it from the newspaper accounts," Holmes continued, "you were responsible for reading the Bible to him and praying over him during the worst of his illness."

Again, I detected a slight trepidation in her reaction, but she remained silent until Holmes resumed his questioning.

"I find it rather remarkable that an independent young woman such as yourself, who would venture forth alone to London and live in the home of such a man as Jedidiah Enright, would also be a strong woman of tradition and faith. You are quite an enigmatic creature, I must say."

Holmes's disarming smile helped soften the sting of his insinuation, but it still stood, and both Miss McKendrick and I felt incensed at his words.

"The mystery is simple, Mr. Holmes, as you doubtless are aware. Your professional client would have already paid for you to snoop into my background. I have no reason to deceive you, nor have I done anything that should cause me shame. I admit, quite proudly, to my independent nature. It was at the root of my estrangement from my family in County Kildare. And yes, Mr. Holmes, very few traditional church people are willing to accept a suffragette in their flock without preaching and judging her harshly, without sufficient cause or knowledge of any misdeeds."

Just as her temper seemed ready to get the best of her, it quickly dissipated, and a calm serenity seemed to descend upon her in a most favourable fashion.

"I was quite fortunate in having my own brush with ill health last winter. I was seriously ill, and it was considered no longer safe for me to be around Jedidiah . . . Mr. Enright."

She blushed as she showed him the same familiarity she showed the old servant earlier. I admit to not holding with such women, but this particular example of the species was undeniably captivating.

"I took my convalescence at the home of an aunt in County Cork. It was there, through her care and Christian example, that I came back to the Lord in the fullness of my faith. I had only just fully recovered and begun to think of settling in County Cork, as my Aunt Margaret implored me to do, when McCarron wrote to me and begged my return. Mr. Enright had taken a turn for the worse, and it was believed he had mere months left to live. I required no further persuasion and hurriedly returned to take up residence here once more as his nurse for those final weeks."

"And how did you find him upon your return?"

"He was notably weaker, Mr. Holmes. There was little I could do but make him comfortable. I read the Bible to him. At first, only when he slept; but later, when his breathing became laboured and he was too weak to argue against it. That was when the remarkable change came over him, gentlemen. He seemed to be at peace and his incessant wheezing began to calm. Some days, he sat up in bed for a few minutes at a time. He spoke to me often and asked questions about a passage I had read. We talked about the Lord a great deal and about salvation, and how a wicked man might yet find forgiveness if his heart was sincere. Mr. Holmes, Jedidiah Enright died in the presence of the Lord. I will go to my own grave believing that, and if anyone doubts the truth of his conversion, then I truly pity them for their cold, cold heart."

I resisted the urge to stand and break into applause. Holmes cleared his throat slightly and cast a glance in my direction as if anticipating my reaction.

"Thank you so much for your time, Miss McKendrick. I am sure you have told us quite enough. Are you going back to County Cork?"

The question seemed to startle her as if her mind were lost in the emotion of the moment she had so vividly described for us.

"Yes, yes, I am."

"And what happens to this old place?" Holmes asked, indicating our surroundings.

"I . . . I'm not sure. McCarron will see to it with Mr. Enright's solicitor, I suppose."

"Well, we shan't detain you any longer. Have a safe trip. Come along, Watson."

My head and my heart were a jumble of feelings after that unexpected meeting, so I kept my thoughts to myself until Holmes and I returned to 221b Baker Street.

"Well, Holmes," I said as I took my seat opposite his, "I am most curious to hear what you have made of the tale related by that charming young woman."

Holmes loaded his briar and was silent for a few moments as he seemed occupied with his pipe.

"I'm not certain it matters, Watson. You were certainly satisfied with all she relayed to us. Surely that is enough, is it not?"

"Oh come now, Holmes! If you were mistaken, then be man enough to admit it. She told us the truth. Jedidiah Enright did undergo a miraculous change of heart on his deathbed. It is an inspirational story, and is the very lesson you should be taking to heart this very season."

"My dear Watson, I fear you fancy Mr. Dickens' works of fiction a bit too much for my liking or your benefit. As it happens, I am quite certain the young lady in question did not tell us the truth, and Jedidiah

Enright did not repent his sinful ways on his deathbed as she claims. I admit I was uncertain before, but now having questioned the young lady, there is no doubt whatsoever in my mind that she is a liar, and a poor one at that."

I was literally speechless at the boldness of his statement.

"Oh, very well, Watson, I shall walk you through the matter until you see it as well. You were there with me. You had all the same clues I did, but you chose to ignore them and believe her, because it was the conclusion you already determined you wanted to reach. So it is with so many well-meaning Christians, I fear. A healthy bit of scepticism would do wonders to reduce the success of swindlers among the many God-fearing people of this country."

"Holmes, I would stake my reputation on that girl's honesty. She admitted her own failings and had the humility to face them and acknowledge that her family was correct. That same humility saved a rotten man's soul from damnation. I will not stand to hear you try to twist the facts to suit your cynicism. I am sorry, but there is no room for your deductive reasoning this time."

Holmes was silent, but he seemed in good humour rather than ill, in spite of the sting of my words.

"Watson, you are a good man with a kind heart. You are also a very talented physician. You will, however, never be a detective, despite the lessons I have tried to impart. Let us start with the beginning, shall we? Miss McKendrick scheduled her luncheon appointment with us, well aware she would be on her way to the station at that time. A simple refusal to see me was not as appealing a prospect as deceiving me into believing we had an appointment she knew she could never keep. That is your first clue, Watson. Her intent to deceive was with us from the start.'

"Next, you will recall her attempt to deceive us when we arrived unexpectedly by claiming she was just leaving and did not have time to meet with us. Had we not overheard her exchange with McCarron, we might have believed her, but she was in fact waiting for the cab to arrive, and stated it would have been early if it had arrived so soon. Again, she proves herself a woman to whom deception is second nature. She holds people in contempt, or she would never have formed a habitual desire to deceive them out of sheer convenience.'

"Then there is the matter of her familiarity with both McCarron and her late employer. She addressed both of them by their Christian names before catching herself. There was another peculiar slip when she referred to McCarron as being 'our' servant rather than Mr. Enright's. In doing so, she placed herself on a near equal footing with Mr. Enright, as if she had been the lady of the house . . . or perhaps I should say the mistress.'

"Now we come to the bits you wouldn't know, Watson, unless you had busied yourself into making enquiries into Jedidiah Enright's . . . shall we say, less respectable interests. You may recall my disingenuous claims that I was acting for a sceptical client. You may also recall Miss McKendrick's belief she knew precisely which old business associate of Mr. Enright's would question his change of heart. That was a significant remark, as was her mentioning she trained to be a nurse in Dublin."

"I must admit, Holmes, you have completely lost me this time."

"Yes, I thought as much, Watson. It seems good Mr. Enright was the *eminence grise* behind a certain disreputable – but highly profitable – establishment in Dublin known colloquially as Lily's Bordello. The business associate in question is one Annie Levant, alias *Annie the Levantine*, alias *Ragtime Annie*, alias the infamous *Lily* herself. Hardly an Irish rose, Miss Levant is what is generally referred to as a 'madam'. Miss McKendrick's familiarity with her is because Lily's Bordello is another part of that chequered past of hers that she assures us she is not ashamed of."

"Great Scott, Holmes!"

"Kindly let me finish, Watson. When we were first introduced by Stamford, lo those many years ago, where did you say your medical degree was obtained?"

"Barts, of course, as you know very well."

"Indeed. Why didn't you simply tell me London?"

"Why, I . . . ." I paused for a moment considering his meaning. "I see what you mean Holmes. The young lady said she trained to be a nurse in Dublin, rather than say Trinity College, for example."

"Precisely, Watson. She did learn to nurse and care for a man in Dublin, but she is not a nurse herself in any professional sense of the word."

"Then why the devil did McCarron . . . ."

"McCarron did not send for her. Her patron did. Jedidiah Enright specifically requested one of Ragtime Annie's girls be sent to him."

"Why, that wicked old scoundrel!"

"He treated her like a grandfather, remember? One wonders just what sort of grandfather our Miss McKendrick had."

"So she is a fraud."

"Yes and no, Watson. She likely did take ill and stay with an aunt in County Cork while she convalesced. Her family is likely from County Kildare and are estranged from her, as she stated. Every liar knows when to retain the truth. Nothing is ever fully fictional, even from the lips of the most practiced of storytellers. Of course, she misled us as to the nature of her illness, but that is only logical."

I paused for a moment.

"Holmes, you don't mean . . . ."

"It is hardly surprising, Watson. She is not the first young lady to stay with an aunt out of town when she is with child and then return after the baby is born, leaving the aunt to care for the child. It is doubtless her destination now that the matter is settled."

"Then . . . Jedidiah Enright is . . . ."

". . . the baby's father, yes. One of scores of bastard children he has doubtless sired and done nothing to provide for. Such reprehensible behaviour is quite common among such men."

"Why on earth would she return when he sent for her?"

"He didn't send for her that time, Watson. It was McCarron."

"I don't understand at all, Holmes," I said, shaking my head in consternation. "First she tells us McCarron recommended her for the position of nurse, when it was Enright requesting one of the bordello's girls as a companion. Then she says Enright asked for her as he lay dying, and you tell me McCarron actually sent for her of his own volition."

"Certainly, Watson. Eoghan McCarron came to Mr. Enright from Dublin. He was very familiar with Annie Levant and her girls. The 'family friend' she called him, if you'll remember. He would have despised Jedidiah Enright, as all who knew him did. He stayed with him for the money, or possibly for fear of whatever secret knowledge Mr. Enright held over him. Blackmail is the currency for men like Enright, as it is for that loathsome swine, Charles Augustus Milverton. He would have promised to call her back before it was too late. Perhaps they thought they could convince him to do right by the girl and his child and leave the home to them. It was not to be, of course and so the matter ends."

"So her story of his deathbed conversion was just that . . . a story and nothing more. Just as you said, Holmes."

My old friend looked at me and smiled warmly.

"No, Watson, there was a part you had correct. A girl such as Claire McKendrick did not come from a good home. Her mother was likely the black sheep of the family. Her mother's sister, the aunt in County Cork, is likely a good sort who has prayed for her sister and niece's souls all these years. Sometimes it takes being brought to one's knees before one is finally willing to listen to the very word they washed their hands of throughout their life. Miss McKendrick probably did find solace in the Good Book, and likely shared it with Jedidiah Enright as he lay dying.

292

The sincerity of his regret for a lifetime of debauchery was the part that was likely just wishful thinking. A story she sold to the newspapers and related to the constabulary and everyone else. There was no reason to doubt her and every reason to believe. After all, she had everything to lose if anyone looked too closely into her background, as I did. That is why she feared my visit, knowing of my reputation, of course."

"Of course, of course. Holmes, there is one question nagging at me. How can you be certain that she wasn't lying about her own conversion, as she did about Jedidiah Enright? What if all of it was an elaborate story from a young woman wishing to give herself and her child a new identity?"

Holmes set his pipe down and looked me squarely in the eye.

"My dear Watson, the answer to your rather cynical question is that sometimes it is best not to judge an unwed mother harshly without having first-hand knowledge of her circumstances or of her disposition. You helped teach me that lesson, so kindly do not forget it so soon yourself."

"Yes, Holmes," I smiled. "Well said. A Happy Christmas to you."

He nodded at me as he took up his pipe again.

"To you as well," he replied, "and Watson, remember me kindly to Mary, won't you?"

The Adventure of the Christmas Surprise
by Vincent W. Wright

The cold of London can have a curative effect on the nerves as well as a damaging one on the mind. There are those who lavish in its restorative power when staying in by a warm fire, but others who suffer from a sort of enclosed sickness that causes them to nearly go mad. Sherlock Holmes is the latter, and I the former.

It was not long after my marriage that I made it a point to spend a winter evening with my friend and discuss those things one does when not involved with a case. My wife was visiting some acquaintances in the north, and I would be along after her in a day or so. Holmes was happy to accept my sudden appearance, but I knew something was amiss with him. His fame had taken a decidedly upwards turn after revealing the involvement of the Vicar of Stowmarket in the disappearance of the Spanish trade ship *El Menear*, but Holmes wanted no part of it. He had told me once that the work itself had rewards which transcended glory, and I never doubted his conviction.

1890 was a particularly busy year for Holmes, and I had done my best to go along with him every chance I could without neglecting my callers. But December had been unkind to his thirsty brain, and ennui had set in. He sat puffing at his newest churchwarden while I read the agony columns and enjoyed a bracing cup of tea. Outside, the occasional winter gust pressed against the walls of our building, and intermittent swirls of snow blew past the window panes, but Holmes was unaware of such things. As he stared longingly into the fire, I decided to break the silence.

"Here's a line from someone in Croydon talking about his lost copy of *The Sign of the Four*, Holmes," I said from the comfort of my old chair. "Seems he left it in the lobby of an East End hotel called The Bard's Bed, but when he returned, it was missing."

"A book?"

"Yes. Why do you ask?"

"Watson, it was only *The Sign of the Four* in the magazine. It was without that dreaded second 'the' in book form."

"You're right, Holmes. Forgive me for getting it wrong," I said with less than an honest tone. "And let me once again thank you for writing to the different publishers about it."

"I did convince some of them to change it. Seems my name carries some weight," he said as he rose from his seat. "Besides, it makes for a better title."

The number of visitors to the door had certainly increased with each published narrative. Calls could come at any time of day, and it usually kept Holmes busy. Lately, the weather had given him fewer cases, and though the calm could be a welcome change, I knew he would not fare well without some mental stimulation. The quietude was broken that evening, however, when the sound of a light knock caused us to look toward the door.

"Who would be out on a night like tonight?" Holmes said with a scoff.

I rose and stepped over to crack the door open. Standing outside of it was a thin, smartly dressed man with a thick black mustache and hair to match, leaning against the frame. His face was flushed, and he was breathing very hard. With one final step he was inside but suddenly slumped forward.

"Holmes! Help me!" I cried as the man fell into my arms.

He leapt forward and we grabbed the man, helping him to the nearest chair. As I opened his collar, I saw that the man's lips were moving. He seemed to be muttering something.

"Quick, Watson, some brandy," said Holmes

I dashed to the tantalus and grabbed a bottle.

"Tilt his head back, Holmes," I said, dribbling some of the liquid into his mouth. "What kind of fool goes out into this weather without a coat of some kind?"

The man coughed several times.

"He seems to be coming around," I said, grabbing a blanket from the settee. "Sir, can you hear me?" I spread the blanket over him as Holmes went to stoke up the fire. The man coughed again after I gave him a small slap on the cheeks. He opened his eyes, coughed once more, and cleared his throat. After blinking several times, he was alert enough to pull himself forward.

"Oh, dear me, did I make it before him?" the man asked in a weak voice.

"Make it before whom?" Holmes asked.

"Mr. Holmes," the man said, grasping at my friend's lapels. "We are in danger, sir! I beg of you to lock your doors as quickly as you can."

"Please, sir, try and calm yourself," said I.

"I cannot, Doctor. He will be here any second."

"You were followed?"

"More chased than followed, Mr. Holmes."

"Who is this mysterious aggressor?" Holmes asked.

A loud pop in the fireplace caused the man to jump. "I'm afraid I don't know his name. Oh, please sir, lock your doors or we will all die," he begged.

Holmes stepped over to the window and looked down at the street.

"There doesn't appear to be anyone down there."

"He was right behind my cab. I don't understand." The man's face turned ash white. "Perhaps he's already in the stairwell. Yes, yes . . . that's it! He must be just outside!"

Holmes looked up at me. "Watson, my revolver is in the top right drawer of the bureau."

I grabbed the pistol from the drawer and walked to the door, putting an ear to it. I listened with all my power for many seconds, but heard nothing. Looking back I shook my head.

"Sir, might I suggest we move to the far corner," Holmes said.

Once they were as far from the door as possible I twisted the knob and pulled it open with as close to one movement as I could manage. I aimed, but there was no one there.

"Empty. I think we're safe," said I, shutting the door.

"I tell you he was just feet behind me," the man said, his hands shaking with fear.

"I truly appreciate your warning, but there seems to be no danger."

"But . . . ."

"Don't worry, Mr. Mallory. If he comes in, I'll make sure he's stopped cold," I said while slipping the gun in my pocket.

"Watson, how could you possibly know this gentleman's name?" Holmes asked, his eyes wide open.

"Oh, well it's very simple. I, uh, I saw his picture in the paper yesterday."

"I don't recall that."

"Well, you read the same paper as I. Strange that you don't remember him in it."

"Nothing escapes me, old friend. But, perhaps this did. Forgive my question."

"Again, Mr. Holmes," Mallory broke in, "our lives are in danger. You seem to be taking this rather cavalierly."

Holmes stepped forward and stared hard into our guest's eyes. "Mr. Mallory, I assure you that this is not the first time that someone has threatened to kill me, whoever this person may be. I get something by post seemingly every month with a threat of some kind. I have even had attempts made on my life, but as you can see, I still exist."

"I do not think you should take this lightly, Mr. Holmes. I believe my information to be quite good."

"I have no doubt you think so," Holmes said, re-taking his seat. "Now, aside from the fact that you are married, have a taste for caviar, knew someone named Julian who has died, and most likely walk with a cane, I know nothing about you. Please take a seat again."

The man forced a smile and shook his head. "I am familiar with your ability to deduce. I must admit I feel rather stupid, for I am at a loss about everything except the married part."

"I never tire of making the deductions," Holmes sighed, "but I do grow weary of explaining them. Yes, the married part is easy. You are wearing a wedding band. As for the rest – you have a small piece of caviar tucked between your lateral incisor and canine on the left side. There is a letter in a woman's hand sticking out of your jacket coat pocket, and the few words I can make out read 'the death of Julian.' It also appears that your right leg is about an inch shorter than your left. Add that to the circular dry patch on your palm, and I'd say you've used a cane with some regularity."

"Perfect, sir, but it seems you left out how I make a living," he said. It did not go unnoticed by me or Holmes when he tried to hide pushing the note farther into his pocket.

"I confess that I see nothing to help with that."

"That's because there's nothing to see," Mallory said. "My family is quite well-off, Mr. Holmes. Coal mining in Donnington. Investing in wheat. That sort of thing. I have never had to work. That wealth has allowed me to live comfortably," he said, looking down at his milky palms. "This evening, my wife and I were attending a party in Mortimer Street. It was the regular meeting of the Fitzrovia Idealists Society. Every 22nd of the month. Caviar was on the tables."

"And your leg?" I asked.

"I fell from a horse when I was nine. Severely broke my leg. Left it shorter, but I have never liked using a cane. I have managed just fine without one, except on nights like tonight when it aches so. Damn thing chaps my palm, though. This weather is no help."

"I understand all too well," I said. "My leg throbs in this weather. Pressure changes."

"And yet, you don't seem to have a cane with you," Holmes said, looking around the floor.

"I don't, but I did. I lost it somewhere in the chase."

Holmes rested a forefinger on his lips. The flames reflected in his intense stare as he held back a curious smile. "Tell me about the note."

"Well . . . ."

His words were interrupted by the sound of someone dashing up our stairs. Seconds later, the door burst open and a large man in a dark blue suit and black overcoat and hat stood with a pistol pointed at us.

"Good evening, gentlemen," the man said with a toothy grin. "Would you all mind standing, please?"

We rose silently, but after a moment Mallory let out a small whimper and buried his face in his hands.

"Thank you," the man said. He stomped the snow from his boots and unbuttoned his coat with his other hand, never taking his eyes off of us.

"I see you failed, Mallory," the man said as he removed his hat. "Mr. Holmes. Dr. Watson."

Mallory looked up with a confused look on his face and furrowed his brow. "Failed? I don't . . . ."

"My good man," Holmes interrupted, "you seem to have an advantage over us. You know us, but we have no idea who you might be."

"They call me Snook."

"Unusual. Perhaps you could tell us why you're here."

"Suppose it won't make a difference, since you'll all be dead soon. I'm here to make sure you are never a pain to my boss again. She is tired of your meddling."

"She?" asked Holmes calmly.

"Lady Miriam Carlyle, that's the she."

Mallory took a step forward, and the man concentrated his gun on him.

"How dare you say such a thing? Miriam is a wonderful person. She isn't involved in anything Mr. Holmes would have to be a part of."

"All I know is what she hired me to do, Mr. Mallory. I don't have any care for what you say."

"You were at the meeting tonight," Mallory said, pointing a shaking finger at him. "The one standing in the back of the room."

"Good memory, sir. Yes, I was."

"And you were the one who attacked me," he said, taking another half-step forward.

"If I had done so proper, you wouldn't be talking or standing, sir. I held back because of my orders."

"Your orders from her to kill us?" asked my friend.

"No, Mr. Holmes. Told me to kill Mr. Mallory here at this address if he didn't do his job. But, I'll just take care of the lot of you since he didn't."

"I don't believe a word of this!" Mallory said through clenched teeth. "How dare you slander her name like this."

"Are you calling me a liar, Mr. Mallory? 'Cause if you are, I don't appreciate it."

Mallory turned to Holmes. "It has to be lies. Miriam would never do anything like this. She is incapable of harm. I swear it."

"You know her one way, and I another," said Snook. "Now, gentlemen, if you'll all step over by the fireplace we can make short time of this."

"Your hat appears to need relined, and your gun is at least ten years old," said Holmes. "Further, you are missing a button on your overcoat. It looks as though things have been somewhat rough lately. If it's money for which you're doing this, I assure you I can pay you more than she will," said Holmes.

"Yes, whatever you want," said I.

"You needn't take notice of any of that, sir," Snook said. "And if you have that kind of scratch here, I'll be looking for it after, don't you worry."

Mallory took another step toward the man.

"Easy there, Alden," the gunman said, refocusing his aim.

"I just want to ask you a question."

"No harm, I suppose."

"Why does she want *me* killed? I have been her loyal friend for twenty years."

"No idea," Snook said with a shrug. "Just know that's what she paid me for."

"This doesn't make any sense," Mallory said, shaking his head. "She never let on anything was wrong. The meeting was wonderful. Everything went just perfectly. And our friendship . . . I am so confused."

"No concern of mine, Alden. Now, over to the fireplace like I said."

Holmes and Mallory slowly stepped in front of the screen.

"Doctor, please join them," he said, motioning with his gun.

I walked over and stood behind them, making sure to hide putting my hand in my pocket.

"Fine. Anything you'd like to say before? It is Christmas-time and all."

"Just that if you're going to do this you might want to close the door. Guns make a terrible noise. Besides, that wind is cold, and it nearly extinguished our fine fire," Holmes said, allowing me to cock the gun without notice.

Snook reached back and pushed the door closed.

299

"Should I pull the shutters, sir? It will diminish the sound, as well."

"I'll take care of that, Mr. Holmes," Snook sneered. He walked past us with the barrel still at our chests. At the window, he turned briefly, and in that moment I jumped out and fired. He let out a short yell and fell prone with a sickening thud. He struggled to get up but failed, and his body went limp.

Holmes ran over and grabbed his gun. "Excellent shot, Watson. The campaigns served you well."

I stood motionless for a moment staring at the body. It had been a long time since I had taken a life. The sensation was familiar, but still unpleasant.

"Mr. Mallory, you look like you need to sit," Holmes said.

"Just for a moment, please. You understand that this isn't the sort of thing I'm accustomed to."

"Of course. Do you need me to get you anything?"

"I could use a drink, I think."

"Certainly. Watson, can you assist Mr. Mallory here while I check on our visitor?"

"I think I should do that, Holmes."

"Nonsense. You've had quite a shake from this. Have a seat and collect yourself. I'll see to him."

I sat and took several deep breaths, then placed the still warm gun on the table.

"Please give me a moment, Mr. Mallory, and I'll get something strong for both of us."

"He's dead," Holmes said, kneeling over the body. "It appears the threat is gone."

"I still don't understand this," Mallory said. "No one will ever convince me that Miriam had anything to do with this."

Sherlock Holmes sat on a dining chair and crossed his legs. "This is something the police will have to bother with now."

"Holmes, you're not just going to let the man lie there, are you?"

"My dear Watson, it will be nearly impossible to find anyone to locate an officer for us at this hour, and even harder to find an officer on our own. The man will be no less dead in the amount of time it takes me to find out everything I need to know about tonight's events. Besides, his heavy clothing will soak up any blood."

"It just seems particularly callous."

"I understand your position, Doctor, but for now I wish for Mr. Mallory to continue with his story."

"But this man tried to kill us!" Mallory cried.

"And I am not surprised. Lady Carlyle runs a vast criminal organization. It was inevitable that she would figure out who was causing her such grief. I have been on her trail for years. Now I can pin her for attempted murder . . . with your help, of course."

"I shall not say a word against her until I can speak to her."

"Then perhaps you could tell me what happened tonight?"

Mallory looked from Holmes to me, and then to the body.

"Never mind him, sir."

Mallory rested his elbows on his knees and took a deep breath. "This can't be happening. It wasn't supposed to be like this."

"Like what, sir?"

Mallory sat up, closed his eyes, and ran his hands over his hair. "Nothing, Mr. Holmes."

"Very well. You were saying?"

"Well," he said after clearing his throat, "I arrived at the party early, as I usually do. Miriam wasn't there yet, and I did my usual job of seeing who was present and determining the mood of the crowd. It's helpful to Miriam to have a feel for things before she enters. What of that drink, Doctor?"

"Yes, of course," I said.

"When did she arrive?" Holmes asked. He tilted his head back and closed his eyes.

"About twenty minutes after I did. She made her way around the room, and I was never far behind. I kept one ear on the room and the other on her conversation. By all appearances, it was a normal function. No troublemakers, no reporters, that sort of thing. Just before the official meeting was to start, I noticed the man in the blue suit at the back of the room."

"Him?" I asked, motioning toward Snook.

"Yes. He never moved. Didn't talk to anyone that I saw. He was out of place. Once I realized he was going to remain in that same spot, I lost interest in him. Oh, thank you, Doctor."

"When was the meeting over?"

"It started at 7:30 and ended about nine. Standard business. Same as always."

"And the man?"

"Well, I never saw him again. People began leaving. I figured he went out with whomever he came with."

"But he hadn't, had he?"

"No," Mallory said, glancing over at him. "I was getting my coat after I had placed Miriam in a cab. The place was dark. I prefer to leave last just to be sure all is well. As I was making my way toward the front door, I thought I heard a sound. Like a boot scraping along. I turned and looked, but saw no one. I called out, but nothing. I assumed it was the wind. As I turned once again, I heard quick steps behind me, and before I could look around to see who it was, I was being held. He had pinned my arms to my back with one hand. It happened very fast. His other arm was around my neck. He wasn't choking me, but I still had trouble breathing. Fear, I suppose."

"That's only natural," I said.

"His breath was hitting my neck. I wasn't in any pain, but terribly scared."

"Did he say anything?" I asked.

"He did. He said to have fun in Baker Street."

"So, you were coming here tonight?"?" Holmes asked, his eyebrow arched.

Mallory stared blankly at him for a moment and then swallowed. He looked over at me with fear in his eyes.

"Given all that has happened I suggest you tell him everything, Mr. Mallory," I said.

Mallory looked back at Holmes. "All I'll say is that I was going to be in the area."

"I see," said Holmes. "Anything else?"

"He said to do what I was told or we would all die."

"And you don't know this man?"

"No. I swear it."

"This is most unusual, wouldn't you say, Watson?"

I had been preoccupied. My mind had been back and forth between the body and Mallory's account. What had started off as a peaceful evening had spiraled into horror.

"Watson?"

"Dreadfully sorry, Holmes," I said, snapping my head around. "My concentration is divided."

"Stop worrying about him, old boy."

"It's just that I can't believe there's a dead man lying here. In front of us. And I killed him. This is not the kind of evening I was hoping for."

"What specifically *were* you hoping for?"

"As always, I prefer a visitor. A chase, or a puzzle of some kind. But this . . . this is too much."

"Come now, Watson. Chances are good that in the next few days no one would stop in. People will be pre-occupied with the holiday. It would likely have been a week before we had a knock. All of this has made it an exciting evening, wouldn't you say?"

"Not the word I would choose, Holmes. Now a man is dead, and at this time of year. No, this is not what I was expecting."

"Not much we can do about it now. Once we are finished with Mallory, we'll try to get an inspector here to help sort all of this out. Now, Mr. Mallory," Holmes said, turning back to him, "please continue."

"Well, sir," Mallory said while looking at the deceased, "I ran toward the door. I could hear him coming, but I was some feet ahead of him. I beat him to the door and tried to close it on him, but he managed to push it open. I ran down the sidewalk and saw a cab. I called for it. As I leapt in, calling out your address, I looked back and saw that he had found one, as well. It must have been a sight, this chase."

"My address? Why my address?"

Sweat had formed on Mallory's forehead and he wiped it away with his sleeve.

"Well," he said, looking back at Holmes,' "this is the most famous address in Baker Street. Must've just naturally come out."

"Thank you for the compliment," Holmes said with a grin. "Did you come straight here?"

"I did. The other cab kept up. Mine stopped and I jumped out. I knew he wasn't far behind. I made for the stairs, but found my legs had nearly given out. I heard him yell at the cabbie that he wouldn't be long and not to go too far. What I recall next was being in here. I can't imagine why he didn't follow me up."

"Mr. Mallory," I broke in, "what do you think this all means?"

"I'm not sure. Obviously I'm aware of you both, but I had no plans on ever coming here."

"Of course you didn't," said Holmes. "Pray continue."

"I have a good life. No problems or controversies. And I don't believe Miriam is this evil person you and he referred to. It simply isn't possible."

"But it is possible that she could have a life of which you are unaware, is that not true? You don't spend every moment with her. You can't be sure of her activities all the time."

"Fair enough, Mr. Holmes, but I've known her for so long and with such closeness. I just can't see it."

"Were you two ever romantically involved?" I asked.

"Oh no, sir. Never. I don't see her that way. Besides, she is twenty years older than me. She's a beautiful woman, but my heart belongs to another."

"Did she write the letter that's in your pocket?"

303

Mallory stared down at the floor for a moment as if ashamed. He pulled the folded paper out.

"May I see it?"

"These are words between friends, Mr. Holmes. I would prefer you didn't."

"When did she give it to you?"

"Tonight, just before the festivities."

"Has she written to you before? And why couldn't she have just told you what she wanted to say? She knew she was going to see you."

"She has only penned something once before. It was a congratulatory piece about my upcoming wedding. I assumed this was also important if she took the time to write it."

"So it's been some time since she last did so."

"Yes. I admit it's confusing, but I still believe it harmless."

"Have you read it?" asked I.

"I didn't have time."

"Sir, I think it's imperative that I look at it. This can't all be a coincidence. And if you say you don't have any kind of a romance with her, then there can nothing too personal in it. If there's business, I'll ignore and forget it. But you must allow me."

Mallory turned it over and over in his fingers before handing it to Holmes.

"Watson, be a good man and toss another log on the fire."

As I rose, Mallory settled back in his chair with a heavy sigh and a frown.

"Watson, this has just taken a most incredible turn," Holmes said.

"What is it?"

"Yes, what does it say? It's my letter and I have a right, damn you."

Holmes turned the paper toward us. Written across it was the message *"You must kill Sherlock Holmes tonight. Avenge the death of Julian. M."*

"What? How did . . . I don't understand."

"Well, it looks to me as though you were to be the one doing the killing tonight. Had you read the letter beforehand, then that man wouldn't have had to come up and do it."

"No. I swear I wouldn't have. I am not capable of it."

"Not even if your beloved Miriam asked?"

Mallory sat quietly for a moment looking down, his eyes darting back and forth. "No. Not even then, Mr. Holmes," he said, shaking his head.

"It seems to me the man you saw at the meeting tonight was there to keep an eye on you. To see if you would read the letter. To see if he was going to have to get involved and do what you couldn't. He didn't follow you up because he was waiting for you to come down after."

"Who is this Julian?" I asked.

"Lady Carlyle's son," Holmes said. "He died last month at the hands of a man she had hired me to stop. He was killed before I could catch my prey."

"I knew nothing of this, Holmes!"

"My dear fellow, I have been involved in many cases without you. There are several that will never be known, as they exist only in my memory, and there they will stay."

"This is incredible! Why would you not involve me?"

"Often it is simply out of fear for your life. Other times I am hired to do a job by myself. I promise you that I have always wanted my companion's assistance, but sometimes it wasn't feasible."

"This hurts our friendship," I said sternly. "I want you to know that."

"I never intended for you to find out. Please don't be angry with me, my friend. I did what had to be done."

"I'm afraid you're mistaken, Mr. Holmes. Julian died in a horse riding accident at Oxford."

"That was the story given to the world, sir."

On the street below we could hear the sounds of a carriage. Holmes stepped to the window and gave out a short laugh.

"The night just keeps getting more interesting," he said, rubbing his hands together.

"Another visitor, Holmes?"

"Precisely, old chap. And a surprising one."

Mallory and I stared at the door while Holmes retook his seat. We could hear the sounds of two people coming up the stairs, one a light step and one heavy. A moment later the door opened to reveal a beautiful woman dressed in a blue evening gown, white gloves, and fur stole. Standing behind her was a large hulk of a man.

"Ah, Lady Carlyle," Holmes said, as we all stood to greet her.

"No time for pleasantries, Mr. Holmes," she said. Upon seeing her former ruffian lying on the floor her jaw tightened and she cursed through clenched teeth.

"Pay no attention to him, ma'am. He's dead."

The woman looked at her companion and nodded toward the body. He stepped past us and grabbed the corpse. With a grunt he slung it over his shoulder and headed outside.

"To what do we owe this pleasure?" Holmes asked.

"You need not worry yourself with reasons for my whereabouts or doings, sir." She looked over at Mallory, who was standing at my side. He wrung his hands and looked down.

"Mir . . . Lady Carlyle. I have heard the most awful things tonight. Things that cannot possibly be true."

"Alden, you and I will speak in my carriage. Go wait for me outside."

"Yes, ma'am," he said, his head still bowed like a regretful child.

"Now, gentlemen, I'll be going. I'm sure our paths will cross again, Mr. Holmes."

"What of Mr. Mallory?" I asked.

"I think that is something we should not ask, Watson. I am curious, however, as to how you knew to come here tonight, Lady Carlyle."

"Again, it is none of your business, but I'll humor the question," she said. "This whole thing was supposed to be done quickly. Since it wasn't, I decided I needed to see to it myself. Now, I'll bother you no more." She turned and disappeared down the stairs.

Holmes closed the door behind her. He motioned for me to follow him to the window where we both crouched down under the sill.

"What are we doing, Holmes?"

"In just a few minutes I shall have all of this taken care of. You and I will be able to put all of this out of our minds and go back to a quiet evening."

"What?" I asked, astonished. "How can we act as if nothing happened? I killed a man tonight, you and I were almost done in together, and then there's Mr. Mallory. I fear for his life."

"Please, Watson, trust me."

"If you say so, Holmes."

Upon hearing shouting, Holmes jumped up and pressed against the window. I stood next to him and strained to see what was happening.

"There!" Holmes pointed down at the street. Lady Carlyle's carriage had just pulled away when a large policeman turned the corner, blowing his whistle and chasing after them.

"That puts an end to all of this, my friend."

"Wait just one second, Holmes! How did you know to have a policeman here? And how in God's name did you signal him?"

"I'm afraid I can't reveal that just yet. In time, I promise."

"If you had access to the police, then why did you allow this Snook to remain upon our floor?"

"All I can tell you is that once you know, it will be something you'll never forget. Until then I have to again insist that you trust me. This whole affair is not over yet."

"This whole evening has been utterly unbelievable. Confusing, as well. But, I'll take your word that you'll tell me everything."

"Thank you, my friend."

"The deception is hard for me to accept, Holmes. Secrets and lies and all. It's not something we've done in the past."

"Have a brandy, old chap. Then get some sleep. Tomorrow will bring answers and peace."

I rose the next morning after a restless night. The events of the previous evening had weighed heavily upon my mind. But, I had a busy day before me. I needed a strong cup of coffee and a good breakfast before starting off. Upon reaching the table, I found I would be eating alone. My meal was laid out, and a fresh newspaper lay folded on my chair. As I opened it, a small slip of paper fell from between the pages and into my lap. After reading it I let out a tremendous laugh.

My dearest Watson,

I must admit to you that I figured out the ruse you had arranged for me for the holiday. Having someone come over to kill me and leaving me to figure out who he was and why he was doing it. It would have been splendid if it had worked. I heard of your plot days ago through an acquaintance – Snook. He was only recently hired by Lady Carlyle – who does NOT run a vast criminal organization! – and happened to overhear you talking to Mr. Mallory. He is an old acquaintance of mine, and came to me with the information. From there the counterplot was born.

Snook is fine, by the way. I had loaded blanks into the revolver. He was not harmed. In fact, he was the policeman who appeared on the street last night. Quite the versatile actor, I must say. I'm afraid Mallory was not terribly convincing. He didn't even bring a weapon with which to threaten me. You must try harder on the details, old chap. I set out to return the gift by having yours compromised. It all worked out beautifully. Everyone (all were people I know) was in on the ruse except for you and your friend, Mr. Mallory, but I am sure that by now Lady Carlyle must have told him. I truly appreciate the thought, and I hope now that you know you can enjoy all of this in hindsight.

Happy Holidays, my friend.

Sherlock Holmes

Upon finishing my breakfast I turned over Holmes's note and wrote on the back. I slipped it back into the re-folded newspaper and sat it on his chair before leaving. It read simply . . .

Happy Holidays, Holmes

A Bauble in Scandinavia
by James Lovegrove

For most of the winter of 1890 Sherlock Holmes was in subdued mood, morose and taciturn. I did not yet know it, but he was brooding on the problem of Professor Moriarty, whose malign influence over our nation and over Holmes himself would reach its apex – and climax – the subsequent spring. Other affairs troubled my friend's mind, including an engagement by the French government to attend to matters of supreme political significance, but principally, as I now see in hindsight, it was Moriarty who cast a shadow over him and dampened whatever pleasure the season might have brought him.

During Advent I took it upon myself to call by at 221b Baker Street as often as I was able, my medical caseload and my domestic demands permitting. I attempted the best I could to cajole Holmes out of his gloom. "Surely," I would say, "you can allow a chink of Yuletide light to pierce this shroud of darkness which surrounds you." In response, all I would receive was a noncommittal shrug of the shoulders and a twitching moue of the mouth, as if I had suggested he fly to the moon and eat green cheese there. He was imperturbable and inscrutable. My efforts to elevate his spirits rebounded like bullets off armour plating.

What a contrast with Christmas 1889, when he and I had memorably been engaged in the pursuit of a villain who had concealed a stolen jewel in the crop of a goose, a jaunty episode I have chronicled as "The Adventure of the Blue Carbuncle". Then, Holmes had been particularly light of heart, even to the point of letting the felon go free in the hope that forgiveness, rather than punishment, would be the salvation of the man's soul. I wondered whether the Holmes of late 1890 would have been quite so lenient.

As Christmas Day itself loomed, I was loath to visit him any more. Until he bucked himself out of the trough he was in, how did it benefit me to seek out his company? He, it was clear, had no wish to consort with me. Why, therefore, might I wish to consort with him?

It was my wife who insisted I should drag myself over to 221b on Christmas Eve, contrary to my own desires. I would far rather have stayed at our cosy home – which she had adorned in splendid festive finery, including numerous paper chains and a heavily ornament-bedecked tree – and enjoyed a night in by the fire, reading a book and indulging in pleasant conversation. My dear Mary, however, was adamant that I not spurn Holmes. Thus, with the utmost unwillingness, I traipsed through the gas-lit dark from Paddington to Baker Street, bearing a gift.

My friend, as had become his wont, did not seem pleased to see me. If anything he was sullener than ever. I found him ensconced in his armchair by the window, legs drawn up, frowning intently over a telegram.

"Watson. What brings you here this cold, blustery evening?"

"Nothing," said I, "save the inclination to offer you a small token in keeping with the time of year."

"Hmm? Oh, a present. Yes. Put it there, would you?" He wafted a hand idly at the dining table before resuming his perusal of the telegram.

I laid the package, which my wife had wrapped very elegantly, where indicated. Inside was a calabash pipe. Holmes was wedded to his briar and his clay, with the occasional diversion to his cherry-wood when he was in a disputatious frame of mind, but I fancied he might find the large bowl and curved stem of a calabash congenial. I had expected him to tender some sort of reciprocal offering, but there was, it would appear, none.

"What do you have there?" I enquired. "The germ of a new case, maybe?"

"This?" He tapped the telegram. "Not as such. Nothing that need concern you, old fellow."

"You are quite absorbed by it."

"It exerts a fascination, I confess."

"Then tell me more."

"So that you can make it the basis of another of your trifling little sketches?"

"I am merely expressing polite curiosity," I said, bristling somewhat. "You could do me the courtesy of satisfying it."

"Well, since you insist. The telegram in fact pertains to an investigation which is already in train. I have a northern Scandinavian client whose business is in danger of suffering a grave setback."

"You have mentioned, more than once, that you are presently being of assistance to the Royal Family of Scandinavia. Is this related to that case?"

Holmes did not reply, instead fixing his keen gaze on the slip of paper. He ran his forefinger along the words, his lips pursing slightly.

"Would you care to read it aloud?" I persisted. "Perhaps I might offer some insight."

He gave vent to a brief and ever so scornful laugh. "You overrate your usefulness, Watson, or else underrate my mental powers."

At that, I picked up my hat and quit the apartment. I do not mind reporting that I was in high dudgeon. I do regret to relate, however, that I was short-tempered with Mary when I got home and that I went to bed thinking some fairly uncharitable thoughts about Sherlock Holmes.

I awoke on Christmas morning still chagrined, still resentful, and although I strove to remain civil and good-humoured over breakfast, I failed. Mary, indefatigably gracious when I was disgruntled or ill at ease, urged me to return to 221b forthwith and make amends.

"I will not have you full of gripe and crotchetiness on this day of all days, John," she said. "Go and clear the air between you and Mr. Holmes. It is the only way I shall get to enjoy Christmas."

I refused, but she was determined. Like the tide eroding the shore, she wore me down, so that by eight o'clock I was exiting the house, clad in Ulster, cravat, and gloves, and wending my way through the London streets. The city was quiet, the pavements empty, the roadways bare of traffic. It was the only day of the year that the capital's constant hubbub dwindled and peace prevailed. The sky sent down a sleety drizzle which, had the temperature been a couple of degrees lower, would have been transfigured into a light snowfall.

I rapped on the front door of my former address, and Mrs. Hudson ushered me in with an expression of surprise. "Doctor, I was not expecting you."

"I did not anticipate being here. Your lodger is in, I presume."

"No. He left an hour ago, and in something of a hurry, too."

"Where might he have gone? Whatever could have summoned him from home on Christmas Day?"

"I'm sure I have no idea. Mr. Holmes is a law unto himself, you know that as well as I. He may have been exercising some whim."

"Or pursuing a lead in a case. He gave you no indication as to his destination?"

"Not in the least."

"Nor as to when he might return?"

"None."

"How singular."

"You sound concerned, Doctor."

"A little."

"What if you were to look about his rooms? There is a chance you might find some clue to his whereabouts there."

"It would seem impertinent."

"But if you are worried about him . . . ."

I assented to her proposal. I could not put my finger on why I thought Holmes might be in jeopardy. I knew only that his behaviour had lately been off-kilter and that, with his tendency towards obsessiveness and single-mindedness – towards mania, even – he could often be his own worst enemy.

Upstairs, I cast an eye around the sitting room. I noted that my gift still sat on the table exactly where I had placed it. It had not been touched. Holmes's breakfast, which Mrs. Hudson had laid out for him, likewise had not been touched.

"He said nothing to you, either this morning or last night, regarding an appointment today?"

"He said nothing to me at all this morning, other than the briskest of goodbyes as he went out the door. As for last night . . . . Well, I do recall him making a comment that I found queer. Queer even by Mr. Holmes's lights. I was taking away his supper tray and he said, 'Mrs. Hudson, I shall just give the ashes a riddle, shall I?' He was kneeling by the hearth at the time with the poker in his hand, preparing to scrape at the grate, and I thought to myself why make such a statement? It was obvious that that was what he was doing, riddling the ashes. Why draw unnecessary attention to the fact?"

"Of late he has been acting rather oddly."

"You would be the better judge of that than I. I could swear, though, that he had been busy doing something else in the fireplace immediately before I entered. He looked . . . furtive, I suppose the word is, and all that talk of riddling was to divert my attention from some other deed."

"Furtiveness? That is not like Holmes. He can be secretive, but never furtive."

I bent beside the hearth and examined the cold ashes in the fireplace. It seemed unlikely that I might find therein some explanation to Holmes's abrupt-seeming departure, but I felt it was worth a look. Almost instantly I spied a scrap of paper standing proud amongst the clinker and the fragments of charred wood. It was the corner of a telegram, and I could not help but assume it belonged to the selfsame telegram which had so preoccupied him yesterday.

I plucked the scorched remnant out and held it up to the light to examine it. Just three words were legible, printed out in the telegrapher's neat hand:

ICE
TRADE
RD

312

Mrs. Hudson read over my shoulder, and together we puzzled over what these meagre morsels of data might signify.

"'*ICE*'?" I said. "Holmes referred to a 'northern Scandinavian client' in connection with the telegram. Ice is undoubtedly a feature of Scandinavian climes almost all year round. '*TRADE*' is less easily analysed. It might, I suppose, refer to an exchange of some sort, of goods or perhaps of contraband."

"What about '*RD*'?" said Mrs. Hudson. "Might that be someone's initials?"

"Or the common abbreviation for 'road', shortened here so as to save the sender of the telegram a penny or two. Each of the words lies at the end of its respective line, but we must not infer that each is complete. The '*RD*' could be the final two letters of a longer word."

"By that token so might '*ICE*' and '*TRADE*'."

"A good point. Were Holmes here and the telegram previously unknown to him, by now he would have extrapolated the entirety of its message from the scant available evidence, and doubtless also the sender's occupation, hair colour and preferred brand of snuff."

"It is unlike you to sound so churlish. Has Mr. Holmes done something to cause offence?"

"He has, but now my anxiety overrides my feelings of affront. I believe I ought to – "

I broke off, slapping my forehead as inspiration struck.

"Mrs. Hudson, there is one obvious interpretation. I am amazed I did not think of it sooner. As you yourself just said, '*ICE*' and '*TRADE*' might also be the ends of words, like '*RD*'. What if those words are '*POLICE*' and '*LESTRADE*'?"

"That would also account for the '*RD*', would it not?"

"How so?"

"'*SCOTLAND YARD*', Doctor."

I made haste to Scotland Yard. I could scarcely believe I was chasing so slender a thread. There was no guarantee I had intuited correctly the import of the telegram from those few isolated characters. In the absence of any other course of action, however, it was all I could do.

That Inspector Lestrade was on duty was perhaps predictable. He was unmarried and faithfully devoted to his job. Few others of his brethren would have given up their Christmas Day to sit at their desks, but Lestrade seemed positively glad to be there. I imagine he found it preferable to staying at home, alone, while all the world around him celebrated in the bosom of family and friends.

"Gone, you say, Dr. Watson?"

"Without warning, without explanation, without trace."

"You are his great intimate, but even I know that Mr. Holmes is liable to vanish at a moment's notice. He is as contrary and unpredictable as a cat. What makes you so certain the reason for this absence is sinister?"

"He has not been himself in recent days. He has been . . . difficult."

"Well now, it's funny you should say that," remarked the sallow, rat-faced official. "Only yesterday he paid us a visit, out of the blue, and I noted then that he seemed distracted. I put it from my mind, thinking it just another facet of a complex personality."

"In what manner distracted?"

"He had called to see Athelney Jones and discuss the affair of the Red-Headed League. The case is shortly coming to trial, where I suspect the jury will have no trouble finding John Clay and his accomplice guilty as charged, and Holmes averred that he had a couple of minor details to clear up. Inspector Jones was not in, however, so I had the pleasure of his company, but not for long. We exchanged pleasantries, but Mr. Holmes's thoughts were elsewhere. He kept muttering to himself."

"Muttering?"

"Yes. I had the impression he was only vaguely aware of my presence, even as we chatted. He returned again and again to a single short phrase."

"What was it?"

"'Greek philosopher in translation'."

"I beg your pardon?"

"That was it. Over and over he mumbled those words: 'Greek philosopher in translation'."

"But it makes no sense."

"Did I say it did?" Lestrade shrugged his shoulders. "I am simply relating the facts of the matter. I assumed it pertained to some investigation he was busy with."

"It must refer to a book. Off the top of my head I can only think of Jowett's *Plato*, but there are countless others. I recall from my schooldays an English version of Aristotle's *Nicomachean Ethics* that induced panicked bewilderment in me every time I opened it, but I cannot remember the translator's name. Memory has drawn a veil over the trauma."

"Possibly it was some clue he was mulling over. Hence the repetition."

"Yes, but if only I could make head or tail of it."

"You're sure this telegram referred to me?"

"I am sure of nothing right now, Inspector, other than that I am in the dark, floundering."

I paused on the front steps of the building, in the lee of the arched doorway, and pondered. How did a Greek philosopher relate to this Scandinavian client of Holmes's? Was there any connection at all? The randomness of it unsettled me. I began to fear that the balance of my friend's mind had been severely disturbed. Had overwork placed too immense a burden on him? Had he cracked under the strain? Worse, had he overindulged in cocaine? He was apt to flee into the embrace of the drug both when he was bored and under-stimulated and when he was under pressure. Its detrimental effects on the psyche were well-known to those in my profession, and Holmes was no casual user of it.

I decided to run through the names of every Greek philosopher I could think of, hoping against hope that this might furnish me with an answer to my predicament. The Classics were not my field of expertise, and once past Plato, Aristotle, Socrates, Pythagoras, and Zeno I came unstuck.

Then one further name popped into my head: *Diogenes.*

A quarter-of-an-hour later, I was knocking on the door of a certain exclusive gentlemen's club on Pall Mall. I could not escape the feeling that I was grasping at straws, but it was better to try something, however desperate, than do nothing.

The Diogenes Club was considerably better attended that day than it had been when I previously passed through its hallowed portals some two years earlier. Its members, united in their antisociality, had flocked there in preference to enduring Christmas at home with their kin. They thronged its panelled libraries and other nooks and chambers, observing the strict code of silence that was the club's unique and primary rule. The one concession to the season was a single small sprig of holly attached to the front of the reception desk in the hall – more an ironic joke, I felt, than a decoration.

I was soon able to inveigle a meeting with Mycroft Holmes in the Stranger's Room, the only place on the premises where conversation was allowed. My friend's corpulent older brother chuckled when he learned of the wayward path that had led me into his presence.

"What an absurd and *outré* conundrum," he declared. "'Greek philosopher in translation'. What on earth is Sherlock up to?"

"You do not think I am right in seeking you out to consult you?"

"On the face of it, you are. The club does of course derive its name from the philosopher Diogenes of Sinope, whose espousal of Cynicism,

315

specifically the rejection of social norms, informs our own practices. Furthermore, do you not recall the circumstances under which you and I first met, Doctor?"

"It was during the affair involving the interpreter Melas and the kidnapping of Sophy Kratides."

"Quite so. Hence the 'in translation' part of that quaint ditty – an oblique nod towards Melas. It seems Sherlock is revisiting old haunts, old cases."

"That rather confirms the unfortunate theory I am forming. Your brother has succumbed to an infirmity of the brain. He is wandering the palaces of his mind, becoming lost."

"That is as may be," said Mycroft, "but I meant literally what I said about revisiting old haunts. Yesterday lunchtime Sherlock was in this very room."

"You don't say! How did he strike you?"

Mycroft Holmes puffed out a sigh of airy indifference. "Much as he usually is. A touch offhand, I thought."

"But lucid?"

"More or less."

"What was his reason for coming here?"

"He gave none. I presume it was to bid me a Merry Christmas, but in the event he neglected to do so. We Holmeses don't really go in for that type of thing. For the most part, he and I chatted inconsequentially while Sherlock leafed through a newspaper he had brought. That very newspaper there, as it happens."

He gestured to a folded copy of the *Daily Telegraph* which lay on the cushions of the window seat. I picked it up to discover that it was open at the advertisements sheet, and moreover that one advertisement had been carefully and emphatically circled in red ink.

"Your brother's handiwork?" I enquired, pointing to the circle.

"Perhaps. I can't swear I saw him do it."

I knew well that Holmes was an aficionado of the advertisement columns, as he was of the agony columns. He liked to clip out certain entries and paste them into his voluminous commonplace books for future reference. They were to him a map of modern civilisation in all its multifarious yearnings and hungers, and frequently afforded him clues to crimes both past and present.

The one he may or may not have singled out as notable read as follows:

Watson – I give generously in northern Scandinavia

316

"My goodness!" I ejaculated. I was more than a little taken aback to see my own surname printed on the page.

"Whatever is the matter?"

I showed Mycroft Holmes the advertisement. "It is beyond coincidence, surely, that your brother found this when he is currently in the service of a client from northern Scandinavia. Some nefarious conspiracy is afoot."

"It does seem somewhat irregular," Mycroft opined.

"But how am I a part of it? Why does my name feature? I am at a loss to account for it. I have no knowledge of the client's identity. Holmes has vouchsafed to me almost nothing about the person."

"'Give generously' could conceivably be construed as sly criminal slang for causing harm, even murder. Could it be that Sherlock believes you are, without your realising it, in danger?"

"It is more than plausible. It might well explain his recent behaviour. I am the unwitting target of some villain's plan – an old enemy of ours, maybe – and until such time as he can ensure my safety, Holmes is pushing me aside, out of the line of fire. By warding me off, keeping me at arm's length, he has been protecting me. With much the same justification, he himself is on the move. He has been crisscrossing London, travelling hither and yon, in order to throw the miscreant off the scent."

"Then there is logic in his apparent illogicality. Nothing irregular about it whatsoever."

It was the second time in the space of a minute that Mycroft had uttered the word "irregular", and all at once a thought occurred to me. I studied the wording of the advertisement again, closely this time. An idea had snagged in my brain, one that was bizarre, fantastical, too ridiculous to be true – and yet the solution lay in front of me, hiding in plain sight, right before my eyes.

The bells of Westminster Abbey were chiming. Londoners from near and far filed through the huge oaken Anglo-Saxon doors for the Christmas service. All were in their best dress and eagerly anticipating a panoply of carols and good cheer.

Lounging beside the entrance to the Abbey was a young man of scarecrow-like appearance and nonchalant bearing, who looked as if he were there just to admire the well-heeled congregants as they paraded by. Really, though, he was eyeing them up with a view to robbing them.

This was how Wiggins, of the Baker Street Irregulars, liked to spend his Christmas Day. The putative leader of Sherlock Holmes's gang of street Arabs was not woven from the purest cloth. When he was not running errands on Holmes's behalf, he was wont to revert to criminal ways, supplementing his honest income with ill-gotten gains.

As I approached, I debated inwardly the rationality of my being there. Was I deluded? Or had the advertisement genuinely contained a cryptic intimation, steering me towards Wiggins? Holmes was adept at spotting patterns in things and extricating secret messages from the most abstruse texts and artefacts. What if the advertisement was a coded reference to a threat which imperilled not just my life but that of another of his associates as well? It could be no accident, I thought, that the initial letters of the words "Watson – I give generously in northern Scandinavia" spelled out Wiggins.

No sooner was I within hailing distance of the youngster than I saw him lurch forward from his position and barge shoulder-first into a stooped, elderly gentleman coming the opposite way. Wiggins apologised profusely to the white-haired, bewhiskered figure, and the other assured him that he was unhurt and no harm had been done.

How wrong he was. For I had spied Wiggins's hand darting inside the man's overcoat and relieving him of a plump calfskin wallet.

"Hullo!" I cried. "Wiggins! I saw that!"

Wiggins turned towards me, and his face fell, his expression lapsing into consternation and alarm. Without further ado he took to his heels, sprinting off in the direction of the Houses of Parliament and the Thames.

I saw no alternative but to give chase.

He led me a merry dance, did Wiggins. For fully half-an-hour he threaded through byways and backstreets, and several times nearly gave me the slip. He was younger than me by a good couple of decades, but I had a stamina tempered by my service in Afghanistan, and many an afternoon on the rugby pitch. I stayed upon his tail, even though I was panting hard and my lungs burned. After a while I forgot about the elderly gentleman's wallet or the advertisement. I ran on, consumed by the simple desire not to let this rascal get the best of me.

Up through the West End I pursued him, and into the doctors' quarter around Harley Street and Wimpole Street, until we were in Marylebone and only a stone's throw from Baker Street.

That was when I at last had to concede defeat. I slowed to alleviate the ache in my chest and the soreness in my legs, and finally stopped altogether while Wiggins trotted unattainably and irredeemably out of my sight. I braced myself on a railing until I caught my breath. I needed a rest and something restorative, and since I was so close to 221b, I made my way there, planning to throw myself on Mrs. Hudson's mercy and beg a cup of tea and a snifter of brandy.

To my utter astonishment, who should I see entering the house but the very same elderly gentleman whose pocket Wiggins had picked.

In a matter of seconds I, too, was inside and climbing the seventeen stairs to Holmes's apartment.

I had a fairly good idea who would be awaiting me within.

I was both correct and incorrect in my surmise.

Sherlock Holmes tugged off the white wig and whiskers of his disguise and straightened up so that he no longer affected the bowed back of old age. He was smiling broadly, his grey eyes twinkling.

Beside him was Wiggins, looking inordinately pleased with himself. Mrs. Hudson was there too, setting the table for dinner. So – and this was the first great surprise – was my old army friend Colonel Hayter, with whom my readers may be familiar from his appearance in the story "The Reigate Squires". The second great surprise was the presence of my own darling Mary.

Holmes led a prolonged round of applause.

"Well done, old friend," said he. "Well done indeed."

Hayter shook my hand warmly, while Mary linked her elbow with mine and planted a brief, affectionate kiss on my cheek.

I shook my head, weary but wise. "You scoundrel, Holmes," I said. "The nerve of you."

"Have you had fun?"

"The answer to that is both yes and no. You had me going there, with that sham of yours. The dark mood. The introspection. The disaffectedness."

"Not wholly feigned, as you will soon learn," said my friend, "but exaggerated certainly, for effect."

"And then this whole elaborate rigmarole, starting with the telegram . . . . The chain of clues and puzzles . . . ."

"A game. A charade in which Mrs. Watson, Mrs. Hudson and Wiggins all had roles and played them admirably, as, I trust, did Lestrade and Mycroft. We are expecting the latter two to arrive shortly, by the way. As you can see, Mrs. Hudson has laid places for seven, and that smell you may detect permeating up from the kitchen is the aroma of a turkey of sizeable proportions roasting in the oven. The bird is big enough to satiate six average appetites as well as the exceptional appetite that is my brother's."

"I am myself more than a little famished, after the wild goose chase you have sent me on."

"A metaphorical wild goose chase, compared with the actual one last Christmas."

"And all in aid of . . . ?"

"Come, come, Watson. Can't you tell? This has been my Christmas gift to you. A mystery of your very own to solve. How many times have you doggedly accompanied me on an investigation, required to do not much more than be a sounding-board and a Boswell? I devised something that would give you a taste of the limelight for once, putting you centre stage, while I stood, for the most part, in the wings."

"There is no 'northern Scandinavian client', is there?"

"Not unless you count a certain jolly, red-cheeked fellow who resides in the Arctic Circle and makes his annual rounds at this time of year."

"Holmes, you have a well-buried sentimental streak."

"You concoct amusing confections out of my cases, Watson. It seems only fair that I should concoct an amusing confection for you in return. In truth, this has been nothing more than a mere Christmas bauble, I think you'll find. But then there's your story title, should you ever choose to set this escapade down in print: 'A Bauble in Scandinavia'. You will doubtless appreciate the wordplay."

I treasured the memory of that Christmas Day throughout the three years that followed, when Holmes was missing, presumed dead. It kept me warm during some very cold, long, mournful nights. The seven of us round the table – friends, colleagues, kin – and food aplenty and fine wine flowing.

Holmes never did take to that calabash pipe, though.

The Adventure of Marcus Davery
by Arthur Hall

As I review my notes, I see that it was no more than a few weeks after the trial of Colonel Moran in 1894 that another extraordinary affair was placed before my friend Sherlock Holmes.

There had been little to occupy Holmes in recent days, and as Christmas approached I saw the signs of boredom that had once driven him to the cocaine bottle slowly reappearing. We were about to repair to the fireside armchairs when his keen ears detected a coach sliding to a halt in the piled snow beneath our window. At once, he dropped his newspaper and stared down into Baker Street. Instantly, and I thought a little desperately, he adopted his habit of rubbing his hands together in anticipation of a visit from a new client. A moment later the door-bell rang, and we heard Mrs. Hudson descend the stairs. After a brief discussion she returned with a gentleman of normal height, but who was made to appear taller by the high top hat he wore. His black moustache seemed to bristle as he took in first the room, and then Holmes and myself.

"Which of you is Mr. Sherlock Holmes?" He asked in a rather clipped tone.

"It is I that you seek," said my friend, before introducing me. He called to our landlady, who was closing the door as she retreated. "Tea, please, Mrs. Hudson, for our guest and ourselves."

"Not for me," our visitor responded as he removed his hat. "Thank you, but I have little time."

"Very well." Holmes gestured to tell her to disregard his request. "But pray sit down, my good sir, and tell us how we can be of assistance."

"You have not seen the papers?"

"We were about to peruse the morning editions, as you arrived."

Our visitor sighed, and lowered himself into the empty chair. "Then what I have to say will mean nothing to you."

Holmes looked at him carefully. "Let us first ascertain the subject of our discussion, before we decide on our understanding of it. I know nothing of you, sir. You have not yet given your name, or it would have been announced as you entered. Apart from the facts that you are not long out of the army, have been roughly handled recently, and suffered

321

great distress, I can deduce little, save that you left your home rather hurriedly."

It did not surprise me that our client showed some astonishment. Holmes's deductions always had a confusing and puzzling effect on those unaccustomed to his methods.

"How the deuce do you know these things, sir? Have I been spied upon, in addition to all else?"

"Not by us," my friend assured him. "All my conclusions were based on the most casual observations, and are easily explained. Your excessively brisk manner and movements betray the fact that you have recently seen military service, as does the emblem forming the handle of your walking-cane. The discolouration around your eyes and mouth indicate that you have recently been beaten, since your general appearance does not suggest boxing or similar sporting activities. Your distress, which I presume to be the reason for consulting me, is evident from the grief in your eyes, and I know you rushed out of your house because your cravat is badly askew."

Our client bent forward in his seat, placing a hand over his eyes. "I see that your reputation is not exaggerated, Mr. Holmes. Forgive me for not introducing myself, and for my brusque manner. My name is Caine Barnett, and I referred to the newspapers because my son's death is on the front pages of them all."

Holmes and I expressed our sympathy, and Mr. Barnett nodded a grim acknowledgement.

"Suicide, I know, is deeply hurtful to those left behind," I said after a glance at the newspaper on the side-table before me. "I have seen it before. The pain lessens with time, but you must endure and exercise patience."

"Suicide?" Mr. Barnett fixed me with a fierce, direct stare. "Yes, that is what the newspapers are saying. Gentlemen, my son, Stephen, was murdered yesterday!"

"Have you consulted Scotland Yard with this claim?" Holmes asked.

"I have come directly from there. Inspector Lestrade has told me that the case will be fully investigated, but I am not satisfied."

Holmes showed no surprise. "Mr. Barnett, pray take a few moments to compose yourself, and then tell us of these events from the beginning. If it is at all possible, I will do all that I can to help you."

Mr. Barnett sat with his head bowed, but when he lifted it I saw at once the emptiness from which Holmes had deduced his loss.

"Six months has passed since I left the army," he began. "I had fulfilled my commission and wanted no more of the life. On returning to

Essex, I found my wife glad to see me, of course, but my son was strangely remote and indifferent. I soon discovered that his surly attitude sprang from an association he had recently formed. Although our conversations were sparse, I managed to drag out of him that he was spending much time in the company of one Marcus Davery, a disreputable character who is well-known on the gambling and horse-racing circuits. He is apparently quite notorious. Perhaps you have heard of him, Mr. Holmes?" The name was unknown to me, but my friend answered without hesitation. "I have. He is the discredited son of the Marquis of Langandale. His history is colourful."

"That does not surprise me," Mr. Barnett said. "For Stephen came to me on returning home one evening, much disturbed and with a tale to tell of how this man had persuaded him to gamble using money he did not possess. Consequently, the house held his notes for a sum he could not possibly repay, and he sought my help."

"Is yours a wealthy family?" I enquired.

"Not at all. I think that Davery miscalculated here, possibly because my son's groundless boasting misled him. We live on my army pension and a few small investments, and so I was quite unable to accede to Stephen's request."

"Trapped in this way then, it was supposed that he took his own life?" Holmes ventured.

"I have no doubt that Davery seized upon this to his own advantage, to excuse his own actions. Stephen's last words to me, before he went to confront Davery, were to the effect that the incident was a deliberate ploy. He suspected that Davery and the gambling house were in league, in a scheme to defraud customers that he introduced to the tables."

"He had proof of this?"

"That is what he told me, the last time I saw him alive."

"But it was never brought to light?"

"I imagine, whatever its form, it was destroyed after Stephen's death. It was his intention to expose them all. The gambling house also has gone, the premises abandoned, and the operators and clientele scattered."

Holmes took on a thoughtful expression. "So, Mr. Barnett, it is your contention that your son was murdered or induced to take his own life by this man Davery, and the given reason was that he found himself inescapably trapped in debt?"

"Debt that he was certain he had not actually incurred."

"Quite so. Did he indicate to you anything of the nature of this deception?"

323

"He mentioned only that he had discovered that several others had been trapped similarly."

"Did he reveal the outcome of these incidents?"

Mr. Barnett nodded, with an expression of despair. "In every case the money was paid. The victims, or their families, wished to avoid the scandal."

"Did you, yourself, take any action in this matter?" Holmes asked after a short silence.

"As I mentioned, I consulted Scotland Yard earlier. News of Stephen's death reached me late yesterday morning, and I confess to feeling anger before grief. I went straight round to see Davery – Stephen had mentioned often enough that he lived off Oxford Circus – to confront him. To my surprise, the fellow practically admitted his responsibility for my son's death, saying that he had become a 'dangerous liability'. He bragged that he was quite immune to the law and retribution of any kind. I threatened him, and he replied that I would be sorry for doing so, and acted almost as if the whole thing were humorous. At this point I could no longer restrain myself, but my attack was repelled by Davery's manservant, who is an ex-prize fighter. Last night I went for a short walk to clear my head, and two ruffians attacked me. I gave a good account of myself but," he indicated his discoloured eyes, "they were too much for me."

"I have no doubt that they found their task difficult," Holmes murmured, "and I imagine that Davery's claim to be beyond retribution is because, although discredited, he has powerful friends. However, we will see if he remains unscathed by the end of my enquiries. Now, Mr. Barnett, is there anything more that you wish to tell us?"

"It remains only for me to say that I am greatly indebted to both you gentlemen, for undertaking to set things right on my behalf."

"You should hear of the outcome shortly," Holmes said. "Pray be good enough to write down the address of Mr. Marcus Davery, before you leave."

Our visitor took the pencil and pad that I produced, and after more expressions of gratitude, he took up his hat and left us.

Holmes sat like a statue for a few moments, and then his expression changed. His eyes glittered, and I saw that he was filled with the extraordinary energy that I knew of old.

"Hand me my index if you please, Watson."

I extracted the volume from the bookshelf, and he began turning the pages eagerly. He studied an assortment of newspaper cuttings, impatiently dismissing one after another until at last he gave a cry of triumph. "Aha! As I said, his career has been colourful."

"Is his notoriety as great as Mr. Barnett implied?"

"Most certainly." Holmes held the sheets up to catch the light. "You will be astonished to hear that this is, in fact, the fifth suicide with which our Mr. Davery has been concerned, apart from the misery he inflicted with the gambling scheme. It appears that anyone who gets in his way chooses it voluntarily, conveniently solving his problems."

"Clearly he has some sort of strong hold on his acquaintances. Has nothing been done before now?"

"As we have already observed, he has powerful friends."

"Are they powerful enough to place him above the law?"

"He is not the first to believe that it can be so, but we shall see how things turn out."

"For how long has this been happening?"

Holmes scanned the pages with a grim expression on his face. "He appears in my index about seven months ago, but I have no doubt that his misdeeds extend back much further. It seems that, at that time, there was some sort of indiscretion involving a Mrs. Elizabeth Velner. Davery somehow discovered and threatened to disclose this to her husband unless she paid him a substantial sum, which she did. Of course, in such situations that is never the end of the matter. After repeated demands, the lady was practically penniless and would have been forced to confess everything, but decided to take her own life instead, or so says the official report. Then we have Mr. Andrew Byncroft, to whom Davery was heavily in debt, until, again, suicide made repayment unnecessary. Next was Mr. George Cornhurst, of whom we have no details other than that he threatened Davery with exposure of some past dishonesty, or worse. Finally, Mr. Benjamin Selter took his own life after discovering Davery in the act of burgling his house. An extraordinary pattern of events, wouldn't you say, Watson?"

"It is appalling," I replied in disgust. "What kind of man can he be, Holmes? How does he induce his victims to end their own lives?"

"Perhaps this can be determined, during the investigation."

"Could it be Mesmerism?"

"There is no mention of Davery possessing hypnotic skills, either in the official report, or elsewhere in my index. Nevertheless, at this stage we cannot rule it out. I know that you have to attend to your patients this morning, Doctor, so I will visit Davery alone. If you would care to hear the outcome of this, I should be back by three."

At that, we took up our hats and coats and left Baker Street together. Outside, much of the snow had been cleared, but the traffic was heavy, so that Holmes had difficulty in securing a hansom. We were about to separate when a boyish figure emerged from the passing crowds to accost us.

"Mr. Sherlock Holmes and Doctor Watson, I presume?" He said with a humorous air.

"Indeed," replied Holmes. "And you, sir?"

"You will know of me already, for Mr. Caine Barnett has consulted you. I am Marcus Davery."

I immediately took stock of him, for he was not in the least as I expected. Dark-skinned and tall, but not of Holmes's height, and clad in a rather flamboyant morning-coat and narrow-brimmed top hat, he had an engaging smile. His eyes shone with amusement, as if he saw everything before him as some light-hearted jest or schoolboy prank, and my first impression of his youth was contradicted only slightly upon closer inspection.

"Do you wish to discuss your dealings with my client?"

Marcus Davery laughed shortly. "Nothing could be further from my mind, Mr. Holmes. The only reason that I am spending a few minutes of my time here is to do you the service of warning you against wasting yours. You will achieve nothing, sir, with any pursuit of my affairs. What is done is past, to Mr. Barnett's detriment, but to my advantage. I am a man who makes his way through life without the burdens of regret. I fear nothing, nor any man. You would do well to remember that."

I felt my temper rising at the man's impudence, but Holmes put a hand on my arm to indicate that I should stay silent.

"This is not the first time I have heard such words from those who feel they are above the law," he said then. "I have been threatened often, yet here I am. However, since you had the foresight to follow Mr. Barnett here, Mr. Davery, I acknowledge that you are a force to be reckoned with."

"You would do well to consider me as such. Mr. Barnett threatened me and was punished for his pains. Naturally I kept track of him to determine his future intentions, and he led me to you."

"Are you not afraid that such outrageous conduct might attract the attention of Scotland Yard?"

Marcus Davery gave a contemptuous snort. "That place exists to keep the little men and women, the inconsequential rabble of the capital, in order. It is a protection for the ruling class against the legions of the unwashed. No sir, I am unafraid of these blundering oafs who are employed to restrain their peers."

"Thank you, Mr. Davery," Holmes stare was expressionless. "You have made things very clear."

"See that you remember my warning. Be aware that my vengeance comes from high places."

"I assure you that I will forget nothing about you."

Davery gave us a long cold look, and I saw that his eyes were blank like those of a mannequin and without sentiment or feeling. Abruptly he turned and walked away, swinging his cane and singing softly to himself.

"That man is criminally mad," I said to Holmes. "His impertinence is almost unendurable."

To my surprise, my friend laughed. "Your diagnosis is doubtlessly correct, Doctor. But we shall see where his view of the world leaves him, in the end." He signalled a passing hansom. "We have met his kind before."

We went our separate ways. It was a little after three when I returned to our rooms through a flurry of snow, but there was no sign of Holmes. I settled into an armchair to read when the front door opened and closed noisily, and I heard his familiar tread upon the stairs.

"Ah, Watson!" he cried as he burst into the room. "I have had a most successful day. Kindly ring for Mrs. Hudson, and I will tell you all over tea."

I had spent a mundane day at my surgery, and so was keen to hear of my friend's experiences.

"My first destination was the docks," Holmes began presently as he pushed away his empty cup. "In fact I visited several harbour masters with the same request, until I found a description of a certain voyage in the records."

"But what has this to do with Davery?" I enquired.

"You will recall that his complexion was rather dark, but not so much so as to be recently returned from the tropics. I deduced from this that he had returned from such a journey some months ago, and postulated that the suicides began since his return."

"Did you confirm this?"

"I did so by consulting the Port of London journals that are maintained by every harbour master. Marcus Davery returned from East Africa via Mombasa, less than a month before his first victim took her own life. I knew where to look because I noticed his signet ring, which bore a design typical of the native art of that region."

"You believe that his strange control over others originates there, then?"

"It appears likely, but we shall see. From there, I went to one of those little places I keep around London, where I changed my appearance to that of an unemployed labourer. I then kept a watch on Davery's house until I was certain that he was still absent, and that the maid had left for the day. The manservant, Manners, is indeed an ex-prize fighter, as Mr. Barnett surmised, but he is not such a bad fellow after all. Pretending to look for work, I engaged him in conversation and managed to learn his hours of service, those of the maid, and about Davery's regular haunts and movements. I am convinced, however, that Manners knows nothing about his master's crimes or how they may have been committed. The encounter ended with him recommending another household where he thought there is work to be had."

"You have done exceedingly well, Holmes, but I fail to see how Davery could have kept his misdeeds a secret from his manservant so successfully."

"I imagine he would have related the facts to him, if he thought it necessary, justifying his own actions in every case. Davery strikes me as a man who covers his tracks well, but Manners seems to be a man who would leave his position rather than involve himself in anything dishonourable."

"Did you learn anything further?"

Holmes began to stuff one of the pipes from his rack with coarse black shag. "I did. After resuming my own appearance, my final destination was the British Museum. There I sought out Professor Egbert Faye of the Department of African Studies. I discussed with him several possibilities that have occurred to me, since learning of Davery's apparent ability to confer suicide on others. As a result, I have eliminated all likely methods but one. Nevertheless, before I proceed, I must have proof that Davery actually works in this way. I propose to obtain such proof tonight."

"If you need me Holmes, I am with you."

"As I knew you would be. Where would I be, without my Watson?"

No more snow fell that day, but when darkness fell it was accompanied by a bleak, bitter cold. I kept warm by walking up and down in front of Davery's house, beating my hands together in their thick leather gloves and watching my cloudy exhalations.

Holmes had assured me that both Davery and his manservant would be absent, and the maid also, as she worked only part-time. My function was to rap upon the door at the sight of a constable or any other threat but, unsurprisingly in this weather, I had seen no one.

The front door opened and the shadowy figure of my friend emerged. He left the house as silently as he had entered it, expertly using his pick-locks, not long before. In moments he was beside me and we were striking out down the gas-lit street.

"You have said before now, that had you not been a consulting detective you might have been a successful cracksman," I reminded him. "That skill does not seem to have left you."

"And glad I am of it. I have in my pocket five envelopes, each containing a possible solution to our problem. When I have analysed these, we should know much more."

"I am relieved that you found what you sought, without leaving Davery any indication of your visit."

Holmes laughed shortly. "Much to the contrary, Watson. If Davery is at all astute, he will quickly realise that he has been burgled, even if little has apparently been taken. I have left some small indications. It will not take him long, I think, to deduce the identity of his visitor."

"My dear fellow!" I cried in astonishment. "I cannot understand you placing yourself in needless danger! Is it wise to invite Davery's vengeance? Did not Mr. Barnett suffer for doing so?"

"Calm yourself, Doctor, and try to have patience. I intend to force Davery into a position where he can do nothing against me, despite my being a continual trial to him. I have no reason to think that this stratagem will prove difficult but it will be as well if you continue with your practice for the time being, and play no part in this."

"If that is what you wish, but it does not sit well with me."

"I know, old friend, but it is for the best. You will see, I promise you."

Holmes spent most of the following day at his work bench. On returning from my practice, I was greeted with a thick and pungent atmosphere, alleviated only by his cheerful announcement of success.

"I must apologise for the smell in here, Watson, but I have at least opened the window. I can now say that Davery's extraordinary power to induce suicide is a mystery no more. After testing the contents of my five envelopes, one sample stands out as a drug that dissolves the will-power. Professor Faye was right, in every respect."

"So, it remains only to prevent Davery from committing more outrages."

"Indeed, and I shall set out upon that course tomorrow."

Holmes was as good as his word. His first act was to secure two prize fighters, much larger and uglier brutes than Manners, through McMurdo, whom he knew of old. The three followed Davery's every move for the next ten days, even watching his house at night. They made no effort to conceal themselves, so that their presence always hung over him. At no time were they approached, although Davery did at first fling a few sneering glances in their direction, and as things progressed

Holmes was able to observe repeatedly the absolute arrogance of the man.

His treatment of his tailor, for keeping him waiting for a fitting, bordered on violence, while he actually struck his wine merchant on discovering that his favourite vintage was sold out!

My friend achieved his objective with superlative success. As he had predicted, he had become an inconvenience that Davery could do nothing about.

Then, as we repaired to our armchairs after an evening meal of Mrs. Hudson's fish pie, a visitor arrived.

"Lestrade!" Holmes cried, as Mrs. Hudson closed our door behind the inspector. "Take a chair and sit with us. Watson, a brandy for the inspector."

"No, thank you, Mr. Holmes." Lestrade brushed snow from the shoulders of his greatcoat. "I will stand if you don't mind."

"I perceive from your rather glum expression that you are here on official business."

"I am, and I take no pleasure in it."

"Pray tell us then."

I saw that the little detective was clearly embarrassed, as if he were about to deliver a message that he personally disapproved of. He stood for a moment, hat in hand, in silence.

"This afternoon I was called to see the Assistant Commissioner," he said then. "It seems, Mr. Holmes, that you have been hounding a member of the aristocracy quite without cause. My superiors, in recognition of the help you have given us before now, have instructed me to warn you of the possible consequences, before charges can be laid."

"Ah, we are talking of Marcus Davery," my friend responded. "That man has murdered several times, Lestrade, and I believe that you know that as well as I. Did he perhaps send a friend or relative who is acquainted with the Assistant Commissioner to make this request of him?"

"His cousin, Sir Stephen Taranet".

"To put your superior in a position where it was difficult for him to refuse, obviously. I should think that Sir Stephen is the only member of Davery's family still in social contact with him, since he was discredited. Come, Inspector, after all these years I know you well. You feel the injustice of allowing the privileged to escape the law as keenly as I."

"I do, but what am I to say? I am caught between what I feel to be right and my orders."

"He is trapped in a difficult position, Holmes," I said.

"He is indeed," Holmes put a paper spill into the fire and lit his pipe from it, "and I have no wish to add to the situation. Yet I cannot, in good conscience, allow a man who I know to be guilty to escape in such circumstances."

I nodded thoughtfully. "A dilemma, then?"

Lestrade looked at both of us. "I have to see the Assistant Commissioner tomorrow, with your answer."

"You may tell him," Holmes blew out a cloud of fragrant smoke, "that in any case my investigation is almost complete. I do not expect it to extend beyond Christmas. Ask him, for he must feel as you and I, and he is in the same position, to turn a blind eye for the next few days. In exchange, I give my word that I will not lay a finger on Marcus Davery, at any time."

Lestrade looked relieved. "Thank you, Mr. Holmes."

"Now will you stay for a brandy, or perhaps a cigar?"

For the first time, the inspector smiled. "I regret that I cannot. From here I go to look into a disturbance in Whitechapel."

"Goodnight then, Inspector."

Lestrade turned and made for the door. Before he reached it he stopped and faced us again. "Merry Christmas, gentlemen!"

Before we could reply, he had gone out into the snow.

For four days more, Holmes continued his observation of Marcus Davery. It was after that, by the early post on Christmas morning, that the letter arrived.

"A message from Davery," my friend explained. "He is of stronger stock than I thought, for I had expected something from him before this."

"He knows now that his attempt to use Scotland Yard against you was not wholly successful," said I.

"Undoubtedly. He suggests a meeting, tomorrow afternoon at the Agora Club, to set things straight between us. His language is exceedingly polite."

"The Agora Club? I cannot say that I know it."

"It is in Pall Mall, at the opposite end to the Diogenes Club, but very different. A meeting-place for political discussion with, I hear, its fair share of lunatics and fanatics. I thought it had closed temporarily, for repairs to its inner structure,"

"So, the building will be deserted? This is a trap, Holmes."

"Oh, I am quite sure of that," my friend agreed, "but who will fall into it?"

"You cannot trust that man. It would be tantamount to suicide."

"You choose your words well, Watson."

I was obliged to visit an elderly patient, which took up most of the morning. When I returned, Holmes was dragging out a dusty old chest from his room. He opened it near one of the armchairs, where he sat while examining the contents. I saw bundles of papers marked "Montague Street", a short crowbar, a naval officer's cap, and several other small items that must have had some significance for him. Finally, he produced a pistol that was much larger than the weapons we usually carried, placed it to one side and returned the chest to whence it came.

Soon after, Mrs. Hudson appeared. As befitted the season, she was full of good cheer as she served our roast duck and plum pudding. Holmes behaved like someone forced into endurance for the sake of propriety, and was clearly glad when the ritual was over.

"Watson," he said as we sat with glasses of port in our armchairs afterwards, "I fear that I must leave you to enjoy the next glass or two of this excellent vintage alone. However, I will be no further away than my workbench, and it will not be for long."

With that he drained his glass and went to the far side of the room, taking with him the pistol he had found earlier. He stood thoughtfully among his chemical apparatus, then I saw him raise a hammer and strike several times. I concluded that he had decided to use this weapon against Davery, if it became necessary, and was repairing it.

The remainder of the day was spent talking of our past adventures, and in general conversation. Holmes produced a box of cigars that he had saved, so he said, for a special occasion. We finished the bottle of port, this interrupted by the wine we shared with Mrs. Hudson when she brought a plate of sandwiches in the early evening. We retired early.

The next day saw me complete the responsibilities of my practice with unaccustomed haste. Holmes had mentioned that his appointment with Davery was for three o'clock, but after battling with a new snowfall I arrived back at Baker Street not long after two.

I found him ready to depart, staring from the window. "Halloa, Watson. I trust your morning went well?"

"It was uneventful," I told him, "but I am more concerned about you. At least take me with you, for there is no telling what this man is capable of."

Sherlock Holmes turned to me and smiled warmly. "You have always been the best of friends to me, Watson. No man could have expected better. If I am going into mortal danger it is not something new to me, as you know well. I have every reason to believe that I will return here later with this affair completed and Davery unable to continue his callous ways but, in case things should take a different turn, let us shake hands now and always remember the adventures we shared. Goodbye, old friend, for however long."

With that he turned abruptly and left, leaving me stunned and with my hand still extended. As I looked down through the swirling snow, watching Holmes board a slowly-passing hansom, I was gripped by despair. The memory of his apparent demise at the Reichenbach Falls was still fresh in my memory, and his exit now after refusing my help in the face of danger, and with so little ceremony, caused my spirit to plummet.

I sat in my usual armchair for a little while with my elbows on my knees, staring at the carpet but seeing nothing but the imagined tragedy that I was convinced would shortly take place. A dark depression swept over me.

Inevitably, my thoughts strayed to the past, to the mysteries we had unravelled together. Was this to be the end, by means of a man like Davery?

Then I saw a light in the blackness! It occurred to me that I had disobeyed Holmes before, sometimes actually helping him towards success. In a moment I had put all doubt out of my mind and, pausing only to collect my service revolver and the crowbar from my friend's chest, took up my hat and coat and went out.

The inclement weather had greatly reduced the traffic. Both passers-by and horses made their way with difficulty, but a cab put down a fare across the street and I ran for it, slipping and sliding. Progress was naturally slower, through streets with indistinct white figures and the strange quality that snow gives to ordinary sounds.

It was almost a quarter past three, when I stood at last opposite the Agora Club. Pall Mall was all but deserted and I realised then that I had no means of entry, when a short man in the uniform of a waiter came out through the high double-doors and hurried away. When he was lost from my sight I crossed the street. The footprints on the steps showed clearly that the snow had been disturbed three times – by Davery, Holmes, and the departing waiter, I concluded.

The doors, of course, were locked. Regardless of the snow, I considered forcing them, in such an exposed position, to be a last resort. The side of the building seemed a better prospect, having a narrow door which was probably a service entrance, and I used the crowbar after ensuring that I was not observed.

I was faced with a small hallway with two doors leading off, both securely bolted. Before me was a flight of curving stairs, which I ascended with great stealth. They led to a landing on the first floor, from which it was not possible to proceed further because, as Holmes had mentioned, part of the inner structure was under repair.

I peered cautiously over the thick oak bannister. Below was a table, set with white napkins. Holmes and Davery sat on opposite sides, facing each other, under a gas chandelier. A crystal glass stood before each man, half-filled. The waiter had fulfilled his function, and departed.

"Thank you so much for coming, Mr. Holmes." Even from this distance I recognised the voice and the boyish smile that I remembered. Davery was dressed immaculately, his hat at the side of the table near that of Holmes.

"I was curious to see what it was that you believe we have to discuss."

"Of course, it is natural that you would be. I am anxious to show you that your recent pursuit of me is without purpose. You are wrong to believe the slanderous things about me that newspapers and others are so quick to lay before the public."

Holmes looked at him curiously. "Have you forgotten your admissions, when you intercepted Doctor Watson and myself, in Baker Street?"

"Oh, that." Davery adopted a comic expression, like a disobedient child who tries to make light of his misdemeanours. "There I must apologise. Mr. Barnett had angered me with his accusations, and put me to the inconvenience of following him in order to discover his intentions. But wait, I am being a poor host! Let us drink to misunderstandings, possible reconciliation and, of course, our Queen."

To my amazement I saw Holmes, without the slightest hesitation, take up his glass and drink. I felt a shudder pass through me, because even with my lesser deductive powers I realised that this was undoubtedly Davery's way of administering the drug that Holmes had identified.

My conviction was strengthened by the relief that clearly showed in Davery's expression.

"Mr. Holmes," he said then, "you really must allow for my point of view."

"Under the law, we are all equal," my friend reminded him. "There can be no distinction for position, nor privilege. Are not the higher orders looked upon to set the example? But you, sir, have abused your position in life with murderous intent. Your conduct cannot be excused!"

"I have done only things which I considered necessary for my own continued welfare. You surely cannot equate the obstacles that I have removed with the importance of that?"

334

I expected a sharp reply to such an outrageous statement, but Holmes was silent. I knew then that the drug had done its work.

"Well, Mr. Holmes, what have you to say to that?" Davery knew the signs, and triumph entered his voice.

Holmes was silent. Davery walked around the table and approached him. For an instant I thought he would strike my friend, but he simply stood gloating and smiling with triumph.

"Ah, yes, this will be useful." He took Holmes's pistol, from where it was displayed with curious prominence in the pocket of his ulster, and laid it on the table before my friend.

Holmes sat unmoving, as if he were asleep, although his eyes were open.

"I know that you hear me, Holmes, because I am familiar with the properties of the compound that I instructed Gibbons, our waiter, to mix with your drink. I shall have no fears of him running to Scotland Yard when your death is discovered, since I intend to arrange a convenient accident for him before then. You are unable to move, as I am sure you have already found, except at my command. The substance responsible is used by witch doctors in East Africa, where I observed its application during my travels. You will have realised that I have used this to remove various impediments from my life, including those you were investigating. I feel that I have been exceedingly patient in your case, since I went to the trouble of warning you through slight acquaintances in the official police." He raised his hands and shook his head, as if in hopeless resignation. "However, it has all come to this in the end." He turned abruptly, and resumed his place at the table.

There was a few minutes of absolute silence, save for the faint howl of the wind through the building. I let my hand fall to the pocket of my coat, to feel the reassuring presence of my service revolver, and waited.

Davery drained his glass. "Well, I see no purpose in prolonging the matter. Stand up, Holmes, and face me."

I watched with a curious fascination, as my friend rose obediently.

"There is a pistol on the table before you. Reach out and pick it up."

Holmes did so.

"Put it to your head."

Holmes did not move.

"Put it to your head." Davery repeated. "I command you."

Holmes remained still.

"Do as I order," Davery's voice was rising and although I could not see from where I stood, I knew that his eyes would now hold the emptiness that I had noticed in Baker Street. I remembered also his instability that Holmes had described witnessing.

Holmes replaced the pistol on the table and turned away.

For a moment Davery stood in amazement, then he brought his fist crashing down on the table. *"Obey Me!"*

Holmes walked stiffly, like a sleep-walker, towards the door.

"Come Back! Do as I say, this instant!"

Holmes did not falter, but Davery was enraged. He snatched up the pistol and flung the table away from him. I drew my own weapon, but Davery had moved out of my sight. I turned and ran for the stairs, but I knew the situation was hopeless as the report filled the building. I was outside in a moment, running and sliding for the front of the building as I prayed that Holmes's wound was not fatal. I swore to myself that Davery would not leave this place alive, if he had killed my friend.

I came to an uncertain halt outside the high double-doors. I whipped out the crowbar from my pocket and was about to force my way in, when the doors opened and Holmes stepped out, alert and unscathed.

"Ah, Watson," he said in a matter-of-fact tone. "I was quite sure that we would meet here".

"Holmes! What happened in there? Are you injured?

"Not all, old fellow," he said with a grim smile. "However, I fear the same cannot be said for Mr. Davery."

Without understanding, I made to enter the building. "I will see if I can do anything for him."

"I really would not take the trouble. He lies dead on that dusty floor with half his face and a good portion of his right arm missing."

I stared at my friend in astonishment. "He was about to fire at you. At that distance he could not have missed."

Holmes closed the doors, took my arm and guided me away. We began to walk along the street with the snow sticking to our coats, watching for a hansom.

"It is very difficult to shoot, with a firearm that has a metal bolt hammered into the barrel," he explained.

"That was what you did to the pistol, in our rooms? I thought you were repairing it."

"It was a souvenir from an affair with which I was concerned before your time. I considered it to be more useful used like this, rather than getting rusty in my trunk."

"But I saw the drug administered to you. How did you escape its effects?"

A cab emerged from a cloud of snow. We climbed aboard and Holmes gave our destination, before he continued as if our conversation had gone uninterrupted.

"You will recall that I first learned of the compound from Professor Faye. He told me also that an antidote was known, and easily obtained. Fortunately, the necessary ingredients were already present among my chemicals, so I was able to mix and test the tincture in advance."

We lapsed into a short silence as we watched a small crowd, appearing as ghostly figures in the wind-driven snow, enter the lighted doorway of a tavern.

"You do realise, Holmes, that some would consider you a murderer?"

He leaned back in his seat and sighed. "We have had this conversation before, Watson, at the conclusion of the Roylott affair. My answer is unchanged. Davery's death will rob me of no sleep, I assure you. When he is discovered, it will appear as suicide, which is both appropriate and ironic. It is doubtful that my presence at the Agora Club will come into it since the only witness, the waiter, lived in fear of Davery for some reason and will surely not come forward. Consider also that I was nowhere near either Davery or the gun when he pulled the trigger. But, old friend, on such a grim day let us talk of brighter things. We can certainly look forward to the warmth of a glass of spirits in our stomachs upon our return to Baker Street."

The Adventure of the
Purple Poet
by Nicholas Utechin

I am a light sleeper in normal circumstances, but I must have been in a deeply unconscious state when first I felt a hand pulling at the eiderdown upon my bed. As I gradually roused myself, I became aware of Holmes's eager face.

"What the blazes is going on?" I asked, fully awake in an instant as befitted my military training years earlier. "Are we on fire, or is it another of your demanding clients appearing at an ungodly hour?" Holmes smiled.

"Neither, Watson, but it is eight in the morning on Christmas Eve and we are summoned to Oxford. Do prepare yourself and throw some clothes in a bag: Mrs. Hudson has laid out a basic breakfast and we should be able to reach Paddington for the half-past-ten."

It took but a few minutes for me to be down at our hearth. Sherlock Holmes was pacing up and down, his chin upon his chest in thought. I busied myself with the dishes and coffee.

"What is going on at your old University city," I ventured at last, "especially in the depths of the holiday period?" Holmes tossed a telegram to the table in front of me. I picked it up and folded down the creases.

"'Univ in uproar,'" I read, "'Please attend. Baffled by Shelley. Macan.' Holmes, what on earth does this mean? How can the university be affected by a poet who died seventy years ago?" My friend laughed.

"I know as much or as little as you do, Watson. But Macan is an old acquaintance of mine and he would not waste my time, especially at Christmas, if the matter was entirely unimportant. And, by the by, *Univ.* is not the whole University. I shall telegraph to tell him when we shall arrive."

Fresh snow had fallen in Baker Street, and the relative earliness of the hour meant that the white blanket had not yet been ruined by too many passers-by and dirty traffic. There was a peace and a calm about the place which I enjoyed for a moment before a cab was hailed and we were on our way to the station, barely a ten-minute ride away.

On our arrival at Paddington, Holmes crossed to the telegraph office, and within a few minutes, we were ensconced in a first-class carriage. Only when the steam was up did Sherlock Holmes finally relax, lying back upon the thick embroidered cloth of his seat. He lit his pipe.

"One or two background facts, Watson. *Univ.* is the shortened form for University College, the oldest college at Oxford. Macan I have known since the '70s, when he was a scholar there and our paths occasionally crossed. He is now a college fellow and a classicist, with an expertise on, if I am not mistaken, Herodotus. As I told you in Baker Street, Reginald Macan is not going to worry about a trifle, and so I am prepared to travel to Oxford on what must be one of the last trains to venture out before the line is closed before tomorrow's full holiday. I fancy we shall be staying in the rather attractive city of spires for two nights. And we shall see what we see and hear what we hear."

Holmes closed his eyes and I could see that conversation was at an end.

The view from the carriage window as we travelled was as picture-perfect as one could have wished. Snow-covered fields spread to the horizon, occasionally interrupted by slight hints of cottages and church towers. There was a wonderful country calmness, lit by a sun blazing down through a crisp blue sky. It was a glorious December morning and I could only guess at what lay ahead.

We drew to a halt at Oxford Station at midday and a cab took us quickly into the city's main street, where we alighted across from the college. A be-gowned gentleman was waiting at the great oaken door, and I was somewhat surprised to see how Holmes and the man greeted each other, in the highest of spirits. I crossed the street, dodging my way through the heavy traffic.

"You are Dr. Watson, I presume," said the scholar, shaking me firmly by the hand. "It is a delight to meet the man whose tales of my old friend so often interrupt my tedious studies. I am Reggie Macan. Come into Univ., both of you, and let me explain why I have asked you to be here."

The three of us passed into the front quadrangle of the college. There was a wide pathway running straight before us, the snow impacted by the passing of feet; but on each side lay lawns untouched by any stray mark, a pristine white. At the far end were two old adjoining buildings, which I took to be the chapel and hall. Gnarled bare wisteria vines twisted their way along the stonework of the four sides of the quadrangle, with arches cut into the walls that led to student staircases.

Sherlock Holmes stood quietly, taking in the view. He was not by nature an emotional man, but I could see that he embraced the atmosphere of peace and quiet.

"It is some time, Macan, since we stood on this spot as undergraduates. But Watson and I are intrigued as to why you think it so vital that we break into what was going to be an exuberant Christmas celebration in Baker Street?" My friend smiled slyly at me. "And what is baffling about Percy Bysshe Shelley? I have always found his poems most congenial." Macan slapped Holmes upon his shoulder.

"Time enough, Holmes. Let us first go to the common room. I shall ask the porter to have your bags taken to your rooms." He signalled to the servant, who had been hovering behind us, and gestured us to follow him over to the right side of the quad.

A moment later we had passed beneath the lintel of one of the stone arches and were hanging our coats upon pegs provided for the purpose. The scholar opened a door and ushered us into a most beautiful panelled room. A festive tree stood at the far end, covered with coloured balls hanging from pieces of twine which caught the flickering light from the candles that stood upon the central oak dining table, on which places were already laid. A fire already glowed gently in the grate and a cluster of decanters shone in the corner

"This is where we shall be dining later, but for now there is a cold collation in the summer common room on the other side of the corridor."

There was a less formal style to this second chamber, with a variety of comfortable looking sofas and armchairs, upon which a number of what were clearly senior college fellows were spread. Macan waved an arm in our direction.

"Gentlemen, may I present my guests Sherlock Homes and Dr. Watson, who I have invited to try and shine some light on our poet's problem. I shall introduce you all properly in due course. A glass of burgundy, Holmes?" he asked, already holding a bottle. A general murmur from the assembled fellows implied that my friend's name was immediately recognised

I felt that Holmes was restraining himself from speaking out, but that he was unwilling to impose himself too quickly upon the sedate traditions of the academic common room. We settled ourselves around a small table in the corner of the room and only then did he show some impatience.

"Macan, I ask again: I enjoy a Christmas puzzle as much as anyone, but . . . ." and he left the obvious question hanging in the air. Our host leaned forward.

"I apologise, Holmes. I shall show you the evidence after lunch, but let me explain what has occurred."

"I should be more than obliged," my friend replied drily.

"You may be aware that Percy Bysshe Shelley came up to this college as an undergraduate in the year 1810. You may also be aware that he left, and was indeed sent down from the university, but a year later, having published a pamphlet extolling atheism. It was a famous story and one that, perhaps, did not redound well on the reputation of University College when, in ensuing years, Shelley became one of this country's finest romantic poets. It took many decades, but we seemed to right some kind of wrong two years ago when almost all of us accepted the offer of a fine memorial – a figurative statue of the man, then only twenty-nine, when his drowned body was washed up on an Italian shore. It had been commissioned by Shelley's daughter-in-law to stand at his grave in Rome, but its plinth was considered of too great a weight to lay upon the churchyard soil, and thus last year – while you, Holmes, were still missing presumed dead yourself – it found a proper resting-place in a special domed structure in the college. It is a glorious sculpture in pure white marble by Onslow Ford, an example of the most superb delicate design and workmanship. In a sense, it demonstrates that Univ. has accepted that an error was made too quickly so many years ago."

Sherlock Holmes responded in some exasperation.

"An informative, but hardly vital, history lesson, my dear Macan."

"Then it will interest you that Shelley's head is entirely purple today."

The others in the common room heard Macan's words clearly, and newspapers and wine glasses were lowered in anticipation. Holmes glanced across at me and raised an eyebrow.

"At last!" Our host's face remained serious.

"Holmes, I suppose this is indeed some sort of Yuletide puzzle, but it is an extremely serious matter. A major work of art has been despoiled and it would be far too tedious, I fancy, to involve the local police force – a force which, it must be said, tries to involve itself in college and University affairs as little as possible. No, there has been no murder or other serious deviltry done, but the story will undoubtedly come out, which will be highly detrimental to the college and could contribute to an element of distrust, and thereby fewer young men choosing to attend here for their further education."

"When you say his head is purple," I ventured, "what exactly do you mean?" Macan was about to answer, but Holmes intervened decisively.

"I cannot but be intrigued, as you thought I would be, old friend. I think you had better show us the scene of the crime – a phrase which is almost certainly a touch too serious in this case. But, come, Watson, we are relaxing in Oxford: let us see how white has turned to purple.

341

Gentlemen," he said, addressing the others in the room, "while you do not exactly appear to be in the uproar that Macan indicated to me in his wire, I hope that by the time you sit down for your Christmas repast on the morrow, there will be no further shilly-shallying over Shelley." With that, he motioned me to follow Macan.

We stepped back into the quadrangle, and our guide led us back towards the lodge, then turned to his left through a corner archway, kicking the snow from his shoes. A short corridor suddenly opened out into a domed area of perfect dimensions, dominated by an ornately carved block of black marble upon which lay the life-size, pure white sculpture of the great poet, of such subtle shaping that it seemed nigh on impossible that it could have been hewn out of Carrara.

Yet, as we approached it, it became apparent that something was badly amiss, for there were blotches and streaks of a deep purple and crimson colour upon the face and head. Holmes descended the two steps and went up to the sculpture.

"Some sad student prank, no doubt," I suggested to Macan, who immediately shook his head.

"Under normal circumstances, Dr. Watson, that is precisely what I should have assumed. But it is Christmas Eve: we have not had an undergraduate on the premises for nearly a month. And there are few of us dons in college at this time of year."

"Seven, including yourself, I should say," came from Holmes, now busy sniffing the sculpture. "Nine places are laid for dinner, I think. This is most interesting, Watson. I should value your opinion." I approached the tainted sculpture in some surprise.

"I am more used to dealing with live bodies, actually," I retorted. My friend smiled, almost impishly.

"Tell me, Macan, when you found the sculpture in this state?"

"After dinner yesterday evening. My rooms are up this staircase, and so I have to pass Shelley."

"Did you tell the other fellows of your discovery?"

"Yes. I hurried back to the dining room, where I found Dr. Rowley and Professor Teasdale. They were appalled, of course. I naturally waited until early this morning to send you a telegram."

"Quite so. Well, Watson, what do you think?"

I had been examining the purple portions closely.

"I don't know what you want me to say, Holmes," I replied, in some exasperation.

"Sixty-three or seventy?" I think the set of my eyebrows must have indicated that I had no idea of what my friend was talking about.

"Macan, I presume the college has a good cellar?"

"Of wines?" the academic asked, uncertainly.

"Well, of ports, to be precise. Watson, did you not smell? Even after a good few hours, there is no doubt that it is port that has settled into the marble. I merely wondered if you recognised the vintage."

"I am more of a Madeira man myself, as you well know," I said to Sherlock Holmes, as a few minutes later we settled ourselves once more in the college common room. We were the only occupants, the other dons having disappeared, and Dr. Macan having held back to ask staff about cleansing matters.

"I don't think we must take this affair too seriously, Watson," Holmes remarked languidly, "but it is a decided waste of Ferreira sixty-three – for that is what I fancy it was. Why should any man hate Bysshe Shelley enough to desecrate such a wondrous sculpture?"

I was about to express agreement when the door flew open and Macan appeared as if shot from a cannon.

"I don't believe it! I simply don't believe it!" he cried, as he slumped into an armchair. "They have done it again, and it is worse, so much worse." He tapped his fingers in exasperation and a vein stood out upon his forehead. "Now it is brandy."

"Surely not spirits as well as vintage wine?" I said. Macan stared at us in agitation and then drew a deep breath.

"There is the most delicate tinge of light brown across the toes. They certainly had not been assaulted thus last night, and I had not noticed this disgrace when we were there just now." Holmes furrowed his brow.

"Nor had I," he admitted with some chagrin. "Show me. Watson, you need not come: relax and think of the Malvasia grape."

I busied myself with the pile of newspapers that lay upon the central table and helped myself to another small glass of white burgundy. Some fifteen minutes later, Holmes and Macan returned, my friend holding a handkerchief.

"Here, you can smell cognac quite clearly, and Macan thinks it must have been done during the few minutes he was waiting at the college gate onto the High Street for our arrival before lunch. Oh, and, Watson, I have just checked: there is a half-filled decanter of the Ferreira in the adjacent dining room."

"I had wondered if it might be a college staff member who could have perpetrated these outrages, if it were not a student," I said. "But perhaps we need to investigate the fellows, if port and brandy are involved." Homes intervened suddenly.

"What was that word you used one moment ago, Watson? What is brandy?"

"A spirit, Holmes," I replied, a touch wearily. "One of many."

"Of course: thank you, my friend. Macan, tell me of the six other Univ. fellows at present residing in the college over this Christmas period."

"Well, we are a college strong in the arts and classics, as you know. Wilson is a historian of the first order, who concentrates on the Whigs of the last century. Teasdale and Kerr are classicists, Rowley and Seton specialise in ancient and more modern literature respectively, while Dix has been immersed in Goethe for as long as I myself have been a Fellow here. All of us are of broadly similar age, in our fifties and sixties.

"By the by, gentlemen, we shall dine early this evening, to permit the steward and the other servants to leave the college at not too late an hour, to be home with their families for the start of Christmas Day. You are both in rooms on Staircase One, and the porter will show you to them. May I suggest we gather here again at half-past-six? Perhaps, Holmes, by then you may have some theories as to what we are facing here, bizarre as it may seem?"

Holmes looked up at Macan from his chair in relaxed fashion.

"I already have one very specific theory. But I need to know what liqueurs you have available? And I should like to see the College Register – would that be possible?"

"It is held in the Master's Lodgings, but he is away at present and there would be no harm in my bringing it over this evening. And all available drinks are over there in the walnut cabinet – apart, that is from the decanters you have already seen in the dining room."

Holmes crossed the room and swung open the doors of the chest, quickly surveying the contents. "I thought so," he announced triumphantly. "An entertaining evening lies ahead for us, I fancy, Watson."

"Do please share some of your thoughts. Which drink has particularly caught your eye?"

"Don't worry, my friend: you will be present at the *denouement*. I must pay one further visit to the sculpture, smoke a contemplative pipe in my room, and be back down here at the time proposed." With that, Sherlock Holmes strode from the common room, whistling, somewhat to my surprise, a jaunty version of "God Rest You Merry, Gentlemen".

"Oh, and by the by," he said, turning abruptly, "hail to thee, blithe spirit!"

I was somewhat surprised at this exhortation, but was glad to see that, however complex the matter of Shelley's head and feet appeared to me, Holmes seemed confident.

Having spent a restive half hour rambling through the snowy streets of Oxford and watching myriad last-minute Christmas gifts being purchased by anxious-looking townspeople, I changed in my room and was down in the common room at the appointed hour. Holmes and Macan were already seated at a side table, poring over a volume, while fellows drifted about with glasses of sherry in their hands. I crossed to my friends.

"Ah, Watson, we were just going over the Register from eighty-three years past. Here is the relevant entry." said Holmes, swivelling the great leather-bound tome towards me and pointing a thin finger at a written entry. "This is why Shelley left University College."

I peered at the ancient scratchy writing: "At a meeting of the master and fellows held this day it was determined that Thomas Jefferson Hogg and Percy Bysshe Shelley, Commoners, be publicly expelled for contumaciously refusing to answer questions proposed to them," I read slowly, "and for also repeatedly declining to disavow a publication entitled 'The Necessity of Atheism'." I looked up at Holmes and was about to speak.

"Stubbornly, or perversely, Watson."

"Hogg was a close friend of Shelley's," Macan explained. "They were both what you might call intellectual rebels and, with the publication of this pamphlet in March 1811, were frankly mocking the very foundations upon which the University – let alone this college – rested at the time. Another student, a contemporary of the miscreants, reported that the two of them had made themselves as conspicuous as possible in the days leading up to their expulsion – walking proudly and blatantly up and down the centre of the quadrangle."

I could see that one or two of the academics were trying very hard to hear what was being said. Holmes intervened:

"Interesting, my dear Macan, that you yourself have just used the word 'miscreants' to describe Shelley and his confederate?"

"It is, of course, another world today, and I used the term lightly. But the fury at their actions apparently ran very deep at the time, Holmes, and certain of the fellows held much rancour against Shelley for years. It would seem that the Master might have had mercy if the young man had been, er, less contumacious, but was livid when he gave no ground. The Dean said that the student could never ever be forgiven for having brought the college into such disrepute, and apparently even forty years later, eyebrows were raised if any undergraduate expressed an interest in the poet's works."

"And yet the college did indeed forgive in the end," I suggested, "as the acceptance of the monument indicates."

345

"Indeed," replied Holmes. "Yet troubled waters run just as deep as those that are still, as we see from the desecrations of that monument we are investigating, the source of which I expect to be discovered before the dawning of Christmas Day. Aha, dinner is being called. And Watson, by the way, I should have drawn your attention to the names of the college fellows in 1811."

I was naturally slightly thrown by this aside, but forbore to reply as the nine of us filed across into the dining room, where three college stewards waited. There was a low murmur of gossip as we took our allotted seats around the long oval table. Holmes was in deep conversation with his friend Macan, and I exchanged words with the classics scholar Professor Teasdale to my right, a man of thin features and a nose upon which a pair of wire spectacles was loosely balanced. He was intrigued by our presence and wanted to know what lines Holmes and I were following, especially since only he and one other don had been present when Macan reported the first discovery of Shelley's ruined head. Since I understood so little of the case myself, we moved on to other topics as a splendid fillet of fish was placed before me, and something rather special was poured into my wine glass.

As the evening wore on and two further festive and fascinating courses came and were consumed, Sherlock Holmes became the centrepiece of the dinner. Macan could but shrug his shoulders and grin in my direction as my friend held court. Truth to say, I had heard some of the tales before and his extraordinary summing-up of the recent and intriguing correspondence between Florence Nightingale and William Rathbone came as little surprise to me. But it was a most enjoyable repast, and by the time the port and Madeira decanters had circled for the final time – the table having already been cleared and the servants departed – we all agreed that it had been a most delightful way to spend a Christmas Eve.

The air in the dining room was thick with cigar smoke and the embers in the fireplace were just beginning to die down when Holmes was suddenly at my side.

'Come, Watson, now, and do not appear surprised," he whispered urgently, then passed from the room. I downed my glass in contemplative fashion, rose and bid my friends a good night and compliments of the season. As I too left, I saw Macan giving a slight nod in my direction.

Holmes was outside in the quadrangle, shifting his weight from foot to foot in anxious fashion as a light fall of snow wafted down. He laid a hand on my shoulder and near pushed me to the left and thus, I surmised, towards the corner archway that would lead to the Shelley sculpture.

There was only the light of the moon to guide us the few yards before we ducked into the complete darkness of the short corridor.

"Holmes, what are we doing?" I whispered. His grip on my shoulder tightened.

"You have correctly surmised that this is not an important case, Watson," he replied in a low voice, "but it is Oxford, it is Christmas, and it is fun. I should like to see that matters turn out as I predict. Here, now, is the statue, and there is room for the two of us in the right-hand corner of this space in front of the Shelley to wait and see what may transpire. I have a shaded lamp here and am trusting to have a poetic outcome tonight. Silence, please."

Over the years, I have shared with Sherlock Holmes long waits during the watches of the night, the cases involving the infernal spotted snake and the league of red-haired men springing immediately to mind. Despite his words, however, that he believed this case not to be one of the most serious he had entertained, no pitch black wait can ever be entirely relaxed if one has no idea of what to expect; and thus it was that I sought some refuge in the fact that Holmes had not asked me to bring any weapon from Baker Street to Oxford.

Perhaps twenty minutes had passed when suddenly Holmes tautened. I became aware of the slight flickering of a candle from our left, the light brightening as it advanced upon the statue area. A dark figure stepped down towards the plinth.

In a second, Holmes released the lamp shutter and moved towards the form. I heard a strangled epithet and the sound of smashing glass, a sweet and somewhat sickly odour immediately suffusing the enclosed space. There was, however, no resistance from our quarry, a man revealed immediately to be the white-haired Doctor Rowley. He quickly collapsed in Holmes's arms, seeming to sob.

"Back to the common room, old man," said Holmes. "It's a sad story and too many decades have passed for you to make such foolish gestures. He's a broken man, Watson. Could you go ahead to the common room? Reggie Macan should be waiting."

"My goodness, two generations pass, and still the affair rankles," said Holmes, as the gas lights came on and the four of us sat back in comfortable seats, Rowley cowed and shivering. "Can your family never forgive?" The old man pursed his lips and remained silent.

"It was the green Chartreuse tonight, was it not?" Holmes persisted. The broken man nodded. Macan smiled, as if he had begun to understand what had occurred. Holmes addressed his words to me.

"What we have here, Watson, is a story of intractable unforgiving, lasting over too many years. It is a tale of misplaced familial loathing,

347

with a trite and alcoholic end. Dr. Rowley, it is a pathetic tale, would you not agree?" Rowley winced.

"I am at a loss to know how you discovered it was me," he said in limp fashion.

"A simple linking of surnames. You are the grandson of Dr. George Rowley, Dean of this college at the time of the Shelley scandal, and later to become its Master. Your grandfather signed his name in the register on the date that Hogg and Shelley were thrown out. A deeply religious man, he loathed the concept of atheism and anyone who promoted it. This carried through to your father and then to you. Macan tells me that you alone of the fellows voted against accepting the offer of the sculpture to this college.

"And then, once it had been installed, having lost the intellectual and historical argument, you began to concoct a bizarre plan of desecration. For a man of your distinction in the university – you are, I believe, one of the leading experts on ancient literature here at Oxford – you made one flawed decision and one psychologically interesting one. For some reason, you chose to make your mark, quite literally, when the undergraduates were out of college during this vacation: had the attacks on the sculpture been made in term time, they would undoubtedly have been put down to student high jinks. You also decided to play what you thought was a pretty little game, by running to a work by the very man you loathed. Watson, how well do you recall Shelley's lines in his poem 'To a Skylark'?"

"A question I regard as striking somewhat below the belt at this hour, after all we have been through, and indeed imbibed, this night," I responded. Holmes laughed.

"A fair enough answer, Watson! Let me, then, draw to your attention the first lines of the fourth verse. *'The pale purple even melts around thy flight'*. The purple of port, perhaps? I even gave you earlier a hint of the direction of my thoughts, when I gave you part of the opening line of the whole poem – and one of the most famous in all poetic history: *'Hail to thee, blithe Spirit'*. See what Rowley was doing? Brandy is as good a spirit to hurl at white marble as any. That is what we were already faced with by this evening.

"What further alcoholic beverage might be chosen next? There is mention by Shelley, of course, of *'the blue deep'*, but I am not aware of any drink of that hue. And I discarded for the same reason, his use of the words *'that silver sphere'*. But eventually the line *'In its own green leaves'* led me to ask Macan here what liqueurs are held in the common room, and when I saw a full bottle of the superb drink created by monks in their Chartreuse monastery near Grenoble, I was fairly sure of Dr. Rowley's next weapon. And it turned out to be so."

Rowley was a pathetic sight, his thin body almost fading into the folds of his academic gown and his hands clasped in anguish. Macan stood up with an air of finality.

"What you have done is despicable, Rowley. The Master will be told on his return to college, and I have no doubt that he will call a meeting of fellows – just as that held in 1811 to decide on Shelley's fate. The result, I fancy, will be the same."

Sherlock Holmes leaned forward in his armchair.

"I wonder, Macan, whether you are perhaps being a touch severe on your colleague? Despicable his actions have certainly been, and I sincerely regret the uses to which fine port, cognac, and liqueurs have been put. But I fancy your college authorities will provide funds towards Shelley's cleansing, with no lasting damage done, unless it be to Dr. Rowley's own conscience. I have no powers in this matter, but Christmas Eve seems to me to be a time for forgiveness and understanding."

Macan smiled and shrugged his shoulders, his anger clearly receding. Holmes turned towards me.

"What a very curious Christmas we are spending, my dear Watson, when events of nearly a century ago have returned to haunt this ancient seat of learning. I think we shall allow ourselves to enjoy a festive day tomorrow in this lovely city and then return to Baker Street and hope for less bitter, twisted tales to come before us.

"So far as you are concerned, Rowley, you should have considered the closing two lines from another of Percy Shelley's poems: '*The world is weary of the past. Oh, might it die or rest at last!*'"

The Adventure of the
Empty Manger
by Tracy Revels

The adventures of my good friend Sherlock Holmes were vast and diverse. In his many years of active practice, he came to the assistance of titled nobility, decorated military heroes, and industrial tycoons. He recovered stolen art and artifacts of incalculable value, tracked down assassins and world-famous felons, and prevented scandals that would have disgraced royal dynasties on three continents. Yet, in glancing back over the hundreds of cases which I have never published, I often find that the small problems my friend resolved were more fascinating than the cases which brought significant financial reward and the gratitude of monarchs. Crimes which took only moments to unravel were, in their way, as exciting as mysteries that required months of strenuous activity on Holmes's part. And as the years of retirement creep steadily upon me, I recall my friend's dignity and kindness far more than his celebrity. Indeed, the memories that are most intense to me are not those of breathtaking escapes or dramatic revelations, but of the times when the heart, as well as the mind, of Sherlock Holmes was revealed. Therefore, I offer to my long-suffering readers this brief account of an incident that gave me a startling insight into the very soul of Sherlock Holmes.

It was Christmas Eve of the year that Holmes returned to London. I had, at his insistence, abandoned both my medical career and my home, and resumed residence in that famous suite of rooms on Baker Street. While the young Doctor Verner had purchased my small Kensington practice, I did, on occasion, receive a summons from a former patient and could not in good conscience refuse to come to his aid. Lady Amelia Hildeborne was one such sufferer, a chronic invalid – at least by her own diagnosis – who would admit no other physician to her bedchamber. The note that she was dying from a hemorrhage had roused me from a winter's nap and sent me scurrying to her mansion in one of London's more fashionable neighborhoods. The lady proved to have only a slight nosebleed, and I was just buttoning my coat and shivering in the bitter wind on her doorstep when a sharp halloo caused me to turn my head. There, bundled in a long coat and muffler, smoking a cigarette with an air of nonchalance, was my friend.

"Holmes? This is a strange coincidence."

He favored me with a look of impatience. His scowl asserted he had once thought more highly of my intelligence.

"It is not a coincidence, Watson," he said, flicking away the cigarette. "I am here because I followed you here."

"But how?" I demanded. "I received the note from Lady Hildeborne at seven, long before you were awake. And do not tell me that you had my destination from Mrs. Hudson, because the note she brought up to me was sealed, and I tossed it into the fireplace before I left Baker Street."

Holmes smirked. "There is no great mystery to the thing at all. When my friend Watson is roused from hibernation at such an ungodly hour of the morning – and I am made well aware of this fact because I can hear his muttered army oaths even through the walls of my own bedchamber – and then carelessly shaves and departs on a medical errand, it can mean only that he is destined for this fine address."

"I confess I hurried but – "

"You clattered on the stairs and slammed two doors. There was blood on the razor and in the basin, and there is spot of plaster on the left side of your jaw, just where I suspected it would be. Your medical bag, which you leave near the sofa, was missing. There was no other possibility."

"But why this address?" I asked. "I could have gone to any of the patients who remain rather inexplicably attached to me. You knew only that I was off on a medical case."

"That, I confess, was a subtle calculation," Holmes said, with a low chuckle. "But it is Christmas Eve, and just yesterday I heard you complain that you wished you had more funds for holiday libations. A particular bottle of French wine prominently displayed at Number 3, St. James Street, was mentioned. And I know that of your half-dozen former patients, only Lady Hildeborne rewards you in cash when your services are rendered. Knowing also that she is, in your own words, a 'miserable hypochondriac', but one whose 'payments are princely', it was easy to imagine that such a summons would be very hastily answered, especially since the desire for a holiday treat is upon you."

I shook my head in amazement. I had not realized just how much I had missed Holmes's gift for making fantastic actions seem so obvious. "You make it all simple."

Holmes shrugged, then turned and gestured to a waiting cab. "Life is appallingly simple, for those with sharp eyes and well-honed brains," he said, without a trace of modesty.

"But there remains a bigger question," I noted, as Holmes opened the door and then slid in beside me. "Why did you follow me?"

Holmes gave the driver orders to take us to Oxford Street. Leaning back in the seat, he frowned, mulling over my statement. For an instant, he appeared oddly puzzled, as perplexed as one of his own clients. "I can only assume that I wanted company."

I tried not to let my amusement show. Holmes could make all the deductions he pleased, work his magical trick as often as the opportunity presented itself, but I felt that in this one area I was the more observant partner. In the months since he had returned, I had noticed a change in him. He was less likely to disappear for long evenings, or to spend endless hours brooding over his index, or simply smoking his pipe in somber reflection. Instead, he had more frequently insisted that I come along with him, whether for a ramble in Regent's Park or to attend a concert of violin music at St. James's Hall. Every case that had come his way, no matter how insignificant or obvious, had required my assistance. It had become the exception, rather than the rule, for one of us not to be at the table when the other was seated. In my view, the deduction seemed rather straightforward. Whatever Holmes had been doing in the three years that the world presumed him dead, it had been a lonely occupation. He had returned to London almost starved for companionship and spiritual connection. His brief accounting of himself given on the day of his return – a tale of covert travels in Persia and Tibet, of wondrous explorations made under the name of Sigerson, and of painstaking work in a chemical laboratory in Montpellier – had never been mentioned again. I had come to believe that my friend was purposefully lying to me about his adventures, but I easily forgave him any falsehood that was required to maintain his dignity. Whatever had happened, it was clear to me that it had been a harsh time for him, and that my duty as his closest associate was to help him resume as normal a life as possible.

"So you plan to do some Christmas shopping?" I asked, as our cab rattled toward London's famous commercial district.

Holmes shook his head. "I plan to do some watching. The combination of holy days and heathen capitalism is always amusing and occasionally instructive. Or would you prefer to return home?"

"No, I'll accompany you. I'm certain that I can find something to spend my 'princely payment' on," I said, patting my waistcoat pocket and feeling the weight of the coins within it.

Holmes began to talk of other things, and I lost track of both direction and time. But suddenly there was a sharp cry and a black robed figure came dashing out of an ancient, grime-covered edifice. The man's shouts and squawks, along with the way he waved his arms and danced about at the edge of the street, gave him the appearance of an ungainly and agitated crow.

"Help! Robbers! Thieves! Help!"

Holmes twisted and gave me a predatory smile. Then, with the agility of a hound over a hurdle, he sprang from the cab. By the time I paid our fare to the startled and swearing driver, Holmes had the hysterical gentleman in his grip, shaking him firmly.

"Courage! Calm yourself." The elaborate cassock clearly denoted the hysterical gentleman as an Anglican priest of the High-Church persuasion, but Holmes showed little respect for his holy status until the clergyman ceased screeching and began to take deep, steadying gasps of air. "Now," Holmes ordered, "tell us what has happened."

The clergyman blinked, as if just awaking from a nightmare. He peered from one to the other of us with tiny, watery blue eyes. He was a diminutive person, barely over five feet tall, with small tufts of white hair just above his ears. A pair of silver spectacles swung from a chain on his neck, clanking against an ornate gold cross. His bald scalp glistened with sweat, and his thin lips trembled as he struggled to master coherent speech.

"Are you detectives?"

"Something of the sort," Holmes answered. "You say you have been robbed?"

The clergyman twisted his boney hands together. "Yes. It – it will be a scandal. A disaster! The parish shall never recover. Oh, how could it have been stolen? Why did I ever walk away, turn my back, leave the door unlocked?"

"What has been stolen?" I asked. Our new client raised trembling hands.

"Our Lord himself. The holy infant of Bethlehem! The Christ Child!"

I noted how one eyebrow rose skyward on Holmes's face. His lips twisted into an expression of chagrin. For just an instant, I thought he would turn on his heel and leave the man babbling on the sidewalk. But instead, Holmes heaved a martyr's sigh.

"Come . . . you must show us the scene of the crime," Holmes said, and the priest motioned for us to follow him inside the sanctuary.

"My name is Morley," our new client gasped as we stepped into the deep shadows of the central aisle. "I have been the vicar of St. Rita's Parish for almost twenty years. Never have we had such a catastrophe. Whatever will I tell the faithful, when they arrive for services tonight?"

As the clergyman continued to whine, I took in our surroundings. Though small, the church was lavish, with exquisite stained glass windows and plush carpeting. The smell of bay-scented candles mingled pleasantly with the aroma of ancient woodwork. Just beyond the pews were ancient marble crypts, complete with effigies of knights and ladies. I guessed that sometime in the distant past, this sanctuary had been the private chapel of a noble family. Though the neighborhood currently surrounding it was unmemorable, the little church clearly had a distinguished history.

The vicar led us to a spot just to the left of the altar. There we beheld a remarkable sight of the holiday season: a nativity scene housed in a hut made of paper and plaster, populated by nearly life-sized dolls. Each figure, from Mary and Joseph to the shepherds, wise men, and angels, was constructed of cloth and held in a realistic pose by nearly invisible wires. Animals, including a donkey and lamb, were likewise cleverly crafted from wool and burlap and positioned in attitudes of adoration. While the shepherds and the holy family were clad in simple tunics and drapes, the wise men glittered with cloaks of gold and silver tissue, their diadems winking with false gems. I was so amazed by the display's novelty and artisanship that for a moment I missed the central problem it posed.

The manger was empty.

"It is a special gift," the vicar explained, "from Mr. Harold Whitestone. Perhaps you have heard of him? No? He owns the Whitestone foundries and mills, in Yorkshire. He was born and raised on this street, a poor lad, but very devout. Since he made his fortune in trade, he has become a generous patron – he paid for our new windows and all the carpets. Just last week he presented us with this tableau."

"It is certainly a striking decoration," I said. The vicar's blue-tinged lips pulled tight in a painful rictus, the expression of a man awaiting the dentist's drill.

"Yes, it is, but such trouble for us – not that I am ungrateful, heaven forbid. Mr. Whitestone has been most kind! But, you see, Mr. Whitestone felt that we should keep the sanctuary open around the clock. He believed that people should be able to admire his gift at all hours – to aid them in their Advent meditations. But, of course, that meant my curate and I were forced to take shifts, to guard it carefully, lest someone be tempted into devilment."

I could not resist a slight chuckle. "Surely making off with the Christ Child is more of a choirboy lark than a serious felony."

The poor vicar's trembling returned with such severity that I thought he might pitch himself onto the stone floor. "Oh no! This is not a prank! A thief has taken the doll for his eyes!"

Holmes had been slowly circling the scene, inspecting the thin wines that kept several of the characters upright. He halted beside the manger. "What was unique about the figure's eyes?" he asked.

354

"They were sapphires, sir. True gems, not bits of paste. They were perfectly matched and said to be worth a thousand pounds each. That is why we have guarded our tableau so carefully. Everyone in the parish knows about the beautiful eyes of the baby."

Holmes cut a sharp glance at the vicar. "And the rest of the doll?"

"It was of no particular value. It had a porcelain head, but the body was cloth, stuffed with sawdust and fragrant herbs. It was wrapped in a blue silk gown."

Holmes dropped to his knees and pulled his lens from a pocket of his coat. He began to crawl around in the straw, closely examining the floor beneath the figures. "Tell me what precautions you took," Holmes said. "Clearly they failed, for such a theft to occur."

The distraught clergyman began to whimper. "I or Mr. Jones sat in the pews whenever the doors were unlocked. I watched the scene all morning – a few ladies and gentlemen came by, and I was forced to shoo away some rapscallion children. An hour ago, Mr. Jones was to relieve me, but he was running late and I fear I had a case of . . . indisposition." He clutched his belly, his face turning purple with shame. "I had no time to lock the doors, and I was in the washroom for nearly ten minutes. When I returned, the Christ Child was gone. Sir . . . sir, what are you doing?"

Holmes had dropped completely to the floor and appeared to be working at the cracks of an ancient burial slab that the nativity scene surmounted. I suspected the vicar was regretting allowing a clearly insane man to try to help him.

"Aha," Holmes called, "we are in luck! The babe has sprung a leak!"

"What?"

"See here – the traces of sawdust and the scattered herbs. For us, the trail will go cold within a few paces, but for another . . . Watson, would you be so kind as to hail a cab and once again pay a visit to my old friend Mr. Sherman at Number 3, Pinchin Lane?"

"Shall I ask for Toby?"

"No, I fear that Toby's best days are behind him. Request Patches instead – it is time that he proved his worth in the field."

I set off immediately on my task, recalling with some humor the journey I had made to Mr. Sherman's odd menagerie during the adventure of the Sign of the Four. It took me well over an hour to reach my destination and return, for the streets were horribly congested with last-minute shoppers, carol singers, snowball fights between street arabs, and general holiday mayhem. As I rode along, I tried to apply Holmes's methods and reconstruct the scene in my mind. Holmes had frequently recommended employing one's imagination in the early stages of detective work, and I gave mine full rein.

Clearly, the thief had learned of the doll's value, either while attending worship or from the idle talk of parishioners. The vicar struck me as a man who would brag about the value of a patron's gift, especially as the neighborhood around the sanctuary was a poor one and the benefactor of the dolls had once been among the lowly of his flock. But how had the thief succeeded? Had he lurked in the shadows or somehow hidden himself beneath a pew? The church was exceptionally small, making such a concealment unlikely. The vicar seemed to believe his curate was trustworthy, but was he? Could the vicar himself be a criminal? For an instant my mind ran wild, considering the web of illegal activities organized by the late Professor Moriarty. Had Holmes failed in his task of bringing them all to ground? A man who would despoil a church had no respect for any creature, and might be the most desperate character imaginable. I suddenly found myself wishing that I were carrying my revolver instead of my medical bag.

Patches proved to be a dog of promiscuous pedigree. He had the long, trailing ears of a basset, the general compact body of a beagle, and the soft, curly coat of a spaniel. His eyes were bright, and his tail wagged madly. He was clearly eager to be released from his kennel and showed no concern for the inclement weather as we returned across the city. The vicar of St. Rita's gave a sharp cry when we entered the sanctuary, protesting the dog's presence.

"Very well, we shall retire," Holmes said. "Do give my best to your patron, and be sure to explain to him that his gift could have been found, if not for your refusal to allow Patches a small sniff of the evidence."

With an annoying whine, the vicar stepped back and motioned for Patches to approach. The dog dropped his nose to the straw, sniffing eagerly. He then whirled and made an unholy braying. I tossed the leash to Holmes, and we were off.

Respectable Londoners cleared a path as we sped down the street. Patches tugged hard, and Holmes was pressed to keep up with the canine. I, likewise, had difficulty keeping up with Holmes. More than once I slipped on the ice and toppled into a dirty snowbank, but I was always able to find my companion's trail by the harsh looks and murmurs of outrage from offended pedestrians.

A man sitting among a collection of spilled packages alerted me to the fact that "a crazy fellow with a dog" had turned the corner. I followed, just in time to spot Holmes ducking into an alleyway. Gasping for breath, I picked up my pace, dipping into the lane behind them.

I suddenly was in a new and repulsive environment. Gone were the cheerfully decorated streets, the warmly glowing windows. I had entered a warren of dingy alleys and narrow pathways, a hive of grim and stench. Walls were dark and stained, filth of all descriptions was piled near narrow doorways. We were stranded among some of the most squalid tenements of London, trapped in a vast rookery of disease and vice. Spectral figures wrapped in rags and cast-off coats hovered around fires set in barrels, and a sharp-ribbed, feral dog growled at Patches as our strange procession passed. I felt the weight of angry stares, the bitterness of resentment in the lean and dirty faces that turned as we moved through them. Patches stopped before a door that was half off its hinges. He squatted down and gave a sharp bark.

"I think we have reached our destination," Holmes said. "My apologies for such a brisk jog, Watson. I trust your leg has stood the test."

I glanced over my shoulder at a party of ill-clad men who had drawn together, whispering and staring at us. "I am much more concerned for my back. In this neighborhood, I might find a knife in it."

"Not a scenic area of our great city, though I hear that tours are regularly organized for the curious – a pastime quaintly referred to as 'slumming'."

I could hardly share Holmes's wry amusement at our predicament. At that moment, however, the flimsy door opened and a young boy emerged. Much to my horror, he was barefoot, despite the bitter cold, and was in the process of applying a match to an old pipe.

"Excuse me, young man," Holmes said, "but could you tell me if you have seen a girl enter this house only a few hours ago, carrying a rather large doll?"

The boy favored Holmes with an appraising look. "What's it worth to you, Guv'nor?"

Holmes held out a shilling. The boy raised his hand and waggled his fingers, indicating a demand for more. Holmes started to place the coin back in his pocket.

"Wait! I know her! I can tell you!"

Holmes dropped one shilling into the boy's grubby palm. The coin disappeared with the speed of a conjurer's trick.

"That's Betsy – she's third floor, in the rear. What's she done? Are the blue bottles after her?"

Holmes shook his head. "Thank you for that information. If you will be so good as to watch my dog for a few minutes, there's a guinea in it for you."

The boy eagerly seized Patches's leash, squatting down to call the pup to him. In the ways of dogs and boys everywhere, Patches began to lick the lad's face, perhaps the first good scrubbing that countenance had known in months. Holmes signaled for me to follow.

"Holmes," I said, as we began ascending a narrow flight of stairs in almost total darkness, "how did you know it was a girl who took the doll?"

"Elementary, Watson. There were some indications of a small, delicate boot-print on the sanctuary carpet around the nativity scene. But even before I saw those marks, I theorized that it was a young girl who committed this crime." He turned as we reached the door of the final flat in the rear of the building. "Who else would impulsively steal a pretty doll?"

Holmes knocked gently. After a moment, the door swung open, revealing a girl who was no more than ten. Her pale face and sharp cheekbones spoke of a life of suffering. Her greasy brown hair was fixed in long, unkempt braids, and her dress and smock were ragged. Great holes gapped from her torn stockings, and her little boots were held together with pieces of string.

"Yes?" she whispered, clearly alarmed at the sight of two official-looking gentleman at her threshold. Holmes removed his hat. His entire persona changed in an instant. Gone was the stern enforcer of justice, the apprehender of felons; Holmes was suddenly a paragon of benevolence. "Miss Betsy, we have been asked to come here by the vicar of St. Rita's church. We believe that there has been a terrible mistake made, and that you have taken something from the sanctuary that did not belong to you."

The girl gasped and stepped backward. Her chin lifted and moisture filled her eyes, but she made no attempt to deny her actions.

"I only took it for Ellen. It was all she wanted, a dolly for Christmas. I went to church, to pray for her. She's so sick, and there's no money, and Father is gone and Mother . . . ."

The child dissolved in tears. I started to speak, but Holmes signaled for silence. The girl gasped against her sudden emotion.

"I didn't think . . . the Christ Child would mind if I took him. Ellen is so sick. I thought maybe . . . having a dolly . . . would make her better. Like a miracle."

"Miss Betsy," Holmes said, "my friend is a doctor. Will you allow him to treat your sister?"

She sniffed and stared down at her twine-laced boots. "I can't. There's no money."

I held up my bag and quickly borrowed a phrase from Holmes. "My dear little girl," I said, "my work is its own reward."

She looked up, the skepticism of a hard existence making her momentarily wary of my offer. Then she grabbed my hand and towed me into the only other room in the flat, a close and miserable chamber with a mattress on the floor. An even smaller girl was laid upon it, covered in an array of thin blankets and scarfs. The Christ Child was tucked beneath her arm, held as tightly as her pitiful strength would allow. Betsy reached down and gently removed the doll, passing it to Holmes with a murmured apology and then making room for me to kneel at her sister's side to begin my examination.

Holmes's way with children was always remarkable – his tone was firm, yet kind, and in no way scolding or patronizing. In just a matter of moments he was able to coax the girl's story from her. Her father, it seemed, had died from an injury sustained in a local factory, forcing her mother to go to work at an unwholesome sweatshop. The girls were left alone, and they tried to help their family by mud larking. Ellen had fallen ill while climbing about in the dregs of the Thames, looking for whatever bits of cast-off junk the children could sell. Their mother was at work, and Betsy had slipped away to the church while her ailing sister napped, at first to pray but then, upon spotting the vicar, to ask for aid. The clergyman had ordered the girl out of his sanctuary, but the moment his back was turned she had returned and stretched out along a pew. When he made his brief exit to the washroom, she scampered up to the altar and purloined the doll from the manger.

"I knew it was wrong," Betsy said, "but I couldn't stop myself."

The little sister had a high fever and was congested, but I felt that we had arrived in time to save her. I was about to say as much when I noted the expression on my friend's face. I had never seen him look so troubled.

"Watson, I must step away for a few moments. Miss Betsy, do pay attention to the good Doctor and do all that he requires."

She nodded solemnly. From long experience, I knew better than to inquire where Holmes was going or what his sudden errand might be. For almost an hour, I schooled the little girl in how to best care for her sister, instructing her on when to administer the medicine I provided, and how to prepare some plasters to keep her chest warm and aid her breathing. We gave her a quick wash, then changed her coverings and her meager gown, wrapping her properly. By the time we finished our tasks, Holmes appeared in the doorway.

"Ah, I see that the sickroom has been cleared of debris," Holmes said. "And this, I think, shall cheer it up."

He removed a package from inside his coat. It was wrapped in bright red and green paper, and topped with a spring of holly. Betsy stared at it.

"Sir, what is that?"

"Something you and your sister will enjoy. No, no, you must not open it until Christmas morning! You cannot wait? Very well. Ah, and I see that my trusty porters have arrived!"

As Betsy freed the box from its paper, a small troop of young boys and girls followed Holmes inside, each carrying a paper bag filled with groceries. One child tripped, spilling out a sack of oranges and nuts. Holmes merely laughed, rewarded each of his helpers with a shiny coin, and herded them out through the doorway.

I heard Betsy gasp. At last the box was open, and inside was the loveliest doll I had ever seen. It was a perfect replica of a young girl, complete with a pink satin dress and embroidered Chinese silk slippers. It had bright blue eyes, and its brown hair was set in enticing curls. I was struck by how much it would resemble Betsy, if life and circumstances had treated her with more kindness.

"Oh, she is wonderful! Ellen will be so happy!" Betsy's gaze took in all of the foodstuffs as well. "But – we cannot pay you."

"Father Christmas never expects payment," Holmes said. "I am merely his delivery man."

Betsy was old enough to know the truth of such matters. Yet she nodded sagely and agreed to tell her sister that they had been visited by Saint Nicholas. Holmes handed the girl a card.

"On Boxing Day, you must come to this address. A kind lady named Mrs. Hudson will give you more treats, which you will share with your sister and your mother."

"But sir," the girl sighed, "shouldn't I be sent to jail? I did a bad thing."

Holmes knelt, meeting her gaze at her level. "It is true, you did a naughty deed, but Christmas is the season for forgiveness. I think you have learned an important lesson today – and perhaps taught a greater one to two old sinners."

The girl nodded solemnly, then bobbed a curtsey. Holmes reclaimed the Christ Child doll, which had been pushed against a wall. We chuckled when we noticed that a seam along its right leg had opened, spilling out sawdust and herbs, withering the limb until the infant Jesus was lamed by his adventure. Holmes wrapped the doll in his coat, then we descended the stairs and reclaimed Patches. Holmes paid his helper, who was somewhat loathe to surrender his charge, as he had been training Patches to fetch a stick. We journeyed first to Pinchin Lane, where Mr. Sherman required a recounting of our adventure, and Patches was duly rewarded for his services with a large bone. We returned to St. Rita's at a much slower pace than we had departed it, and found the frantic vicar waiting for us at the door.

"Thank heavens! By all that is wonderful, you have saved me!" He seized the doll from Holmes's hand and raced to return it to the manger. "I cannot imagine the damage that would have been done. My career, my reputation would have been ruined. But . . . but who took it? How did you find the villain? Is he under arrest? Where should I go to file the charge against him? Tell me his name and I will have him prosecuted to the full extent of the law!"

"You will do no such thing," Holmes snapped. "You hired me only to retrieve the figure, not to find the thief."

"But – "

One icy glare silenced the clergyman. Holmes folded his arms. "Now, there is the matter of my fee."

"Fee?"

"Do you think I race around London for my health? Do you think that solving mysteries, producing stolen articles from thin air, is some variety of magic trick? Of course I demand compensation."

The vicar's brow became a virtual Niagara. Sweat streamed over his bushy eyebrows, dripped from his chin, and stained his collar. He pressed clenched hands against his breast.

"Oh, of course. How . . . how much, sir? What will it cost me?"

"Some human compassion," Holmes said. "I demand that you show some care for the people who live at this address. They are to receive food, clothing, and medicine for their sick child." Holmes thrust a card into the clergyman's hand. The vicar peered down at the address and gave a gasp of recognition.

"I know them. The father died of drink, I believe, and the mother is a harlot – the oldest girl will be a slut as well, in time. Surely there are more worthy recipients."

In a sudden motion, Holmes seized the wretched clergyman by the front of his cassock. The vicar's feet quivered in mid-air. "This family will receive aid, or your patron will be informed of how his gift was nearly lost by your irresponsibility. Is that clear to you?" Holmes hissed.

The clergyman bobbed his head. Holmes dropped him to the ground and bid him good day. We departed just as the first of the Christmas Eve worshippers came streaming into the sanctuary.

Later that evening, Sherlock Holmes fell into a black mood. He barely exchanged words with me over dinner, other than to complement the choice of vintage wine that I had purchased on the way home. He stood smoking his pipe, staring out the window onto Baker Street.

"Watson," he said, "are you familiar with St. Rita, the worthy for whom the church was named?"

I confessed my ignorance as I poured myself another glass of wine and joined him at the window. Outside, a few intrepid carolers were making their rounds, and more than one obviously intoxicated reveler staggered down the sidewalk, bobbing from doorway to doorway and trying without success to hail a cab.

"She is a patron saint of impossible causes. I am beginning to think that it is all impossible . . . or at least pointless."

A fresh, heavy snow began to fall, forcing those of goodwill and too much holiday cheer to abandon the street. Holmes withdrew his pipe. His face was a mirror of sadness, and his eyes seemed not to be gazing out at the snow, but deeply into the past.

"What kind of world do we live in, Watson?" Holmes asked. "What type of man would create gilded statues and dolls sewn with gems while ignoring starving orphans in the shadows? What kind of faith would place more emphasis on the letter of the law than the spirit of compassion? We say we live in an age of progress, but what progress have we really made?"

Something in his stance, his tone, brought me to a powerful realization. My friend was hiding something beneath his innate brilliance. Over the years, I had caught glimpses of it in the way Holmes treated his Baker Street Irregulars and in his general comradery with children. It illuminated him whenever he fought for justice for the weak and oppressed. My friend had never refused a case for lack of payment, and he could be as gallant to an old charwoman as to a duchess. In that very moment, as Christmas Eve became Christmas Day, I began to wonder if what little Holmes had told me about his youth might be as much of a falsehood as I suspected the tales of his hiatus were. What secrets was he protecting? What might have been his true origin?

But I dared not voice my suspicions. Holmes's sudden despair alarmed me, and I tried to draw him out of his dark thoughts. "Where did you find the doll that you gave to Betsy and Ellen?"

"In a toy shop not five blocks from where those poor girls resided. They must have passed it on display in the window, every day on their way to the Thames." He turned and went to the fireplace, knocking out the debris on his pipe into the grate. "I have never set foot in such an establishment. No wonder parents dread this season. Do you have any idea of how much such a babble costs?"

"Yet you did not hesitate to pay it," I said. Holmes made a face and provided a pithy description of the nearly murderous crowd in the store, all squabbling over dolls and trains and sets of building blocks. Perhaps it was this sudden spark of humor, or possibly it was the second glass of wine that I had consumed, but something caused me to blurt out the thoughts that his amusing tirade inspired.

"Holmes – you do the world a disservice by remaining a bachelor! You should marry and become a father. Your talents with children are exceptional – imagine how rewarding a family would be."

"A family! Then heaven help London!" Holmes said, with an excess of alarm. "Can you envision the Holmes tribe set loose upon the metropolis? Running amok, trying to solve every puzzle and unravel every mystery among the juvenile set? My children would be inquisitive little savages with magnifying glasses and cloth caps and pipes – even the girls! They would make the Baker Street Irregulars look like angels. No, my friend, the offspring of Sherlock Holmes would be a story for which the world would never be prepared!"

I laughed fully and poured yet another libation for us, passing a glass to my friend and thinking that, of all the gifts of the holiday, the best one of all was to have him back. "Happy Christmas, Sherlock Holmes."

The Adventure of the
Vanishing Man
by Mike Chinn

While it would be more than unfair to consider my friend Sherlock Holmes an embodiment of a modern Scrooge, I think it reasonable to observe he often appears immune to the Spirit of Christmas. He is not averse to the notion of exchanging gifts. Indeed, each year he presents me with some excellent cigars, whilst it has become customary for me to give him a pound of decent tobacco, in the hope of weaning him from his usual noxious weed. On each occasion Holmes has attempted, quite successfully, to deduce just what the package contains before unwrapping it. Indeed, the exchange has grown into something of an annual contest. For Christmas, my tobacconist had provided me with a mild golden shag from the Lake District which, unlit, had little aroma. I was confident that even Holmes's skills would be undone on this instance.

On reflection, I suspect it was the anticipated conviviality and all that entails which he found irrelevant and, thus, objectionable. When Mrs. Hudson declared she would be inviting a selection of friends and relatives to a lunchtime Christmas Eve gathering in her parlour, it was only with the greatest of difficulty that I persuaded him to attend. I was feeling rather low at the prospect of spending that Christmas alone, and it was my opinion that both of us would benefit from genial company. As it was, while half-a-dozen of us partook of a rather sprightly punch and exchanged the season's greetings, Holmes stood in a corner, clutching his cup and looking distinctly unengaged by the proceedings.

"Is the drink not to your taste?" I enquired, joining him.

Holmes gazed at his cup, swirling the contents lazily. After a moment he raised it to his nose and inhaled, working his lips as though he was actually tasting the concoction.

"It is vodka, I think," he said after a moment.

I resisted an urge to laugh. "You think Mrs. Hudson has included vodka in her punch?"

"Not she." He indicated the festive bowl where it stood, surrounded by unused cups, on a table by the parlour window. "Our good landlady is a creature of tradition. Clearly there is baked apple and sliced lemon, and judging from the colour, she has used heated cider as a base. The smell alone tells me that it is spiced with cinnamon, cloves, and nutmeg. But there is an overall astringency, a heat, which is entirely due to another ingredient."

I took another sip of my own drink; I have already remarked upon its vigour. "But vodka?" I said.

"Gin would add to the bouquet, whisky, brandy, or rum to the palate. Vodka, although not entirely tasteless or odourless, may pass unnoticed among more aromatic elements."

I glanced around the small party of faces familiar as Baker Street neighbours or visiting acquaintances of Mrs. Hudson as Holmes continued.

"And although I normally find it repugnant to theorise with such a paucity of data, I think, on this occasion, I may indulge myself." He indicated a pale-faced, sulky youth in dark clothing, a cap pulled low across blond curls. "Jerzy Krakowski, the nephew of Mrs. Krakowski whom, so I am informed by Billy, has been staying with his aunt these past seven weeks. I understand the boy has already acquired an admirable reputation for ill-directed high spirits."

At that moment there was a loud, urgent rapping upon the front door. Mrs. Hudson, fussing loudly, answered it, returning with a distraught figure clutching his hat brim in white fingers, his dark hair uncombed, and eyes staring behind round spectacles which had fogged over in the parlour's warmth.

"He wishes to speak with you, Mr. Holmes," spoke our landlady, brusque at the interruption.

My friend instantly put down his cup. "I am Sherlock Holmes," said he.

"Mr. Holmes!" Our visitor pulled off his spectacles, revealing eyes of a most extraordinarily pale blue. "Oh sir, you must help me – !"

"I shall do what I can." Holmes paused. "Mr – ?"

"Edwin M'Gurk, sir."

"But first you must compose yourself, Mr. M'Gurk. Mrs. Hudson. Bring our guest some of your most excellent punch, for I perceive he is in need of a restorative." He glanced towards me, thin lips quirking as at a private joke. "And some of your mince pies, if you please. Mr. M'Gurk has travelled far and with reckless despatch. I fancy he has not eaten for some time."

Mrs. Hudson offered the newcomer a plate well laden with seasonal delicacies, along with a brimming cup.

"When you have gathered your wits, Watson and I shall be awaiting you in our rooms." Holmes took my arm, guiding me towards the parlour door.

"Really, Holmes," I said as we climbed the stairs. "Did you have to make it so obvious you wished to be elsewhere? I fear you will have hurt Mrs. Hudson's feelings."

He barked a laugh, throwing open the door to our sitting room. "Our esteemed landlady knows me well, my dear fellow. She is more likely to be more amazed that I endured her *soirée* for the time that I did." He went straight to the mantelpiece, taking down his pipe and packing it with tobacco. I settled myself in an armchair, lighting a cigarette. "Besides, for a man to leave the comfort of his hearth on such a cold night, in a hurry, and travel no small distance . . . ." He lit his pipe, allowing the words to tail away as he puffed.

"Very well," said I, rising to the challenge. "I agree he has travelled in haste. His hair is a fright and the buttons of his waistcoat awry. Signs of a man in an all-consuming hurry. But the distance?"

"Did you not observe the recent traces of mud upon his boots, Watson? The cold of the past days has left our streets crisp, but dry. Only in the countryside, where deeply rutted tracks contain water sufficient to remain liquid, might he obtain such contamination."

The study door swung open and M'Gurk, tailed by Mrs. Hudson, entered. His punch cup was again full and I imagine the landlady had kept him well plied to ward off the cold. Certainly there was a hint of colour returned to his cheeks, although his features remained pinched with worry. Holmes indicated a chair with his pipe stem and the man sat, placing his hat on a side table.

"Thank you, Mrs. Hudson."

With a final stare at my friend, the good lady retreated, closing the door loudly in her wake.

Holmes fell back into a third chair and fixed M'Gurk with a keen eye, puffing hard on his malodorous pipe. "Now, sir, if you would be so good . . . ?"

M'Gurk took a deep pull on his drink. I offered him a cigarette, which he initially refused with a shake of his untidy head. "As I began to explain downstairs, gentlemen, I am valet to Mr. Wenman Higgins of Corvin House, Norfolk. Mr. Higgins is a wealthy gentleman, with a tidy fortune amassed by prudent investment and part ownership of a small fishing fleet sailing from Cromer – "

Holmes nodded slowly, half-closing his eyes. "Norfolk? No small distance indeed."

M'Gurk frowned at my friend's remark. "Indeed not." He took another drink and cleared his throat. "Mr. Higgins disappeared, sir."

"He has failed to return home?" I asked. The man shook his head.

"No, sir. He disappeared. Right before my eyes!"

366

Holmes raised his shaggy eyebrows. "Explain yourself."

M'Gurk glanced my way. "I'll have that smoke now, sir, if you don't mind."

I passed him my opened case, lighting the cigarette which quivered between his lips.

"Yesterday afternoon, I was up in Mr. Higgins's room, preparing his suit. He was expecting guests for an early Christmas dinner, for it has always been his habit to spend Christmas Day with his sister and her family near North Walsham."

"Yes, yes," Holmes sighed, waving a hand.

"My employer was out walking in the grounds at the rear of the house. There is a lawn there and a mature garden. From his room I could clearly see him through a small bay window." M'Gurk drew shakily on his cigarette. "As he crossed the lawn, he simply vanished. One moment I saw him, striding out with his stick, cigar smoke forming a great cloud about his head. Then, he had gone. Vanished before my eyes."

Holmes leaned back in his chair. "Intriguing. You had clear sight of him at all times?"

"As clear a view as you have of Baker Street from your window, there."

"Your eye was not distracted; not for the briefest instant?"

"No, sir."

"At what time was this?"

"Somewhere between three and four o'clock, I think."

"That will not do, Mr. M'Gurk!" Holmes barked. "Was it three or was it four? We are not so far removed from the year's shortest day. A mere fifteen minutes can mean the vital difference between daylight and evening."

The valet blinked his pale eyes. "I think it must have been closer to four – but the day had been one of exceptional sunshine. The sky a cloudless and steely blue. Visibility was excellent; unusually so for, as you say, the time of year."

"You have the poetic turn of your Celtic ancestors, Mr. M'Gurk." Holmes puffed on his pipe a moment longer. "Was there anyone else abroad in the garden?"

"I saw no one, sir." M'Gurk took a moment of his own to consider. "No – he was alone. The garden is bordered by a tall hedge. If there had been a soul beyond that I cannot say, but the garden was deserted except for Mr. Higgins."

"Excellent, Mr. M'Gurk. You went outside, of course?"

"Immediately, Mr. Holmes. I called for all the staff to assist me. We searched the entire grounds but found no sign of our employer."

"How long did it take you," I asked, "from the moment you saw Mr. Higgins – disappear – to reaching the grounds?"

He thought a moment. "Ten seconds, perhaps. No more than twenty, certainly."

"Have the local constabulary been informed?" asked Holmes.

M'Gurk looked uncomfortable. "It was agreed that – for the sake of Mr. Higgins's business associations – news of his disappearance, no matter how literal, should be suppressed for now."

Holmes's gimlet eye speared the man. "Who exactly decided this? Not you?"

"It was Mr. Jocelyn Barrington, my employer's lawyer and closest friend. He was one of the dinner guests and arrived before word could be circulated that the evening was cancelled."

Holmes sucked on his pipe, brow furrowed in thought. "When did you leave Corvin House?"

"I caught the earliest morning train to London, although Mr. Barrington was very much against my engaging you, Mr. Holmes. He felt that involving another party might encourage news to leak. I had to assure him of your discretion."

"You were right to do so. I take it the search for Mr. Higgins did not cease overnight?"

"No sir. We searched every inch of the house and grounds I don't know how many times. Not so much as a hair could be found."

"Forgive me if I say that is unlikely." Holmes arose from his seat. "Mr. M'Gurk, you have provided me with the perfect Christmas gift. Although the case is not so difficult as you imagine, there are points of interest. Watson and I will be delighted to investigate."

"Holmes. Tomorrow is Christmas Day." I protested.

His response was the briefest flicker of a smile. "And I believe spending Christmas in the country is just the tonic you need, Watson. Away from London's contaminated air and its associated memories."

I was struck dumb by my friend's words. It is all too easy to forget that Holmes's perceptive intellect can be used to pierce more than just a criminal's heart. Silently, I nodded agreement.

M'Gurk was also on his feet. "I have taken the liberty of instructing a cab to await me outside, Mr. Holmes. At your convenience it will take us to Liverpool Street Station. I will be happy to accompany you back to Corvin House."

Holmes and I quickly donned overcoats, scarves and hats – for myself ensuring the tobacco intended for my friend was safely in a pocket – and followed M'Gurk downstairs. We paused only to make our farewells to Mrs. Hudson and her guests, Holmes murmuring something in the good lady's ear. Through the closing parlour door, the indignant cries more than hinted to me what his words had conveyed. In that moment, I would not care to have been Jerzy Krakowski.

We shared an unheated compartment to Norwich, all of us thankful for our heavy coats and scarves. To warm ourselves, we smoked as Holmes questioned M'Gurk further. The man had been in Higgins's employ for a little over ten years, during which time he had found him temperate, generous to his staff, and with a robust sense of humour. Higgins had never married, but doted on his nieces and nephews to the point where his sister, Mrs. Whitside, despaired that he would ruin them. The lawyer, Barrington, tended to his investments, whilst the Cromer-based fishing fleet was managed by a local man. At weekends, as his neighbours took to the water and decimated the local wildfowl, Higgins preferred instead to arm himself with sketchpad and pencil. Indeed, he had a local reputation for being an excellent watercolourist, although he was reluctant to exhibit his work.

"And none bore him any ill will?" asked Holmes.

M'Gurk mournfully shook his head. "He was universally loved, Mr. Holmes. But this is all by the by, for he was not abducted, nor assaulted. He vanished into the thin air!"

"So you say. And I have no doubt that you believe wholeheartedly in what you saw. But you must concede that your statement, as it stands, smacks of the impossible."

"I know . . . I know . . . ." The wretched man stared out of a fogged window at the speeding countryside.

"People go missing all the time, Holmes," I interjected, moved by M'Gurk's obvious misery.

"So they do, Watson – but rarely in sight of an observer." He leaned back, closing his eyes. "In 1763 one Owen Parfitt – a man paralyzed to immobility by a stroke – disappeared from outside his sister's Shepton Mallet home on a warm June evening. In 1809, British diplomat Benjamin Bathurst was said to have vanished in sight of his companion after stopping for dinner in the town of Perelberg."

M'Gurk took his eyes from the fogged window. "There was an observer in that case," said he.

"Indeed," agreed Holmes. "But I caution against accepting these accounts at face value. When committed to newsprint, vital details are frequently omitted, all the better to spice the anecdote. And it is not unknown for a newspaper editor with column inches to fill, or a travelling salesman with nothing better to occupy his time, to concoct the most lurid flights of fancy."

M'Gurk sank back into staring glumly.

"However, I accept that sometimes there is a genuinely mystery," said Holmes. "Four years ago, the pioneering French photographer Louis LePrince boarded a train in Dijon and retired to his compartment. There were no noises from LePrince's cabin; the door was locked and window tightly closed. Yet when the train arrived at Paris, not only was LePrince entirely absent, but his baggage – kept in a separate compartment – was also missing."

I confess I laughed. "I was unaware you took an interest in the colourful fictions to be found within *The Illustrated Police News*, Holmes."

"A scientific mind must be open to all possibilities, Watson, no matter how ridiculous they may initially appear. I have no personal belief in ghosts, yet I concede that there have been many reported sightings, and by sober witnesses. It is my assertion that every case may be easily explained by taking each on its own merits and weighing the evidence. And if not now, then at some future date when the Laws of the Universe are better understood. The LePrince disappearance, for instance: I have been conducting my own research for many months, and hope to soon present my conclusions. Ones that will not invoke the supernatural."

"I look forward to reading them."

Holmes inclined his head at my enthusiasm. "My point is, M'Gurk, that I do not accept that people disappear willy-nilly into the ether. Although you believe whole-heartedly in what you saw, I hope you will take no offense when I say that you almost certainly did not see it – "

"Mr. Holmes!" M'Gurk bristled.

My friend held up a calming hand. "You observed precisely what you were meant to observe. Nothing more."

"You have solved it already?" I said.

"Although I am far from a satisfactory explanation, let us say I have constructed a yet untested hypothesis which goes some way towards a solution. I am satisfied that we may find all our answers at Corvin House"

"I am cheered to hear you say it, Mr. Holmes," said M'Gurk, "for we are minutes away from Norwich Station."

Evening was upon us when we stepped from the train. M'Gurk was well known to the station staff and lost no time securing a horse and trap for the final leg of our journey. Snow fell in a desultory manner as we left the town and plunged into an unlit countryside. Neither of my companions spoke as we clattered along the uneven roads, Holmes no doubt mentally examining and evaluating his hypothesis, M'Gurk sunk in a deep study from which he did not rouse until Corvin House was in view. In the darkness, it was little more than a forbidding black hulk with soft lights glowing from three first floor windows, and above the main door. Never has a single lamp been so inviting.

M'Gurk paid the driver as Holmes and I made our way towards the front door. It was opened while we were still some distance away by a young girl in a maid's uniform. Her fair hair tumbled in disarray from beneath her cap, and bright, feverish spots burned high on her cheeks. She curtsied to us both, although it was our companion she addressed.

"I'm so glad you're returned, Mr. M'Gurk. Mr. Barrington has had word sent to Mrs. Whitside, and I feared she would arrive before you."

M'Gurk touched the girl on the arm with an intimacy I could not fail to notice. "I'm here now, Connie," said he. "This is Mr. Sherlock Holmes and Dr. Watson of London. They will soon have the master back with us."

Holmes arched his brows at such a wild claim. "I cannot promise anything so definite," said he stiffly. "But I shall do everything that I can."

We were ushered indoors out of the cold. The maid, Connie, took our overcoats, asking if we required warming drinks. I would have agreed, but Holmes insisted that he examine Wenman Higgins's room without further delay. M'Gurk led us upstairs, whilst the girl was sent to prepare a pot of coffee.

Higgins's room was in a rearward-facing corner of the house. It was plain but comfortable, with a large bed, wardrobe, dresser, and stand for water jug and bowl. Several watercolours hung upon the panelled walls and, if from the brush of Wenman Higgins, he was indeed a talented man. There were two windows, a wide picture window along the side, and a small three-sided bay – the one through which M'Gurk had observed his master. Both contained diamond-paned leadlight glass. The bay formed a curtained alcove, with a window seat running inside its circumference. It was too dark to see the garden of which M'Gurk had spoken.

Holmes sat himself on the window seat, pulling a small lens from his waistcoat, and examined the bay windows thoroughly. As he bent closely over the wooden window ledge, he murmured, "Have shutters ever been fitted?"

M'Gurk shook his head. "Perhaps in earlier times – this house is almost two hundred years old – but never in my recollection."

Holmes drew back and glanced at the patterned drapes. "And these curtains? How were they positioned?"

"They were partially drawn, much as you see them now, leaving the alcove itself in shadow. But not enough to obscure the view through the windows."

"Excellent!" Holmes pocketed his lens. "Well, we may do no more until daylight, so I suggest we partake of that coffee you mentioned. Friend Watson here looks positively grey with cold!"

Corvin House was blessed with more rooms than the small household would ever need. The staff of valet, cook and maid was, unconventionally, given rooms on the first floor, rather than within the spacious attic. That area, I was given to understand, stood unused except for storage. Only the gardener slept elsewhere, in a small brick lodge adjoining the garden. I could see why Higgins's staff loved him so – such egalitarianism is rare.

I awoke and dressed early. It was still dark outside, with an hour or more to go before any decent examination of the grounds could begin, so I decided to ensure myself of a decent breakfast. When I entered the dining room, there was no sign of Holmes, but a tall, saturnine fellow sat at the table enjoying kippers and scrambled eggs. He arose at my entrance, offering his hand.

"Jocelyn Barrington," said he in a jolly voice, quite at odds with his gloomy appearance.

"Dr. Watson." I took his hand.

"Ah yes, companion to the redoubtable Sherlock Holmes." His dour expression flickered with what I interpreted as mild annoyance. "Join me, Doctor, please. Wenman has always provided a good table."

I thanked him, filling my plate from an admirable selection laid out on the sideboard as he once more sat. I took a seat to his left.

"I would offer the compliments of the season," I said, "but under the circumstances . . . ."

"Ah yes, Christmas Day. Never has it felt less so." He took a sip of coffee. "I am sure M'Gurk has passed on my misgivings about Mr. Holmes becoming involved."

I nodded.

"It's just that I feel, at this point, such as step is unnecessary . . . ." Barrington leaned back, his glum features growing more morose. "Wenman has always demonstrated a keen – if sometimes individual – sense of humour. He may reappear at any moment, laden with a sack of gifts, and laughing 'Merry Christmas!' at us all."

"His valet does not share your optimism."

Barrington sighed. "M'Gurk, if you will forgive my saying so, occasionally embodies all the superstitions of his forefathers. Vanishing

372

before his eyes, indeed. He has quite infected the household with his mania. I had to send for Laura, of course. She arrived late last night, quite beside herself."

"Laura?"

"Mrs. Whitside – Wenman's sister. Thanks to M'Gurk, she is convinced her brother has been abducted."

I ate a final morsel of spiced sausage. "And you do not, Mr. Barrington?"

"As I have indicated, Doctor, I believe Wenman is playing another of his strange jokes – "

"I hope that will prove to be the case." We both looked up to see Holmes entering the room, brushing from his coat what resembled lengths of cobweb. "Although I suspect events have taken a darker turn than a simple joke."

Barrington stood, offering a reluctant hand. He seemed unnerved by the effluvia still flowing from Holmes's arms. My friend squeezed the proffered fingers in the most perfunctory manner before sitting himself across the table, facing me.

"Have you breakfasted, Holmes?" I enquired, already certain that he had not.

He waved a hand. "I will take some coffee when you refill your own cup." He glanced at our companion. "Mr. Barrington, friend and lawyer to the disappeared Higgins. Am I correct in assuming the police are still to be informed?"

"I did not – "

"Did not wish the news to be broadcast and so damage your friend's business interests. Quite so. Thank you, Watson." He took a sip from the coffee I placed before him. "The predictable actions of a lawyer, but far from those of a close friend."

"Mr. Holmes – !"

My friend was unperturbed by Barrington's outburst. He took another sip of coffee. "Never fear. I have despatched M'Gurk to the closest constabulary with a message from myself. I do not anticipate him returning soon. The police take it very ill when a personage such as Wenman Higgins disappears and no one seeks to notify them."

"I have already explained to your colleague – "

"You may offer explanation upon explanation, Mr. Barrington; it will not make them true. Please – no more bluster. This case is, at its heart, quite simple, once the gaudy theatrics are put aside. That you continue to obfuscate rather than assist suggests you know more than you admit – if you are indeed not actively involved in the disappearance of your friend and client."

For a moment I imagined Barrington would erupt into a violent rage. Then his dour face collapsed. His entire body seemed to shrink and sag in his seat.

"Bring your police, Mr. Holmes. I will answer any question."

"Naturally. But first, kindly confirm for me that Mr. Higgins's finances are not at all what both you and he have led everyone to believe."

The lawyer nodded silently.

"Excellent. Come, Watson. Daylight is finally upon us!"

The morning was dull, the sky filled with low, threatening cloud. Our condensing breaths hung listlessly, unperturbed by air which held not a trace of breeze. Holmes and I repaired to the rear garden and stood directly in sight of the small bay window in Higgins's room. It would certainly have afforded a wide view of the tiny estate, even to someone standing well inside the room as M'Gurk had. The garden was not large – a square lawn running the width of the house – but it was artfully laid out with paths running between four small plots which, during the growing season, would undoubtedly have been filled with flowering plants. The space was bounded to the sides and rear with a box hedge.

"What do you expect to see out here?" I asked. "The staff will have been walking back and forth in their search for Higgins. Their tracks will have destroyed any trace of his steps."

"Your reasoning is faultless, Watson. No, I am in search of other evidence, if the perpetrator has not already destroyed it – " He straightened abruptly with a cry, pointing towards the demarcating rear hedge. "There! Do you smell it, Watson?"

"A bonfire?"

"Quite, and at this time of year. All of autumn's fallen leaves are already swept up and destroyed. What else might the gardener be burning? Make haste, Watson, make haste!"

We fairly sprinted across the lawn, circling around squares of black soil where only the hardiest of plants stood skeletal in the cold earth. Beyond the box hedge was a stretch of bare ground, upon which stood a simple two-storey brick cottage, flanked by greenhouses and cold frames. The gardener's home and workplace. A small fire burned sullenly on the ground, but it was neither leaves nor twigs which smouldered there. Rather, it was what appeared to be a pile of rags.

Holmes rushed forward, kicking at the fire, impulsively dragging the burning pieces of cloth from the flames with his boot tip. I found a length of dead branch and joined him, raking the bonfire apart and stamping out the surly flames. Someone cried out – the gardener, emerging from his cottage. For a moment he stood, imploring us to cease, before taking to his heels and racing – I was surprised to note – away from Corvin House and not towards it.

"Leave him, Watson," said Holmes, crouching over the smoking rags. "He cannot run far, and the countryside affords few hiding places."

Once the last glowing embers were extinguished, we took up the rags and carried them to the house. We were met at the door by Barrington and a young woman whom I guessed to be Higgins's sister, Mrs. Whitside. Chestnut hair framed a heart-shaped face that was presently a ghastly white. When she saw what Holmes and I bore, one hand flew to her mouth and she clutched at the lawyer with the other. She groaned piteously.

"I beg you, madam," spoke Holmes, "do not leap to any conclusion. Give us five minutes before coming to your brother's room. The truth is not as grave as you imagine, but nevertheless, prepare yourself."

Although I had questions of my own, I followed Holmes silently up to Higgins's room, where we laid out the smoky remains upon the bed. Like a charred jigsaw, they came together after a few moments' pondering. Although significant areas had been consumed by the bonfire, the remaining pieces were clearly from a tweed jacket, heavy trousers, and the peak of a flat cap.

"Higgins's clothing?" said I.

Holmes had turned away and was looking intently towards the small bay window. "Mrs. Whitside must confirm it but, yes, I believe so. And unless I am much mistaken, that is her tread upon the stair."

I opened the door to allow in both Mrs. Whitside and Barrington. The woman's eyes strayed to the clothing upon the bed and again she reacted with shock. The lawyer led her to the room's only chair, where she sat, ashen faced, gaze still locked upon the charred rags.

"From your response, I see you believe these to be your brother's clothes," said Holmes.

She nodded, her eyes glistening with the onset of tears. "Does this mean . . . ? Is he murdered, Mr. Holmes?"

"Far from it." He glanced towards the lawyer. "Barrington, might I ask that you favour us with a short walk across the garden, there. Within sight of the bay window, if you please."

Wordlessly, Barrington left the room.

"Mrs. Whitside, may I crave your indulgence for a moment?" Holmes held out a hand. She took it and came to her feet. All three of us stood near the foot of the bed and looked out upon the garden through the bay window. The partly drawn curtains cast the alcove into shadow, further emphasising the cold, grey light coming through the leaded panes.

"Ah – here he comes!" exclaimed Holmes.

I glanced aside. Through the picture window, I saw Barrington walking alongside the house and turning the corner. Returning my attention to the bay, I watched as the lawyer appeared in the left window, treading morosely. As he came parallel to the central pane he glanced up, although it is impossible for him to have seen us. Then he reached the right side of the bay – and promptly vanished.

Mrs. Whitside gasped. I am certain that I exclaimed in surprise. Holmes simply clapped his hands. A moment later, Barrington reappeared just as magically, retracing his steps.

"How is this possible?" cried Mrs. Whitside. A brief smile tugged at Holmes's lips and he stepped into the alcove, reaching for the right hand side of the bay. It came away in his hands and he spun to face us, holding a faultless replica of the window: the diamond panes, the portion of garden beyond.

"Is this not perfection, Watson?" he laughed. "Wenman Higgins is not only a consummate watercolourist, but an illusionist superior to many a tawdry music hall magician!"

It was certainly a wonderful piece of stage craft. Close up it became an oblong of painted wood, but at a distance of two feet or more the deception reasserted itself.

"Remarkable," I agreed. "Where did you find it?"

"In one of the attic rooms, carelessly hidden. You will have noticed my disreputable appearance earlier this morning. Those rooms have not enjoyed a duster's flick for many a month. I imagine the plan was to eventually destroy it, but events ran too quickly for the perpetrator. When the excitable M'Gurk told us back in Baker Street that he had seen Higgins simply disappear, it was obvious that a device such as this must have been employed. And where best to quickly hide it than in the one area of the house so seldom visited?"

"Ingenious," said I.

"Quite, and yet not without inherent risks." Holmes placed the false window upon the bed just as Barrington returned to the room. "Viewed from the wrong angle, the illusion fails; the horizon skews. Yet Higgins knew his man. I'll wager that M'Gurk has long made a habit of standing in the light of both windows to brush down his master's dinner suit, even in the darker winter hours. Even so, if it had snowed or was raining heavily, the artifice would be instantly revealed."

"M'Gurk indicated that on the day the weather was fine and bright."

"Exactly, Watson! Perfect conditions for the illusion. Higgins was either exceptionally lucky, or he was experienced enough to be able to predict the local weather in advance. Such a talent would serve him well in his artistic strolls."

"Mr. Holmes." Mrs. Whitside was returned to her seat, her nerves almost certainly near breaking point. "Are you saying that Wenman arranged his own disappearance?"

"Just as Barrington has asserted, although for the wrong reasons. He was, of course, party to the whole deception, and keen to delay any form of investigation until his client should be far enough away."

Mrs. Whitside raised her pale features. "Jocelyn, is this true?"

The doleful lawyer nodded. "I cannot say I was happy with the arrangement, but you know how damnably persuasive Wenman can be. He would have contacted you presently, to assure you that all was well."

"But why?" Anger was returning colour to her cheeks, and her eyes sparked.

"Because he was destitute," Holmes answered the question. "There are few reasons a man will stage his own disappearance. When I heard of how profligate your brother could be, I reasoned that he had, ultimately, outspent himself. Barrington confirmed my suspicions. Higgins did not have the strength of character to admit his circumstances, either to you or your family, so he chose to vanish. To spirit himself away like a character in a seasonal ghost story. The plan was that while Barrington prevaricated, and the excitable M'Gurk sowed alarm in the household, Wenman Higgins would flee to Europe."

"That is monstrous!" cried the lady. "To subject his own family to such distress, merely so that he might escape!"

"Do not judge him too harshly," said Holmes. "Many men in such straits, who can see nothing but ruin ahead, have chosen a far more permanent route from their woes."

"But how did he get away?" I wondered. "M'Gurk said it was less than twenty seconds between him witnessing the vanishing, alerting the household and rushing outside. Higgins could not have fled too far a distance in that time – particularly as he appears to have changed his clothes."

"The figure M'Gurk observed walking across the garden was obviously not his master. I would dearly love to meet and talk with your brother, Mrs. Whitside. He has an excellent brain. Every aspect of the plan relied on the single witness seeing only what was expected of him. A window instead of artfully painted wood, his employer instead of the disguised gardener."

Mrs. Whitside and I expressed our incredulity at that, while Barrington maintained a brooding silence. Holmes indicated the charred remains on the bed.

"It was afternoon, the light starting to fail. M'Gurk sees a figure dressed in these clothes. Who would he think it to be except his employer? When the alarm is raised, the gardener quickly rids himself of the disguise, most likely stashing in under a hedge, and races to join the search. We were fortunate in catching him before he could burn the evidence, Watson."

"And my brother?" asked Mrs. Whitside.

"Already gone that morning. Fled to Cromer, his fleet of fishing boats, and a crew no doubt as loyal as Corvin House's staff. From there it is a short trip to the continent."

"Then Wenman is gone . . . ."

"Not at all, madam." Holmes fairly glowed with satisfaction. "The message that M'Gurk bore to the local police in my name was for them to immediately contact their colleagues in Cromer. No fisherman will be risking the seas on Christmas Day when they have families and warm hearths. If Higgins is not already in custody, he will by the day's end."

"And what will become of him?"

Holmes glanced towards Barrington. "That is for the courts to decide. His crimes are small. With an eloquent lawyer, it is quite likely he may avoid a custodial sentence."

Barrington nodded.

"And we shall stand by him." Mrs. Whitside came to her feet, stiff with resolve. "Mr. Whitside is far from rich, but he has contacts in the City. If my foolish brother had but asked, I am certain we might have averted all of this. With the help of those who love him, we shall come through."

I was warmed by her words and gladdened that, even though Wenman Higgins had lately been foolish, the goodwill he had engendered in those around him might save him yet.

Holmes rubbed his hands together. "Capital. Then we may return to Baker Street, Watson – "

"I will not hear of it, Mr. Holmes!" said Mrs. Whitside. "It is Christmas Day. You and Dr. Watson must dine with us at North Walsham. You too, Jocelyn. Wenman may not be with us this year, but he will be present in our hearts."

And so it was that Sherlock Holmes and I celebrated Christmas with the Whitsides. It should have been a sad affair, but the family would only look forward to better times. And as evening fell, the Cromer police delivered an extraordinary Christmas gift: Wenman Higgins, bailed into his sister's care until the New Year.

Holmes – after reminding me of the tobacco I had so signally failed to smuggle undetected in my overcoat pocket – once more correctly deduced its origins, before presenting me with a box of first-rate *Principe de Gales*. In all, Christmas that year unfolded into an exceptionally happy and a reassuringly traditional one.

A Perpetrator in a Pear Tree
by Roger Riccard

Chapter I

As we sat in our rooms at 221b Baker Street on that cold winter day, Sherlock Holmes lit his churchwarden pipe with a hot coal he had retrieved with the fireplace tongs. The city had been snowbound for several days, a condition which curtailed my friend's profession as the world's first consulting detective.

Having finished the breakfast provided by our landlady, Mrs. Hudson, we were indulging in our pipes and reading the morning papers when there came to our ears the sound of heavy footsteps on the stairs.

Before the knock came to our door, my companion cried out, "Come in, Inspector Lestrade!"

Slowly the door opened and the Scotland Yard Inspector entered with a quizzical look upon his face. "How'd you know . . . ?" he started to ask, then changed his mind, remembering that Holmes had done this to him before. "It's the footsteps again, isn't it? It's devilish, I say! I don't know how you can distinguish mine from anyone else's."

Holmes smiled and waved the man to a seat by the fire, for his coat was quite damp and snow still clung to his bowler.

"Your footsteps were heavier this morning," Holmes admitted. "However, the pattern was its usual cadence. Combining that with this headline from *The Times*, I was able to logically expect a visit from one of our friends at the Yard."

He held up the front page with his finger pointed at the first column, which read:

IMPOSSIBLE MURDER IN MUSWELL!

The Honorable Judge Jameson Mason, of Fortis Keep in Muswell Hill, was found dead yesterday under mysterious circumstances. Upon receiving no answer when called upon for breakfast, the Judge's son, Edgar Mason, sent for assistance. Servants were required to open the tower room where the retired Judge had retreated the night before to work upon his memoirs.

The Judge appeared to have a mortal wound to the heart. However, no weapon has been identified and no trace of an intruder has presented itself.

Sergeant Mossgarden has ordered an exhaustive search of the area for any persons of interest or clues to the manner of death.

The story went on with more details and some speculation as to the possibility of former convicts who may have sought revenge upon the Judge, who was known for his strict sentencing.

"Yes," replied the inspector. "The reports from Sergeant Mossgarden indicate some unusual aspects that I believe you would find to be of interest."

Holmes leaned back in his chair and steepled his fingers in front of his chin, gazing intently at our visitor.

"I shall be happy to accompany you, Lestrade," he responded after a few moments. "If you will explain the *real* reason you wish my presence on this case."

The Scotland Yarder feigned ignorance and started to protest, but Holmes cut him off.

"No, no, my friend. Do not deny it. You have another motive for wanting me along."

Lestrade's shoulders sagged in defeat. Finally he cast his eyes down and made his admission.

"Sergeant Mossgarden is a very formidable individual, Mr. Holmes. He is stubborn and bitter that he has not yet received a promotion to become an inspector at Scotland Yard. He will do all he can to take the credit for this case and attempt to make anyone from the Yard look foolish, to prove he is more worthy than they."

I could not believe my ears and spoke up at this confession. "Surely, Inspector, you are not afraid of such an individual? I've seen you in action on many occasions and you are one of the bravest men I've met. I've never known you to kowtow to anyone. Even in those instances when Holmes disproves your own methods or theories, you accept them with grudging respect, without apology."

Lestrade looked me in the eye and answered, "It's kind of you to say, Doctor, and normally I believe I can stand up to most any man alive. But this fellow . . . ." He shook his head in exasperation. "This fellow has the most irritating character that I've ever come across. He's a conceited, arrogant bully who won't listen to reason if it contradicts his own thoughts. I wouldn't be a bit surprised if he was a descendant of Captain Bligh himself!" [1]

Holmes stood and announced, "Then we shall gladly accompany you, old friend. For we cannot have you so exasperated that you break the law yourself by throttling such a lout."

We bundled ourselves against the weather and the three of us caught a train for East Finchley. From there, we acquired a trap and set off for Fortis Keep. The weather was cooperating, for there had been no snow for twenty-four hours, but the temperature was still frigid.

Thus, it was that less than two hours from Lestrade's knock on our door that we arrived at the scene of the crime. Fortis Keep is an ancient castle with a single tower and high walls surrounding the living quarters, courtyard, and stables. At some point in its past, an adjacent stream was partially diverted to create a moat some twenty feet wide surrounding the structure. The drawbridge we crossed over appeared to have not been raised for decades. judging by the rust on the chains.

A groom took charge of our trap and led the horse to the stables while we advanced upon the main door. Lestrade announced us to the butler, Carson by name, and requested to see Edgar Mason.

After allowing us in from the cold, Carson turned to us, hesitating as to his next action. He was an elderly gentleman, tall with a full head of wavy grey hair. A pair of silver rimmed spectacles protruded from his breast pocket. Finally he spoke.

"I am afraid Master Edgar is unavailable, Inspector. Your man, Mossgarden, came and arrested him this morning for murdering his father."

Chapter II

"Good Lord!" I cried, "What was his evidence?"

Carson hung his head, "I've no knowledge, I'm afraid. He merely arrested him and took him away. We were all shocked at his actions and none of the staff believe Master Edgar was capable of this act."

Holmes spoke up, "As long as we are here, Inspector, I believe we should examine the scene of the crime for ourselves."

"Quite right, Holmes," agreed Lestrade. "Carson, would you please take us to the room where this murder took place."

The inside of the keep had been upgraded to modern lighting and plumbing, yet still retained the ancient tapestries and trappings of a medieval castle. We passed a dining hall with a large stone fireplace engraved with the motto: *Veritatem et iustitiam in omnes,* [2] and an armory where suits of armor and armaments still lined the walls. A glass covered case also held smaller weapons: knives, flintlock pistols, and molds for projectiles and early lead bullets. The gentleman's gentleman led us up a long flight of circular stairs to the Tower Room, where Judge Mason had set up a study for himself.

Before entering, Holmes questioned Carson.

"Who had keys to this room?"

"Judge Mason, of course, and he habitually locked himself in so as not to be disturbed while he was writing his memoirs. There is also a set of master keys which I keep in the butler's pantry. Only the Judge and I have . . . rather, *had* the pantry key."

Holmes nodded, "From the newspaper accounts, I understand that you were summoned by the Judge's son when he failed to get a response from his father?"

"Yes, Mr. Holmes. Master Edgar had gone to call his father for breakfast, which was a common occurrence. The Judge often lost track of time when he was writing. When there was no answer and no sound from within, he came to me and we both returned here so I could unlock the door."

Holmes bent to examine the lock with his lens. Satisfied, he bid Carson to go ahead and open the door. Once we could see the interior, the detective held up his hand to indicate we should not yet enter.

Turning again to the butler he asked, "What did you observe when you first opened the door?"

Carson thought back, visualizing the scene in his mind. "Judge Mason was lying on the floor over there." He pointed toward a spot away from the desk, near the window. "He was face down, and the carpet at his feet was disheveled."

The "window" referred to was actually an archer's slit, only about a foot wide and four feet high. There were three of them allowing light into the room from various angles.

There was also a fireplace, a suit of armor, and a floor length tapestry of the family crest. Holmes bent to examine the carpet, which was an oval shape with a maroon and gold pattern.

"The area has been trampled by too many feet to yield any clues. What happened when you opened the door? Please be precise."

Carson cleared his throat and pointed toward the spot he had indicated before, "The Judge was lying there, and his son immediately cried out and ran to him. He turned him over and said, 'My God, he's been shot! Carson, send for a doctor!'

"I ran downstairs and out to the courtyard, where I called for one of the stable boys to ride for the doctor. I then returned to the Tower Room with towels, bandages, and water. When I arrived, young Edgar was slumped on the floor against the desk. His father still lay where we found him, his chest covered with blood."

The memory seemed to affect him deeply. He grew pale and quickly sat in one of the chairs by the fireplace, lowering his head into his hands.

I knelt at his side and encouraged him to keep his head down and breathe deeply to avoid fainting. Lestrade strode over to the window and looked out while Holmes examined the spot where the body lay.

The inspector looked from the window to where Holmes knelt on the floor and made an observation.

"See here, Holmes," he said, as he pointed outside. "There's a tree opposite this window that would make a fine perch for a shooter."

Holmes nodded, hesitated a moment, and then joined our comrade at the archer's slit. There, about fifty yards away, was a good-sized tree, bare of leaves but tall and sturdy.

"Such a shot would require a considerable marksman," observed the detective. Turning back to the butler, who had somewhat recovered, he asked, "Did anyone hear a shot?"

Carson summoned the strength to stand again and replied, "No, Mr. Holmes, it was a quiet night. There was a light snowfall and a full moon occasionally broke through the clouds. I could observe it from my quarters where I was polishing the silver."

Holmes digested that remark, called Carson over to the window and asked, "Is that tree visible from your quarters?"

"Not from where I was sitting, sir. I have to be standing by the window to observe that particular tree."

Holmes nodded, then he suddenly went to the floor, lay down and asked, "Is this approximately where the body was when you first saw it?"

Carson suggested a slight adjustment and Holmes complied, then enquired further, "Could you see the wound when his son turned him over?"

Carson answered immediately, "Sergeant Mossgarden asked me the same thing. I could not originally see it. Master Edgar was kneeling between the Judge and where I stood frozen at the door. I did not see the actual wound until I returned."

Holmes contemplated that and stood. "Now, about the carpet, can you show us how it was disturbed?"

The butler knelt and curled the edge of the rug back toward where the body's feet would have been.

Holmes took in the scene and closed his eyes. I strode over to where Lestrade had remained by the window and looked out at the aforementioned tree. Holmes was correct. It would have taken someone with the skill of Colonel Sebastian Moran [3] to make such a shot. As he was safely locked away in Newgate Prison, I could not imagine who else could achieve the task from that distance at the upward angle required.

Holmes put his hands on his hips and asked one more question, "What was the state of the fireplace when you opened the door?"

Carson, hesitated at the incongruousness of the question, then answered, "It was down to just a few smoldering coals, Mr. Holmes. The room was much colder than the Judge usually kept it."

"Yet there was plenty of wood in the rack, was there not?"

"Yes, Mr. Holmes, it was half full. The stable boy refills it every day."

Holmes strode over to the desk and observed the papers, books, and writing utensils lying there. At last he announced, "I believe I have gleaned all I can from inside this room, Lestrade. I should like to examine that tree now."

We made our way out across the drawbridge and approached the tree that Lestrade had noted. Holmes carefully eyed the snowy ground surrounding its base. He then walked around the tree, studying its bark. Suddenly he reached up and pulled himself up into its branches. He seemed to be observing the limbs until he reached a high perch. From there he looked toward the castle tower through a fork in a branch. He examined the fork with his magnifying lens and then made his way quickly back to the ground beside us.

"What did you find, Holmes?" enquired Lestrade.

The great detective brushed the snow from himself and replied, "It is a pear tree, not a prime choice for a climber. As you can see the branches thin out quickly and one cannot ascend to great heights. However, the fork where I stopped does enjoy an excellent sightline to the window where the Judge was standing."

Lestrade clapped his gloved hands together, "So, it could be the shooter's perch!"

Holmes cocked his head to one side as he looked back up at the branch in question and replied, "Our perpetrator very likely climbed this tree. There are scuff marks on various limbs and several broken twigs. However, there are no marks at all on the fork, which would have been the ideal place to steady a rifle. Surely, the weight of the gun and the recoil of the shot would have left some scraping along the bark. There is also the fact that no shot was heard. I do not believe a silent air gun could have the range necessary to perform a killing shot at this distance. For now, I suggest we continue on to the police station and question Edgar Mason and Sergeant Mossgarden.

"Wait, Holmes" I stated. "Aren't you going to question the staff? Search the grounds? Look for alternative suspects?"

"All in good time, Watson," he replied. "At this point, I have insufficient data to contradict Sergeant Mossgarden's actions. Once we meet with him and Mr. Edgar Mason, I shall be able to determine our next steps."

Chapter III

As we drove on to the Muswell Hill Police Station, Holmes asked us a question. "How many possible weapons did you note in the room, gentlemen?"

I answered quickly, "I saw no gun of any kind. Just the lance next to the suit of armor and the swords on the wall."

Lestrade thought a moment before speaking up. "There was also the fireplace poker and the letter opener."

"But wasn't Judge Mason shot?" I asked.

"We do not know that," answered Holmes. "We only know his son made that statement. In addition, if the newspaper reports are correct, which I do not assume, there was no projectile found. This points more likely to a stabbing. There were also a pen, pencil, the pointed end of the axis of the small globe on his desk and the scissors under the folders of court cases in the center of his blotter.

"I trust, Inspector, that you will permit us to view the body itself. Dr. Watson's examination could prove most useful."

The Scotland Yard man nodded emphatically, "Certainly, Holmes. I'll make sure you get access to all the evidence collected."

The Muswell Hill Police Station is a three-story brick structure on a corner in a residential area, approximately a quarter-mile from the East Finchley Underground Station. Upon entrance, Lestrade introduced us and asked to see Sergeant Mossgarden. We were shown back to an office, where he sat filling out paperwork.

Looking up to see whose shadow darkened his door, he bellowed, "Lestrade, what the hell are you doing here? And who are these men?"

Our inspector stood his ground and replied, "This is Mr. Sherlock Holmes and Dr. John Watson. We are here about Judge Mason's murder."

"Oh no, you don't!" cried Mossgarden, rising abruptly from his chair, the sudden motion causing it to fall backward to the floor. "This is *my* case and *my* arrest. I'm not letting you, or this amateur lapdog of yours, come anywhere near it. You can just turn right around and go back the Scotland Yard. I've got my man and you're not taking credit for it!"

I must admit, the size of this red-faced, red-haired officer, with his long muttonchops curling into a thick moustache, was quite imposing. He was taller than Holmes, possibly even six-and-one-half feet. His weight was in his barrel chest and tree trunk arms that threatened to burst the seams of his uniform.

"I'm not here for credit, you bloody fool!" Lestrade answered evenly. "You know as well as I that C.I.D. [4] is required to investigate all crimes involving members of the court. I was ordered here by my superintendent."

"I've investigated and I've got the murderer. It was his son. No doubt about it."

Holmes cleared his throat and interrupted this debate.

"If, I may, Lestrade," he said, and the inspector nodded. "Sergeant Mossgarden, I've no doubt you have made a reasonable investigation and come to a common sense conclusion. One does not reach your rank by making false accusations. As you say I am not an official policeman, but much of my small success has been due to the observations I have made while accompanying Lestrade, Gregson, Bradstreet, and other seasoned members of the Yard. I would sincerely appreciate the opportunity to glean what lessons I can from the way you solved this case so quickly. It may also interest you to know that Dr. Watson here, in addition to his little entertainments for the masses regarding my work, also writes reports worthy of publication in various newspapers around London. He would be happy to act as your agent in giving your career the type of boost it most certainly deserves."

Following Holmes lead, I pulled out a pencil and notebook and nodded at the giant before me. Although I had never *actually* written such reports for the press, technically Holmes hadn't lied, only saying my reports were 'worthy enough'. The effect on the sergeant was quite phenomenal. His balled fists loosened, his puffed up chest relaxed, and the fierce expression on his face turned into a calculating smile.

"Hmm, maybe I'll give you a try. But my name must appear prominently in every report, even those Lestrade has to sign," he ordered, as he picked his chair off the floor with one hand and sat back down behind the desk.

Holmes smiled, "I promise you, Sergeant, your name will figure distinctively in the accounting of this case."

The sergeant handed Lestrade a copy of his report. As the inspector perused it, Holmes asked Mossgarden, "How did you come to the conclusion that Edgar Mason killed his father?"

The big sergeant huffed, "It was obvious. The room was locked from the inside. No secret passages. The windows were too small for anyone to enter, yet there was no bloody weapon in the room. When I questioned the butler, I knew there was only one solution. The old Judge had tripped on the rug and while he lay unconscious, the son saw an opportunity to do him in. With his body blocking the view from the butler, he stabbed his father in the chest. When the butler went for help, he tried to dispose of the murder weapon by throwing it into the moat. That was the clincher. The moat was frozen over. The knife, which has been verified as belonging to the younger Mason, buried itself into the thin layer of snow on top of the ice. It was easily found when I searched the grounds below the windows."

"Have you ascertained a motive?" I asked as I made notes.

Mossgarden leaned back in his chair, which squeaked in protest, hooked his thumbs in his belt, and proclaimed, "Take your pick. Come New Year's Eve, he was about to get married to a woman of whom his father did not approve. Fortis Keep, while nowhere near the value of Alexandra Palace down the road, is located on prime land which certain developers are clamoring after. But the old Judge wasn't willing to sell. As the only heir, Edgar can make a killing. Ha, ha!"

His laughter at his own pun was disturbing, but before I could protest, Holmes spoke up.

"I should like to see the murder weapon. I am making a study of knives, swords, and other cutting weapons for a monograph on the subject of murder by blade."

"It's with the body at the coroners in St. Pancras. Just a formality of course, but he needs to match it up with the wound for his report."

Lestrade then spoke up again, "I'll need to see the prisoner before we leave."

The big sergeant leaned forward again, hands on his desk, "He'll just deny everything."

"Nevertheless . . . ." parried the Scotland Yarder.

"Very well," countered Mossgarden, "he's in a cell in the back. The guard's name is Fredericks."

His beefy hand pointed in the general direction of the cell block, indicating that he did not deign to go with us. We soon found Constable Fredericks, and he unlocked the cell so that we could interview young Mason.

Edgar Mason was in his late twenties, clean shaven, with wavy brown hair. His appearance was a bit disheveled, as we learned that his arrest had come early that morning while he was dressing. The jacket of his grey wool suit hung on the back of the chair in his cell, where he sat in his waistcoat, but no necktie. He stood upon our entrance. I gauged him to be about five foot six inches tall with a stout body, leaning toward flabbiness that came with too much sedentary work.

Holmes took the lead in the conversation and made introductions. As there was only one chair in the cell, I sat on the bed to rest my aching war wound, which is always exacerbated by cold weather. Holmes indicated that Mason be seated while he stood over him. Lestrade leaned against the cell door.

The interview was brief. We learned that the younger Mason, like his father before him, had entered the practice of law. His studies and work as a beginning lawyer in a well-known legal firm in the City, had left him little time for social activities, but recently he had met the daughter of one of the firm's partners and become engaged.

His father, exhibiting his prejudices against that particular law firm without ever having met the young lady, was opposed to the marriage on the face of it. They argued over that issue, but it had never become violent.

"Did your father ever threaten to disinherit you?" asked Holmes.

The young man seemed startled by the question. "The subject never came up, Mr. Holmes. I am his only heir. I can't imagine he would do such a thing."

"How do you explain your knife being found out the window in the snow?"

"I only carry my knife when I leave the house. It's a small multiplex pocket knife, hardly suitable as a murder weapon. I thought I'd lost it when I was out riding the other day."

Holmes mulled that over, and in the brief silence I spoke up and asked a question which had been bothering me. "Forgive me, but since apparently your father has been stabbed, why did you exclaim to the butler that he had been shot?"

He shook his head, "I can only assume my mind jumped to that conclusion based upon the circumstances. He was near the window and the room had been locked. There was no knife. There was just . . . ." He hesitated and caught his breath. "A hole in his shirt with a large blood stain."

He put his head in his hands.

Holmes knelt down, "Just one last question. Are there any current enemies in your father's life? Anyone with whom he was having a dispute?"

The young man took a handkerchief from his pocket and wiped his eyes, then looked at Holmes's face.

"My father made many enemies as a judge. Any man who has finished his sentence or is out on parole could hate him enough to do this. The only current dispute I am aware of is the land developer who wants to buy Fortis Keep."

Obtaining this person's name, Holmes stood and turned to Lestrade, suggesting, "That is sufficient for now. Let us be off to St. Pancras and see what we can learn there."

Chapter IV

The Coroners Court was next to the St. Pancras Hospital, where the autopsies are performed. Being only two-and-a-half miles south of Muswell, Lestrade and I barely had time to eat the box lunches we purchased at the station. Holmes, sustaining himself with tobacco, was silent during the short ride.

Upon arrival, we were led to the laboratory of the Coroner, Dr. Donald Drake.

He welcomed us with open arms when I introduced myself.

"I've heard good things regarding your work with the police courts, Dr. Watson. I should be happy to assist you in any way I can."

It was obvious that my rapport with him as a fellow physician suggested I take the lead, so I asked to see the body of Judge Mason and the evidence pertaining to the case.

While he showed me the body, Holmes and Lestrade busied themselves with an examination of the clothes and the knife. The Judge's shirt was marred by a large pool of blood, the shade of red varying from light to dark as the stain ran downward from the hole. The knife was as young Mason had described, a multiplex knife with the largest blade being less than four inches in length.

On discussing the body with Drake, I discovered he had determined a very significant fact. "As you can see, Doctor," he prompted, handing me a lens to examine the wound, "the blade which made this wound was double-edged. The knife sent down with the body could not be the murder weapon."

I explored the wound and agreed. Then I noted something else. "This wound is remarkably thin and straight," I pondered. "There is also a bulge in the center."

Holmes head snapped up at that and he crossed the room to the autopsy table in a flash. Snatching the lens from my hand, he bent down and examined the laceration minutely.

"Did you find anything inside the wound?" he demanded.

Drake replied, "I was just about to probe the wound when you gentleman arrived."

Holmes handed the lens back to me, "If my surmises are correct, Doctor. There will be nothing to find. Had you done so earlier, there may have been trace elements of the weapon."

The Coroner stiffened at this admonishment. "Look around, Mr. Holmes. I've two other cases demanding my time as well. Sergeant Mossgarden's report stated that he had already made an arrest. That put this case as lowest on my priorities."

"That is unfortunate, Doctor. I do sympathize. However, Mossgarden has the wrong suspect, and it would be a shame to have an innocent man spend Christmas in gaol and possibly miss his New Year's Eve wedding."

Holmes went on to ask if Drake had certain chemicals, and the Coroner pointed to a cabinet. Holmes then took up the bloody knife and went to a table where he performed some delicate tests.

In the meantime, the Coroner probed the wound in the Judge's chest. As Holmes suspected, he found nothing. My friend, though, made an interesting discovery.

"The blood on the knife," he stated with certainty, "is bird's blood, not human."

Lestrade spoke up, "Then Edgar Mason is not the killer."

Holmes waved his statement away. "I knew that the minute the sergeant proposed his theory of the crime. The evidence we have gathered now, however, tells us the weapon used and narrows our suspect list considerably."

"What weapon could leave a wound like that?" I asked.

"A most diabolical one, I assure you, Watson."

On the ride back to Fortis Keep, Lestrade insisted Holmes reveal why he was sure Edgar Mason wasn't the killer.

"Inspector, it is simplicity itself," exhorted Holmes. "If the son stabbed his father in the chest after he turned the body over, the blood would only be on the father's shirt. In actuality there was blood on the carpet corresponding to where the body lay face down *before* it was turned over.

"Furthermore, young Edgar is not athletic enough to have climbed that tree. However, I am convinced that our perpetrator did climb the pear tree in order to see if he could make a shot from there. He determined that such an act would likely have roused the house and he would have had to flee for his life. Instead, it was while in the tree he realized another method he could apply. One which would be silent, and which he could use to manipulate evidence against the son, thus ruining both the Judge and his heir."

"So who is it, Holmes?" I asked. "And how did he do it?"

Holmes pondered a moment, "That is yet to be determined precisely," he finally replied. "However, I am certain it is a member of the staff, and that the weapon is in the armory."

Chapter V

Arriving back at Fortis Keep, Holmes had Carson show us the way to the ramparts and we ascended to the top of the tower, where archers could shoot down between the battlements.

First, he explored the snow covered surface while Lestrade and I watched. Then he examined the area directly above the arrow slit where the Judge was standing when he was killed. Finally, he called out.

"See here," he said, pointing to some fresh marks on the wall. We joined him and saw some small strands of hemp caught in the cracks, as well as areas where the snow had been compressed or brushed away. "This is where the murderer tied off a rope and lowered himself to the window where he made the fatal shot."

Lestrade protested, "I thought we'd established that he's been stabbed."

"That takes us back to the armory, gentlemen. If you please."

We went back downstairs, and Holmes requested that Carson assemble all the staff members in the armory. While the butler went to attend to that, Holmes opened the glass case and began examining the various molds. Picking out one at last, he held it out for the inspector and me to see.

"This is the mold used by our murderer, gentlemen. Normally filled with molten lead. Now however, you can see where it has already started to show signs of rust."

I took it from his hands. It was old and tarnished, but he was right. There were fresh signs of rust upon it.

Lestrade accepted it from my hands and enquired, "Isn't this is for a crossbow bolt?"

"Indeed, Inspector," answered Holmes. "If you will just step over here."

We both joined Holmes at the wall where several weapons were on display.

"Note the level of dust upon these items. Yet this," he said, picking a crossbow off its pegs, "is perfectly clean and freshly strung. Here is your murder weapon."

He handed the medieval contraption to the inspector, who began examining it. Holmes, while our attention was on the weapon, surreptitiously made his way over to stand by the armory door. Several staff members started to enter and we turned at the sound. Suddenly, one of them, seeing us with the murder weapon in hand, turned on his heels and bolted for the door. Holmes blocked his path and put him down with a sharp jab to the solar plexus. As the man lay gasping on the floor, we joined our friend who explained, "Our killer, gentlemen. Judge Mason's gamekeeper."

Having finally regained his breath, the man spoke out in protest as he raised himself up on his elbows.

"I didn't kill no one!" he shouted.

"Then why did you run when you saw we had the murder weapon?" sneered Lestrade.

"I weren't runnin'," he replied in his low level English. "I just remembered I left somethin' on the stove an' thought it best to take it off when I saw how big this meeting was goin' t'be."

Holmes chided him, "The game is up, my man. Your boots left tracks in the snow around the pear tree and on the roof. The snowfall hasn't been heavy enough to obliterate them as you hoped."

Holmes reached down and lifted the man's right foot off the floor, causing him to fall off his elbows and lay prone again.

"This boot has a distinct wear pattern to its heel. Much like that found among prisoners who have been chained while doing hard labor. It would have been easy for an old con like you to snatch Edgar Mason's knife and to plant blood on it from one of the birds you shot as the gamekeeper. Only you could have wandered the grounds outside the castle without arousing suspicion, as it was an element of your duties. You had access to this room to steal the weapon, and the privacy of your supply shed to create the bolts you needed.

"Once your weapon was ready, you chose a night cold enough to maintain the integrity of your ice bolts. You lowered yourself from the battlement by a hemp rope, attracted Judge Mason's attention by some pretext to get him to come to the window where you were hiding just to the side. Once he was there you swung into place and shot him through the heart. You tossed his son's knife toward the ground below the window to implicate him, but your aim was off as you hung there and it landed on the frozen moat. You then climbed back up, returned the crossbow and mold to the armory, and went about your business."

Holmes dropped the man's foot to the floor. Being in such a vulnerable position, surrounded by accusing on-lookers and faced with such a detailed accounting of his actions, he couldn't hope to deny his guilt. He slowly got to his feet and faced us.

"All right, you've got me. But I'm not sorry for it. Not one bit. The old Judge deserved what he got and more. I'll tell you my story, and you see if I weren't justified in what I done."

Holmes had Carson dismiss the rest of the staff and sat the prisoner down while Lestrade handcuffed him. He then began his tale.

"My real name is Pete Silcox. Twenty-two years ago, I was an orphan on the streets of London. My father was a sailor whose ship sunk when I was just seven. My mother died of consumption when I was twelve, and I was turned over to St. Mary Magdalene's workhouse. It was a filthy place and I run away the first chance I got.

"I lived by me wits and odd jobs here and there. Got handy at pickin' a pocket or purse to get by from time to time. One day I got me a rich haul. Found a gentleman's wallet in an alley outside the rooms of a certain lady who was known for her favors. Well, it had over a hundred pounds in it, and I thought I'd died and gone to heaven. But then this gent comes back and catches me with his wallet. We struggle over it for a bit when a policeman comes along and grabs me by the collar. Naturally he takes the gentleman's side when he lies and says I picked his pocket and he chased me into that alley.

"So off to court I go. I'm only sixteen at the time, so I figure worst case, it'll be back to the workhouse for me. But this Judge Mason won't listen to my story about finding the wallet. Says because I stole an amount of such 'grand proportions' as he put it, he's sentencing me to fifteen years!

"I was lucky to survive the beatings and the abuse, and I vowed if I ever got out of that place alive, I'd make that Judge pay as dear a price as I could.

"When I was finally released, I got me a job on a farm as a gamekeeper's apprentice. I'd changed my name to 'Jack Fox' so none of my old prison mates could find me, and my criminal record wouldn't follow me. I learned my new trade well, and also did some pokin' about to find out where Judge Mason was. I found he'd retired and was livin' in this place, and I eventually was able to hire on here two years ago with a good reference from my former employer.

"I waited for my chance. I learned the habits of the household, and when the Judge took to writin' his memoirs late into the night, I began makin' my plans. It's true, those footprints by the pear tree were mine. I had realized it would make a fair perch for a shot at one of the windows of the Tower Room. But there were too many problems to deal with. I'd have to wait for the leaves to come back out in the spring to avoid being seen before I took the shot, and who knew if the Judge would still be writin' up there by then? The noise, of course, would draw people out here, since nobody normally hunts at night, and I'd risk gettin' caught. Then there was the problem of getting the Judge to come to that particular window. Besides all that, it was a difficult shot to make. Fifty yards uphill at night into a target only a foot wide? I've gotten to be a pretty good shot, but those odds weren't in my favor.

"But while I was up in that tree, I saw an old owl take off from the roof of the tower. That gave me the idea of lowering myself down to the window. I got to thinkin' maybe I could pull this job and not get caught. I'd have the satisfaction of gettin' my revenge and still keepin' my new life.

"At first, I thought I could kill him quietly by stabbing him with a sword, or spear. That would make for a silent killing and give me lots of time to get back to my shack. But I realized it would be awkward, and I might only wound him if he had time to jump back out of reach before I could position myself for a fatal thrust. That's when I decided on the crossbow."

I interrupted at this point, for there was a glaring error in this scenario.

"But we found no bolt from a crossbow in the wound. It looks more like a stabbing."

"Ah, that was the genius of it," he smirked. "Earlier this winter, I saw the icicles form along the roof lines and realized what a formidable weapon they could make if delivered properly. So I stole the mold and made up some arrow bolts during the cold nights when they'd freeze up good and firm. I practiced with the crossbow until I was sure of myself, then put my plan into action.

"I lowered myself down next to the window around midnight. Then I started hootin' like an owl to attract the Judge. I knew he wouldn't be able to concentrate and he'd come to the window to shoo an owl away. Soon as I heard him, I swung around with the crossbow and fired. He stumbled back and tripped on the rug. But I saw his face before he fell and I'll cherish that look for the rest of my days."

Lestrade had the next question. "But why frame the Judge's son? He'd done nothing to you."

Silcox slammed his manacled fists down on the table. "He had the life I should have had! He was the free son of a rich man, and about to marry a beautiful woman and live happily ever after. That should've been me! So I decided to take my revenge on both father and son!"

Holmes spoke up again, "I think we've heard enough, Lestrade. It's time to visit Sergeant Mossgarden and conduct a prisoner exchange."

Chapter VI

It was nearly nightfall when we arrived at the Muswell Police Station. Sergeant Mossgarden was not happy to see us. He had obviously heard from the Coroner. He stared menacingly at Lestrade.

"So, you've come to shanghai my case after all," he accused. "And who's this fellow?"

Inspector Lestrade shoved Silcox forward. "This is the real murderer of Judge Mason. He's confessed it all. Now it's time for you to free Edgar Mason."

Mossgarden reluctantly led us back to the cells and locked up our prisoner. When we went to free the son, we found he had visitors.

The big sergeant unlocked the door, but it was Lestrade who announced, "You are free to go young man. We've caught your father's killer."

He had been sitting on the bed with an elderly man at his side and a young lady on the chair opposite. Upon hearing the news, they all stood immediately and Edgar spoke.

"Charlotte, Mr. Anderson. This is Inspector Lestrade of Scotland Yard, and Sherlock Holmes and Dr. Watson. They're the men I told you about."

Anderson, a portly fellow with an expensive suit and balding head, who was a partner at the law firm where Mason worked, stepped forward and immediately shook hands with Lestrade.

"Thank you, Inspector. I'm glad to see *some* member of the official police force who knows what he's doing," he said, glaring at Mossgarden as he did so. "My daughter and I are sincerely grateful for your help, all of you."

He shook hands with each of us in turn while Mossgarden left us, mumbling about Mason picking up his things on the way out.

Charlotte Anderson was an attractive woman in a cherubic-like sense. Her plump face beamed with a smile that could melt a man's heart. She walked over to us and shook hands with Lestrade and me, then suddenly, overcome by emotion, she threw her arms around Holmes and began sobbing her thanks.

"You saved our wedding and our Christmas, Mr. Holmes! Oh, thank you, thank you, thank you!"

Peeling himself away, Holmes replied, "You are quite welcome, Miss Anderson, I assure you."

Edgar Mason came up and put his arm around his fiancé, who turned her full attention back to him.

"I cannot thank you gentlemen enough. Who was that fellow who killed my father?"

Holmes gave a brief summary of Silcox's actions and motive, and we soon left the police station with Mason a free man. He invited us all back to Fortis Keep for dinner, but Holmes declined, stating that we needed to get back to the city. Anderson brought up the subject of Holmes's fee, but my friend merely nodded toward the happy couple climbing into a cab and said, "Let this one be a Christmas present for their sake."

The three of us returned to Baker Street, where Mrs. Hudson had a warm fire going and prepared hot toddies for all of us. As we sat by the fire and drank, I asked Holmes to explain his reasoning in the steps he took.

"It was obvious from the start, Watson that the killer had to be someone familiar with the Judge's habits and who could access that room in some fashion. That narrowed the suspects to family or staff members. I determined that the lock had not been picked and thus, even though it was improbable, the arrow slit seemed the only method of delivering the fatal blow.

"After examining the pear tree which our perpetrator had climbed, I deduced that it was impossible to make the shot from there, except by using a high-powered rifle, which would have been heard. It also offered no cover for the shooter and no guarantee that the Judge would come to the window. Why would he, during a cold night when his desk was by the fire?

"The state of the fire was also critical to debunking Mossgarden's theory of the crime. Remember Carson said that it had burned down to its embers. That meant the Judge had been dead for some time, unable to maintain the fire, and not killed by his son upon that morning."

Lestrade spoke up, "That still doesn't mean the son couldn't have done it during the night."

Holmes lit his pipe and blew out a puff of smoke before he answered, "It's true that the timing does not exonerate young Edgar, Inspector. Remember, however, I noted the athleticism required to climb the pear tree and to later descend from the rooftop, are quite beyond the young man's capabilities. As were the size of the footprints 'round the tree, and later on the roof."

"How did you determine the weapon used?" I asked.

He smirked, "Simple deduction, Doctor. The only weapon which could have silently delivered a projectile made of ice with sufficient force had to be a crossbow, which I observed the first time we walked through the armory."

"How did you know it would be ice?" asked Lestrade.

"Our killer had decided to frame the son by leaving the knife in a compromising position, which would look like Edgar had tried to get rid of it. Thus, he needed the real instrument to be one that would disappear. There have been theories about ice bullets, which would melt away and leave no trace. But such items are impossible due to the explosive nature required to deliver them. Firing an ice bolt with a crossbow however, would work over a short distance. When I examined the Judge's shirt, the bloodstains were lighter in color close to the wound, this is where the melting ice diluted the blood. That confirmed my theory and I knew you would find nothing in the body, and that there would be a clean cut with no distortion caused by the inevitable twisting removal of a knife or sword."

Lestrade, working on his second toddy, spoke up, "When did you decide that it was the gamekeeper?"

"I don't *decide* these things, Lestrade. That was Mossgarden's mistake. A man seeking an easy solution will find it, even if he has to make it up. I *deduced* that our suspect was a staff member and had narrowed it down to either the gamekeeper or someone who worked in the stables, since they would need privacy and the proper tools. That is why I had Carson summon the whole staff to the armory. I hoped that the sight of us with the murder weapon in hand would create a reaction, which is precisely what happened when Silcox attempted to flee."

The inspector rose to his feet, a trifle unsteady now as he worked on his third rum toddy, and we followed suit. He raised his glass to the detective and declared in a slightly slurred voice, "You are a brilliant man, Sherlock Holmes. Thank you for joining me on this case."

Knowing such unbridled praise was probably a result of intoxication, Holmes and I took his remark in stride. We clinked glasses with him and the detective returned Lestrade's compliment.

"Thank you for another little mystery to solve, Inspector. It is as fine a Christmas gift as I could ask for."

And together we drank to a Happy Christmas for all.

NOTES

1 – Lieutenant William Bligh, Captain of the *HMS Bounty*, whose despotic rule so enraged his crew that they mutinied near Tahiti in 1789.
2 – "Truth and Justice for All"
3 – Colonel Sebastian Moran, famous big game hunter, attempted to assassinate Holmes with an air rifle in "The Empty House".
4 – Criminal Investigation Division

The Case of the Christmas Trifle
by Wendy C. Fries

It is not difficult to imagine myself to be Sherlock Holmes.

It's long been a habit of mine to try to put myself inside my friend's head. When at a loss for where a case is leading, I will sometimes pause to more closely examine footprints and ash, the untouched dust on a mantel, a carelessly placed cushion, as if seeing these things through my friend's eyes.

I know I'm not the only one who does this, for I've watched countless constables, loosely at attention in the corner of a room, tilt their heads as they strain to catch a better view of a vase over which Holmes is leaning, to peer at a chair that has caught his attention or, more often than not, to frown as Sherlock Holmes stares at something that isn't there.

Even Lestrade will boldly look over Holmes's shoulder, squinting at scatterings of dirt or a half-peeled orange, and I imagine he too wonders the same things I do. What is there? What's there that we're missing?

We always find out later, of course, when Holmes is sure of his solution. As often as not, he unveils it with a bit of theatrical pomp that annoys some, but amuses others, mostly Holmes himself.

Of course, it's easy to understand what Sherlock Holmes has seen in those moments of explanation afterward, and each time I think the skill of deduction is really quite simple and surely we won't all be so far behind next time. Then next time comes and behind we are.

I say all of this by way of saying that, though it's not difficult to imagine myself as Sherlock Holmes, it is impossible for anyone else to actually *be* Sherlock Holmes. The reality of this came home to me in a case we had near Christmastime a year or so after Holmes returned from his long three years away. It was then I had a chance to be impressed afresh by my friend and what he does: Taking the smallest of trifles and deducing from them revelations. However, my certainty that we would none of us ever learn to be the man himself came when I observed in Holmes a rare trait I think few realise he has: Humility.

It was not quite noon and not quite a week before Christmas when I entered our Baker Street rooms, finding Holmes in his dressing gown, stretched out upon the sitting room sofa, one arm over his eyes while the other conducted a phantom orchestra.

A quick glance around showed no beakers smoking or bubbling, no stack of papers teetering at the edge of a chair, not a single book placed on its belly on the floor. I felt safe in making a deduction. "The Inspector did not come by, and you still have no cases on."

Holmes uncovered one eye, though he did continue conducting. "After this morning's post, I have quite a few cases actually, but they're neither pressing nor interesting." Holmes sat up but only barely, slouching so that his long legs stuck out across the hearth rug. "The Spanish royal family has another small matter they wish me to look in to, and I still expect Inspector Lestrade by at any time with that case giving Scotland Yard a bit of a fit. Also, I have a chemical puzzle I'm worrying through on paper, but Watson, there isn't anything of interest." Holmes fixed me with his keen eyes and slowly leaned forward. "Though I do suspect you're about to change that."

I'm no longer surprised when my friend reads me so easily, but I continue to be impressed. "Was it the tilt of my hat or the turn of my cuff that gave me away this time?"

Holmes smiled, "Oh Watson, if you could see your own face, you'd know anyone could deduce you now. You're practically beaming."

"Obviously I've lost whatever poker face I may have once had, but you're right." I rubbed my hands together and took a seat across from him, delighted to have something of interest to share. "I just met a young lady in the same building in which my publisher has his offices – "

"Ah, an enthusiast of your writing."

"How on earth could you know that?"

Holmes rested his heels on the edge of the sofa and his chin upon his knees. "Watson, you're a very serious man when you enter your publisher's establishment. You get a certain no-nonsense air to you. I expect that's partially my fault for teasing you so much about your stories of our little adventures.

"So it is obvious that, on a mission to deliver your latest manuscript – was this the one about the coffee baron or the one about the horse?" Holmes waved away his own question. "On such an important errand I doubt very much that you'd have spoken to anyone – that is, unless they spoke first to you first. In that case, you would of course reply, if for no other reason than you are a far more courteous man than the world deserves. Now, why would a lady approach you in an office building? In the case of Dr. John Watson, it is most likely one of two things. She is a patient, or she recognised you from your writing, which not unoften includes a likeness alongside your byline. You said you had just met her, so she is not a patient. Therefore she is likely a reader of your work, which she enjoys, and approached to tell you so. That much is clear from your smile, Doctor."

I executed a small bow from my chair. "Just so. However, though Miss Sarah Bartram was indeed very complimentary of my stories, she had more than praise to offer. She has a little problem I thought might interest you."

Before I said another word, Holmes popped up from his chair and flew toward his bedroom.

"Where are you going? You haven't heard the problem yet!"

Holmes paused in his doorway. "It's two minutes to twelve, Watson, or can't you hear Mrs. Hudson rattling up the stairs with a tray laden with tea things? Being as she only brings noon-time tea when one of us requests it, I presume we've a client coming and that you've made an appointment for Miss Sarah Bartram to meet us here in just under a minute!"

With that Holmes began to shed his dressing gown, and I again wondered why I try to tell Holmes anything, as he seems already to know everything. Still, I called after him, "Indeed!" as I let in our landlady. "Mrs. Hudson, it seems a man could set his watch by you!"

Our landlady smiled, but before she could reply, the bell went and she hastened to answer it.

By the time I'd set the tea out, Holmes was standing by the sitting room window, neat as a pin and hands clasped behind his back as if he'd been standing there all afternoon.

Mrs. Hudson showed in Miss Sarah Bartram. She was a fresh-faced woman and quite petite, which made her look even younger than her years. Though old enough she was, she hastened to assure me when we first met. "I am of age, Dr. Watson, and so is my fiancé. Have no doubt that this is a matter between adults, do you understand?"

I had assured the young lady that I did, and though Miss Bartram was not yet twenty, her serious demeanour, straight-backed posture, and intensity made her seem a woman twice her age. I gestured to Holmes. "Sarah Bartram, may I introduce Mr. Sherlock Holmes."

Our guest nodded at Holmes, who bowed and invited her to take a seat. As she settled, the young lady removed hat and gloves but kept her exceedingly serious expression.

"First, thank you for your time, Dr. Watson, and thank you, Mr. Holmes, for considering my case."

Holmes leaned back in his chair, finger steepled, ankles crossed, and said, "And what pray tell is your case, Miss Bartram?"

She sighed, sat straighter still, and said, "I have had a letter from my fiancé saying that he doesn't wish to marry me."

I glanced at Holmes, but he said and did nothing. I was curious, having at my publisher's received only the briefest of sketches from Miss Bartram. "So this is a romantic matter then?"

I knew of Holmes's fondness for small cases, the minutiae of which he far prefers. As a matter of fact, if given the choice of solving the problems of a potentate or those of a peat farmer, I knew my friend would be far more interested in the humbler case. International intrigue held no fascination for Holmes, and yet neither was he fond of a wholly domestic sphere.

Sarah Bartram turned to me and said, "Not at all, Dr. Watson. This is a case of kidnapping."

It was then Holmes became quite lively, leaning forward until his elbows were on his knees. "Very interesting. Now start from the beginning, Miss Bartram, and understand that there is no bit of information too small, no trifle worth withholding."

Our client looked to me with a smile, "Ah yes, just as in your stories, Dr. Watson."

Though Holmes had perhaps ruefully admitted to teasing me about my tales, he was disinclined to encourage praise just now, and so, with a dismissive wave, he said, "Yes, yes, now please set out the particulars."

With a confidence that her case might intrigue, our client began.

"I am rich, sir, and always have been. All my life, I've been the doted-upon child of a self-made man who, after mother died in childbed, wanted nothing more than to ensure my happiness. For all of my life, he did exactly that. That is, until six months ago, when I lost him to a lingering heart complaint. He left me everything, Mr. Holmes, and his building interests were extensive. It's why I was in the City today, speaking to his solicitors. Even father's hobbies brought income, though I know few would classify a copse of trees as particularly entertaining. My father did, however, and in the last few years he'd began buying up old growth here, there, everywhere. To be honest, it seemed more the pastime of a child hording toys."

Holmes rose, looked around the room curiously for a moment, then went to the small table beside my desk. In its little drawer he found a pile of newspaper clippings, which he shuffled through impatiently. "I've meant to file these," he said, collapsing again in his chair and waving a half-dozen pieces of paper in the air. "One never knows what will come of what, and when I noticed in the business columns that one man was purchasing extensive acreage in Kent, I rather thought something might come of this particular something."

Holmes tossed the papers to the floor, as if they now meant nothing. "Of course, you'll have something more relevant for our investigation?"

As if waiting for just this question, our visitor pulled a piece of paper from her purse, and read to us its contents.

Dear Miss S,

When you get this note my father and I will have taken our leisurely leave of London. I can not quite bring myself to apologise for departing without saying goodbye as I feel this leave-taking is for the best. That is because I think you may have misunderstood my intentions toward you and, had I stayed any longer, I believe things would have only turned for the worse. Despite what I may have said on several occasions, in fits of unreasoned passion, I do not wish to marry you. After I complete my longed-for studies, I will happily be joining my father in business.

This, then, is to be our very final contact Miss S and under no circumstances are you to attempt to find me.

Alas, I can not sign myself yours.

Mr. Stephen Hessian, Jr.

Sarah Bartram looked from one of us to the other, her gaze keen. "This note was written to me by my fiancé, Mr. Holmes. When I went to see him today, the landlord told me that he and his father had left the premises. Then he handed me this letter. When I asked to see what I could not believe, the man was kind enough to let me into the apartment."

Miss Bartram seemed to wilt, but didn't remain so for long. "Everything was gone, Mr. Holmes. Everything. I may have overstated when I said Stephen was kidnapped, but not by much. Though he is a few months my junior, he is every bit as focused, as mature. I believe he was coerced into leaving London, and it's this letter that tells me I'm right. It also tells me that he wants to be found." Again she fixed us with her sharp eyes. "It's quite unusual, this note, don't you think? Please be honest."

I waited for Holmes, who seemed to wait for me. With hesitancy I said, "Well, it is a touch . . . over-written."

Miss Bartram smiled, and at that Holmes let loose with a laugh. "Thank heavens the writer said it and the prospective bride agrees!" Holmes clapped his hands and rubbed them together. "A melodramatic missive, it's at once rude, self-aggrandizing, and vague. I trust there's something in its vagaries that is entirely clear to you, Miss Bartram?"

Our client's young face lit with admiration as she handed Holmes the letter. He scanned it quickly, passed it to me. I read it through then returned it to its owner, feeling no more the wiser.

"Stephen Hessian and I met almost two years ago, soon after our fathers became acquainted through business. Stephen's father was in timber and it was, for him, a very serious work. Though he and my father had a grudgingly respectful acquaintance, there was no love lost. I think Mr. Hessian resented both my father's wealth and his carefree ways.

"What they thought of each other didn't matter to Stephen and I. We fell in love and swore ourselves to each other just months after we met. However, we agreed it made sense to delay getting married until Stephen finished his law studies.

"Well, I'm afraid recently our will got the better of our resolve. Knowing there would still be more than a year to wait, we made plans to marry sooner. Next Friday as a matter of fact."

"Christmas Day."

"Yes, we both thought it a fitting day to marry. It pleased Stephen that every anniversary it would feel like the whole city was celebrating with us."

"A sentimental sort, your Stephen."

"He is kind and quiet and sentimental, yes, but he's also strong-willed and he means what he says."

"And yet, you know that he does not mean what he says in this letter," said I.

"On the contrary, Dr. Watson, he means every word of it."

"Do explain," said Holmes.

Our client stood, gathering the hem of her jacket as she gathered her thoughts. She gazed at the mantel, looked idly at Holmes's pipes, a scattering of tobacco, a willy-nilly stack of papers. I wondered that Mrs. Hudson hadn't been tutting at the mess.

"We've always had a bit of a game, Stephen and I, and it started as a result of Mr. Hessian, Stephen's father.

"He is a bumptious man, Mr. Holmes, and seems always to be talking out both sides of his mouth. His truths sound like lies, his lies like truths and, well, somehow Stephen and I, to hide the depths of our feelings and even our plans from him, we began saying the very opposite of what we mean."

Our client laughed. "It seemed so logical to us, but as I tell it to you, it sounds silly. Nevertheless, 'I'm very sorry I'll be missing that dance, Miss Bartram', of course meant that Stephen would meet me at the dance. 'I would like to complete my schooling', meant that Stephen was anxious to keep to our plans to elope. I'm aware this all sounds confusing and open to misunderstanding but Mr. Holmes, I know Stephen."

Sarah Bartram took the small piece of paper from her pocket, spread it on the mantel, and was silent so long she could only have been reading the note again and again. Eventually she folded it, tucked it away, and turned to us. "I know this note is as straightforward a love-letter as he could write to me under his father's watchful eye. He wants to marry me, Mr. Holmes, he wants me to find him. Will you help?"

Though I, like half of Scotland Yard, may fail to *think* like Sherlock Holmes, I believe that I have learned a bit how to *read* Sherlock Holmes. Though he didn't answer our client's question for long moments, I saw his shrewd gaze. I knew he'd take this curious case, and that he likely already had a strong idea as to its solution.

He stood. "We will, Miss Bartram, but I have three questions that need answering. The first: Did Stephen's father knew of your plan to elope?"

"I believe he learned it somehow. Perhaps he overheard us talking."

"My second question: How did you and Stephen signal to one another when you were, for all intents and purposes, lying?"

"Quite simply. He would call me Miss S and I would call him Mr. S."

Holmes nodded as if he'd suspected just this. "My final question will be answered at the offices of *The London Sentinel Times*."

My friend showed our client to the door. "I would like to see that empty apartment today, Miss Bartram. Would three p.m. suit you?"

It did. and shortly our client left. "Will you meet us at Barons Court at three, Watson?"

I reached for my coat as Holmes did for his. "I wouldn't miss it. In the meantime, I promised a friend I'd come by so he could show off his new surgery."

We left the flat together, but before we went our separate ways, I asked Holmes if he had an idea about where Miss Bartram's fiancé might be.

"Not a one, but I'm confident we'll find something of use in that flat. The young lovers seem quite adept at their odd form of communication, so I have faith the young man found a way to make matters clear for his fiancée."

At my doubtful face Holmes clapped me on the back. "Have a little faith, Watson," he said gently. Then he climbed into a cab and was gone.

Having sold my own medical practice, I found myself keen to have a look into the newer surgeries of my acquaintances. Which meant I thoroughly enjoyed spending a few hours in my friend's fancy West Kensington digs.

As he showed me around, we talked over the newest tools and the oldest maladies, and by the time I left I was in high spirits. I walked with a jaunty step the short distance to Barons Court.

I arrived early and found that so had our client, though within a few moments Holmes's cab arrived as well. Shortly the landlord let us into the Hessian's apartment and indeed, the place was stripped bare, as one would expect when lodgers leave.

To be sure there were a few scattered items, paper ephemera, a crumpled Christmas stocking amidst a few business cards.

Holmes prowled the flat silently, collecting all of this detritus and, when he was done, he joined Miss Bartram and myself in the sitting room. He tossed his pickings onto the bare table, then began to look over each item carefully, peering into the empty little stocking, flicking through the newspapers, going so far as to take out his magnifier to peer at the business cards and a tattered college prospectus.

Finally he sighed. "These are useless."

Sarah Bartram worried the hem of her jacket. "Oh no! I had hoped there was something I wasn't seeing."

"This is entirely too much evidence." Holmes picked up the half dozen newspapers in one sweep. "All of them are from Glasgow. All of them have an advertisement for lodging circled. This card is for a Glaswegian solicitor. The prospectus for a Scottish college. Mr. Hessian Senior does not want to be found, so I find it hard to believe he would have left so much information behind. This is meant to confuse us. There must be something else."

"Did you find nothing useful at the newspaper office?" I asked.

"Not enough. I suspected Mr. Hessian and Mr. Bartram might have overlapping interests, that perhaps the root of this was literally . . . roots. Trees, forests, a clash of some sort. But while they shared a profound interest in purchasing land, the business columns for the last year show that neither bought in the same places and certainly neither bought in Glasgow."

Never even entertaining that this could be the end of the case, I was as surprised as our client when Holmes said, "Miss Bartram, there is nothing more I can do."

Holmes busied himself with experiments the rest of that day, though I could tell his mind was not on what he was doing. He muttered occasionally and tutted twice. When I asked what was wrong, he mumbled something about acids and improperly mounted specimens.

I knew he was worrying over the particulars of Miss Bartram's case as he paused during supper to wave his fork, on which was speared a roast potato. "There's more to this Watson, I'm sure of it. That letter was particular. Young Mr. Hessian left some other clue."

With nothing more to go on, Holmes spent the rest of the night smoking his pipe and conducting his unseen orchestra. Eventually he retired in silence.

The next morning he was in better spirits.

"Ah, you're finally up, Watson! I expect we'll be seeing Inspector Lestrade sometime soon. That case that's got Scotland Yard in an uproar?" Holmes waved the morning paper at me. "It's gone a bit darker with last night's passing of the duke. If London's best and brightest were up to their necks before, they're surely in over their heads now!"

While my friend crowed, I reached for the tea and one of our many daily papers. I had just settled in to enjoy the morning when the post arrived, and with it a small package addressed to Holmes. It bulged a bit in the middle, and as soon as Holmes noted Miss Bartram's return address he hooted, "This is it!"

He upended the envelope and the "it" turned out to be a small lump of coal, barely as big as a lady's thumbnail. Holmes snatched it up and went right to his desk, hunting for a magnifying glass. I picked up the card that had fallen out with the coal.

"*Dear Mr. Holmes,*" I read, "*It occurs to me that there was one more thing in that empty flat and though I can't imagine what it could tell you, I know what it tells me. This small item, found in an abandoned Christmas stocking, is a diamond. I know that is what Stephen meant for me to see. I hope that you see in it something that only you can see.*"

By the time I had finished reading, Holmes was grinning by the window, peering at the new bit of evidence.

"As you know, Watson, I make a point of studying my surroundings, no less so than when we travel for some of our little cases. While I only dabble in geology, it is in itself a fascinating field of study. Just as mud on a shoe can tell you from which part of London a man has come, a bit of coal can also betray its origins. I recognise this particular coal, Watson, because I've *studied* this particular coal! Do you remember that case we had in Kent awhile back, the one with the lady and her pigeons? No matter. The thing is, this inclusion here tells me exactly from whence this nugget comes."

Holmes strode over, handing me the magnifying glass and the small black lump. "Do you see?"

407

The bell chimed downstairs as I looked at the coal. I rose, brought it to the window, and had a question, but it was then that Mrs. Hudson showed in Sarah Bartram and, right behind her, came Inspector Lestrade.

"Ah, two birds and one stone. Thank you, Mrs. Hudson!" Holmes said gleefully. "Come in, Inspector. Please, Miss Bartram. Watson, do we have more tea?"

Only after everyone was situated did Holmes finally settle, long legs crossed and a sly smile on his face.

"I presume you come about the business with the pearl earrings, Inspector?"

Hat on one knee, teacup on the other, Lestrade nodded. "I know we should've been by sooner, Mr. Holmes, but it really did seem as if we had him."

"Well, you did have him, didn't you? Just the wrong him. No matter, we'll find your man, and I have a few ideas on exactly where."

Holmes turned to our other guest. "Just as I have a quite certain idea as to where we shall find yours, Miss Bartram."

Our client pressed steepled fingers to her lips, her relief obvious and extreme. "Oh Mr. Holmes! Was it the coal?"

Holmes pulled the small lump from his waistcoat pocket, held it high. "It was indeed." He turned the coal a bit, until there was a brief and brightly metallic flash.

"I was just telling Watson that I have made a small study of coal and the various other minerals sometimes found within it. That small shine you can just barely see is pyrite, a mineral found in abundance in Kent. Pyrite has a far more common name, did you know? It's called 'fool's gold'."

And with just those two words, the elder Hessian's circumspection became clear. "Stephen Hessian's father thinks he's discovered a gold mine!" I exclaimed.

Holmes tossed the rock into the air, caught it, then leaned over to drop the little nugget into Miss Bartram's palm. "Mr. Hessian can't have much knowledge of geology if he mistakes that deceptive flash for the real thing. I think everything's becomes clear now, however, and your search quite narrow Miss Bartram. Your beau is in or quite close to Canterbury."

"Mr. Holmes, why would he have gone to all this trouble? Neither Stephen or I care one whit for his business dealings."

"Plainly put, he didn't trust his own son to keep his interests quiet, and he did not trust you, Miss Bartram. I expect he thought that if you got wind of this, you would carry on with your father's buying spree in that area. Mr. Hessian believed the only thing he could do until his land deal was done was separate his son from his prospective bride." Holmes laughed without mirth. "Clearly, he's doubly a fool, or else he'd have known that such endeavours have historically proven quite impossible."

Sarah Bartram lifted her chin. "Oh, Mr. Holmes, I must apologise. You said that no fact was too trifling, and still I didn't think something as trifling as this – " She held out her clutched fist, inside which her gem nestled. " – mattered. I'm so sorry."

Here is the moment in my tale for which I've written these several thousand words. While Holmes could have agreed with Sarah Bartram just then, making her an object lesson before the captive audience of the often-doubting inspector, Holmes did not. Instead he reached for a pipe and said, "Faith in your own judgment is what rightly led you to seek help to begin with." Holmes leaned toward me for a light, and as I struck a match, he finished. "Sometimes we must learn to have the same faith in others that we have in ourselves."

It had been more than two years since Holmes's resurrection and return, and it had been only a little less since I had said to him petulant words about faith and trust. At the time, I thought he hadn't heard me, but as Holmes inclined his head in thanks for the match, he smiled and said, "Me most of all, I expect."

Then, with a flourish of his pipe Holmes asked, "Inspector, Miss Bartram, more tea?"

Our client clutched her "diamond" tight. "I think I have a trip to Canterbury, Mr. Holmes, and I want to leave before the last train. Thank you so much." She looked to me. "And thank you Dr. Watson. Perhaps Stephen's and my story might be worthy of a few pages in one of your magazines some day."

With that, we saw the last of Miss Sarah Bartram. Though it was not the last we heard from her.

It was the day after Christmas that Holmes came upstairs with the post, all of which he threw onto a table as was his careless way, excepting one slim envelope which was addressed to us both. This he handed to me, and when I opened it I found a cheque.

"One thousand pounds!" I exclaimed. "From Miss Bartram. And there's a note." I read the letter aloud.

Dear Dr. Watson and Mr. Holmes,

I wish I could thank you for your aid in that trifling matter of which we so recently spoke. Alas, I can not. Christmas Day was a shambles.

I handed the cheque and the note to Holmes. "I trust she means the opposite of what she says?"

My friend pocketed the cheque and tucked the letter into a drawer; he has a habit of keeping an item or two from most cases. "So the signature tells us." With that, Holmes marched energetically across the room, threw open our door, and shouted down the stairs.

"Mrs. Hudson! Mrs. Hudson, where in London might a man order a nice Christmas trifle? The good Doctor and I know a newly married couple who would very much enjoy one!"

Holmes once said that a bit of selection and discretion must needs be used in producing a realistic effect and, though he was endeavouring to teach the police the art of deduction, his words are also true from a writer's point of view.

In truth, I've failed to report half the fantastic things Sherlock Holmes has done, for the certainty that no one would believe me. I've had readers question how a bloody fingerprint could tell Holmes that a man thought dead was quite amongst the living, so how can I tell them that a lump of coal – a mere trifle – when peered at through his magnifier could tell a woman where to find her one true love?

The answer, of course, is that I can't. It's all a matter of selection and discretion, and the knowledge that, while we may each of us occasionally imagine ourselves to be Sherlock Holmes, there is certainly only the one.

The Adventure of the Christmas Stocking
by Paul D. Gilbert

That Christmas had proven to be one of the coldest in living memory. The temperature had not risen above freezing for many a long day, and the snow that still lay upon the ground had been compacted into a deep shell of ice.

The bustling throng of Londoners that were going about their last minute festive preparations were huddled under a mass of mufflers and overcoats. Desperate to escape the biting cold, many found it difficult to maintain their footing on the ice as they made their way towards the warmth of a glowing fire and an expectant family.

By the time that I had completed my own arrangements and finally arrived back at 221b Baker Street, the threatening snow had restarted in earnest, and I was grateful for Mrs. Hudson's fussing and sympathetic welcome. She helped me with my parcels and coat, and by the time that I had thawed off in front of the fire upstairs, she had arrived with a steaming pot of tea. Our rooms were festooned with holly, and I was surprised to note that upon the table lay a brightly wrapped gift, addressed to me from my friend and colleague, Mr. Sherlock Holmes.

I say surprised because Holmes was not normally a man who enthused upon making any form of yuletide celebrations. It was not that he objected to such activity – he was certainly no Ebenezer Scrooge – but this time of year normally found him engaged upon one case or another, and he would barely set foot over the threshold when he was so involved. Conversely, if he found himself singularly unemployed, a dark mood would descend upon him from which no amount of festive cheer would rouse him. For reasons best known to him alone, this year seemed to be an exception to the rule. We had not seen a client since the Fairweather suicide case of early November, when Holmes had deduced a subtle and despicable form of murder by analysing the scrapings from under the victim's thumb nails! Yet this dearth of work had done nothing to dampen his enthusiasm for the imminent celebrations. He was delighted to discover a new Persian slipper beneath the wrappings of a gift that I had presented to him, and I, in turn, was overwhelmed by a large box of my favourite cigars within mine.

We were encouraged by the sounds of activity emanating from our landlady's kitchen, and we knew that a veritable feast would be forthcoming by the following lunch time. Holmes and I took our ports and cigars over to the cheery, crackling fire and barely gave a thought to the arctic conditions that were prevailing outside. A vicious northerly wind had suddenly picked up and had whipped the steady snowfall into a treacherous blizzard. Therefore, our surprise at hearing the sound of the bell-rope being pulled on such a night should be easily understood.

Mrs. Hudson appeared to be greatly put out by this interruption to her preparations, and equally embarrassed at having to interrupt our convivial evening.

"I apologise, Mr. Holmes, but the gentleman downstairs just simply will not be put off. Christmas Eve, indeed!" she protested.

"Well, I must say, the effrontery of the fellow!" I exclaimed, while setting a light to one of my most excellent cigars.

Holmes leapt up from his chair and over to the window, where he summoned me to join him. I was aghast to see the conditions that were now prevailing. The volume of the snow had reduced visibility to almost zero, and the empty street below seemed to be suffocating beneath a veritable avalanche.

"Your attitude surprises me, Watson. Surely anyone motivated enough to venture out on such a deadly night must be about to present us with a problem at least worthy of our consideration. I am not advocating goodwill to all men, but surely someone in such a plight must be deserving of a glass of port and a few moments of our time?" Holmes proposed.

"Well, of course he is!" I agreed with a guilty smile. "Please show the gentleman up, Mrs. Hudson."

Mercifully, our visitor had removed his outer garments in the hallway below; otherwise, I fear that our rooms would have been drenched beyond redemption. As it was, his suit was ruined, and he huddled over to the fire without affording Holmes and I even a second glance. He was clearly frozen to the core, and he apologised at once for his oversight and the large puddle that his overshoes had created on our rug. He rubbed his hands together voraciously before the flames, and I moved our visitor's chair further forward for his convenience.

"I was about to offer you a glass of port, but I see that you have already partaken of a rather generous libation," Holmes declared, while replacing the decanter onto the table.

"I should not let that fact prevent you, Mr. Holmes, for I fear that the events that I am about to recount to you would not be erased from my mind were you to offer me a dozen such decanters! Although, in truth, I did not imagine that my condition was as obvious as that." Holmes was so animated by our visitor's promise of intrigue that he poured out the glass of port without a moment's further hesitation.

With a nod of appreciation, the gentleman retreated from the fire to his chair while gratefully caressing the glass.

"Mr. Holmes, you should know from the outset that there is not another living soul who knows of the events that have befallen me on this inauspicious Christmas Eve. I have come directly from my home to lay before you the facts, prior to them becoming perverted by others."

"Well, at least you did not have far to travel." Holmes impishly suggested.

I saw upon our visitor's face the same look of astonishment that I had observed upon those of so many who had come before him, and Holmes was not slow in offering him an explanation for his conclusion.

"I can see from the absence of tracks in the snow that not a single vehicle has passed beneath our windows in more than an hour, for they have been inhibited by the depth of the snow. If you had been walking through these conditions for any considerable distance, I assure you that the water mark on your trouser legs would have climbed considerably higher than your hem! That much a trained mind can tell from a single glance, although a dull mind would not have reached those conclusions given an hour's study. However, there are limits even for the keenest observer!" Holmes invited the man to begin his story by way of a dramatic gesture with his right hand, while he encouraged me to take out my notebook and pencil.

"Gentleman, I cannot apologise enough for my apparent rudeness, although I am certain that you will excuse such behaviour once I have offered an explanation for my disturbed state of mind. My name is Sloane Cartwright, and my wife and I do occupy a comfortable town house in nearby Portman Square, from where I have hastened to you this very evening. I beseech you for your help and assistance, Mr. Holmes, for I greatly fear that my liberty may shortly be under threat!"

Mr. Cartwright's agitation caused him to sink back into his chair in an acute state of breathlessness, and Holmes waited patiently while Cartwright finished his drink and slowly regained his composure. Holmes studied Cartwright with an amused leer, but I could see nothing remarkable in his appearance. He stood at an inch or so above average height and a small paunch, which told of immoderate indulgence, protruded from an otherwise slim frame. His saturated suit was tailored from the finest worsted and cut from a roll of City chalk stripe. I placed his age at no more forty-five years, and his thick black hair shone with pomade.

"You must calm yourself, Mr. Cartwright, for I can assure you that you are amongst friends here. Outline the nature of your dilemma to me in precise detail and we might do some good, even on such a night as this. Dr. Watson will attest to the fact that I am very rarely inconvenienced by the constabulary. I beg you to be brief, in case they are more efficient than is their custom!" Holmes emitted a short sarcastic laugh as he considered such an unlikely prospect. He sacrificed the cigar for his cherry-wood pipe, closed his eyes, and leant forward in a state of intense concentration.

"The facts then are these. A dozen years ago, I assumed control of a large, but failing, import export business in the City of London, and I would not be unduly singing my own praises when I tell you that in that short time, I was able to transform it into one of the foremost companies if its kind. The achievement of such success does come at a price, and more than its share of sacrifice.

"In my own case, the sacrifice has come in the form of domestic neglect. My wife, Olivia, and I have not been blessed with any offspring, so it is even more inexcusable that I have spent so much of my time engaged in the running of my business. Olivia has born this situation well enough. However, the past few months have seen a marked change in her manner towards me. She has become distant and cold, and the interest that she once showed in the running of my company has diminished to the point of indifference."

At this point, a shield that Cartwright had erected around his emotions suddenly broke down, and he found himself unable to continue. He suppressed an outpouring of his grief with heroic effort and finally, aided by the draining of his glass, he came to his inevitable revelation.

"I apologise, gentleman. I really must stop referring to my wife in the present tense . . . ."

"Steady your nerves, Mr. Cartwright, steady your nerves." Holmes had never been comfortable when faced with a display of raw emotion, and he was clearly agitated by this untimely interruption to Cartwright's interpretation of the events of that evening. "It is absolutely vital that you continue with an accurate précis of all that occurred prior to your wife's untimely demise." Holmes indicated that I should replenish Cartwright's glass, and Holmes arranged himself cross-legged with his eyes tightly shut. All the while, his pipe continued to emit its soothing fumes and he attained a state of absolute concentration.

My reassuring smile prompted Cartwright to continue with his story, although now his tone was somewhat hoarse and hesitant.

"It was more than I could bear, to see Olivia so unhappy and remote, and the servants reported to me that she had taken to the habit of

414

going off for long and lonely walks for hours on end, each afternoon, often extending well into the early evening! I was resolved to put matters to right. With Christmas rapidly approaching, I decided to pay a visit to her favourite jewellers, Caldecott and Tyler, where I purchased an elaborate gold pendant festooned with a clutch of lustrous diamonds and rubies. This was an important piece, rumoured to have once adorned the neck of Marie Antoinette. There is no provenance for this, but it was nonetheless an expensive and beautiful piece of jewellery.

"Each Christmas Eve, it is our habit to hang a pair of stockings over the morning room fireplace. Normally they are filled with nothing of more value than candied almonds and the like. I decided to heighten Olivia's excitement and pleasure this year by secreting this pendant in the stocking intended for her. I placed it there before leaving for work this morning, and I spent the day in anticipation of her delight upon making this discovery on my return.

"As you correctly concluded, Mr. Holmes, I was somewhat the worse for wear by the time that I had reached my front door. It is my custom to thank my staff for a successful year with a lavish party within our extensive offices each Christmas Eve. I spare no expense on the food and drink and I always participate with the celebrations." Cartwright appeared to be satisfied that this explanation excused his inebriated condition. Holmes was clearly indifferent to this aspect of his story and eyed him quizzically before closing his eyes once again. As a result, Cartwright hastened to continue.

"I finally arrived home about an hour ago, and I was surprised to find that the house was in complete darkness. It is my practice to dismiss our staff from their duties on Christmas Eve, so that they might celebrate with their families. It is . . . or rather, was, our habit to dine with friends on Christmas Day, so their absence was only a minor inconvenience. I was surprised that Olivia had not turned on the gas herself, and equally that not a single fire in the house had been started. The interior was unbearably cold, and I immediately set the matter to rights in the drawing room.

"It was only as I had approached the fire in the morning room that I realised that the absence of fire and light were not the only omissions. Of the two stockings that we had hung over the fireplace, only one still remained. I hauled it down with some urgency and realised with horror that it only contained a small cluster of sugared almonds. The stocking that had contained the pendant was gone!

"It was inexplicable to me that anyone, other than my wife, would have bothered searching in her stocking, especially as mine had remained untouched. Furthermore, the house is full of fine works of art and pieces

415

of porcelain, and there were no indications of an intruder. Equally, there was no sign of my wife!

"I repeated this process throughout the entire house, firing up the gas and then starting a fire within every room of my progress. I tried to ensure that Olivia returned to a warm, comfortable, and safe house. However, when I finally turned on the gas in her dressing room, on the first floor, I realised the futility of my actions. There in the centre of the floor lay my poor Olivia, stretched out as if she had been trying to haul somebody back!

"Clearly, some sort of struggle had taken place. A low occasional table lay on its side, and a pair of fine ginger jars had been shattered into a thousand pieces. The very stocking that had contained the pendant was now tied viciously around Olivia's slender neck and seemed to have been the cause of her death. I cursed myself for having devised the plan in the first place, and then concluded my tour of the house, but in a more urgent fashion.

"I assure you, gentlemen, that each door remained locked and secure, and that every window and shutter was in place. I returned to the front door and found there to be only one set of male footprints, barring my own, of course, leading away from the front door, but there were none leading in. I concluded that my wife had invited this person into the house, prior to the first snow storm, and that the blackguard had remained until its conclusion.

"The whole thing is inexplicable to me, Mr. Holmes, and so I have hastened to you in the hope that you might help me escape this dilemma. I trust that I have not overstated the precarious nature of my situation?"

Holmes sat in a silent stillness for what seemed to be an eternity. He placed his pipe upon the arm of his chair and stared at Cartwright with an overwhelming intensity as he gravely shook his head.

"Mr. Cartwright, I would be doing you a grave disservice were I to deny it. Under the circumstances, I must say that you have reached your conclusions most admirably. If anything, you have probably understated the gravity of your position. After all, the footprints of that mysterious third party have since become obliterated by the second and heavier fall of snow. What other conclusion can the authorities possibly draw? Your servants can attest to the strained nature of your marriage, and the missing pendant is only your hearsay." Holmes avoided Cartwright's mournful glare and leapt to his feet with some urgency.

"Was there somebody else that you can think of who might have had knowledge of your purchasing the pendant?" I asked.

Holmes prevented Cartwright's reply with a loud grunt of irritation.

"That much is obvious Watson, and I, too, still have a myriad of questions for Mr. Cartwright, many of which are actually pertinent! Our priority must be to return to Portman Square with as much haste as our legs can muster on such a night. Perhaps we might yet retrieve a dire state of affairs before they become irretrievable."

With that, we all pulled on our heaviest coats and our strongest boots and made our way towards the ghost lands of Baker Street.

"Gentlemen, the journey begins!" Holmes announced as he opened the front door and departed with his customary, cursory wave to Mrs. Hudson and with a strident farewell.

As we made that long and painful journey towards Portman Square, I was struck by the manner in which the stark white background had accentuated the dark and derelict shapes of the dormant trees. Thin strips of snow that were stuck tenuously to the naked branches highlighted this extraordinary vision, and black and white seemed to be the only colours of our spectrum.

The trudge through the knee-high snow was an exhausting and strenuous affair. Under normal circumstances, it would have been a short walk indeed. But each step of our progress required a lunge, and Portman Square seemed to be a million miles away, even after a twenty minute trek. Only Holmes seemed to be oblivious to this impediment as his long thin legs pumped up and down with the regularity of a hydraulic piston, while his breath remained regular and determined.

By the time that Cartwright and I had reached his front door, Holmes had been waiting impatiently upon the front step for a full ten minutes! The lightly churned snow told of a right foot that had been ceaselessly tapping and I could see that he had already consumed two of his cigarettes. He held out his eager hand for Cartwright's key and then indicated that we should both retreat by a foot or two. Cartwright and I exchanged a look of confusion, but we immediately followed his advice.

Holmes pushed the door open, but he sank to his knees before he had even crossed the threshold.

"Mr. Cartwright," he called up. "I do not suppose that you recall the size and the shape of the footprints that you had observed earlier with any degree of accuracy?" Holmes asked in a most unenthusiastic tone.

"On the contrary, Mr. Holmes, because of the similarity that they bore to a pair of boots of my own, I remember them most clearly. They were made by a large pair of square toed boots, and their soles boasted an unusually deep tread." Cartwright seemed to be proud of his recollection, while a deadly scowl upon Holmes's brow soon dampened his eagerness.

417

"They sound like they are almost identical," Holmes growled. "I expect that your boot selection is still intact?"

"I could not be sure without an inspection." Cartwright strode towards the doorway as if to satisfy his curiosity.

"Stand back, Mr. Cartwright!" Holmes cried, but he soon remembered himself and added, "If you do not mind, it is of extraordinary importance that neither of you pass through until I have concluded my examination."

With that, Holmes brought out his glass and began a thorough inspection of the door mat. He extended this scrutiny to the edge of a very fine hallway carpet, and he only rose to his feet once a look of satisfaction had floated briefly across his face.

"I would now like to view the room from which the stocking was originally removed." Holmes stated while moving onwards.

"You surely mean the room in which my dear wife still lies?" Cartwright was understandably moved by the thought, but Holmes had no such considerations.

"Mr. Cartwright, I feel sure that you have not required your staff to return until after tomorrow's celebrations?" Cartwright nodded his affirmation. "Therefore, we have ample time in which to extend our search to the upper level."

Reluctantly Cartwright acquiesced and led us down the hallway to a morning room that was now paradoxically warm and cheery. The sight of that solitary stocking hanging forlornly above the glowing fire somehow induced an air of melancholy to fall upon Cartwright and myself. On the other hand, my friend was not so affected.

He threw himself to the floor in an instant, and he was now working feverishly with both a tape measure as well as his glass. He appeared to be reasonably satisfied with the results of his investigation, for an enigmatic smile was now playing upon his lips. A moment later, Holmes was back onto his feet, and to our great surprise he demanded to see Cartwright's cigarette case!

Cartwright handed this over with an air of bewilderment, and he was agog when Holmes ran his nose along the rim of the case's interior. Instead of offering an explanation for his behaviour, Holmes merely went on to quantify the gravity of our client's circumstances.

"You must understand, Mr. Cartwright, that the police will merely formulate their conclusions based upon the facts that are immediately obvious to them. Who else but you would have had prior knowledge of the presence of the pendant? There is no evidence to support the notion of an intruder, nor even a sign that there had been a third party here at all! Of course, once they have interviewed your servants and thereby ascertained the strained circumstances of your marriage, they will regard their case against you as complete."

Cartwright sank listlessly into a chair by the fire and gazed unrelentingly towards my friend.

"Is there no hope that you can offer me, Mr. Holmes? You seemed to attach a great deal of importance to my cigarette case, for example, even though I had given you no evidence of my being a smoker up to that point."

"I observed the shape of your case quite clearly through your sodden jacket back at Baker Street, and my hasty examination was nothing more than a little experiment of mine."

"Well, I am certainly glad that my dire circumstance is allowing you the opportunity to carry out some research!" Cartwright responded bitterly and with not a little sarcasm.

Holmes ignored Cartwright's understandable retort.

"I would now like to examine your square toed boots. Perhaps you would lead the way?" Holmes suggested while pointing towards the stair case.

Cartwright's dressing room was adjacent to that of his wife, and after measuring the width of the toe of one of Cartwright's boots, Holmes finally condescended to visit the crime room.

The situation was much as Cartwright had already described. The table was still resting on its side, the remnants of the jars were strewn across the floor in every direction. Cartwright's wife lay on her side, where she had fallen, and the long grey stocking still rested upon her bruised neck. She had been a tall slim woman with fine blonde hair and impeccable taste. Holmes's attention was not drawn towards the dead young woman, for his keen eyes had fallen upon a tiny key that was sitting upon the dressing table.

"I see that you have purchased some luggage recently, perhaps for a forthcoming trip?" Holmes suggested, although he was actually examining a small pile of dust while he made this assertion.

"We had no such plans, I promise you, Mr. Holmes. Furthermore, I cannot for the life of me understand why you should make such a suggestion." Cartwright was clearly becoming agitated by Holmes's inscrutable behaviour, and even I was finding his methods just as unfathomable.

"Very likely not, but I assure you that there is a perfectly sound reason for everything that I do and say. My method and manner might not meet with your approval, Mr. Cartwright, but my work here today will certainly save you from the gallows!" Holmes made this astonishing declaration without affording either of us even a single glance, and a moment later he was gone, leaving Cartwright and I equally bemused!.

"I shall be able to produce your wife's murderer within forty eight hours. In the meantime, I suggest that you should notify the police," Holmes called out as he strode through the front door and into those arctic conditions once again. I followed haplessly in his wake with a huge swathe of questions bursting within my head.

Miraculously the dense and forbidding snow clouds had dispersed during the short time that we had spent within Cartwright's house. The winter constellations now shone like clusters of lustrous diamonds, and the three-quarter moon penetrated and illuminated this darkest of nights. As a consequence, the temperature had tumbled considerably, and the soft snow through which we had struggled earlier was now more traversable, thanks to a hardened icy crust that had formed upon its surface.

Nevertheless, I still made a far slower progress than my friend, and by the time that I had arrived at our rooms, Holmes was already wrapped within his purple dressing gown and a large woollen blanket. He was on the point of lighting his cherry-wood pipe with a burning ember caught within the fire tongs when he caught sight of me standing breathlessly by the door way. He could not suppress a brief, strident laugh.

"Oh, my dear fellow, for heaven's sake warm yourself by the fire and calm yourself with a pipe and port. I assure you that by the time that we retire I shall explain everything that I have observed and deduced this night. For now, however, I must be allowed to sit in an absolute silence for a full thirty minutes."

Holmes had obviously sensed that I had been about to bombard him with a myriad of questions, and he had deflected that threat with a single sentence. I nodded my agreement and maintained my vow of silence whilst Holmes meditated upon his chair. My smoking and the port certainly had the desired effect, and I was on the point of drifting into a stupefied slumber when Holmes suddenly jumped up to his feet and clapped his hands loudly in triumph. I could not comprehend the cause of his elation and I told him so.

"I simply do not understand why you would have made such grandiose claims and assurances when matters appear to look so bleak for our client. After all, you summed things up quite accurately a while earlier, although I thought a little harshly."

"Once again, Watson, you have made that most fundamental of errors. You have assumed without being in possession of the facts. Whilst it is true that you did not have the advantage of my tape and glass,

I am equally sure that even if you had, the likelihood of your being able to put them to their correct use is remote at best.

"You might have gathered that my brief examination of Cartwright's front hallway revealed the presence of a third person. Although this mysterious visitor sported an identical pair of boots to that of our client, they were also a half-a-size smaller than his. Cartwright's prints were obviously the fresher of the two sets, so we can easily deduce that this visitor was invited into the house before the onset of the first of the storms. Before you ask, we know that he was invited in because there was no trace of a forced entry, and Olivia Cartwright seems to have led her visitor quite calmly from room to room.

"Had our visitor been interested in the jewel alone, there would have been no need for him to have made his way upstairs at all. There were no traces of the stocking having been forced from the mantel, and it was on the upper level that the murderer did the majority of his smoking. I observed only a single stub upon the drawing room floor, and the ash had accumulated in a neat single pile. In the dressing room, the ash was strewn haphazardly, as if he had been pacing about while consuming several more of his Turkish cigarettes."

"Ah, now I understand the reason behind your examination of Cartwright's case!" I exclaimed. "Obviously, with your profound knowledge of cigar and cigarette ashes, you were able to eliminate at once the likelihood of Cartwright having been the smoker." Contrary to my expectations, Holmes was not the least bit irritated by my interruption.

"Oh, that is excellent, Watson. I could tell that whatever interaction had taken place between the two had caused the murderer great agitation. Indeed, the only occasion that the ash fell on a single spot was when he stood over the woman after he had carried out his callous crime. I would not speculate as to its nature, but I am reasonably certain that she had agreed to some sort of romantic tryst and then went through a sudden change of heart. I observed the beginnings of a pile of items being readied for packing upon one of her shelves, and one other notable item."

"Of course! The key!"

"Exactly, Watson. You may not have noticed that the key bore no traces of ever having been used before. Mrs. Cartwright must have purchased new luggage this very day, to avoid arousing her husband's suspicions. Obviously the killer took exception to Mrs. Cartwright's rebuttal, but he became even more passionate once she threatened to declare herself to her husband. I am in no doubt that his primary motivation was the procurement of a most valuable piece of jewellery."

Holmes sank back into his chair with an air of justifiable triumph and satisfaction.

"I really must congratulate you, Holmes," I declared with due sincerity. "Once again, each link in your chain of deductive reasoning is pure and flawless, and you have surely saved Cartwright from conviction. Nonetheless, you have given no indication of how you intend to carry through your bold declaration. Tomorrow is Christmas Day, after all, and you promised to identify and apprehend the killer within forty-eight hours!"

Holmes was obviously inspired by this unfeasible challenge, for he suddenly leant towards me with his eyes aflame.

"The identification of this individual should not present us with too much of a dilemma. After all, there are only three people who could possibly have known about the existence of the pendant and one of them, of course, is Sloane Cartwright himself. Although I do not frequent the establishment myself, I am fully aware of Caldecott and Tyler and have passed it on many occasions. The place is run by an elderly gentleman, presumably one of the original partners, and his smart young assistant. I am reasonably certain that it was this devious individual who wormed his way into Mrs. Cartwright's affection and then hatched his plot to procure so valuable an item.

"In order to apprehend him, I shall require the services of the butcher's boy, and the only acquaintance of ours who will not be perturbed at having his Christmas interrupted"

"Ah, so you are sending for Menachem Goldman!" I ventured.

I should mention here that Goldman was Holmes's primary conduit into the iniquitous world of stolen jewellery. Neither a single gem nor a gold candelabrum could be sold or acquired without Goldman having prior knowledge of its movement. His eyes and ears seemed to be everywhere, and his knowledge was vast. When he was plying his trade upon the streets, he was the epitome of an orthodox Polish Jew. However, during his private transactions, he could drop this at a moment's notice and become a humble East End tradesman. He had proved invaluable to Holmes on several cases, but most notably during the recovery of the legendary Goblet of Ephesus.

"Goldman doubtless knows of the availability of the pendant, even as we speak, and I intend that he should let it be known that the best price for it can be obtained at this exact address!"

"Oh, I am sure that Mrs. Hudson will be glad to hear of this arrangement." I complained sarcastically.

"Do not overly concern yourself, Watson, for I will ensure that the matter will be conducted swiftly and securely. By the time that Goldman has managed to set things in motion, Scotland Yard's finest will have already been called to Portman Square, and will doubtless be at our door a short while later. I am sure that the promise of a prominent arrest will dissuade them from incommoding our client, and the real murderer will be caught red handed!"

"You are so certain that he will come?"

"Menachem Goldman and the promise of a handsome price will both prove to be very persuasive, and in the meantime, we can spend a most pleasant and restful Christmas right here in our rooms."

Reluctantly I accepted Holmes's arguments, although I felt uncomfortable at the thought of keeping Mrs. Hudson totally ignorant of our scheme. Christmas Day passed in the way that Holmes had predicted, and I must say that in the preparation of our goose, Mrs. Hudson had really surpassed herself.

"Holmes, I really cannot comprehend how you have managed to spend such a relaxed day, knowing full well the potential drama that could unfold between these walls tomorrow," I admitted once we had completed our feast.

"I can assure you, Watson, that you will hear and see enough to satisfy both your curiosity and that of your long suffering readers before the day is done." Holmes smiled mischievously as we took our glasses over to the fire.

I had long found it a futile experience to protest the merits of my chronicles to Holmes, to whom they presented nothing more than a romanticised dilution of his craft and science. On this occasion I did not even attempt it, and I sank silently into my chair with my port.

We were relieved to awake on Boxing Day morning to discover that there had been no further falls of snow overnight, and that there was nothing, therefore, that could inhibit the smooth culmination of our plans. We took a hurried breakfast, and for Holmes this consisted of little more than a cup of coffee and a cigarette. Before too long our guests began to arrive.

The first to arrive was Goldman, and he was suitably attired for the occasion, in a large rimmed black hat and a long black coat. He took a seat by the table, and soon he was joined by our understandably nervous client. He protested at the prospect of remaining cooped up inside Holmes's bedroom throughout the proceedings, until we explained that it was the only room within earshot, and that his discovery would jeopardise Holmes's ploy.

It was no surprise to discover that the next arrival would not be so easily persuaded. Inspector Lestrade and my friend hadn't always enjoyed what one might describe as a congenial working relationship.

Holmes had frequently chastised the man from Scotland Yard for his lack of imagination and intuition, while Lestrade had always found it difficult to reconcile Holmes's unconventional methods with good police work. However, the Baskerville Affair upon the moors had gone some way towards instilling in each of them a reluctant mutual respect, and the sight of his weaselly expressions did not fill me with the abhorrence that they once did.

"So, Mr. Holmes, it would seem that you have now added the crime of harbouring a primary suspected felon to that of withholding evidence!" Lestrade brusquely declared as he marched purposefully into the room.

Holmes greeted this with a cheery smile.

"I wish you the greetings of the season, Inspector Lestrade! I do hope that you are not referring to Mr. Goldman here, for he has kindly given up his time to help me with my little experiment"

Lestrade twisted up his lips in frustration at Holmes's attempts to charm him.

"Mr. Holmes, you know perfectly well why I am here, and the gentleman to whom I am referring. I have conducted an extensive examination of Cartwright's house and questioned his staff at length. Consequently, I have come to the inevitable conclusion that he is guilty of the murder of his wife, Olivia."

"Surely, Inspector, you could spare a moment or two of your most valuable time in listening to the results of my own examination of the house, at least until the arrival of my final guest?" Holmes proposed persuasively.

"I suppose a moment or two would not do any real harm. I will require certain assurances as to the situation of Sloane Cartwright and the identity of this final guest of yours."

"I can assure you that Mr. Cartwright is quite secure and close at hand, while my final guest will prove to be none other than the murderer of Olivia Cartwright!" Holmes concluded with a dramatic flourish of his right arm and he then proceeded to recount every step of his process at Portman Square.

Lestrade remained still and silent throughout, and slowly his sly and cynical expression gave way to one of disbelief and wonder.

"You are certain that you can produce this individual?" he asked.

At that precise moment, the unmistakable sound of the bell rope pierced the stifling atmosphere of our rooms, and we all became rooted to the spot in a stunned silence.

"Gentlemen, if my purpose here is to be fulfilled, may I suggest that you now retire from the room without delay." Goldman assumed his very best Polish accent, and he placed a slim case upon the table that was supposedly full of bounty.

Silently, Holmes ushered us into his room to join Cartwright, who was hovering nervously by the door. Holmes smiled reassuringly at him to allay any fears he might have been harbouring because of the presence of Lestrade. Holmes invited him to sit on the bed and the two detectives took up a position within earshot of the activity in the room beyond.

We heard the door close behind the unknown visitor and then the sound of the chair being moved while he took a seat opposite to that of Goldman. A professional of Goldman's status did not stand on ceremony, nor did he waste any time on pleasantries.

"I take it that you have brought the merchandise with you?" he asked coldly, and we heard him indicate where he wanted to see it by tapping the table with his finger. We heard the guest fumbling in his pocket, but before he revealed its contents, he insisted that Goldman expose the contents of his case.

The sound of the locks snapping back was unmistakable as Goldman assured the visitor of his financial integrity. We later discovered that a thin covering of bank notes obscured the fact that the majority of the case was full of nothing more than neatly folded newspaper sheets! Goldman did not risk any further investigation and he closed the case in an instant.

Evidently the visitor fulfilled his side of the arrangement, for Goldman declared, "It is a most beautiful object indeed, sir! May I ask you how you came by such a treasure?"

"I do not think that it is necessary for you to know that. After all, a man in your dubious line of work cannot reasonably expect to see a written form of provenance." The man had a far younger voice than I had expected to hear, but he was obviously well educated and spoke with a modulated tone.

"Oh, but sir, even one such as myself has a certain moral code and a reputation to uphold. For example, there are certain aspects of my work to which the authorities turn a blind eye in exchange for information that I might feed them from time to time." We could hear Goldman tap his case enticingly while he attempted to coax more information from the stranger.

There was an excruciating silence while the young man weighed up his position, but eventually the lure of a case full of money seemed to degrade his sense of discretion. We could hear Goldman force the man's hand by standing up suddenly, as if to leave the room with his case. Goldman's bluff achieved its purpose, for the stranger began to laugh nervously as he bade Goldman to return to his seat.

"You are being far too hasty, Mr. Goldman. Although I am not at liberty to reveal certain facts to you, you may be assured that the previous owner of the pendant actually invited me into her home on the night that I came by this."

"Are you telling me that she actually gave you so precious an object?"

"Not exactly gave, Mr. Goldman, not gave. We are clearly alone here, and we are both men of the world, so I will tell you that the lady in question went back upon her word to me, and I decided that the pendant presented to me an adequate form of compensation." There was a malicious tone of arrogance to his voice now that Cartwright found to be totally unbearable, and without warning he burst past Holmes and Lestrade into the next room!

"You are an absolute blackguard, sir!" he exclaimed and he strode towards the table with a violent intent that was obvious to us all.

Holmes managed to grab Cartwright by his wrists before he could do any harm, and Lestrade calmed him down by assuring him that he had already heard enough for him to be absolved. Cartwright, however, was shaken to the core when he finally recognised the rogue with the pendant and the implications of this realisation.

"Why, Mr. Holmes, this devil is none other than Andrew Gill, Mr. Caldecott's young assistant!"

"I was in little doubt that it would be," Holmes stated. Then, in response to a room full of questioning glances, "Who else would have known that you had purchased the pendant in the first place? After all, and with all due respect, Mr. Caldecott himself is far too old to have stolen your wife's affections."

Cartwright sank to his knees, stricken inconsolably with grief. While all eyes and attention were upon Cartwright, Gill decided to make a bolt for the door. He would probably have made it but for the timely intervention of Goldman, who pushed the table firmly into the villain's midriff. Gill fell breathlessly to the floor and in an instant, Lestrade moved across the room and lashed a pair of handcuffs to Gill's wrists.

"My own selfish neglect pushed my poor Olivia into the arms of this devil!" Cartwright cried, whilst still on the floor.

I helped him slowly back up to his feet and tried to console him with the thought that his wife's involvement with Gill had been her choice nonetheless. My ill chosen words had the opposite effect from my intention, for he would have rather blamed himself for this tragedy than his beloved wife. To make matters worse, Gill did not offer even one word in his own defence; he just sat there smugly, smiling maliciously as if pleased at the distress that he had caused.

"You should not chastise yourself, nor your wife, too severely, Mr. Cartwright, for she did have a dramatic change of heart at the last. But for this creature here, her brief indiscretion would have remained as nothing more than that." It was surprising to hear Holmes speak such soft and poignant words, but Cartwright understood them and slowly nodded his head in recognition. He removed himself from the room, a stooped and broken man. Only weeks later did we receive a note of thanks and appreciation from him.

Holmes slapped Goldman on the back as he took his leave and ironically wished him a Merry Christmas! Lestrade was not exactly temperate in his handling of Gill as he hauled him to his feet by the cuffs, and he nodded to Holmes in gratitude.

"Inspector Lestrade, once you have removed this person to Scotland Yard, you are more than welcome to join Dr. Watson and I in the conclusion of yesterday's most excellent and enormous goose!"

I do not know if Lestrade was more surprised than I at Holmes's uncharacteristically jovial invitation. He managed a confused half smile and he saluted casually to my friend as he led the despicable Andrew Gill from the room. Gill would certainly not be having a Merry Christmas!

The Case of the
Reformed Sinner
by S. Subramanian

*Among the unfinished tales is that of Mr. James Phillimore, who, stepping back
into his own house to get his umbrella, was never more seen in this world.*
– "The Problem of Thor Bridge"
The Casebook of Sherlock Holmes

It was on the bitterly chill morning of December 22nd of the year '98, as I
see from my notes for that twelve-month period, that the attention of my
friend Mr. Sherlock Holmes was first drawn to the singular affair –
which I have elsewhere recorded as one of his notable failures – of Mr.
James Phillimore. This was a deliberately misleading assertion on my
part, one which I resorted to for reasons which I trust the present account
will render clear. It is only now, some twenty-three years after the events
described here, that news of the demise of this story's protagonist
releases me from the implicit obligation of silence on the matter which
has bound me all these years.

The remains of our breakfast had just been cleared, and Sherlock
Holmes and I had lazily retired to our respective armchairs, he to light
his pipe composed from the dottles of the previous day's smokes, and I
to read the newspapers.

"All of fashionable London, my dear Holmes," I said, "seems to
continue to be in the grip of one, and only one, event: the disappearance
from his home in Kensington, the day before yesterday, of the justly
celebrated star possession in Lord Haileybury's distinguished collection
of jewelry, the sapphire known as the *Noor Jehan*. I see from the papers
that his lordship has announced a reward of five-thousand pounds for its
restitution to its rightful owner. Our friend Lestrade is in charge of the
case, and reading between the lines of *The Times'* report that 'the canny
Scotland Yard detective is reliably learnt to be approaching the problem
from all possible angles', I take it that he is in his customary state of
bafflement over the mystery."

"There is no particular mystery in the matter, Watson," responded
my friend in a bored voice. "I have been anticipating the event over the
last few months, and I knew that it was only a matter of time before it
happened. It is my strong belief that the facts underlying the case point in
the direction of a prosaic theft involving a careless peer, and an alert
butler who is a member in good standing of a well-established jewel-

stealing outfit. For some time now, I have had my eye on the Camberwell Gang, headed by the notorious ruffian Edward 'Bandy' Benson. I have brought the imminent possibility of the sapphire's theft repeatedly to the attention of Lestrade, but if he and his minions at the Yard will insist on taking their flat-footedness to hitherto unexplored depths of ineptitude, then there is little one can do to save the situation. It is that old adage about leading the horse to the water. I am convinced there is no great intellectual puzzle involved in the affair. All it calls for, to bring it to a successful resolution, is to display some urgency in following the movements of Mr. 'Bandy' Benson. But what have we here? The bell, the step, the knock: we are in luck, Watson. Surely it's a Christmas gift – a client!"

I opened the door to admit a tall, strapping, fair-haired and fresh-faced young man.

Sherlock Holmes waved him to a chair, with the query, "What can my colleague Dr. Watson and I do to help you?"

"Mr. Holmes," said our visitor, "I hope very much that I am not here upon a fool's errand, and that I do not waste your precious time with some trivial and inconsequential problem. But I thought I must lay it before an expert to determine if it is a serious matter or not when a man steps into his own house to fetch his umbrella, only to vanish, thereafter, like a puff of smoke!"

"Come, this is a most agreeab – that is to say, distressing – state of affairs," said Holmes, rubbing his hands together. "Pray sit down now, and explain, in your own words, the circumstances which have brought you here."

"You should know that my name is Sebastian O'Connor, and that I am a junior clerk with the well-known stock-broking firm of Thurston and Ayres, which has its principal office in Camberwell. My presence here has to do with the sudden disappearance, yesterday morning, of my friend and professional colleague, James Phillimore. It has been our daily practice, over the last two years of our clerkship with T. and A., to walk each morning to our place of work, to have a pint of beer together at the end of each day's work at The Camberwell Arms, to walk back from the public house to our respective diggings which are but a stone's throw apart, and to offer worship, every Sunday morning, at the local Catholic Church (for we are of that persuasion). It is a life, as you can see, of ordinariness and routine – as ordinary and commonplace and non-descript and universal and same as our daily collars and hats and rolled-up umbrellas and briefcases!"

"The local Catholic Church at Camberwell," interjected Holmes. "Would that be St. Francis Xavier's Church, by any chance?"

"Indeed, yes," replied our client.

"Ah! Pray forgive the interruption, and proceed with your most interesting narrative."

"Well, yesterday, as on other mornings, I ambled over from my digs to Phillimore's modest quarters. It was our invariable practice to walk together to our office. He would usually wait for me at the gate of the somewhat grandiosely-named Alexandria Mansions, which houses his own, and a dozen other similar two-room quarters. Yesterday, I found him apparently seeing off a couple of men of somewhat rude description, though the conversation was polite enough. I heard the older of the two men tell my friend, 'I am grateful, guv'nor, for the return of my possession, what's a 'umble enough thing but of the greatest value, speaking sentimentally of course, to me.' 'No, no,' said Phillimore. 'It is no big thing – just one of those accidental mistakes which any of us is capable of making in a moment of absent-mindedness.' The man made a hurried departure, holding his hat in his hand and his umbrella under his arm, after favouring my friend with what was no doubt intended as a smile of gratitude, but was rendered somewhat sinister by the unfortunate scar, running from chin to ear, that disfigured his face."

"Scar from chin to ear, did you say?" interposed Holmes sharply. "May I enquire if the man was also noticeably bow-legged?"

"Why, yes!" said O'Connor in surprise. "How – ?"

"Never mind!" said Holmes, with a chuckle. "My apologies again for interrupting your narrative. Pray continue."

"Well, there isn't much left to report. Phillimore greeted me, and begging me for a moment's time to fetch his umbrella, he went back through the front door of his house, closing it shut behind him. The seconds ticked over into minutes, and when there was no sign of his returning, I rang the bell at his door several times, but to no avail. Eventually, I had to get the porter to open the door with a key from his bunch of spares. We searched the quarters thoroughly, but there wasn't a sign of Phillimore anywhere in that house. We could only surmise that he had given me the slip through the back-door, which is self-locking. Since then, he has not returned home, nor have I heard nor seen anything of him. Before alerting the police, I thought I should lay the problem before you, Mr. Holmes, for your opinion."

"You have done wisely to consult me, Mr. O'Connor," said Holmes. "Can you think of no reason why your friend should desert you so abruptly, if that is what has happened?"

"Not a single blessed reason that makes any sense, sir," replied our client emphatically.

"Very well. Before I proceed in the matter, let me ask you just one more question. Have you ever encountered our scar-faced, bow-legged friend on any earlier occasion?"

"Indeed I have, Mr. Holmes," replied Sebastian O'Connor. "On more than one occasion. He has been a frequent visitor, over the last few months, at The Camberwell Arms. He has even, on occasion, sought to make desultory conversation with us, with queries on where we worked and lived. Indeed, now that you ask me, he dropped in at The Camberwell Arms the night before last, which was the last occasion on which Phillimore and I had a drink together. It was an evening like most others, and the street was crowded as it usually is at that hour. It is a somewhat rough neighbourhood, and I had just been jostled by an unsavoury-looking character when I caught sight of a couple of burly constables walking down the street. I remember thinking – though I am quite capable of looking after myself – that this was a distinctly welcome sight. However, the matter passed off without incident. We had just entered the public house and seated ourselves on a couple of high stools in front of the bar when Mr. Bow-Legs walked in after us, sat on the stool next to Phillimore, had a quick drink, and departed. I am not even sure if my friend was aware of the man's presence by his side, but I was, because I caught sight of his reflection in the strip of mirror in front of us."

"All of this is most suggestive, Mr. O'Connor," remarked Sherlock Holmes. "I am hopeful that we may find a solution to the problem of your missing friend, though I must prepare you for a life, henceforth, in which he does not figure as your daily companion at work or in leisure. Rest assured that when the matter is cleared up, you will have word of what has transpired from a mutual friend of ours."

After our client had been ushered out, my friend turned to me. "Well, Watson," said he, "What do you make of it?"

"I make nothing of it, Holmes," I replied. "It is all an impenetrable fog to me."

"Come, Watson, surely it is not so hopeless as all that. Indeed, if you do not allow yourself to be distracted by those suggestions of the bizarre and the *outré* which permeate the case so thoroughly, you should be able to see your way clearly through to its really rather straightforward solution. In my own case, I have the distinct advantage over you of knowledge regarding the identity of the gentleman whom our client referred to as 'Mr. Bow-Legs'. The facial scar and the bent legs of a Camberwell *habitué* can belong to but one man – the Edward 'Bandy' Benson, of dubious repute, whom I mentioned to you before our client arrived.

431

"I have already acquainted you with the fact that my earlier investigations provoke the strong conviction that Benson has had a major hand to play in the theft of the *Noor Jehan* jewel. As the head of the Camberwell Gang and the principal planner of the sapphire's theft, he would be the most likely recipient of the jewel. Understandably, and in the event of a swoop by the police, he would not wish to be found with the jewel in his possession. Let us begin with the eminently reasonable working hypothesis, then, that the sapphire entered Benson's possession, presumably through some other member or members of the gang in a chain beginning with Lord Haileybury's butler, sometime after its theft the evening before last.

"That was also the evening when our friend O'Connor saw him (or his reflection in the mirror) at The Camberwell Arms. An admirable receptacle for a stolen jewel is the handle of any umbrella that can be fashioned into a detachable knob. That, let us suppose, is where Benson secreted the sapphire. His umbrella, we may assume, is one of hundreds of identical ones in the city of London, with perhaps a mark of distinction such as his engraved initials on some part of the umbrella where no-one would think to look, and which would assist with reclaiming it when the time for that should come. It is reasonable to believe that he too saw the constables mentioned by O'Connor walking down the street, with, for all one knows, no specific immediate object in their minds. However, it is very likely that he panicked at the sight of the two policemen. In case they were looking for him, the last thing on earth he would have wanted was to be found by them with the umbrella in his hand. Given the circumstances, he needed to be quickly rid of the umbrella and to find a safe lodging place for it for the night, away from him.

"What simpler, then, than to enter The Camberwell Arms and sidle up to the stool next to Phillimore's, have a quick one, and imperceptibly substitute his umbrella for Phillimore's, which is conveniently leaning against Phillimore's stool? Do you recall O'Connor's wry reference to the artifacts of his and his friend's daily apparel – their hats and collars and umbrellas and briefcases – as belonging to an indistinguishable mass of similar artifacts? Benson could count on Phillimore carrying his (Benson's) umbrella home, thinking it was his (Phillimore's) own. He could then reclaim it the next morning from Phillimore, without running the risk of the jewel being found anywhere in his own proximity on the evening and night after the theft. And that, precisely, is what our client found Benson doing at his friend Phillimore's doorstep the following morning.

"Let us now shift our attention to Phillimore himself. It is entirely conceivable that he, like O'Connor, had registered Benson's entry into The Camberwell Arms the previous evening. I would go further and say that he was perfectly aware of the little umbrella-substitution stunt that Benson pulled when sitting next to him at the public house. Phillimore's interest, curiosity, and suspicions were by now, we may imagine, thoroughly aroused, but he kept them to himself. Back in the privacy of his quarters, he no doubt subjected the umbrella to thorough investigation, and discovered the *Noor Jehan* in the hollow of the detachable knob.

"Our friend James Phillimore is, I believe, a man of some considerable pith and enterprise. He resolved he would not turn his back on what chance had laid at his doorstep. He removed the jewel from its receptacle in the umbrella and screwed the false handle back on again. He must have contemplated doing a bolt that night, but Benson would have posted himself all night in front, and a confederate at the rear, of Phillimore's quarters, just as a measure of abundant caution against the possibility of precisely such an exit by our friend. The two men would have been visible to Phillimore from his front and rear windows. Benson and this confederate were no doubt the two men to whom O'Connor saw his friend speaking at his doorstep yesterday morning.

"Having seen them off and greeted O'Connor, Phillimore knew that it would be only a matter of seconds before Benson discovered the loss of the sapphire and got after him. He had to act, and act with the greatest dispatch. Shouting something to his friend about fetching his umbrella, he entered his house and bolted through the back door, and then out of Alexandria Mansion through a rear exit. I would wager that he ran all the way to the Brixton Road or Camberwell Green Underground Station, clambered on to the earliest departing train, and then lost himself in the teeming millions of the city of London. 'Bandy' Benson would have been just that little bit too late to stop Phillimore."

"Extraordinary, Holmes," I exclaimed. "But what next? Must we not lay Phillimore by the heels?"

"Ah, Watson," remarked Holmes. "Ever the man of action! I am wiring the contents of my recent little exposition to a young and quite brilliant man I know in Camberwell, in the hope that it will not prove too late for him to track down Phillimore and recover the sapphire from him. We shall know by tomorrow morning."

And not another word would he say on the subject all the rest of the day.

Next morning, when I came down to breakfast, I was surprised to see that we already had a visitor, in the form of a diminutive individual dressed in the habit of the Roman clergy, his feet shod in a pair of comically rounded shoes, and carrying a somewhat disgracefully worn and over-sized umbrella in his hand.

"Watson!" cried Sherlock Holmes, "I would like you to meet my young friend from Camberwell, of whom I told you yesterday – the Reverend J. Brown of St. Francis Xavier's Church. He has news for us!"

"Well, yes, Mr. Holmes," said the priest, blinking in a somewhat vacant fashion. "I managed to track down young Phillimore without too much difficulty. I had a long talk with him – on this and that, don't you know. The upshot is that he surrendered the *Noor Jehan* to me. It was just one of those temporary moral aberrations which the most virtuous of us are not always proof against. But he repents his error with genuine remorse. He is already on a boat, on my suggestion and with my help, to America, where he will start a new and honourable life with a new and honourable name. I suppose you would call it abetting a felony. I would call it helping a sinner."

"I believe, my dear padre," said Holmes good-humouredly, "that I would call it both – but Watson and I, I am sure, would heartily approve of abetting a felony in the cause of helping a sinner. We have occasionally cast ourselves in the role of a jury, acting on the principle '*Vox populi, vox Dei*'. What is more, and as I have had occasion to observe in a similar context earlier, it is the season of forgiveness."

"But how did you track him down?" I asked. "And how did you persuade him to surrender the jewel?"

"Oh," said the priest vaguely. "One's little flock, you know. One knows the haunts of both their physical and spiritual geographies. I caught him as an angler catches his fish, but with a line and a hook made of reason and suasion rather than wire and iron. I hope that doesn't sound awfully conceited to you. It's the sort of thing we're trained to do, you know. As to how we do it – well, we have our own little professional secrets, too! By the way, thank you, Mr. Holmes, for undertaking to return the sapphire to its rightful owner. Here it is, before I forget, and walk away with it."

With that, the priest handed over the sapphire to my friend, and stumped out of our room. But we were destined to see him again, and quite soon at that. He was back in our room the following morning, with a radiant smile upon his amiable face, and the news that he had received a cheque for five thousand pounds from Lord Haileybury, made out in favour of St. Francis Xavier's Church.

"This is your doing, Mr. Holmes. The benefit to the struggling school and hospital which our little Church has been endeavouring to support will be incalculable. How do I thank you?"

Sherlock Holmes laughed heartily. "By desisting from doing so, Reverend," he said. "Surely, we are united by the common bond of seeking and finding fulfillment in helping those less fortunate than ourselves. I am no theologian, but I am hard put to it to find a purpose for life which is, at one and the same time, both humbler and grander than this ambition. In some hours from now it will be Christmas Eve, and we should indeed be rather sorry specimens of humanity if we did not allow its spirit to prevail with us. May the peace and goodwill of Christmas be with you, on this and every Christmas henceforth.

"And now, my dear Watson, since duty beckons, I must ask you to be so good as to stretch out a hand and pass me the papers of the Flint-Clerihew case, from the painfully routine and uninspiring rigours of which the sudden disappearance of Mr. James Phillimore has provided us with such a brief but engagingly welcome break."

The Adventure of the
Golden Hunter
by Jan Edwards

Christmas was an odd time at 221b Baker Street, given that neither Holmes nor I were in the habit of celebrating in any grand manner. At Mrs. Hudson's insistence, we had draped swags of greenery on mantels and picture rails and placed a decorated tree in the window, but none of it could be considered elaborate. And as Mrs. Hudson herself had left to spend the Christmas period with her sister, our plans had evolved no further than dinner at The Criterion.

London sparkled beneath a recent snow fall, and the cold snap brought the inevitable flurry of influenza and worse to my patients. It was on returning from one such visit that I found a handsome woman of some thirty years seated by the fire, speaking earnestly with Holmes. Her velvet coat and hat of deepest blue, which perfectly complemented her dark auburn hair, were of the best quality and taste, marking her as a woman of means.

"Allow me to introduce my colleague, Dr. John Watson," Holmes said. "Watson, may I present Lady Alicia Havingham."

She turned to study me, intelligent grey eyes meeting my gaze with confidence. I decided immediately that I liked her and strode forward to shake her outstretched hand. "Lady Havingham. Good morning."

"So pleased to meet you, Doctor Watson." She smiled, almost apologetically, as if she had grown used to excusing her American cadence.

I glanced at Holmes for some explanation for her visit, but having made his introductions, he seemed pre-occupied. Holmes could be unspeakably rude at times, but his manner toward clients was usually impeccable, especially the fairer sex, though he admitted them to be a mystery to him. "Have you come far?" I asked her.

"No, not far. Do you know Rhyton Hall at all? It is just outside of Winchester," Lady Havingham replied. "I have asked Mr. Holmes, and of course your good self, to come and investigate a matter for me. It would mean Christmas in the country, if you can bear it."

"At the Hall?"

"At Rhyton, yes, though the family are all spending the festive season with my parents at the Dower residence, Rhyton House, which is on the edge of the estate. There are workmen renovating the Hall, and it would be simply impossible to entertain in such chaos."

"I've heard of Rhyton. A substantial estate."

"It is. My parents rented the Dower House when we first arrived in England, which is how I met my new husband." She smiled at me, though not entirely happily, if I am any judge at all. "Rhyton House is beautiful," she said. "Positively ancient. Why, it must be a hundred years old at least."

"Rhyton's Dower House is over three hundred years old," Holmes said. "Built in 1573 to be precise. Rhyton Hall was built by the old Duke in 1816, which is when he added the red brick facade to what is now the Dower House. Because of that, I will allow it has a far more recent appearance."

"So you *do* know it," the lady said, her face lighting up in her amusement.

"Indeed I do." Holmes's nostrils flared in mild distaste, and he hid the gesture by crossing to the window to stare into the whitened street.

I leaped in to fill the gap left by his abruptness. "Lady Havingham. May I ask the nature of your enquiry?"

"It is a delicate matter of theft," she replied. "The losses are known within the household, of course, but I very much wanted to keep this matter out of the public eye. I had hoped Mr. Holmes would agree to help, but he seems undecided. Perhaps you might persuade him, Doctor Watson?"

Holmes rocked back and fore on his heels, his back stiff and his gaze fixed on the street outside. I recognised the signs. He was unhappy with whatever business this lady had brought us. "I was just explaining to Lady Havingham that petty theft is not my usual domain," he said, as if reading my thoughts.

"Oh, I realise you would not bother with such a trifle in the normal way. I had several times wished we'd good reason for an illustrious detective such as you to join us. Then, as luck would have it . . . ." The young woman took an envelope from her reticule. "It seems, Mr. Holmes, that we are related, albeit distantly through your French *Grand-mere*, who was cousin to my own Great-*Grand-pere*. Not a strong link, but sufficient for my parents to extend hospitality for the Christmas season. My husband . . . ." She laughed brightly. "Oh my, I am still not used to that. I was married only a few days since."

"My congratulations," I said.

"Thank you. I hope." She sighed heavily and looked toward Holmes. "Things have not been quite as I expected. We are leaving for the Continent in the New Year, and we shall be gone for some months."

She drew breath, obviously considering her next words carefully. "If I may speak plainly, Mr. Holmes? Mine is not a love match. My family very much wanted it to happen, and I was happy to enter into it. That aside – I would prefer that this cloud hanging over him be lifted before we sail. He is my husband, and I'm sure you'll agree any marriage that begins with mistrust between man and wife will never thrive."

Holmes's shoulders relax a little at that assurance. He came to take the envelope in those long slender fingers and flicked it open to peruse the contents. "An interesting family tree," he said at last. "Well researched."

"Why, thank you. I do so like a mental challenge. I'm afraid my love of learning has always governed my heart."

I hid a smile. Holmes so often said such similar things that it was disconcerting to hear them from a woman. It was not hard to imagine them related in some way. "Come now, Holmes," I remarked. "How can you possibly refuse Lady Havingham's request when she is one of your own?"

"How indeed." Holmes refolded the genealogy and laid it carefully on the table next to him, seemingly reaching a decision in that moment. "Before you arrived, Watson," he said, "Lady Havingham was explaining how all of the missing items came from her trousseau. I think you will agree that is quite singular." He turned, tilting his head to view her from an angle. "Tell me, Lady Havingham, were these items of any great value?"

"Not at all. Father has bought a great many pieces since we arrived in England as investments, and he has been generous enough to gift several of them to me. But the stolen objects were little more than trinkets. A small green figurine, Chinese I believe. Two French snuff boxes, and a pair of extremely ugly silver candlesticks. Thirty guineas at most. There was a small Dutch canvas not five paces from the candlesticks, a portrait of a young girl, well known to be worth five times all of those missing pieces together, yet it was left untouched." She sighed. "I am not one to fuss over the losses, and I am privately rather thankful to see the back of those dreadful candle sticks. The gold hunter, however, was a Christmas gift commissioned especially for my husband. Poor Edward will be disappointed not to have it, but I suppose that it cannot be helped now."

"Your husband knows what he is – or perhaps I should say *was* – to receive from you?"

"Lord Havingham had been unfortunate enough to mislay his old pocket watch, and I offered to replace it with a suitable facsimile," she replied. "The original gold hunter had been his father's."

438

Holmes raised a questioning eyebrow. "Is it possible that his old timepiece's loss was a part of this crime spree?"

Lady Havingham paused to consider for a moment and then shook her head. "No, I cannot see any possible connection. That heirloom went missing two whole months before. My brother Henry was with him at the time and he told me how Edward was distraught over its loss. They had been to the races, do you see. Edward is quite the equestrian, though he prefers hunting to the racecourse." She smiled. "I am led to believe they neither of them had enjoyed a successful day."

"They are gambling men?"

"Well . . . Henry abhors gambling. I was surprised to hear that he went at all. As for Edward?" Lady Havingham laughed a little ruefully. "No more than any other man, I suspect."

Holmes tapped his steepled fingers to his lips, gazing at Lady Havingham from beneath beetled brows. "So both took a loss at the races on the day that Lord Havingham lost this 'heirloom'?"

"Oh, please don't think he lost the hunter in a racing transaction, Mr. Holmes. No, no. The timepiece was lost in a hansom cab on their way between the train station and Lord Havingham's London club. Henry assured me they scoured the cab ranks to find the driver, but to no avail. The loss was no more than an unfortunate accident."

"Unfortunate, then, that its replacement should subsequently have gone missing."

"It is. I am so grateful to Henry for supplying a splendid alternative gift in such short order. My brother has always been so very good to me. But if I could get the gold hunter back . . . ." She shuddered. "It seems so ridiculous saying it here, but I can't help feeling these thefts are somehow aimed at me."

"It may well be personal, though not in the way you think," Holmes replied. "In view of our kinship, I believe I could lend myself to your problem after all. I do have a few small matters to clear up before I can leave town, but you may expect us by midday tomorrow, if that is satisfactory?"

The lady took her cue and rose gracefully. "Thank you, Mr. Holmes. I am most grateful." She pulled on her gloves and clutched her reticule tightly in her right hand. "Good morning to you also, Doctor Watson. Until tomorrow, gentlemen."

Holmes escorted her out, returning with a tell-tale spring in his step, and went to stand before the fire. I could only wait whilst he filled his briar pipe at an agonisingly fastidious speed before leaning down to select a spill.

439

"Well?" I demanded finally. "Why a sudden interest in this case? I can't believe it attributed to this distant kinship."

"I am taking the case because I'm certain there is more to it than mere theft," he replied. "Lady Havingham informed me that the replacement gold hunter went missing from her locked bureau, pointing toward someone in the household with access to her private apartments."

"Then it should be a matter for the police," I said. "It has all the appearance of pilfering by a rogue member of staff. Some new addition to the house perhaps? Or one recently dismissed? Any village bobby could question a household over such a trifle."

"Indeed he could. However, the lady requires more delicacy than the local constabulary would provide. My instincts tell me there is more at stake here than a pretty timepiece."

"You are concerned over her choice in husband? A trifle late for that."

"She did not say as much, but I believe she suspects the thief to be her aforementioned groom." He peered at me, his eyes glittering. "I was almost inclined to agree with her."

"Almost – but not quite?"

"Havingham was an unpleasant school boy, and I doubt that he has changed in essence. It is common knowledge that debt has forced Edward Havingham to sell a great deal of his family's assets, but though he is a bully, I do believe common theft would be beneath him. The marriage is political, of course, and a good match in many respects. Ephraim Woodsford wants Havingham's title for his grandchildren, and Havingham wants Alicia Woodsford's considerable dowry, which he will have no difficulty in appropriating, now they are married."

"Lord Havingham means to rebuild the family estate with her money."

"Not an uncommon occurrence. Several wealthy American dynasties have bought their family a place in London society." Holmes clamped the pipe firmly between his teeth, lit it with the spill, and stood gazing at the fire in ruminative mood. "Havingham is a proud and ruthless man when it comes to protecting the family name. It seems illogical for him to risk that name over such piffling trifles. There has already been a steady selling-off of the family silver, so I have no doubt he would sell them quietly but openly. Yet he is also possessed of a violent temper. He was admonished for a particularly brutal flogging of a fag when we were at school, and his name has been linked to a number of unfortunate incidents since then."

"So you do fear for her safety? I'm surprised she had not realised his character before the wedding – she seems a woman of intelligence."

440

Holmes sucked on his pipe for a long moment, examining the bedraggled greenery along the mantel shelf. "Havingham can be a man of great charm when he chooses," he said. "He was described as a 'golden boy' on more than one occasion. Lady Havingham's family doubtless viewed him as quite a catch for a railwayman's only daughter. Even when that railwayman is a millionaire. He would not alienate them. So no, I believe she is safe enough. And I don't doubt she feels capable of keeping Havingham's excesses in check, with the help of this paragon of a young brother. But the fact remains that in that house there lurks a viper, and I could not vouch for the safety of anyone."

"Then should we accompany Lady Havingham back to Hampshire today?"

"I have enquiries to make first," Holmes chuckled quietly. "Have patience, and clear your calendar until the New Year, Watson. I foresee an affair of some complexity before us."

Christmas dawned crisp and bright, and our train journey to Winchester was uneventful. "The Dower House is typical of its kind," Holmes observed as our cab clattered up the driveway. "It was the original family residence. To the casual observer, it has the same Georgian elegance as Rhyton Hall, but dig deeper and you will discover a Jacobean manor. Below stairs retains elements of the Tudor, and the cellars are un-ashamedly Gothic."

"You talk as if you know it well," I said.

"I had occasion to visit in the distant past." He pulled his Ulster close around him and said nothing more until we alighted at the doors of Rhyton House. A cutting wind blew off snow-laden Downs, and though the sky was blue, dark grey clouds limned the white horizon. "Things to come," my companion murmured. "Clouds are gathering, mark my words."

"Snow?" I glanced at him curiously. "It *is* the season, Holmes."

"It is indeed." He smiled one of his tight, fleeting smiles that told me exactly how wide of the mark I was.

The white-and-black tiled ceramic floor of the main hallway was loud under our boots as we entered the house, each step echoing up between ionic columns to a veritable cascade of chandeliers suspended beneath vast plaster cartouches. I had little time to take in much more before we were ushered into a fashionably furnished drawing room.

Lady Havingham rose quickly and crossed to greet us in a flurry of silk and lace. "Gentlemen. So pleased you could join us. Papa, Mama, this is Mr. Sherlock Holmes and his friend, Doctor Watson." She favoured us both with smiles. "Allow me to introduce my parents,

441

Ephraim and Gertrude Woodsford. My brother, Henry," she went on. "And my husband, Edward, Lord Havingham."

"Hemlock. It's been a long time." Havingham advanced with his hand extended, a grin splitting a face that had once been handsome but was rapidly going to seed. The professional part of me recognised a liverish condition. The other half recognised a *bonhomie* toward Holmes that was plainly not reciprocated.

"Hemlock?" I asked.

"One of my first monographs, written whilst at school. *Poisons Common to the English Country Garden*." Holmes affected indifference to his precocious plaudit, raising his chin to view the lord along the length of his nose. "Surprised you remember it, Havingham," he murmured.

"You've met?" Lady Havingham asked.

"Most decidedly. We attended the same prep school not thirty miles from here. Hem . . . pardon me," Havingham bowed mockingly. "Sherlock was a year ahead of me, but we had elder brothers who were the greatest of pals, so our paths crossed often. Tell me, does Mycroft still sit and ignore people in that dingy club of his?" He beamed at us both through slightly yellowed eyes. "He was never one for the sporting pursuits. Speaking of which I trust you will both join us for our Boxing Day hunt tomorrow?"

"Wouldn't miss it." Holmes murmured.

His reply startled me. I knew Holmes to be an excellent shot and admirable boxer, and he had often demonstrated an extensive knowledge of horses, but I had never known him ride to hounds.

"Mr. Holmes, or should I call you Cousin Sherlock?" Mrs. Woodsford insinuated herself between her daughter and new son-in-law, a bird-like woman made smaller by her husband's quiet bulk just behind her. "Enough of sport. You menfolk can talk horses later over your port. The afternoon is for us ladies." She laid a hand on Holmes's arm with that American openness. I watched him stiffen at the contact, but our hostess seemed not to notice as she twittered on disarmingly. "I have read all Dr. Watson's tales of your exploits, and I was just thrilled when Alicia told me we had a connection. I simply insisted Ephraim here invite you to join us for the holiday." She smiled, and I could see where her daughter's vivacity stemmed from. The older Mr. Woodsford smiled affably and bowed.

"The good Doctor and I were pleased to come," Holmes replied. "It is an honour to meet my cousins from the Americas."

"The honour is all ours," Woodsford rumbled. "Gertrude, ring for tea. Now Gentlemen, come – sit. Warm yourselves. Edward hinted at intriguing exploits when you were at school together, and it all sounds most exciting."

"I should have said it rather ordinary," Holmes replied. "And younger sons are seldom remembered."

"Few would forget you," Havingham said. "Holmes made an impression on the entire school. Mostly in the laboratories, which he blew up . . . how many times, Holmes? Two? Three?"

I have seldom known Holmes to be affected by the opinions of others, but Havingham plainly exerted an influence that was not welcomed. My old friend's jaw tightened. "We should not bore these people with 'old boy' gossip, my dear chap." He smiled with a mechanical tweak of the lips that was belied by steely grimness in his eyes. "Mrs. Woodsford, it is a pleasure to meet you. I am sure brother Mycroft will be fascinated by this new connection. Tell me, where are you from?"

"Boston," Mrs. Woodsford said, quite emphatically, as if there were no other place it could be. "Why did your brother not come with you? I should very much like to meet him."

"Mycroft seldom leaves London," Holmes replied. "I shall be sure to pass on your good wishes."

The afternoon and evening passed quickly, giving Holmes the opportunity to study the family at his leisure. In particular, he watched Havingham unwrap the gauze and crepe ribbons from his gift. The man had stared at the handsome silver flask for a long moment. "A hip flask?" he murmured. "How will I ever be on time with a snoot full of good brandy?"

Holmes watched without expression, but the flexed muscles in his jaw hinted to me that Havingham had surprised him in some way. The couple only laughed, and the moment passed as tokens were exchanged by the rest of the gathering.

There were thoughtful gifts for the both of us. A handsome pipe for Holmes and a leather writing case for me, which made me glad I had persuaded Holmes to include additional bottles of good port in the hamper we had brought for the household. I noted, however, that after their initial exchange, the old school chums continued to avoid each other as the identical poles of a magnet will do.

Boxing Day dawned near perfect for its traditional hunt. The clouds of the previous day had not lived up to their promise, and laying snow was already melting beneath a cloudless sky on a far warmer day than was expected. The thought of a few hours in the saddle filled me with some trepidation, yet I was looking forward to this event far more. I had not ridden to hounds since returning from the Afghan Wars and missed it a great deal.

The local hunt sported a full pack of hounds and some forty riders, and the taking of the stirrup-cup was a boisterous affair. Serving staff from the hostelry to one side of the green wove their way between animals and people, offering trays of warming tots of brandy, sherry, or port. I was surprised to find that neither the older Woodsfords nor Lady Havingham had joined us, but Lord Havingham held centre stage, dressed in full hunting pinks, chatting loudly with the great and good of the country set, and sipping from the handsome flask that was his wife's gift to him the previous day. The younger Woodsford, by contrast, hung back, his horse skittering at the noise around us.

"What do you expect to see, Holmes?" I asked.

"I'm not certain." He scanned the crowd and frowned. "Something is afoot. We must watch and wait, my friend."

There was an order forming in the chaos as the Master of the Hunt sounded the pack-off, and we were on our way. Trotting at first, following the hounds at a clipped pace along slushy roads before we turned off into the fields, heading for a stretch of woodland high on the Downs. When the *Tally ho!* sounded, the entire pack took off at a gallop. riders and hounds streaming across the snowy hillside in full tongue. I galloped after them, but very soon found myself lagging behind even the stragglers. The older mare I had been lent possessed a smooth gait, but I was unable to stand into the saddle for more than a few seconds at a time before the pain of my old injury became too much.

I paused at the top of the combe to watch their progress with some regret as the distance between us grew ever wider. The baying of hounds and braying of horns and the hunters hallooing came clearly to me, but there was no chance of my ever making up the lost ground.

They had reached the lower meadow and split into distinct order. The less headstrong riders veering left toward the gate, whilst the rest pulled right, plainly intending to take the hedge at its lowest point.

One rider seemed a lesser horseman than the handsome dark bay beneath him deserved. He swayed and bumped in the saddle like a stuffed sack, his head flopping from side to side. The horse plunged gamely on, emboldened by the chase, eager to run with his compatriots and not be left behind. Then it leapt forward without warning, its front quarters rising in an awkward half-rear before stumbling almost to its knees. The rider lost his seat and was thrown in a flurry of limbs, hurtling into the whitened headland at fatal speed, where he lay motionless. Too tight against the obstacle now for safety, the horse refused the hurdle and bolted, rider-less, along the line of the hedge.

I held my breath, just for a second, willing the rider to rise, before the instincts of a military medical man took hold. Gritting my teeth against the pain of my leg, I urged the mare in a headlong downhill charge, reaching the rider before the pack realised he had taken a fall. I dismounted to kneel in the churned up snow and search the prone huntsman for a pulse, though I had seen enough death in far warmer fields than this to know that the rider was beyond help before I had ever started down the slope.

I turned him over and let out an involuntary sigh. Just as I feared, it was Lord Havingham's fleshy features staring back at me. My hand moved from checking his carotid to closing his lids over stark, misting, eyes.

"Is he badly hurt?" The Master of the Hunt appeared at my side and stood gazing at Havingham's body.

"Dead," I replied.

The Master respectfully removed his hat. "Oh, dear God. Tragic when any rider comes a cropper, but Havingham had a good seat. Never known him take a fall at such an easy jump."

"I was watching from up there." I gestured up the slope. "His horse shied and took fright. He was taken by complete surprise."

The man nodded. "Some horses will see tigers behind every bush."

I sensed movement at my side and Holmes was there, adding softly, "Poor Havingham. He was a difficult sort, but I had thought to prevent this."

"Holmes," I said. "You caught his mount already?"

"It was more provoked than spooked, and could not run far with reins dragging around its fetlocks." He nodded at the Whipper-in and handed over the bay's muddied reins. "When Havingham dropped back from the head of the pack, I knew something was amiss." Holmes bent suddenly to sniff at Havingham's lips. "No odour of any significance," he muttered to me. "Yet all the signs are there."

His words chilled deeper than the weather. "You suspect foul play?" I said. "Surely not."

"I always suspect." Holmes leaned across to shield the body from onlookers and surreptitiously slid something from Havingham's pocket into his own.

"Holmes . . . ."

"Say nothing, Watson," he replied, and held a gloved finger against pursed lips as more riders clattered to a halt around us.

"Is he dead?" Henry Woodsford demanded.

"He is," I replied.

Woodsford nodded, his face passive but for the small "V" of concern forming between his brows. "Poor Alicia," he said at last. "All this coming around again. If I believed in such things, I'd swear she'd had a curse laid on her."

Holmes eyed Woodsford up and down as a mongoose would a cobra. "Co-incidences are seldom what they seem," he said. "I am certain your sister's spiritual well-being has no bearing on this sad affair." He remounted and turned his horse back the way we had come. "Watson, I must get to London immediately. Give Lady Havingham my apologies and tell her I hope to return by the last train. Question the staff whilst I am gone. This shock may loosen a few tongues."

Holmes did not return to Rhyton that evening as promised, but appeared at my bedroom door just a few minutes before the breakfast bell. "My room, Watson. You must bring me up to speed whilst I change."

"I don't have a great deal to report," I said as I closed his door behind me. "I questioned the staff, but none had any idea what could have happened. And the magistrate ruled Havingham's death as misadventure before the sun had set. He released the body for interment within hours."

"I am not wholly surprised," Holmes replied. "In dealing with a man of Havingham's stature, a local magistrate would be eager to avoid any hint of foul play, and hunting accidents occur often enough to rouse little suspicion. That is not important at present. Before we left London, I sent an associate to check the pawn shops of Winchester, in case a relative of a maid or footman had been commissioned to pawn the missing items." He sipped at the tea the maid had brought him and offered me a dark smile. "I had similar enquiries made in Town."

"So you *do* think he was murdered? But why?"

"I *know* he was murdered," Holmes replied. "It is the *how* and the *by whom* that are the burning questions. It was the theft of the hunter watch that aroused my suspicions."

"Why would it be so significant? I should have thought a gold watch was a temptation for any thief."

"Targeting that trinket in a house filled with wedding gifts of considerably higher value? And stealing only those items new to the Havinghams? Come, Watson. You can do better than that. I suspect these petty thefts were committed merely to muddy the waters. The target, my dear chap, was never the gold watch, but our unfortunate fox hunter."

"But I saw Havingham fall. There was nobody within yards of him."

"As you rightly say, nobody was close, yet something caused his horse to shy. When I examined the animal yesterday I found a small cut on its rump in the exact spot that I expected, made by a projectile fired from something like a powerful slingshot. It would not discombobulate an experienced rider such as Havingham in the normal run, but when that rider is under the influence of a mild narcotic, it would require little more than a sudden lurch to unseat him."

"How can you be sure?"

"He was an accomplished horseman. His being drugged was the only plausible answer." The smile Holmes adopted was genuine this time. "I am surprised you missed such obvious signs, Watson. Your medical instincts are slipping. Did you not notice his constricted pupils? His clammy skin? Laudanum is not an indulgence of my own, but I recognise its effects well enough. It was administered to him in that spanking new silver flask – knowing that Havingham would not be able to resist flaunting it."

"So all that would be needed was to have his horse take off at a gallop and unseat him?"

"Precisely."

"If you don't mind me saying, Holmes, had someone wanted to do away with him, it was a plan that left a great deal to chance."

"It was a serious attempt nevertheless. Conveying the concept of accidental death was paramount, and the perpetrator was plainly comfortable in the knowledge that if this bid did not succeed, there would always be other opportunities. Ergo, it must be someone within the household."

"Do you know who?"

He nodded. "The same person who, amongst other things, stole the hunter and other gee-gaws. I await a few final pieces to confirm my hypothesis, but yes, I believe I do."

"And of course, you are not going to tell me anything."

He glanced at me and grunted surprise. "You wish me to cast aspersions on any one of the party without proof?" He rose suddenly. "When the Irregulars have furnished me with final pieces to this puzzle, I shall reveal all." Holmes stripped off his tie and collar as he advanced on the washstand to pour water from ewer to bowl. "I am certain that the thief was not Havingham, which will please her Ladyship no end."

"You're very certain about that."

"His surprise at the gift Lady Havingham had given him was obvious."

"Because he was expecting the hunter?"

"Lady Havingham told us as much when she came to Baker Street. And recall what Havingham said as he opened it. 'A hip flask? How will I ever be on time with a snoot full of good brandy?' Plainly a private joke between our newlyweds."

"He could have been covering his tracks."

Holmes shook his head. "Havingham did not have the wit. With luck my final proof will arrive this very morning, and we shall be home for New Year's Day. Now, excuse me whilst I ablute, Watson. We shall reconvene over our kippers and eggs."

I was surprised to see the widowed Lady Havingham appear at the breakfast table, eschewing a tray in the seclusion of her room, as her parents had not. She looked composed, despite her complexion being made pallid by austere mourning dress and her hair scraped back into a black snood.

"Gentlemen," she murmured as Holmes and I rose to greet her. "Do be seated. I stand on no ceremony amongst friends." She frowned at her brother Henry, who sat at the far end of the table nibbling toast and hiding behind *The Times*, but did not comment on his manners. Having selected a kipper, she sat peering at it, as if wondering what it might be. "Odd how the eyes of dead things stare so," she said.

"Perhaps you might start with eggs," I gently ventured, "if the fish disturbs you."

She smiled a wry smile. "I am not disturbed, Doctor Watson. I am saddened by Edward's death, but we were not in love."

"Nor was he your first loss," Holmes observed.

She flinched, her fragile composure faltering for a moment.

"Holmes," I muttered, "have a care."

"It's quite all right, Doctor," she said. "It is no secret that I was married once before. My first husband also died soon after our marriage – the result of a tragic climbing accident in the Alps almost eight years ago." A shadow crossed her lovely features. "Henry here survived, as did the guide, but Barnaby fell to his death. He was a good man. A little reckless granted, but I miss him still."

"My condolences, then, for both your losses," I said.

"Thank you, Doctor Watson. I . . . ."

A footman entered with a salver. "A package for Mr. Holmes, M'Lady."

Holmes took the brown paper packet, unwrapped it carefully, and picked a large gold hunter from the folds. "Yours, I believe, Lady Havingham."

She took it from him, turning it over and over, examining every inch in wonder tinged with sadness. "Edward's gift. But how?"

"The Irregulars," Holmes replied. "Combing the back streets around the American Club for jewellers and pawn shops. Such a fine piece was easy to trace. They had it within hours. That it was sold to the establishment in question by a tall, auburn-haired American made it more notable still."

All eyes turned to Woodsford. "I am hardly the only American in London," he drawled.

"You were the only one to sell such a valuable gold hunter. Which, coupled with the slingshot that I have just found in your room, is quite damning." He took the weapon from his pocket and carefully laid it on the expanse of white tablecloth that stretched between himself and the young American.

"Slingshot? A mere toy," Woodsford snapped. "My window overlooks the stables, and I amuse myself taking pot shots at the rats."

"So the head groom informed me, which is why I knew to look for it. On its own, it is no proof. But you also purchased a bottle of laudanum from one Bertel and Sons, Apothecary." Holmes removed a bottle from his pocket and stood it beside the slingshot, and the two men stared at each other across the evidence. "Having retrieved Havingham's flask at the time of the accident, I was able to ascertain that it was laced with laudanum – not sufficient to kill, but more than enough to render both mental and physical reactions dulled. Your target practise in the yard honed your skills sufficiently to fire a chalk piece at Havingham's horse, causing it to bolt. When I saw the welt on the animal's haunch moments after it threw Havingham, and noted white dust around the impact, I had already surmised the missile used was of the calcium carbonate common to these Downs. It was less likely to be noticed in the snow, and would not be out of place after the thaw. I had also noted in passing that the fingertips of your riding gloves were marred with chalk."

Woodsford blanched as pale as his grieving sister, who sat dumbstruck at the revelations unfolding before her. "How would you prove any of that?" he said. "Do you also have this chalk missile in your possession?"

Holmes looked down to examine his cuticles for a moment before continuing, "Apart from the watch, much of what I have amassed so far is pure conjecture. In the same way that the French gendarmerie could not ascertain why the ropes tying yourself to your first brother-in-law were severed in such a very precise manner."

"Henry?" Alicia Havingham's voice caught on the single word. "Henry . . ." she said again. ". . . tell me it isn't so. Mr. Holmes, surely you can't be accusing my brother, of all people?" She stared from him to Woodsford, her hand raised to her lips in horror. "The flask," she said. "You filled it from your own bottle. You told me it was a surprise. You swore me to secrecy. You lied to me, Henry. You lied to your own sister and took me for a fool. And then you murdered my husband? Both of my husbands . . . ." She held the back of her fingers over her lips to stifle a sob. "Poor Edward. Poor, poor Barnaby. Why ever would you do such terrible things?"

Holmes glanced toward her, releasing her brother from his captive gaze. "I regret the need to be so direct, Lady Havingham, but the facts cannot be ignored."

"This is intolerable, Mr. Holmes." Woodsford slapped his newspaper onto the table. "It would be plain stupid to incriminate myself in such a fashion. What reason would I have to do all that you claim? What about those other thefts?"

Holmes snorted quietly. "Each of the missing items, including the original watch belonging to Havingham's father – the catalyst for this whole sorry affair if I am not mistaken – were pawned in different London establishments. By a man signing the slips as Edward Havingham. A clumsy ruse to throw suspicion on your brother-in-law, should the police attempt to trace them. The flaw in that plan, according to my witnesses, is that, despite calling himself an English Lord, the seller was quite clearly American. I am certain the traders in question will be able to identify you. Once both Scotland Yard and the Pinkerton Agency have concluded their investigations, your state of innocence will change quite dramatically."

"They were parasites," Woodsford growled. "Both of them. Using my sister as a . . . as a . . . bank vault!" He got to his feet and paced the space between table and window. "Alicia, did you know Father paid Barnaby's gambling debts before you married? And again after his death? Money drawn from *my* inheritance! Not yours! Your dowry was always safe. And your precious Lord Edward was just the same. When he took me to the races that day and lost a hundred guineas on one wager without so much as a by-your-leave? I knew he was the wrong man for you. He dropped his watch in the cab and I picked it up with every intention of returning it. But I quickly realised he did not give a fig for it beyond its market value."

"You planned this whole thing way back then?" Lady Alicia stared at her brother, incredulity and anquish catching at her voice.

"In part." He reached a hand toward her, and dropped it away when she shrank from him. "I did all of this for you, Alicia. Please believe me. My first intention was to discredit him. But when you ordered the

450

facsimile, at great cost, and at his behest . . . I could not allow you to tie yourself to such a creature. I've gotta say, for an intelligent woman you've mighty poor taste in men." He glanced at Holmes. "It is possible, sir, to do ill for the best of reasons."

"Your motives are not my concern. Of course, I shall require a day more at least to complete my enquiries." Holmes busied himself in buttering toast, the gentle noise of knife against charred bread loud in the silence that followed.

"There is a boat leaving Southampton for New York today," Woodsford said at last.

"The Pinkertons will be watching that ship – at my suggestion." Holmes reached for the marmalade and casually spooned a small quantity of the orange preserve onto his plate. "There is, however, a steamer leaving Liverpool tomorrow, Rio bound."

Woodsford stared at Holmes as the inevitability of the trap was set, and the only course left open to him became clear. "Very well." He moved to his sister's side and planted a kiss on her forehead. "Alicia . . . I . . . Good bye."

"Henry . . . ." She leaped to her feet, grasping his arm to turn him back. "Henry, you cannot just leave us like this. What will I say to our Father? And to Mother?"

Woodsford extricated himself from her grip and touched her lips to silence. "Say nothing. Look out for her, Mr. Holmes, Doctor Watson." He nodded to us both and strode from the room.

"Excuse me, Gentlemen," Lady Havingham said, and hurried after him.

In the quiet that followed, Holmes set toast aside and served himself a large kipper.

"Holmes," I said. "He murdered two men."

Holmes raised a finger and shook his head. "Two men met untimely ends that were declared accidental by the courts," he replied.

"But you can prove them wrong!"

"And when I have gathered all of the facts, I shall offer them to Scotland Yard. Until that time?" He shrugged and lifted a forkful of fish to sardonic lips.

"You cannot take the law into your own hands, man! I see no reason for sparing him the rope. He was no better than the men he killed, looking out for his own account at his sister's expense."

"Indeed." Holmes looked up from his fish to stare me in the eye. "He is a bad seed and should be punished. Yet think about it. Once the facts are known, Woodsford will never be able to return to his family or society, either here or in America. Nor will he ever be able to claim the

451

inheritance he was trying to protect. I would go so far as to hazard that his inheritance will not exist once his father is acquainted with those facts. Under those circumstances, what good would sending him to the gallows achieve? Only to cause pain to a woman who has buried two husbands through his vile acts. No, Watson, I believe his punishment will last a lifetime. And surely that is punishment enough."

The Curious Case of the
Well-Connected Criminal
by Molly Carr

It was a week or so before Christmas, and I was wondering what to give as a present to my friend Sherlock Holmes to mark the occasion.

He would probably give me a box of good cigars (waving away my thanks with a smile and hurrying back to his chemical experiments). But I would have to think hard if I were not to do the same. Retorts, retort stands, petri-dishes, and flasks he had in plenty, and his shelves were full of books, especially books on crime. So it wasn't surprising that I was walking down Oxford Street (in quite a heavy fall of snow and with my umbrella up,) busy wracking my brains, along with crowds of other shoppers with, like myself, no other thought in their minds than the problem of what to buy for their friends and family at this festive season.

I couldn't, as a gentleman, give my friend an article of clothing, not even a pair of socks or something as insignificant as a bow-tie, since we were not related in any way. Even if I defied convention, he had enough deerstalkers, Norfolk jackets, and bowlers to make any such gift from me entirely superfluous! But as I pondered the problem, at the same time gazing at each store for inspiration, I saw reflected in their windows a man whom I suspected was following me. Indeed, he seemed to have been doing so for some considerable time. When I stopped, he stopped. When I crossed the road, he did the same. There was nothing for it but to dodge into Portman Square and make my way back to Baker Street.

When I mentioned the incident to Holmes, he seemed interested and asked for a description of the man.

"Small, thin, and, I think, more of a boy than a full-grown adult."

"Someone you had never seen before, and didn't recognise?"

"Yes, to the best of my knowledge."

"Did he ask you for a touch? After all, it is Christmas, and you look the sort of chap who would take pity on someone short of cash at such a time."

"He never said a word, not even when I turned and stared at him for all I was worth." Flinging my coat onto the nearest chair, I pulled off my boots and reached for my slippers. The room felt comfortably warm, and a good fire blazed in the grate.

"And he didn't follow you into the Square to see where you were going?"

"If he did, I was unaware of it. But in any case, I had shaken him off before I reached Baker Street."

"Could you, perhaps, describe him more accurately? I imagine that part of town was thronged as usual, and probably even more so today, with people too intent on their Christmas shopping to take note of much else."

"It is as you say about Oxford Street. But do you really think that there were scores of undersized and thin urchins wandering about, hoping for charity?"

"My dear fellow, I'm certain of it, all trying to benefit a great deal from other people's generosity, including your own."

"I've already told you that the youth didn't speak to me," I said with a touch of impatience. "He simply followed me around Oxford Street. But if you want a more detailed description, I can tell you he was neatly dressed, as well as intelligent and alert."

"Also, by the look of it, determined that you should know what he was doing, without making it too obvious or bothering to engage you in conversation. What I don't understand is, if he recognised you and wanted you to be aware of him, why he *didn't* speak to you or follow you to our rooms. Or indeed, how did he knew you weren't at home in the first place."

"As to your first observation about following me to our rooms, he may have done so, in spite of what I said earlier. But I was so rattled I didn't notice. The second observation, his knowing that I wasn't at home, appears more baffling. But perhaps he was hanging about on the off-chance of meeting me – something which I admit makes the whole episode appear one of hit-and-miss."

At that moment, our landlady entered the room. Holmes raised an enquiring eyebrow and she said, "There's a boy come knocking at the door, sir. Says he needs to see you urgently."

"Then be so kind as to show him in, Mrs. Hudson, while the Doctor here builds up the fire again, it being such a very cold season of the year."

A minute or two later, I turned away from tending the now merrily jumping flames within the grate and saw a familiar, but not, to me a particularly welcome, face. "So you did follow me after all?" I said angrily.

"I wanted to make sure I had the right man, sir, and had come to the right place."

"Right man! Right place! What on earth would you want with me?"

"I knew you could lead me to this gentleman here."

It was Holmes's turn to be surprised. "Do you mean, young man, that you recognised Doctor Watson and knew not only that we were friends, but that we also shared rooms?"

"The description I was given fitted your friend exactly, and I was told that I only had to find and follow him to get to you eventually, however long he spent out of doors or, as it happened, mingling with the crowds and looking at the shops in Oxford Street."

"And who gave you this description?" I demanded.

"My boss," said the boy simply.

"Who is – ?" said Holmes, relighting his pipe and throwing the spent match into the fire.

"I am not permitted to say."

"Come now," said my friend impatiently. "First of all, you put my colleague out of countenance by trailing him along what must at present be the busiest thoroughfare in the whole of London. This forces him to dodge into one of the main squares in an attempt to shake you off. Then you disturb our landlady, who has to open the door when she could be occupied with more important things, such as preparing our supper. Finally, you invade our private rooms without having the good manners to tell us why, or who sent you."

My medical training made me aware that our visitor was trembling, and I had already made a mental note of how white in the face he looked. "Holmes," I said quietly, "I think that it would be wise if we let the boy sit down."

For answer, my friend indicated one of our armchairs, and the youth sank gratefully into it. "I was told to come here to see you, and to communicate something important," he said. "But on no account was I to tell you the name of the person who sent me, at least not until you had agreed to co-operate with us."

"I'm not sure I care for the term 'co-operate'," said Holmes. "But you had better spill the beans as best you can. Otherwise, we are not going to get anywhere. You have already said you've been at some pains to ascertain that you've found the right place and the right persons to deal with. But so far . . . ."

"So far," I interrupted, "nothing makes any sense whatever. Holmes, you are so famous that nearly everyone in London must know where you live. There would be no need to make sure someone recognised and followed *me* in order to find you, even though you do lead a somewhat retiring life when not on a case."

"An address well-known in London," said the young man suddenly. "But my boss normally lives in Paris."

"So what is he doing here, in the Capital?" demanded Holmes.

"*She* wants you to find her fiancé."

"Not *cherchez la femme* then," said Holmes with a light laugh, "but rather the opposite."

"He went out to buy cigarettes and didn't come back," said our young visitor.

"A common enough occurrence," replied Holmes dryly.

"But," said the youth heatedly, "he is the soul of honour, and they are to be married within a week!"

I got up to put some more coal on the fire and, as I returned the scuttle to its place, thought to myself that this wasn't getting us anywhere. We were talking to someone who was obviously British about a woman who might or might not be French, and who had a fiancé who might be either. I could see that my friend too was becoming restive, and hoped he would quickly hone in on some more useful data.

"If I am to be of help," he said with a touch of sarcasm, "you will have to force yourself to be a little more specific, whatever orders you have received."

Looking closely at him, I saw that the boy had recovered himself somewhat. He no longer trembled, and his face showed a little more colour. But whether from the warmth of the fire or for some other reason, it was difficult to tell. "I don't like to betray my employer," he said in some confusion. "Especially as she . . . ."

"Come now," said Holmes kindly, "I agree to take up the case. Does that satisfy you enough to reveal who sent you?"

The young man glanced nervously in my direction, and Holmes said, "Like your boss's missing fiancé, Dr. Watson is the soul of honour. You can speak as freely in his presence as you can to me."

"I have been instructed by Madame the Marquise de Brinvilliers to tell you that if you agreed to help her, she would like to meet you as soon as possible in her suite of rooms at the Savoy Hotel."

"Marquise de Brinvilliers, the notorious poisoner who's been dead for nearly two-hundred years!"

"I shouldn't worry about that," said the youth suddenly, and with something of a smile. "Just before we left Paris, she was calling herself 'Madame de Pompadour'."

I glanced nervously at Holmes, wondering if we should, after all, have anything to do with the woman, since she was obviously as mad as a hatter. This answer, however, seemed to amuse him and he said, "It's an easy walk to the Strand, so I suggest all three of us get to the Savoy as soon as possible before the lady becomes someone else!"

The person in question turned out to be barely in her early twenties, and when we were introduced, Holmes, with a sly grin at me, gave her the deepest bow I have ever seen in my life. With a gracious gesture, she indicated that we should sit down and rang the bell for some refreshment while my friend, with another mischievous glance, asked how his client wished to be addressed.

"By my name, of course," she said tartly. "The one you have just heard: Constance Cameron."

"Well", I thought, "that sounds genuine enough," and prepared myself to hear what would be said next.

It was Holmes who spoke. "I understand that you need my services to find your fiancé," he said. "This young man has told us that he went out to buy cigarettes and didn't return. But it would be helpful if you could confirm this, and perhaps supply any additional information which may be of use."

The girl had produced a handkerchief. She now dabbed her eyes with it and gave us a most mournful look. "Everything seemed as usual between us," she said. "There had been no disagreement of any kind. In fact, we were happily discussing the wedding arrangements and looking forward to where we were to spend our honeymoon."

"Which would, I suppose, judging by your family name, be somewhere in Scotland?"

"No. I have lived in France for some years. My mother was French, and when she died, she left me not only a considerable amount of money, but a property in Paris, as well as another in the Dordogne. It was there that we planned to stay for a while."

"And this trick of calling yourself by different titles?" asked my friend playfully.

The girl smiled for the first time. "I see that Willie has also told you about that silly habit. It amuses me. But I only do it in private. I assure you the management here knows my real name, and quite possibly the exact size of my fortune!"

This might explain her presence in this very expensive hotel, the magnificent suite of rooms with their wonderful views over the river – and the speed with which a waiter had responded to her summons. But it was more difficult to fathom why she had come to London at all, unless it was to buy new clothes in time for the honeymoon. Surely Paris would be the place for that? Also (I reflected somewhat belatedly) how had she obtained such an accurate description of me that the boy knew whom to follow?

"I saw a photograph of you both in *Le Monde*," she said, as if reading my thoughts, "soon after an attempt to steal the Mona Lisa from The Louvre was foiled. Something which, if I may say so Mr. Holmes, was handled by you with consummate ease."

I noticed with amusement that my friend blushed a little, showing that he was not entirely immune from feminine praise, in spite of what he often said about the inscrutable nature of women's thoughts and actions. After a slight pause, however, he returned to the matter in hand.

"Your fiancé's name?"

"Albert Block."

Prosaic, I thought.

"British then?"

"Yes. He owns a chain of import shops, although he made his money, when he was younger, in a variety of other less staid ventures. Or so he led me to believe. I met him on the Continent, when he was arranging for some deliveries."

"Do you have any idea where your sweetheart might have gone, and why?"

"I believe he has been kidnapped."

"By whom?"

"Albert has led a somewhat adventurous, not to say rackety, life. In fact, we used to laugh about it, and he often said he was looking forward to settling down."

"Would you have liked that? I have an impression that you are quite a spirited young person yourself, and feel that too much 'settling down' might bore you!"

Holmes shifted slightly in his armchair and took several sips of hot chocolate while our client gazed at him in some surprise. At the same time, she lifted her own cup to her lips before saying, "You are obviously a good judge of character. I do like excitement. But surely you realise that I'm more worried than bored at present."

"Certainly I do," said Holmes. "But let me remind you that I asked if there was anything you could tell us which would help to find the missing man. So far you have not done so, but have simply put forward the idea that he has been kidnapped."

"During the course of his life as an adult, my fiancé has made several enemies in one way and another," said Miss Cameron with some distress. "And he recently received a number of peculiar and decidedly unpleasant notes."

"And there was no way in which he could recognise the handwriting?"

"There is no handwriting to recognise. Letters had simply been cut out of a magazine and stuck on cheap paper to form certain words."

"A very tedious procedure, I should have thought," said Holmes taking another sip of chocolate.

"Indeed. But that might explain why the messages were so short. For example, '*Where is your wife?*' and '*Why are you overdrawn at your bank?*' But of course, he has no wife, at least not yet, and he told me that his finances are in perfect order!"

"Could it be a case of mistaken identity? Why didn't he consult someone immediately?"

The young woman's lips trembled slightly. "At first, I think he dismissed the whole thing as some childish prank," she said. "As for the letters being for someone else, his name was printed in block capitals on the envelopes, and the address was the correct one. But it is the latest communication which finally decided him to discuss seeking help."

At this, our informant made a sign to the young man she called Willie. He had been sitting quietly, listening to our conversation, fidgeting uneasily from time to time as the story unfolded. Now he rose and went over to a small desk at the further end of the immense room. Opening it, he brought out a crumpled piece of paper and handed it to the woman that he had called his 'boss' when speaking to us in Baker Street. She in turn handed the paper to Holmes, who smoothed it out and looked at the printed letters which were stuck to it. I saw from over his shoulder that they seemed to have come from a reputable source, since each was clear and easy to recognise. But it was the message itself which startled both of us. "*Be sure wel get you*" and (an inch or two further down) "*before very long*". I looked twice to verify that the third word in the abominable communication read "*wel*," rather than "*we'll*" or "*we will*", and there was, in fact, only one "*l*". However, no-one but an imbecile could mistake what was meant.

Holmes looked at the address on the envelope and said musingly, "It is odd how criminals and other persons never quite appreciate how easy it is to recognise letters printed in block capitals, since that does nothing at all to hide the writer's hand. Any expert could spot who wrote this, given that he had seen other examples of it, in capitals or not. With your permission, Miss Cameron, I will keep this to send to Scotland Yard – "

At that moment, there was an urgent knock at the door. Without waiting for a response, the door burst open and a middle-aged hotel employee, showing every sign of distress, rushed into the room. Miss Cameron jumped to her feet, and much of the hot chocolate in her cup fell precipitately to the floor. A frightened Willie grasped her hand and began to tremble, just as he had done in our rooms.

"That young man has more than a nervous disposition," I thought to myself. "He is evidently badly frightened about something, even allowing for the fact that we are all four of us more than a little surprised at this precipitate intrusion."

"I was downstairs," gasped our unexpected visitor, "in the lobby supervising some of the staff who were just finishing off the decorations that we normally put up at this time, including decorating the huge Christmas tree in the foyer." He swallowed. "A police constable rushed in and asked if a Miss Constance Cameron was staying here. Of course, I answered in the affirmative, and he said – " here the man paused for breath, " – 'Tell her to go as soon as possible to the London Hospital.' I have a cab waiting downstairs, ma'am, and it seems you must use it immediately."

"I am a doctor," I said at once, "and will accompany the lady. Meanwhile – " I added, with a glance at Holmes, " – the boy could go with my friend to Baker Street, as in the circumstances it is impossible for him to remain here alone."

"Willie will come with me," said Miss Cameron firmly.

Holmes was wearing a puzzled frown. Something just wasn't making sense to him. I was used to not appreciating all the facts of many of the investigations we tackled together until he revealed them to me, but I rarely saw my colleague at a loss. However, there was no time for speculation, and the news when we reached the hospital was so devastating it drove everything else out of my head. An unconscious man had just been brought in, and when trying to identify him, the address of the Savoy Hotel was found on his person, together with a note stating to contact Constance Cameron, staying there, should anything happen to him.

"She reminds me of one or two other enquiries in which we have been involved, where men and women have not been what they seemed," said a familiar voice. I was waiting in a chair outside the room into which Miss Cameron had been conducted, along with Willie, immediately upon arriving at the hospital.

Holmes settled himself beside me and stamped his feet to remove some snow from his boots. "I'm not exactly accusing her of anything, but I cannot help feeling that she is disguising herself in some way. However, the real mystery is why she insisted on bringing the boy here with her. He calls her his 'boss', but I suspect a quite different relationship."

"He appears more than a little frightened," I said carefully.

"A brother, perhaps. Or a son . . . ." said Holmes, ignoring my interruption.

"My dear fellow, you remarked yourself on how young she looked!"

"And you, Watson, remarked on how the person who followed you to Baker Street seemed more of a boy than an adult! Women have ways and means of making themselves look younger than they are. But I must confess I incline more towards a fraternal rather than a maternal relationship."

"What about the abrupt summons to this hospital?"

"It *must* be her betrothed, and it would certainly help if we could find out what was behind any attack. I would also be happier if I could discover something more about him. Something perhaps which Miss Cameron might be reluctant to tell us. I don't recall his name, and I didn't have time to check my index."

I glanced out at the still falling snow and noted the few passers-by hurrying in search of shelter. The hospital seemed strangely quiet. There were no nurses moving sedately about, and no sign of a trolley or any patients. No doctor, complete with stethoscope, came out of any door to summon help, and even the clock seemed to have forgotten to tick.

"If those two were really to be married within a week, the Registrar General's Office might help," said I.

"And," replied Holmes enthusiastically, "if we knew the church where the banns should have been called over the last three weeks, that would also get us somewhere."

At that moment, a distraught Miss Cameron, accompanied by the youth I had become used to thinking of as "the boy", came towards us with a handkerchief pressed to her mouth and tears gushing from her eyes. "He is dead," she said simply, and fell to the floor in a dead faint.

Between us, Holmes and I managed to revive her and, along with Willie, we all travelled post-haste back to the Savoy Hotel, where Miss Cameron went straight to her bedroom and the boy sat looking at us from the depths of an armchair, the very picture of the most abject misery. He refused to provide any of the additional information about the girl's fiancé that we needed.

"I hate to say this," said Holmes, "but there is nothing we can do here at present, so I suggest we go back to Baker Street."

Grasping the boy by the shoulder, my friend looked most kindly and compassionately at him and said, "When your 'boss' is sufficiently recovered from such a dreadful shock, I want you to tell her that the doctor and I will be waiting, ready to help in any way we can, and also to do everything in our power to discover what and why this has happened. In the meantime, you must do all that *you* can to help her. But now it would be better for us to leave."

"Due to our somewhat precipitate exit," said I, as we walked towards Baker Street, "there is no way we can tell exactly how this man met his death. The attending physician indicated to me that he was found in an alley several blocks from the Strand. He had died from a blow to the head, but he had numerous other injuries. The initial theory is that he was injured in some sort of road accident."

Holmes snorted. "I think, old fellow, that there must be more to it than that. I wish that I had been allowed to examine the body."

"I'm sure that Miss Cameron would have allowed it, if she hadn't been incapacitated. And as the attending physician professed to have never heard of you . . . ." I added.

Holmes ignored my tweak. "The note on Block's person about getting in touch with Miss Cameron points to his possibly being aware of some imminent danger, perhaps of an entirely different sort."

"Such as?"

"While it is perhaps perfectly natural that he had his fiancée's name and address with him, the note stated that she should be told at once if anything happened to him. Why should he think that something might happen to him, unless he was aware that certain enemies were on his track?"

"Enemies, possibly. But of what kind, and for what purpose?"

"We heard her say that the man had led rather a 'rackety life', and was looking forward to 'settling down'. The question is, what kind of life, and where?"

"And for how long had his enemies have been on his track?" I said carefully.

Holmes bent down to re-tie a recalcitrant bootlace, at the same time as he stamped his feet to remove snow from his boots, just as he had done while we waited in the London Hospital.

"*If* there was anyone on his track," he said.

"My dear chap, there can surely be no doubt that he is dead," I said, striving to keep up with his long stride as we drew nearer to Baker Street.

But all he said was, "Did you see him at all, Watson?"

I had to admit that I hadn't, deeming it more tactful to allow Miss Cameron to go into the room accompanied only by a nurse and young Willie.

"Not one of us has seen him," said Holmes. "The supposed fiancé and the dead man could be two entirely different people."

By the time we reached our lodgings, the snow was falling even more steadily than before. Holmes took out his latch-key and, motioning me inside, followed almost immediately up to our sitting room. "Let us recap," he murmured, sinking into his armchair and ringing for Mrs. Hudson to ask her to bring in tea. "A young man is sent to find our lodgings so that he can deliver a message to me. That message is from a Scotswoman living in France. However, she is about to marry a man, presumably British, who has been receiving threatening messages, and who has now met with a fatal accident. Does anything odd strike you about all this?"

"Only the way the boy behaved," I said. "Following me around Oxford Street so that he could discover our whereabouts."

"Our client mentioned the Mona Lisa theft, if I remember correctly. Since our photograph was also in the French newspaper, it is highly likely our Baker Street address was there too. Truly the plot thickens! But now I have decided, however near we are to Christmas Day, that I must to go up to Scotland, and I imagine, Watson, that at this time of year you will be far too busy to accompany me." He paused for a moment outside his bedroom door while I looked back in amazement at this sudden and unexplained decision. He continued, "By the way, before I forget, congratulations on being elected to The Authors Club. You might try The Travellers Club next, since your family once lived in Ballarat."

"Holmes," I said with a laugh, "I'm a busy doctor with a sizeable number of patients. I write up your investigations for my own amusement, and for the edification of the public. As far as I am able, I help you in these investigations. Isn't that enough? Next you'll be suggesting I stand for Parliament!"

"Not a bad idea. We might get something done then."

"Nonsense. I'd fall asleep in the middle of the first debate."

"Very well, we'll say nothing more about it, if only to protect your undoubted modesty."

Although I was used to my friend's abrupt decisions, I was rather surprised at his going off without any preamble. However, as regards my medical duties, at this time of year my days were (like those of all my colleagues) full to bursting with patients suffering from colds, coughs, and other similar seasonal complaints. So I was obliged to let Holmes proceed alone in any way he pleased, trusting to him to tell me how I might help if the need arose.

Meanwhile Mrs. Hudson, tired of doing it herself on our behalf, had decided to employ a page-boy, Billy, to perform such tasks as answering the doorbell or bringing us our newspapers. She had even gone so far as to provide him with some sort of livery, something I knew she was well able to afford, since her terms had always been high – which was why I had come to live in Baker Street in the first place, to share the cost of the rent with Holmes, although we could now both quite easily pay our own way alone, as my resources had grown considerably since that time, and his services were in great demand in almost every part of the world.

A couple of days later, Holmes was back from Scotland, but all that he would say in answer to my enquiries was that his visit to the North had been most productive. The next morning, Billy ushered a young woman into our sitting room. She was dressed in the deepest black, and we recognised her at once as Constance Cameron.

"In spite of its being so near Christmas," said Miss Cameron, "I have left the Savoy Hotel, and taken lodgings in Camberwell for myself and Willie."

"A bit of a comedown for you," said Holmes brusquely, climbing to his feet. "But appropriate, since you have hardly a penny to your name! And don't think you can deceive me, coming here dressed in that way. You have no fiancé, and have had no fiancé, alive or dead. Before I left here for the Highlands – "

"The Highlands!" gasped our visitor.

" – I ascertained that no banns had been called and no arrangements for a wedding ceremony been made, here or anywhere. The note on the Block's body was to tell anyone who found it to inform you, so that you would know that particular deed (the first of what was planned to be many in my opinion) had been done, and you could then prepare yourself to take part in the next.

"Come now," he continued, "it's time to end this tarradiddle. You remember the note you showed us. It was far too much like an educated writer pretending, rather clumsily, to be an uneducated one."

I recalled the single 'l' in 'wel' and could only silently agree, surprised that the thought hadn't occurred to me before. But Holmes was well into his stride. "A report on that note arrived last night," he said. "Nothing like that has been found by the experts at Scotland Yard. I suggest you had Willie sit down with a newspaper and scissors putting the whole thing together, for reasons yet to be explained."

"That," I thought to myself, "might account for his being so scared. He was certainly more than uneasy about something."

To my great surprise, Miss Cameron suddenly burst into tears. All her self-possession seemed to leave her. She was no longer the sophisticated being we had first encountered.

"I have come here to ask you to rescue me," she wailed. "Me, and my poor young brother."

Holmes shot a triumphant look at me, recalling his speculations about her relationship to the youth. "Rescue you from what?" he asked coldly.

"I am wearing black because I was obliged to attend a funeral. The clothes are not even my own, and I had to pretend the funeral was that of my fiancé in order to keep up a dreadful deception and prevent any harm from coming to Willie or to me."

464

"In fact," said Holmes "the dead man, lonely and without friends, was someone you had been told to lure to the Savoy Hotel."

"But," I protested, "the boy said the man was 'the soul of honour'."

"So he may have been," said Holmes. "Miss Cameron here took care that she didn't compromise herself or him. Her brother was always in the room with her."

"And the idea was . . . ?"

"I'm sure you remember, Watson, that holiday we took in the Highlands last summer? The fishing was good, and I recall that you caught a trout which you threw back into the Loch. When I left you here alone and went back up to that small hotel where we stayed, it was to confirm my suspicions that Miss Cameron had worked there as a chambermaid. When we first met the other day, I was certain that I'd seen her before. In that hotel last year, I had caught a brief glimpse of somebody very like her when we were checking in.

"My questioning revealed that I was right. I found that she had recently attracted the attention of one of the recent guests there, who thought she might be of use to him, and they went off rather abruptly, taking her young brother (who worked as a boot-black at the hotel) with them. Her new friend had heard somehow of a man, Albert Block, a Midland's merchant who was exceedingly rich. Someone who, if the surroundings were right, would believe that Miss Cameron, too, was wealthy. After a plausible amount of time, and once the intimacy had proceeded beyond mere friendship, the woman would then hint at certain (though of course temporary) money troubles."

Here Holmes paused to re-light his pipe and got up to stand in front of the fire. "I found your friend, Elsie, still working as a maid at the hotel." Miss Cameron looked up sharply. "I convinced her to tell me of what happened before your departure. The rest was easy to piece together. You all ended up here in London. After you had been here for several days, it was time to put the plan in motion. Your supposed fiancé didn't go out to buy cigarettes, but to visit his bank," said Holmes, "whereupon he was then set upon and robbed by someone lying in wait for him. Something which, as I said earlier, was planned to be the first of many such episodes involving gentlemen who became susceptible to your undoubted charms."

"Steady the Buffs," I said hurriedly. "Robbed, but why killed? And presumably in broad daylight, since banks have restricted opening hours."

"I rather think the man who committed the murder panicked after leading his quarry to a quiet spot on some pretext or other. Either that, or his victim put up too spirited a resistance. It could be that he always intended to destroy the people he planned to rob, so that they couldn't set the police on him. However, Miss Cameron's swoon in the London Hospital was quite genuine. When faced with the stark reality that she had helped to kill a man, she suddenly realised the horror of what she had done, something which you saw caused her to pass out so dramatically.

"She evidently had no scruples about using her brother to tell us a pack of lies," continued Holmes, "as well as telling us a whole pack of lies herself. Neither did she hesitate when asking him to stick incriminating letters on a piece of paper. I am at a loss why she involved me in the first place, since there was evidently no mystery to find, and no villain she wished to unmask."

Miss Cameron continued to weep, offering no explanation. "Surely," I said, "it was to add verisimilitude to her supposed fiancé's disappearance?"

"Any run of the mill detective would have done for that. There was no need involve the best sleuth in the Metropolis."

I smiled inwardly at my friend's conceit, but was careful not to remark on it. Instead, I said to the woman sitting so near me, "It is scandalous, the extent to which you have involved an innocent boy in your schemes, and I'm not at all surprised that he showed fear in our rooms, as well as on one or two other occasions, such as when we came to the Savoy Hotel. As to employing Holmes in default of another detective, I suppose it was to bolster up the idea of how wealthy you were, although I have known occasions when he has foregone his fee if he thought the investigation interesting and important enough, or knew that his client couldn't afford it. The one occasion I can definitely recall – "

"Please don't mention the Duke of Holdernesse," interrupted Holmes wearily. "Why did you write the kidnap note and pull me into the investigation?"

"Because I *did* know who you were, Mr. Holmes. I was afraid to tell the truth, but I thought that if I created a mystery that was interesting enough, your involvement would spook Edward, and he would drop the matter. In the meantime, perhaps Willie and I could slip away."

"Edward being Edward Stokes, the instigator of this whole plot, and the man who killed Albert Block."

She nodded. "We cut out the letters to make the note. Then, Willie followed Dr. Watson until he was noticed, to make it seem more mysterious. It was all going according to plan, but then we learned that Albert – Mr. Block – had been killed. I knew then it was too late for us."

Holmes was silent for a moment. Then, "Have you seen Edward Stokes since the murder?"

She simply shook her head.

"It is time for you to get back to Camberwell, Miss Cameron, and that unfortunate brother of yours. I will keep you posted. Be careful, and stay out of sight. But on no account must you leave London. Where are you staying in Camberwell?"

She gave him an address, one that I knew to be a mean little place indeed. We saw her to the door, and as she left, Holmes gave whispered instructions to Billy. "He will notify one or two of the Irregulars in the vicinity to follow her, making sure that the address she gave is accurate, and to watch for her safety as well. And now," he added, "it is up to us the find the murderer,"

"And where do we start?"

"Good old Watson! We will begin with the London Clubs. The Turf, for example, since our quarry Stokes, it turns out, is the by-blow of a duke who apparently thinks of himself as one of those often called 'blue blood'."

"Disinherited blue blood, most likely!"

"The Turf," he continued as if I hadn't spoken, "has had its headquarters on the corner of Piccadilly and Clarges Street since 1875 and can be said to be a younger edition of White's. It is also notably well provided with dukes."

"My guess is that if he has gone to the bad, you won't find him there, even if his father is, or was, a duke. It would be much better if we had obtained a full description of him from Miss Cameron."

"My dear Watson! Surely you know me well enough by now to know that I have already acquired that information."

And so Holmes and I toured London together, spending the rest of that day going to both The Turf and a number of other likely places, asking innumerable questions. The one deciding result was a visit from a most unwelcome and dangerous intruder who must have heard of our activities through some sort of grapevine, whether criminal or otherwise.

That evening, Holmes had gone to bed early, whether to sleep or to refresh his catalogue of investigations, I had no means of knowing. I sat up, reading one of my favourite Clark Russell sea stories, keeping the "ungodly hours" I had mentioned to my friend at our first meeting so many years earlier. Just as I was dozing off, I was alarmed to see Holmes standing beside me in dressing gown, brandishing a poker. "There is a stranger in the building," he hissed, "though I cannot say exactly where."

Our landlady was away for the night visiting her friend, Mrs. Turner. I could imagine the two women sitting happily drinking tea together and exchanging stories about Holmes. I was glad that she was out of the house. I knew that Billy would be spending the evening with his young friends, up to all kinds of innocent japes and anticipating Christmas. That was all very well, but this being the Christmas season meant that everyone would be too occupied to suspect a crime taking place in our sitting room. Additionally, many of our neighbours were away visiting relatives and friends. I don't think I ever felt so lonely and unprotected in my life, not even on the battlefield.

I sprang up and prepared to encounter anything which might happen next. The wait was not long. The door of our sitting-room was flung open and a man I had never seen before stood with a gun trained straight at us. "This is what happens when people leave the house without locking the area door," he said with a leer, while I cursed inwardly at Mrs. Hudson's being so anxious to see Mrs. Turner that she forgot this elementary precaution.

Holmes, however, remained cool. "I believe I have the honour of addressing Edward Stokes, peripherally a member of – " here he named a famous Ducal House, " – whose men and women until now have been models of probity, giving much to their time to the advancement of our great nation."

"That's enough of your sneering and your 'until now' and 'models of probity'," said the man angrily. "Don't forget, I'm the fellow with the gun, and I'll make sure you and your friend here don't live to see another day."

"On the contrary," said Holmes with a sudden spring, bringing up his hand and giving the intruder a vicious knock on the wrist with the poker that he had kept hidden until now, so that the gun fell impotently to the floor.

I picked it up at once, pointed it straight at the intruder's head, and said, "Summon the police here as quickly as you can, Holmes, while I stand guard over this blackguard. Even if Inspectors Lestrade and Gregson are on leave and getting ready for the festivities, there will be others holding the fort."

Later (over a breakfast which we enjoyed to the fullest after the night's adventure,) Holmes said, "It is a very disheartening thing when the events we have been through happen at this special time of goodwill to all men. However, I have persuaded Miss Cameron to return to Scotland directly after Christmas and take up a post with the local Laird who, you may remember, was so accommodating when letting us fish on his land. She will be his wife's help, and the boy will be set to learn gardening, eventually taking over from the present man who is due to retire sometime in the next couple of years. There is, I believe, a young

Factor who is decidedly sweet on her and who has often made an excuse to come into that small hotel so that he could see and sometimes speak to her. She has learned her lesson and they will, I am sure, eventually marry and settle down. There will be no more Marquise de Brinvilliers, Madame de Pompadour, or any Lucretia Borgias."

"I wouldn't bet on it," I said, busy cutting into my bacon and eggs. A certain thought had occurred to me concerning Holmes's remark to Miss Cameron regarding an educated writer pretending to be an uneducated one. "Surely . . . ." I said.

Holmes was busy buttering a slice of toast. He looked up and replied slowly, "Contrary to her lowly position as a chambermaid, she had, as you saw for yourself, an aristocratic bearing. She spoke well, as do most Scots, and has had, I am sure, at least the rudiments of a good education."

"Probably as the result of an earlier post as a gentlewoman's companion." I said.

But Holmes was busy opening his mail. "A letter from brother Mycroft," he cried, "inviting us to spend Christmas with him at his Club. So there will be partridge and fine wine, convivial conversation in the Stranger's Room, and a chance to tell him all about our latest adventure!"

"And what a lucky escape we both had from death," I remarked, pouring out a second cup of coffee for myself.

The Adventure of the Handsome Ogre
by Matthew J. Elliott

While I have long been of the opinion that this particular incident occurred late in 1901, I see from my records that it was, in fact, in the December of 1902 that Sherlock Holmes received a telegram summoning us to the chambers of the legal firm of Austin, Freeman, and Redfern. My friend was far from enthusiastic, having only recently accepted a case from Scotland, where Lord Drumforth had somehow managed to misplace the valuable Star of Rhodesia. However, the message assured us that the present matter was an urgent one, and so, somewhat reluctantly, we ventured out.

Holmes refused to be drawn into speculation as to what might await us at Temple Gardens, and thus our cab drive was spent in uncompanionable silence, which at least enabled me to give some thought to the forthcoming festivities at Sir Boris Wyngarde's home, to which we had both been invited. Holmes had churlishly thrown his own invitation into the fire, and I wondered if he was in danger of taking on the characteristics of the famous misanthrope Ebeneezer Scrooge, but he showed some sign of cheer upon sighting the familiar bony frame of Inspector Alec MacDonald, awaiting us in the doorway.

"I'm aware that Cornelius Redfern summoned you, of course, gentlemen," said the Scotsman, as he attempted to light his pipe in a bitterly cold wind. "Believe me, I'm always glad of your assistance, but honestly, I'm not sure that there's much for either of you to do."

"Whyso, Mr. Mac?" Holmes enquired.

"Simply because it shouldn't be too difficult to lay our hands on the fellow who did this."

This was an assurance we had both heard from police officers on many previous occasions, and even though it came from the lips of one of the capital's most competent police agents, I found it difficult to conceal a grin.

"Surely it's fairly easy for a criminal to disappear among this city's teeming millions," I suggested.

"Not *this* criminal, Doctor. All three witnesses are agreed, he was some sort of beast – an ogre, Miss Arundell called him."

In my many years of association with Sherlock Holmes, I could not ever recall hearing the term "ogre" before, but it was as music to the ears of my colleague.

"Perhaps this case will be worthy of my attention after all," he murmured. "A fitting Christmas gift from the Yard to its most reliable helpmate."

"The body's upstairs, sir," MacDonald told us, "in the anteroom."

In all my musings as to the nature of our enquiry, I had not considered that it might involve a murder – Redfern's telegram had certainly not indicated anything of that sort. I asked the inspector whose body we would be examining, and was informed that the unfortunate fellow was Mr. Redfern's junior, a young gentleman by the name of Wellesley Cobb.

At the head of the stairs we found our way into the plain anteroom, blocked by a tall bluff fellow with a broad, clean-shaven face.

"Inspector, this is extremely inconvenient," he complained, and his unexpectedly high-pitched voice grated on my ear.

"Inconvenient for the dead man as much as anyone, Mr. Ratchett," MacDonald replied, unruffled.

"I'm not concerned for myself so much as for my cousin," Ratchett went on, although I sensed that it was indeed his own inconvenience that he was concerned about.

"You can tell the young lady that the body will be removed from the premises as soon as Mr. Sherlock Holmes here has had a look at it."

Moon-eyed with astonishment, Ratchett examined both of us before settling his gaze upon my companion. Holmes gave a slight, stiff bow.

"Your servant, sir."

Emitting a series of incomplete, partially comprehensible exculpations, Ratchett backed away, eventually disappearing into a room to the right, which I imagined contained the office of the gentleman who had summoned us, Mr. Cornelius Redfern. I was struck by Ratchett's unusual gait as he backed away, and wondered aloud whether the gentleman, while a little young for the condition, might not be suffering from a touch of gout.

With his absence, my attention shifted to the corpse of Wellesley Cobb, splayed out before us on the rug. A young man, not quite thirty the inspector told us, but his chubby features giving the impression that he was younger still. His arms were stretched out as though, in his final moments of life, he had been desperately attempting to reach something above or behind him. My first thought was strangulation, but when I loosened Cobb's collar, I saw no indications of violence inflicted upon his throat.

"He was killed by the robber before he entered Redfern's office,"

471

MacDonald observed. "Probably didn't want him summoning the police. The only thing that's unclear to me is just *how* he died. He wasn't shot, or stabbed. He doesn't appear to have been struck on the head."

"Injection, perhaps?" I mused, though an examination of Cobb's exposed skin did not reveal evidence of any punctures, simply a silvery mark on his wrist.

"You have been very thorough, Inspector," said Holmes. "But if you don't mind me saying so, not quite thorough enough. Did you, for example, take a good look at his nose?"

MacDonald and I both frowned at this suggestion. Holmes did not elaborate, but simply handed me his magnifying glass. How he had seen them from such a distance I cannot say, but with the aid of the lens the presence of tiny fibres inside each nostril became clear.

"What does it signify?" MacDonald asked, when I had related my discovery.

"It signifies that the intruder smothered Cobb," Holmes explained, "probably with his cap, if he wore one."

"All three witnesses say he did."

Holmes strode up and down as he spoke, re-enacting the actions of Cobbs' killer, I imagined.

"He came in, found Mr. Cobb in the anteroom. The briefest of struggles ensued – as you see from his frame, Cobb was far from athletic. I wonder if the intruder even meant to kill him, or simply to render him unconscious. Mr. Mac, I take it you noticed the ginger hairs beneath the victim's fingernails?"

The Scot nodded. "I left them there for you to see, Mr. Holmes."

"Really, Inspector, the Scottish variety of policeman is far more cooperative than our home-grown variety. Well, you're quite welcome to give Mr. Wellesley Cobb the attention he deserves."

I sighed loudly. "A death at any time is tragic, but right on top of Christmas, it seems particularly sad," I observed.

"Especially as he had just become a father," Holmes added.

The inspector started. "That's what Mr. Redfern says, sir, but how on Earth did you know?"

"Note the cigar in his breast-pocket. And yet I see no case or any other smoking paraphernalia – it was clearly acquired for a special occasion."

"I wish I could applaud your deduction, Holmes," I told him.

"It's not always gratifying to be correct. Now, if the inspector has no further need of us, we shall be in Mr. Redfern's office."

We entered as Ratchett was again protesting his enforced

confinement. He twisted his body awkwardly to acknowledge us as we entered, as though he feared to move his legs.

"Our apologies, Mr. Ratchett," said Holmes. "Please continue."

"Oh, I was just remarking that I was becoming a little restless," he explained, before introducing us to his cousin, Helen Arundell, a young woman with a clear-cut, sensitive face and an air of self-assurance I might have described as noble.

"Gentlemen, I've read a good deal about you, of course," she said, betraying none of the alarm exhibited by her relative, or even by our client, Cornelius Redfern, a bow-backed gentleman of sixty or so, with an impressive and well-groomed moustache. On the desk before him lay a large, empty wooden box. Similarly empty was the heavy metal safe which stood ajar in one corner of the office. I observed little festive ornamentation, and perhaps it was just as well, considering the grim sight that had greeted us upon our arrival.

"I have absolute confidence in the ability of Scotland Yard, Mr. Holmes," Redfern began, "but I have asked you here to recover the items stolen by this – this *thing*."

"I believe Miss Arundell used the term 'ogre'," I said.

"And an ogre he was, Dr. Watson," she replied. "I've never seen such a mis-shapen face."

I wondered whether she might be referring to an injury or a physical deformity, but realising that the young woman was undoubtedly unqualified to make such a distinction, I decided against asking her that particular question.

"What concerns us is the recovery of Miss Arundell's property," Redfern said. "Five thousand pounds in golden sovereigns."

"This was not, I take it, a normal legal transaction," Holmes remarked. "A small fortune in gold sovereigns is certainly a rather unconventional Christmas gift."

"An inheritance, Mr. Holmes," Miss Arundell explained. "*My* inheritance. You have perhaps heard of Major Harold Beaton?"

I could not speak for Holmes, but I was certainly familiar with the name of one of the heroes of the Siege of Ladysmith. Ratchett interrupted her to state that they were his only surviving relatives.

"And he left the coins to you both?" I asked.

"To Helen," Ratchett said, with ill-concealed irritation. "I inherit his country home – Barwick Hall. Rather a dilapidated old place – it might fall down before I get a chance to tear it down. We are here for the official reading of the will, and for Miss Arundell to take delivery of the coins stored in Mr. Redfern's safe. Hence my presence – to carry the box of coins. Well, drag it, anyway. Fearfully heavy thing."

473

"And empty now, as is Mr. Redfern's safe," Holmes noted.

"The brute-man wasn't too choosy about what he took," said Redfern, his moustache twitching with annoyance. "The contents of my safe, *and* the coins, all went into his Gladstone bag."

I was growing ever more curious about this intruder, whom the young lady referred to as an ogre, while her solicitor called him a brute. I could not help but picture the illustrations I had seen of the unfortunate named Merrick.

Holmes asked if the thief might not have been sporting some sort of gutta-percha mask.

"I think we would all have spotted a mask, Mr. Holmes," Miss Arundell replied. "I tell you the robber was some sort of hideous thing – a ginger-haired ogre! He burst into the room, waving a gun about, demanding that we all raise our hands, as though we were characters in a melodrama. And the way he spoke – as though he hardly knew how to move his own mouth. Even the way he stood seemed out-of-the-ordinary."

Ratchett gave his cousin a condescending pat on the shoulder. "Helen, my dear, I don't think these gentlemen are interested in 'feminine intuition'."

"It wasn't feminine intuition, Gilbert, it was observation."

Knowing that to be one of the few things with which Holmes had any patience, I saw that the lovely young woman had his complete attention. He encouraged her to proceed with her recollections.

"Well, he seemed to hold his right shoulder higher than the other, perhaps another symptom of his deformity."

"And the hand in which he held the gun?" Holmes asked.

"The right. And there was one other thing I noticed, though I couldn't say if it is of any significance whatever, but after he fled, I watched him from the window. I saw him cross the road, and disappear round the corner. But just before he crossed, he did a rather odd thing. He looked in the wrong direction."

This did indeed seem rather odd, but I could not see that it could be of any importance either. Holmes, however, found her remark of considerable interest.

"Miss Arundell," he said, taking her hand as though about to bid her farewell, "were it not for the fact that I am obligated to work with Watson here, I would consider you an excellent help-mate. I have no doubt we will be able to restore your gold sovereigns to you before the Christmas festivities are over."

The head of Alec MacDonald appeared at the door, and he informed us that the body of the unfortunate Mr. Wellesley Cobb had now been removed.

"Thank heavens!" Ratchett exclaimed. "I must say, this has been quite an ordeal! Come along, Helen."

I have previously mentioned the gentleman's unusual gait which caught my attention as we conversed in the anteroom. Now, as he made his way rapidly to the door, I was aware of a peculiar jangling noise. Holmes stretched out a long, thin arm to bar Ratchett's way.

"Just a moment, sir," he said. "I can't help but notice that there seems to be something amiss with your trousers."

Ratchett was aghast. "Really, gentlemen! If you're simply going to resort to personal abuse, I must insist upon leaving!"

Holmes withdrew his arm, but before anyone had a chance to move, he dropped down to his knees and withdrew a gold sovereign from the turn-ups of Ratchett's trousers. "And there are several more in here to match it."

"Good Lord!" Ratchett cried, in the most annoyingly false display of astonishment I have witnessed. "How – however did they get in there?"

"However indeed?" Helen Arundell wondered, and I knew from her withering tone that she was in no doubt that her cousin had seen them fall from the thief's Gladstone bag and picked them up before anyone else in the office had noticed.

In spite of the fact that he had yet to be accused of anything, the bounder insisted on protesting his innocence. "It's clear to the meanest intelligence what must have happened! Some of the coins must have missed the bag as that creature was attempting to fill it, and – and – bounced into my turn-ups. Without me noticing."

"I suppose it's possible, if not exactly probable," observed the lawyer.

"The very maxim by which I live, Mr. Redfern," said Holmes.

Feebly, and while attempting pathetically to smile, Ratchett restored the coins to his unamused relation. "Thank-you, dear cousin," she said through pursed lips. "I think it would be for the best if we took separate cabs. Gentlemen, the compliments of the season to you."

"And to you also, Miss Arundell," I responded.

With Ratchett begging for a few shillings for the fare, the two departed. Holmes and I shared a wry grin. Would that every element of this case could be resolved so amusingly.

Redfern thrust his thumbs into the pockets of this waistcoat, a gesture clearly meant to indicate that he wished to expound.

"Gentlemen, you would be justified in imagining that the theft of my client's property and the murder of poor Cobb would be sufficient cause for concern, and yet I must own that there is something else troubling me, a personal issue. You see, this terrible beast didn't just help himself to Miss Arundell's gold sovereigns. You observe that the door to my safe is open? He cleaned it out. A few papers of negligible value . . . and a parcel."

Holmes's eyes brightened with barely-contained excitement. "I wish to be able to assist you, sir, but I can hardly do so unless you are completely forthcoming."

"It was a Christmas gift. Intended for a married lady whose name, I'm sure you would understand, I would prefer not to mention. The package in question contained a cameo of the lady's likeness. If the thief should, by some remote chance, identify her, then not only might I become a target for blackmail, but there is also the matter of how the woman's husband might react. I freely confess that I am not a brave man when it comes to physical disputes."

I have made no secret of my own colourful romantic history, but not once have I ever become entangled with a married woman, and it troubled me that in assisting Redfern, we might be giving a man license to conduct an illicit affair. I expressed my concerns to him.

"Oh, you need have no fear over that, Dr. Watson," the lawyer replied. "You see, after the theft, I came to realize – well, what a silly old fool I'd been, to be flattered by a pretty young female. I thought I was immune to such things. But if you are able to put the cameo back in my hands, I'll gladly smash it into a thousand pieces and thank my good fortune."

"*And* the efforts of a consulting detective," Holmes pointed out. "I can certainly lay my hand upon the man who took it, and do so without the knowledge of the police. I hold Inspector MacDonald in the highest esteem, but he's on the wrong track entirely if he expects to find the thief based entirely upon his singular appearance. Mr. Redfern, it is very likely that you will hear something from us by end of day."

"Thank-you, Mr Holmes. I should very much like to spend Christmas Day free of all anxieties. Save, of course, for my grief at the loss of my junior."

I had expected Holmes to instruct the cab we took from Redfern's office to return us to Baker Street, but instead he directed the driver to my club, of which Holmes was not a member and had hitherto refused to attend in the role of guest.

"We progress, Watson," he announced.

It was my considered belief, his promises to Cornelius Redfern notwithstanding, that we were as much in the dark as ever. I said as much to Holmes.

"Not while the one person who can shed light on the mystery sits in this cab. No, Watson, I do not mean myself. Rather, I think it exceedingly likely that *you* might shed some light on the mystery."

I guffawed. "You'll forgive my bluntness, old chap, but I cannot possibly imagine how."

"Nevertheless, it's clear to me that the man who stole Miss Arundell's sovereigns and Mr. Redfern's cameo is a medical man. And, yes, I am well aware that there must be several hundreds in this great city, but the gentleman we seek is quite distinguished, I believe."

"If you mean distinguished by his horrific appearance," I said, "then I quite agree, but I cannot think of anyone within our profession who matches that description."

"Oh, the fellow's features are entirely irrelevant. And while his possession of a Gladstone bag is suggestive, it is by no means my sole means of determining the man's vocation. You remember MacDonald remarked upon the silvery stain on the wrist of the unfortunate Mr. Wellesley Cobb?"

Now that Holmes had drawn my attention to it, the inference seemed plain. "Silver nitrate. The killer was taking his pulse."

"As I suggested, Watson, it was never his intention to murder Cobb. And Miss Arundell observed his peculiar stance – one shoulder higher than the other. It's a common condition in those who teach; it comes from reaching up to write upon a blackboard. So our murderous thief is not simply a doctor, but one sufficiently skilled to be in a position to pass that knowledge onto others. I would add that he is a man of exceptional physical strength – five thousand pounds in gold sovereigns is, as Mr. Ratchett pointed out, rather heavy. And there is one final point – when he crossed the road as he fled, he looked in the wrong direction. Now why should he do that? Because he was expecting the traffic to be coming the other way. Ergo, a foreign doctor who teaches. Now, should we be able to locate an individual who meets those exact criteria?"

"I can think of someone instantly," I told him, "Ronald Hatton. He's an American – well, born in this country, but raised in America. He's recently begun teaching physiology at the University of London. But this won't do at all, Holmes."

Holmes said that he was inclined to agree.

"Cobb tore several hairs from his attacker's head did he not? Ginger hairs. Well, Hatton's hair is blonde."

My colleague nodded. "I observed traces of glue on the ends of the strands. He wore a wig for his criminal endeavours."

"Even so, Hatton can't be the ogre. His good looks are much

remarked upon."

Holmes was not to be put off by this, and enquired whether there might be a record of his address at the Hippocratic Club, which – as the name suggests – takes its membership almost exclusively from the medical profession. I said that I thought it exceedingly likely.

"Then you now understand my directions to our driver."

It is probably true to say that, had he not been deemed a foreigner by the club's secretary, obtaining Hatton's address might have been a more torturous affair. As it turned out, I experienced no objection, even receiving the felicitations of the season as I departed, and within the hour, we found ourselves on Elmhurst Avenue, discussing the difficulties that still remained in this case, specifically how a handsome man like Ronald Hatton could have appeared to three people as a hideous beast. Believing him capable of some sort of transformation in the manner of Stevenson's Henry Jekyll was a rather fantastical notion.

Hatton's house, Number 37, had already caught my attention before we had even ascertained that it was indeed the correct address. It had begun to snow quite heavily half-an-hour before, but I could see that condensation had collected on the windows, suggesting that the temperature inside must be ridiculously high, even to combat the cold without.

"Is Hatton maintaining a Turkish bath?" I wondered aloud.

"I believe this might explain the one element of this case that still puzzles you, Watson," Holmes replied, opening the gate.

I made my way to the window and attempted to see what might be occurring inside. Through the beads of liquid running down the glass, I could make out a desk, on which sat a large bowl of steaming liquid – clearly the source of condensation, then – and an open Gladstone bag. My heart sank at the sight of it, and I grew positively alarmed upon realising that lying face down upon the floor before the desk was not, as I had first imagined, a rug fashioned from the skin of some wild animal, but the prone figure of Ronald Hatton. I reported to Holmes what I had seen. I have rarely managed to surprise my friend, and I take no satisfaction in this being one such moment. This was clearly not what he had expected to discover. I prepared to break down the door by putting my shoulder to it, but discovered it instead to be slightly ajar. Holmes indicated the path, and I observed a set of small footsteps in the snow. Someone had been here very recently.

"Proceed with caution, Doctor," Holmes advised as we stepped inside..

I withdrew my service revolver from my pocket, and we entered the room in which Hatton's body lay. He did not move when I called out his name, and a brief examination confirmed that he was, indeed, dead. As with the unfortunate Wellesley Cobb, I detected no signs of injury, and no indication of fibres within his nostrils.

Holmes picked glass of brandy from Hatton's desk and handed it to me. "Sniff, but for heaven's sake, don't taste!"

My friend's senses are considerably more acute than my own, but I could just make out the faint odour of wood alcohol. One good gulp would result in either blindness or death. In the case of Ronald Hatton, it had been the latter. The day was beginning to take on the quality of a nightmare.

Holmes was more displeased with his failure to foresee Hatton's death than his inability to prevent it. "Of course, that man was no career criminal," he said. "He must have been acting under someone else's instructions. Whoever they were, they were not in the least interested in the gold sovereigns." He picked a handful of coins from the Gladstone bag and allowed them to tumble through his fingers. They were of less moment to him also than the present puzzle.

"Holmes," I protested, "in spite of your deductions, in spite of the money, I just don't see how Ronald Hatton could have been the hideous intruder Redfern and his clients described."

"Paraffin, Watson," he responded, by way of explanation. "Heated and injected into the face, it can alter the contours, turning well-regarded features into those of an abomination. One has to admire the ingenuity, if not the use to which it was put."

I looked once again at Hatton. He appeared to me the same as ever.

"I should add that when subjected to hot water and steam, the paraffin oozes from the pores. Hence the state of the windows. I have heard of something similar being done in America, but – "

His attention was diverted by the creak of a floorboard. The sound had not been made by Holmes or myself, and most certainly not by Hatton. There was, therefore, a fourth person in the house. I drew my revolver, and instructed the intruder to make himself known to us.

"You wouldn't shoot a lady, would you, Dr. Watson?" There appeared in the doorway a plump, diminutive woman of thoroughly unappealing aspect, her hands raised in the air. I sensed not fear in her tone, but rather mockery.

"If it should turn out that you provided Dr. Hatton with this glass, my friend may not have to shoot," Holmes informed her. "A noose around your neck will do the job just as well."

She regarded the body on the floor before her. "Poor Ronald didn't know his own strength. Of course, I had to kill him for that."

I was frankly startled by the lady's brazen attitude and her willingness to admit responsibility for the terrible crime.

"I recognise you from the illustrated crime news," she went on. "You're Mr. Know-It-All Sherlock Holmes. But you don't know it all this time."

"The man responsible for killing Wellesley Cobb lies here," I pointed out, "and you have just confessed to the murder of this man. I respectfully suggest that you might supply everything that is presently unknown."

"Not I, sir. My name is Mrs. Eliza Bradley, and I am simply what you might term a 'facilitator'. But I know that you have some sway with the police, sir. If you were to speak to them on my behalf, I'm certain I can lead you to the gentleman with more sins to his name than I can count."

I have never before visited the sort of establishment run by Eliza Bradley, but I was well aware that, during my time in the army, many of my fellow officers frequented similar houses in search of entertainment while on leave. Often, they returned with more than they bargained for, despite my insistence that their free time could be spent more profitably with either a hand of cards or an improving book.

The lady led us to a cramped, bare room with a large window upon one wall, displaying the interior of the room beside it, decorated in the most appalling taste, and presumably intended to reflect someone's notion of what a maharajah's palace might look like. As such, no concessions to Christmas were on display. There was little light to see by, save for what emanated from that other room, in which Mrs. Bradley now sat upon a divan, sipping tea from a delicate embroidered cup. Holmes drew my attention to four regularly spaced gaps in the dust at our feet.

"A camera has been placed here until very recently, in order to photograph the goings-on in the next room. Evidently, some sort of trickery is involved here: a mirror on one side, and plain glass on this. It's still possible that out voices may be heard, so try to remain as quiet as possible, Watson."

I did as I was instructed, hoping silently that we would not be forced to wait for very much longer. As it turned out, less than five minutes passed before an attractive young lady entered Mrs. Bradley's room and informed her that she had a visitor.

"Show the gentlemen in, please, Gwendolyn."

Despite the fact that, during a conversation with Mrs. Bradley on the journey from Scotland Yard to her place of business, I had been apprised

480

of what had occurred, I was still surprised to see Mr. Cornelius Redfern, the solicitor, enter the room.

He refused to sit, and pooh-poohed the notion of a cup of tea.

"I received your letter, Mrs. Bradley," he said, "though I cannot imagine what business you imagine you and I might have. I am aware of the nature of this house, and I wish you to know I find it quite disgusting. How you and your clientèle have avoided imprisonment is beyond me."

Mrs. Bradley set down her cup. "Many gentlemen come here, to indulge their . . . tendencies. And sometimes when they're here, they talk. They're not always careful what they say around my employees. I'm very generous to those employees who bring me any information that might make me some money. So when a visitor mentions a London solicitor who regularly deals in stolen goods, and who happens to have one item of particular value in his safe at the moment, of course I'm thinking of the best way to extract it. Not that I would ever do it myself."

Redfern smiled, but it was evident from his tone that he was far from amused. "Naturally," he said. "That would be quite unladylike."

"Couldn't have put it better myself, sir. But another of my regulars happens to be a doctor – an American, clever sort, important. Open to persuasion. And he says that yes, on reflection, there is a way he could do the job and no-one would ever know it was him. He even plans to steal a few other items to make it look like an unplanned robbery. But then he goes and kills someone, this Wellesley Cobb. My commiserations, Mr. Redfern, I hope he wasn't a close friend."

"Simply an employee, but in a very different line of work from your own staff."

Mrs. Bradley's smile was, unlike that of her guest, quite genuine. "I wonder if he knew about your little secrets, sir. I mean, the number of valuable items that pass from one person to another in your offices! I've never heard the like!"

Redfern turned as though to leave. "I don't know what you're talking about. And our conversation is concluded. Good day."

From behind a cushion, Mrs. Bradley produced a cameo, the very one Redfern had earlier described to us. "You won't want this, then. Don't recognize the lady, don't suppose she even exists. But the funny thing is . . . when I shake it, it rattles, as though there's something inside it. Now, I wouldn't know what to do with something like this, but I expect you have someone waiting for it already. I'm not greedy woman, Mr. Redfern – a quarter of what you expect to make will do me very nicely. I need to buy presents for my girls, you see."

Redfern was evidently prepared for the demand, for he produced a sheaf of notes from his pocket, and tossed them into Mrs. Bradley's lap, snatching the cameo from her grasp as she regarded the money.

"Now, Watson!" hissed Holmes. Without waiting for me, he was through the door of our hidey-hole. I followed, and saw that he had already positioned himself outside Mrs. Bradley's room. The door opened slightly, and I heard Redfern say, "We shall not meet again, madam."

The door opened fully, and the solicitor barged into my friend. The look upon his face was a mixture of surprise and horror. "Holmes!" he cried.

"A very good evening to you, Mr. Redfern," my friend replied. "May I ask what you have there?"

"My – ? It's nothing! Nothing at all!"

Holmes plucked the cameo from Redfern's hand. "It appears to be the stolen cameo. Watson! And it rattles. How peculiar."

"It seems there's something inside, Holmes," I suggested, mischievously. "Perhaps if you were to give it a twist . . . ."

Ignoring Redfern's protestations, Holmes did as I suggested. The cameo split in two, revealing that it was nothing more than an ornate container. And within, a beautifully-cut jewel that could hardly be unfamiliar to anyone with a daily newspaper within arm's reach – the missing Star of Rhodesia.

"Mr. Redfern, how do you account for this?" asked Holmes.

"This cameo is . . . it's not the one I lost," he replied, entirely unconvincingly. "This lady here asked me to look after it for her."

"I suspect that is not entirely true, is it? Everything you have said in this room has been overheard. Inspector MacDonald is awaiting your pleasure outside. Perhaps by the time you gentlemen have been reintroduced, you will have devised a more convincing explanation. My apologies, sir; it seems that your Christmas Day will not be free from all anxieties."

It seems that the inspector's assurance that, in return for assisting in the capture of Cornelius Redfern, Mrs. Bradley would spend the rest of her days behind bars was not a particularly compelling bargain. She evaded capture, fleeing through a hidden exit in her establishment, doubtless used by her most prominent clients. When last heard of, she had resumed her unwholesome activities in Marseilles. It would seem that both Scotland Yard and Mr. Sherlock Holmes are content that she should remain there.

The Adventure of the
Improbable Intruder
by Peter K. Andersson

"Although I am a man of reason, I cannot conceive of any theory that would account for the appearance of the strange little man in Dr. Whittington's library, and the curious turn of events that followed."

Holmes and I leaned forward to make sure we would not miss a word of our visitor's narrative. He was a tall and thin man in his late thirties, sporting a pince-nez and a pencil moustache. His bony hands played nervously with the lower buttons on his waistcoat as he laid his case before us.

"My name is Christopher Petty, and I have been engaged as Dr. Whittington's private secretary for five years. Dr. Whittington is an unsociable and reclusive gentleman who has enjoyed a long and distinguished career as an anthropologist, but who has chosen to spend his retirement away from the public gaze, allowing him to pursue his research according to his own instincts and inclinations. While I have been in his employ, we have together embarked on a highly innovative and original research into the medicinal qualities of certain types of weed native to the Home Counties of England, which Dr. Whittington believes to have played a formative role in the folklore and customs of that region. The work has been quite consuming, forcing us both to neglect our social lives, but earlier this year we made a breakthrough which meant that we found a reason to decelerate the intensity of our work. Dr. Whittington is a widower and has a grown-up daughter who is married and lives in India, so his social life is understandably limited, whereas I am engaged to be married with my childhood sweetheart, Dorothy, in the spring.

"To celebrate our successes, Dr. Whittington kindly invited us both to spend Christmas with him at Cumbersome House, his estate in Buckinghamshire, together with a few of his old colleagues and some local neighbours. The festivities were truly enjoyable, and I was delighted to see Dorothy befriending my noble employer. Dorothy and I were spending a few nights at the house, and as the guests of the Christmas dinner withdrew to their nearby homes, the only people who were left in the house, apart from the servants, were Dorothy and me, Dr. Whittington, and an old collaborator from his days at Oxford, Professor Seemly. Seemly is a frivolous and kindhearted gentleman, but he is quite old – I have not found out quite how old he is – and as a result somewhat forgetful, and suffering of an extreme crookedness in his back. I consider him an eccentric, which is expressed above all in his singular partiality to hazelnuts, a bowl of which he requires each night before going to bed. As we all retired for the night to our respective quarters, the large house was enshrouded in a drowsy slumber, and all was silence and darkness as the snow covered the valley.

"It was nearly two o'clock when I relit my bedside lamp and admitted to myself that I could not sleep. I suffer intermittently from violent bouts of insomnia, and when I am under its spell, there is nothing for it but to rise from the bed and find something suitable to read. Said and done, I impaled the bedroom slippers with my frozen feet and descended the staircase en route to the library. The library of Cumbersome House is vast and ancient, containing a complete collection dating back to the seventeenth century. Over the years, it has been added to by the various owners of the house, however, and I knew it to contain a number of quite current travelogues that I was fond of skimming through. However, stepping across the threshold, I immediately sensed that something was wrong. The room is a long and narrow gallery with windows on one side, and I could see in the moonlight that was filtered through the curtains a small figure moving in the shadows at the far side of the room. I hurried across to turn up the gas, and as I did so, I was perplexed to see the smallest person I have ever encountered, standing upright on top of the large table in the middle of the room. He could not have been more than a foot high, but his body was quite proportionate. He was dressed in a long grey robe and a curious headdress, and when the light was turned on, he turned to me with a vicious stare, made a sound like a snake hissing, and then quickly went down on all fours and scurried across the table, onto the floor, and out through a back-door, faster than a bolt of lightning.

"For a brief moment, I was completely paralysed, but after a few seconds, I ran after him to the door where he had disappeared. I then found the door to be bolted, and the only means of exit was a hole in the wainscoting beside it, where he must have made his escape. I returned to my bedroom, trying to banish the thought of having witnessed something supernatural from my head, but now of course sleep was even more difficult to find, and I laid awake in my bed until the first stream of light came in through my bedroom window, whereupon I ran to Dr. Whittington's bedroom and knocked on his door. Fortunately, he was already awake, and I explained to him my experience as clearly and as soberly as I could. His reaction was naturally one of disbelief, but I saw in his face that he made an effort to take me seriously. He decided that

484

we should make a complete search of the house for any traces of the character I had seen. My next instinct was to go and make sure that Dorothy was unharmed, and I was relieved to find that she had slept peacefully the entire night, as had our other guest, Professor Seemly.

"Our subsequent search produced no results, and as we all sat down to breakfast, I told the others my story again. We began to speculate how we might explain the incident, but no theory managed to encompass all of its strange aspects, until Dr. Whittington started to speak of the local traditions concerning brownies and elves.

"'The old people of the area believe that every house is home to a brownie, a small fairy creature who lives under the hearth and helps out with the chores of the house. He is small of stature, usually dressed in grey, and has quite a temper. If you enrage him or fail to bring little gifts of food to him every now and then, he will punish you. This is a tradition that can be found among the simple people of many different nations, sometimes associating the brownie with elves and fairies, and, of course, leprechauns, all of which are mythical beings of short stature.'

"'Oh, I have heard of this,' replied Dorothy. 'Are they not supposed to come out on Christmas night?'

"Dr. Whittington smiled amiably. 'According to some traditions, yes, but one must not confuse the ancient traditions of brownies and elves with the quite recent fictions that mix elves with Father Christmas.'

"'As in that American poem,' I retorted. '"The Night Before Christmas". Father Christmas there is described, if memory serves, as "a jolly old elf".

"Dorothy giggled. 'Was that who you saw, Christopher? Was it Father Christmas?'

"'Now, don't make fun of Mr. Petty,' mumbled Professor Seemly. 'I remember seeing fairies and all manner of things when I was a boy. I grew up in the country, you see, and if you live long enough in the country, sooner or later you will see one of them, in a barn or a meadow. Quite funny little things they are, too. Nothing to be afraid of. Now, where are my nuts?'

"As you might understand, I did not know quite what to think when faced with these eventualities. Had I been a witness of something supernatural? Was this an event that would prove to be epoch-making, constituting the first encounter with a brownie by a man of science? Or had my time in that part of the country caused me to fall under the same spell as the natives that made them believe in old superstitions? The whole matter made me exceedingly pensive, and pondering over it in the following days, I started to become used to the idea that I had actually seen a fairy. I have now practically accepted that these beings are among us, and I find the thought a gratifying one. The thought of them, even when unseen, will add a charm to every brook and valley and give romantic interest to every country walk. The recognition of their existence will jolt the material twentieth-century mind out of its heavy ruts in the mud, and will make it admit that there is a glamour and a mystery to life. However, there is still in my mind a kernel of doubt, and the consistently sceptical attitude of my mentor, Dr. Whittington, has induced me to consult you, only to hear your opinion on the matter."

Mr. Petty leaned back in his chair and crossed his legs, looking at the two of us with an expectant gaze. I glanced at Holmes, almost fearing that he would bolt from his chair and turn the poor man into the street. His face did betray incredulity, no doubt, but he evidently held back his innermost thoughts.

"Watson," he said, "will you consult the good old index and see what we have on the matter of fairies and brownies?"

I made my way to the shelf and promptly extracted the correct volumes. Holmes received them and placed them in his lap.

"Now then, let us see. Hmm! This is a motley assortment of incidences if ever there was one. 'The Dun Cow of Dunsmore', 'the Vicious Black Mask of the Simpsons', 'the Cotswolds werewolf' . . . Every one of these occurrences proved in the end to have quite natural explanations, as I am sure will be the case in this instance as well."

"Oh, come now, Holmes," I protested. "You cannot be certain of that. Mr. Petty's experience was quite clear and sober. It is only reasonable that there are things in this world that we have not yet explained or discovered. Why, it is only a few decades ago that Chaillu confirmed the existence of the gorilla! Before that, the creature was as mythical as the unicorn."

"I admire your broadminded stance, my dear Watson, but there are some points in this case that need clarification, comprehensible though Mr. Petty's narrative is. I suggest we both accompany Mr. Petty to Buckinghamshire to investigate the matter. I trust you have no objection?"

"I am only too delighted to see that you take my matter seriously," replied Petty.

"Splendid!" Holmes ejaculated. "You will come, Watson?"

Regrettably, I had a prior engagement which prevented me from accompanying my friend on this particular adventure. My announcement appeared to annoy Holmes slightly, as I am sure he had assumed I would take part in the case, but I explained that I was dining with my wife's parents that evening, whereupon he smiled and declared that he quite understood.

"We must not forget our loved ones this time of year! Well, I shall miss your assistance, my friend, but I hope I will have an opportunity to report my findings to you shortly."

Happily, I had a chance to visit my good friend on the following afternoon. I found him hard at work by his chemistry table, from which he looked up briefly to greet me, before resuming his experiment. I sat down with the morning paper and waited patiently for him to finish. Within ten minutes, he was sitting in his easychair in front of me.

"I trust your experiment has some bearing upon the Buckinghamshire case," I said.

"The Buckinghamshire case? Oh that! No, no, I was engaged only this morning by the Earl of Pembroke in a most promising case of extortion. If all goes well, this will keep me occupied through the holidays and save me from having to indulge in plum puddings and mulled wine."

"Do you really abhor Christmas that much, Holmes?"

"I do. Now then, I suspect you came here to learn the conclusion to the mystery of the brownie in the library? A most stimulating little problem. Completely elementary of course, but not without its points of interest."

"Do not leave anything out," I said eagerly.

"There is not much to tell. When we came to the house, it was already dark, but the people who had been in the house on Christmas night were still there. I spoke briefly to the doctor, the professor, and the future Mrs. Petty, and was given a full tour of the house by its owner. It was a spacious and imposing Georgian house with many nooks and corners and places to hide, but it was hardly the type of place that a fairy creature would choose for his home. Dr. Whittington interested me greatly. He was a broad-shouldered and burly man with a winning manner, despite his reclusive habits. As he stepped forward and greeted me upon my arrival, I was provided with a clue that allowed me to form a preliminary hypothesis. He first took me to the library, which I examined without any notable results. The lack of rewarding traces led me to require that I be taken to the upstairs bedrooms immediately. Here, I uncovered the first relevant piece of information, namely that Mr. Petty's and Dr. Whittington's bedrooms were next to each other. I found this worthy of note, especially since there is a ventilator connecting the two rooms."

"Holmes!" I exclaimed. "This is that business of the Speckled Band all over again."

"Ha! Not quite, Watson, but I see how your mind's working."

"But I don't understand. What was the clue you acquired when you were greeted by Dr. Whittington?"

"His breath."

"His breath?"

"Yes. He had a particularly bad breath."

"That is hardly a thing that incriminates a man. Many men have problems with bad breath."

"Yes, but Dr. Whittington's bad breath was caused by himself, and I found the evidence by his bedside. A small ashtray that contained the remnants of cigar ash."

"Nothing strange there. Apart from the foolishness of smoking in bed. But you do that yourself, don't you?"

"This was not the ashes of an ordinary cigar. I only needed to examine them briefly to conclude that Dr. Whittington had been smoking the weeds that are the subject of his researches."

"I see. But what does that mean?"

"His research – as he himself explained to me – concerns the plant known as Goat's Horn, which grows in many parts of Buckinghamshire, and which has well-documented hallucinogenic qualities."

"Good God! Do you mean he willingly drugs himself with that foul plant?"

"When I confronted him with it, he readily confessed, and said it helped him to relax from his work."

"Outrageous. But I fail to see how this has bearing on the case."

"Quite simple. When Dr. Whittington smokes in bed, the smoke comes into Mr. Petty's bedroom through the ventilator in the wall, affecting him as much as it does the doctor."

"So you mean to say that what Petty saw was all a hallucination?"

"That is only part of the picture. I realised when smelling the breath of the doctor that a hallucinogenic fitted into this somehow, but Petty's experience was so distinct and his narrative so convinced, even when he was in a sober state, that I refused to think that the whole matter could be explained this way. He had definitely seen something in the library."

"That was my thought as well. He seemed so certain of it when he told us his story."

"Quite so. I proceeded to tour the house, but despite my exertions I found nothing. It was most disheartening, and to enliven my spirits, Dr. Whittington gracefully invited me to dine at the house. Over dinner, I made the acquaintance both of Petty's delightful fiancée and of Dr. Whittington, who – in spite of his weaknesses – struck me as an intelligent and wise man. But it was also during dinner that I found the piece of the puzzle that was missing."

"What was it?"

"Hazelnuts."

"Hazelnuts?"

"Yes. You remember, don't you, that Petty told us about Professor Seemly and his curious liking for hazelnuts?"

"Oh yes. I thought that was strange from the outset."

"Yes, and Professor Seemly is a strange man, a true eccentric. I did not wish to cause him any embarrassment, so I waited until after dinner, when I followed him up to his room. I gave him time to disappear into his bedroom with his usual bowl of nuts, and after a few minutes I threw open the door. There they were. Professor Seemly, sitting by his desk, with his pet squirrel sitting before him, eating hazelnuts from his bowl."

"A squirrel?"

"Yes. Pondering the professor's nut obsession over dinner, I recalled Petty's description of the brownie, how it had squeaked and how it had leapt across the table, and I thought: Might not a man under the influence of a drug, seeing some small animal from a distance of a few yards, mistake it for something that his hallucinations changed? I was right. Professor Seemly confessed immediately, and he was more than happy to confess it to the other guests, having all the while been unsure of whether his squirrel – who had escaped from his cage on Christmas night – was actually the culprit. Dr. Whittington also confessed his undue use of the weed in his bedroom, and there was a confusing moment of surprise and anger, but after some minutes of explanation and excuses, the spirit of the season was restored, and everyone at Cumbersome House was happy and content again. Mr. Petty was at first reluctant to admit that my explanation was possible, but this was only a brief outburst of pride, which was quickly superseded by recognition when the professor introduced him to his little friend."

"Unbelievable, Holmes. What a stupid and simple solution. A squirrel at large in a country house!"

"Sometimes, my boy, Occam's Razor is not nearly enough. There are times when Occam's Hatchet is more appropriate."

"Quite right, Holmes." I glanced at the clock. "Dear God, is that the time? We had better hurry. Be a sport and go dress for dinner."

"For dinner? What on earth for, Watson?"

"Because you are dining with me and my wife tonight. Come on, the hansom's waiting downstairs."

Holmes sniggered. "I truly abhor Christmas," he said, and bolted from his chair.

The Adventure of the
Deceased Doctor
by Hugh Ashton

It was Christmas of 1916 – that terrible winter following the fighting on the Somme, where so many of our gallant young men lost their lives in the mud of Northern France, and so many had been killed on the Turkish shores of the Dardanelles. For my part, I had re-joined the colours, but my duties were in "Blighty", as we had learned to call our native land, where I worked in a Hampshire hospital treating those who were recovering from the loss of a limb or severe head wounds.

Since providing assistance to my old friend Sherlock Holmes in the matter of the arrest of the German spy, Von Bork, he and I had maintained a correspondence, and from him I learned of his elder brother Mycroft's death some years previously as the result of an aneurism. Sherlock Holmes himself was employed in matters which had previously formed part of his brother's remit, and from the guarded hints that he dropped in his letters to me, he was dividing his time between his bees in Sussex and the Admiralty, where he had dealings with a mysterious organisation in that building which went by the name of "Room 40". Naturally, as a patriotic citizen, I did not enquire further into the nature of his work, and he, by his very nature, was secretive regarding it.

It was, as I say, Christmas-time, and I had invited Holmes to spend the holiday season with me. My fellow-lodger had recently departed for the Front, and I considered it to be a kindness to Mrs. Dalwymple (the landlady of my "digs", whom I discovered after having lodged there for some months to be a distant cousin of dear Mrs. Hudson of Baker Street) to invite Holmes to take the room for a week or so at my expense, as well as providing me (and, I hoped, Holmes) with congenial company.

Much to my delight, he had accepted my invitation, and he arrived, showing signs of age, which I fear were not only due to the passing of the years, but also to the terrible strain and stress that he was suffering as a result of his Admiralty work. He was, as was his nature, reticent about the details, but from my knowledge of Holmes, I could read between the lines that a terrible responsibility lay upon his shoulders as the result of his duties.

"I am delighted to see you, Watson," he greeted me as he entered the house. "And back in harness. You appear to be in good health, though you have lost a little weight. Five-and-one-quarter pounds, I fancy, since I saw you last."

I laughed. "Holmes, I do not have time or the inclination to worry about such things. I dare say you, as always, are correct. Ah, Mrs. Dalwymple," I added as my landlady approached, "may I introduce my old friend, Mr. Holmes."

"Pleased to meet you, sir," she said to him. "Doctor Watson has told me that you used to lodge in London with my cousin, Mrs. Martha Hudson."

"Indeed so. Happy days, were they not, eh, Watson? I hope you will not take it amiss, Mrs. Dalwymple, if I make you a present of these." He held out two jars of honey. "They are from my own hives on the South Downs, and I will wager that it is some of the finest honey you will ever taste."

"Oh, Mr. Holmes!" she exclaimed. "With the rationing and everything as it is now, this is most welcome. You keep bees, then, sir?"

"Indeed I do. Forty hives, forty little kingdoms, or should I say 'queendoms', each busy in the pursuit of sweetness."

"Why, Holmes, you are quite poetic," I laughed.

"Apiculture is a subject fit for poetry. You remember your Virgil, Watson? *The Georgics*, Book Four?"

"A cup of tea, Mr. Holmes?" Mrs. Dalwymple offered.

"It would be most welcome," he answered, and I ushered him into the drawing-room that was used by the lodgers of the house as a common-room. Currently, I was the only lodger, and was therefore able to treat the room as my own.

After ascertaining that my landlady had no objection to tobacco, Holmes filled and lit his pipe, and leaned back in his armchair. "Ah, Watson," he sighed, "you have no idea what pleasure it gives me to see that familiar face seated opposite me. The memories of those days . . . ."

"You are becoming sentimental in your old age, Holmes."

"Am I? I suppose it is a state that we all approach as time passes. But it is true, is it not, that those days which you recorded so sensationally were indeed some of the best of our lives?"

He and I fell into reminiscences, interrupted only by the arrival of the tea-tray, graced with a steaming teapot, and with some scones adorned with some of Holmes's own honey. I learned that Lestrade had recently retired, with the rank of Superintendent, and that Tobias Gregson, one of the Force's more promising officers, according to Holmes, had recently been rewarded with a knighthood.

"And you yourself, Holmes? Why are you not now Sir Sherlock Holmes? The nation owes you that, and much more, for your services over the years."

"The honour has been offered to me on a number of occasions," he said. "What need have I for such a bauble? My fame, such as it is, is the result of your work, and requires no further adornment. As for those who rule us, believe me when I say that they are well enough aware of my little contributions to the security of our realm." He paused, and yawned. "As am I. The work on which I am currently engaged is devilish tiring at times."

"Would you permit me to examine you at some time while you are here?" I asked him. "I am certain that it is some time since you have visited a medical practitioner."

"If it will amuse you," he answered. "You are correct in your supposition, though. I seem to have had little time for such matters recently."

I had detected, during our conversation, various signs of fatigue and strain, similar to those I had observed in our shell-shocked patients. The twitching eyelid and slight trembling motion of the hand were symptoms I had also observed before in Holmes when he had driven his body and spirit to their limits. There was an additional air of "nerves" about Holmes which was remarkably pronounced, even for him.

The evening passed pleasantly enough, however, in friendly conversation, punctuated at times by those silences which can be said to be companionable, and whose existence is only possible with those between whom a deep friendship exists.

"I am for bed," I told Holmes as the clock struck ten. "I must make the rounds of the wards early tomorrow morning, although it is Christmas Eve. I expect to be finished and to have returned by half-past eight, and we may breakfast together on my return, if that is agreeable to you."

"Perfectly agreeable," he answered.

It was five o'clock in the morning as I made my way through the darkened wet streets to the hospital. As I approached, I was surprised to glimpse more lights in the windows than I would expect to see at that hour.

I entered the building and was instantly accosted by the nursing sister who was in charge overnight.

"Doctor Watson!" she exclaimed breathlessly. "Thank goodness you are here. Come with me now!"

"Why, what is the matter?" I asked her. "Surely there is nothing that Doctor Godney cannot manage?" I should add that our patients were for the most part convalescent, and did not require the kind of intensive medical attention that was needed at the Front, for example.

"Doctor Godney," she answered me with a sniff, "is dead. He is sitting there in his office, at his desk, but cold as ice."

I was naturally shocked at this news and expressed my surprise that such a seemingly healthy young man should pass away so suddenly.

"But that is not the worst," she added. "Come and see for yourself."

She led the way to the room, where, as I had been told, Godney was sitting at his desk, motionless. On the floor was visible, protruding from behind the desk, a pair of legs, shod, but otherwise bare to the knee, and female, if the shoes on the feet were any guide.

"Who is that?" I asked, pointing to the legs.

"Nurse de Lacey. One of our volunteers."

I remembered the girl, who was working at the hospital to "do her bit". She was an exceedingly pretty young lady, from one of our old county families, and seemed always willing to help with even the most menial of tasks, which would have turned the stomach of many lesser women.

"She is also dead?" I asked, horrified by this revelation.

"No. Merely unconscious."

"And you have left her there? Why?"

"See for yourself, Doctor," was the reply.

By now it was clear to me that foul play of some kind had been done. I therefore stepped with extreme caution around the side of the room, taking care to cause as little disturbance as possible, and beheld the scene from the far side of the desk.

"You are sure he is dead? What have you moved or touched?" I asked.

"I am sure, Doctor," she answered me. "I have touched as little as possible. Both of them are in the same place and posture as when I discovered them. I did only what was necessary to confirm the presence or absence of life."

"It was you who discovered this scene, then?"

"It was I. One of my patients was coughing, and I came to the office to obtain the key to the dispensary from Doctor Godney. I knocked, and there was no answer, so I let myself in, and saw – this."

"When did you discover this?"

"Not ten minutes before you arrived, Doctor."

"And who else knows of these events?"

"No-one other than you. If you had not arrived when you did, I was about to alert Perkins, the porter, and ask him to inform the police."

"Very well," I told her. I surveyed the scene. Sister Lightfoot was experienced enough for me to be able to take her word regarding the condition of the two bodies. It was clear, in any case, that Nurse de Lacey was alive, but appeared at first sight to be in no danger. However, the garments comprising the upper half of her nurse's outfit, as well as the undergarments beneath, were opened at the front, almost to the waist, and nearly exposing her breasts, which rose and fell gently in time with her shallow breathing. Her skirts had been pulled up to a little above the knee, and it was clear that her stockings had been pulled down. Her body appeared to be lying on a hypodermic syringe, half of which was visible.

"The hussy," said the sister, as she took in my shock at seeing the partly-undressed body lying there.

"It is not for us to judge others, Sister," I told her sharply. "Now listen to me and follow my orders. You are to tell Perkins and ask him to fetch the police, as you were about to do. Having done that, you are to return immediately with a blanket, and use it to cover Nurse de Lacey. You are then to stand outside the door and permit no-one to enter, including the police. We are lucky in that my old friend Sherlock Holmes is presently staying with me. I am sure that he will be able to provide answers to the questions that we all have regarding the death of Doctor Godney, and the unfortunate condition of Nurse de Lacey." I spoke in a tone of voice befitting the nominal Army rank of Captain which had been bestowed on me on my appointment to the hospital. "While you inform Perkins, I will stand guard here until your return with the blanket, and then fetch Mr. Holmes."

"Yes, Doctor," she replied meekly. When she had gone, I moved as carefully as I could to Godney, and satisfied myself that life was indeed extinct. Sister Lightfoot's first words, that he was cold, were mistaken. Given the temperature of the room, which was well heated, I estimated that he had passed away not more than a few hours previously, but it was impossible for me to be sure of that without more precise measurements. However, it was clear that *rigor* had yet to set in, and this likewise confirmed my suspicions.

I had completed my preliminary investigations when Sister returned, bearing a blanket, which I helped her spread over Miss de Lacey.

"Very good, Sister," I told her, instructing her to wait outside until I returned with Sherlock Holmes. "I will be as quick as possible," I told her.

Much to my relief, Sherlock Holmes was awake and dressed when I reached Mrs. Dalwymple's, though it was barely six o'clock.

"Back so soon?" he asked me.

"I am glad to see you awake," I answered.

"I found it hard to sleep, and accordingly arose early. Surely breakfast is not prepared at this hour?"

"By no means. You are needed at the hospital urgently. There has been a death, and I suspect murder."

His face brightened. "How very gratifying. I mean to say that it is gratifying you feel that I may still be of use in these matters," he added hurriedly. "A murder, you say? Well, well. Just like old times, indeed."

He dressed for the chill outdoors, and as we hurried through the streets, I informed him of the circumstances.

"Dear me," he exclaimed, as I informed him of the partially undressed state of Miss de Lacey. "I fear we will be uncovering matters which the principals in the case would best have left hidden."

We arrived at the hospital, to discover Sister Lightfoot standing outside the door, with an elderly uniformed constable beside her.

"I've heard of your work in the past, Mr. Holmes," the policeman informed him, "and I'm no detective myself, being the only man free when the porter came to the station, so I took this lady's word that I wasn't to enter until you came here. I can't speak for Inspector Braithwaite, though, who is our senior detective officer. He's been called, and should be with us shortly."

Holmes introduced himself to the sister, and thanked her gravely for her promptitude and professional conduct in the matter, words which seemed to please her. When he chose to be, Sherlock Holmes could be the most pleasing and emollient of personalities, and it was good for me to see that this faculty had not deserted him.

Without entering the room, he opened the door, and peered inside. "I trust that your Inspector Braithwaite will not be too long in arriving," he said to the constable. "It is important that we examine the scene of the crime as soon as possible after the event, but I do not propose to make an examination without the permission of the police. I have no wish to interfere where my presence is unwelcome."

"Speaking for myself, sir, I am more than happy to see you here. Many of our best men have gone over to France, sir, and Inspector Braithwaite, though he is – Ah, here he is now, sir," he broke off, drawing himself up to attention as a tall figure, accompanied by Perkins, was visible at the end of the corridor, and made its way towards us.

"Thank you, Constable. You may stand easy," said the newcomer, with more than a hint of a Northern accent to his voice. He turned to Sherlock Holmes. "You are Doctor Watson?"

Holmes smiled and shook his head. "No, sir. This man," indicating me, "is Doctor Watson. My name is Sherlock Holmes."

"Indeed? Bless my soul! I had imagined you to be retired from the business of detection. This is indeed an honour, Mr. Holmes. May I ask what you are doing here?"

"I am spending the season with my friend, Doctor Watson."

"I see. And you," addressing me, "discovered the body?"

"It was Sister Lightfoot here who made the discovery, and brought it to my attention when I arrived for the early ward rounds this morning."

"Very good." He proceeded to question the sister, who repeated what she had told me earlier.

"Thank you. Excellent," he said to her. "Constable, go with Sister here to another room, and take her statement, and then return to the station. Now," turning to me, "you have been in the room and seen the body?"

"I have," I told him, and informed him of my actions to date.

"We will require your statement later, Doctor. And you, Mr. Holmes?"

"I was waiting for your arrival before I entered the room. I judged it best that it be left undisturbed as far as possible."

"Thank you for your consideration, but to tell you the truth, Mr. Holmes, I am a relative novice at this kind of work. With the war, and so many of our officers leaving to fight the Hun, we all find ourselves in unfamiliar employment, do we not? I am content to let you work the magic of which we have all read in the accounts by Doctor Watson here, and to watch, and with luck to learn from you."

"Very well, then," said Holmes. "I will endeavour to live up to my reputation."

It was a joy to me to see my friend in his element once more. His eyes fairly glittered as he entered the room and took in the scene. He sniffed the air.

"Do you not smell it?" he asked me.

"What is it?" I answered. At the time I was suffering from a mild cold, and my sense of smell was dulled.

"There is a faint scent of rose water."

"No doubt it is the scent worn by the nurse, de Lacey, is it not?" commented Braithwaite.

"Almost certainly that is not the case," I corrected him. "The nurses at this hospital are under strict instructions not to wear any kind of jewellery or to use cosmetics or scent of any kind while on duty. The matron here strictly enforces these matters."

"The doctor, then?" suggested the policeman.

"I have never known him to wear such," I said.

By this time, Holmes had reached the bodies, and swiftly ascertained that life was extinct in that of Godney. "How long do you estimate he has been dead, Watson?" he asked me.

"Judging from a very rough estimation of the temperature of the body and of the *rigor* that I made earlier, I would say a few hours at the very most."

"I concur," said Holmes. "What would you take to be the cause of death?"

"I have no certain idea," I replied, "but I will undertake that the syringe here that you observe has some connection."

"At what time would he commence his duties?"

"At eight last evening, and he would make two ward rounds in the course of the night until he ceased to be on duty at six in the morning."

"Very well," answered Holmes, and bent to the fallen nurse, removing the blanket with which she had been covered. "Ha!" he exclaimed, following a brief examination of the clothing that now only partially covered the poor girl's body. "Did you examine her?"

"I only ensured that she was alive and not in immediate danger," I answered, with a slight blush.

"Then you did not observe that these garments appear to have been torn open by sheer force? See, here, where two buttons are missing. I am sure your dragon of a matron would never allow a nurse to appear with a missing button."

"Indeed so."

Holmes gently opened one of the girl's eyelids. "You observe the contracted pupil?" he asked me.

"One of the symptoms of opioid poisoning?"

"Indeed."

The inspector had been watching Holmes at work in an embarrassed silence. He now broke in with, "Is it not time that you covered the poor lass and sent her to her bed?"

"One minute, please. Watson, you are a medical man. One last thing. Please ensure that Miss de Lacey's nether undergarments are in place."

"What in the name of – ?" began Braithwaite, but then stopped as the implication of Holmes's request struck him. I was deeply embarrassed at having to perform this task, but a quick inspection was enough to reassure me.

"All appear to be in place and untouched," I was able to report, with a certain sense of relief.

"Very good," said Holmes. "Watson, you are familiar with the workings of this place. I will restore Miss de Lacey to some sort of state of modesty, while you summon aid to transport her to someplace where she can be cared for."

When I returned, with two porters bearing a stretcher, and accompanied by Sister Lightfoot, who had completed her statement to the constable, the stricken nurse was now in a decent state.

"I suppose we are to move this Jezebel to a bed?" snapped the sister.

"I fear you misjudge her," Holmes said gently. "Her upper garments seem to have been torn from her by main force. It does not appear at all possible that she removed them herself. And Doctor Watson here assures me that all is as it should be below the waist, as it were."

"Based on my cursory examination, that is," I added.

"So the poor girl was the victim of an assault by Doctor Godney?" Sister Lightfoot's attitude appeared to change dramatically on hearing Holmes's words.

"She appears to be the victim of an assault, certainly," Holmes answered her. "As to who was the perpetrator, I agree that Doctor Godney would appear to be guilty, but, as I remarked once to Watson, and he has never let the world forget these words, it is a capital mistake to theorise before one has data."

The porters lifted the unconscious girl onto the stretcher and carried her away, the sister following. Holmes carefully picked up the syringe on which she had been lying and placed it on one side of the desk.

"So, Inspector," said Holmes, rubbing his hands together, "what do you make of it so far?"

"I would call it an open-and-shut case," said Braithwaite. "The girl came to the office, he assaulted her, she resisted his advances, and in self-defence she used this syringe here to protect her honour. In the struggle, she also received a dose of the drug with which she poisoned him."

"Good, Inspector. A fair summary of the facts as you perceive them, but not, unfortunately, of the facts that are to hand.

"Consider the following. We are told that under no circumstances are the nurses or staff permitted to wear scent or toilet water or perfume, and yet, when we entered this room there was a distinct smell of rose water. I think we are all satisfied that this did not emanate from Doctor Godney, nor Miss de Lacey.

"Next, we have the evidence of the ripped clothing," he continued. "Two buttons were torn off the bodice. Where are those buttons?"

"Maybe they are still with Miss de Lacey, hidden in folds of her clothing?" I suggested.

"It is certainly possible," answered Holmes, "and you may be sure that if they were, I would not be the one to find them. Watson, I intensely dislike using you as my Mercury, but you are a member of the staff here, and you have the authority to command. Can you please ask the sister to search Miss de Lacey's clothing for the missing buttons or any scraps of torn cloth, or threads? Thank you."

I left on my errand, and returned to discover Holmes examining the hypodermic syringe with his lens. "Well now, what do you make of that?" he asked me, passing me the lens.

"The plunger is halfway down the barrel, and I see some traces of blood on the needle, but yet I see no sign of any liquid having been recently contained in there," I said, a little perplexed.

"Indeed so. And now look at this." With a forefinger he lifted one eyelid of the corpse, to display an eye that appeared perfectly normal. "You recall de Lacey's eye?"

"Indeed I do. We agreed that it showed the symptoms typical of poisoning by an opiate, did we not?"

"We did. And if the doctor here perished by the same means, we would expect to find the same symptoms here. We do not find them, therefore we may conclude that Godney met his end by some other means."

"But the syringe," exclaimed Braithwaite. "What is the significance of that if, as you say, it did not contain a fatal drug?"

Holmes said nothing, as he searched through the papers contained in the wastepaper basket beside the desk. "Aha!" he said, with an air of triumph, holding up two small crumpled scraps of dark brown paper. "I had guessed there would be something of the sort here."

"What are they?" asked the policeman, as Holmes laid them on the desk beside the syringe.

"Smell them," Holmes invited, by way of answer.

Obediently, Braithwaite did so. "Chocolate!" he cried triumphantly. "With a strange bitter aroma added."

"There," said Holmes, "you have the method by which the drug was administered to de Lacey."

He bent to the desk, where Godney's curled hands still rested, and after first requesting and receiving permission from Braithwaite to examine the body, opened the right hand. Clutched within it were two buttons, which matched those I had observed on de Lacey's bodice. Without removing them from the dead man's palm, he applied his lens to them and examined them closely. Abruptly he stood up, with a sudden intake of breath and handed the lens first to Braithwaite, and then to me, inviting us to examine the objects.

"Tell me," he said to me suddenly, "was Godney married?"

"He was, I believe. I did not know him well, but I recall his discussing marriage at some times in the past."

"And was he in favour of the blessed state?"

"By no means," I laughed. "He regarded a wife as a drag on a man's ambitions, and even an ambitious wife as being a handicap to success. He was by no means averse to female company, however." I broke off. "This is merely hearsay, and my word regarding a colleague. I hope you will not regard it as merely idle chatter."

"Let me be the judge of that. I know you too well of old, Watson, for me to dismiss your words lightly."

"At any rate, the story was that the nurses, particularly the younger and prettier ones, refused to be alone in a room with him. There were tales of unwanted words and worse. I repeat, though, that this is merely such gossip as tends to circulate within a small community such as this hospital."

"Nonetheless," retorted Holmes, "it may well prove to be of considerable importance. In your opinion, is it possible that Godney might have attempted to force his attention on Miss de Lacey, after summoning her to his office on some pretext?"

"I must reluctantly admit that such an action would indeed be possible."

"And what, do you think, would Miss de Lacey's reaction be?"

"Without doubt, she would repulse his advances."

"You seem very sure of your answer, Watson."

"I am indeed. There is a precedent."

"Oh?" Holmes arched his eyebrows.

"This is merely gossip once more, you understand, but I have every reason to believe it true. The story is that Godney attempted to steal a kiss from Miss de Lacey about a week ago. She not only refused to accept his attention, but delivered a ringing slap to his face. This latter action was reportedly witnessed by two other nurses who happened to be passing, and the news of the incident was all around the hospital inside an hour. Since that time, Godney had been avoiding any intercourse with others in the hospital, save when his duties demanded his presence."

"Embarrassed, was he, eh?" asked Braithwaite. I nodded.

"Given his misogyny, which is typical, may I add, of many such womanisers, it would seem likely that he would seek his revenge on the woman who had shamed him, as he would see it," said Holmes. He broke off abruptly as there was a knock on the door.

Sister Lightfoot entered in answer to Holmes's invitation. "There were no loose buttons or threads in her clothing, though there were some missing from her bodice."

"Thank you, Sister," answered Holmes. "Then we have them here," and he showed the buttons clutched in the dead man's hand.

She shrank back at the sight of them. "Then he got what he deserved," she said. "I am sorry for the names I called that poor girl just now, but I sincerely believed that she had fallen a victim to his evil ways. Doctor Godney was a danger to any woman near him, Mr. Holmes. I do not flatter myself that I am still young or beautiful, but even I was not immune to his unwelcome attentions. As for the younger nurses," she shrugged, "they refused to be alone with him. Though I complained about him to the Superintendent, nothing was done and he persisted in his ways. Doctors are scarce in this time of war, and good doctors even more so, and Doctor Godney, for all his personal faults, was a good doctor."

"You say that the nurses feared to be alone with him? So when you discovered the two together, you feared the worst?"

"Indeed I did. I do not know if Doctor Watson has informed you of last week's incident?"

"He has."

"My immediate thought was that Godney had invited her to his office early in the morning, while they were both on night duty, on the pretence of making some sort of amends for his earlier behaviour, and she had succumbed to his advances. But the fact that you have found these buttons clasped in his hand would seem to indicate otherwise."

"Indeed so," replied Holmes. "One more question, if I may, Sister," he added as she turned to go. "Watson has informed me that the nurses and other staff here are forbidden the use of scent or toilet water."

She nodded. "That is so."

"So you would have no idea from where the scent of rose water might originate?"

"What a question, Mr. Holmes. It is, as you know, a popular fragrance."

"Of course. But please cast your mind back to when you might last have encountered it."

She appeared lost in thought for a minute, and then came to with a start. "Yes, I do remember," she told us. "It was about three weeks ago. Captain Cardew's widow."

"Pray continue." Holmes by now was occupying one of the chairs in the office, his eyes half-closed and his fingers steepled in that attitude I knew so well.

501

"Captain Cardew was one of our patients. The poor man had been severely wounded by a grenade, and had lost both legs below the knee, and his entire right arm. He was suffering from shell-shock, and his constitution was extremely weak. You will vouch for that, Doctor Watson."

"Indeed. He was not under my particular care, but I attended him on a number of occasions, and it was a source of wonder to me that he hung onto life as he did."

"In any event, he died some three weeks ago, and his widow came here to view him before the undertakers arrived. I distinctly remember the smell of rose water at that time."

"Had she been a frequent visitor to the hospital before her husband's death?"

"Why, yes. She came to see him, even if it was only for a few minutes, almost every day."

"And the doctor responsible for his care was Doctor Godney?"

"Yes, he was. How did you guess?"

"No guessing was involved, Sister. Thank you." It was a clear dismissal, and Sister Lightfoot took herself off.

Following Holmes's orders, I arranged for Godney's body to be removed from the office and taken to the morgue.

"I am baffled," said Braithwaite when the stretcher had left the room. "I see nothing but confusion."

"On the contrary, my dear Braithwaite, the case is now as clear as daylight. And speaking of which, the sun is at last risen, and Watson and I are ready for our breakfast. Come, let us return to the estimable Mrs. Dalwymple's. Will the addition of another guest for breakfast inconvenience her in any way, do you think?"

"It is hard to tell in these days of rationing," I said, "but I am sure that she will manage."

"Thank you," said Braithwaite, "but I fear you are playing some sort of joke on me. I completely fail to see what you have deduced from this?"

"Never mind," Holmes told him. "All will become clear soon."

Following breakfast, which Mrs. Dalwymple provided for the three of us with seemingly little trouble, we made our way, at Holmes's request, to the police station.

"Do you know this Mrs. Cardew, Inspector?" Holmes asked.

"I hardly know her, Mr. Holmes. We move in somewhat different social circles, you understand. Of course I know who she is, and something about her. Her family owns the big house in one of the villages hereabouts."

502

"Send one of your constables to bring her to the station."

"To arrest her?" Braithwaite appeared horrified.

"That is for you to decide when you have heard her answers to the questions which I, with your permission, propose to put to her."

"Very well, Mr. Holmes, but I fear for my position, such as it is, should you be mistaken in this matter."

"Never fear, Inspector," Holmes answered gaily, clapping the man on the shoulder.

It was some thirty minutes later that Mrs. Geraldine Cardew was shown into the room in the police station where we sat waiting. She was a striking young woman, and her widow's weeds did little to obscure the obvious beauty of her face and figure. Her expression, however, was one of stiff arrogance.

As she sat down, I noted the smell of rose water, with which she had clearly scented herself.

"Well, Sergeant," she addressed Braithwaite, "I hope you have a good reason for bringing me here. You could have visited me at the Hall and saved a poor widow the trouble of this visit."

"It is not Inspector Braithwaite, but I who requested your presence," Holmes informed her. "Thank you for your cooperation." He made a small half-bow in her direction.

"And you, sir, are . . . ?"

"The name is Sherlock Holmes." There was a sharp intake of breath. "The name is familiar to you, I see."

"You are the private detective, then? I am flattered that you lower yourself to speak to me." The tone was half-amused, and mixed with sarcasm.

"Firstly, I wish to inform you that Doctor Godney at the hospital passed away last night."

"Why should I be concerned about the death of a doctor there?"

"He treated your husband, did he not?"

She frowned as if in an attempt to remember, but to my eyes unconvincingly. "Yes, I recall him."

"And he also comforted you in the time of your husband's illness, did he not?"

"He was sympathetic, yes."

"And he made himself agreeable to you?"

"If you say so, Mr. Holmes."

"Agreeable enough for you to have your photograph taken together?" Holmes reached in his pocket and produced a pasteboard square which he tossed onto the table.

She blanched at the sight of the photograph which showed her and the late Godney together. "Very well, then. Yes, I loved him, and I believed he loved me." She paused. "Do I have to continue?" Holmes said nothing, but nodded silently. "My poor Giles – my husband – was a broken man. Even if his body ever healed, he would be forever only part of a man. I needed a man, Mr. Holmes, a man to hold me and care for me. Perhaps you have never felt the need of another, but for me it was a necessity, even as I watched Giles slip away from this life. Lionel Godney was that other. He appeared to me to be good and kind, and attentive."

She paused, and dabbed at her eyes with a handkerchief. "Please continue," Holmes invited. "It will go easier on you at the trial."

She started at these words, but resumed her narrative. "Then I discovered from a friend, in the week after Giles had died, that I was not the only one in his life. In fact, he had an unsavoury reputation as regards women. There were tales of his advances on the nurses at the hospital. I heard that he had been forcing his attention on Olivia de Lacey, and that was the last straw as far as I was concerned."

"She is known to you?"

"Her family's lands adjoin those of my family. We have known each other since childhood, though I confess I am a little older than her. At any rate, I was not prepared to lose Lionel to her."

"She rebuffed him, you know," I told her.

"I did not know that last night." She took a deep breath. "You want to know how it all happened, Mr. Holmes. I will tell you, then. I knew that Lionel had the night duty last night, and I knew that he spent most of the time in his office. Earlier in the day I had come to the hospital, and hid myself in one of the unused rooms along the same corridor as his office, from which I could observe the comings and goings. At about four o'clock or a little after, according to my watch, I observed Olivia de Lacey enter his office, and I was filled with a jealous rage.

"I crept along the corridor, and flung open the door, hoping to catch the couple in what I believe you detectives call *in flagrante delicto*. Instead, I found Olivia sprawled on the floor, seemingly lifeless, and Lionel standing over her, a look of horror on his face.

"I forced him to sit down in his chair – "

"Excuse me," broke in Holmes, "but how did you manage that?"

"I had Giles' service revolver in my hand," she replied simply. "It was unloaded, but Lionel Godney did not know that, so it was easy to force him to do my bidding. When I demanded an account of what was happening, he explained that he had lured Olivia to his office on the pretext of apologising for some previous incident, but had intended rather to take advantage of her. To that end, he had prepared some sweetmeats – chocolates – laced with laudanum, but it seemed that he had miscalculated the dose, and she had fallen to the floor, lifeless, almost immediately after eating two of them."

"Her fatigue may also have accelerated the effect," I added. "The nurses are being asked to perform work over and above the call of duty."

"Be that as it may, Olivia was lying on the floor, dead, and Godney, the coward, was shaking in his shoes. I was so angry that I forgot the revolver was not loaded, and pulled the trigger. He burst into laughter which was almost hysterical, and that inflamed me still further. I pushed the revolver back into my skirt pocket, and snatched up the first thing I could find to hurt him."

"The hypodermic syringe that he had used to inject the laudanum into the chocolates and had subsequently cleaned, and left to dry on his desk before returning it to its proper place?"

"Yes, I suppose so. At any rate, it was sharp, and it was in my hand, and it went in under his arm. There was remarkably little blood, I remember, but in a matter of minutes, he clutched at his chest, and appeared to lose consciousness. It soon became obvious to me that he was dead. I was glad, Mr. Holmes. Glad, I tell you.

"My next move was to blacken his name without, I hoped, blackening that of Olivia de Lacey, whom, it seemed, I had misjudged. It hurt me in my heart to do this, but in my frenzy it seemed to me to be the best for all. I opened Olivia's garments roughly, exposing her flesh, not caring if I tore the cloth. I had noticed that for some reason she had pulled her stockings down about her knees. I assumed that this was as a result of her suspender belt having 'gone'." Here she made a wry grimace. "I do not expect you gentlemen to fully understand the mysteries and complexities of these things. You must take it from me that this is sometimes the case. In any event, I wished to emphasise that her upper legs were bare, and I pulled her skirts up so that the fact was obvious to all. I hoped that the implication was that Godney had assaulted her, and she had stabbed him with the syringe, which I tucked under her body."

"Did you not realise that she was still alive?" asked Holmes.

To my amazement, Mrs. Cardew burst into peals of laughter. "She was alive?"

"She lives," I confirmed, "and will recover soon, it is to be hoped."

"So all my ingenuity was in vain, it would seem? Poor Olivia. But I wished that Godney would suffer in death, so I removed some buttons from her bodice and placed them in Godney's dead hand, and curled the fingers over them."

"The intention being to make it appear as if he had ripped open her garments, tearing off buttons in his haste?"

"Precisely."

"You should have torn off the buttons, not snipped them off with scissors," Holmes told her. "Better yet to have left them as they were."

"How do you know that I used scissors?" Mrs. Cardew fairly gasped.

"Elementary. A high-powered lens uncovers many secrets."

Braithwaite, who had remained silent throughout this whole conversation, now spoke. "Geraldine Cardew, I arrest you for the wilful murder of Lionel Godney on the morning of December 24, 1916. I warn you that anything you say will be taken down and used as evidence against you. Take her to the cells," he instructed a constable. "I will take her formal statement later."

Before she was led away, Mrs. Cardew requested and was granted permission to address Sherlock Holmes. Her words were as follows.

"Mr. Holmes, I do not know whether to thank you from the bottom of my heart or to curse your name for evermore for your part in exposing my crime. Yes, I did it, and I am glad that he is gone out of my life and the lives of all the other women he has tormented. I regret taking his life, though. I cannot say that I did it deliberately, and I cannot say that it was an accident. I am sorry for poor Olivia, and I am sorry for Mrs. Godney. I hope that she will thank me for removing Lionel from her life. I hope – I do not know what I hope . . . ." With that, she broke into a fit of sobbing as the constable led her away.

"Well," said Braithwaite as the door closed. "How did you come by all that, Mr. Holmes? I was in the same room as you, I saw and heard all that you saw and heard, and yet I was in the dark, while you were shining light all around. How did Godney come to die, for example?"

"Watson will confirm that the injection of air into the bloodstream will cause a painful and rapid death. When she stabbed at him with the empty syringe, the plunger was depressed. By bad luck, she must have hit a blood vessel, and the air bubble entered his bloodstream."

"So it was an accident?"

"You could make out to be such, certainly. My first clue that a third party was involved came when I noted the scent of rose water. Whence had that come? It must have been from a person who did not work at the hospital. Sister Lightfoot told us of the identity of that person. The fact that Miss de Lacey had obviously suffered from opiate poisoning, and Godney had not done so posed a slight problem, but that was resolved when I examined the syringe and formed the hypothesis regarding his death that I just described to you."

506

"How did you know that the syringe had been used to inject the laudanum into the chocolates and then cleaned and left to dry?"

"A bow drawn at a venture. It proved to hit the target, I think."

"Where did the photograph of the prisoner and the murdered man come from?"

"Ah, there you must forgive me. I abstracted it from his desk drawer while you and Watson were otherwise occupied. I had a fair idea of what I was looking for, after Sister Lightfoot had told us about Captain Cardew and his wife. But the really damning evidence came with the open bodice. It was meant to appear that it had been ripped open, when in fact it had been opened with a little care. And then our fair criminal over-gilded the lily."

"The buttons?"

"Precisely. Cutting them rather than tearing them off was a careless error, but it was ridiculous for her to imagine that had he indeed ripped them from their place, Godney would still be holding them in his hand. The art of the criminal, like that of the painter, consists of knowing when to stop."

"I thank you most sincerely, Mr. Holmes," said Braithwaite at the end of this recital. He rose and shook hands with Holmes. "I am more than grateful to you for your assistance."

"All the credit shall be yours, Inspector," Holmes told him. "I do not wish my name to be mentioned in connection with this case."

"That is uncommonly generous of you, sir," said Braithwaite.

"Nonsense. Consider it my Christmas gift to you. It is, after all, the season of peace and goodwill, and God knows there is little enough of either at this time. Let me attempt to redress the balance in this small fashion. A very Happy Christmas to you, Inspector Braithwaite."

The Mile End Mynah Bird
by Mark Mower

In the days prior to the Christmas of 1919 there remained a general air of despondency in Britain, with the interminable upheavals caused by the aftermath of the Great War. While there had been widespread jubilation at the end of the conflict, the mood of the population had soured with the slow demobilisation of troops from the western front and the influenza pandemic that had continued to sweep across Europe. In the previous month alone, there had been around a thousand deaths in London, and with the significant shortage of medical personnel to cope with such demands, I had felt it my duty to come out of retirement and assist where I could. By day, I attended a number of patients on a private basis, while three nights a week I acted as an unpaid consultant at the Charing Cross Hospital just off the Strand.

I was on duty one evening when a young man was rushed into the emergency ward of the hospital on an orderly's trolley. My first thought was that he was yet another victim of seasonal excess; a merrymaker who had fought or fallen under the influence of too much strong liquor. Yet, the police officer who accompanied him explained breathlessly that the patient had been shot, the result, he said, of what looked like an attempted murder. As fortune would have it, the shoulder wound sustained by the man looked worse than it appeared, the bullet having passed across the top of his collar bone. With some minor surgery we had the patient patched up and sedated for the night within a couple of hours, just before I finished my shift at ten o'clock.

Police Constable Dunning had continued to wait for news of the patient, and when his charge had been transferred to a bed in a quiet side ward of the hospital, had pulled up a chair alongside the sleeping man. Dunning was a tall, fair-haired Scot, with broad cheek bones and exceptionally large hands. He explained that his divisional inspector had ordered him to stay with the injured man as a measure of protection. Curious to know why the metropolitan force was taking such precautions, I asked him who the patient was.

"He told us his name was Jonathon Christie. Beyond that, we know nothing of the man. It was the only information he was prepared to share with us, Doctor."

"Then why the heavy-handed police presence?" I queried.

"The man who shot him was Serang Sayan, a Lascar sailor. He is wanted in connection with a number of assaults which we believe he carried out with his brother, Bhandarry, under the direction of an East End moneylender named Sydney Vulliamy."

". . . And both Vulliamy and Bhandarry Sayan appear to have disappeared, PC Dunning. Neither has been seen for over three weeks, according to my sources . . . ."

Both Dunning and I turned sharply towards the door as the voice came from behind us, my own senses heightened immediately by the familiar timbre. "Holmes!" I cried. "What brings you here?"

"I might ask you the same, Watson, but your attire speaks for itself. Not quite the relaxed retirement you had in mind, I'd warrant."

Dunning looked from Holmes towards me with evident glee. "Dr. Watson! I'm so sorry, sir, I hadn't realised from our earlier conversations that you were *the* 'Dr. Watson'. Mr. Holmes has been with us for the past month. It has been an honour to work with him and now I've finally got to meet you as well."

I smiled at him and then nodded affectionately towards Holmes. "Not much of a retirement for you either, then?"

"No, just can't keep out of trouble. But it is good to see you, Watson. It must be a good six months since we last spoke."

We chatted along for a few minutes, catching up on all that had happened, relaxed in each other's company and almost oblivious to the presence of PC Dunning, who sat quietly by the hospital bed. At sixty-five, Holmes retained a youthful look, his dark hair swept back and showing only a fringe of grey at the temples, his eyes still bright and alert. He stood tall in a fawn-coloured Norfolk jacket with matching waistcoat and trousers and light-brown brogues.

We moved on to the subject of the shooting. Holmes explained that he had been given a short briefing on the events earlier that evening, but asked Dunning to provide his own account. The officer was pleased to oblige: "About six-thirty, we received a telephone call from a Mr. Metcalf, the landlord of the Bancroft Arms on the Mile End Road. He said that a scuffle had taken place in the tap room of the bar and a man had been shot. The gunman had been prevented from leaving the bar by some of the pub regulars, who had taken the small pistol from him. They held him prisoner until we arrived about half-an-hour later.

"I accompanied Inspector Banns and PC Moxon. When we got there, the inspector and I were delighted to see that the man being pinned to the ground by three hefty drinkers was Serang Sayan."

Holmes nodded while Dunning paused and gestured towards Christie. "This young fellow lay face down on the floor of the tap room.

509

We thought he was dead at first, but when we turned him over, we could see that he was still breathing. He looked to have been shot in the shoulder at close range by the Derringer pistol and was probably knocked unconscious as he fell to the floor. Sayan clearly thought he'd killed him, for when the inspector asked the publican for some smelling salts and brought Christie around a short while later, the sailor made a wild lunge at him. Before we separated them, Sayan glared at Christie, held a forefinger to his own lips and then ran it across his throat."

"As if telling Christie to keep quiet or face the consequences?"

"Yes, Doctor, that is what we believe. And it seems it had the desired effect. Christie would only tell us his name and refused to say anything further about the attempt on his life."

At this, Holmes expressed some surprise. "He has said nothing at all beyond that?"

"No, Mr. Holmes. Well, actually, he did say *one* other thing, although it didn't seem that significant. He said: 'Please take care of Delilah'."

"And you have no idea to whom he may have been referring?"

"No, sir. He has been silent ever since. Inspector Banns and PC Moxon left to take Sayan to a nearby lock-up, and I was instructed to wait for the ambulance and to stay with Christie until told otherwise."

"I see. Well, the bad news is that Sayan has managed to escape. Inspector Banns left him at the lock-up in the charge of a constable who was evidently duped. Apparently, Sayan fell to the floor of the cell, shaking violently and foaming at the mouth. The constable unlocked the door, believing him to be suffering some sort of fit, and was immediately set upon by our man, who escaped and was last seen heading along Hanbury Street. Banns has alerted all divisions to keep an eye out and, despite all of the yuletide demands on the force, is confident that Sayan will be retaken. In the meantime, he has asked me to look into Christie's affairs and see if I can make sense of what has gone on and how it might relate to our wider investigations into the affairs of Vulliamy, the moneylender."

"Is this moneylender dangerous then, Holmes?" I enquired.

"Yes, he set up his money-making venture in the East End about three years ago. Those who fall foul of him and fail to repay their loans and the exorbitant rates of interest he charges have been subjected to threats and assaults, perpetrated by his loyal sidekicks, Serang and Bhandarry Sayan. The Hindu brothers have gained some notoriety for their barbaric methods of extracting money from those in debt to Vulliamy.

510

"So far, the gang has managed to stay one step ahead of Inspector Banns' men who were tasked with shutting down the moneylending operation. Scotland Yard fears that Vulliamy is being protected by a high-ranking officer within the force who is receiving bribes in return for intelligence on the unfolding police investigation. The Commissioner, Sir Nevil Macready, asked me a month or so back if I could provide some assistance. As yet, I have seen no evidence of police corruption in the case, but believe that Sidney Vulliamy and Bhandarry Sayan are lying low in the knowledge that we are investigating their affairs."

PC Dunning then asked, "Do you think it possible that Serang Sayan might come here and try to finish Christie, Mr. Holmes?"

My colleague answered him directly. "No. I think that very unlikely. Clearly, you will need to be on your guard, but I suspect our sailor will be long gone."

Dunning look relieved. Holmes then probed whether the constable had taken time to search Christie at any point. Dunning shifted uneasily and admitted that he had not. It was then that I remembered Christie's grey woollen jacket in the operating theatre.

"Actually, Holmes, I had to cut the jacket from Christie before we could patch up his shoulder. I asked one of the orderlies to package it up along with his boots and a necklace and place them in one of the lockers outside the theatre. I could go and retrieve the package, if you think it important?"

Holmes beamed. "Excellent. That would be most helpful."

When I returned to the side ward, Holmes was sat on a chair on the opposite side of the bed to PC Dunning, looking intently at the patient. Somewhat incongruously, a looped paper chain was strung just above his head – the colourful decoration having been made earlier by some of the children unfortunate enough to be occupying beds in the lead up to Christmas. He was puffing away on a pipe, the strong tobacco smoke mingling with the smell of surgical spirit, and reminding me of happier days in the upstairs room of our Baker Street apartment.

"You know, I should tell you to take that pipe outside the ward, Holmes," I said with a broad smirk. "The hospital takes a dim view of smokers on surgical wards these days."

Holmes looked at me absentmindedly and then removed the pipe from his mouth. "Apologies, Doctor. Old habits die hard, as they say."

I passed him the package. He removed the string, undid the bundle, and placed the brown paper on the floor. One sleeve of the grey jacket lay on top of the garment, the result of my earlier work with the scalpel. Holmes glanced over it, and then dropped it onto the brown paper. Lifting the rest of the jacket he then began his detailed examination;

smelling the woollen fibres, checking all of the pockets, removing a couple of items, and scrutinising every point of interest with his familiar magnifying glass. When he had finished, he turned his attention to the necklace which also lay on top of the jacket, and then the footwear: a pair of scuffed black leather ankle boots which had clearly seen better days. It had been some time since I had seen him in action, and I was every bit as fascinated as PC Dunning to watch the consulting detective at work.

After what seemed like an age, Holmes looked up and spoke. "Not much to be gathered, but a few pointers which may be useful. Christie is an apprentice stonemason, left-handed, and twenty-two years of age. He lives in a modest house in Mile End Old Town and is a keen gardener. He also has a nervous disposition, which may be the result of a recent loss, and is a devout Anglican and pacifist."

Dunning chortled. "Mr. Holmes, you are truly remarkable. How any man could presume to know so much, from so little, is beyond me."

I recognised the hint of irritation which passed momentarily across my colleague's face. "Constable, if you had searched Christie you would have been able to discern much of this. He wears a St Christopher's medallion, a clear sign of his faith. On the back there are two separate pieces of engraving. The first is his name and date of birth, probably done when he was given the medal as a child – the engraving being difficult to pick out given the wear on the silver. A much more recent engraving displays the name 'Benjamin Christie' and a date of '2nd November 1919'. It suggests the very recent death of a family member – a father, brother or uncle, perhaps – which may account for his nervousness. His nails are ragged and bitten to the quick, and yet this is not a long-standing habit, for he has well-formed cuticles.

"In his pocket is a three-year old document which announces his official status as a 'conscientious objector'. It tells us that he was successful at his wartime tribunal in seeking to be excused from bearing arms, but was required to undertake some trade or profession in support of the war effort – clear proof of his pacifism and again suggestive of a strong religious conviction. The document also identifies his address on 'Louisa Street', about half a mile from the Bancroft Arms. I know the area. It is a road of well-appointed terraced houses which have small gardens to their rear, and is a refuge for many tradesmen and professionals of the middling order."

"But how do you know Christie is a stonemason – and an apprentice at that?" quizzed Dunning.

"A close examination of the fibres on his jacket reveals evidence of a fine white dust, unmistakably tiny fragments of Portland stone. His left hand bears the scars of his profession: the hard skin on the fingertips, the engrained dust on the palm, and a slight swelling around each of the knuckles. In muscular terms, his right arm is the more fully developed – confirmation that it is used to wield a stonemason's mallet. At twenty-two, he is unlikely to be a master stonemason, so alongside the other discernible facts, I would suggest that he is still completing his apprenticeship. And if I had to be pushed on the nature of his work as a non-combatant during the war, I would submit that he was most likely engaged in preparing tombstones and memorial plaques for those who died fighting on foreign soil."

PC Dunning looked on in awe. Holmes concluded his deposition with a few final words: "As for the gardening, the underside of his boots testifies to the frequent use of a spade. There are clear ridges on the left hand sole where the ball of the foot has been used to tread down on the spade. The ridges are absent from the other sole. We know that his house has a garden. I would expect it to be well-tended."

"Bravo!" said I. "And what do you propose to do now, having learned so much about our mystery man?"

"Why, visit his home, of course. There is no time like the present, my friend."

"Splendid. I have just finished my shift, so if you have no objection, Holmes, I would be pleased to accompany you."

PC Dunning looked crestfallen. "I wish I could join you, gentlemen, but duty compels me to stay here until I am relieved by PC Moxon. Good luck with your endeavours."

It was surprisingly mild that evening as we walked out onto the Strand in search of a taxi. There was a strong and welcome aroma of ground coffee and a hint of roasted chestnuts in the air from one of the many cafés that had sprung up now that the war had ended. Lanterns and glittering decorations adorned some of the shop fronts, and while it was busy on the thoroughfare with flurries of festive revellers, it took us little time to find a taxi rank and a cabbie willing to drive us the three miles into Mile End Old Town.

Sat in the back of the taxi, Holmes announced suddenly that he had not been entirely honest with PC Dunning. "There are some features to this case which are, for the moment, somewhat baffling, Watson. I did not wish to set hares coursing by mentioning it, but it was clear to me that Christie had gone into that pub for a specific reason. He is no drinker. In fact, in an inside pocket of his jacket was a signed 'pledge' in support of his abstinence. Close to it was another item I failed to point out to Dunning – a sheathed hunting knife made by J. B. Schofield of

Sheffield. Hardly the sort of weapon we might expect a pacifist to be carrying. Until I am in possession of some further data which may shed light on these apparent anomalies, I would prefer to keep the matters from the police."

"Understood, Holmes – as you wish."

It was a little after eleven o'clock when we alighted from the taxi at the entrance to Louisa Street. The gas lamps along the street cast a warm glow on the yellow brick terraced houses, which were nicely proportioned with a front entrance door, single downstairs window, and two upper sash windows comprised of six-over-six panelled glass panes. Christie's property was some way along the street to our right. Unlike many of the homes nearby, it appeared to have no Christmas decorations on view. Just before we reached it, Holmes whispered that we should be discreet in our business. I noted that he had already withdrawn from his pocket a set of keys.

"A stroke of luck, Watson – a standard Davenport rim lock," he said in a hushed tone. His fingers worked quickly as he sought out the correct skeleton key and inserted it in the lock. With a faint click the lock was undone, and Holmes turned the doorknob. We wasted no time in entering the house and closing the door behind us.

For a few seconds we stood in darkness. I heard Holmes returning the set of keys to his pocket and then saw a slim shaft of light stretching out before us and illuminating the narrow hallway of the house. Holmes held in his hand a small silver canister, from which the light was emanating.

"A new toy?" I whispered.

"Yes, indeed – a Winchester pocket flashlight. A small gift from a grateful American client. It is powered by two small electric batteries. I wouldn't be without it."

On the right, a short distance along the hallway was a closed door. Holmes opened it and we stepped into the room to find that it was the front parlour. Illuminated by a gas lamp across the street and the more telling beams from the flashlight, it looked to be sparsely yet luxuriously furnished, the wallpaper a dark red colour with an intricate floral pattern. Either side of a small fireplace and hearth on the opposite wall there were tall mahogany bookshelves filled with volumes of all sizes. Set in the far corner against the window was a small green leather armchair with an accompanying side table. It was the full extent of the furniture.

"Mr. Christie is clearly a man of modest means," I ventured.

"You forget that he is still completing his apprenticeship. This is a desirable property for someone of his age and profession. I would venture that he inherited the house from his parents and until recently lived here with an older brother."

I expressed some surprise. "Why do you say that?"

"The décor is too florid and fussy for a working man in his early twenties. On the mantelpiece is a photograph of an older couple and beside it another of two dark-haired men, unquestionably brothers, the younger looking of which is Jonathon Christie."

". . . With the other being the recently deceased 'Benjamin Christie'?"

"My thoughts exactly," chimed Holmes.

As we were about to step out of the parlour and back into the hallway, there was a loud shriek from elsewhere within the house. We both froze, the beam from the flashlight playing out into the empty hall and giving us no clue as to the identity of the screamer. A chilling voice then uttered: "I'll kill him! I'll kill him!"

Holmes strode out of the room and passed quickly along the hallway. I followed behind, noting a stairwell to our right, as we entered the main downstairs room of the property. In the uncertain light, we relied on the flashlight to make sense of what now lay before us: a mirror on one wall, a large table in a corner on which sat a piece of white stone, another bookshelf, and a couple of wooden dining chairs. A space no bigger than fifteen feet square with a window directly ahead of us and a further closed door to the right. And yet, nowhere within the space could we see any human form. As my eyes began to scan around the floor for anyone lurking near the wainscot, the same screeching voice echoed around the room, "Two down and one across! Two down and one across!"

The next noise came from Holmes, who broke suddenly into an uncontrolled chuckle and guffaw. It left me with a discomforting sense of bewilderment. *What exactly was going on?*

My gaze followed the beam of his flashlight into the corner of the room to our right. It was then that I saw the reason for his mirth. Hanging from a chain, on a hook fastened into the ceiling, was a cage some three or four feet in diameter, in which I could see perched a striking, stocky-looking bird of oriental appearance. The blue-black sheen of its feathers was tinged with a purple hue, and I could see distinct bright orange patches along its wings. In contrast, the legs and bill of the specimen were a bright yellow and it was around ten inches in height.

"My God, Holmes! It's a damned parrot!"

"Hardly – this bird is something far more impressive. You are looking at a Mynah bird, a creature which can imitate the human voice." He moved closer, angling the beam of the torch away from the cage, so as not to shine the light directly into the bird's eyes. "A most remarkable specimen, eh? And another mystery solved . . . ."

"Yes. I'm thinking that this must be Christie's 'Delilah'?"

The Mynah bird seemed to chirp in confirmation.

"It seems we all concur!" laughed Holmes. "And I'm pleased to see that the ravages of war and early retirement have not dulled your senses, Watson. Now, let's see what other clues we can find."

It was good to be back at his side. I had quite forgotten just how much I had missed Holmes and the adventures we had shared for so many years. He seemed to be in fine fettle and, having scanned the rest of the room with the flashlight, walked across to examine the white stone on the large corner table.

"This is very nearly completed – a grave marker, no less. But why would Christie labour on this at home, rather than at work? He seems to have fashioned it here on this very table, with just a few basic tools." His hands worked their way around the stone cross, touching its contours, feeling the fine dust which covered each surface. "I may not be a master stonemason, but this looks like a pretty basic piece of work, with little finesse. I would say that Christie produced this at some speed and with little enthusiasm."

"Perhaps he picks up the odd private commission, outside of his day to day work, to earn a bit of extra money?" I suggested.

"Hmm . . . Possibly."

"Two down and one across! Two down and one across!" Delilah's piercing squawk filled the room once more.

"Is it conceivable that our rare avian has a penchant for those strange word puzzles that you used to delight in, Holmes?" The comment was made in jest, but my colleague responded positively.

"That is not so far-fetched. You may remember that the first 'word cross' puzzle appeared in the *New York World* five or six years ago – the invention of a Mr. Arthur Wynne, a journalist originally from Liverpool, I believe. Since that time a number of American newspapers have included weekly or daily 'crossword puzzles' within their pages. I confess that I still find them diverting in the absence of any other mental stimulation. It is possible that Christie enjoyed the same leisurely pursuit, although it's hard to imagine him shouting out the elements of a puzzle he may have been struggling with."

"Yes, I imagine the bird will only remember and repeat short phrases which are said over and over again."

"I'll kill him! I'll kill him!" shrieked the Mynah.

"Indeed," mused Holmes, his eyes narrowing as he scrutinised the bird afresh, "how true."

Our continued investigation of the downstairs living room threw up no further clues. Beyond the room was a small kitchen, again sparsely furnished, with a small side door from it leading to the rear garden of the property. The set of skeleton keys again proved useful.

In the narrow beam of the flashlight, we stepped quietly outside the back door and into a short passage which ran along the length of the kitchen. To our left was the wall of the neighbouring property. Beyond the passageway, paved slabs, laid end to end, ran down the length of the garden to the left, ending in a wide gate set within a wall at the bottom. To the right of this I could just make out a small wooden shed. The remainder of the land was given over to soil, most of which had been overtaken by weeds. The garden was flanked on both sides by tall brick walls, shielding us from view.

Holmes edged forward in small steps, doing his best to examine all areas of the garden in the uncertain light. I tucked myself in behind him so as not to impede his progress.

Two-thirds of the way down the garden he paused and turned to me, whispering, "This patch of earth has been dug recently. But the rest is something of a mess. Christie may be less of a gardener than I imagined." I nodded in agreement, noting a spade, still upright, in the soil beside a long open trench.

When we had reached the end of the garden, Holmes spent some time looking in through the window of the wooden shed. He held the flashlight above his head and played its beam down at an angle into every part of the interior, standing on tip toes at one point to ensure that he had seen everything he could from his vantage point. With a quick look over the smokehouse lock on the outside of the door, he had apparently seen everything he needed to.

Before returning to the house, Holmes spent some minutes examining the paving slabs and soil close to the green-painted garden gate. With some excitement, he pointed down at a number of distinct muddy tracks on the first half dozen paving slabs. I nodded again in confirmation as he brought the torchlight up to see my reaction. I had seen the tracks, but had no idea why Holmes felt them to be so significant.

It was only when we were back in the kitchen and he had successfully relocked the rear door that we began to speak. I followed him through to the living room, where he lit a candle on the table and switched off the flashlight.

"Well, what do you make of it all? Casts a new light on the case, don't you think?"

I had to confess to being none the wiser. "I'm sorry, Holmes. I did see the tracks you pointed to near the gate and the recently dug earth. I also saw the contents of the shed – a few tools hanging on the rear wall and the painted boards and advertising signs stacked up on the floor nearby. But I have no clear idea what it tells us."

"What did you see *on the signs*?" asked Holmes.

"Some painted pictures of fruit and vegetables, and some prices for various produce."

"Precisely – you saw everything I did, and yet you seem not to have grasped its significance. Christie is clearly a stonemason as we suspected. However, it seems reasonable to conclude that his recently deceased brother was a greengrocer, who plied his trade from a hand cart. The signs and track marks tell us as much."

I felt a tad slighted. "Well, I saw no hand cart. How do you explain that?"

"That is a lead which we have yet to follow. But you cannot doubt that a hand cart was involved. You saw the tracks yourself. A larger vehicle would not have fitted through the gate."

"Granted. But what significance does this have for the case and the attack on Christie?"

"Two down and one across!" It was Delilah, reminding us of her presence in the corner of room.

Holmes smirked. "That clever bird has just given you the answer, my friend."

"No, I don't see it at all."

"Cast your mind back. Sidney Vulliamy and Bhandarry Sayan appear to have disappeared. Serang Sayan had attempted to kill Christie. It is possible that the two acts are linked. Let us suppose that Christie wished to kill the moneylender."

"Hence the Mynah's repeated call: *I'll kill him! I'll kill him!*"

"Exactly," replied Holmes. "Christie is a man of faith, a teetotaller and a pacifist. A resort to violence would not ordinarily be part of his *modus operandi*, and yet we find him carrying a hunting knife and involved in an altercation with a violent offender in a public house a few days before one of the most significant events in the Christian calendar. Serang Sayan does not usually resort to firearms. The attacks he has carried out for Sidney Vulliamy have been vicious, but he has always stopped short of murder. Why is he also acting out of character?"

"You suspect this has something to do with Christie's older brother?"

"Yes – that is the key to this. It cannot have been easy trying to eke out a living as a greengrocer, with all of the deprivations that we continue to experience here in London, despite the end of the war. It is not fanciful to imagine that the man may have found himself in debt, paying over the odds for a limited supply of fresh produce, while his customers struggle to find the cash to pay for the fruit and vegetables he has on display. In desperation, he is reluctant to fall back on the limited earnings of his beloved younger brother, so turns instead to Vulliamy, the local moneylender. From there it is a slippery slope into debt and the unwanted attentions of the Sayan brothers."

At last I could see where he was heading. "So you believe that they murdered the greengrocer and Christie has been seeking to exact his revenge?"

"That is possible, although it is more likely that their heavy handed tactics led to his suicide. Either way, I do believe that they were responsible for his death and Christie has indeed been out for revenge – with some success, I have to say."

"I'm not sure I follow."

"Come on, Watson! You must know where this is leading. I was right to suggest that Christie has been doing lots of digging recently, but a look at the back yard tells us he is clearly no gardener. If I am not mistaken, that freshly-dug section of earth towards the end of the garden is now the resting place of Sidney Vulliamy and Bhandarry Sayan. He murdered them and transported their bodies here using the greengrocer's cart. It was the perfect way to move them without attracting attention."

My surprise was palpable. "Really – how can you be so sure?"

He turned towards the bird cage. "It was Delilah here that confirmed the matter. She is well named. Was it not Delilah, a woman in the valley of Sorek, who betrayed Samson in the *Book of Judges*? This Mynah bird has done the same for young Christie. Not only has she told us of the man's deep-seated hatred of Vulliamy and his intentions to '*kill him!*', but she has provided us with testimony on Christie's thoughts after the murders. The bird can be forgiven for misquoting the stonemason. '*Two down and one across!*' was no reference to a crossword clue. What Christie actually said was, 'Two down and *for one a cross*! Meaning that he had only managed to despatch two of the three men he sought and felt obliged to provide a Christian burial for Vulliamy."

"The crudely carved stone cross which sits on the table here!" I added. "Perhaps he believed that as a Hindu, Bhandarry Sayan would not require the same treatment."

"That is my supposition."

"And the confrontation in the Bancroft Arms – was that Christie's attempt to assassinate the last of the trio?"

"No, unlikely, I would say. It seems more plausible that Serang was pursuing Christie, in the full knowledge that the stonemason had murdered Bhandarry and Vulliamy. He was carrying a loaded gun, after all. Christie would not ordinarily have gone into a public house. I believe he entered the establishment in fear of his life, having been chased by Serang. That working hypothesis also helps to explain why Christie has, so far, been tight-lipped about the whole affair."

"He is fearful of being exposed as a double murderer!"

"Yes – the Lascar's finger across the throat gesture seems to confirm that. He was telling Christie to hold his tongue. Serang will stop at nothing to avenge the death of his brother, but he will not risk involving the police. He has too much to lose. We must be wary, Watson. This man is extremely dangerous. It is not the first time we have faced such an adversary. You might remember the Lascar sailor we encountered in the case you so lovingly embellished as 'The Man with the Twisted Lip'?"

Had it not been for the wry smile that accompanied his words, I might have taken the remark as a criticism, but knew that not to be the case. I ignored the taunt and turned instead to our plan of action. "Where do we go from here?"

"I have a suite at the Grosvenor Hotel in Victoria. There is more than enough space for the two of us. I suggest we take advantage of a decent meal and a good night's sleep and then set out first thing tomorrow to track down our elusive sailor."

I was taken aback. "Really – is there not a case for acting while the iron is hot, so to speak?"

"Serang Sayan is going nowhere, my friend. He has half the metropolitan force out looking for him, an East Bengal sailor far from home. I know exactly where he will be hiding, and it will not hurt to keep our powder dry for a dawn assault."

With that, he extinguished the candle and resorted once more to the flashlight. As he reached the door of the living room, he turned to me and nodded towards the corner of the room. "Don't forget Delilah, Watson! We can't leave the poor creature here, especially as she has been so helpful in our enquiries!"

It was close to five-thirty the next morning when I was woken rather sharply by Holmes in the luxurious surroundings of the Grosvenor Hotel. Our arrival the previous night had sparked a considerable flurry of activity. Holmes had left the Mynah in the care of a bemused night porter with full instructions to ensure that the bird was fed and watered and properly accommodated. The concierge had arranged for a bed to be made up for me within Holmes's suite, and some ten minutes later, a salver of turkey sandwiches, a side plate of mince pies, and a bottle of Burgundy had arrived in the room. It has been sometime since I had enjoyed such extravagance.

"Good morning, my dear fellow! I trust that you slept well? A maid has just returned your shirt, washed and ironed, and these trousers have been pressed to within an inch of their lives! I took the liberty of ordering room service – a small cooked breakfast to help us on our way."

My response was heartfelt. "Holmes, it is a pleasure to be back in your company. While it seems slightly bizarre to be investigating grim murder at such a festive time, I cannot tell you how much I have missed our adventures together."

I could see that my comments had touched him, but he turned away, avoiding my gaze, busying himself with the tray of breakfast items and the large tea pot at its centre. Our conversation thereafter was focused on the case.

Evidently, Holmes had been busy during the few hours that I slumbered. He told me that he had managed to reach Inspector Banns by telephone a short while earlier and had arranged for a team of detectives to meet us later that morning at a point of rendezvous. He had also pinpointed the location where he believed Serang Sayan would be hiding.

I expressed my disbelief at this rapid rate of progress. "How on earth did you manage to find the hideout without leaving the hotel?"

"Eyes and ears! You remember the old days when we made good use of the Baker Street Irregulars, that proud group of itinerant ragamuffins that I valued so highly. Well, while the Irregulars are long gone, their erstwhile leader, the indomitable Charlie Wiggins, has always stayed in touch, and prior to the War ran a successful business as a private investigator. Having been called up for war service, he has now returned to London, keen to resume the profession. This is the first opportunity I have had to involve him in a case and he has clearly lost none of his talents. I called him by telephone last night and set him to work. Only half-an-hour ago he rang back to say that his discreet enquiries had enabled him to locate the hideout close to the Mile End Road."

"But how did he know which area to concentrate upon? You cannot tell me he has the ability to search the whole of London in one night?"

"No – but it was clear that the search would be more limited. Our hypothesis was that Christie's brother had worked as a greengrocer using a hand cart, and that Christie had used the cart to transport the dead bodies back to Louisa Street. The tracks on the garden path indicated that more than one journey had been made. I therefore concluded that he moved the bodies one at a time."

"I see. So you were working on the basis that with the weight of the bodies, Christie had travelled a relatively short distance?"

"You have it in one. I told Wiggins to focus his attention on the streets close to Christie's home. He found what he was looking for on White Horse Lane."

"And what was he looking for?"

"The missing cart. Having taken the second of the bodies back to Louisa Street, I believe that Christie returned to the murder scene a final time. The more I thought about it last night, the more convinced I was that he would only have done that for one reason."

"Which was?"

"To collect a third body to fill that one remaining trench in the garden. I believe that he thought he had killed all three men and was returning for Serang Sayan. However, when he got there, he found that the Lascar was still alive and waiting for him. Christie flees, leaving the cart, and is pursued by Serang. He tries to escape into the Bancroft Arms and is shot by the sailor and left for dead."

"It sounds remarkable, but fits the facts as we know them. And if Wiggins has found the cart at the hideout, it lends further credence to your theory."

"Indeed. And with our breakfast finished, we can now put our theory to the test."

It was just past seven-fifteen that morning when our taxi dropped us off at a quiet location along White Horse Lane. Waiting there was Inspector Banns and six uniformed constables, all armed, we were told, with standard issue Webley revolvers. Holmes quickly briefed the men on what we had found out and Banns confirmed that he knew exactly where to find the hideout. Some minutes later the police had the three-storey brown brick building surrounded. Holmes and I stood at a safe distance across the street watching the drama unfold.

At a given signal, two of the officers were sent to the rear of the house to affect an entrance. Less than a minute later we saw a man stagger from the front door of the dwelling. He had not reached the gate of the front garden when he was brought down in a rugby-style tackle by one of the larger constables. The officer retained his grip and kept the sailor pinned to the floor until the others came to his assistance.

Inspector Banns seemed delighted with the arrest, having said earlier that he feared Serang might be in possession of another firearm. But as the officers searched the prisoner, he was found to be carrying only a short knife, some three or four inches in length. The man was no taller than five feet in height, but looked extremely strong and muscular. His bright penetrating eyes fixed on Holmes as we approached the officers, a look nothing short of pure hatred. Holmes smiled back at him, impervious, it seemed, to any threat the man posed. The prisoner then seemed to shake violently and vomited at the feet of one of the constables.

Banns stepped aside from the others and shook us both by the hand. "Thank you, gentleman, I forgot to mention it earlier, but it seems you were right about the garden in Louisa Street. I sent two men there immediately after your telephone call this morning, Mr. Holmes. Two bodies were uncovered, and a pathologist is now at the scene. He tells me that there are no obvious signs of violence on either man. So it seems we have some further questions to ask of Jonathon Christie."

"I wonder, in that case, Inspector, if you would permit the two of us to have a short interview with the man, before your formal interrogation. It may help to prepare the ground for you if he knows that the police are already aware of the crime he has committed."

Banns narrowed his eyes slightly while looking at Holmes and then cast a quick glance in my direction. "I'm sure that would not be a problem, sir. You have been invaluable on this investigation and I trust your integrity. Christie is now out of hospital and currently detained in Bow Street Police Station. I will make the arrangements as soon as I return to the station. Would two o'clock this afternoon be soon enough?"

"That would be perfect," replied Holmes. "I am very grateful to you."

I left Holmes shortly afterwards to return home and attend to one of my private patients. He appeared to be on the mend and imbued with more than a little festive spirit, insisting that I accept a plump turkey from him as some recompense for the many days I had spent nursing him back to health. The consultation lasted about an hour, and after preparing a light luncheon and catching up on some correspondence, I made my way to Bow Street. Holmes was pacing up and down in the lobby of the building when I arrived.

"Is everything alright?" I asked, concerned by the look on his face.

"Yes – just a few odds and ends I cannot fathom. Christie seems curiously ill-named. One wonders how he could have countenanced multiple-murder at this time of year given his apparent faith. I have had a subsequent telephone conversation with Inspector Banns. He tells me that Serang Sayan has been admitted to the Royal Free Hospital suffering from severe stomach pains. As yet, they are unsure whether this is another ruse on his part, but Banns is taking no chances and has two armed officers sat beside his hospital bed. I believe he is genuinely ill and may well have been on the earlier occasion when he escaped custody."

"What makes you say that?"

"Firstly, that I find it hard to imagine he could have faked the foaming at the mouth stunt. And secondly, I have been considering how Christie – a small man not given to violence – managed to overpower three vicious men armed only with a hunting knife. He must have been convinced that he had killed all three to have the confidence to move their bodies one by one in the grocer's cart. And yet, the bodies of Vulliamy and Bhandarry showed no signs of violence. The only plausible explanation is that a powerful gas or poison may have been involved – one that was administered by Christie himself."

A few minutes later we were seated in a large ground floor interview room facing Jonathon Christie. He was still heavily bandaged around his upper body, but the colour had returned to his face. The stonemason was the first to talk. "I understand that one of you is Dr. Watson, the surgeon who operated on me last night?"

"Yes," I replied, "that's me."

"I just wanted to say how grateful I am for your assistance, Doctor. I genuinely believed that I was going to die, as the pain in my shoulder was excruciating."

"In the scheme of things, a routine piece of minor surgery. I have seen much, much worse in recent times, Mr. Christie."

My veiled allusion to some of the wartime casualties I had dealt with was clearly not lost on Christie. "Yes, I cannot begin to imagine how anyone coped with the carnage of the Great War. It left many scars."

"Like those on your brother Benjamin?" Holmes's question bypassed any pretence of courtesy and hit Christie hard, just as my colleague had intended.

Christie took a second or two to readjust before responding. "I have, of course, heard of you, Mr. Holmes, and read many of the good Doctor's tales of your adventures. Meeting you under these circumstances does not seem quite so inspiring. I imagine you already know every facet of this case and have come here to present your deductions in a theatrical denouement designed to pamper your ego and send me to the gallows."

Holmes appeared to take no offence from the remark and responded with admirable composure. "On the contrary, Mr. Christie, Watson and I have made good progress in piecing together various leads and observable facts, but we are still unclear on a number of significant details. We know that you are a man of faith who has struggled with his conscience since the death of your brother. We believe you set out to murder the three men you blamed for his death – Vulliamy, the moneylender, and his two accomplices, Serang and Bhandarry Sayan. My supposition is that you gassed or poisoned all three men and then sought to bury their bodies in your back garden. Had it not been for Serang Sayan, who clearly survived the poisoning, you may well have succeeded. In the event, when you returned to White Horse Lane for the third time, you found him alive and out for revenge. He chased you along the Mile End Road and into the Bancroft Arms, where he then shot you. Until the police arrived, he was convinced you were dead, and having realised that you were not, gestured for you to say nothing about the events that had led to the attack."

"That is accurate in every respect. Although I am still bewildered as to why he should have wished for both of us to remain silent."

Holmes nodded. "Serang operates according to an ancient criminal code. He would rather go to his death than inform on another law breaker. He also believes in a tenet that you may now share, namely, 'an eye for an eye'. He will stop at nothing to avenge the death of his brother."

"Then we are not so different after all. As brothers, Benjamin and I were raised in a devoutly Christian family. He held firm to his faith, as did I, but found it increasingly difficult to adhere to the strict pacifist ideals of my parents. When war was declared, he announced that he was enlisting to fight overseas and within weeks left us for his regiment. My father died soon afterwards, and my mother a year later. I was left to run Benjamin's greengrocer's stall until I faced the call-up.

"I thought long and hard about my decision, but applied for conscientious objector status and then appeared before a tribunal. I was granted an exemption from bearing arms but told that I would have to take up a trade or profession in support of the war effort. With the grocery business struggling to pay its way, I enrolled as an apprentice stonemason. It was tough living alone and making ends meet, but I survived until Benjamin returned home in 1917. He was suffering from shellshock and spent six months recovering.

"Having little else to support us, I continued with my apprenticeship and Benjamin did what he could to resurrect the greengrocery business. Within a couple of weeks, it was clear that it was never going to provide us with a reliable income, and Benjamin began to drink heavily, spending whatever meagre earnings he had made. I did not feel I could voice any objection, as I felt like a fraudster, having stayed at home, refusing to enlist.

"Sidney Vulliamy had been at school with my brother, although it would be stretching it to say that they had ever been friends. But in need of a few pounds and developing an expensive taste for alcohol, Benjamin turned to the moneylender. Vulliamy was only too happy to assist, spending time drinking with Benjamin and showering him with gifts – one of which was 'Delilah', the Mynah bird, who had originally belonged to Bhandarry Sayan.

"It took some time for Benjamin to realise he had been deceived and that all of the money he had been lent would need to be paid back in short-order, along with a considerable sum of interest. Unwilling to saddle me with his debts, and terrified about what the Sayan brothers would do given his obvious inability to pay, Benjamin took his life. For once, I was not prepared to sit back and turn the other cheek.

"I knew enough about Vulliamy's operation to realise that he operated out of the White Horse Lane address. I also recognised that I would stand no chance of fighting all three men if it came to violence. So I hatched a different plan. I found it was surprisingly easy and cheap to buy tartar emetic over the counter. I purchased small amounts from chemists all over the capital, so as not to attract attention. The yellow crystals seemed to dissolve easily in alcohol, which I hoped would also mask any taste it had. Knowing the three to be keen drinkers, I mixed a large quantity of the antimony with decent Scotch and then arranged to meet them in White Horse Lane.

"Vulliamy welcomed me into the house, saying how upset he had been to learn of Benjamin's suicide. It was all I could do not to attack him with the hunting knife I had hidden in my pocket. But I was not to be outwitted. I maintained that my brother's death had come as something of a shock, particularly as we had significant debts, and said I had heard that Vulliamy had occasionally lent money to people in the neighbourhood and asked directly whether he would consider extending me some credit.

"The man seemed to relax instantly and invited me to sit at a table in the centre of the room. He must have believed to that point that I had arranged the meeting to challenge him about the way he had treated Benjamin. With more than a hint of irony, I indicated that I would be forever indebted to him and had brought the Scotch as a goodwill gesture.

"Just imagine that, gentlemen! I'm in the lion's den and yet I have become the hunter – my greedy prey happy to distribute the whisky glasses and drink a toast or two to our financial transaction. So greedy were they that they didn't even realise I wasn't drinking with them. I watched as all three downed the first glass and Vulliamy poured a second. It was only on the third glass that the bottle stayed on the table. Serang was the first to fall, landing heavily on the floor and clutching his stomach. He began to be sick immediately. Vulliamy never rose from his chair. His face turned ashen and within five minutes it was clear that he was dead. Bhandarry attempted to get up and make it to the kitchen. After only a few steps he slumped against the table, sending the whisky bottle and the glasses scattering across the floor.

"I sat and watched for twenty minutes, the only sound coming from Serang, who continued to lie on the floor. I guessed it would only be a short time before he too slipped away. I left the house and walked back to Louisa Street. I had the cart ready at the back gate and wheeled it the short distance to White Horse Lane. Using the rear door to Vulliamy's house, I first dragged his body to the cart, covered it with a tarpaulin and transported him to my home. His body went into the first of the three trenches I had already prepared, and I quickly covered the corpse with soil. I then did the same for Bhandarry Sayan.

"On returning to the house for a third time, I knew instantly that something was amiss. As I entered the back door, Serang fell upon me, but in his weakened state I managed to fend him off, pushing him against a dresser. As he came at me again, I realised he had a gun in his hand and retreated back through the door, expecting to be shot any moment. I ran from the house, turning briefly to see Serang tripping over the abandoned cart. He seemed to be gaining in strength, and as I ran out onto the Mile End Road, I could see that he was still following. In desperation I entered the Bancroft Arms. The rest you seem to know already . . . ."

Christie slumped back in his chair. He looked visibly relieved as if recounting the tale had somehow lightened his burden. I made an observation in the sudden silence that had engulfed the room. "It is not unusual for antimony poisoning to affect people in different ways. Some, like Vulliamy, will decline very rapidly in the face of such toxicity. Serang was probably saved because he began to vomit straight away. This would have expelled the contents of his stomach immediately, the poison acting very much like its own antidote. Of course, it remains to be seen whether he will survive the ordeal. From what I hear, he is still very ill."

Christie shrugged. "What is done is done. I still cannot find it within me to feel any remorse. So, what will happen to me now, Mr. Holmes?"

I could see there was no point in pretending that anything positive could ever come from the predicament that Christie now faced. Holmes clearly felt the same. "There is no easy way to say this, Mr. Christie, but there seems little doubt that you will be tried and found guilty of murder. If you are willing to cooperate fully with the authorities and freely admit

527

your guilt, there is some chance that your sentence might be commuted from one of execution to life imprisonment. That decision rests with you."

Christie did not seem perturbed by Holmes's words and had but one final request. "I know I am in no position to request anything further from either of you, but must ask. Would it be possibly for a decent home to be found for Delilah? I have a curious affection for that bird. She has been my only companion for some weeks now, and the only living creature I felt I could talk to throughout all of my troubles."

Holmes smiled at Christie and then turned to me with a sly wink. "Dr. Watson and I understand completely. Rest assured I will be pleased to look after the bird myself. Her conversation has already proved to be most enlightening."

It was on Christmas Eve that I next saw Holmes. I had arranged to meet him for lunch at the Grosvenor Hotel and arrived a few minutes early. To my surprise, he was already waiting in the reception area, and as soon as I had entered the hotel, he grasped me by the elbow and led me back out again to a waiting taxi.

"No time to waste, Watson. I'm afraid our luncheon will have to wait."

He bundled me into the back of the black cab and gave the driver our destination before continuing. "You might remember that at the start of the Christie case, I mentioned that I had been asked to investigate whether there might be a high-ranking officer within Scotland Yard who was taking bribes to protect Vulliamy. I feel confident that I will be able to reveal who that officer is in the next hour – a revelation likely to send shock-waves throughout the organisation."

I could not resist taunting him: "So this time we are looking for a mole, rather than a bird."

Holmes laughed out loud. "I've missed have your acerbic wit and welcome repartee, Dr. Watson. Lest I forget, as I am often prone to do at this time of year, a very Merry Christmas to you!" And with that, he slipped back into a short period of intense introspection, as only the great detective could. For the first time in over five years, it felt like a very joyous occasion indeed.

About the Contributors

The following contributors appear in this volume
The MX Book of New Sherlock Holmes Stories
Part V – Christmas Adventures

Peter K. Andersson is a Swedish historian specialising in urban culture in the late nineteenth century. He has previously published two collections of Sherlock Holmes stories, *The Cotswolds Werewolf and Other Stories of Sherlock Holmes* and *The Sensible Necktie.*

Hugh Ashton was born in the U.K., and moved to Japan in 1988, where he remained until 2016, living with his wife Yoshiko in the historic city of Kamakura, a little to the south of Yokohama. He and Yoshiko have now moved to Lichfield, a small cathedral city in the Midlands of the U.K., the birthplace of Samuel Johnson, and one-time home of Erasmus Darwin. In the past, he has worked in the technology and financial services industries, which have provided him with material for some of his books set in the 21st century. He currently works as a writer: novelist, freelance editor and copywriter (his work for large Japanese corporations has appeared in international business journals), and journalist, as well as producing industry reports on various aspects of the financial services industry. Recently, however, his lifelong interest in Sherlock Holmes has developed into an acclaimed series of adventures featuring the world's most famous detective, written in the style of the originals, and published by Inknbeans Press. In addition to these, he has also published historical and alternate historical novels, short stories, and thrillers. Together with artist Andy Boerger, he has produced the *Sherlock Ferret* series of stories for children, featuring the world's cutest detective.

Brian Belanger is a publisher and editor, but is best known for his freelance illustration and cover design work. His distinctive style can be seen on several MX Publishing covers, including *Silent Meridian* by Elizabeth Crowen, *Sherlock Holmes and the Menacing Melbournian* by Allan Mitchell, *Sherlock Holmes and A Quantity of Debt* by David Marcum, *Welcome to Undershaw* by Luke Benjamen Kuhns, and many more. Brian is the co-founder of Belanger Books LLC, where he illustrates the popular *MacDougall Twins with Sherlock Holmes* young reader series (#1 bestsellers on Amazon.com UK). A prolific creator, he also designs t-shirts, mugs, stickers, and other merchandise on his personal art site at *www.redbubble.com/people/zhahadun.*

Derrick Belanger is the author of the #1 bestselling book in its category.y *Sherlock Holmes: The Adventure of the Peculiar Provenance*, which was in the top 200 bestselling books on Amazon. He also is the author of the *MacDougall Twins with Sherlock Holmes* books, the latest of which is *Curse of the Deadly Dinosaur*, and he edited the Sir Arthur Conan Doyle horror anthology *A Study in Terror: Sir Arthur Conan Doyle's Revolutionary Stories of Fear and the Supernatural*. Mr. Belanger has recently started the publishing company Belanger Books, which released the Sherlock Holmes anthology *Beyond Watson*. Derrick Belanger also is a frequent contributor to *I Hear of Sherlock Everywhere*. He resides in Colorado and continues compiling unpublished works by Dr. John H. Watson.

S.F. Bennett was born and raised in London, studying History at Queen Mary and Westfield College, and Journalism at City University at the Postgraduate level, before moving to Devon in 2013. The author lectures on Conan Doyle, Sherlock Holmes, and 19th century detective fiction, and has had articles on various aspects from The Canon published in *The Journal of the Sherlock Holmes Society of London* and *The Torr*, the journal of *The Poor Folk Upon The Moors*, the Sherlock Holmes Society of the South West of England.

Bob Byrne was a columnist for *Sherlock Magazine* and has contributed to *Sherlock Holmes Mystery Magazine* and the Sherlock Holmes short story collection *Curious Incidents*. He publishes two free online newsletters: *Baker Street Essays* and *The Solar Pons Gazette*, both of which can be found at *www.SolarPons.com*, the only website dedicated to August Derleth's successor to the great detective. Bob's column, *The Public Life of Sherlock Holmes*, appears every Monday morning at *www.BlackGate.com* and explores Holmes, hard boiled, and other mystery matters, and whatever other topics come to mind by the deadline. His mystery-themed blog is *Almost Holmes*.

Molly Carr has been writing articles (paid and unpaid!) for many years on every conceivable subject for a wide variety of magazines and newspapers, and once had a tale accepted for the BBC's *Morning Story* slot. But it wasn't until she discovered MX Publishing that she attempted a whole book. In fact, she has written five books: *The Sign of Fear* and *A Study in* Crimson, which are meant to be funny, a semi-academic *In Search of Dr Watson*, a collection of pieces with the title *Sherlock in the Spring Time*, and *A Sherlock Holmes Who's Who* – which one critic said would do in lieu of anything better, and another called "excellent". She lives in a beautiful part of the country, which unfortunately is sometimes disturbed by the very noisy lawnmowers of landscape gardeners. This makes her long for a cork-lined room in which to compose something readers might see as really worthwhile.

Mike Chinn has published almost sixty short stories, from westerns to Lovecraftian fiction, with all shades of fantasy, horror, science fiction, and pulp adventure in between, along with a tale of the good Professor in *The Mammoth Book Of The Adventures Of Moriarty* (2015, Robinson). The Alchemy Press published a collection of his Damian Paladin fiction in 1998, whilst he has edited *Swords Against The Millennium* (2000) and *The Alchemy Press Book Of Pulp Heroes* Volumes 1, 2, and 3 (2012, 2013 and 2014 respectively) for the same imprint. 2015 saw the publication of his short story collection *Give Me These Moments Back* (The Alchemy Press), and a Steampunk Sherlock Holmes mash-up, *Vallis Timoris* (Fringeworks). A new Damian Paladin collection, *Walkers in Shadow*, and a Western, *Revenge Is A Cold Pistol*, are to be published by Pro Se Productions.

Bert Coules wandered through a succession of jobs from fringe opera company manager to BBC radio drama producer-director before becoming a full-time writer at the beginning of 1989. Bert works in a wide range of genres, including science fiction, horror, comedy, romance and action-adventure but he is especially associated with crime and detective stories: he was the head writer on the BBC's unique project to dramatise the entire Sherlock Holmes canon, and went on to script four further series of original Holmes and Watson mysteries. As well as radio, he also writes for TV and the stage.

Sir Arthur Conan Doyle (1859-1930) *Holmes Chronicler Emeritus*. If not for him, this anthology would not exist. Author, physician, patriot, sportsman, spiritualist, husband

and father, and advocate for the oppressed. He is remembered and honored for the purposes of this collection by being the man who introduced Sherlock Holmes to the world. Through fifty-six Holmes short stories, four novels, and additional Apocryphal entries, Doyle revolutionized mystery stories and also greatly influenced and improved police forensic methods and techniques for the betterment of all. *Steel True Blade Straight.*

C.H. Dye first discovered Sherlock Holmes when she was eleven, in a collection that ended at Reichenbach Falls. It was another six months before she discovered *The Hound of the Baskervilles*, and two weeks after that before a librarian handed her *The Return*. She has loved the stories ever since. She has written fan-fiction, and her first published pastiche, "The Tale of the Forty Thieves", was included in *The MX Book of New Sherlock Holmes Stories – Part I: 1881-1889.*

Jan Edwards is a British author. She was born near Horsham, Sussex, UK, but now lives in Staffordshire Moorlands with her husband, Peter Coleborn, and the obligatory three cats. She has a life-long passion for folklore and the supernatural, and draws on this for her fiction. To date, forty-plus of her short stories have seen publication in magazines and anthologies, including *The Mammoth Book of Dracula, The Mammoth Book of the Adventures of Moriarty,* and *Terror Tales of the Ocean.* Much of her published short fiction is reprinted in the collections *Leinster Gardens and Other Subtleties* and *Fables and Fabrications.* Jan won a Winchester Slim Volume Prize for her rural novel *Sussex Tales,* was short-listed for a BFS Award for Best Short Story as an author, and short listed three times as editor of anthologies. She edits anthologies for the award winning Alchemy Press and also for Fox Spirit Books. In a previous existence she has been Chairperson for both the British Fantasy Society and Fantasycon. Other works by Jan Edwards include *Leinster Gardens and Other Subtleties, Sussex Tales, Fables and Fabrications.* Anthologies edited by Jan and Jenny Barber include *The Alchemy Book of Ancient Wonders, The Alchemy Press Book of Urban Mythic, The Alchemy Press Book of Urban Mythic:2,* and *Wicked Women.* Jan's World War II crime novel *Winter Downs* is due for publication in 2017. For more details on Jan and her fiction visit *http://janedwardsblog.wordpress.com/*

Matthew J. Elliott is the author of *Big Trouble in Mother Russia* (2016), the official sequel to the cult movie *Big Trouble in Little China, Lost in Time and Space: An Unofficial Guide to the Uncharted Journeys of Doctor Who* (2014), *Sherlock Holmes on the Air* (2012), *Sherlock Holmes in Pursuit* (2013), *The Immortals: An Unauthorized Guide to* Sherlock *and* Elementary (2013), and *The Throne Eternal* (2014). His articles, fiction, and reviews have appeared in the magazines *Scarlet Street, Total DVD, SHERLOCK,* and *Sherlock Holmes Mystery Magazine,* and the collections *The Game's Afoot, Curious Incidents 2, Gaslight Grimoire, The Mammoth Book of Best British Crime 8,* and *The MX Book of New Sherlock Holmes Stories – Part III: 1896-1929.* He has scripted over 260 radio plays, including episodes of *Doctor Who, The Further Adventures of Sherlock Holmes, The Twilight Zone, The New Adventures of Mickey Spillane's Mike Hammer, Fangoria's Dreadtime Stories,* and award-winning adaptations of *The Hound of the Baskervilles* and *The War of the Worlds.* He is the only radio dramatist to adapt all sixty original stories from The Canon for the series *The Classic Adventures of Sherlock Holmes.* Matthew is a writer and performer on *RiffTrax.com,* the online comedy experience from the creators of cult sci-fi TV series *Mystery Science Theater 3000* (*MST3K* to the initiated). He's also written a few comic books.

Steve Emecz's main field is technology, in which he has been working for over twenty years. Following multiple senior roles at Xerox, Steve worked for platform provider Venda, and Fintech startup Powa Technologies. Steve is a regular trade show speaker on the subject of mobile commerce, and his time at Powa took him to more than forty countries – so he's no stranger to planes and airports. He wrote two novels (one bestseller) in the 1990's and a screenplay in 2001. Shortly after, he set up MX Publishing, specialising in Neurolinguistic (NLP) books alongside his day job. In 2008, MX published its first Sherlock Holmes book, and MX has gone on to become the largest specialist Holmes publisher in the world, with over one hundred authors and over two hundred books. Profits from MX go towards his second passion – a children's rescue project in Nairobi, Kenya, where he and his wife, Sharon, spend every Christmas at the rescue centre in Kasarani. In 2014, they wrote a short book about the project, *The Happy Life Story*.

Melissa Farnham, Head Teacher of Stepping Stones School, is driven by a passion to open the doors to learners with complex and layered special needs that just make society feel two steps too far away. Based on the Surrey/Hampshire border in England, her time is spent between relocating a great school into the prestigious home of Conan Doyle, and her two children, dogs, and horses, so there never a dull moment.

James R. "Jim" French became a morning DJ on KIRO (AM) in Seattle in 1959. He later founded *Imagination Theatre*, a syndicated program that is now broadcast on over 120 stations in the U.S. and Canada, and also heard on the XM Satellite Radio system all over North America. Actors in French's dramas have included John Patrick Lowrie, Larry Albert, Patty Duke, Russell Johnson, Tom Smothers, Keenan Wynn, Roddy MacDowall, Ruta Lee, John Astin, Cynthia Lauren Tewes, and Richard Sanders. Mr. French states, "To me, the characters of Sherlock Holmes and Doctor Watson always seemed to be figures Doyle created as a challenge to lesser writers. He gave us two interesting characters – different from each other in their histories, talents and experience but complimentary as a team – who have been applied to a variety of situations and plots far beyond the times and places in The Canon. In the hands of different writers, Holmes and Watson have lent their identities to different times, ages, and even genders. But I wanted to break no new ground. I feel Sir Arthur provided us with enough references to locations, landmarks, and the social conditions of his time, to give a pretty large canvas on which to paint our own images and actions to animate Holmes and Watson."

Wendy C. Fries is the author of *Sherlock Holmes and John Watson: The Day They Met* and also writes under the name Atlin Merrick. Wendy is fascinated with London theatre, scriptwriting, and lattes. Her website is *wendycfries.com*.

Mark A. Gagen BSI is co-founder of Wessex Press, sponsor of the popular *From Gillette to Brett* conferences, and publisher of *The Sherlock Holmes Reference Library* and many other fine Sherlockian titles. A life-long Holmes enthusiast, he is a member of *The Baker Street Irregulars* and *The Illustrious Clients of Indianapolis*. A graphic artist by profession, his work is often seen on the covers of *The Baker Street Journal* and various BSI books.

Paul D. Gilbert was born in 1954 and has lived in and around Lindon all of his life. He has been married to Jackie for thirty-nine years, and she is a Holmes expert who keeps him on the straight and narrow! He has two sons, one of whom now lives in Spain. His interests include literature, ancient history, all religions, most sports, and movies. He is currently employed full-time as a funeral director. His books so far include *The Lost Files of Sherlock Holmes* (2007), *The Chronicles of Sherlock Holmes* (2008), *Sherlock Holmes and the Giant Rat of Sumatra* (2010), *The Annals of Sherlock Holmes* (2012), and *Sherlock Holmes and the Unholy Trinity* (2015). He has recently finished *Sherlock Holmes: The Four Handed Game*.

John Atkinson Grimshaw (1836-1893) was born in Leeds, England. His amazing paintings, usually featuring twilight or night scenes illuminated by gas-lamps or moonlight, are easily recognizable, and are often used on the covers of books about the Great Detective to set the mood, as shadowy figures move in the distance through misty mysterious settings and over rain-slicked streets.

Arthur Hall was born in Aston, Birmingham, UK, in 1944. He discovered his interest in writing during his schooldays, along with a love of fictional adventure and suspense. His first novel, *Sole Contact*, was an espionage story about an ultra-secret government department known as "Sector Three", and was followed, to date, by three sequels. Other works include three Sherlock Holmes novels, *The Demon of the Dusk*, *The One Hundred Percent Society*, and *The Secret Assassin*, as well as a collection of short stories, and a modern detective novel. He lives in the West Midlands, United Kingdom.

Dr. John Hall has written widely on Holmes. His books includes *Sidelights on Holmes*, a commentary on The Canon, *The Abominable Wife* on the unrecorded cases, *Unexplored Possibilities*, a study of Dr. John H. Watson, and a monograph on Professor Moriarty, "The Dynamics of a Falling Star". (Most of these are now out of print.) His novels include *Sherlock Holmes and the Adler Papers*, *The Travels of Sherlock Holmes*, *Sherlock Holmes and the Boulevard Assassin*, *Sherlock Holmes and the Disgraced Inspector*, *Sherlock Holmes and the Telephone Mystery*, *Sherlock Holmes and the Hammerford Will*, *Sherlock Holmes and the Abbey School Mystery*, and *Sherlock Holmes at the Raffles Hotel*. John is a member of the *International Pipe-smoker's Hall of Fame*, and lives in Yorkshire, England.

Narrelle M. Harris is a Melbourne-based writer of crime, horror, fantasy and non-fiction. Her books include *Fly By Night*, fantasies *Witch Honour* and *Witch Faith* (both short-listed for the George Turner Prize), and vampire books *The Opposite of Life* and *Walking Shadows*. The latter was nominated for the *Chronos Awards* for Science Fiction and Fantasy, and shortlisted for the *Davitt Awards* for crime writing. Narrelle also writes erotic romance. Find out more at *www.narrellemharris.com*.

Roger Johnson BSI is a retired librarian, now working as a volunteer assistant at Essex Police Museum. In his spare time he is commissioning editor of *The Sherlock Holmes Journal*, an occasional lecturer, and a frequent contributor to the Writings About the Writings. His sole work of Holmesian pastiche was published in 1997 in Mike Ashley's anthology *The Mammoth Book of New Sherlock Holmes Adventures* (and in script form in *The MX Book of New Sherlock Holmes Stories – Part IV – 2016 Annual.*) Like his wife, Jean Upton, he is a member of both *The Baker Street Irregulars* and *The Adventuresses of Sherlock Holmes*.

Jonathan Kellerman is the author of 48 books, 83.3% of them best-selling crime novels.

James Lovegrove is the author of more than fifty books, including *The Hope, Days, Untied Kingdom, Provender Gleed,* the *New York Times* bestselling *Pantheon* series, the *Redlaw* novels, and the *Dev Harmer Missions.* He has produced three Sherlock Holmes novels, with a Holmes/Cthulhu mashup trilogy in the works. He has also sold well over forty short stories and published two collections, *Imagined Slights* and *Diversifications.* He has produced a dozen short books for readers with reading difficulties, and a four-volume fantasy saga for teenagers, *The Clouded World,* under the pseudonym Jay Amory. James has been shortlisted for numerous awards, including the Arthur C. Clarke Award, the John W. Campbell Memorial Award, the Bram Stoker Award, the British Fantasy Society Award, and the Manchester Book Award. His short story "Carry The Moon In My Pocket" won the 2011 Seiun Award in Japan for Best Translated Short Story. His work has been translated into over a dozen languages, and his journalism has appeared in periodicals as diverse as *Literary Review, Interzone,* and *BBC MindGames.* He reviews fiction regularly for the *Financial Times.* He lives with his wife, two sons, cat, and tiny dog in Eastbourne, not far from the site of the "small farm upon the South Downs" to which Sherlock Holmes retired.

David Marcum plays The Game with deadly seriousness. He first discovered Sherlock Holmes in 1975, at the age of ten, when he received an abridged version of *The Adventures* during a trade. Since that time, David has collected literally thousands of traditional Holmes pastiches in the form of novels, short stories, radio and television episodes, movies and scripts, comics, fan-fiction, and unpublished manuscripts. He is the author of *The Papers of Sherlock Holmes Vol.'s I* and *II* (2011, 2013), *Sherlock Holmes and A Quantity of Debt* (2013, 2016) and *Sherlock Holmes – Tangled Skeins* (2015). Additionally, he is the editor of the three-volume set *Sherlock Holmes in Montague Street* (2014, recasting Arthur Morrison's Martin Hewitt stories as early Holmes adventures,) and most recently this current ongoing collection, *The MX Book of New Sherlock Holmes Stories* (2015-   ). He has contributed stories and essays to *The Baker Street Journal, The Watsonian, Beyond Watson, Sherlock Holmes Mystery Magazine, About Sixty, The Solar Pons Gazette,* and *The Gazette,* the journal of the Nero Wolfe *Wolfe Pack.* He began his adult work life as a Federal Investigator for an obscure U.S. Government agency, before the organization was eliminated. He returned to school for a second degree, and is now a licensed Civil Engineer, living in Tennessee with his wife and son. He is a member of *The Sherlock Holmes Society of London, The Occupants of the Full House* (a Scion of the Baker Street Irregulars), *The John H. Watson Society* ("Marker"), *The Praed Street Irregulars* ("The Obrisset Snuff Box"), *The Solar Pons Society of London, The Diogenes Club of Washington, D.C.,* and *The Diogenes Club West (East Tennessee Annex),* a curious and unofficial Scion of one. Since the age of nineteen, he has worn a deerstalker as his regular-and-only hat from autumn to spring. In 2013, he and his deerstalker were finally able make his first trip-of-a-lifetime Holmes Pilgrimage to England in 2013, with return trips in 2015 and 2016, where you may have spotted him. If you ever run into him and his deerstalker out and about, feel free to say hello!

William Patrick Maynard was born and raised in Cleveland, Ohio. His passion for writing began in childhood and was inspired by an early love of detective and thriller fiction. He was licensed by the Sax Rohmer Literary Estate to continue the Fu Manchu thrillers for Black Coat Press. *The Terror of Fu Manchu* was published in 2009 and was followed by *The Destiny of Fu Manchu* in 2012 and *The Triumph of Fu Manchu* in 2016. His previous Sherlock Holmes stories appeared in *Gaslight Grotesque* (2009, EDGE Publishing), *Further Encounters of Sherlock Holmes* (2014, Titan Books), and *The MX*

Book of New Sherlock Holmes Stories, Part II (2015, MX Publishing). He currently resides in Northeast Ohio with his wife and family.

Julie McKuras ASH, BSI discovered Sherlock Holmes at the age of eleven through the late night magic of the Basil Rathbone and Nigel Bruce films. It was a bonus to learn there were actually books written by Sir Arthur Conan Doyle. She served as the President of the *Norwegian Explorers of Minnesota* for nine years, and has been on the board of *The Friends of the Sherlock Holmes Collections* since 1997, editing their quarterly newsletter since 1999. Julie was the first editor of the *BSI Trust* newsletter as well. She is a frequent contributor to the *Friends* newsletter, and has had articles published in the *Baker Street Journal*, London's *Sherlock Holmes Journal*, *Through the Magic Door*, and *The Serpentine Muse*. Her essays have been included in *The Norwegian Explorers Christmas Annuals*, *Sir Arthur Conan Doyle and Sherlock Holmes: Essays and Art on The Doctor and The Detective*, "A Note on the Sherlock Holmes Collections" published in *The Horror of the Heights*, *Violets and Vitriol*, and *Sherlock Holmes in the Heartland: The Illustrious Clients Fifth Casebook*. She is a co-editor of *The Missing Misadventures of Sherlock Holmes*, and with Susan Vizoskie, she co-edited *Sherlockian Heresies*. Julie has been a speaker at a number of conferences and events, such as *The Sherlock Holmes Society of London*'s Statue Festival, Holmes Under the Arch, the Newberry Library, From Gillette to Brett, and the 2014 Reichenbach Irregulars Conference in Davos. She lives in Apple Valley, Minnesota with her husband, Mike, and with her children, their spouses, and her three grandchildren nearby.

Mark Mower is a crime writer and historian whose passion for tales about Sherlock Holmes and Dr. Watson began at the age of twelve, when he watched an early black-and-white film featuring the unrivalled screen pairing of Basil Rathbone and Nigel Bruce. Hastily seeking out the original stories of Sir Arthur Conan Doyle and continually searching for further film and television adaptations, his has been a lifelong obsession. Now a member of the *Crime Writers' Association* and the *Sherlock Holmes Society of London*, Mark has written numerous books about true crime stories and fictional murder mysteries. His first Holmes and Watson tale, "The Strange Missive of Germaine Wilkes" appeared as a chapter in Volume I of *The MX Book of New Sherlock Holmes Stories* (MX Publishing, 2015). His own collection of pastiches, *A Farewell to Baker Street* (MX Publishing, 2015) appeared shortly afterwards. His non-fiction works have included *Bloody British History: Norwich* (The History Press, 2014) and *Suffolk Murders* (The History Press, 2011). Alongside his writing, Mark lectures on crime history and runs a murder mystery business. He lives close to Beccles, in the English county of Suffolk.

Sidney Paget (1860-1908), a few of whose illustrations are used within this anthology, was born in London, and like his two older brothers, became a famed illustrator and painter. He completed over three-hundred-and-fifty drawings for the Sherlock Holmes stories first published in *The Strand* magazine, defining Holmes's image forever after in the public mind.

Ashley D. Polasek, PhD, FRSA, BSB, ASH, is an "Aca-Sherlockian", happily living at the crossroads of academia, traditional Sherlockiana, and contemporary fandom. Ashley holds a doctorate in the study of Sherlock Holmes on screen. As an internationally recognized authority on Sherlock Holmes adaptations, she has spoken on the subject at academic conferences and Sherlockian events across the U.S., the U.K., and continental Europe. She has published in peer reviewed journals and academic texts relating Holmes to literary and film studies topics as diverse as postcolonialism, feminism, postmodernism, historical period, costume, war propaganda, performance theory, copyright, and fan studies. With Lyndsay Faye, Ashley is the co-editor of *Sherlock Holmes: Behind the Canonical Screen* from BSI Press, and as a guest emeritus at *221B Con*, she has spoken on over two-dozen panels since the convention's inception in 2013. She has been interviewed about Sherlock Holmes on CNN International and CBS *Sunday Morning*. When she is not writing and speaking about Sherlock Holmes, Ashley spends her days teaching composition and literature and her evenings training in Historical European Martial Arts. She lives in Upstate South Carolina with her husband, Mr. Hyde, and her Wheaten Terrier, Jekyll. Ashley can be found on Twitter *@SherlockPhD*.

Tracy J. Revels, a Sherlockian from the age of eleven, is a professor of history at Wofford College in Spartanburg, South Carolina. She is a member of *The Survivors of the Gloria Scott* and *The Studious Scarlets Society*, and is a past recipient of the Beacon Society Award. Almost every semester, she teaches a class that covers The Canon, either to college students or to senior citizens. She is also the author of three supernatural Sherlockian pastiches with MX (*Shadowfall, Shadowblood,* and *Shadowwraith*), and a regular contributor to her scion's newsletter. She also has some notoriety as an author of very silly skits: for proof, see "The Adventure of the Adversarial Adventuress" and "Occupy Baker Street" on YouTube. When not studying Sherlock, she can be found researching the history of her native state, and has written books on Florida in the Civil War and on the development of Florida's tourism industry.

Roger Riccard of Los Angeles, California, U.S.A., is a descendant of the Roses of Kilravock in Highland Scotland. He is the author of two previous Sherlock Holmes novels, *The Case of the Poisoned Lilly* and *The Case of the Twain Papers*, as well as a series of short stories in two volumes, *Sherlock Holmes: Adventures for the Twelve Days of Christmas* and *Further Adventures for the Twelve Days of* Christmas all of which are published by Baker Street Studios. He has another novel, a new series of short stories, and a non-fiction Holmes reference work in various stages of completion. He became a Sherlock Holmes enthusiast as a teenager (many, many years ago,) and, like all fans of the Great Detective, yearned for more stories after reading The Canon over and over. It was the Granada Television performances of Jeremy Brett and Edward Hardwicke, and the encouragement of his wife, Rosilyn, that at last inspired him to write his own Holmes adventures, using the Granada actor portrayals as his guide. He has been called "The best pastiche writer since Val Andrews" by the *Sherlockian E-Times.*

Denis O. Smith's first published story of Sherlock Holmes and Doctor Watson, "The Adventure of The Purple Hand", appeared in 1982. Since then, numerous other such accounts have been published in magazines and anthologies both in the U.K. and the U.S. In the 1990's, four volumes of his stories were published under the general title of *The Chronicles of Sherlock Holmes*, and, more recently, a dozen of his stories, most not previously published in book form, appeared as *The Lost Chronicles of Sherlock Holmes* (2014) and *The Lost Chronicles of Sherlock Holmes Volume II* (2016). He also wrote a new story for the anthology, *Sherlock Holmes Abroad* (2015). Born in Yorkshire, in the north of England, Denis Smith has lived and worked in various parts of the country, including London, and has now been resident in Norfolk for many years. His interests range widely, but apart from his dedication to the career of Sherlock Holmes, he has a passion for historical mysteries of all kinds, the railways of Britain and the history of London.

S. Subramanian is a retired professor of Economics from Chennai, India. Apart from a small book titled *Economic Offences: A Compendium of Crimes in Prose and Verse* (Oxford University Press Delhi, 2012), his Holmes pastiches are the only serious things he has written. His other work runs largely to whimsical stuff on fuzzy logic and social measurement, on which he writes with much precision and little understanding, being an economist. He is otherwise mainly harmless, as his wife and daughter might concede with a little persuasion.

Amy Thomas is a member of the *Baker Street Babes* Podcast, and the author of *The Detective and The Woman* mystery novels featuring Sherlock Holmes and Irene Adler. She blogs at *girlmeetssherlock.wordpress.com*, and she writes and edits professionally from her home in Fort Myers, Florida.

Nicholas Utechin BSI joined *The Sherlock Holmes Society of London* in 1966, aged fourteen. Ten years later he became Editor of *The Sherlock Holmes Journal* – a position he held for thirty years. The year 1976 also saw the publication of two Holmes pastiches he co-wrote: *The Earthquake Machine* and *Hellbirds.*. He is a *Baker Street Irregular*, an honorary senior member of the *Sons of the the Copper Beeches* Scion society, a founding member of the *John H. Watson Society*, and has contributed extensively to Sherlockian scholarship over the decades. The fact that he is related to Basil Rathbone could have something to do with this madness. In another life, he was a senior producer and occasional presenter for BBC Radio in the field of current affairs. Now retired, he lives in Oxford, U.K., with his wife, Annie, follows the careers of their two sons with interest, and the lives of their two grandchildren with love. He believes he knows quite a lot about fine wine and silent films (meeting and interviewing Lillian Gish was something special,) and is lucky enough to own a Sidney Paget original (sadly not one for a Sherlock Holmes story.)

Marcia Wilson is a freelance researcher and illustrator who likes to work in a style compatible for the color blind and visually impaired. She is Canon-centric and her first MX offering, *You Buy Bones*, uses the point-of-view of Scotland Yard to show the unique talents of Dr. Watson. She can be contacted at *gravelgirty.deviantart.com*

Vincent W. Wright has been a Sherlockian and member of *The Illustrious Clients of Indianapolis* since 1997. He is the creator of a blog, *Historical Sherlock*, which is dedicated to the chronology of The Canon, and has written a column on that subject for his home scion's newsletter since 2005. He lives in Indiana, and works for the federal government.

Also from MX Publishing

The MX Book of New Sherlock Holmes Stories
Edited by David Marcum

Part I: 1881-1889
Part II: 1890-1895
Part III: 1896-1929
Part IV – 2016 Annual

MX Publishing
The World's Leading
Sherlock Holmes Book Publisher

www.mxpublishing.com

MX Publishing

MX Publishing is the world's largest specialist Sherlock Holmes publisher, with several hundred titles and over a hundred authors creating the latest in Sherlock Holmes fiction and non-fiction.

From traditional short stories and novels to travel guides and quiz books, MX Publishing caters to all Holmes fans.

The collection includes leading titles such as *Benedict Cumberbatch In Transition* and *The Norwood Author*, which won the 2011 *Tony Howlett Award* (Sherlock Holmes Book of the Year).

MX Publishing also has one of the largest communities of Holmes fans on *Facebook*, with regular contributions from dozens of authors.

www.mxpublishing.co.uk (UK) and *www.mxpublishing.com* (USA)

Lightning Source UK Ltd.
Milton Keynes UK
UKOW02f2331071116

287120UK00001B/97/P